For Hannah
Always in my heart

Acknowledgments

Writing a book is a team project and I would like to thank some of the members of my team who worked hard on this book. Rosalind Noonan and John Scognamiglio both gave hours of their expertise on the novel. Everyone at Kensington Publishing has been incredible and of course, I would like to thank Nancy Bush, Ken Bush, Alex Craft, Matthew Crose, Niki Crose, Michael Crose, Kelly Foster, Darren Foster, Ken Melum, and my agent, Robin Rue. There are others, of course, but these people come to mind.

WITHOUT MERCY

"So someone came in, hit Drew Prescott, kicked him through the hole in the floor of the loft and then hung Nona?" Jules asked.

"No weapon was found," Trent said. "The cut on the back of Drew's head was deep, probably from a sharp rock, but the police haven't found it yet. Until the storm breaks, they might never. For all anyone knows, it could be at the bottom of the lake or buried under two feet of snow." He hesitated, as if unsure how much he should divulge, and then continued. "I suppose if you're going to stay here, you should be armed with the truth." He told her of the severity of the attack on Nona.

"What kind of sick mind would do that?" she asked, almost wishing she didn't know the truth.

"Someone extremely disturbed." Trent let his boot scrape at a wad of hay and they both watched as golden strands of straw tumbled through the opening and fluttered down to the stable floor far below. "Someone here at the school . . ."

Paperbacks and Pieces
429 Mankato Ave.
Winona, MN 55987
507-452-5580
www.paperbacksandpieces.com

Books by Lisa Jackson

SEE HOW SHE DIES
FINAL SCREAM
RUNNING SCARED
WHISPERS
TWICE KISSED
UNSPOKEN
IF SHE ONLY KNEW
HOT BLOODED
COLD BLOODED
THE NIGHT BEFORE
THE MORNING AFTER
DEEP FREEZE
FATAL BURN
SHIVER
MOST LIKELY TO DIE
ABSOLUTE FEAR
ALMOST DEAD
LOST SOULS
LEFT TO DIE
WICKED GAME
MALICE
CHOSEN TO DIE
WITHOUT MERCY
DEVIOUS

Published by Kensington Publishing Corporation

WITHOUT MERCY

Lisa Jackson

ZEBRA BOOKS
KENSINGTON PUBLISHING CORP.
http://www.kensingtonbooks.com

ZEBRA BOOKS are published by

Kensington Publishing Corp.
119 West 40th Street
New York, NY 10018

All Kensington titles, imprints, and distributed lines are available at special quantity discounts for bulk purchases for sales promotion, premiums, fund-raising, educational, or institutional use.

Special book excerpts or customized printings can also be created to fit specific needs. For details, write or phone the office of the Kensington Special Sales Manager: Attn. Special Sales Department. Kensington Publishing Corp., 119 West 40th Street, New York, NY 10018. Phone: 1-800-221-2647.

Zebra and the Z logo Reg. U.S. Pat. & TM Off.

ISBN-13: 978-1-4201-0274-1
ISBN-10: 1-4201-0274-5

First Kensington Books Trade Hardcover Printing: April 2010
First Zebra Books Mass-Market Paperback Printing: March 2011

10 9 8 7 6 5 4 3 2 1

Printed in the United States of America

Author's Note

There is no Blue Rock Academy, nor a sheriff's department whose jurisdiction included the academy. But there is an incredibly beautiful stretch of country in the mountains of southern Oregon, so while the institution isn't real, the landscape is and let me tell you, it's phenomenal!

CHAPTER 1

"Help me . . . Oh, God, please someone help me. . . ." The voice was a desperate plea, barely audible over the sounds of a familiar song and the steady drip of liquid splashing, like a single drop of rainwater hitting the ground. Over and over again.

Her heartbeat pounding in her eardrums, Jules Farentino, barefoot and wearing only a nightgown, made her way toward the den where a fluttering blue light was barely visible through the sheers on the French doors.

"Hurry . . . there isn't much time. . . ."

She wanted to call out but held her tongue. The feeling that something was wrong here—something dark and evil—caused her to creep silently along the icy floors.

Slowly, she pushed open the door to the den and peered inside. The L-shaped couch and a recliner were illuminated by the weird, flickering light of the muted television.

Michael Jackson's voice sang about Billie Jean through the speakers.

Above the melody:

Drip. Drip. Drip.

So loud.

Like rolling thunder in her aching head.

Liquid warmth splashed on the tops of her bare feet, and she looked down quickly. Her eyes rounded as she saw the blood dripping from the long blade of the knife in her hand, the red stain spreading into a pool.

What?

No!

She tried to scream but couldn't, and as she looked toward the open French doors, she saw her father lying on the floor near the coffee table.

"Help me, Jules," he said, lips barely moving. He stared up at her, eyes unblinking, a jagged gash on his forehead, a stain spreading on the front of his rumpled white shirt.

Blood gurgled from the corner of Rip Delaney's mouth as he stared up at her, whispering in a wet rasp, "Why?"

Transfixed, her hand now sticky with blood, she started to scream—

"Seven forty-five in the morning. It's a chilly thirty-seven now. That's only five degrees above freezing, you know, but temperatures will climb until midafternoon, topping out near fifty. It's going to be a cold, wet one today, a major storm expected to roll in later this morning. Now for the traffic report . . ."

Jules awoke with a jerk.

Her heart was pounding, her head splitting, the radio announcer's voice an irritant. She slapped off the alarm and shivered. Her bedroom was freezing, her window open a crack, wind rushing inside, rain beating a steady tattoo against the roof.

"Damn," she whispered, wiping her face, the vestiges of her ever-recurring dream slipping back to the dark corners of her mind. She glanced at the clock and groaned, realizing with a sinking feeling that she'd forgotten to reset her alarm.

Rolling off the bed, she disturbed her cat that had been

sleeping in a ball on the second pillow. He lifted his gray head and stretched, yawning to show off his needle-sharp teeth as she snagged her bathrobe from the foot of the bed and threw it on. She didn't have time for a shower, much less a jog.

Instead, she threw water over her face, tossed a couple of extra-strength Excedrin into her mouth, and washed them down by tilting her head under the faucet. After yanking on jeans and an oversized sweatshirt, she found an old Trail Blazers cap. Then she searched for her keys, scrounging in her purse and in the pockets of the jacket she'd worn the day before.

Her cell phone rang, and she found it plugged in to the charger on the floor near her bed.

Flipping it open, she saw Shay's face on the small LED screen.

"Where are you?" her sister demanded.

"I'm on my way."

"It's too late. We're almost there!"

"Already?" Jules tugged on one sneaker as she glanced back at the clock. "I thought you were leaving at nine."

"The pilot called. There's a storm or something. I don't know. He has to fly out earlier."

"Oh, no! Make him wait."

"I can't! Don't you get it? She's really doing it, Jules," Shay said, and some of the toughness in her voice disappeared. "Edie's getting rid of me."

That was a little overly dramatic, but so was Shay, through and through.

Jules finished lacing her running shoes. "Then tell *her* to wait."

"You tell her," Shay said, and a second later Jules heard her mother's voice say, "Look, Julia, there's no reason to argue with me; this is beyond my control. I told Shaylee that she has to go whenever the pilot can fly her safely to the school, and he says they need to go earlier because of the storm."

"No, Mom, wait. You can't just send her to—"

"I damned well can. She's underage. I'm her guardian. And she's got a court order. We've had this conversation before. Let's not rehash it."

"But—"

"It's either this or juvenile detention again. This is her last chance, Julia! The judge ordered her to make a choice, and she, smart as she is, took the school. It was also *her* choice to hang out with that criminal and take part in a crime. Her boyfriend wasn't so fortunate; he didn't have a rich father to get him a lawyer. Dawg will be going to prison for a long time, so your sister should count herself lucky!"

"Just wait!"

The connection was severed, leaving Jules to worry from the middle of her messy bedroom. She couldn't believe her mother was actually shipping Shaylee off to a distant school for troubled teens, one that was in the middle of no-damned-where. She flew out of her condo and waved to Mrs. Dixon, her neighbor, as the woman carried her wet newspaper into her unit.

Once inside her old Volvo, she drove toward Lake Washington and the address she'd gotten from Edie earlier, the spot from which Shaylee was to be picked up by seaplane for her ride to Blue Rock Academy in southern Oregon. Edie had given Jules the address the day before.

Jules floored it.

However, the freeway was a parking lot, and the latest traffic report blaring from Jules's radio didn't make her feel any better. Apparently everyone who owned a car in the state of Washington was sitting on the I-5 freeway in the drizzling rain, as evidenced by the line of blazing taillights stretching ahead of her Volvo. Jules peered wearily past the slapping windshield wiper as the traffic crawled north. Still fighting a headache, she drummed her fingers on her steering wheel and wished she knew a faster way to get to Lake Washington.

She'd battled rush hour down in Portland, Oregon, when she'd worked at Bateman High, but since losing her teaching job last June, she'd been spared the annoyance of rush hour. In her current position as a waitress at 101, a high-end restaurant on the waterfront, she covered the night shift and usually avoided traffic. One of the few perks of the job.

The radio did little to calm her nerves, and the windshield wipers slapping away the rain only added to her case of jitters. Jules was too late. Shay was going to fly off without a good-bye, and there was nothing anyone could do about it. Not even Edie could fix this. A judge had ruled that Shay was to be sent away for rehabilitation.

She tuned the radio to a station where songs from the eighties were peppered with rapid-fire traffic updates from Brenda, the serious reporter who rattled off trouble spots on the freeway system so fast it was hard to keep up.

Not that it helped.

Basically, it seemed, every freeway was a snarled mess this miserable February morning.

"Come on, come on," Jules muttered, glancing at the clock on the dash of her twenty-year-old sedan. Eight-seventeen. The height of rush hour. And she was supposed to be on the dock by eight-thirty, or it would be too late. She flipped on her blinker and bullied her way into the lane that was curving toward the Evergreen Point Bridge that spanned Lake Washington.

A semi driver reluctantly allowed her to squeeze in, and she offered him a smile and a wave as she wedged her way into the far right lane and nosed her car east. She was nearly clipped by a guy in a black Toyota who was talking on his cell phone.

"Idiot!" She slammed on her brakes and slid into the spot just as the first notes of "Billie Jean" by Michael Jackson filled the interior of her Volvo. "Oh, God." She pushed the radio's button to another preset station, but the strains of the song reverberated through her head.

In her mind's eye, again she saw her father, lying in a pool of his own blood, his dying eyes staring upward as the song played over and over.

Jules nearly smashed into the pickup in front of her.

"Oh, Jesus." *Calm down. Don't kill yourself getting there!* Adrenaline from the near wreck sang through her veins. Jittery, she took three breaths, then, with one hand, fished inside her purse for a bottle of painkillers. The stuff she'd taken earlier hadn't worked.

She found the bottle and popped off the cap with her thumb. Pills sprayed over her, but she didn't care, washing two tablets down quickly with the remains of yesterday's Diet Coke that she'd left in the car's cup holder.

The bad mix of caffeine-laden syrup and headache medicine made her wince as the refrain of "Billie Jean" kept pounding through her brain. "You're a head case," she told her reflection in the rearview mirror. "No wonder you're out of work." Well, technically she had a job waiting tables, but her teaching career was over. Her recurring nightmare and blinding headaches had taken care of that.

In the mirror, beneath the bill of her cap, she caught a quick glimpse of gray eyes that held a hint of rebellion—that same disguised mutiny that was so evident in her younger sister.

At least Shaylee wasn't a hypocrite.

Jules could hardly say the same of herself.

A siren wailed in the distance; then she spied an ambulance threading through the clogged lanes of freeway traffic, going in the opposite direction.

God, her head throbbed.

Even though it was a cloudy day, the glare got to her.

She found her pair of driving shades tucked in the visor and slipped them on.

"Come on, come on," she muttered at the truck belching exhaust in front of her.

It took another twenty minutes and one more near collision before she reached her exit and eased along a winding road that hugged the shoreline of the lake.

She rounded a sharp curve and pulled through the open wrought-iron gates of a private residence. With a long, brick driveway, the building that appeared through the spruce and fir trees was more castle than house, a huge stone and brick edifice that rose three full stories on the shores of the lake.

She parked near the front door, next to her mother's Lexus SUV. Then, without locking her car, she dashed through the spitting rain to the porch. Under the cover of the porch, she rang the bell and waited near the thick double doors.

Within a few seconds, a fussy-looking, wasp-thin woman answered. "Can I help you?" The woman was dressed in black slacks and a sleek sweater tied at her tiny waist. Ash-blond hair, salon cut and teased, increased the size of her head and masked her age. Perfectly applied makeup accentuated her sharp features. Her smooth skin screamed face-lift, and she glared at Jules as if she'd been interrupted from doing something *very* important.

Jules realized that in her decade-old jeans topped by her favorite UW sweatshirt, sunglasses, and faded baseball cap, she probably looked more like a bank robber than a worried family member. But, really, who cared? "I'm looking for Edie Stillman. She's with her daughter, and they were going on a seaplane to—"

"I believe they're at the dock," the woman said with a smooth, practiced smile that didn't hide her disapproval.

Nor did she ask for any kind of ID or what Jules's part in Shaylee's departure was. She waved a disinterested hand toward a stone path leading around the house. "But I think you may be too late. The plane's about to take off."

Over the steady beat of rain, Jules heard the distinct sound of an engine sputtering to life. *Hell!* She was already running in the direction the woman had pointed as the engine caught and roared with the sound of acceleration.

CHAPTER 2

"**D**on't let the dogs out!" the impossibly thin woman warned loudly as Jules, desperate to stave off the inevitable, dashed through the rain, over the uneven stones, and around the corner of the majestic house where rhododendrons shivered in the wind. She flipped up the hood of her sweatshirt, though cold rain was already dripping down the back of her neck.

Not that she cared.

She just wanted a minute with Shay.

A tall wrought-iron gate stopped her for a second, but a key was in the lock, so she pulled the gate open and heard it clang shut behind her as she flew down a series of steps.

The dogs—two black standard poodles—raced up to her. She barely gave them a second glance as she hurried to the dock and boathouse, where Edie stood under an umbrella that trembled in the wind. Beyond her, a seaplane skimmed along the top of the steely water, then made its ascent into the gray Seattle sky.

"Great!" Jules's stomach dropped. She was too late. Damn it all to hell. "You put her on the plane?"

"I said I was going to. For the love of God, Julia, she's

just complying with a judge's orders!" Edie Stillman, dressed in a blue silk jogging suit, turned to face her oldest daughter. Her expression said it all as she eyed Jules's clothes with distaste. "Didn't you have anything to wear?" she said, obviously embarrassed. "You look like some kind of thug."

Rain battered the hood of Jules's sweatshirt, dripping down the bill of her baseball cap. "Just the look I was going for."

"I can't even tell that you're a woman, for God's sake!"

"What's that got to do with anything?" Through her shaded lenses, Jules looked up to the sky and saw the seaplane vanish into the clouds. "Damn it, Mom, I said I'd take her in!"

"And Shay said . . . let's see, what was that darling little quote?" Edie touched the edge of her lips and pretended to think as raindrops peppered the decking and pimpled the lake. "Oh, now I remember. She said, 'I'd rather puke up dead dogs than live with Jules!' Wasn't that just the sweetest way of saying, 'No thanks'?"

Jules bristled. "Okay. I know she wasn't crazy about the idea, but, really, this place you're sending her, it's like a prison."

"A pretty nice 'prison.' It looks more like a camp or a retreat. Have you seen the brochures?"

"Of course, I looked online, but they've got guards and fences and—"

"Then maybe she'll learn the value of freedom." Edie was unmoved.

"At what price?" Jules demanded as rain drizzled down her cheeks and stained the shoulders of her sweatshirt. The sound of the seaplane's engine faded into nothing. She remembered the articles she'd pulled up on the Internet when she'd first learned of the plan to ship Shaylee off to Blue

Rock Academy. "I've done some research, and they've had their share of trouble. The school's gotten some bad press in the past year. A girl disappeared last fall, and there was something about a teacher being involved with a student and—"

"As for teachers and students, it happens everywhere—not that I condone it, of course. At least he was found out."

"She," Jules corrected. "The teacher was a woman."

"That seems to be the new crime du jour, doesn't it?" Edie scowled. "As for that girl, Lauren Conrad—"

"Her name was Conway."

"Whatever. She was a runaway," Edie said, lines cracking her evenly applied makeup. Though in her early fifties, she worked hard at looking fifteen years younger than her age. Today, with the stress of sending her wayward child away, all her carefully applied makeup and semiannual injections of Botox weren't doing their jobs.

"No one knows what happened to Lauren Conway, Mom," Jules objected. "I know because ever since you told me Shay was going there, I've done some research. Lauren still hasn't turned up."

"I think she had a history of taking off and disappearing. Really, Jules, it *is* a school for delinquents."

"And that makes it okay for a student to go missing? Even if she did take off, isn't the place supposed to be secure? Isn't that the whole point of the school? To keep at-risk kids safe?"

"Give it up." Edie's lips pulled tight, as if from invisible purse strings. "I can't quote their mission statement, but trust me, this is what's best for Shaylee and me. You know I've tried everything and nothing worked. I took her to counselors when she was depressed, got her into tae kwon do and even kickboxing to help her deal with her aggression. I gave her art, dance, and voice lessons to support her creative expression. Beading. Remember that? Beading, for the love of God! And how did she pay me back? Huh?"

Edie's temper was sizzling now. "I'll tell you how. She got into drugs. She's been picked up for theft and vandalism, not to mention being kicked out of three schools." Edie held up a trio of shaking, bejeweled fingers, which she shook in front of Jules's face. "Three!" she huffed. "With an IQ in the stratosphere and all the privileges I could afford, this is what she does? Goes out with a criminal named Dawg?"

"She's a kid. Maybe she just needed some special attention."

"Oh, give me a break. I lavished attention on her. More than I ever did with you!"

Jules wasn't sure that was necessarily true.

"This isn't about mother love or father love or the lack thereof, so cut that pseudopsychological garbage, Jules. It's not working on me!"

"Just calm down."

"No! You saw her latest tattoo, didn't you? The bloody dagger on her forearm? What was she thinking?" Edie threw her arms up, nearly losing her umbrella. "I can't count how many times Shay came home with a tattoo or a piercing or a stolen CD. And that mouth . . . full of filthy back talk . . ." She let her thoughts drift away.

"Who cares about a few tats and nose rings? She didn't hurt anyone."

"Tattoos are self-mutilation, indicative of deeper problems!"

"I don't think so."

Edie's eyes blazed. "Then what about all her trouble with the law? I just can't take it!"

"Did you think about finding her a new psychiatrist?" Jules suggested.

"She's had half a dozen."

"Give her a break." Jules hated that their mother was so hard on Shay. "She was there that day, remember? She was in the house when Dad was killed, for God's sake."

Edie's expression turned hard. "So were you."

"And look how it messed me up. Shay was only twelve, Mom!" Jules was close to hyperventilating now. "Twelve! Just a baby."

"I know, I know," Edie said quietly, and some of her self-righteousness evaporated. "That was a bad time for all of us," she admitted, adjusting her umbrella.

For a fleeting second, Edie appeared sincerely sad, and Jules wondered if Rip Delaney had been the love of her mother's life. She quickly cast that question aside, because she knew better; it was just her stupid fantasies, the dreams of a daughter who always thought her parents should have stayed together, who had been ecstatic at their reunion, only to have her dreams turn to dust. Rip and Edie should never have reunited; the mercurial moods and fights that had abated during the years they were separated started up again once they were in close proximity. Weeks after they said their vows, Edie burst into a jealous rage, certain Rip was seeing another woman. And it was true. Rip Delaney simply was not cut out for monogamy, though Jules had always hoped he would change.

"I should never have married him," Edie had admitted not long after the second marriage ceremony. "A leopard doesn't change his spots, you know."

That image of her mother, eyes red and swollen with tears, had haunted Jules since long before her father's death. If relationship skills were passed down from parents to their children, Jules figured that she and Shay were doomed to lead some very lonely lives.

Turning away from the lake, Edie tipped back her umbrella and sighed theatrically. "Sending her away isn't punishment. It's just the last straw. She needs help, Jules, help she wouldn't allow you or me or any of her psychiatrists to give. Maybe they can help her at this academy. Lord, I hope so. Isn't it worth a shot?" She glanced up at the sky, where dark clouds were being chased by the wind. "Oh, well, it's over and done now. She's someone else's problem. Pray that this works!" Edie attacked the steps from the dock, a slim woman hell-bent in her convictions.

"Wait a sec. Why was Shay picked up here, at this mansion? Doesn't that seem a little off to you?" Jules followed right on her mother's heels.

"Not really, no."

"Really, Edie?" Jules couldn't believe it. "You mean it's not odd to you that you didn't drive her down there or that . . . that she wasn't flown by a commercial carrier to an airport nearby, like in Medford?"

Edie didn't break stride. "This is the way it's done. This house is owned by the school."

"You're kidding!"

"No, I'm not. I think it's used by the director, Reverend Lynch."

"Really?" Jules was floored. "A preacher lives here?"

"Part-time, I think. When he's not at the school."

Jules took in the expansive grounds with its trimmed lawns, sculpted shrubbery, and manicured paths that sloped down to the wide concrete dock and a stone boathouse. The estate was insulated from neighboring mansions by a high stone fence and was buffered with towering fir trees, long-needled pines, and white-barked birches devoid of leaves. The only other homes in view were distant, situated on their own acreage a mile across the flinty waters of the lake.

To Jules, the reverend's estate was truly spectacular. Not exactly pauper's quarters.

"I guess he doesn't buy into the whole shedding-of-earthly-possessions thing."

"Well, maybe the school owns it and he just stays here; I'm not sure."

Jules whistled under her breath. "I take it Blue Rock Academy isn't cheap."

Edie's lips pursed. "You get what you pay for, Jules; you should know that. In the case of your sister, money's not the issue. I've talked to Max. He's agreed to help." Max Stillman was Shaylee's father, or at least the sperm donor and heir to the "Stillman Timber fortune" that Jules had heard about ever since her mother had met him nearly nineteen years ago. Theoretically, Shaylee was next in line for the money, except that Max had never been close to his daughter, and what little interest he'd had in Shaylee had waned since the birth of Max Junior, his son with his second and much younger wife, Hester. Max had come into the world about four years earlier, not long after the time Shaylee had become "a handful." Shaylee's title had morphed, of course, from "a handful" to "a problem."

Jules adjusted her cap against the heavy drizzle. "It just doesn't feel right . . . Shay getting hauled off to the middle of nowhere."

"I'm doing what the judge ordered," Edie said, marching up the last few steps toward the main house, where one of the black poodles was pacing along the wide back porch. Its companion was busy sniffing a sodden azalea. "Let me remind you that Shay's about out of options. It was this or a juvenile detention center, and that's only because of her age. She'll be eighteen in June, and then she won't be eligible for any get-out-of-jail-free cards." Edie shuddered. "I just did as the judge ordered: checked out the school, filed the paperwork, got Shay admitted. I even talked to your cousin Analise. She went there, you know. A junkie. Turned her life around and is in nursing school, so please don't give me any grief about it, Jules. The school is legit."

"What about Lauren Conway?"

"If she's missing, well, then I'm sorry, but it sounds like a matter for the police." Edie sent her a dark look. "You need to move on, Julia. It's time you take charge of your own life and pray that your sister makes the most of this opportunity to turn her life around." Edie touched Jules's wet sleeve, and her expression softened. "I swear, sometimes you take on the whole world. You're not even twenty-five; you're at the point where you should be having the time of your life. Instead you act like you're pushing forty, worrying about Shaylee, when it doesn't do any good."

The wind kicked up, teasing at Edie's hair. "I know it's because of Rip, honey, and God, I wish you hadn't been there that night. . . ." Her voice lowered. "I wish none of us had been. Oh, damn." She blinked rapidly, fighting tears. Turning quickly, Edie hurried up the remaining stairs, leaving Jules, stunned at her mother's glimmer of understanding, alone on the patio.

"Wow," she whispered, clearing her throat.

Suddenly she wondered what had happened to the dogs. She hadn't seen them slip inside, but they were gone, the backyard feeling suddenly barren and lonely, brittle tree limbs rattling in the wind.

Jules followed her mother through the side gate and along the path to the front of the house, where Edie was digging through her purse. She snagged the keys and, all motherly concern erased from her expression, gave Jules the once-over. "I thought you had a job interview this morning."

Jules tensed. God, it was hard to keep up with her mother's shifting moods. "I called and canceled. I thought this was more important."

"That was foolish." Edie scowled as she climbed into her vehicle. "And you can't afford to throw away an opportunity like that, Julia. There aren't a lot of job openings for teachers at this time of the year." Edie spoke as if she were an employment expert when, in truth, she'd worked barely a day in her life.

"I think they were hiring from somewhere within the district," Jules said, stretching the truth a bit. "I have a friend who works at the school as a secretary, and she said someone was transferring in."

"Well for God's sake, Jules, get the transferee's job! Unless you just love being a waitress. And why can't your 'friend' help you?" She made air quotes to indicate she thought Jules was lying.

She was.

"Can't your *friend* put in a good word for you?" Edie persisted.

"Maybe."

"Oh, Lord, Jules, I just don't get you. You're educated, you had a great husband—"

"Who cheated on me. Not so great, Mom. Let's not talk about Sebastian. Not now. Okay? We've got more pressing issues."

With a flip of her wrist, Edie turned on the ignition, then rolled down the window to continue the conversation. "I know you care about Shay, Julia. I do, too. But it's time for each of us to take responsibility for our own actions. Not just Shay, but you, too." With that, she shoved the Lexus into reverse, backed up, then rammed the big SUV into drive and roared off.

Soaked to her skin, Jules flipped off the hood of her sweatshirt as she slid behind the wheel. The old sedan sparked to life on her first try. Like her mother, Jules headed away from the big house. But as she flicked a glance in the rearview mirror, she spied the fussy woman with the forced smile looking through the windowpanes surrounding the massive front doors.

A shiver slid down Jules's spine, and her teeth began to chatter.

It had been a helluva day.

And it wasn't yet noon.

CHAPTER 3

Cooper Trent crossed the campus quickly, bowing his head against the sharp wind, heavy with the promise of yet more snow. The ground was still white from the last storm, an icy blanket that covered the dry grasses and clung tenaciously to the branches of nearby trees.

Trent had only fifteen minutes between his classes, and he'd been summoned by his boss: Reverend Tobias Lynch. He knew what to expect; there had been talk of another student being accepted by the academy. He or she was on the way, though Trent hadn't yet heard the details. No one had.

That was the way this place worked—a public face of earnestness, congeniality, kindness, and openness, but behind closed doors, Lynch ruled the place with an iron fist. Oh, in all the groups, there was always lots of talk about personal freedoms and open discussions and working through problems, but the truth of the matter was that here, at Blue Rock Academy, there were more closed-door meetings and secret agendas than anyone could guess.

Hence, the rumor mill was always pumping out gossip, and there had been mention of a new student arriving midterm. As he passed the flagpole in front of the administration building, he guessed that his number was up. No doubt he'd been chosen as the group leader to catch the new pupil.

Which was just as well. As the latest teacher hired, he needed more responsibility, more trust, and he wanted to blend in. He couldn't risk that anyone would guess his true reasons for applying for the job at the academy. Though he had all the credentials he needed for the position of physical education teacher, he was really working undercover, a private investigator searching for clues in the disappearance of Lauren Conway. The local sheriff's department had exhausted all their leads, according to Cheryl and Ted, parents of the missing girl.

He hurried up two broad steps and through glass doors to the admin building, where warm air and the smell of some kind of cleaner greeted him.

He winked at Charla King as he passed her desk and was rewarded with one of her frosty glares. Hell, she was uptight. Charla was school/church secretary and accountant, and she took her job seriously. All the time. In her fifties, with close-cropped hair, rimless glasses, and a tightly set, if sagging jaw, she believed it was her personal mission from God to balance the books to the penny and see that the academy was always in the black. Bean counter to the max.

She turned her attention back to her computer and the grid of numbers on the screen as he made his way through the glassed-in cubicles where others were working diligently at their assigned tasks.

His boots, now wet with melted snow, rang up the short flight of stairs to Lynch's business office, the place where he dealt with secular business. The director also kept a smaller, cozier office in a room within the chapel complex. That book-lined cranny was relegated for conversations about faith, personal problems, or spiritual matters. Dr. Lynch also used it to meditate about all things theological.

Or so the company line went.

Trent rapped on the half-open door with his knuckles, then stepped inside the pine-paneled room. Tobias was seated at his oversized desk.

"Trent!" Lynch said, smiling widely and waving at one of the visitor chairs. "Here, take a seat."

Crossing toward the desk, Trent noted Adele Burdette, looking distracted as usual. The headmistress for the female students stood at the window, resting a hip on the sill as she stared at the roiling waters of Lake Superstition. In her midforties, Adele was trim and strong, a sour woman who never bothered with makeup. Her curly red hair was scraped back from her head in a perpetual ponytail that was starting to silver.

"We've just got a few minutes," Lynch said, "but I thought I'd bring you up to speed about a new student." A tall, thin man whose posture reminded Trent of a modern Abraham Lincoln, Lynch seemed to hunch over his desk. Behind his tinted glasses were eyes as dark as obsidian, eyes that, Trent guessed, didn't miss much. "It's short notice, I know, but sometimes that's how things work around here." He offered a brief smile, stretching his mustache and soul patch. Lynch fulfilled many roles at Blue Rock: religious leader, theology teacher, headmaster for the boys, and dean of faculty. "So, I just got all the paperwork this morning via fax. Her name is Shaylee Stillman, and she goes by 'Shay.'"

Every muscle in Trent's body tightened. No way. Not Jules's sister. He must've heard wrong.

"She's had her share of run-ins with the law, and her mother is worried that once she turns eighteen, things will only get worse."

Burdette was nodding, agreeing. "The mother's right; I read all the reports."

"Where's she from?" Trent forced himself to lean back

in his chair, feigning nonchalance. If the new student was Shay Stillman, things were going to get a lot more complicated. A lot.

"Seattle," Burdette supplied.

Son of a bitch!

"Your neck of the woods," Lynch said.

"I'm from Spokane."

"Oh. Right." Lynch rubbed his tiny beard with one finger as he studied the top sheet of a stack of papers.

Burdette was equally distracted, her eyes on the window again.

So much for their concern about the new girl, Trent thought.

"Anyway," Lynch went on, "I've added her to your pod." He slid the faxed documents across the wide expanse of his desk. "Here're her records. Check out the questionnaire."

"Classic," Burdette muttered.

"When is she due to arrive?"

"Within the hour."

"Today?" Trent tried to keep the concern from his voice.

"She's on her way. Last report was that the plane was just north of Eugene."

Trent kept his face impassive, but inside he was fighting a full-blown panic. If she was one and the same Shay Stillman—and it sounded as if she was—then she was Jules's half sister and a holy terror. The age was right, the attitude was toxic, and she was coming from the Seattle area. It all added up to trouble for Trent. Big trouble. "You sure my pod's the best?"

"Why not?" Lynch frowned. For all his outward talk of open discussions and being respectful of others' opinions, Tobias Lynch was about as bending as an oak tree. The reverend didn't like being opposed. In Trent's short time here at the academy, he'd learned that much. Though Lynch saw himself as a kind, judicious, fair-minded leader who guided with a steady but thoughtful hand, in truth, the guy considered himself the only person capable of making the "right" decision. His word was etched in stone.

Still, Trent had to fight this one; he couldn't be in close proximity to Jules's sister. It was just too damned dangerous. He picked his words carefully. "Sometimes a troubled girl needs a strong female leader, someone who can relate to what she's going through."

Lynch disagreed. "Not this one—female dominated, confused about father figures." He smiled. "Perfect for you."

Burdette added, "Both Rhonda's and my groups are full, and we've always had mixed-gender pods. It's no big deal. Until we can hire another teacher and leader, we all have to pull our weight—more than our weight, actually. If there's a problem, you know that any of the girls can talk to us individually, and there are female counseling sessions." As she looked at him over her shoulder, tiny lines emerged between her eyebrows. "Do you have a problem with taking on this one?"

Oh, yeah, a major problem. "Not at all," he lied, and hoped to hell he sounded convincing. "Just talking aloud, wondering what's best for her."

"Good." The reverend seemed relieved. "We always put the students' needs first. Since you're in line for the next new student, she'll be in your group." He was nodding to himself, silently congratulating himself on a job well done. "Should be interesting."

More than interesting. He noted that the tiny lines of suspicion on Burdette's forehead hadn't disappeared. There was stress here at the school, more than anyone let on. Being down a teacher was just one of the problems.

Lynch forced a smile and rose to his feet, signifying that the meeting was over.

Trent couldn't wait to leave. He needed time to think

about how he was going to handle Shay. Would she recognize his name? They'd never met face-to-face, but there was a damned good chance that Jules had mentioned him.

And not with fondness.

Nope. Their breakup had been anything but amicable.

Great.

Just. Damned. Great!

Shaylee Stillman was a complication he didn't need. He left the building and half-jogged to the gym, where his office was nestled on the far side of the locker rooms. He tossed Shaylee's file onto the desk and flipped it open, and sure enough, Jules's little sister stared up at him from a photo. He suspected it was a candid shot; the girl's eyes glimmered with rebellion, anger, and mistrust.

With one eye on the clock, he skimmed through the file, all the while knowing that Shaylee Stillman could blow his cover and damned well ruin everything.

Clicking on the computer's mouse at her desk, Jules half-listened to the radio while she searched online for information about Blue Rock Academy. Ever since Edie had announced she was shipping Shaylee down to Oregon, Jules had been consumed by the desire to learn everything she could about the school.

Then she heard the commercial. Between songs on the radio came a sincere woman's voice, a woman at the end of her rope. "I didn't know what to do," she lamented. "I was out of options. My daughter was getting into trouble with the law, with drugs, with the wrong crowd, and she wouldn't listen to me. Her attitude was affecting my marriage and my other children. I thought I had nowhere to turn, but then I learned about Blue Rock Academy, a forward-thinking school that knows how to deal with troubled teens."

Jules stopped surfing the Net and listened as the testimonial continued. The mother's voice was stronger now. "So I enrolled my daughter at Blue Rock Academy. Ten months later, she returned with a new attitude, great grades, and a healthy lifestyle. She's now an honor student on her way to college." There was just so much pride in the woman's voice. "Thanks to the caring, intelligent staff members at Blue Rock Academy, I got my daughter back."

A younger, bright voice chimed in, "And I got my family back. Thanks, Mom. Dad. I love you guys!"

Really?

No way.

Disbelieving, Jules stared at the computer as a serious, deep-timbered announcer gave some information about the institution, including the Web site and phone number. "If your teen is troubled, call Blue Rock Academy. It's a phone call that could save your marriage, and your child's life."

"Oh, give me a break," Jules said, rolling back her desk chair as music resumed. There was something about the radio spot that felt false, a facade. She thought of Shay, probably already touching down on the campus of the academy tucked into the southern Oregon wilderness.

What was it about the place that bothered her? Why couldn't she just accept it as the haven for at-risk teens it was touted to be?

She turned back to her keyboard and clicked on a link to the school's Web site. On Blue Rock Academy's home page, she viewed pictures of cedar and stone buildings flanking the shores of a pristine lake—Lake Superstition, said the caption. Teens smiled as they canoed through the sapphire water. A large church dominated the landscape. Its windows rose to the high peak of a sharp roofline, and the framework of those glass walls was supported by beams in the shape of a magnificent, three-storied cross. Snow-laden mountains rimmed the campus, their spires sparkling in sunlight.

In a montage of photographs, groups of laughing teenagers were photographed doing a variety of activities: astride horses on wilderness trails, navigating challenging white-water rapids in rafts, pitching tents near glowing fires, or strumming guitars at sing-alongs under the stars. In the winter shots, some students snowshoed while others skied cross-country.

Blue Rock appeared a veritable Eden.

Of course, there were serious shots of earnest teachers leaning over students' shoulders as they sat in front of computers. Other pictures of teens avidly studying test tubes and peering into microscopes. Still others were seated in a large carpeted pit in front of a massive stone fireplace. The students cradled open books, camaraderie evident among the good-looking, clean-cut kids. Bibles were in evidence in several of the shots, and not one tattoo or pierced body part or colorful Mohawk was seen. No, sir.

Everyone in the pictures was model-beautiful, teachers, students and aides alike. There was a politically correct mix of Asian, Hispanic, and African American students and staff.

Most of the photos could have been published to advertise a resort rather than a school. The buildings were new and clean, the grounds well kept, the entire campus surrounded by pristine forest. Jules half expected to see a couple of Bambis and Thumpers peering curiously from the woods.

She clicked to the preapproval questionnaire and quickly skimmed some of the questions and answered them aloud as she thought of her sister.

Yes, Shay was angry.

Yes, she disrupted the family.

Hell, yes, she'd threatened a family member, more times than Jules would care to count.

Yep to Shay being in trouble with the law as well as using drugs and alcohol.

Shay had admitted as much. Had she made statements about suicide?

Only to get Edie's goat.

All in all, there were thirty questions, some general, some specific, all, when applied to Shay, answered with a big yes.

Maybe she shouldn't be so jaded. Maybe Blue Rock was on the up-and-up. Maybe the counselors there would get through to Shay.

"I hope so," Jules said to Diablo as the cat trotted into the room and hopped up to her lap. "But I just don't believe it."

CHAPTER 4

Trent watched the seaplane descend.

Engines roaring, the aircraft landed noisily. It bounced over the roiling water of Lake Superstition, then motored over to the dock. Steely dark clouds reflected in the shifting water as the pilot, Kirk Spurrier, cut the engine and climbed out of the cabin. With the help of an eager student who'd been summoned by Reverend Lynch, Spurrier tied the plane to the cleats at the end of the dock. Once the plane was secured, Spurrier ducked back inside and Blue Rock Academy's newest student emerged.

The muscles in the back of Trent's neck tightened.

Sure enough, Shaylee Stillman, Jules's younger half sister, was Blue Rock's new student.

Bad luck all the way around.

Trent hoped Shay didn't recognize him. If she did, he was counting on her to keep her mouth shut until he had a chance to speak with her alone.

What a damned small world, he thought as he stood with seven of his colleagues on the beach that rimmed the lake. In matching Windbreakers emblazoned with the Blue Rock

Academy logo, they were an impressive group: Reverend Lynch was in the lead, with Dr. Burdette a step behind him. Dr. Tyeesha Williams, the women's counselor with a doctorate in psychology, stood with her arms folded, blinking against the wind. Rhonda Hammersley, dean of academics, spoke quietly with Wade Taggert, a psychology teacher, and Jacob McAllister, a youth minister. At the end of the line, Jordan Ayres, the school's nurse and medical authority, waited to greet the newest student.

She didn't keep them waiting.

Shay emerged from the plane with her attitude firmly in place. Smaller and thinner than he remembered Jules ever being, Shay wore a gray sweatshirt and tight jeans. Her hair, a dull, fake black, was mussed and shaggy, falling over big owlish eyes rimmed in thick, dark pencil. Several braided cords encircled one of her wrists, and she wore flip-flops despite the frigid temperatures. Black nail polish on her toes matched the chipped color on her fingernails.

Trent had the feeling that her I-don't-give-a-damn, rebellious look actually took a lot of work to achieve.

Hauling her backpack over one shoulder, she eyed the group of authority figures waiting for her, and, if possible, her white complexion paled. Still her mouth was set, pale lips determined. It was obvious she would rather be any other place on earth than here.

Trent didn't blame her. His own gut clenched as Lynch stepped forward. This was the moment of truth.

"Welcome to Blue Rock Academy, Shaylee," Lynch said, hand extended.

She didn't respond, just stared at his outstretched fingers with indifference.

Lynch didn't miss a beat. "This is Mr. Trent. He's in charge of the students in your group, or pod, as we call them."

"Pod?" she repeated, her eyes even rounder. "Really? Like whales? Maybe I'll get lucky and end up with the orcas."

Trent ignored the sarcasm. "Hi, Shaylee." He thought, for just a second, she narrowed her eyes at him. Or maybe he was being paranoid.

Lynch motioned to the woman at his side. "This is Dr. Burdette, the dean of women here. She'll be your counselor."

"Welcome to Blue Rock," Burdette said, and Shaylee rolled her eyes.

While Spurrier unloaded a small suitcase and a bedroll, other introductions were made hastily to Wade Taggert and Jordan Ayres. Whereas Taggert was tall and lean with a perpetually worried expression, Nurse Ayres was a force to be reckoned with. At nearly six feet, she looked as if she could've once been a part of the German Decathlon Olympic team. Short blond hair, startling blue eyes, and a muscular frame. Determination fairly radiated from her.

Lynch herded everyone along the dock, toward the cluster of buildings rimming the shore. "Come on inside and we'll get you registered and settled in."

"Settled in?" she repeated. "You're kidding, right? I'm *not* settling in."

No one argued. Her reaction was expected. Typical. The staff had heard it hundreds of times.

Shaylee eyed the cedar, stone, and glass buildings that resembled a resort more than the locked-down institution it was. Trent followed her gaze and caught a few students looking through the windows as they tried to get a glimpse of their newest peer.

"You're in the girls' dorm," Burdette said. "But before you're allowed into your room, you have to go through an evaluation and detox at the clinic."

"Detox?" Shay repeated, her cool mask cracking. "Why? You think I'm hopped up on something? That I'm using? Oh, for God's sake, I'm *not* on drugs! *Any* drugs! Unless you count the caffeine in Red Bull! What did Edie tell you?" She threw an arm up angrily, fingers grasping the air. "What? That I'm a crack addict? On meth?!"

McAllister stepped forward and offered the frightened girl a smile. "You'll be okay," he said.

"Oh, yeah? How do you know?" She wasn't buying it.

"I have an in with the man upstairs," McAllister joked. "He told me."

Shay rolled her eyes as McAllister backed off, while Dr. Williams and Nurse Ayres led the way to the clinic at the back of the admin building.

"This way," Burdette said calmly. She gestured toward the group, giving Shaylee no choice.

Frightened, Shaylee glanced over her shoulder, her gaze chasing after the youth minister, but he was already crossing the campus.

She found Trent staring at her. There was fear in her angry glare and something more—a question. Her forehead puckered and her eyes narrowed as she sized him up.

Trent guessed she wasn't sure if she knew him or not.

"So you would describe your experience as positive?" Jules asked as she sat on the edge of her cousin's couch in Analise's postwar cottage in West Seattle.

"Of course." Analise wiped her daughter's face with a warm rag. "Yeah, it was great."

Chloe, all of twenty-four months, was protesting from her high chair, shaking her head and shouting, "No! No, Mommy!"

"Blue Rock really turned me around." To her daughter, "Okay, okay, you're clean now."

"Down!" Chloe ordered.

"You got it." Analise released the toddler who, with a mistrustful eye cast in Jules's direction, waddled over to their chunky bulldog. A moment later, the dog took off like a shot, nails scrabbling on the hardwood floor, rather than being subjected to the two-year-old's curiosity and pokes and prods.

"I just have a bad feeling about the place," Jules admitted.

"Why?"

"All this secrecy and isolation. I can't even call her."

"That's to keep everyone focused. But she'll be able to call you once a week or so, depending. As soon as she finishes the introductory phase."

"When is that over?"

"It's different for everyone, but Shaylee will be able to reach you in a week or so, and then you'll see that you're all worried for nothing. Hey, would you like a cup of coffee or tea? I think I've even got an ancient Diet Dr Pepper in the fridge."

"I'm good." But she followed Analise into the small kitchen, where a glass pot was warming in a coffee machine. Outside, the day was gray, twilight gathering through the bare branches of a lilac bush just starting to bud. Rain spattered the glass, the chill of March seeping through the panes that had been installed sometime in the late forties.

"Why are you so freaked out about Shaylee?" Analise poured herself a cup of coffee, then held up the pot as a second offering. "Sure?"

"Uh-uh." Jules shook her head. "It just feels wrong."

"Why?" Analise asked, then lifted a hand to cut off any

explanation. "Look, despite the advertisements to the contrary, Blue Rock is far from perfect, but I was a mess when my dad shipped me down there. Into weed and boys and even dabbling in meth and E. My grades were in the toilet, so I ended up at the academy, alone, with no friends. It was hell at first. I won't kid you. There's definitely a pecking order there, just like at any school, but I had to fend for myself and . . . and I made it." She was heading back to the living room where Chloe had the dog cornered behind the couch.

"Doggy!" she cried happily, apple cheeks red, her tiny teeth showing as she grinned. "Bent-ley!"

"Give Bentley a break. Come here, you." Analise set her cup down, then swept her child off her feet and lifted her into the air until Chloe giggled uproariously. The dog hurried from the back of the couch and lay in his bed, where he peered worriedly at the child. "They're best of friends, really. Bentley adores Chloe, here, but he's eleven and not as spry as he used to be." She sat in the rocker, daughter in her lap. Leaving her coffee untouched, Analise grabbed a blanket and a favorite book of Bible stories. She kept talking with Jules while she flipped through the pages. Surprisingly, Chloe didn't scramble to get down.

"That's where you found God, right? At Blue Rock."

"It was the turning point, yeah."

"Is it optional? The religion thing?"

"Uh-uh. It's required. And not just God-as-any-supreme-power, but the real Christian God."

"Well, real if you're a Christian."

"You can knock it if you want, Jules, but for a lot of kids, *moi* included, we find God and listen to his word and teachings. It helps us with our addictions. With our lives."

And it was true, Jules guessed. Analise seemed happy, at peace.

"Substituting one obsession with another. Trading drugs for religion."

"Only the truly jaded would look at it that way." For the first time, she seemed a bit nervous. Agitated. "Look, Jules, I don't know why you're so dead set against the school. It helped me; it might just be the answer for Shaylee. Lord knows she needs it. As I did. I might be dead now if I hadn't gone to Blue Rock, and I never would have found Eli."

"Baby Jesus!" Chloe cried, pointing at a page.

"That's right; there's Jesus," Analise said.

"So do you know anything about Lauren Conway?"

"Who's she?"

"The girl who disappeared a couple of months ago. From Blue Rock. I've searched the Internet and all the newspapers. As far as I can see, she's never been located."

Analise's smooth forehead puckered. "I don't know anything about it. While I was there, a boy tried to leave, but one of the TAs convinced him to return."

"TAs?"

"They're like grad students who stay on and work at the academy. Each 'pod'—that's the group you're assigned to when you enroll—has a teacher for a leader and at least one TA to help the teacher and kind of, oh, you know, connect with the members of the pod. Bridge the generation gap, I guess. TAs are people you can talk to, people who have endured what you've gone through and are a lot closer to your age, so it's easier to confide in them."

"And they report back to the teachers."

"No . . . not really. Eli was my TA and look, I ended up marrying him." She smiled proudly.

Jules didn't share her enthusiasm. In her opinion, Eli Blackwood was a sanctimonious know-it-all who seemed to quietly control his wife. There was something snaky about him, something that bothered her. Analise seemed to adore him; he seemed to quietly bully her. But she wasn't going to bring it up now. Instead she asked, "Wasn't getting involved with your TA frowned upon?"

"Oh, yeah. We didn't actually get together, well, not openly, until I got back here and he finished his term."

"How did that go over?"

For the first time, Analise looked away and appeared more than a little anxious. "Not great," she admitted. "Since Eli was, well, 'chosen,' for lack of a better word, to be one of the special TAs, it was expected that he'd stay there until he was out of college."

"Special?"

Analise shrugged. "Students showing the most promise, I guess, are pulled into an elite program. The school has an online program they worked out with a local university in southern Oregon. Eli actually fulfilled that requirement, but he decided to do his graduate work here, in Seattle." She bit at the corner of her mouth. "That didn't fly so well," she admitted. She was fingering Chloe's gold curls as she spoke, but she seemed far away, in another world.

Jules asked, "So what were the ramifications of his leaving?"

"Nothing. We got married as soon as I finished nursing school, and we adopted Bentley from a bulldog rescue shelter, bought this house, and had Chloe."

"And you have nothing bad to say about Blue Rock."

"Nothing," she said quickly. Almost too quickly. Then she added, "Do you think maybe you're tilting at windmills, Jules? I know you and Shaylee were tight when she was growing up, but you've both changed, and Shay might not be the sweet little innocent she once was."

"I don't think she's innocent or naive," Jules admitted. "Not anymore. But it's tough out there for kids."

"I know, and you've always felt that it was kind of you and her against the world."

"Sometimes."

"And, come on, you and I aren't that old; it was tough for us, too."

Chloe squirmed on Analise's lap. "Uh-oh, someone's getting sleepy," she said, and though the kid looked anything but ready to go down for a nap, Jules got the hint.

"I'd better go anyway." She stood, then grabbed her coat and scarf from the hall tree by the front door. "Oh, wait. Was there a teacher named Maris Howell on the staff when you were there?"

Analise was hauling Chloe to her feet. "I don't think so."

"She taught social studies, I think."

Analise shook her head. "I was there eight years ago, Jules, but the name isn't familiar. Why?"

"She was let go. Some scandal with a student."

"Really?" Analise pulled a face. "Was she fired?"

"I'm not sure."

"Teachers and students—taboo at Blue Rock."

"Taboo anywhere, but sometimes it still happens."

Jules slung her scarf around her neck. "I thought you might know what happened, who the student was."

But her cousin was shaking her head as she opened the door. "Neither Eli nor I have had much contact with the academy since he left."

"Bye-bye!" Chloe said, as if to push Jules out of the house.

"Bye, Chloe. Analise, thanks."

"Not at all. See ya later." Analise stood on the porch for a few seconds as Jules hurried down the steps to her car, parked on the street. Her Volvo was wedged between a Chevy Suburban and a minivan, but she was able to pull away. In her rearview mirror, she watched as Analise carried her daughter inside.

Analise was a fan of Blue Rock. And truthfully, the academy had really helped turn Analise around. Jules should have felt better about the school after her visit with her cousin.

Instead she felt worse.

CHAPTER 5

Shaylee glanced around the living area where she was being held. Scattered comfy chairs, a few tables and lamps, even an aquarium. And all securely locked.

Only a moron would stay here, she thought, and one thing was certain: According to every IQ test she'd ever taken, Shaylee Stillman was no moron.

She didn't know how that was possible, considering her gene pool, but, hey, she was fine having more brain power than her mother and father put together. Edie and Max—could anyone have a worse combination for parents? Shay didn't think so. Well, maybe Jules. Rip Delaney had been the lowest of the low. Shay had spent way too much time thinking of her loser parents as she bided her time in the initiation area of this screwed-up school. One day and night at Blue Rock Academy was all she needed to know that the place was a friggin' nightmare. No cell phones, no e-mail, no television except as a group for four hours on Sunday. No iPods, no Facebook, no MySpace. No friggin' destressors. She wasn't supposed to contact anyone, couldn't, in fact, even make a phone call unless it was an emergency and supervised by one of the brainwashed staff of this neo-concentration camp.

She'd been given a schedule of her classes and the names of her instructors—something to look forward to. Getting physical in phys ed with hottie Cooper Trent. This G.I. Joe Hispanic guy named DeMarco taught chemistry and trig. Perky Dean Hammersley for the cheerful side of English and world history. Psycho Wade Taggert taught psychology, and, of course, she'd be studying all the reasons she'd be going to hell with the oh-so-reverend Lynch. Too bad she didn't get to have sessions with the youth minister she'd met on the dock. He was interesting, his blue eyes warm, his smile sincere. But of course not. Her counseling sessions were scheduled with Reverend Lynch and Dr. Tyeesha Williams, who was hardly a soul sister. And something called *outdoor activities* with a drill sergeant named Flannagan. Oh, yeah, *Mister* Flannagan. All in all, her days were filled with classes, then chores with her "pod."

It was all such a disaster. What had Edie been thinking?

Shay ran fingers through her hair and knew she had to get out. Find a way to go home. It wouldn't be easy, though. This place really was the edge of the earth.

If you didn't get out by seaplane, the only other route was a narrow, winding one-lane access road that sliced through the mountains. She'd seen it from the air on the day she arrived. A steep road that hugged the cliffs. Scary but passable. Of course, there was a massive gate and guard-house about a mile or so from the heart of the campus. Good luck getting past that. But still, if there was a way for supplies and the staff to enter, surely someone with any brains at all could escape.

Pacing across the wood floor, Shay scratched absently at her arm where a bandage covered the needle marks from the tests. Nurse Ayres had punctured her and filled a syringe big enough for an elephant.

But Ayres was just doing her job. Carrying out the judge's orders and buying Edie her freedom. Anger burned hot at the thought of Edie's decision to send Shay here. Shay was supposed to have had a choice in the matter—the judge had allowed them to pick an institution—but Edie had taken Shay's rights away.

Leave it to Edie to jump at the first school she found, just to get rid of the problem. Pain knifed through Shaylee's heart, the same old pain of rejection that she'd always felt with her parents. Max and Edie Stillman, a short-lived union that had ended in divorce and her father walking away. The hard part was, he'd never really looked back. As if he never thought about Shay. She always said she hated him, but deep down, she wished he'd show he cared. Just once. That was all.

Maybe his rejection of his only daughter was because of Edie. Shay hoped so. You didn't need a degree in psychology to realize that Edie was a mess. The fact that she had married Rip Delaney twice was proof enough that she always had to have a man in her life—no matter what.

Again, Shay thought of her father. Rich, affable, quick with a joke, and "as handsome as the devil," Edie had often said, though Shay now suspected her mother's fascination with Max was probably due to the Stillman Timber fortune that Shay had heard about all of her life.

Shay pushed Max's image from her head and blinked against the heat behind her eyelids.

She couldn't let herself give in to tears.

No matter how miserable she was.

Her throat was thick, though, and she had to clear it.

Her family. If you could call it that. She only hoped she never, ever turned out like her mother.

She's been married only three times, two times to the same guy. Is that so bad?

Maybe not, but if Edie had her way, dear old Mom would be adding Grant Sykes, her young golf-enthusiast fiancé to the list. Again, she felt that pain deep inside, and again, she tamped it down and hoped some stupid hidden camera didn't see her wipe her eye carefully so that she didn't ruin her mascara.

Shaylee had just about had it with the small living room behind the locked doors of the nurse's station, and she knew her only hope to get out of the place was Jules. Her half sister would see this school for the sham it was—little more than a prison. First, though, she had to find a way to communicate with the outside world, to contact Jules, and that would prove tricky.

And then there was Dawg. His real name was Jensen Wolfe, and they'd been dating a while. At twenty-three, he was just so much more mature than boys her age. And now, because of that stunt they'd pulled of robbing a convenience store, he was on his way to prison. She wished she could talk to him. Dawg might be the only person on earth who really "got" her.

She sighed and sat on the arm of a small love seat. Less than twenty-four hours here and she was still stuck in quasi-isolation pending her drug tests, which would come back—gasp!—clean. She'd only smoked a little weed this year and had had one hit of cocaine, but that was months ago. Despite what Mommie Dearest thought, Shaylee wasn't a druggie. But then, Edie wasn't the sharpest tool in the shed. You had only to look at her choice in men to figure that one out.

But she couldn't worry too much about her mother right now. Not while she was in this hellhole. Detox, Burdette had called it. Ha!

Where would they send her next? Her counselor, the tall,

black woman named Dr. Williams, had said she would be moved to semipermanent quarters with a roommate so that she could "socialize" and "feel comfortable" before being allocated a private room of her own. Translation: until we can trust you and don't have to have someone spy on you twenty-four/seven. It was lame, lame, lame. To the max.

But she was stuck, at least for the moment, and the roommate, a girl she was introduced to at dinner, seemed about as interesting as one of those foreign films Edie was forever going on about. The roommate's name was Nona Vickers, from somewhere in the Midwest.

Shaylee hadn't gotten to talk to Nona yet, but already she suspected it was going to be a stiff, uncomfortable pairing. She'd been the new kid in school enough times to know what the drill was. At first she'd be isolated, looked upon with curiosity, and a few do-gooders might try to take her under their wings, but she would have to prove herself if she wanted to have any real friends, which she wasn't sure she did. Not yet. Not until she'd scoped out this place.

If she was here that long.

She crossed her fingers. Hopefully, somehow, someway, Jules would get her out of here.

Shay got to her feet and yanked the bandage from her inner elbow, where that moose of a nurse had stuck in the syringe to take her blood. Walking around the perimeter of the room, she ignored the reading material scattered about. All that God stuff and self-help garbage that she had no use for had been fanned neatly on the coffee table.

Under a shelf holding books like *The Answer* or *With Jesus in My Life* an aquarium bubbled, its brightly colored fish swimming around fake rocks and grass. Shay had spent an hour watching a shy, tiny eel hide in its little cave near a clump of coral. Every once in a while, it would dare to stick its head out, only to retract it quickly.

"I know how you feel," she'd confided to the timid fish.

At the sound of her own voice, she looked over her shoulder, certain someone was watching her, listening to her, noting her every move. From the moment she'd stepped onto the seaplane, she'd felt hidden eyes observing her, eyes that were as malicious as they were curious.

Paranoid, Shay, you're sounding paranoid. Any more of this and you'll end up like Jules, fractured to the point of emotional paralysis. Oh, yeah, like you could ever live with her! Jules is a wreck.

And yet Shay knew, deep down, her sister was her only chance of salvation. The one person who would help her get out of this creepy institution.

No one she'd met here was going to be much help. The first person she'd come into contact with was the pilot, Spurrier. Around forty or so, with dark hair and eyes that forever scanned the horizon as he'd steered the plane. At least he'd been quiet, his headset in place, only making a little bit of small talk every now and then. From their brief conversation, she'd found out that he not only flew the seaplane but also was part of the teaching staff.

She'd also seen some of what she thought of as "the inmates" looking out windows as she'd passed through the campus. Then there were two guys in the clinic, around twenty years old, who had special privileges. One was Asian, the other Hispanic, and they seemed to work here. Through the glass wall separating the reception area from her "lockdown," she'd observed the Asian guy working at a laptop, all business. His friend wasn't quite as focused on work. He'd caught her eye a couple of times, even smiled slightly, but that look was quickly hidden whenever anyone else showed up. Nurse Ayres, the bruiser, was definitely the authority of the clinic.

Shay picked at the tiny scab on her arm and wondered if

she could enlist the Hispanic boy's help. He'd definitely been interested in her. She needed an ally, and he was the first potential friend she'd seen.

She considered the others she'd met here, mostly members of the staff, but cast them all aside until she remembered the guy who was going to be her "pod" leader, whatever that meant.

His hair had been a little longer than that of the others, his skin dark from hours in the sun, though it was still frickin' winter. There was something about him that bothered her. What was his name?

Mister Trent?

Huh. The name Trent rang distant bells, but she was pretty certain she'd never met him. She would've remembered, because he was kind of hot.

Who was he? She sat on the arm of the couch, crossed her legs, and absently drummed her fingers on her thigh.

He was kind of sexy in that rugged, cowboy way so many women went for, but he was old. Definitely over thirty. Maybe thirty-four or thirty-five.

And then the youth minister. McAllister. She wondered where he was . . . if she'd see him soon. There was something about him that was at odds with his clerical collar. . . .

The glass door to the living area opened suddenly.

Startled, Shay looked up to find Dr. Williams and her big smile sweeping through. With her was Nona, a pale girl with big doe-eyes and stringy brown hair that was so thin, the top of her ears parted the strands.

"Hi, Shaylee," Dr. Williams said in that syrupy friendly voice Shay already hated. "I thought you and Nona could get to know each other a little better."

"Hi," Nona said with one of those ingratiating grins Shaylee detested.

Shay didn't respond.

"Nona's from Indianapolis," Williams continued.

Big whoop.

"She's been here, what, ten months?"

Ten months? No way! Shaylee shriveled inside. She would die if she had to stay here that long.

"Almost eleven," Nona corrected, fingering a slim silver cross dangling from a chain around her neck. Though she had a shy way of turning her head, there was something in her expression at odds with her meekness, a glint in her eyes that bespoke of a strong person beneath the church-mouse facade.

Shay asked, "So why are you still with a roommate? I thought everyone here moved up to a private room. Isn't that what you told me?" Shay turned her gaze from Nona to their counselor.

"Nona's considering staying on as a TA after she graduates," Dr. Williams said proudly.

"Why?" Shay could not imagine staying on campus one millisecond more than required.

"Opportunity," Nona answered. "Here at Blue Rock Academy, I've found incredible opportunities, a new way of life. A new faith in God and country." Her mouth curved into a smile, as if she'd been filled with the divine truth.

Or brainwashed.

Shay felt nauseated. Nona was a puppet performing a well-rehearsed act. The whole place was surreal, so out of touch. "You don't want to go home?"

"Not until I'm ready."

"I'm ready now," Shay announced, and Dr. Williams laughed a little, a knowing laugh that bugged Shay. The conversation went on, meaningless small talk meant to draw Shay out of her shell and make her feel all warm and fuzzy and secure. Fat chance!

Dr. Williams beamed. "We have to run now, Shaylee, but tomorrow, I think you'll be in your own room with Nona!"

"Wow. Like a slumber party? From the fifties? And I didn't pack my poodle skirt!"

"Ouch," Dr. Williams said, but laughed.

Nona the Pious stared at her. Was it Shay's imagination or did Nona work hard to swallow a smile?

Shay watched them leave and felt as if something was out of whack with Nona Vickers. Though her new roommate didn't show a hint of resistance to the program here, Shaylee sensed there was more to the girl than silver crosses and meek obedience.

Beneath her malleable, mousy exterior, Nona Vickers might just be a force to be reckoned with.

From his hiding spot in the loft of the chapel, the Leader waited for another glimpse of her, the new girl, another student added to the ever-growing enrollment of Blue Rock Academy. Watching from the soaring window of the chapel, he stared into the windows of the nurse's station, hoping to see her.

His intrigue with her was insane. He should have learned his lesson with the last one and knew deep down that women were his weakness. From the time he'd hit puberty, his fascination with the opposite sex had become his blessing as well as his curse.

Lauren Conway had tempted him.

In a quicksilver memory, he saw her: tall, athletic girl, a beautiful girl just on the threshold of womanhood, or so he'd thought. But, of course, he'd been wrong. Her treachery had been so disguised in innocence he'd come to trust her.

And that had been his fatal flaw.

So why now would he even be tempted by this new one?

Getting close to her would be a mistake.

He knew it.

The problems with Lauren were testament to his lapse in judgment. Her beauty had bewitched him, and he'd let down his guard. Smart and sassy, she'd caught his eye from the first second he'd seen her. With eyes as blue and seductive as a mountain lake, sculpted cheekbones, and a small pouty mouth that promised the most intimate of favors, she'd been a seductress. Her hair was brown, thick and dark, almost black, as it had waved past her shoulders.

He'd been a fool.

Forgotten his mission while entranced.

He couldn't make the same mistake twice. Besides, he had enough disciples, didn't he? Another would make the group too large, would increase the chance of exposure.

Or would it? Wasn't there always room for another, more beautiful and seductive initiate?

He caught a glimpse of her in the window. Pacing. Like a caged animal.

God, she was beautiful in that rebellious way he found so intriguing. Sharp-witted, with an IQ rumored to be near genius, Shaylee Stillman had fire and looks, a lethal combination. Her eyes smoldered and narrowed, and she wasn't going to accept her forced admission into the academy easily. Maybe she was ripe for the plucking; he could offer her a position that would elevate her status, give her some special privileges over time. She was young; she could be molded.

He rubbed the tips of his fingers together in anticipation and felt a rush of heat on his skin, the warmth of his blood flowing through his veins. His cock twitched, coming to life at the thought of her soft, supple, willing body.

He imagined himself leaning on his elbows, staring down into her wide hazel eyes. They would be round with anticipation. Hungry with need. She'd moan as he touched her hair and kissed the crook of her neck. Her sinuous body would respond, her back curving upward as his knees parted hers. She would be his willing servant, offering up any sexual favors he requested.

Shaylee. Even the sound of her name caused a rush of blood in his ears.

Don't do this . . . you can't. Remember Lauren? Didn't you learn your lesson? What if she denies you? Throws your advances back in your face? Worse yet, what if she talks? Lauren made it easy, but this one, what if she calls you out?

Who would believe her?

He watched Shaylee walk to the fish tank, and all of his concerns faded.

In his mind's eye, he saw her naked body lying beneath him, her full, firm breasts waiting to be touched, to be kissed, to be teased with his teeth. . . .

His knees went weak at the thought. He would have her; he would. And she would want him, her desire fanning his. He wouldn't make the same mistake he had with Lauren. And he'd make room for her to be a part of his secret disciples, to warm his bed.

His throat was dry, his erection hard. He reached for his fly, just to take the edge off until he could be with her. His fingers grazed his zipper.

Creeeaaak.

A door opened in the rooms below.

Damn!

He couldn't be found!

Not like this.

His cock shriveled instantly.

With one final glance through the window, he saw her toss her dark hair over her shoulders before looking upward, through the glass, as if she knew instinctively that he was watching her every move.

His breath was lost in his lungs for just a second before he convinced himself she would never be able to see him in the shadows. Then, without making a sound, he stole down the back staircase and wondered how long it would be before his erotic fantasy became reality.

CHAPTER 6

"Hey, Jules!" Eli's voice boomed through her cell phone as she pulled into her parking spot at the condo. "Analise said you were here. Sorry I missed you."

"No big deal." She pulled on the emergency brake and cut the engine, wondering why Eli was calling. This was the first time ever. He'd always been friendly enough at family gatherings, but he'd never taken the initiative and called her or dropped by. "What's up?" She juggled her purse and phone as she climbed out of the car and locked it. Rain was drizzling from the gray sky and running down her neck.

"You wanted some info on Blue Rock, right? Because Shay's enrolled?"

"Uh-huh."

"So . . . why all the questions?"

"I wanted the inside scoop on the place."

"Analise said you weren't crazy about Shay being sent there."

She snorted as she dashed to her front door. "I'm not."

"Why?"

"I thought there might be other options." She bent down

to pick up a flyer someone had left on her stoop. It was a wet advertisement for carpet cleaning.

"The way I hear it, Shay needs some straightening out."

"Or guidance?" she offered. There was something about Eli, an air of superiority that had always gotten under Jules's skin.

"That's what I meant. A little tough love. There wasn't a lot of it in your family, what with Max leaving your mom and all that trouble with Rip."

"Trouble?" she repeated, irritated.

"Yeah—"

"He was murdered, Eli," she reminded him tightly as she straightened and jabbed her key into the lock. "Killed by an intruder." She felt a rush in her ears, a thunder that always precluded the same vision of Rip lying on the floor, staring, gasping up at her, his lips crimson as she stood over him. . . .

Had the knife been in her hands?

Or was that image only in the nightmare that haunted her?

"Hey, don't take this the wrong way. I'm just saying Shaylee grew up without a real strong father figure."

"And Blue Rock Academy will supply one?" She twisted the knob.

"It will give her a good, solid base. Rules to live by. Counselors to talk to. Strong Christians who will show her how to live her life to her full potential."

"You sound just like some of those testimonials I read online."

The door was stuck again. Swollen with the rain. With an effort, she shouldered it open and made a mental note to talk to the handyman for the condos.

"Blue Rock is a great place. Perfect for Shaylee."

Tossing the soggy brochure onto a table near the door, she said, "Glad to know. Thanks."

"So . . . then . . . we're good, right?"

"Haven't we always been, Eli?"

"Yeah, but . . . Well, Analise was afraid that you might go poking around—"

"Poking around?"

"Making trouble."

"There's that word again: *trouble*. For whom?" Where the hell was this going? "You?"

"Analise told you that we didn't leave the school on the best of terms, right? But it was our idea. No fault of anyone at Blue Rock Academy."

"I don't understand," she said, leaning against the wall, feeling the hem of her coat dripping onto the rug near the door. Diablo stretched on the top of the couch, claws extended, back legs stiff. "What're you getting at, Eli? Are you saying that someone from the academy might give you some kind of trouble? Is that it?" She couldn't believe this. "And you're afraid that you wouldn't be invited to the class reunion?" The cat hopped off the couch and hurried over to greet her. Jules bent down and scratched his chin with her free hand.

"That's *not* it!"

"Then what is it, Eli? Huh? Why the hell are you so rattled about me discussing the academy with your wife—"

"It's not that," he cut in. "I just don't think you know Shay. That girl is trouble, Jules. She needs this kind of structure. She needs to learn respect."

"I think I know my own sister, and don't turn this around to Shay," Jules argued. "What is it that you're afraid of?"

"Nothing. We're . . . I'm not afraid of anything."

She didn't buy it. The silence was thick. She straightened as Diablo did figure eights between her wet feet.

"Look, Jules. I was just concerned. Do whatever it is you have to do, okay? But don't say I didn't warn you."

"Of what, Eli?"

He hesitated, then his voice lowered to a whisper. "Of whatever it is you find, Jules. You might not like it." With that, he hung up with a loud and final click.

"Bastard," she hissed as she hung up. The cat was looking up at her expectantly. "Not you, okay?" She slid out of her coat and hung it on a peg near the door, allowing the water to drip onto the tile of the entryway. "Let's get you some dinner, eh?" she said, heading into the kitchen.

What was it about Blue Rock Academy that made everyone so jumpy? For all their praises of the institution, Analise and Eli were scared. But of what? They were both well out of it.

"It gets stranger and stranger," she said to the cat as she found a half-full can of cat food and forked some into his dish. Diablo ignored the bowl and trotted after her to the living area, where she switched on the gas fire and flopped onto the couch. She needed time to think. To figure out what to do.

Everyone was telling her to let Shay be, to leave her alone. The consensus was that her half sister was getting what she deserved and would come out of the experience all the better. But Jules, ever protective of Shay, just didn't see it that way. Others, those who weren't close to her, and even Edie, didn't see the inner child within Shay. Sure, she was acting out, but she was scared of going to the academy. What seventeen-year-old wouldn't be?

But then the world hadn't had the glimpses into Shaylee's life that Jules had. She remembered Edie returning from the hospital with the fussy, wide-eyed bundle. From the minute Shay had entered Jules's life, she'd been fascinated by the cooing baby, then the curious toddler who had puppy-dogged after her. She and Shay had been together throughout the rocky marriages, rough divorces, and awkward reconciliations of their parents.

Jules had been close to her father. Rip had adored her.

Not so with Max Stillman. Deep down, Jules had felt a little guilty that her dad had treated her like a princess and, really, done a poor job of taking Shaylee under his paternal wing as well. Not that Shay would allow him to.

While Jules had been in grade school, Shaylee had waited by the window, looking for her older sister to return home; then, chubby toddler legs flying, she'd run out the door when the bus's squealing brakes had heralded Jules's arrival.

"Sissy!" she'd cry happily, her little face aglow.

"Shh!" Jules had been embarrassed as she'd taken Shay's little hand in hers. "Call me Jules."

"Sissy!" Shay always had the last word, and she had happily run away, giggling so that Jules would give chase.

Later, when Shaylee had entered school, they'd taken the bus together, even sitting across the aisle from each other, as Jules knew it wasn't cool to share a seat with a kid seven years younger, especially her sister.

In junior high, they'd grown farther apart, and then in high school Jules didn't have much time to spend with her kid sister; she had better things to do. Especially when she discovered boys and ultimately Cooper Trent.

Whoa! She put on the mental brakes.

She didn't want to dredge up memories of the one man who'd gotten a good hard look at her soul.

Diablo curled into a ball on her lap and began to purr. Jules stroked his smooth fur and stared at the flickering flames. Her headache had receded a bit, thank God, and after a few minutes and no answers, she ended up in the kitchen again, where she made herself her favorite budget dinner: ramen noodles with frozen vegetables heated in the microwave.

"Yummy," she told Diablo. "Just like in college. Consider yourself lucky to have Tasty Tuna Treats."

The cat didn't seem impressed and followed Jules, carrying her bowl, upstairs to her desk and computer. She wasn't much of an investigator, but there had to be a way to learn more. Analise and Eli hadn't been much help, but she had faith in the Internet. If there was dirt on the academy, she'd find it.

And then what?

"One step at a time," she reminded herself as she set her bowl on her desk and ignored the steaming broth. "One step at a time."

So this was the room. Shay's new "home."

Twin beds separated by a wide aisle, two minuscule closets, two L-shaped desks that met in the middle of the room beneath the single window. Neat. Clean. Sleek. And with all the personality of a jail cell.

Home sweet home, Shay thought sarcastically, but really her room was just about what she'd expected. So far, Blue Rock Academy, or BRA as she'd begun to think of it, wasn't disappointing.

"This is your bed," Dr. Williams said, pointing to the empty twin. Nona's bed was neatly made, a navy blue quilt stretched with military precision over her thin mattress. A cross was mounted over her bed, a well-worn stuffed pink koala propped on the pillow. Otherwise there was no wall decor. "You can put your things in your closet, and Nona can answer most of the questions you have, but if there's anything else you need, I'm available day and night." She offered her fake-o brilliant smile before giving a few last instructions about wake-up calls, prayer meetings, and class schedules. Then with a wave she said, "I'll see you at morning service," and left the two girls alone.

Once the door closed, Shay tossed her backpack onto the bed. "Is she a workout or what?"

"Actually, she's great," Nona said, sticking to the company line. "Talented and smart."

"If you say so."

"All of the professors are dedicated. Really into helping kids."

Shay just stared at her. Was this girl for real?

Nona walked to her desk chair and offered her sickly smile, then glanced to the top of the door. Shay followed her gaze to what appeared to be a sprinkler set into the ceiling. Or was it? She glanced at Nona, who casually lifted one eyebrow. "I've been here since last May, and I can tell you that I was really messed up. Drugs. A boyfriend who, now I see, was abusive. I hated it here for the first few weeks. But after a while . . ." She shrugged. "I lost my bad attitude and saw this academy for what it really is."

"And what's that?"

"Salvation. I was on the wrong path. I would have been dead before I was twenty-five if I hadn't come here."

Shay wasn't buying it. She glanced up at the cross.

"You come here with Christ or is he a new friend?"

Nona winced. "I took Jesus into my heart once I realized how much I needed him, how he was there for me, how through his love, I was brought here."

"Uh-huh."

"I don't expect you to believe me. Not now."

Not ever!

"But you will. Don't you believe in God?"

"Of course I do," Shay said without a trace of sarcasm. "But in my world, God isn't judgmental. Isn't the old fire-and-brimstone, vengeful and wrathful God you know."

She expected Nona to shake her head, but it seemed she'd hit a nerve. "I know. Reverend Lynch is . . ."

"Old school."

"Traditional. But Reverend McAllister, who everybody calls 'Father Jake,' he's a lot more today. More relevant, I think. Spent time working in the inner city. You'll like him. Everyone does."

"*Father* Jake? Is he a priest?" Shay asked, thinking about the freckled, sandy-haired clergyman with the dimple in his chin and a smile in his eyes.

"No," she said, smiling again, "but he did try it for a while, went to seminary school, I think, and discovered that he liked girls, so he switched."

"Just like that?" Shay said.

"Who knows." Nona shrugged. "Ask him. I'm sure he'd tell you."

Shay said, "Anything here you don't like? Anything not"—she made air quotes with her fingers—"perfect?"

"Sure. I hate Mrs. Pruitt's tomato casserole. It's gross."

"Mrs. Pruitt?"

"She's the head cook; everyone has to work with her, just like the other jobs around the school. We spend a week in the kitchen, a week in the barn, a week cleaning the dorms, and a week working outside around the grounds every month."

"Free labor," Shay said.

"It teaches us respect and responsibility and—"

"Yeah, yeah, I heard the drill already. The brainwashing starts from day one."

Again Nona glanced to the sprinkler head. A warning? Or just a nervous habit? "So everything here is awesome?" Shay asked, and walked over to the desk. "Every little thing? I don't think so." She pushed herself onto the desktop and sat, her legs dangling as she looked at Nona. "I mean, other than the cook's casserole?"

Nona shook her head, but there was hesitation in her gaze, a tiny bit of fear. As she glanced out the window, she shielded her hand with her body, blocking it from the doorway, then opened her fist where a short message was inked onto her palm: *Camera & mic recording.*

"Most of the food is okay," Nona said, cutting Shay off before she could say a word, "but some of the chores are disgusting, like cleaning out the horse barn." She exaggerated a shiver, but once more she glanced back to the doorway, then rolled her chair to the closet where she found a jar of hand cream on a shelf. With the aid of a tissue, she quickly erased the warning from her hand. When she glanced at her roommate again, her gaze said it all: *Be careful. This place is dangerous*. "Even mucking out the stalls is okay once you get used to it."

"Don't think I ever will."

"It just takes time." She tossed the smudged tissue into a trash can tucked under her desk. "Look, I'd better get to my homework. We've got a paper due in English tomorrow, and I need to study for a chemistry test."

Shay nodded and tried not to stare at the phony sprinkler head. Wasn't it against the law to have a camera and listening device set up without a resident's consent?

She considered the myriad of papers she'd signed in the past few days, some of which she hadn't bothered, in her agitated state, to read. Then there was everything Edie had put her John Hancock on while being so damned hell-bent on sending Shay down here. Dear old Mom . . . Edie would have signed anything to get her out of Seattle so she could be with that worm of a fiancé. It was all just sick.

Suddenly claustrophobic, Shay felt as if the walls were closing in on her. She could barely breathe. When she looked over her shoulder to the sprinkler head, her blood turned to ice. Who was on the other side of the small camera? Who was watching her every move? Listening to anything she had to say? She wasn't one to scare easily, but there was something off about this place, something evil.

Stop it! That's paranoid!

But as she glanced out the window to the darkening

night, the towering hills seemed dark and forbidding, barriers to the rest of the world. She felt small and helpless.

Don't go there! That kind of thinking is just what they want to break you down.

As Nona snapped on her desk lamp and opened a thick chemistry textbook, Shay continued to stare out the window. She saw her own pale image shimmering in the reflection and Nona's as she looked up and met Shay's gaze in the glass.

Her eyes were a warning.

A warning that underlined Shay's desperation. She had to find a way out of here and fast.

CHAPTER 7

"What do you mean, you haven't heard from her?" Jules demanded as she sat at her desk, cell phone jammed to her ear.

"That's the way it works, Julia. You know that," Edie explained, her voice tight. "There's to be no contact for two weeks. Then just a short phone call. If she wants."

"But she's your daughter. Underage. You should get a report."

"I can talk to the counselors at any time, just not your sister."

"That's nuts."

"It's their policy."

"Well, it's crap. Shay's just a kid." But it was basically the same thing Analise had told her.

"We've been through this. Blue Rock Academy knows what it's doing. I trust them."

"But I want to talk to her."

"You can write a letter in care of the school."

"A letter? What is this, the Dark Ages?" Jules shoved back her chair and paced from one end of her small office to the other. "What about cell phones or e-mail or Face-book?"

"Not allowed."

"Of course. The place is starting to sound Draconian, Mom."

"And you're starting to sound like a drama queen! The very thing you accuse me of. Just slow down, give the school a chance. And, please, don't go bothering Analise anymore."

"What?"

"Eli called me, you know," Edie said.

Jules's heart sank.

"Of course he did." What a pansy, running to Aunt Edie and tattling. Like a three-year-old.

"You're stirring up trouble," Edie charged.

"I'm looking for answers."

"Maybe you should worry more about your life and where it's not going rather than obsess about your sister."

"What's that supposed to mean?"

"You tell me, Julia. You're the one who's divorced and not working. Right?"

"Maybe I learned from the best," she said quickly, and heard her mother gasp. Edie's track record in marriage was always a forbidden subject.

"Look, I didn't mean that the way it sounded, but you've got to quit attacking me, Mom. I just care about Shay."

"Well, believe it or not, that makes two of us. Oh . . . I've got another call. It's Grant. Gotta run. Bye." She clicked off.

Jules let out a sound of frustration. Shay had been in southern Oregon for three days, and Jules was even more convinced that Blue Rock Academy wasn't the right place for her sister. Sure, Shay had a bad attitude and needed *some*thing to shock her out of her sullen, rebellious ways.

But a boarding school where one girl had gone missing a few months back and a teacher had been let go because of sexual misconduct with a minor or something akin to it?

Having read every article she could find on the Internet about Blue Rock, Jules had learned that it was founded in 1975 and was not associated with any other school. Blue Rock had been named for the color of some of the rocks in the caves nearby. It was an independent institution, was fully accredited, and—if the quotes from satisfied teens and parents printed all over its Web site were true—was "a godsend." The testimonials were effusive. If Jules were to believe Blue Rock's own advertising, then Shaylee had been sent to her utter salvation somewhere deep in the Siskiyou Mountains.

Jules still wasn't buying it. Everything seemed too slick, too perfect.

She read the academy's mission statement, a letter from Reverend Lynch, and a few glowing testimonials. It seemed so scripted.

Her eyes glazed over as she clicked on the faculty page. It seemed like a small list, and she didn't recognize any names. Maris Howell's name was conspicuously absent. A note at the bottom of the page stated that the Web site was being updated.

"I'll bet," she said aloud. "Have to update the Web site so it doesn't show one damned flaw." Everything about the school seemed too good to be true.

"Just your suspicious nature," she said, echoing her ex-husband's accusations when he swore on his mother's life he wasn't having an affair. But then Sebastian Farentino was nothing if not a liar who would call up any excuse to save his own pathetic hide. She'd learned that soon enough. And as for the accusation of him having an affair? How long had it taken him to marry wife number two? Five or six weeks from the minute the divorce papers were signed.

"Fast work, Sebastian," she said under her breath, though, in truth, most of her anger and hurt had dissipated in the past three years.

The worst part of the whole betrayal was that his new wife, Peri, had once been Jules's best friend. The whole scene reeked. "So cliché," she told herself as she clicked off the school's homepage and checked the status of her ever-shrinking bank account. From there, she clicked on the Web site she'd been using to find a job. She scoured the listings, read over the few responses she'd received—all negative—and convinced herself that as an out-of-work third-year teacher, she would never find a teaching job. For now she would have to stick with waiting tables.

Discouraged, she pushed back her chair and headed down to the kitchen, where she placed a pot of tea on one of the two working burners. She had rented this two-story condo near the university after moving back from Portland. She'd envisioned herself going back to school, then maybe someday buying a place of her own. So far it hadn't happened.

When she'd taught at Bateman High School, her debilitating headaches had caused her to miss a lot of class time. Those headaches were the direct result of sleepless nights, nights of suffering from recurring nightmares. "Insanity are us," she said sarcastically as the teakettle shrilled, and she reached for a cup.

She found a tea bag she'd used that morning, stuck it into a cup, then filled the cup with steaming water. What if her waitressing job dried up? High-end restaurants were closing daily in Seattle and its suburbs.

Her dwindling bank account was testament to the fact that she needed another source of income. She'd considered taking in a roommate, a situation she'd heretofore avoided. But things had changed. Since there was no chance of Shaylee moving in, Jules could cram her desk into her bedroom and rent out the other two to college students. Yeah, it would cut into her privacy, but at least she'd have help with the rent and utilities. Maybe then she wouldn't worry about losing her home.

She thought fleetingly of the house she'd shared with Sebastian, a sleek contemporary set on a wooded hillside with a view of Mount Hood. A lumber broker, Sebastian still lived in that house in the west hills of Portland, now with Peri and their one-year-old daughter.

Surprisingly, she didn't miss him. In truth, she probably missed her friendship with Peri more. As for the house, it had always been "his," all glass and wood and high ceilings and flat-screen TVs. Bought with his money, decorated according to his taste. No, she didn't miss Sebastian Farentino, nor did her mother's disappointment that she'd let such a good catch "slip through her fingers" really bother Jules. What really killed her was that Peri, a friend since the sixth grade, had traded their relationship for one with Sebastian.

That had been the sharpest knife in her back.

But then, Peri had known about Jules and Cooper Trent.

And that fateful knowledge had apparently given her carte blanche when it came to flirting with her best friend's husband.

Lost in thought, Jules carried the tea back up to her office. If it hadn't been Peri, some other woman would have convinced Sebastian to stray. He was a player and would be until he was six feet under. Jules was better off without him.

You never really loved him; come on, Jules, admit it.

She didn't want to go there. She'd *thought* she'd loved him at the time she married him, had *intended* for the marriage to be her first and last.

She kicked her chair into position in front of the desk.

"What does it matter now?" she asked herself, sipping her tea. It was all water under the bridge.

Back at her keyboard, she clicked on the Web site for Blue Rock Academy again and looked at the pictures of the campus. Boy, were those "at-risk" kids having fun with their guitars, canoes, horses, hiking boots, and fishing poles. She scrolled through photos of apple-cheeked students, lodgelike buildings, a sparkling mountain lake, and snow-glazed mountains that spired to a clear blue sky.

What a crock.

She clicked through the different areas of the Web site and came to a menu with options that included "Employment Opportunities." With another touch of her finger, she found that the school was looking for a kitchen worker, a maintenance man, and a teacher.

She was a teacher. An unemployed one, at that. One with a teaching certificate good in Oregon. Not believing for a second that she'd actually try for a job at the school, she printed out the application. Why not?

The last thing Shay needs is you messing things up. She's there for a reason, under judge's orders, and she's made it crystal clear that she doesn't want you anywhere near her.

Jules scanned the questions. Did she still have a résumé? She tapped a finger on her desk. The school wouldn't hire her if they knew she was related to one of their students.

So she'd have to lie.

And not just one lie, but a lot of them.

She'd have to use her last address in Oregon, which would work out, as she hadn't yet bothered to change her driver's license to Washington. That would be good. More distance between herself and Shay, whose place of residence was Seattle.

She'd also have to lie to Edie, but that wouldn't be too

tough; Jules had lots of practice from her own years as a re-bellious teen.

What would she accomplish if she did get hired? So she would see Shay every day, so what?

You would be able to see for yourself that the academy is on the up-and-up; that all those testimonials are, in fact, true. If not, you could help get Shay released, right? Find out the dirt—if there is any—and spring your sister. On top of that, be pragmatic: There's a bona fide teaching job at a private school. Even if you don't stay for more than a year, it will look good on your résumé that you're still working in your field as an educator.

Well, not if it was found out that she'd lied, and Shay would make certain of that.

What the hell had she been thinking?

That she could kidnap her sister?

That she could expose the school for being a sham just because it all looked too perfect?

"Stupid." She took the pages she'd printed out and, one by one, flipped them into the trash.

"What did you mean about the microphone and camera?" Shay asked her roommate the next day after class. She'd already suffered through a prayer service, four classes, a pathetic group meeting after lunch, and now was scheduled, with the rest of the losers in her "pod," to do the assigned chores. Today they were cleaning out the horse stalls. Tomorrow they'd repaint some of the canoes. The next day back to cleaning the stalls and maybe fixing and polishing saddles and bridles and the rest of the tack. The fun just didn't stop here at Blue Rock.

"In the sprinkler heads," Nona whispered as they lagged behind the rest of the group walking briskly toward the barns. No one else could hear, not even smarmy Kaci Donahue, the leggy brunette TA who seemed to be everywhere, or her sometimes friend Drew Prescott, a mean-faced dude who Shay guessed had some kind of inferiority complex from the snide comments he made about nearly everyone.

"Who's watching?" Shay asked.

Nona shrugged. "Who knows? Lynch? Burdette? Some pervert?" She slid Shaylee a knowing look.

"Someone in particular?" Shay asked.

Nona hesitated. "More than one."

"Who?"

"I, um, I dunno," she said quickly, as if wishing she'd held her tongue. Shaylee wasn't letting her off that easy.

"You do."

She didn't respond as ten pairs of boots crunched in the snow and a flock of geese flew overhead, a wavering, uneven V heading north through steely clouds.

Shaylee tried again. "So we're always being spied on?"

"Nah. Not always." Her voice was low, hard to hear over the rush of the wind. "There are some places that aren't covered."

"And you know where they are?" Shay guessed.

"Oh, yeah!" Nona nodded her head, obviously proud of herself. "But you still have to be careful," she whispered; then her lips twitched. "It makes it really hard to have a boyfriend."

"You have one? Here?" Shay was dumbfounded. She hadn't seen Nona with a guy at all, and there were no pictures on her desk, no mention of him. In fact, up until now, Nona had only mentioned an abusive ex-boyfriend back at home. Though it wasn't allowed, Shaylee had seen some of the kids flirting with each other. But Nona? "Who?" she asked.

Nona just grinned like a cat who'd eaten a canary, and Shay ran through a list of potential candidates. Ethan Slade? He was cute as hell. Or Eric Rolfe, the kid with the military cut and sharp blue eyes. Maybe Tim Takasumi or Roberto Ortega, the two boys who had access to the nurses' station. Shay had learned their names, along with everyone else's, during the lame introduction ceremony.

"So who is it?" she urged as they walked together.

"Guess."

"I'm not guessing! I don't even know anybody yet."

Nona giggled, then looked up and her smile faded. "Shh! Not now!"

One of the boys in the group, the tall blond kid named Zach, looked over his shoulder, and Nona ran like a frightened deer to catch up with her friends Maeve and Nell, two girls who hadn't yet given Shay anything but icy stares.

Shay was left to bring up the rear. It figured. Not that she gave a damn. Shay watched Nona hurrying away, as if glad to be rid of her. Was Nona lying, bragging about some fantasy boyfriend? Like those little kids who have an imaginary friend, maybe Nona had an imaginary boyfriend. Or maybe it was Zach.

Shay decided it was a waste of time speculating.

Who cared?

But suddenly Shay was more interested. As Nona ran, something started to fall out of her pocket—something dark and slim, like a cell phone or an iPod or a camera, all of which were strictly forbidden. Nona nearly stumbled, then shoved the object deep in her pocket, glancing at Shay.

Their eyes locked, Nona silently pleading with Shay to keep quiet.

Shay held her stare. No way would she rat her roommate out, but she wanted to know what was in the pocket and how Nona had pulled it off.

Nona caught up with her friends, and she was suddenly giggling again with Maeve Mancuso and Nell Cousineau. Maeve, the reddish blonde from Rhode Island, was a bit of a basket case, as far as Shay could tell, a deep-seated romantic. She'd heard the girl was a cutter, that she had the scars on her wrists to prove it. And Nell, a sixteen-year-old from a small town in Marin County, north of San Francisco somewhere, seemed to have been blessed with a sharp wit and an extremely wicked tongue that Shay found intriguing.

Now, Nona glanced over her shoulder and, casting a quick, almost naughty look over her shoulder at Shay, smiled slyly. So maybe the story about the boyfriend had all been a joke. Tell a big lie to the new girl, suck her in. Shay had been on the losing end of that prank more than once.

But this, today with Nona, wasn't quite the same. And then there was the phone—that's what she thought it was, some kind of cell phone, here in the middle of nowhere. Would it even work?

There was something going on with her roommate, but she couldn't put her finger on it.

What she did know was that she was an outsider.

In a school of outsiders.

Big surprise.

It was friggin' cold, and Shay would have liked a smoke. She hadn't had a cigarette since leaving Seattle, and though she really didn't think she was hooked, it would have helped ease her nerves. When she'd been admitted to this hell, the big nurse had informed her that all tobacco products, along with alcohol and all recreational drugs, were banned.

Seriously?

Hadn't Shay smelled a whiff of tobacco smoke on a couple of the teachers? Dr. Burdette and Mr. DeMarco came to mind, as did some of the TAs. Shay was pretty damned sure that Roberto Ortega and Missy Albright, the tall, platinum blonde, had both reeked of tobacco just yesterday after returning to the chemistry lab after doing something with the rest of a group of the teacher's aides.

She couldn't believe that no one on campus had a pack of cigs on them. Come on! There had to be eighty teenagers as students and over twenty members of the staff. Surely some of them smoked.

Well, maybe this was her time to quit. At seventeen. When she'd barely picked up the habit.

Gusting, the wind rattled through the surrounding trees and churned up the surface of Lake Superstition. She really had landed at the end of the world.

At the head of their group was her team leader, the rugged-looking guy with the familiar name. There was just something about Mr. Trent that got under her skin. He was twenty feet ahead, near the front of the line. His leather jacket, lined in sheepskin, was stretched over his broad shoulders, and his jeans were faded, even frayed a bit. Leather gloves and well-worn cowboy boots . . .

Why the hell did she think he was familiar?

"Okay, everyone, listen up." He turned, his breath fogging in the air. "You all know the drill, except for Shay, so someone buddy up with her. You, Ethan, show her the ropes." He pointed to a dark-haired boy who, without a word, walked over and put his hand on her shoulder.

"Ethan Slade," he said, though she recalled his name from the embarrassing introduction ceremony that had happened earlier this morning. She remembered Ethan Slade because he was just so damned hot. With near-black hair and a quick grin, he was friendly enough, though he probably wouldn't give up many secrets about the place. His skin appeared permanently bronzed, as if he had some Hispanic blood in him, and Shay was drawn to the whole dark-side vibe to the guy. Add to that the interlocking tattoos on his left arm. Very cool.

A few of the students turned to look at her. Most seemed curious, but two of the girls pissed her off. Tiny Maeve with her perpetual pout, and her BFF Nell, the athletic one. Those two threw her glares that could cut through steel, as if she'd dissed them.

Get a life, she thought before turning away from their harsh gazes and completely ignoring them.

Which was likely to piss them off even more.

Exactly the point.

Shay wasn't looking for a new set of friends anyway. If these girls in her pod didn't like her, fine. They'd made that perfectly clear the moment Reverend Lynch had introduced Shay to the campus.

Directly after the first prayer in the predawn hours at the chapel, Lynch had announced, "Everyone, we have a new student with us. Shaylee, come on up here." To her utter mortification, she'd been escorted by Dr. Williams to a spot in front of the podium, where she'd faced the congregation of staff members and students. "This is Shaylee Stillman, from Seattle. I expect you all to introduce yourselves at breakfast and do everything you can to make her feel at home." Reverend Lynch had placed a fatherly hand on her shoulder, then led them in a final prayer that included thanking God for sending Shaylee to Blue Rock Academy. As the group had whispered "Amen" in unison, Reverend Lynch had squeezed her shoulder a bit, and she'd looked at him sharply, only to see him smile benevolently at her.

Now, though, it was Ethan who had his hand on her shoulder. A nice feeling.

"I'm Shaylee," she said to Ethan, and was a little mesmerized by the gleam of his white teeth.

He was muscular and compact, like a wrestler. "I guess I should say 'welcome.'"

"Don't. I've heard it enough."

"I bet." He stifled a grin, and his dark gaze glinted, as if he understood. Maybe things wouldn't be so bad around here after all.

From the corner of her eye, she noticed Maeve, Nell, and Nona whispering and sending her dark looks.

Shay was used to it.

She'd been the "new girl" before. She knew the drill. They'd eventually warm up, or not. But if she was buddied up with Ethan, she'd become public enemy number one, the new bitch in town. That might not be so smart.

"Okay, grab your equipment inside the door, and let's make this stable shine," Mr. Trent said. "Last week, Dr. Burdette's team got special mention for how clean it was after her team cleaned it. I think we should show them up."

Shay stepped closer to Ethan, murmuring, "Oh, don't tell me they give out gold stars for shoveling horse poop."

Ethan didn't bother hiding his smile, that heart-stopping flash of white against his dark skin. "Better than that. Credits. Toward using the Internet or phones."

"They allow you to communicate with the outside world? Wow." She widened her eyes as if awestruck. "Finally. A reason to live."

Is that how Nona had her cell phone? If so, then why was she hiding it?

"Sure," he said as they walked inside the building that smelled of horses, dung, and oiled leather. He grabbed a pitchfork from the wall and tossed it to her, tines pointed upward. She caught the fork on the fly.

He added, "You just have to play by the rules."

"I have a little trouble with that."

"You won't," he predicted, and there was an edge to his voice that she hadn't noticed before. And the glint in his eyes hardened a bit.

Yeah, sure. The guy talks nice for a second and you think he's into you?

Stabbing the pitchfork into a clump of hay, Shay wondered if there was a reason their team leader had picked Ethan to show her around. Maybe it was Ethan's job to watch her a little more closely. He would probably report back to the pod leader or maybe Reverend Lynch.

He was probably a spy, faking that he liked her.

Shaylee shivered inside and didn't let it show. But she suddenly felt more alone than she ever had in her life.

From the reading loft in the education hall, the Leader watched Trent's group head to the stables.

Shaylee Stillman brought up the rear, and he couldn't help but notice how she walked, the way her hips moved slightly. Her forced bravado—but he believed that her mask was slipping. All that sassy, dark attitude would give way.

It always did.

Except for Lauren, right? She'd managed to keep her sarcastic tongue and glint of daring in her eyes, no matter how she was put to the test.

A classic mistake.

And stupid.

A student of history, he'd known better than to trust any female completely. Cleopatra, Mata Hari, Wallis Simpson. Prime examples of seductresses who changed the course of the world. And yet, he had let down his guard.

Not that she'd been any woman, Lauren Conway. Oh, no.

And he'd fallen for her allure.

Completely.

Madly.

Stupidly.

He'd allowed her into his inner circle.

For all the wrong reasons.

Mainly because of his ego.

And his dick. His damned dick.

Just like all those screw-ups in history who'd lost wars, given up thrones, changed the course of civilization: all for a woman.

She was Eve with the apple.

Delilah with her shears.

Jezebel with her idolatry and witchcraft!

He'd been forced to deal with her, and it had been painful, a reminder from God that despite his intelligence and his honed body, he was, in fact, only human.

And he couldn't make the same mistake again.

Not with Shaylee Stillman.

Not with any woman.

CHAPTER 8

Everything was distorted.

Colors off. Light shifting. A headache thundering behind her eyes.

Jules blinked. She was home . . . right?

In the house she shared with her parents and sister?

Or was she?

Things were a little off, the rooms so dark.

In the den, the French doors were ajar. Wind whispered through the crack, causing the gauzy curtain to flutter. It moved like a dancer, gracefully gliding over the wood floor, its hem stained a vibrant ragged scarlet as the sheer fabric swept over a dark, congealing pool of blood.

Jules's heart pounded in fear.

She felt the knife in her hand, saw drops of blood sliding down the blade to fall and splatter around his body. . . .

Brrriiinggg!

Jules awoke with a start. Her cell phone was jangling, her computer screen dark, as it had gone into hibernation mode. She must've dozed off searching for hits on the academy, Lauren Conway, and Maris Howell. Snagging the phone before it rang again, she said, "Hello?" and tried not to sound too groggy.

"Hey, it's me." Erin Crosby had been Jules's friend since college. Although they had been education majors together, Erin had found that being a teacher wasn't her thing. These days, she sold cell phones and service plans. Erin had also made the fateful mistake of introducing Jules to Cooper Trent. Somehow Jules had forgiven her for that one.

"Thought you might want to go out for drinks tonight. Or sushi," Erin suggested. "You're not working, are you?"

"Got the night off, so just let me check my social calendar," Jules said dryly. Her lack of social life since her divorce was well known, and Erin had been privy to the entire Peri/Sebastian debacle. Once upon a time, they'd all been friends.

"How about six-thirty at Oki's?"

Jules glanced at the digital clock on the monitor of her computer. Four twenty-seven. Just enough time for a run, a shower, and, if the gods of Seattle traffic were on her side, the trip into downtown during rush hour. "I'll be there."

"Good. Gerri's already on board. Gotta run. I'm getting the evil eye from my manager." She hung up.

Jules wasted no time. She stripped off her jeans and sweatshirt, threw on her running gear, and was on the jogging path just as the streetlamps began to glow. Dusk came early this time of year, and with the oppressive cloud cover, gloom had settled deep into the city. A heavy mist seeped through her clothes. Though the temperature was somewhere near fifty degrees, Jules broke a sweat within five minutes. Cars and trucks sped past, tires humming through puddles, engines rumbling, windows fogging. Jules slogged through the puddles and around pedestrians and dogs, tackling the hill that marked the midpoint of her circuit. She was breathing hard, and her waterproof running shoes were leaking. *Just another couple of miles,* she told herself as she angled toward the university, through the skeletal trees shivering as the rain thickened.

She thought of her father and the night he died, how she'd found him in the den, the weapon that had taken his life lying in a thick red puddle beside him. Or had it been still in his body? Her dreams were confusing and sometimes her memory jumbled. Some people had speculated that Edie had killed him, the man she'd married twice. Others suspected that nineteen-year-old Jules, who had picked up the knife when she found him, had used it to stab him viciously. Even Shay had been a suspect, but the footprints outside the house and the open door that appeared forced had convinced the police that the intruder who had stolen Rip Delaney's wallet had also taken his life.

The intruder had never been found, and though the cloud of suspicion over the family had slowly lifted, life had never been the same.

No amount of counseling sessions or antianxiety pills had stopped the horror of the recurring dream that robbed Jules of sleep, creating debilitating migraines that had often forced her to spend days in bed.

Even after five damned years.

So she ran.

Every day.

Rain or shine.

Taking a respite only if the snow was ankle-deep or the sleet so severe that ice froze solid on the streets.

It kept the demons at bay and helped with her sleep.

She rounded a final corner and sprinted downhill. From this vantage point, she usually caught glimpses of the lake, but not today. It was too foggy, too dark.

By the time she reached her doorstep, she was breathing hard and covered in sweat. She leaned down to stroke Diablo, then flew through the shower, washed her hair, and twisted it into a topknot. Slapping on some lipstick, she called it good.

On her way out the door, she grabbed her cell phone and tucked it into her pocket. Through some searching on the Internet, she'd found Lauren Conway's parents' number in Phoenix. She'd phoned twice, left a short message each time, but so far her calls hadn't been returned. She figured if anyone had the dirt on Blue Rock, it would be the Conways. Either they'd want to discuss their missing daughter, or they'd shut Jules down, but she had to give it a try. She hadn't been so lucky at tracking down Maris Howell.

Yet.

She locked the door behind her, then headed for the Volvo. The car's windows began to fog as she wended her way toward the restaurant near Pike Place Market. When she turned onto Pine Street, she lucked out and spotted an older Cadillac vacating a spot. She nosed into a parking space, glad that she'd have to pay for just a few hours' street parking. That would save her some money. Flipping up the hood of her jacket, she jogged the four blocks to the restaurant.

The sushi bar was all metal and glass, dim lights, and aquariums filled with strange-looking fish that Jules hoped weren't on the menu. Most of the small tables were occupied, and muted conversation hummed. Erin was waiting, waving frantically from a booth in the back. Gerri sat across from her.

"We've already ordered," Erin announced as Jules slid into the booth beside her. "Edamame appetizer, California rolls, shrimp tempura."

"And dragon rolls," Gerri added.

"Sounds good."

"We just didn't know what you wanted to drink."

"With this?" she asked. "Saki. No question." She scoffed

at Erin's glass of white wine and Gerri's martini. They'd known each other since their freshman year in college, all ending up in the same dorm, none pledging a sorority, all education majors. Gerri was from Washington, D.C., while Erin had grown up around Spokane. It was Erin who had first met Cooper Trent through her older brother, who trained horses.

They drank, ate, and laughed. Erin's sarcastic sense of humor helped chase away the sense of foreboding that had been with Jules ever since she'd first found out that Edie and a judge were sending Shay to Blue Rock. Eventually the conversation wound its way to the academy.

"What's going on with you? You look depressed," Erin said, dipping a slice of rainbow roll into mustard sauce. "Don't tell me it's Sebastian."

Jules frowned at the mention of her ex. "No."

"Of course not," Gerri said skeptically.

"I believe you." Erin eyed her friend as she bit into the slices of tuna and salmon. To Gerri she added, "You know Sebastian was just a rebound thing."

Gerri lifted a shoulder. "Rebound thing that turned into marriage."

Jules saw no reason to hide what was going on with her family, and she had drunk just enough saki to let down her defenses. "It's my sister," she said with a sigh. Then, while finishing the remainder of her meal, she launched into the story.

Gerri and Erin only broke in to ask a question or two, but for the most part, they were rapt, spellbound by Shay's problems, not particularly sure Jules was looking at the situation the way she should.

"So . . . I can't shake this really bad feeling about the whole thing. I think it's a big mistake," Jules admitted. "I hate the fact that there's no communication between the students and their families."

"All those rehab places are like that," Erin offered. "They have to cut off negative influences."

"But that's not me," Jules defended. "I support my sister."

"I know, but it's all part of the treatment."

"Maybe the doctors and teachers and psychologists at Black Rock—"

"*Blue* Rock."

"Okay, whatever. The people there are professionals. Has it ever occurred to you that they know what they're doing?" Gerri offered. "Shay was getting herself into trouble. It sounds to me like the judge was lenient, giving her another chance. Come on, Jules, you *know* she's got problems."

"We all got into trouble," Jules said. "We all experimented with drugs, alcohol, and sex."

"Just weed," Gerri clarified, "and nothing after college."

"Shaylee was arrested a couple of times, right?" Erin touched Jules's sleeve. "I know you worry about her, and I hate to agree with Gerri, but maybe this place is the best thing for her. You've got to quit mother-henning her; she's almost eighteen. Believe me, she can handle whatever that academy dishes out." She took a swallow of her wine and effectively changed the subject. "So, let's talk about you. How's the job hunting going?"

"Dismally."

"Sorry that I can't help you out. They're laying off teachers at my school," Gerri said. "I think I'll be okay, but the first-year teachers are really worried."

"The economy sucks," Erin agreed. "My company's cutting hours."

"There's a job opening at Blue Rock." Jules sipped her drink, letting it heat her from the inside out.

"Uh-oh. Don't tell me you're thinking of applying?" Erin smelled trouble.

"No, I don't think so," Jules said, though, in truth, the idea kept taunting her. "One of the teachers there was let go."

"Maris Howell, right?" Gerri asked thoughtfully. She wiped an imaginary spill from the black lacquer tabletop.

Jules was surprised. "How did you know?"

"I know her . . . well, kind of. We met at a seminar the first year I was teaching, and we kept up for a while, then lost touch. I saw her name in the paper a while back, and I tried to contact her, but no answer. The phone number I had wasn't hers any longer and same with her e-mail."

"You know what happened?"

"Uh-uh." Gerri frowned into her empty martini glass. "Not really. But I was surprised about the scandal. It doesn't make sense. Maris seemed like a real straight arrow. Into her church. Big on her family. She did lose her fiancé in Afghanistan, though, and that could have changed things. She could have flipped."

"Innocent until proven guilty," Erin reminded them all as she twisted her wineglass in her fingers and turned to Jules.

"So you're down because of Shay?" Gerri said skeptically. "It's not a man thing?"

"Of course not!" Jules shook her head. "Let's not go there."

Gerri tapped a fingernail on the lacquer table. "If you ask me, she never got over Cooper."

"What!" Jules said, nearly choking on a swallow of saki.

"The rodeo guy." Gerri wrinkled her nose. "He was sexy, but really, he rode Brahman bulls, for God's sake. What kind of a weird macho thing is that?"

"It's cool. Sexy. And there's big money in rodeo if you're good," Erin said.

"Yeah, well, there are other ways to earn a living." Gerri

pulled out the small plastic pick and sucked an olive into her mouth.

"You're just too urban to understand," Erin said. "The whole cowboy imagery and legend, the loner on his horse, is part of most females' fantasies."

"Not this girl," Gerri said.

Erin lifted a shoulder. "But it is for me, and maybe for Jules—"

"Hey, you don't have to talk about me as if I'm not here," Jules cut in. "And I am so done with cowboys. I'm through with anyone remotely associated with the rodeo."

"Uh-huh, sure. Once a cowboy groupie, always—"

"No way." Jules shook her head.

"If it's any consolation, I think Trent gave up the whole bull-riding thing, too." Erin twirled the stem of her wine-glass between her fingers.

Jules looked away, trying like crazy not to express interest when, the truth of the matter was, she still found Cooper Trent a little interesting, still a bit dangerous. There was something about him, a fearlessness that had intrigued her, but she'd tried, oh, God, she'd tried to forget him. To the point that she'd married someone else.

A mistake.

"So he's not a cowboy anymore. Bully for him." Gerri smiled at her own little joke as laughter erupted at one of the nearby tables, where two couples were huddled together, each trying to outtalk the others. "So what's Cooper moved on to? Calf roping? Pig wrestling?"

"Funny," Erin said, wrinkling her nose. "Last I heard, he finished some training and was hired as a deputy in Colorado somewhere. No, that's not right. It was Montana, I think. Some little town I never heard of . . . not Great Falls, but something very similar." She shrugged. "Grizzly Falls, maybe? Not that it matters."

"A cop? Trent's a cop?" Jules said, disbelieving.

"Or was . . . I'm not sure. I lost touch. I could ask my brother if you're interested."

"I'm not!" Jules was firm.

"Then I guess you haven't talked to him since the two of you broke up?"

"Not once."

"In five years?" Gerri was surprised. "Why not?"

"No reason." What she and Trent had shared was ancient history. So why was it that she still had dreams about him? Erotic dreams that left her breathless and sweating— that is, when she wasn't experiencing the recurring nightmare, that horrid, disturbing dream of her father's murder.

"She's moved on," Gerri said, but Erin didn't seem convinced.

Jules wasn't interested in rehashing her love life, so she turned the conversation around. "What about you two?"

Erin's eyes flashed, as if she'd been waiting for someone to ask. "You won't believe this, but I actually found someone online."

"Craigslist," Gerri offered.

Erin rolled her eyes. "Not quite."

"Close enough. His name is Franklin, and he's *all* she ever talks about," Gerri said, shaking her head. "I'm surprised it's taken so long to get to the subject."

Erin sighed. "Franklin is the best."

"Despite his name," Gerri teased.

"It's a great name." Erin wasn't about to hear one bad word about the new man in her life.

"So what about you, Gerri?" Jules persisted.

"Nothing. Just broke up with a guy I dated all of six weeks." She rolled her expressive eyes. "He definitely wasn't *the one*."

"I don't know if there is such a thing," Jules said, glad

the conversation had shifted away from the unsettling topic of Cooper Trent. "So, come on," she urged Erin, "tell me about Franklin."

The waitress paused at their table. "More of the same?" she asked, and they ordered another round.

"So . . . back to Franklin." Erin waxed poetic and went on about the new love of her life, a car salesman who was taking classes to become an accountant.

Gerri rolled her eyes, an unspoken B-O-R-I-N-G in her gaze, but Jules enjoyed the easy exchange among friends, catching up as they talked and laughed over the next two hours.

By the time she returned to her car, Jules felt better, more balanced. Luckily, she hadn't collected a parking ticket, though the meter had run out, and she drove home without incident.

"Things are looking up," she told herself as she locked her car and stepped through a puddle on her way to the front door.

Inside, she shook off her wet jacket and spent a few minutes playing with Diablo when she found his one-eyed catnip mouse under the couch. "Right where you left it," she admonished as he slunk off, carrying the shredded thing between his jaws.

"Fine, be that way," she kidded, then walked to the kitchen to check her messages.

There was only one. No caller ID.

"Jules," Shay's voice, a whisper, quivered on the recording. Jules froze, staring at the answering machine.

"Are you there?" Shay asked. "Jules? Oh, God, please pick up! It's Shay . . ."

Jules's heart was beating in her eardrums as she tried to hear Shay's soft, frightened voice.

"You have to get me out of here, Jules," Shay whispered frantically. "This place is horrible. But you can't call. I'm not supposed to be on the phone. Just please, *please* find a way to get me out of here! Uh-oh—"

The line went dead.

CHAPTER 9

Anxiously, trying not to make a sound, Shay clicked off the phone. Was it her imagination, or was someone on the other side of the door to this darkened office? It was supposed to be empty, but Shay had sneaked through a back way that didn't quite lock, the entrance used by cleaning staff.

One of the students, JoAnne Harris, the girl who was never far from her banjo, mandolin, or guitar, had clued her in. That JoAnne went by the name of Banjo was just plain lame. But at least, while they had sat near each other cleaning tack earlier today, Banjo had let it slip that there was a secret way to call out to the real world. If you could sneak into the admin building, you could get through with a special code that one of the students had found while cleaning Charla King's desk. That was how Shaylee had been able to reach Jules, who hopefully would find a way to spring her.

The codes changed monthly, Banjo had confided, but Charla King kept the list taped to the inside of a desk drawer that she sometimes forgot to lock.

So, even if Banjo's name was stupid, at least she was willing to give up a few secrets of this place.

Again, she thought she heard voices in the hallway.

Damn!

Wasn't that just her luck?

No one was supposed to be patrolling the halls of the administration building at this time of night. And if they found Shay here, what punishment would those dorky TAs dream up? So annoying, those überstudents who'd been brainwashed into believing they were superheroes or something. The TAs would act like she'd committed a major crime, just because she strayed from the rec hall next door.

Now the voices were louder. A man and a woman.

Shaylee shrunk into a dark corner, but bits of a heated argument seeped through the glass door with its blinds snapped shut.

"Let's not go there, okay? I get it. I should have known she was going to bolt. My mistake!" A high-pitched, girly voice hissed through the hallways. Shay had heard it before and knew in a heartbeat it belonged to Missy Albright, one of the TAs. Was she talking about Shay and the fact that she'd slipped away from the group that had congregated in the rec hall?

Damn!

She had to hide, and fast!

Noiselessly, she dropped to her knees and crawled around the corner of the desk, using it as a screen if anyone walked through the main doorway. Even so, she felt like a dead duck.

A male voice responded to Missy. He sounded angry, but Shay couldn't tell who it was or even what he was saying.

With a loud click, the door opened and the lights flipped on, offering wobbling illumination as the fluorescent tubes overhead flickered on.

Shay held her breath.

She couldn't be caught here!

"See? Nothing!" the male voice said. "No one's here."

"I swear—"

"Just calm down."

"Like I should have calmed down with Lauren?" Missy challenged.

Shay felt the blood rush through her head. They were talking about Lauren Conway, the girl who had disappeared one night. She'd already heard the rumors about her. No one knew if Lauren was dead or alive. Had she escaped? Had she met with some accident and died? The weirdest theory was that someone had killed her and she'd returned to haunt the school. Maeve Mancuso, a twit if ever there was one, was certain she'd seen Lauren's ghost lingering in the gazebo under a full moon.

"Don't patronize me, okay. It's not cool." Missy was really riled.

Shay squeezed her eyes shut and prayed the blond TA wouldn't step farther into the room.

"We should get back," the man said.

The lights clicked off.

Shay wasn't fooled. They hadn't left.

She waited.

A few seconds later, the door closed with a soft thud.

Still, she wondered if Missy, after winking to her companion, had stayed inside to flush Shay out. Shay didn't move. Slowly and silently, she counted out the seconds: *one thousand one, one thousand two,* until she'd clicked off a good five minutes. There was no sound in the room aside from the soft rush of air through the heat ducts and the wild hammering of her heart.

When she could stand the tension no longer, she peeked around the corner of the desk, and deciding Missy hadn't stayed behind in a ruse to catch her, Shay climbed to her feet.

Her pulse was jumping, her nerves as tight as bow-strings.

Now, wondering if her actions were being filmed by hidden cameras, Shay eased out of the room quickly. In her haste, she banged her thigh into the corner of a desk and bit her tongue to keep from crying out.

Her pod leader and Ethan thought she was in the restroom, so she had to hurry back to the rec hall, where everyone gathered after dinner. She bit her lip and grabbed the handle of the door. God help her if anyone saw her slip into the hallway.

Now or never. She opened the door and found the hall empty. With a loud click, it shut behind her. Barely breathing, she hurried to the main corridor that, beneath the roof of a breezeway, led back to the rec hall.

She was nearly to the door when she heard footsteps behind her. What? She had thought she was alone.

Glancing over her shoulder, she saw Dr. Wade Taggert, one of the psychology teachers and counselors, following her. Shay's heart nosedived. Wade, with his thin goatee, was somewhere around forty years old and seemed always a little edgy, tweaked. At his side was that stupid Missy Albright, the platinum-blond TA with the squeaky voice who had nearly caught Shay in the admin building.

Great.

"What're you doing in here?" Wade's voice boomed down the hallway.

Was it the same male voice she'd heard while she'd been hiding, the same guy talking with Missy? Shay wasn't sure, but now she had no choice but to stop and turn.

"Isn't this where the restrooms are?" she asked innocently.

Missy's eyes narrowed.

"I mean, why are you in this building?" Wade explained.

"There are restrooms in the rec hall, and that's where everyone's supposed to be at this hour."

Except you two, Shay thought, but held her tongue. She decided to go with confusion rather than say something that might land her in trouble. "Well, I thought so, but I couldn't find one, and I knew there was one here, because I'd used it the first day when I was being registered. I really had to go, so . . ." She left the rest for their imagination and tried to look sheepish and flustered.

Missy obviously wasn't buying it. "Really?" she mocked. "There's a set of bathrooms just down the hallway from the conversation pit. You must've walked right past them on your way out." God, her voice was grating.

Shay shrugged as if she knew she'd been an idiot. "I didn't."

"Well, now you know. Come along." Wade was glowering at her as if he didn't know what to believe. Beneath his goatee, his lips flattened over his teeth in irritation. "Didn't your pod leader assign you an escort?"

"Yeah," she said, thinking of Ethan Slade. "But, you know, he's a guy." If only she could blush! That would help. Instead she tried to appear uncomfortable, staring down at the floor. She hoped this was all worth it, that Jules would show up.

As Wade reached for the door, Shay saw movement from the corner of her eye. She turned just as "Father Jake" appeared from the shadows, walking rapidly, long strides moving him along the breezeway toward the admin building. "Is anything wrong?" he asked, quickly sizing up the situation as Wade opened the door.

"Miss Stillman apparently got lost."

"Easy to do." Father Jake didn't appear worried.

"She couldn't find the restroom," Missy supplied, her little-girl voice disbelieving as she rained one of her I'm-just-so-darned-cute smiles on the handsome preacher.

"But she found one. So we're all okay?" Father Jake said with an easy smile. "Right?"

"Right." Shaylee couldn't help liking him a bit.

Father Jake grinned. "Good, good. Then you'd better join the others."

"Let's go." Taggert's eyes had slitted. He held the door open, and the girls passed through.

"I'll be there in a minute," Father Jake said, then continued walking swiftly toward the chapel. Shay wanted to follow him, the preacher in jeans and a thick down jacket. He, at least, seemed real.

During the walk along the breezeway, Missy sent Shay a withering I've-got-your-number look, but Shaylee ignored it and opened the door to the rec hall. Inside, she walked briskly along the short corridor, past the clearly marked restrooms, and into the wide expanse of the common area.

Kids were studying and talking, and Banjo was fiddling around on her guitar while a few others from their pod listened.

Ethan was flopped in a worn chair, while Lucy Yang sat next to Banjo in the same grouping of rust-colored furniture. Lucy was one of the few people Shay liked here at the academy. Obviously smart, Lucy was as unbending as steel. She still had the tough-girl thing going with her spiked hair, untrusting eyes, and hints of the irreverent attitude that had forced her to the academy.

Thank God not everyone had been converted to freakin' robots. Shay cast a casual glance at Nona, who leaned over her open book to chat with Maeve and Nell. Despite the differences in their looks, those three tried to be cookie cutters of each other with similar clothes, hair, and attitudes. The three girls glanced up at Shay as she walked past. When Shay returned the stare, Nona and Nell looked away, but Maeve sent Shay the same frosty glare she'd been giving her since her arrival.

When he caught sight of Shay being escorted across the cavernous room, Ethan straightened and bolted out of the chair. "Hey! I was just starting to wonder about you."

Maeve looked peeved.

"She was in the admin building," Wade announced.

"What?" Ethan's gaze clouded. "Why?" he asked Shay.

"She couldn't find the women's room here," Missy said, her pale eyebrows shooting up to indicate she smelled a lie.

Ethan got the message. "But—"

"Yeah, I know," Shay said, cutting Ethan off. "I missed it, okay? Geez, everyone's acting like I committed some major crime or something. I just needed to pee!"

Wade's scowl deepened. "Just keep an eye on her," he told Ethan, then went across the hall, toward the thermoses of tea and hot cocoa.

Shay wasn't exactly sure of all the dynamics, but it was obvious Maeve was pissed. Did she have a thing for Ethan?

Missy leaned close to Ethan. "If you can't watch her, I will."

"Hey! I *don't* need a keeper!" Shay had heard enough. She didn't want any more attention thrown her way. "I made a mistake. Sor-ree. Let's not make a federal case of it."

"I got it!" Ethan said to Missy, and the girl actually smirked a bit, as if she couldn't wait to put Ethan in his place. In a hit of recognition, Shay decided that these two had once hooked up, but something had gone wrong. Maybe the woman-scorned thing? Missy was all about rubbing Ethan's nose in his mistake.

A few heads turned. Nona's group was suddenly all ears, and Keesha Bell, the sole African American girl in Shay's pod, quit paying so much attention to Benedict Davenne. Keesha had big brown eyes that didn't miss much and cornrows so perfect they reminded Shay of an aerial view of suburban streets. Keesha and BD were tight, and even though there was a rule against getting romantically involved with anyone on campus, it was broken all the time. But now, for once, Keesha and BD were tuned into something besides each other.

"Is there a problem?" Shay's group leader, Cooper Trent, cut away from the bunch of boys he'd been talking to and strode across the room.

"Yeah." Shay held up her hands in surrender. "I guess I broke the rules."

"We caught her in the admin building," Missy said smugly.

"I was looking for a bathroom, didn't see the one in here, went next door, and got caught in a fu-frickin' toilet sting."

Missy gasped.

A couple of kids chuckled.

Shay was surprised to see Nell actually grin.

Dr. Burdette shook her head as she passed by, frizzy red hair sprouting from her ponytail, but she didn't stop to chastise.

"It's all my fault," Shay continued. "I don't know what the punishment is for using the wrong bathroom, but I'm guilty as charged."

Keesha giggled, then put a hand over her mouth to keep from laughing out loud.

"It's getting a little loud over here." Wade strode over, a steaming cup in hand. "Let's pipe down."

"Yes, let's move on." Trent said to Shay, "Why don't you go back to studying? You know where the restrooms are now, right?"

Shay nodded. So this dude had her back. Or did he? Maybe his ass was on the line because he was her pod leader. If he really wasn't on her side, she was pretty sure she could count on Father Jake. Or was she kidding herself? Sheesh, this place was nuts!

"Good." Trent glanced up at Ethan, a quick, silent reprimand, then said to Shay, "If you have questions, talk to me or Ethan . . . unless you'd prefer to have a female TA."

Like Missy Albright? Save me! "I'm cool with Ethan."

Keesha swallowed a smile, and Lucy Yang actually had the nerve to give her a thumbs-up.

"Good." Trent met Taggert's unhappy glare. "No harm, no foul, right?"

Taggert looked about to argue, but the main doors opened and Reverend Lynch walked in on a gust of cold air. Wearing a long black coat, he strode to his favored spot in front of the oversized fireplace. He stretched his arms out like an eagle spreading its wings—the motion for everyone to gather closer.

"Sorry I'm late." He glanced at the clock. "It's nearly time for lights-out. So, quickly now, let's lift our voices in praise, then close with a quick prayer." He motioned toward the piano in the corner while finding the English teacher with his gaze. "Dean Hammersley," he said to the woman with the body of a marathon runner, "if you could please accompany us?"

Shaylee squeezed into the space between Banjo and Lucy. Ethan, properly chastised, was only a step behind her and was next to Zach Bernsen, the TA whom Shay had silently christened the Viking God because of his Nordic features.

A few feet away, Drew Prescott smirked, as if he felt some satisfaction with her discomfiture, but then she'd already pegged him for a loser. He was good-looking enough, despite his acne. With his dark hair and eyes and with the build of a soccer player, he was always smug, like he knew her innermost secret.

Another one to avoid.

Near Reverend Lynch, Mr. DeMarco, her new chemistry

teacher, stood as if he were some kind of sentry. Black haired, swarthy skinned, face set, he stared at the group as a whole, but Shay was certain she was in his sights. He had what she thought of as a lizard's gaze, one you couldn't follow.

She tried not to stare at him and looked at the floor, but that didn't help much.

From the corner of her eye, she saw Missy glaring at her, but she pretended not to notice. When Father Jake returned to stand a few feet behind Shay, somehow she felt a little safer.

As the first few notes of the hymn reverberated through the hall, Shay hoped that Jules had taken her seriously and was finding a way to get her out of this madhouse.

Later, after the final prayer in the rec hall, the Leader slipped outside to stand in the shadows. A few steps out of the lamppost's circle of illumination, he was hidden behind a copse of saplings while a stiff winter breeze ruffled his hair and cooled his blood.

Surreptitiously, he watched as Shaylee left the rec hall, just as he'd observed her when she'd lagged behind her group on their way to clean the stable. There was just something about her that intrigued him.

Now, Shaylee followed the shoveled path along with the group of students heading to the women's dorm. While the other girls were talking and laughing under the glowing security lamps, Shaylee hung back from the crowd, the lonely new girl who had no friends. She looked worried, fragile, though he knew better. If nothing else, Shaylee was a fighter.

Even the strongest warrior needs an ally.

Smiling inside, he knew it was nearly time to strike. To

take advantage of her frayed emotional state. He would offer her comfort. Solace. A friendly ear and a strong shoulder to lean on.

Shaylee Stillman.

He rolled her name through his mind as she walked beneath the lamp, her features caught in the light.

Surly.

Sexy.

Sultry.

Sassy.

Over the past few days, he'd spoken with her, of course, welcomed her. After all, it was expected. But he hadn't yet shown his hand; he didn't dare. Not until he was certain she would be a willing candidate.

He needed to learn more about Shaylee, test her, find out if she was ready.

He couldn't afford another mistake.

CHAPTER 10

With cell phones that connected to the Internet and beamed up to satellites around the world, Jules knew there must be a way to reach her sister. She called Erin, who knew a few tricks to retrieve numbers because of her job working with cell phones. They tried a few tacks, without success. When Jules called the school, no one answered and a recorded message advised her that someone would be in the office the next morning.

It was closing in on ten when Jules called her mother. In response to her concern, Edie laughed. "Really, Julia, what did you expect? Of course she called you, because she thought she could get to you. Reverend Lynch advised me that this would happen; it's totally normal."

"It is not normal, Mom."

"You have to get over this."

"I can't. She called me."

"She can only blame herself for ending up there."

"Then let's talk about Reverend Lynch. What about that mansion on the lake? That's not normal, either. Preachers—at least upstanding Christian preachers—don't normally live in houses worth several million dollars."

Edie sighed dramatically. "Of course they don't. I already explained that the school owns it, and I think it was bequeathed by someone connected to the academy, or maybe some grateful grandparent; I'm not really sure."

"Grateful *rich* grandparent."

"It's not a crime to have money," her mother admonished. "Why do you have to be so negative, Julia?" The conversation went downhill after that.

Jules hung up feeling even worse. Was she really putting her own negative spin on this? For all her help, Erin had warned Jules that the way Shaylee was being treated was normal. "All rehab centers cut off communications," Erin had said. "They have to break negative patterns."

Maybe Jules was taking this too seriously. Shay was, and always had been, the princess of high drama, waiting to become queen, but so far, Edie wasn't giving up her crown.

Jules tossed her pen onto the desk and told herself to give it a rest, consider the fact that everyone seemed to think Shay was in the best place for her.

Diablo jumped onto the desk. His long tail flicked, and his gold eyes stared at her fingers as she took another turn at the keyboard of her computer. "Don't tell anyone," she whispered, and Googled Cooper Trent. Ever since having drinks with Erin and Gerri, she'd wondered about him. It was stupid and she knew it, but she couldn't stop herself.

"Oh, great," she muttered, seeing that there were dozens of articles about him. Photos, too. She weeded through them all, searching for the most recent information, and found that a few years back, he had signed on with the Pinewood Sheriff's Department in Grizzly Falls, Montana. He was listed as the arresting officer in a few articles, but those had been several years before. When looking at the Web site for the county, Deputy Cooper Trent's name wasn't listed, his picture missing.

So either he was fired or he quit and was now off the radar.

Not that she should care. The cat hopped into her lap, looking up at her and meowing. "I know," she admitted, stroking his sleek head. "I'm an idiot. So what else is new?"

Trent locked the door of the equipment storage shed and gave it a tug, hearing the metal bolt rattle as it held fast. Used as storage for the canoes, snowshoes, kayaks, and hiking and fishing gear, this outbuilding near the boathouse was one of his responsibilities. Satisfied his gear was secure, he turned his collar up against the wind and headed across campus to his cabin, one of several that housed the staff. His place was a long haul from here—over a quarter mile away, on the far side of the dorms and rec hall, closer to the kennels, stable, and barns.

But he wasn't complaining. He figured he'd gotten lucky. He didn't have to have a roommate, mainly because of the state of repair of his particular bungalow. It was not only the smallest, but was also the oldest on the campus, one of the few buildings that remained from the years when this isolated spot had been a haven for hunting and fishing. Built in the early 1900s, the original lodge had been demolished and the gravel access road had washed away in spring thaws and flooding. But a few small cabins were still standing. Barely.

Trent could deal with a leak in the bathroom ceiling and plumbing that screeched when he twisted on a tap or flushed the toilet. He'd take a dilapidated old cabin if it meant privacy. The newer staff quarters were like town houses, big enough for two with common walls, each unit identical to the next.

No thank you.

Being near the stable was a plus for him. He had always felt more comfortable with animals than most people, to the point he'd been considered a loner by some, a cowboy by others. Not that he gave a rat's ass.

When he wasn't teaching sports like basketball and volleyball in the gym, Trent was the go-to guy for wilderness survival and a backup for Bert Flannagan, who was the horse and dog handler. All his years on the rodeo circuit had been on his résumé when he'd applied for this job. His experience had convinced Reverend Lynch that he should spend time with the animals, which, Trent thought, shoving his hands into the pockets of his denim work jacket, was far more preferable than working with his peers.

The kids he liked.

Sure, a lot of them had attitude problems, and some were seriously on the way to becoming criminals, but for the most part, they could be challenged and changed. He couldn't say the same for some of the teachers and counselors here.

Was Tobias Lynch, the reverend, theologian, head administrator for the school, as pious as he portrayed himself to be? His wife, Cora Sue, spent little time on campus, preferring the mansion on the shores of Lake Washington, just miles from the civilization of Seattle. Trent didn't blame the woman, but it was an unusual setup for a high-profile guy like Lynch.

And what about Salvatore DeMarco, the math and science teacher, who was as quick with a knife as he was with a smile? Trent had seen DeMarco gut a fish in seconds, snap a rabbit's neck, and take down a buck with a bow and arrow. DeMarco was an ex-Marine who'd served in Afghanistan. With a master's in chemistry, he taught science and math, but also gave lessons in self-defense and survival.

Adele Burdette, headmistress for the girls, was an enigma; Trent hadn't learned much about her, but she rubbed him the wrong way.

Bert Flannagan was another curiosity. True, Flannagan had a way with the animals, but Trent suspected the man had a cruel streak. In his midfifties with a military haircut and eyes that were often slitted in suspicion, the guy was leather-tough and well-read, more fit than most thirty-year-olds.

Trent had overheard Spurrier and Flannagan talking once, and there was mention of Flannagan once being a mercenary. The truth? A joke? A lie to impress? Trent was betting there was at least a kernel of truth to it; the guy just had that look about him. Trent had never seen him mistreat an animal, though Flannagan reprimanded students all the time. Most recently, Trent had seen him rip into Drew Prescott and Zach Bernsen, two of the TAs, who had tried to pawn off the chore of cooling their mounts to underlings. The boys had deserved the dressing down they received.

As the latest teacher hired—the new kid on the block— Trent wasn't yet privy to a lot of the inner workings of the school, but he'd done his homework before he applied for the position, and it hadn't taken him long to figure out that some of the counselors and teachers here weren't on the up-and-up.

Like you?

He felt his mouth twist in self-deprecation. He, too, was a phony, getting this job on a trumped-up résumé. But he didn't feel bad about the lies on his application, the deception he was perpetrating. It was necessary if he was ever going to find out what the hell had happened to Lauren Conway. The sheriff's department in this county was stretched thin. A handful of deputies struggled to cover hundreds of miles of deep forest; rocky, mountainous terrain; and long stretches of curving, dangerous highways. Power outages occurred regularly, hikers or campers got lost, and the snaking roads winding through the rugged Siskiyous presented ample opportunity for accidents.

On top of all that, Blaine O'Donnell, recently elected to the position of sheriff in Rogue County, wasn't the brightest bulb in the chandelier. As far as Trent knew, the guy wasn't really crooked, just lazy and inept.

So what had happened to Lauren Conway?

Trent wasn't certain.

Yet.

But he had a feeling her disappearance wasn't the act of a runaway, as the school administration purported. And the sheriff's department seemed to have written it off with little investigation. Trent couldn't help but wonder who from the school had lined O'Donnell's pockets and campaign war chest in the last election.

Lauren Conway's disappearance was the reason he'd taken the position at Blue Rock, though, of course, the administration didn't suspect that he had a hidden agenda, that he was working undercover hoping to discover the truth. He had the feeling that someone here knew more than they'd admitted; he was working on finding out what that something was.

And he was making inroads as the staff and student body began to trust him.

He hoped to keep it that way.

So far, in the past few months, he didn't think he'd raised much suspicion, but that could change on a dime. Especially if Shaylee Stillman decided to open her mouth and make some noise.

As he passed the interlocking corrals near the stable, he

slowed, his gaze scraping the darkened landscape for anything out of the ordinary. Rustic wooden fences, slats gray in the moonlight, bisected fields of glistening snow. Peaceful. Serene. A few thin clouds moving with the breeze.

And then he heard voices.

Arguing.

Near the garage where the tractors and heavy equipment was stored.

Rather than shout his arrival, he eased slowly along the edge of the stable and under the overhang where the horse trailer was parked. From there he looked across an expanse of parking lot to the shed.

"I told you not to panic," one male voice said in a harsh whisper. "Just stay cool."

Who was it? He should know.

"But we have to do something! Who knows who could be next?" A female voice. But again the hissing whisper disguised the true tenor of her voice, making it impossible for him to identify her. Should he show himself and demand answers? Or wait?

"Just be patient, okay? I won't let anything happen to you. I promise."

"How can you promise me? This is getting out of hand. I mean, when I agreed to this, to be a part of it, I thought it would be fun, a thrill. And I believed in him. But now . . . Oh, God, I don't know. I just don't know!"

"Shh! You have to have faith," the male voice insisted.

Trent decided to sneak closer when he heard a sharp neigh from the other direction, on the far side of the stable.

"Oh, no! Someone's coming!"

The horse let out a high whinny again, but Trent was already crossing the parking lot to the garage. He heard footsteps running frantically on the other side of the building.

He gave chase, keeping close to the garage and rounding a corner.

No one.

The back of the garage area was undisturbed, the snow piled on its asphalt apron, unmarked, the huge, rolling doors shut tight.

Trent dashed to the far side and once again was faced with an empty expanse of parking lot, though tire tracks and footprints were visible in the snow. Whoever had been meeting here was long gone, and the tracks he found—two sets of bootprints, one smaller than the other—led toward the heart of the campus. He followed them until he hit the shoveled sidewalk, where they disappeared.

Students?

Counselors?

Who?

He looked toward the dorms and saw someone pass under the lights between buildings, a glint of gold showing, as if the person were wearing a yellow cap or had blond hair. From this distance, he couldn't be certain. Nor could he prove that the person was either of the two he'd heard whispering behind the garage. Even if he could, so what? They were talking. Breaking curfew if they were students, not so if they were TAs or members of the staff.

The horse neighed again, clear and harsh in the night air. Other animals responded. One dog in the kennels started barking and was joined by others, but the noise was muted by the walls of the kennel. As were the answering neighs of the horses.

Knowing that he'd lost his quarry, he backtracked around the garage and crossed to the stable. On his way there, he spied a yearling named Nova for the star burst of white on her forehead. The filly whinnied, shivering in the cold. She was locked out of the building.

"Son of a bitch," he muttered under his breath. He opened the door and found a lead, then snapped it onto the filly's halter. "Come on, girl," he said softly, clucking his tongue and leading her inside the stable. Warm air that smelled of horses, saddle soap, and urine greeted him. Horses shuffled in their stalls, hooves swishing in the straw, an occasional nicker reaching his ears.

"You caused a stir, Nova," he told the sorrel filly, who tossed her head and nervously danced. "Hey, come on. You're okay. Here ya go."

Other horses stretched their heads over the rails of their boxes, and he rubbed the gray's nose before he settled the sorrel into her stall. After filling her manger with a ration of grain and hay, he brushed her shivering coat until it gleamed red under the stable lights. That seemed to have calmed her. "Better?" he asked kindly, though inside he was burning, pissed as hell that someone had left the filly outside when the temperature was well below freezing. *Idiot!*

The dogs were going crazy now, their soft woofs having escalated to serious barking.

"No!" a man said firmly, and the noise stopped instantly. Flannagan.

Several horses raised their heads and looked expectantly at the door.

It opened a second later, and Bert Flannagan, his face set in a scowl, a rifle gripped in his right hand, strode in. "What the hell is going on?"

"Nothing that requires a gun, Bert."

"You never know."

"What were you gonna do? Shoot someone, probably a student, in the stables, and maybe hit a horse or two? Scare the rest of them so that they kicked out of their boxes and injured themselves? Put the damned thing away."

Flannagan hesitated, glaring at Trent as if he wanted to

shoot him on the spot, but he set the rifle, butt on the floor, near the door. "Okay, so I asked before, what the hell's goin' on?"

"You tell me. I found Nova outside."

"Outside?"

Trent explained how he'd found the filly in the field while heading to his cabin. He left out the part about the voices he'd heard for now, until he got a bead on Flannagan. But as he told the older man about the filly, Flannagan's face grew hard. His nostrils flared, his mouth stretched tight over his teeth.

"That's the problem with leaving kids in charge," he said through lips that barely moved. "They have no sense of responsibility, no sense of purpose."

"Isn't that what we're supposed to be teaching them?"

"Impossible with the mambie-pambies that we get— rich kids whose mommies and daddies don't want them to suffer the consequences of their actions. Just ship 'em out, pay a buttload of money, and have someone else teach 'em how to grow up." He eyed the filly and shook his head, his short silvery hair in deep contrast to his tanned face. "I'll tell ya what. If the parents would let those damned kids face up for what they did, let 'em go cool their jets in jail for a while, it would save them all a whole lot of money and you and me a whole lotta time."

"And you wouldn't have a job."

Flannagan threw him a dark look. "There are better jobs, believe me. I didn't put in twenty years with the marines to end up here, wiping the noses of these kids. For the love of God, who leaves a horse out in the middle of the winter?" He walked into the filly's stall and ran knowing hands over her muscles. She flicked her ears but otherwise didn't object.

"Who was in charge tonight?" Trent asked.

"That's the hell of it." He rubbed the horse's forehead and she snuffled loudly. "Bernsen and Rolfe were in command, but they had kids from your pod, that girl who's always with her damned guitar." He snapped his fingers and the filly snorted.

"JoAnne Harris."

"She's the one. Along with the Asian girl with spiky hair—Yang—and Bell. And I don't care if it's PC or not, but Bell doesn't know a damned thing when it comes to horses."

"I don't think it's because she's black."

"'Course not. It's cuz she grew up in the middle of god-forsaken Detroit! How many horses you think they got in the Motor City?"

"Wasn't Missy Albright supposed to be part of this group?"

Flannagan nodded. "Always thought she was all right, aside from that annoying voice. Hell, she's smart, that one, good with animals."

And a blonde. As was the person he thought he saw dash between the dorms. What had the woman said? *We could be next.* She sounded frightened and had been told not to "panic" by her companion, but Trent didn't know what "next" meant. It could have been anything from disappearing like Lauren Conway to failing a class. He hadn't heard enough of the conversation to come to the right conclusion.

Besides, Missy was not the only blonde at Blue Rock. Off the top of his head, he came up with half a dozen, and that was just the students. The school nurse and the cook could be added to the group.

Even if he could identify the two people he heard outside the garage, so what?

"I'll deal with Bernsen in the morning. He was the TA who should have been in charge."

Another blonde. "Let me talk to him," Trent said. "Most of the students he was overseeing were in my group."

Flannagan was already walking to the door of the stable. "Fine with me. Just make sure he understands the severity of leaving a horse outside." He grabbed his rifle at the door, then looked over his shoulder with some final, sage words of advice. "And don't take any lame-ass excuses that he delegated the work. Doesn't mean jack shit. He was in charge; it's his ass on the line."

CHAPTER II

"Look, there's nothing more I can tell you," Cheryl Conway said over the wireless connection. Jules had tried one last time to reach the missing girl's parents before leaving for work. Finally, Lauren's mother, who lived in Phoenix, had taken the call. "Lauren's still missing, but we're holding out hope that she's okay, that we find her soon. Oh, God." Cheryl Conway's voice broke at the thought of losing her child, and Jules felt like a real jerk for having forced the woman to talk about it.

"I'm sorry," she said, gesturing with her free hand, though she knew the other woman couldn't see her. "I hope she comes home soon."

"We all do."

"I'm calling because my sister's a student at Blue Rock Academy, and I'm concerned about her."

"I . . . I don't know what to say." Jules heard another voice—deeper and definitely male—say something in the background, but she couldn't make out the words, just the admonishing tone. Was it Lauren's father? Or an older brother? Some authority figure.

"Mrs. Conway?" she said.

"Uh . . . please . . . Look, I'm sorry . . ." Cheryl's voice became a squeak as she tried to control herself and failed. "I . . . I really can't talk about this. I shouldn't. If you have any other questions, take them up with the sheriff's department."

Cheryl Conway hung up, and Jules stood in the hallway near her front door, her cell phone still clamped to her ear, feeling that she was missing something. Cheryl Conway had wanted to tell her more, but her husband had admonished her.

Why?

She slipped her phone into her purse.

What had she hoped to learn by tracking down beleaguered, frightened parents who, though "holding out hope," were worried sick that their daughter was already dead? The phone call had provided little information. It just reaffirmed Jules's fears about the school.

"Nancy Drew, I'm not," she told Diablo. Aside from working for a collection agency as a file clerk while going to college, she had no skills at being a detective of any kind.

Still, she felt an urgency to spring Shay from Blue Rock, and some of her anxiety sprang from Shay. Lord knew she was manipulative. Jules snagged her keys and checked her reflection in the narrow mirror by the front door. Her hair was piled on her head, her white blouse pressed, black skirt straight. Her makeup hadn't smeared, so she was ready for work at a job she really didn't mind but wasn't in love with. There was always Tony, the manager, with his sexual innuendos to deal with. Then there was Dora, a whiny waitress who loved to complain. "But it pays for Tasty Treats," she told the cat before grabbing her coat for the night shift at 101. The hours were long, the crowd noisy, the prices steep, and the tips great. The best thing was that it was a night gig, so if a migraine interrupted her sleep, or the nightmare returned, she could ignore the alarm clock in the morning.

She was lucky to have the job. "I'll see ya later," she promised the cat, then, outside, waved to her neighbor Mrs. Dixon before dashing through the drizzle to her sedan. The car, sometimes stubborn, started on the first try, and she was halfway to work when her cell phone rang. She wouldn't have picked it up and risked a ticket for driving while talking on a cell, but she recognized the out-of-area number as the one she'd last dialed—Lauren Conway's parents in Phoenix.

"Hello?"

"This is Cheryl Conway again," the woman whispered. "I couldn't talk earlier, not really. My husband doesn't approve. He wants to do everything by the book, but I can't stand to think that someone else's daughter might end up missing if I don't help. The sheriff's department . . . it's not enough; they don't have the manpower. Sometimes you have to do more."

"Do more how?" Jules asked.

But Cheryl ignored her question and just kept talking. "I don't know you or your sister, but trust me, something's very wrong at that academy. They have a program that breaks kids down or builds them up or something, but the students are left alone in the wilderness to find themselves and learn to rely on themselves. Sometimes for days. You know, some of the schools do that, leave the kids to fend for themselves for twenty-four or forty-eight hours in the forest to teach them to survive. I . . . I can't help but wonder if that's what happened to Lauren. If she was left in the forest and there was an accident, and the school's decided to cover it up."

"They wouldn't," Jules said automatically, not really believing that the school would cover up something so horrid.

Not the school, but someone in the school. It just takes one person with a secret agenda or an owner who could lose millions in a scandal and a lawsuit. Jules thought of the huge mansion on Lake Washington. Worth millions. Someone was living the high life and wouldn't want to risk it.

Suddenly Jules felt as cold as death.

"Who knows what 'they' would do?" Cheryl said. "All I know is my daughter is missing, and the last time I talked with her, she confided that the school wasn't what people thought it was, and she was going to prove it. She isn't a teenager, you know. She was recruited, yes, but not to be a student; it was to be a part of some counseling program, a teacher's aide of sorts. She'd get her college paid for while helping troubled kids, and she jumped at the chance.

"I tried to talk her out of it, to stay here at the university, but Lauren was always looking for an adventure, a challenge, pushing herself to the edge. That's why she was recruited and I think . . . I mean, it's possible that the very reasons she was chosen are the reasons she's missing." There was desperation in the woman's voice. "Reverend Lynch insists that she left by choice, of course, but I know my daughter. She wouldn't let us worry like this."

"I'm so sorry."

"We're going to find her." There was a renewed conviction in her tone. "No matter what it takes, we're going to find her. I'm not trusting the sheriff's department or that Reverend Lynch to do what it's going to take. Just because Lynch is supposed to be a man of God means nothing these days."

Didn't Edie say the house on the lake was owned by a preacher? No, that wasn't right. The school owned the property and a preacher lived there part-time. She'd mentioned Lynch by name.

"I'm serious," Cheryl continued. "If you value your sister's life, then get her out of Blue Rock Academy. But do not call my house again. My husband is very upset."

For the first time since she'd heard of the school, someone was confirming Jules's worst fears.

"I have to go," Cheryl said.

"Wait! If I need to get in contact with you—"

"I have a cell phone." Cheryl rattled off the number, then hung up. Repeating the number over and over again, Jules found a pen and wrote the ten digits on a gas receipt she'd tossed into her empty cup holder. After she parked her car on the street three blocks from the restaurant, she would punch the number into the contact list of her cell phone.

She thought about everything Cheryl Conway had told her, and her blood ran cold. Shay was at the academy, alone. Remembering Shay's last phone call, her desperate plea, Jules knew she had to do something; she couldn't just let her sister meet with the same fate as Lauren Conway.

Jules glanced at her watch. Late again! As Jules fed the meter for the next few hours and hurried into the restaurant, Cheryl Conway's warning chased after her: *If you value your sister's life, then get her out of Blue Rock Academy.*

Jules would.

And she knew just how she would go about it.

"And you left your last teaching job because the school was cutting positions?" Dr. Rhonda Hammersley asked over the soft sound of classical music wafting through the room.

"I was one of the last teachers hired, the first to be let go," Jules said, and she felt her palms begin to sweat. She sat across from the dean and kept her trembling hands under the polished wood table to hide her nervousness.

After taking Cheryl Conway's advice to heart, Jules had applied to Blue Rock Academy online. Within two days, she'd been called for an interview, not at the school, but, here, at the house on the lake where the two poodles were lying by a fire, heads on their paws, dark eyes staring at her as if silently accusing her of lying. This had been a quick process, with the people interviewing her flying up from southern Oregon. "The district was also eliminating art and music in the school with the budget cuts. Since my major was in art, I was let go."

"Oh, yes, there've been so many job losses with the falling economy. Your minor was in history and you have a credential to teach it, according to your résumé." With short brown hair and a runner's build, Hammersley struck Jules as a serious woman, though a hint of compassion shined through.

"That's right."

Hammersley studied Jules over the top of her reading glasses, then glanced down at Jules's application and credentials spread out on the table. "I have to admit, I like what I see, though I'm just part of the committee."

The committee had been interviewing Jules for more than an hour. Hammersley was the third person to come to the polished table. First she'd been grilled by Dr. Burdette, the dean of women for Blue Rock Academy. Wearing a smart black suit, Burdette had been all business, crisp and distracted. She looked at her watch three times during the interview and wound a finger in her kinky reddish locks before catching herself and stopping abruptly. Permanent frown lines were beginning to form at the corners of her mouth and between her eyes. Jules had guessed that Adele Burdette, Ph.D., was not a happy person.

The following interviewer had been Dr. Williams, a tall, slim, black woman who was as friendly and warm as Burdette had been uptight and icy.

Mutt and Jeff, Jules had thought.

"Please, call me Tyeesha," Dr. Williams had insisted while shaking Jules's hand and flashing a megawatt grin. Nearly six feet tall and dressed in a rust-colored sleeveless dress and multicolored bracelets, she seemed as comfortable in her own skin as Burdette had been itching in hers.

Finally, she'd met Rhonda Hammersley, the woman seated across from her. Solid yet kind, Hammersley seemed intent on wrapping up the meeting.

"Of course, Dr. Lynch has final say. He's reviewed all your documents." She leaned closer, elbows on the table. "You know we have a stellar reputation as a school that can do miracles for troubled teens. We offer kids without any other option a new lease on life, so to speak."

The door behind Jules opened as if on cue. The poodles rose to their feet and started wiggling. A man's voice said, "Jacob! Esau! Sit!" The poodles quit moving and planted their rear ends on the floor near the hearth.

"Oh, Reverend Lynch," Hammersley said, standing. She was practically beaming.

Jules followed suit and rose to her feet, turning to find the reverend towering over the tiny, prim woman Jules had met at the door of this house about a week earlier.

"You must be Julia," he said warmly, and extended a big hand. "I'm Dr. Lynch, and this is my wife Cora Sue."

Mrs. Lynch also reached forward, the diamond on her right hand glinting in the firelight. "Pleased to meet you." Her eyes glittered like the rocks on her fingers as she studied Jules with cool gloss. "You look familiar. Have we met?"

"Not that I remember," Jules lied, hoping her appearance had changed enough to fool the woman. She'd taken the trouble to add blond streaks to the curls that fell around her shoulders. She'd also bought a pair of high heels she couldn't really afford, though the slim skirt and matching blue jacket hadn't been worn since she'd graduated from college. Conservative blouse, strand of pearls her grandmother had willed her, and makeup that had been missing in their last meeting. Jules had done her best to alter her looks, and still Lynch's wife wasn't certain.

"I'm sure I would remember you, Mrs. Lynch," Jules said, and sounded almost sincere.

The knit of Cora Sue's eyebrows relaxed; she seemed satisfied.

"I know this interview isn't traditional, but at Blue Rock we like to think of ourselves as family, so I ask people to interview here, rather than at the school. Let's talk about Blue Rock. Come on into my study. Cora, dear, could you get us some coffee? Or tea?" Lynch asked Jules.

"Coffee," she said decisively. The last thing she wanted to appear was wishy-washy. She knew instinctively that an I-don't-care attitude wouldn't fly, and she was desperate to see her sister again; this was her best chance. Maybe her only chance.

"Coffee it is, Cora. But tea for me, please."

Cora Sue nodded stiffly.

The reverend paused to pet the expectant dogs on their heads, then with a quick "Go with Momma" and a snap of his fingers, he sent the poodles down the hallway to pad after Cora Sue and Dr. Williams.

Jules's stomach was jumping, her nerves getting the better of her. Her four-inch heels clicked loudly on the marble floor while cutting into the top of her foot as she walked with Dr. Lynch under a glimmering crystal chandelier that hung from three stories above the foyer. While the other women and the dogs headed toward an archway to the far side of a sweeping staircase, Jules followed Lynch through double doors to a study near the rear of the home. Inside, floor-to-ceiling bookcases flanked a massive fireplace where a gas fire hissed over "charred" ceramic logs. This room overlooked the lake where the seaplane that had taken Shay to southern Oregon was tied to the dock.

Lynch followed her gaze as he settled behind a carved desk big enough to serve six for lunch. "The plane," he said with a chuckle. "I guess it's a bit of an indulgence, but it does make things easier. Our academy is remote, as you know, though there is a road that's open most of the year. It's impassable sometimes with the snowfall in the winter. If the weather warms too quickly in the spring, the runoff from the mountains tends to wash the road out."

Again his softly amused chuckle. "Not to worry, though, we have the seaplane and a helicopter pad. Only in the very worst weather are we completely isolated, and even then it's not a problem. With our own generators, live-in staff, and stores of supplies, we can get through any catastrophe God sees fit to send us." He waved Jules into a visitor's seat at his desk and settled into a leather executive chair opposite her. "Well, I guess we might not survive the ten plagues of Egypt as they were described in Exodus."

"Right." Jules knew nothing of the plagues but kept it to herself and made a mental note to bone up on Exodus. Attempting to appear comfortable in the stiff wing-back chair, she listened while Lynch, obviously in his element, began a diatribe about the school, its history, the good it had brought the community and youth across the country. Nothing negative, no bad vibes at Blue Rock. An orator at heart, Lynch explained how the school, "a little bit of heaven here on Earth," attained its goals. Aside from academics, the eighteen-month curriculum included eight moral-value workshops, four drug and alcohol sessions, and gender-specific classes that dealt with sexual issues. The students were divided into peer groups and were encouraged to work together to solve interpersonal problems.

Lynch went on about the school's mission, about the good Blue Rock Academy was doing in turning around young lives.

Jules would have loved to believe it—what an incredible and altruistic vision! However, she knew it was just too good to be true. Lynch, however, seemed to be buying what he was peddling, his dedication sincere.

After a tight-lipped Cora Sue brought in the tea service, he even went so far as to play a CD about Blue Rock Academy wherein several people gave their testimonials.

The first was a graduate of Blue Rock. He had been a famous soap opera star, according to his sincere message, "strung out on heroin and on the verge of suicide" before he was twenty. His "totally self-destructive" behavior would have killed him if not for the faith and self-respect he found at Blue Rock Academy.

The next familiar face was a popular and handsome TV evangelist who praised the academy for its good works of showing the nation's youth the "true and glorious" path to Christ and saving young lives.

What about Lauren Conway? Jules wondered, but managed to hold her tongue. She couldn't afford to blow her cover before she was hired. *If* she was hired.

The third testimonial was by a husband and wife team of authors who published self-help books. The covers of *You Are What You Believe* and *The Answer* were flashed upon the screen.

He clicked the television off after the infomercial and after pouring a bit of cream and lots of honey into his tea, stirred the concoction and said, "We have had our share of detractors, of course, and though most of the charges are completely unfounded, there have been a couple of black marks—blemishes, if you will—on our reputation."

Here we go, Jules thought, sipping her black coffee and waiting to hear the spin on the "blemishes."

"One of our students went missing last fall." He sighed loudly as he stared into the depths of his teacup, as if he could read the leaves or come up with some answer. "We don't know why, nor has she been found. Yet. I have my ideas of what happened, but I can't even begin to speculate. It wouldn't be fair to her family."

Translation: The lawyers for Blue Rock Academy advised anyone associated with the institution to clam up.

"I heard about that," Jules said, realizing that anyone who applied to work at the school would have done his or her research about the institution.

"Then you probably know that the reason we're looking for a new teacher is that one of ours was accused by a student of taking . . . liberties. Again, I wouldn't want to comment on that except to say these two little situations are to be expected, I suppose, people being what they are. But"— he held up a long, judicious finger—"I would remind you that the students we work with aren't mainstream; they have issues. Problems. The reputation of Blue Rock Academy speaks for itself." He paused then, cocking his head as if hearing the music for the first time. "Is that Bach?" He closed his eyes and moved his hand as if waving an invisible conductor's baton in rhythm to the softly flowing notes from the string section.

"Excuse me." He opened his eyes at the end of the interlude. "Sometimes . . . Well, music moves me." Then, straightening, he asked, "How quickly could you take a position with the academy?"

Jules's heart began to beat a little faster. "The information on the Web site indicated a position was open immediately."

"And you could do that?"

"Yes," she said easily. "I could be ready tomorrow."

"Really?" He looked surprised, and she inwardly kicked

herself. She didn't want to appear too eager or raise any suspicions.

"I could arrange it, yes, though, of course, it would be best to have a few days," she admitted.

His eyes narrowed thoughtfully; then he checked the wall clock over the fireplace. "I'll get back to you, Ms. Farentino," he promised. "Soon. Either way."

"I appreciate it." She stood and extended her hand, looking him squarely in the eye. "Your school sounds very interesting. Cutting-edge. A necessity for so many of our disenchanted youth." The words nearly stuck in her craw with what she knew, but she managed a smile.

One of his eyebrows lifted a bit as he held her hand just a millisecond too long. Did his gaze slip a little, down her neck to her breasts?

A moment later, they were both facing the door, Jules wondering if she had imagined things.

She might have been mistaken.

The interview over, Lynch escorted her to the foyer. Dr. Williams and Burdette waited there with another man, whom Lynch introduced quickly as the pilot for the academy.

Kirk Spurrier shook her hand. Tall, with dark hair and eyes that matched, he was all business. "Nice to meet you."

"You, too," she said.

He flashed a smile, then turned to Lynch. "If possible, I'd like to fly back in daylight," he said.

The reverend nodded curtly. "I think we're finished here."

"Thanks for applying to Blue Rock," Tyeesha Williams said, clasping Jules's hand in both of hers. Her smile was wide and gleamed as brightly as the silver bracelets on her wrist.

Adele Burdette gave her a cursory nod, and Cora Sue ignored her altogether.

A disingenuous group, Jules thought as she drove off in the rental car she'd used as part of her ruse. She'd been concerned that Cora Sue, mistress of the biblically named poodles and seemingly unhappy wife of the reverend, might recognize her battered Volvo four-door.

Jules could be found out easily enough, of course, though any communication from her old address in Portland was currently forwarded to her in Seattle. If asked, she'd admit to moving up here but that she just hadn't gotten around to all of the paperwork, and she could claim that her car was in the shop. She only hoped that it wouldn't come to any darker deception. She didn't really have a moral qualm against lying—not while trying to save her sister—but really, she wasn't very good at it. Jules was a lousy liar, a novice in schemes and deceptions.

Then again, she was a quick study.

CHAPTER 12

Rhonda Hammersley just wanted to hire the woman and be done with it, but that, of course, wasn't Reverend Lynch's way. No, siree, Lynch prided himself on looking at "all sides of the issue." Snap decisions were *not* his forte.

They were seated at the library table where Julia Farentino had been interviewed less than an hour earlier. A fire glowed in the corner where Cora Sue, knitting needles softly clacking, sat on a love seat, the poodles at her feet. The reverend's petite wife never spoke in these meetings, but she listened. Oh, boy, did she listen. The woman gave Rhonda the creeps, but, of course, she never admitted as much. If the money from Cora Sue's family had started Blue Rock's endowment, then Rhonda could keep her mouth shut. Blue Rock was worth it to her.

Waiting impatiently in the doorway to the foyer, Kirk Spurrier shifted from foot to foot. The pilot was always in a hurry, always had an eye to the sky, edgy about the weather.

Hammersley could tell that Adele Burdette was satisfied with the interview and ready to move on. "Let's hire her," Burdette suggested as she flipped through the pages of Farentino's résumé one last time. "At least until the end of the school year. If she doesn't work out, we'll terminate her contract." She looked to Williams and Hammersley for support.

"Sounds good to me," Hammersley offered. "She's certainly qualified."

Lynch lifted a staying hand. "We can't be too hasty."

"But we don't have any other prospects," Burdette argued. "And we can't be too picky. Everyone else we approached either had trouble with our location or they've been scared off by the Lauren Conway business."

Lynch actually winced, but Burdette wasn't finished.

"It doesn't help our credibility that she's never been found."

"She was a runaway. I can only assume that she met with some kind of accident or is in hiding."

"Maybe. The truth is, we don't know," Burdette argued, "and that's not good."

"Of course it isn't." The reverend's face collapsed into a mask of concern as he agreed, just as he had a hundred times before. "Unfortunate thing, that." He looked away. "Tragic."

Hammersley was nodding; she'd liked Lauren. So bright. So inquisitive. An athlete with keen intelligence and a sharp wit; Lauren Conway had been a natural addition to the college program in which the older students became teachers' assistants in the high school classrooms. Lauren hadn't been jaded or scarred, a refreshing change from some of the TAs at Blue Rock. It bothered her on a very basic level that the girl had gone missing, and she didn't want to think too much about what might have happened to her. If Lauren truly had tried to run away, how far could she have gotten in the wilderness that surrounded the academy? And why run at all? That didn't seem like Lauren.

Had she gone hiking and fallen? Come across a bear or a cougar? Or had she met some other deadly fate? Hammersley wouldn't let her mind wander down that treacherous path again; she'd gone there before and every time had come up with no answers.

Burdette was still pressing her point. "Maris Howell was no accident, and no teacher wants to be associated with *that* scandal."

Lynch scowled, as if he'd bitten into a lemon.

Spurrier tapped his watch. "We have to go."

"Can't you fly at night?" Burdette asked, obviously agitated.

"I'd rather fly in daylight." Spurrier was calm but firm. "It's safer."

"But it's not convenient." Burdette's eyes closed to shiny slits.

What was it that bothered the headmistress about the pilot? Hammersley wondered. Spurrier was a loner by nature, but affable enough. Not only was he trustworthy in the cockpit, but he was as an educator as well.

"If you didn't notice, we're trying to conduct business here," Burdette groused.

Hammersley had seen this before, an undercurrent of tension, some kind of petty power struggle between these two. Both were just too competitive, in Hammersley's opinion.

His eyes sparked, but Spurrier tamped down his temper. "I'm just saying it would be best if we left soon."

"Okay, we get it," Burdette said.

"Back on topic?" Williams's brows rose, the chastising face that academy teachers all wore so well. "I'm with Adele. We're only talking about a few months, but the staff is stretched thin. Things were already tight before Maris left."

"She was fired," Burdette cut in.

"Whatever." Williams sighed, obviously tired of the argument. "Julia Farentino has the qualifications and certifications; she could be just what we need. Her criminal background check came back clean, credit's okay, though it looks like she could use a steady job. We know why she's not teaching right now, and she's single. There's no husband or children to stop her from taking the job. She's also willing to move down temporarily. That's always difficult to find. If, in June, we . . . *you* change your mind about her, then don't renew her contract." Then, deferring to the director, Williams offered a smile. "But, of course, this is your decision, Reverend."

"I know." He smiled benignly and tented his hands, then nodded curtly. "Fine. Let's do it. Rhonda, give her a call, advise her the job is temporary, get the paperwork together, and see when she can get down to Blue Rock. The sooner, the better. Everything can be handled by e-mail, right?"

"Yes."

"Good!" He slapped his hands on the arms of his chair. "There, that's done. Let's get out of here."

As they gathered their documents, stuffing them into briefcases, Spurrier dashed outside and jogged toward the dock where the plane was moored.

Lynch's wife straightened from her chair and proffered her cheek as her husband passed.

"I'll see you this weekend, darling," he said. "You're coming down?"

"Of course."

Hammersley tried not to stare as Lynch and his wife walked to the French doors. Domestic bliss? The reverend and Cora Sue always looked amiably photogenic, but Hammersley never observed anything to indicate that a real love burned in their hearts. There seemed to be some invisible barrier between them, as if they were acting out their affection. Not that it was her place to judge. First Corinthians told her to "judge nothing," and she knew good advice when she saw it.

The dogs stretched and nuzzled at the glass to get out. Hammersley thought the poodles might walk them down to the dock, but Lynch had other plans. A firm "Stay" from the reverend was all it took to convince the poodles and their tight-lipped mistress not to follow.

Jules tossed her floor-length apron into the hamper near the back door of 101's huge kitchen and snatched her purse from its locker. It had been a long night, and her feet ached, but the tips had been good. She might actually have enough for her rent this month, along with a Costco-size box of ramen noodles.

Sometimes she thought if it weren't for the meals she boxed up here at 101—steaks that hadn't been cooked perfectly, a dressed salad that was supposed to have its vinaigrette on the side, a piece of salmon that was "just too dry"—she might just starve. She turned on her cell phone and headed out, passing several waitresses, the sous-chef, and a line cook having a final cigarette in the damp night air.

Making her way to her car, she listened to her messages and saw that Rhonda Hammersley had called just before five. "Ms. Farentino," her message said, "we're offering you the position at Blue Rock Academy according to the terms discussed with Reverend Lynch this afternoon. Please call me back and let me know that you'll accept. You can reach me on my cell till eleven-thirty tonight. Otherwise you can leave a message. Thank you."

Jules was floored.

It was really going to happen; she was being hired. Suddenly her palms were sweaty, and she wondered if she could pull off her plan.

She replayed the message, and then, looking at her

watch, noting that it was already eleven-twenty, she placed the call.

Rhonda Hammersley picked up on the second ring.

"This is Julia Farentino. I got your message and, yes, I accept. Thanks!"

"Good!" Hammersley sounded genuinely pleased. Within minutes, the deal was done, at least preliminarily.

Jules was to drive down to the school by the end of the week, meet with Lynch, and sign all the appropriate documents. She'd have a few days to settle into quarters and meet the staff and students before starting work the following Monday.

Jules did an about-face, walking back into the restaurant where she found Tony, the manager, in his small office. She let him know that she needed some time off for a "family emergency" but didn't elaborate. Tony gave her the what-are-we-gonna-do-without-you? routine, but she worked it out with Dora, another waitress, who wanted more hours. Dora would be willing to cover her shifts for the next few weeks.

Anticipation fluttered in her chest as she drove home. By the end of the week, she would see Shay. She only hoped that her sister wouldn't give her up and ruin the entire ruse.

Nona checked her watch. Twelve fifty-three in the morning. She'd pretended to fall asleep earlier, waiting for her stupid new roommate to finally turn out the light. Shaylee Stillman didn't play by the rules and refused to obey the lights-out order at eleven. She'd gotten away with it. Probably because there were some kids who had to stay up later to get all their homework done. Lights-out was the one rule that could be bent a bit, especially if you stayed awake in the name of education.

Now the dorm was quiet aside from the soft hum of the furnace blowing warm air through the building. No one was talking in the hallway, no footsteps passed by their door on the way to the bathroom.

She sneaked a peek at the sprinkler head. She wasn't even certain that all of her actions were being followed, though that was the rumor. But who knew for sure? Tim Takasumi, the TA who worked with a lot of the electronic equipment for the school, had made it sound like there were cameras in the sprinkler heads in each room, but she'd never seen one, and she wasn't sure she could trust Tim. He was beyond geeky and really bought into the whole Blue Rock Academy rah-rah routine.

It would be just like Tim to start a rumor about hidden cameras to keep the myths about this place going. Rather than leave the program, Tim had stayed on after "graduation" and was working on some sort of accelerated college program via the Internet with the professors here. That's what the TAs did; they stuck around. Nona figured that they were part of some kind of secret group; she'd overheard Missy Albright whispering to Eric Rolfe about a meeting late at night in some freakin' shelter of some kind. Whatever that was.

Not that Nona could be bothered with whatever cult was happening. She didn't care if the kids involved were dropping acid or drinking blood. She had more important things to think about.

Specifically, her boyfriend. No, make that her first real boyfriend. She didn't count the creep back home who had hit her so hard he'd knocked out one of her teeth; that hadn't been love. She knew that now. And, boy, were things heating up. She was still a few months shy of sixteen and in love!

Her boyfriend had vowed that he loved her, that he needed her, and he knew just where to sweep his fingertips to leave her quivering. When she thought of what his lips and tongue and fingers could do, touching her in places that she'd never even dreamed about, she started melting inside. She had to close her mind to all that now. She couldn't start breathing fast or thinking about him and what they would do, not until she'd gotten out of the dorm.

For now, she had to concentrate.

She'd been certain she'd be a virgin until sometime in college, if she went on to school, but all that had changed a few months ago, right after Lauren Conway disappeared. Nona had been getting noticed, and she liked it. The feelings had scared her at first, as she remembered the first time he'd kissed the crook of her neck, letting his teeth nibble and even bite her. That had scared her a little at first. But soon, quicksilver heat melted away any fears, and she'd found she'd liked it; the rougher he was, the more exciting.

That didn't make her a slut, did it? Or some kind of sex freak?

Of course, it didn't mean that she had low self-esteem or any of that psychological garbage that Dr. Williams and Reverend Lynch were always spouting. It just meant she liked life exciting. On the edge. When he stood behind her, rubbing his cock up and down her spine and buttocks while his hands massaged her breasts and he held the back of her neck in his teeth . . .

Oh, God, she was going to do it! Everything!

Until now, she'd not allowed him to penetrate her with his dick, probably because of some holdover from her "good girl" days when she'd wanted to only please her father. She didn't want to become a "slut" or a "dirty whore" like her mother. At least, that was what her father had said. All Nona knew was that her mother had taken off when she was young, leaving her father to raise her alone, and her father had nothing but horrible things to say about her mother.

But then, Peggy Vickers had never called or written or sent a birthday card or Christmas wishes to her only daughter. Nona knew she'd been foolish enough to think that each year would be different, that she would hear from her mom.

Which made her think that her father was probably right.

But she didn't believe that there was "bad blood" running through her veins or that she'd better be careful or she'd end up a "filthy tramp just like your mother."

Tonight she intended to ignore all her father's warnings. He'd sent her here, hadn't he? When Catholic school hadn't stopped her from sneaking out and smoking and drinking and experimenting with meth and Ecstasy and a few pills. The shoplifting had been the straw that broke her father's back, and he'd found the means, probably borrowed from Grandma, to send his wayward daughter here.

It was Blue Rock or foster care or juvenile detention, he'd sworn, and she'd agreed to this quasi-reform school in the sticks. Wouldn't Daddy Dear be surprised to know how his plan had backfired? Despite all his attempts to keep his daughter a lily-white virgin, he'd sent her to Blue Rock, where she fit in with delinquents just like her.

And she'd found the perfect boyfriend.

Tonight, she thought, considering her all-too-burdensome virginity, she might just give in. What was she clinging to? That old Catholic rhetoric about being chaste?

What a crock!

In the dark, she reached under her bed, grabbing her jeans and a long-sleeved sweater. She didn't want to bother with her bra, as it was about as far from sexy as you could get, but she snapped it on because she didn't want her breasts to be flopping around as she ran to the stable, where she was supposed to meet him. She could ditch the bra before they actually started making out. . . .

She smiled in the dark as she located her down jacket

with the Blue Rock Academy logo emblazoned upon it, then silently slipped her arms through the sleeves. Wouldn't "tough" Shaylee be surprised if she knew. Nona had read the disbelief in Shaylee's eyes when Nona had intimated that she had a boyfriend. Shaylee thought she'd been lying.

As if she thought it would be impossible for any boy, make that any *man,* to show interest in Nona.

Just showed what an idiot her new roommate was. At the door, she checked Shaylee's bed. She was shifting around again, always restless, but the girl didn't wake up.

Just before she left, Nona slipped Shaylee's Oregon Ducks baseball cap off its hook and tucked her hair inside it. She'd done it before, using it for a disguise in case she got caught by any cameras or roving teachers. Ha-ha to Shay.

No one would consider Nona capable of breaking the rules, least of all anyone on the staff. She had them all believing that she was buying into their regimented Christian doctrine and was a conscientious student. To that end, Nona had ended up with the dubious privilege of babysitting Shaylee Stillman, a wacko if ever there was one. It was bad enough that Nona's mom had gone out for cigarettes and never returned, but Shaylee's stepfather had been murdered or some such shit. No wonder she was a loner!

God, Nona hated the new girl. Okay, she felt a *little* sorry for her, being the new kid on campus who people just pretended to like, but that was about it. Shaylee Stillman didn't inspire friendship.

Always acting so tough, with her tattoos and bad attitude. Rumor had it she was smarter than most, but Nona had yet to see it.

In the shadowy darkness, she saw the lump that was her new roommate, head under the covers, breathing regularly, *finally* asleep.

Okay, it was now or never!

Without making a noise, Nona slipped out the door and sneaked down the dimly lit hall. Nerves thrumming, heart a wildly beating drum, afraid that at any second someone on the floor would open a door and catch her, she eased to the staircase.

According to the dorm gossip, this was probably the route Lauren Conway had taken the night she escaped from the school. Nona was certain that was what had happened. She left and disappeared, end of story. All of the talk about her being killed, or accidentally dying, or reports of people seeing her ghost, were just hype, a means to keep everyone else in line. If she'd really died, where the hell was her body?

It didn't take a rocket scientist to figure out that Lauren had just not wanted to return home, that she was looking for a way to escape whatever problems she had in Arizona or wherever it was that she was from. All that talk about her "wanting" to be here to become a TA was a lie. *No one* ever came here voluntarily. So she had disappeared and was probably in Mexico somewhere with dyed hair, tropical sunshine, and a pissant job and loving it. No more studying, no more parents with all their rules, no more lame Blue Rock Academy.

Using the beam of her wilderness flashlight, Nona slunk through the creepy basement and tried to ignore the fact that spiders and rats probably nested in the cracks and crevices. The place smelled of dust and mildew, and the constant drip from a sink near the stairs grated on her nerves.

Cautiously, she found the window she'd learned didn't latch. Supposedly it had been fixed months ago, but the repairs had been half-assed, and it hadn't taken long for one of the students to jimmy it loose again. Probably that awful Crystal Ricci girl with the tail of a dragon tattooed around her neck. Oh, yeah, like *that* was attractive! What a lowlife.

The trunk that people had used as a step had been removed, but nearby, just around the corner, was an old writing desk that had been discarded. It took no effort to move the small table and climb atop. With the tiny screwdriver that was hidden in a niche over the windowsill, she quickly popped the faulty lock and—voilà—the window creaked open.

Cold air immediately rushed inside, the snap of winter invading the musty basement as Nona crammed her flashlight into the pocket of her jacket. With gritted teeth, she gripped the sill, stuck her feet out, and propelled herself through the window to freedom.

Well, relative freedom.

Once outside, she crept over the deep, crusted snow to the path. From there she scurried ahead, keeping to the shadows, though the moon and stars were already cloaked with a thick layer of clouds. More snow was predicted, and she was sick to death of it.

She reached into her inside pocket for her cell phone, the one she'd gotten on the Blue Rock black market. Each week, when the van went into town for supplies, a few of the TAs were allowed to go on the shopping spree, and one of them was running a banner business in contraband. She'd ordered and received one of those prepaid cell phones, and it was a lifesaver.

Except it wasn't in her pocket.

But it had to be. She was always so careful with it. If it was ever found, she'd be in big, big trouble. She patted down each of her pockets, then turned them inside out. Damn! It must've fallen out of her pocket, like it nearly had on the way to the barns when she was running to catch up with her friends.

Panic crawled through her guts. She couldn't lose it. She looked back at the path she'd just taken, searching for the slim phone, but didn't spy any small black rectangle on the snow. Nothing. Not even when she swept the beam of her flashlight quickly along the edge of the bushes where she'd hidden.

So . . . if it had fallen out inside, probably as she'd pushed her way through the window, she'd find it when she returned. Right?

She tried to calm down.

It would be okay.

And if it was found, it couldn't be traced to her, not unless the school was into fingerprinting.

It wasn't a problem.

Just an inconvenience.

And it was worth it.

Anything was.

As long as she could be with *him*.

CHAPTER 13

The Leader's breath shuddered in the cold night air, disturbing the snowflakes that were falling steadily. He couldn't sleep, was too keyed up. There was a snap in the air, a tension that fired his nerves.

Outwardly, everything appeared as it always had.

Serene. Peaceful.

But a change was coming.

He would see to it.

His passion would guide him.

If he didn't allow it to rule him. That was the trick. Passion was a double-edged sword. Especially when it came to women.

Shaylee Stillman's face came to mind as he turned his gaze to the dorms and the window of her room. She was the challenge, the one he wanted. He would love to tame the mutiny he saw rising in her big hazel eyes, love to let his fingers graze the white, white skin of her side to linger at her waist. He'd surround it with a hand, his thumb poised right above her pubis, his fingers pressing hot near her spine. Making her hot inside. Making her wet.

He licked his lips and told himself to be patient. Careful. His weakness was sex.

Always had been.

It had started with his mother, he knew now. She'd caught him with his tutor, a high school girl who had the most incredible breasts he'd ever glimpsed. Secretly, from his upstairs window, he'd watched her sunbathe in her backyard.

Lissa Harvey.

She'd oftentimes taken off her bikini top while the sun's rays had been the most intense and caressed her skin, causing sweat to collect. Dark nipples had pointed upward at the sky. Perfectly round. Making him hard. Chocolate disks that were larger than he had expected. God, how he'd wanted to suckle and lick and bite at them.

Better yet, sometimes, when she was alone and the family minivan wasn't in the drive, she'd slip her hand under her polka-dot bottoms and, closing her eyes, pleasured herself while baking in the warm summer sun.

He'd touched himself as well, timing his orgasm with hers. And he had fantasized about her in those sultry summer nights when no breeze had stirred the curtains and wasps, trapped inside, had beaten themselves to death on the windows.

She'd turned bronze over the summer, her nipples seeming to fade as her breasts darkened. She'd been a scholar, without a boyfriend, a college-bound student with long dark hair who understood math, algebra in particular.

He hadn't cared about school at the time, and his mother had been worried, hiring Lissa in late July before she took off for university.

That's when the affair had started.

In the musty basement with its low ceiling and tiny windows. On a futon reserved for guests, in front of the cold hearth of an unused fireplace with books and notes spread over the coffee table, they'd first kissed. First touched. First made love.

It had been fast.

Embarrassingly so.

But Lissa had been patient.

Intent on teaching as well as learning.

It hadn't hurt that he was good-looking, physically mature for his age, developing muscles and shaving before most of the boys in his class. They'd explored every orifice, tried new positions, worked on titillating and turning on. There in the musty old basement, on the futon his grandparents slept on when they'd visited.

And then she'd left.

Gone off to college.

Never written, never called.

Nor had she returned one phone message.

It was as if she'd erased him from her life.

The bitch.

His blood boiled as he thought of her, but then again, she'd gotten hers, hadn't she? Been found out fucking her professor, a married man with two small children. And her next lover, an engineering student, had one day opened his mail to find photos of Lissa in a compromising position with a kid. Did he realize she could be jailed for what she'd done with a minor?

The engineering student left her and married someone else. The professor had been replaced, and Lissa, poor, poor Lissa, had been exposed for the Jezebel she was. She lost her scholarship and was forced to return home, to attend the local junior college.

He'd never spoken to her again.

Refused eye contact.

After all, he'd been the victim, right?

Oh, Lissa, sexy little seductress, payback stings like a bitch.

Lissa had been his first, and she'd opened so many doors for him. Some portals to ecstasy, others doorways to hell.

He'd made a few mistakes.

He couldn't afford another, no matter how he was tempted.

He had only to think of Lauren Conway and feel the burn of his own foolishness climb up the back of his neck.

Through the falling snow, he caught a glimpse of movement, a shadow tracking along the wall of the rec building.

What the hell?

Who would be out at this time of night? More importantly, why? He felt a tingle of anticipation sing through his blood.

On silent footsteps he followed.

Nona ducked beneath the frigid leaves of a rhododendron and along the well-trodden path away from the heart of the campus to the barns. Here, it was tricky. She had to be super quiet. Any noise would wake the dogs, and they'd start baying, barking, and raising hell. That could wake all the stupid animals in the sheds—God, those chickens! Squawking, noisy, dirty things. Although she gave the kennels a wide berth, one of the dogs barked sharply and another took up the cause.

No, no, no!

Curling her fists, she waited by a storage shed, mentally counting off the seconds as the dogs growled a bit, then settled back to sleep. She gave them a good ten minutes or more as she shivered in the dark. Maybe they'd heard her . . . but she'd been so careful.

Not you, Nona. They heard him! He's never as cautious as you are, you know that. Don't be a ninny.

She gave the dogs another minute or so, then crept

stealthily to the stable. All the while, she had the odd feeling that she was being watched.

Her scalp crinkled with gooseflesh, and she glanced over her shoulder.

Nothing seemed out of place.

No dark figure was huddled against the cedar walls of the rec room or hiding in the overhang of the garage. It was just her own nervousness getting the better of her.

She reminded herself: *He* was here somewhere, too.

Nothing to worry about.

And yet . . .

Did she hear footsteps?

Breathing?

Her insides curdled and she froze, ears straining, eyes searching the darkness. There was the tiniest light in the chapel, behind the soaring windows, but that light was always visible, supposed to represent Jesus's claims of being the "light of the world," a quote that was similar from the book of John.

She kept walking, her skin freezing, her mind running in circles of anticipation and fear. No one was following her, of course not. She was just anxious because she knew she was breaking the rules.

The kennels remained silent as she reached the stable. Without a second's hesitation, she opened the creaking door and stepped inside.

Greeted by the warm air smelling of horses and dung, dust, and oiled leather, she turned on her flashlight again, careful to keep the beam away from the windows.

A few of the geldings and mares moved in their stalls, hooves rustling the straw. She heard an occasional disturbed huff from nostrils as she passed, and one soft nicker of disapproval reminded her she wasn't where she was supposed to be.

She reached the ladder to the hayloft and started climbing. "Hey," she whispered, pausing on the fifth rung. "Are you here?"

She waited, ears straining.

Nothing. She squinted in the darkness, daring to run her flashlight over the floorboards and around the barrels of feed and slats of the stall rails.

More disgruntled snorting.

"It's me, Nona," she hissed.

Damn it, he was always playing games with her. Stretching her patience, making her wait, often jumping out at her to startle her and get a reaction. Tonight, she wasn't in the mood. She just wanted him to grab her and kiss her hard and rip her clothes off so he could nibble at her breasts. Oh, God, she was getting herself hot just thinking about what he would do to her.

She climbed up the remaining rungs and hoisted herself upward. Hay bales were stacked high, nearly to the rafters. Above the tallest stacks, a single round window was cracked to let in a breath of frigid air and what little light the night sky had to offer. She heard the sudden, wild flap of wings. A barn owl? Or . . . what? Desperately, she tried to hold on to her cool, to keep herself from freaking out.

Damn it, you ninny, it was just a bird.

But what had made it panic and flutter so crazily?

Who knows, probably you! It's just an owl, Nona. It's what they do. For the love of Christ, pull yourself together! He's not interested in a silly goose of a girl. Take off your clothes. Surprise him. Show him you're a real woman.

She crawled up to the top of the hay bales, to the false front, behind which he had carved out an impression, like kids did when they made a hay fort. Bales were stacked all around her, creating walls around the old sleeping bag that was tucked over the floor of their little nest. Inside the hideaway, she killed the flashlight and waited. Where was he?

On her knees, she tossed off the cap and sweater. Then she unhooked her hated bra and slithered out of it. Lord, she had to buy something sexier, one of those push-ups from Victoria's Secret if she could ever get out of this place. They would both leave Blue Rock Academy and be together forever. . . .

She heard his muffled footsteps below as she bit her lip and wiggled out of her jeans, tossing them and her cotton panties onto the heap of clothes.

"Hey." His voice. So close.

But . . . how did he get up here so quickly?

"I like this," he said, and suddenly he was in front of her, completely dressed, his face barely discernible in the darkness. He ran a hand down her side and she trembled.

"Wait," she whispered.

"Nuh-uh. I've waited too long as it is." He pulled her close, a big hand splaying over her back, fingers digging into the flesh around her spine as his lips found hers, and he kissed her hard.

His tongue pushed past her teeth, and his free hand grabbed her breast, moving it, mashing it, kneading it. She gasped as he pushed her back onto the hay. Down, down, down. They tumbled onto the sleeping bag, and she closed her eyes, reveling in his touch, loving the way he explored her.

"You taste so sweet," he said, and bit at the corner of her mouth before sliding lower, kissing her breast, sucking on her nipple, teeth scraping her skin.

God, she was ready for him.

Though a virgin, she knew that this was desire; she felt it lick at her very core. Her hands tore at his clothes, stripping him of his shirt, pushing his pants over his hips. Her nails scratched across his buttocks so deep he sucked in his breath.

"You want me." It was a statement.

"Yes."

"You want it!"

"Y—yes," she admitted as he moved his hand across her abdomen and lower, his fingers parting her legs as he toyed with her.

"God, you're hot!" he whispered.

And he was right. Heat rocketed through her body. Her blood fired through her veins, and she could barely breathe. Here, in this hayloft, she couldn't wait for him to do it to her, to change her life forever. . . .

And he did. Breathing heavily, rubbing himself on her, he said, "I can't wait any longer."

"I know."

She felt his knees push hers aside. "Oh, baby," he whispered, his hunger evident in his voice, his first thrust so painful she cried out. But he didn't stop. Just kept moving inside her, creating friction, making heat, so damned much heat. She heard herself moan over his grunts and rapid, shallow breaths. She clung to him as the world spun out of control.

"You like this, don't ya?" His voice was low, guttural. He thrust harder. Faster. "Tell me."

"Yes," she whispered. "Yes, oooohh." The pain was still there, a burning deep inside, but there was pleasure, too, an ache being salved.

She couldn't think, could barely catch her breath.

The world centered on his hard, nearly vicious thrusts.

Closing her eyes, Nona moved with him, ignoring the pain, losing herself in the moment.

She felt him stiffen and cry out. In ecstasy?

From the floor below, one of the horses nickered nervously, then stomped a hoof.

"What was that?" he asked breathlessly, turning his head, his body suddenly still. "What the fu—"

Clunk!

What?

Something cracked and Nona blinked beneath him, trying to see. She called out his name as he fell against her. "Ooof," he moaned, slumping forward, pinning her, a dead weight.

"Hey!" she cried, her face pressed against his neck. "Are you okay?" She reached up to cradle his head, her fingers threading through his hair and coming away wet and warm and sticky.

Blood?

What?

Her insides crawled. She attempted to push him off her. Tried to scream, but suddenly hands were at her throat. Squeezing. Cutting off her air.

What was this?

Panic jettisoned through her. This wasn't happening. Couldn't be. But even as denial swept over her, she was fighting. Kicking. Clawing. What the hell . . . Oh, God, she couldn't breathe. Couldn't draw a damned breath.

How? Why? Questions piled with sheer, dark terror assailed her.

She was trapped. Her boyfriend was unmoving. She tried to roll away, squeeze out from under him. As she did, she caught a glimpse of the person whose hands circled her neck, cutting off her air.

Squeezing!

Tighter and tighter!

No!

Thumbs dug deep into the hollow of her throat. Pressing. The world spun, the smells of horses, dust, and dung deep in her nostrils, the fear of death clawing at her brain.

Using all her strength, Nona arched her spine. Tried to roll away.

Her boyfriend slid off of her, or was kicked aside; she didn't know which, couldn't think. Her head was exploding, darkness rising before her eyes.

Fight, Nona! Save yourself! Oh, Jesus!

She scrabbled, trying to dig at her attacker's wrists, force him off her, gain a little room so that she could drag in a breath. Just one. Anything!

But it was no use. The horrid hands tightened.

Help me. Please, someone help me.

Her lungs were on fire. Silently shrieking for air.

No! No! No!

Nona tried to yell, to scream, but no sound escaped, the air in her airway trapped and burning like all hell. She needed to breathe! To gasp. To cough! Anything!

If only someone would hear her, but the noises coming from her throat were only sick, frightening gurgles.

She writhed, frantically trying to buck the maniac off her, the sleeping bag bunching beneath her, bits of hay clinging to her hair. But the more she struggled, the stronger and more determined were the fingers at her throat.

"Die, bitch!" The words, a low growl, reverberated through the hayloft.

Oh, God.

No!

Blackness swam before her eyes. Pain ripped mercilessly through her body.

No! No! Oh, dear God, no!

She clawed desperately. Wildly.

Help! she silently cried, kicking, writhing. *Oh, sweet Jesus, someone please, please help me!*

Pain rocketed through her. Light splintered behind her eyes. Bursts of horrid, brilliant color. Her lungs were so damned tight, and she couldn't think, could barely flail.

Please . . .

But it was too late.

She felt her life oozing away, blackness creeping over her.

Her hands fell limp at her sides.

The fingers around her throat clamped even tighter, crushing her airway.

Somewhere high overhead, the owl hooted and flapped his great wings, but she couldn't see or hear him. The only sound was the rush of blood in her ears. The only vision was the shadowy face of her assailant.

In those last few seconds of consciousness, Nona Vickers realized that she'd lost more than her virginity this night; she'd also given up her life.

CHAPTER 14

Cooper Trent woke up in a foul mood.

After a restless night, he gave up, rolled out of bed, and slammed shut the window he'd cracked open, thinking that the cold mountain air would help him sleep. Not that it mattered, as this old cottage was so poorly insulated that the elements tended to seep right through the walls.

Daylight was hours from splitting the night sky, but that was just too bad. He wasn't going to spend another second tossing and turning and wondering what the hell he was doing here. He thought about what he'd discovered in the past few months, and it wasn't much. Something was going on beneath the surface of this institution, but he hadn't been able to put his finger on it.

Some of the students had opened up to him about Lauren Conway. In his phys ed classes, he'd done a few lectures about stress and relaxation, leading students to talk about things that bothered them. In two classes, the topic of Lauren's disappearance had come up. Student opinion seemed to fall in two categories: those who thought she had been killed by the school while trying to escape, and those who'd thought she made it. "I like to think that she got away from this school and away from her parents. I can just see Lauren living in some city somewhere with a job and her own apartment. She's living a life and laughing at Blue Rock," Maeve Mancuso had said, and her friends Lucy and Nell had agreed.

"Even though she was a TA and had come here voluntarily?" Trent hadn't been able to follow Maeve's reasoning.

"Yeah, well, that was probably the first step into breaking away from her family."

"She was twenty. Of age."

Maeve's frown had indicated he didn't know anything. "Some parents run your life forever. Just ask my older sister!"

Maeve had an unrealistic theory, one that lacked foundation. If Lauren had escaped these mountains last November, she would have been spotted by someone in a nearby town or seen hitchhiking on the interstate.

Trent hadn't pressed the issue with Maeve and her friends. To argue vehemently or in any way remind them that he was an authority figure would undermine their trust, and he needed the kids to open up to him if he was ever going to find out what had really happened to Lauren, which was, of course, his real reason for taking the job at Blue Rock.

Trent had also overheard a few conversations suggesting that a group of students had formed some kind of secret club. "They meet after dark, and you have to be hand-picked to join." This he'd gathered from the buzz in the boys' locker room. It sounded like a fraternity, but he'd found no evidence that the school was involved. Though he didn't agree with all of Blue Rock's policies, so far the teachers and staff seemed to be true to their mission. Blue Rock was a school dedicated to helping at-risk kids find their way back to their families and God. Some of their practices seemed extreme, but no school activity could account for Lauren Conway's disappearance. Kidnapping and murder were not a part of the curriculum.

And the faculty was tight-lipped. Stiff. Which didn't help him at all.

Trent wished he had something more definitive to report back to the Conways, since they'd hired him to find their daughter, but so far, he'd come up pretty damned empty-handed.

Scraping a hand over his whiskered jaw, he walked to the window, then snapped the shades open. What was the story with those dogs, barking in the middle of the night? They'd shut up after a while, but they'd shot all chances of sleep to hell.

He tossed on yesterday's jeans and his faded flannel shirt. Then, before making a pot of coffee, he pulled on a pair of comfortable boots, worn and battered from his rodeo days years ago.

Sometimes, when he was restless, he'd visit the animals. He would stop at the horse barn first, then wander through the pens of chickens, goats, and pigs before stopping at the kennels. He missed having his own small herd of horses, or, at the very least, a dog. So far, he hadn't replaced Buster, a dog that had been part German shepherd, part boxer, and God knew what else. Loyal and true, Buster had been known to be afraid of his own shadow.

Stretching, he heard his back pop, reminding him of how many times he'd been thrown into the dirt of a rodeo ring. He missed that life. Once, living among horses, cowboys, dust, and leather had been a part of his future, but then things had changed abruptly when his femur had snapped in two places.

So, now, here he was, living a life that wasn't what he'd planned, lying through his teeth as he did it. His leg had healed, his wounded pride not so much, and though he was healthy, athletic again, he'd hung up his spurs.

Who cared?

It was all ancient history.

Right there with Jules Delaney, and he'd been reminded of her a lot lately, what with her half sister now in his charge. What were the odds of that?

He snagged his jacket from a peg near the door and patted a pocket out of habit, forgetting for a split second that he'd given up smoking years before.

At Jules's insistence.

He felt his lips twist wryly when he thought about how he'd almost started the habit again once they'd broken up. Then sanity had prevailed. Withdrawal from nicotine was a bitch; he never wanted to go through that again.

No stars this morning.

No coyotes yipping or howling.

Not even a bat flying by as he pulled on his work gloves and headed toward the darkened stable.

Calm and peaceful, a light snow was falling in thick white flakes to drift against the buildings and catch in the eaves, where icicles had already formed. The place looked like a Christmas card.

But that sense of serenity was short-lived.

The second he opened the door to the horse barn, he knew something was wrong. The energy inside was all wrong. He flipped on one row of lights. The gray mare, Arizona, was snorting and shifting in her stall, and Plato, a Tennessee walker, usually a calm gelding, had pushed his head over the top rail of his box. Plato's eyes were wide and white-rimmed, his chestnut coat quivering.

Creeeaaaak. The noise was soft and low, unnatural.

And there was a smell that didn't belong here.

Over the powerful, warm scent of horses and the acrid odor of urine was another, underlying smell of something darker. Blood?

Trent scraped his gaze over the interior, past the sacks

and barrels of grain and the walls where bridles, halters, and pitchforks hung. Nothing was out of place. And yet . . . He started toward the ladder leading to the hayloft, then broke into a run.

"Shit!"

Just beneath the opening to the upper floor was the crumpled, naked body of a man. Trent hurried around the body to examine the face. Prescott. One of the TAs, Andrew Prescott. Blood had pooled around his head, and he wasn't moving.

"No. Ah, Jesus!" Bending on one knee, Trent felt for a pulse and found the faintest of beats at the kid's neck. He was breathing, his heart beating, but he was in bad shape, the gash on the back of his head gaping, one arm bent at an impossible angle from his fall. "Hang in there, kid," Trent said, and scooped up the wireless phone cradled near the stalls. He punched in 911 and hoped to God help would arrive in time to save the boy's life.

"Come on, come on," he said, praying the connection would go through.

"Nine-one-one. What is the nature of your emergency?"

"Send an ambulance!" he ordered. "Better yet, life flight. I've got an injured student at Blue Rock Academy, and I'd say it's critical. We need to airlift him to the hospital. He's unconscious, a lot of blood, maybe bleeding internally." He rattled off the address of the school, gave the operator his name and position, then barked out, "Tell them to hurry!"

"Sir, stay on the line and—"

"I can't. Just get a medical team to the school, fast!" He hung up and punched the number of the clinic, and the call was forwarded to a groggy Nurse Ayres. "It's Trent. Get to the stables ASAP. Drew Prescott's been injured, bad."

"Have you called Reverend Lynch?" she asked, her voice thick with sleep.

"Hell, no! I've called nine-one-one and now you, so haul ass with your medical supplies over here, now. He's fading fast."

Trent hung up before she had time to argue, then hovered over the boy. He knew first aid and CPR and various emergency procedures, but he also recognized death when he saw it coming, and Prescott was damned close.

"Hang in there," Trent said to the injured kid as he found a saddle blanket to cover him. "You just hang the hell in there. Come on, Drew. You can do it. I know you can."

But he was lying.

The kid was slipping away. Fast.

Within minutes, Ayres arrived, toting a hefty first-aid kit. She was on her knees at Drew's side in an instant. "Did you find a pulse?" she asked Trent.

"Very slight, but it's there." Trent watched as she gloved up and set to work examining the student.

A moment later, Lynch's long strides carried him into the stable. His clothes still looked pressed, his damned hair combed, though his beard shadow gave his usually neat soul patch a ragged appearance. "What's going on here?" he demanded, seemingly outraged at the sight of the injured student.

Trent shook his head. "I wish I knew."

"Why in the world is this boy out here? And where are his clothes?" Lynch turned his face away from the unconscious student, his gaze scraping the interior of the stable. "What's this?"

"What?" Trent looked up from Drew Prescott's bloodless face to see the spot where Lynch was looking, a smear of blood mixed with straw. In his concern for the boy, he hadn't noticed the stain that was separate from the wide puddle of blood beneath Drew's head. "Don't touch it," he said to the director, who was bending low over the stain. "Leave it for the police."

"I could use some help here!" Ayres said. Kneeling beside the boy, she was lifting Drew's arm from under the saddle blanket to take his blood pressure. Trent took the corner of the blanket while Lynch, worry lining his brow, closed his eyes and, lips moving silently, appeared to pray.

"What happened here?" Ayres asked.

"I found him when I came to check on the horses." Trent gave her a quick rundown of what he'd discovered.

"Why were you out here so early?" the director asked as he opened his eyes again, his prayer finished. Silent accusations hung in the musty air.

Hell! Trent didn't have time for this, not now. "Look, our first priority is to take care of this guy, get him the medical attention he needs." Trent wasn't afraid of being a scapegoat. Let the reverend, so quick to point blame, think what he wanted.

"He's breathing at least." Nurse Ayres talked through her inventory. "ABC. Airway, breathing, circulation. Wound seems to be clotting, but he needs oxygen. More blankets. Hydration. I need the neck brace in case there's spinal injury, and the backboard. We can't move him anywhere until his cervical spine is immobilized."

The stable door banged open.

Bert Flannagan, all five feet ten inches of suppressed fury, swept inside with a rush of wintry air. Rifle in hand, he marched down the aisle between the stalls. "What the hell is going on here?" he asked. "I saw the lights—" His breath whistled between his teeth as he caught sight of Drew Prescott's motionless body. "For the love of Saint Jude, what happened here?"

"We don't know," Trent said.

Flannagan's hard expression didn't alter. "Is he alive?"

"Barely." Ayres was all business as she carefully applied pressure to the patient's open wound.

Trent's jaw tightened. Time was of the essence. "Life flight is on its way."

Lynch's head snapped up. "You phoned for help?"

"That's right. Couldn't stay on the line, though."

"Call them again!" Ayres ordered, her voice urgent.

The reverend's cool facade cracked. "You should have spoken to me first; this wasn't your call—"

"Shut up, Tobias!" Ayres's eyes flashed angrily. "Trent did the right thing. This boy needs to get to a hospital, fast."

Lynch argued, "But there's a protocol."

"Screw protocol!" The nurse's face was beet red with fury. "This kid's got a broken ulna and radius, a helluva head injury, and God only knows what else inside!" She shook her head in disgust. "Let's not have a student die on us if we can help it. Especially while we're discussing protocol."

Lynch cupped his chin in one hand and closed his eyes in surrender. "Fine."

Disgusted, Ayres turned to Trent. "We need to get him warmed up and stabilized until the medevac copter gets here. We need a backboard and oxygen from the clinic. Yes, it would be easier on him to bring those things here. Oh, and I can start an IV line."

"We could drive him to the nearest hospital," Lynch suggested, beginning to understand the severity of the situation.

"Two hours away? With a head wound?" Again she pinned Trent in her stare. "You're sure they're sending a helicopter?"

"I told them it was necessary. No other quick way in here."

"Those flights get grounded in foul weather, and there's already some snow falling, a storm predicted." Flannagan strode to the windows where the first streaks of gray light penetrated the night sky.

Ayres took charge. "Then phone again." She sent a killing glare up at Lynch. "Better yet, since you're the director, you handle it. You call nine-one-one." She reached into her first-aid kit as Lynch, no longer arguing, found the phone. "If they're on their way, we'll get him on a board and stretcher and wheel him over to the helipad." She pointed to Flannagan. "What the hell are you waiting for? I need that backboard, blankets, and oxygen. STAT!"

"You got 'em!" Flannagan was out the door as fast as he'd swept in.

Lynch was already dialing 911. Within seconds he was connected. "This is Reverend Tobias Lynch," he said solemnly. "I'm calling to check on the status of a life flight to Blue Rock Academy."

The reverend sounded cooler than he looked, Trent thought as he watched Ayres place a tourniquet around Drew's arm and swab it, searching for a vein to start an IV line. At least Ayres seemed to know her job.

"Yes, I'll hold," Lynch said as the door opened again.

This time Jacob McAllister strode in. His face was set and hard, all the boyish charm he usually radiated cut off.

"What happened?" he said, dropping to a knee at Prescott's side.

"They're on their way?" Ayres asked without looking up from the procedure, not giving the young preacher an answer.

"The dispatcher says it's in progress." Lynch cringed when he dared to look down at the boy, who was still hanging on, his skin pallid.

"How did this happen?" McAllister demanded.

"We don't know," Trent said.

Lynch was shaking his head. "Why would he be here alone? And naked?"

Trent scowled as he thought. "Was he alone? I wouldn't bet on it." He met the questions in McAllister's eyes.

"Oh, dear God, there could be others," Lynch whispered, running a shaking hand over his neatly combed hair, mussing it, no doubt his thoughts on the reputation of the school.

Creeeaaak!

The unworldly sound again. Like a ghost moaning.

Trent felt a whisper of dread crawl up his spine.

"What's that?" Lynch stepped back, squinting up toward the opening to the hayloft.

A knot in his gut, Trent was already on the first rung of the ladder.

Was someone else in the loft?

Injured?

Oh, hell.

He climbed, his boots ringing through the stable, one of the horses letting out a worried neigh. The minute he hoisted himself into the upper story, he knew something was wrong. He looked down. Yeah, obviously Drew had fallen through the opening around the ladder; blood showed on the rough edge of the board where the kid had hit his head when falling through. And there was more—evidence of someone being dragged through the scattered straw.

What the hell had gone on here?

Who had Drew met? Or had the kid walked in on something he wasn't supposed to see?

He stepped closer to the stacked bales, noticing a dark stain in the thinly strewn hay at his feet, hearing someone following him up the ladder.

A trail of blood.

Drew's?

Creeeaaaaak!

The sound was louder, gave him the willies. He looked up to the darkened rafters, then jumped backward, nearly falling through the hole in the floor himself.

"Jesus!" he whispered as his eyes grew accustomed to the darkness.

He thought he might be sick.

A young woman's naked body swung gently from a rope tied to a crossbeam. White and ashen, her eyes bulging, she twisted slightly as a breeze blew through the open window.

"Goddamn it!" He couldn't believe what his eyes were telling him as he stared at the details of her face, puffy and pale.

Nona Vickers was hanging from the rafters, her bare skin blue in the half-light.

"Son of a bitch," he muttered under his breath, questions cutting through his brain.

"For the love of the father." McAllister was standing next to Trent, staring up at the dangling corpse, his hand to his mouth as if he might be sick. "Saints be with us."

Who had done this? Trent wondered.

Why?

Drew?

Had he, after stringing Nona up, fallen through the opening by mistake?

No, no. It didn't make any sense.

Two pinpoints of light in the dark rafters startled him . . . the eyes of an owl, roosting above the girl's body.

"What is it? Did you find something?" Reverend Lynch's voice boomed upward, through the opening to the floor below.

Oh, yeah, Trent thought, still staring at the girl. He'd found something all right. And it looked like the work of the devil.

CHAPTER 15

"I don't know anything!" Shay insisted, her eyes round with fear.

Watching her, Trent felt bad that the girl had been rousted from her bed and hauled into Reverend Lynch's office in the middle of the night.

Trent stood near the window, watching the road, listening. He didn't like what was happening here; it seemed more like an inquisition than a casual questioning, but the stakes were high. Someone had killed Nona Vickers, and until that person was caught, fear and terror would haunt everyone on this campus.

Adele Burdette leaned against the door as if to block it, just in case Shaylee decided to bolt.

And run where? Trent wondered.

"What's going on?" Shay asked. "Where's Nona?"

Lynch was calm, his voice even. At least he was trying to keep things under control. "You and Nona share a room. When did she leave?"

"I didn't know she did!" Shay's skin was sickly white against her black hair. "She was still up when I fell asleep. And . . . and the next thing I know, she"—Shay hooked a thumb at Burdette—"bursts through the door like there's a police raid and orders me to get dressed." Outraged, Shay turned furious eyes on the dean of women. "Then she waited in the room while I put some clothes on. What are you? Some kind of lesbo perv?"

Burdette's jaw tightened as she folded her arms over her chest, but she didn't rise to the bait.

"Let's not resort to name-calling," Lynch said, but his own equanimity was obviously rattled.

"What happened?" Shay asked. "I saw the helicopter. Someone was airlifted out of here. Is that what happened? Is Nona hurt?" Her eyes were round and wide. Scared. "Look, she was my roommate. I deserve to know."

Trent agreed.

"I'll be making a statement shortly," Reverend Lynch said.

"A statement about what?" Shaylee demanded.

Trent had heard enough. It was time they quit beating around the bush. "Nona's dead."

"What?" Shaylee nearly jumped out of her chair. "Dead? No. Dead? Oh, God . . . no. You're wrong. She was there in the room last night and . . . and . . ." She turned horrified eyes to Trent. "They wouldn't take her body out in a helicopter. She has to be alive. She has to!"

"That was Drew Prescott." Trent walked closer to her, resting a hip against the desk, leaning closer.

"What? Drew?" Shay squinted. "I don't get it."

"We found him in the stable, along with Nona. She was dead; he's in critical condition."

Shaylee shrank into her chair. "Jesus Christ. How? I mean, where . . . Oh, God, she said she had a boyfriend, but I didn't believe her." She drew her legs up on the chair and wrapped her arms around her knees. "They snuck out and there was an accident?" She shook her head in disbelief.

"Did she tell you she was sneaking out?"

"No."

"But she told you about Drew."

"Just that she had a boyfriend . . . that was all; she wouldn't tell me his name. It was like some big secret or something."

"So the last time you saw her was—"

"In our room. She was there when I went to bed, and next thing I knew, there was all this pounding on the door, and here I am."

"Your baseball cap was near her body."

"What?" Shaylee's head snapped up, and she clamped two hands atop her head as if to locate the hat in question. "No, it wasn't." She was shaking her head again, as if in so doing she could change everything that was happening.

Trent nodded. "In a pile with her clothes."

"She . . . she wasn't wearing her clothes?" Shay whispered, and bit her lip. "Why not?"

"Why was your hat there?"

"I don't know! The last time I saw it, it was on the hook by the door in our room. That's where I put it. How it got . . . wherever she was." She looked at Trent. "Where was she? In Drew's room?"

"In the stable."

"That's enough," Lynch said. "We'd better wait for Sheriff O'Donnell before we question her further. He promised to come out personally, with the detectives."

"The sheriff? Detectives? This was an accident, right? They got themselves trampled or fell or . . ." Shay's eyes were huge, dark with fear.

Trent felt for her. "They always look into accidents." He didn't want to panic the girl, but it seemed too late.

"Police officers, yeah. Accident-reconstruction people . . . but that's not what he's saying." Shaylee sank down in the chair.

Trent said, "Detectives are called when someone dies."

But Shaylee would not be reassured. "Wait a minute, you don't think that someone . . ." She swallowed hard, blinking back tears. "Wait a friggin' second. Do you think that I . . . ?" She looked from Lynch to Trent, and some of the color returned to her face. "The talk about my hat—you think I'm responsible for whatever happened to Nona and Drew? Do I need a lawyer or something?" She was more than scared now. Terrified. "What the hell happened to Nona?"

"A lawyer?" Burdette repeated, her eyebrows rising as if she were truly surprised. "Shaylee, you've been watching too much TV."

"This is over," Trent said. "When the sheriff gets here, he's going to want to talk to a lot of us, so for now, let's just wait."

But Shaylee lowered her head into her hands, a gesture of surrender. "Don't you have cameras everywhere around campus? In the dorm rooms? In the hallways? Even in the stable?" She turned accusing eyes at Reverend Lynch, who blanched visibly. "Then everything's on tape, right? So why the hell am I here being treated like some kind of criminal? Look at your sicko—probably illegal—tapes and let me go." Finding Trent as her only ally in the room, she turned big, pleading eyes up at him. "And I don't mean back to the dorm. I want out of here. Someone call my mother. Tell her what happened, that kids are dying, okay? I want to go home. And I want to go now!"

Jules was hungry and tired, and her butt was starting to ache like crazy from hours of sitting behind the wheel of the car.

Still, she drove, eyeing the road ahead. This part of I-5 was a treacherous gray snake that curved and twisted through the steep, forested mountains of southern Oregon.

Having been behind the wheel for over seven hours through most of Washington and Oregon, she stepped on the accelerator, her Volvo's tires singing as she passed semis that crept up the hills, then barreled down steep inclines.

Her stomach was rumbling, her mood decidedly souring. Sleep had eluded her this week, the recurring nightmare of her father's death creeping through her subconscious, images of Cooper Trent interspersed with the horror of blood seeping over the hardwood floor.

After popping a couple of headache pills with two cups of black coffee this morning, she'd only stopped for a burger and a Diet Coke from a drive-through outside Portland. No wonder her stomach was roiling.

She'd drunk most of the bottle of water she thought to pack, and her headache was back, inching its painful way through her skull.

In the past few days, she'd cleaned out her refrigerator, prepaid her rent, and settled Diablo in with her neighbor, Mrs. Dixon, who'd been delighted—actually clapping her hands—at the prospect of caring for her favorite cat. Jules had also squared things with Tony and Dora at the 101, left messages with Gerri and Erin that she would be "out of town" for a while, then offered up a flimsy excuse to Edie about a possible teaching job in Northern California.

Now, with her head throbbing, Jules had to look ahead to her ultimate goal. If Blue Rock Academy was all it was cracked up to be, then fine, Shay would have to do her time. But, if Jules's suspicions that the school wasn't the shining institution for youth it claimed to be turned out to be true, then Jules intended to spring her sister and let the whole world see the academy for the sham it was.

Edie would have to deal with her daughter and find Shay a day facility. Or, if that didn't work, Shay would have to swallow her considerable pride and attitude and live with Jules.

As the miles sped away, doubts assailed her.

What if you're wrong? What if everything down at Blue Rock is totally on the level? What if you're, as your ex so often said, an alarmist, a person looking for a good conspiracy?

"I'm not," she said aloud as the radio station she'd picked up around Eugene started to fade. Rick Springfield's "Jessie's Girl," part of the station's playlist from "the eighties biggest hits" was rapidly being replaced by crackling static.

She hit the SCAN button and heard the remnants of an old Waylon Jennings and Willie Nelson tune about mamas not letting their babies grow up to become cowboys.

In her mind's eye, she saw Cooper Trent's rugged face: crow's-feet fanning out from deep-set eyes that shifted from green to gold in the sunlight. Straight hair, forever mussed, streaked by hours in the sun. A nose that had been broken more than once and a jaw that could be set so hard a pit bull would be envious. Not Hollywood handsome by any means, but strong and sexy and a major pain in the rear.

"Damn it!" She clicked off the radio. "Go away," she muttered, not allowing her mind to linger on that son of a bitch. What had she been thinking, falling in love with a bull rider and, as it turned out, a bullshitter? What was the saying? When the going gets tough, the tough get going. Yeah, well, that's the way it had been with Trent, and she was ticked at herself for even having the tiniest thought of him.

"A long, long time ago," she reminded herself, and flipped on her wipers. Rain mixed with snow had begun to fall.

She didn't have a GPS, so she was using a map she'd pulled off the Internet. So far, the trip had been easy: Drive onto I-5 and head south for over four hundred miles. But now things were getting a little dicier, as snow was beginning to fall, fat flakes skittering over her windshield and gathering along the edges of the highway.

Great, just great.

She slowed down, though fifty felt like a crawl. With relief, she saw the sign to exit the interstate. She turned off the expressway onto a county highway, a narrow road that traveled a serpentine path through steep canyons. Her knuckles ached from gripping the steering wheel. The small towns wedged into the hills were little more than four-way stops in the road. Such a deserted, lonely stretch of road, now white with snow.

Her cell beeped from its spot in the unused cup holder. She answered but kept one wary eye on the road. "Hello?"

"Ms. Farentino?" a vaguely familiar voice asked. "This is Dr. Hammersley of Blue Rock Academy."

Jules's heart sank. The school had figured out that she was a fraud, and the dean was calling to say they would not be hiring her.

Hammersley went on. "I'm afraid I have some disturbing news."

Oh, God. As the windshield wipers slapped the snow away, Jules looked for a place to pull over, but the road was too narrow, no wide spots or driveways allowing her a space to park. "What is it?"

"There's been an accident."

Shay! Her heart stopped. You're too late! Something horrible has happened to your sister!

"I don't want to alarm you," Hammersley went on.

Too late!

"But I was afraid you might hear it on the news, so I wanted to tell you that one of our students has died, and another is in critical condition at a nearby hospital."

Jules let out a little squeak of protest.

"The doctors are not certain that he'll make it."

Not certain that *he* will make it, Hammersley had said, meaning a boy. *Not* Shaylee.

Hammersley cleared her throat as Jules's mind raced with scenarios of horrid accidents befalling her sister and a friend. Boating, horseback riding, wilderness hikes, rock climbing—all dangerous. All potentially deadly.

"Who?" Jules forced the words out as she noticed a turnout for a logging road and pulled the car onto the frozen shoulder. Her tires slid to a stop, and she pushed the gearshift into park.

"I really can't give out the information until next of kin has been notified. School policy."

"But I'm on the staff," Jules said, panic blooming in her chest, her heart thudding out of control. Not Shay, oh, please God, not Shay!

"Don't worry, you'll hear everything when you get here. You're on your way?"

"Yes, not far . . . maybe twenty or thirty miles, but it just started snowing."

"Yes, there's a storm hanging over the mountains. Take it slow. Did you bring chains?"

"They're in the back." But Jules had never used them. She wasn't even sure how to chain up.

"You'll need to park in the lot near the gatehouse," Hammersley said. "There's an area marked for all staff vehicles. I'll have someone meet you at the gate, get your name on the clearance list, and make sure you get in without any trouble."

"Thank you," Jules said weakly. She hung up and let her shoulders sag as she drew in several deep, calming breaths. The windows of the Volvo had fogged during the short conversation, the white hills closing in. Half an inch of snow already coated the hood of her car. Apprehension and isolation tugged at her, and she tasted fear, so bitter on the back of her tongue. Even if Shay wasn't hurt, one student was dead, one was hurt; two families would be as frightened as she was now.

As frightened as Shay was to be shipped off to the academy?

With trembling hands, Jules pushed the gearshift lever into drive and pulled onto the road again, her tires sliding just a bit. What, she wondered, had she gotten herself into?

Rhonda Hammersley walked into the rec hall where the students had been asked to assemble. The detectives from the sheriff's office wanted to talk to each of them, and while deputies did the first round of interviews, separating the wheat from the chaff, the rest waited.

The room was somber and ghastly quiet. No one cracked jokes. No one strummed a guitar. All the students sat with books open, though the dean suspected that no one was studying.

Who could blame them?

Beyond the windows, snow floated down as it had all day. Big, fluffy flakes swirled lazily from the heavens, adding a serene blanket of white to the grounds, capping the trees, coating the walkways.

The campus looked idyllic and peaceful, though it was anything but calm. The students were freaked, and already, Charla King, the school secretary, reported that a few frantic parents had phoned. Someone had leaked the information. Perhaps it was an employee of the school, the sheriff's department, or the hospital where Drew Prescott now lay in critical condition.

Whatever the source of the leak, the word was out. Hammersley had helped Reverend Lynch field a few calls from the media. One television van was parked at the main gates, and if the weather improved, helicopters would be buzzing overhead, trying to film the campus. In fact, the weather was the one thing staving off eager reporters, terrified parents, and scads of law enforcement agencies. Old tragedies like the Conway girl's disappearance and Maris Howell's alleged sexual involvement with a student would be revisited.

Dark times ahead for Blue Rock.

Worry consumed her as she walked across the open area with the conversation pit and stone fireplace, where a fire was burning low, hissing softly in the grate. Despite Blue Rock's faults, she loved this place; she believed in its mission. Over the past few years, she had seen much good come of the counseling and positive leadership provided to the kids who came here. They arrived jaded and burned out, some so lost it was hard to see a glimmer of hope in their eyes. Turning these kids around was not an easy task, but she'd always believed that nothing worthwhile came easily. They needed help, and by the grace of God, she was here to give it.

Keeping watch over the students, pod leaders pretended to work quietly, their books and notes scattered around them. Which pod leader should she send to pick up the new teacher at the gate? She scanned the group and decided on Cooper Trent, who had already been questioned by deputies and detectives. In his absence Wade Taggert and the other pod leaders, Adele Burdette and Tyeesha Williams, could ride herd over this dejected group. Besides, those three had also already given their statements.

Reverend Lynch had retreated to his office, where he juggled complaints and inquiries from the sheriff's department, students, staff, and parents. Rhonda was relieved that it had fallen on Lynch's shoulders to handle Nona Vickers's grief-riddled father, as well as the parents of Drew Prescott, who were driving to Medford to join their son. If it weren't for the beast of a storm, parents would be pulling their kids out or demanding they be flown out, which was impossible in this snow. The seaplane was grounded until the snowstorm lifted, although Lynch was so intent on getting Cora Sue on campus that he'd booked her on a commercial airliner and sent Spurrier to retrieve her in the school's Jeep, once she landed in Medford.

With all of the impending scandal and media attention, the reverend was desperate to have his lovely, dedicated wife at his side for comfort and, of course, for appearances in front of the media.

Again, Hammersley glanced outside. The weather service had predicted that this would be the mother of all storms, up to three feet of snow to be dumped in the next two days. That meant isolation. The school had generators and snowplows, but even so, the roads would be treacherous if not impassable for a while. Lack of access would certainly stymie the homicide investigation and exacerbate the isolation of the campus.

It was a wonder that Julia Farentino was still ready to take the job, though no one would want to turn back through that storm in the mountains.

Cooper Trent sat on a bench near the fire, his hands clasped between his knees. He looked up as Hammersley approached. "Any word on Drew?" he asked.

She shook her head, then sat on the bench next to him. "I don't know anything more than before—surgery, then, if he pulls through, he'll be in ICU. His parents have been notified; his mother and stepfather are driving to Medford from Bakersfield, California. Reverend Lynch left a message for the biological father in Las Vegas, but that's all I know."

Trent nodded, his thoughtful scowl intact.

She asked, "How about doing me a favor?"

"Depends on what it is."

"I've got the new teacher coming in, and I haven't been interviewed yet. Could you pick her up? I think it would be better than having her wait in the guardhouse for the supply van."

"You finally hired someone?" Trent asked, obviously surprised. Lowering his voice, he asked, "You're bringing someone into this hornet's nest?"

Hammersley shrugged. "She was already on her way, though I warned her that there's been an accident."

"An accident?" Trent frowned as he rubbed the back of his neck. "Hell, that's really whitewashing it, don't you think?"

"I couldn't really say anything until I was certain that the next of kin had been notified."

"Nona's dad?"

Hammersley nodded. Whit Vickers was a single parent, Nona's mom long out of the picture. An only child, Nona wasn't a bad kid, just offtrack. Poor girl.

"You just didn't want to lose the new recruit," he said, eyes accusing. "If I pick her up, I'll tell her the truth."

Of course he would. He never sugarcoated anything. He usually wasn't harsh, just a straight shooter. Even so, Hammersley thought something about him didn't ring quite true; she wouldn't be surprised if Trent had a skeleton or two hidden away in his own closet.

So join the club.

"I'm not keeping secrets," he said, as if reading her mind.

"Fine, tell her." Why not? The minute Julia Farentino drove into the parking lot by the main gate and saw the television van and county vehicles, she'd know that the incident was something more than just an "accident." Hammersley handed Trent the keys to one of the school's Jeeps. "Normally, Reverend Lynch would want to handle the details, but all things considered . . ."

Trent glanced at the room where the kids were being interviewed, nearly a hundred of them, all in the reverend's charge. "Looks like he'll be busy for a while."

"That's why you've got the job. Tell her."

Trent stood, stretched his shoulders. "She here yet?"

"Not quite, but she's on her way, should be arriving within the next half hour or so."

"She got a name?"

She appreciated Trent's sense of humor, considering the grim circumstances. "That she does: Julia Farentino, from Portland." Was it her imagination or did the corner of Trent's mouth tighten a bit? Hammersley added, "Julia's young, not quite twenty-five, so she should relate to the kids. I feel, if things ever calm down around here, she's going to fit in just fine and be a real asset to the academy."

"I hope so," Trent said, but for some reason, his words held more than a trace of sarcasm. He snagged the keys from Hammersley's hand and added, "I can't wait to meet her."

CHAPTER 16

Hammersley had to be kidding or mistaken, right? But Trent didn't see one glimmer of levity in the woman's eyes. She was dead serious. And, of course, she had no idea that Trent and Jules Delaney, aka Jules Farentino, had once been lovers.

Right?

For the love of Christ, what the hell did that mean?

Nothing good.

Not one damned thing!

Every muscle in his back tightened, but somehow he kept his face impassive, snagged the keys, and headed to the garage where the Jeep was parked. Instead of cooling off, with each step he grew more infuriated, more incredulous. Jules? Here? Less than a week after her sister had become a student at Blue Rock?

Nuts, that's what it was. Goddamned, frickin' nuts!

He reached the garage but found the Jeep parked outside. With one of his gloves, he swiped snow from the windshield, worked on the ice, then slid inside.

"Son of a bitch," he growled as he jabbed the key into

the ignition, and wheeled onto the long road leading to the main gate. "Son of a goddamned bitch!"

Why Jules? Why now?

The last time he'd seen her, she'd been falling into a million pieces. When he'd stupidly tried to help her pull herself together, she'd broken it off. Quick. Simple. Her parting words had been, *Don't touch me. Don't call. Just get the hell out of my life! Got it, Cowboy? Leave me the hell alone.* Then tears had filled her eyes. *I never want to see you again.*

He hadn't believed her. He'd even gone so far as to take a step forward, and she'd slammed the door in his face before twisting the dead bolt shut.

That resolute click had echoed through his brain.

He'd pounded. Yelled. Told her that she was making a mistake, that she shouldn't shut him out, that he loved her, damn it, but she hadn't responded.

Burned, his pride trampled to a pulp, he gave up. He'd gotten the message.

Loud and clear.

Much as he sometimes wanted to, he never picked up the phone or drove by her house again. If that was the way she wanted to play it, damn it, he wasn't going to grovel. He wasn't the send-flowers-after-a-spat kind of man, and she knew it. The next thing he'd heard, she was engaged, then quickly married. A divorce had eventually followed, or at least according to B.J. Crosby, who, after a few beers somehow always needed to impart whatever he'd learned about Jules from his sister, Erin.

So now Trent was going to face her again?

What a frickin' disaster.

Snow was falling steadily, keeping the wipers busy as he drove.

Trent had spent most of the day trying to figure out what had happened in the hayloft, what had created the gruesome scene. His hands tightened on the wheel as he thought about Nona Vickers's naked body swaying from the rafters.

Suicide?

He wouldn't bet on it. If Nona had wanted to off herself, swallowing a bottle of pills would have been a whole lot easier, and though all prescriptions were carefully monitored, there was a black market on campus, just as there was in most prisons. If someone wanted something badly enough and was willing to pay, trade, or barter, they could get it. Despite what all the glossy literature about Blue Rock Academy claimed about being drug-free, there were cracks in the shiny veneer.

There had been discussions of how to curtail the problem but no permanent solutions.

If Trent were to bet on the source of the black market, he'd probably pick some of the TAs. They seemed to get far more privileges than just a year or two of good behavior should warrant. Roberto Ortega and Tim Takasumi spent a lot of time in the clinic and computer lab, areas restricted to the regular students.

And they knew a lot about the kids who were enrolled here—not only by hanging out with them and working in the classroom, but also through other means, or so Trent concluded. Assistants such as Missy Albright, Kaci Donahue, and Ethan Slade worked in the counseling offices, too, close to sensitive files. Zach Bernsen and Eric Rolfe had access to the stables, water craft, and weapons used in survival skills. Yeah, the rules were decidedly loose for the group of kids who'd elected to stay on after graduation. Privileges granted.

Andrew Prescott was being considered, after his graduation, to become one of the youngest teaching assistants, a new recruit. Reverend Lynch had mentioned it in the last staff meeting and had indicated that Andrew's parents were interested in him being a part of the program. What Andrew had thought of it, Trent didn't know and wondered if he, or anyone else, ever would.

Because Andrew was now fighting for his life.

What the hell had happened in the hayloft? Trent asked himself for the millionth time as the tires crunched through new snow and slipped into icy ruts. From all appearances, it seemed that Nona Vickers had met Drew Prescott for the express purpose of sex. Their clothes were piled together. The unzipped sleeping bag in the loft had been mussed, the flannel lining probably stained with blood and semen.

So if it started as a romp in the hay, something had gone wrong.

Something had happened.

He'd considered and discounted various theories involving rape, a gang bang, or a suicide pact. But he kept getting back to the fact that these kids had been found in a love den, and they were both naked.

Were they having sex when a third person had discovered them in the hayloft?

But who?

And why?

What other person had been skulking around the stable deep in the night?

Trent remembered Nona's body. There were no contusions other than the bruising around her neck, no cuts or scrapes or broken fingernails. If the hanging didn't kill her, she had died by a means that didn't leave other visible damage. And it had been no quick snap of the neck, as evidenced by the petechial hemorrhaging. He'd made sure that the detectives on the scene, Baines and Jalinsky, had noted the tiny broken blood vessels in Nona's eyes. It pointed to a slow suffocation.

As for Drew Prescott, he, too, had been naked, so it seemed unlikely he was leaving the scene. Even if he'd been scared away, his natural instinct would have been to grab his pants. Right?

No matter how you sliced it, the evidence pointed to a third party in that loft.

He thought of Shaylee Stillman's hat. The only clue connecting her. He discarded the cap as a plant, left to point the guilt her way. If Shaylee had gone to all the trouble of stringing Nona from the rafters and getting rid of Drew, she would have snagged her yellow cap rather than leave it as a beacon shining the blame right on her.

Unless she'd been too freaked out and made a mistake.

She could have gotten careless.

Hell. He flipped the wipers onto a higher tempo as the snowfall increased.

And what was Shaylee's motive for killing Nona?

Privacy? A room to herself? Was her roommate an easy target? Then what about Drew? And how could she pull it off?

No, it just didn't make sense.

But nothing did.

There were so many threads dangling and no way to tie them together.

Scowling as he stared through the windshield, he remembered seeing the flash of yellow-blond hair or a light-colored cap the night the filly had been left out. Shaylee's University of Oregon hat? Missy Albright's platinum hair? Something else? The woman he'd overheard had worried that something would happen to her.

Who knows who could be next? she'd worried aloud.

Had she been talking about Lauren? That would be Trent's guess. Had the speaker been Nona Vickers, predicting her own demise?

I thought it would be fun. A thrill. I believed in him, the girl had also said.

Believed in who?

Lynch? Or someone else?

What would be fun?

Something dangerous, some kind of web where, once they were caught in it, the willing participants couldn't break free.

He slowed for a sharp corner, downshifting, and tried to put it all together. The Jeep's gears strained on the winding road, the four-wheel drive fully engaged. At an altitude of nearly fifty-two hundred feet, the campus was nearly a thousand feet higher than the gatehouse, this access road steep in even the best of conditions.

How did the grisly scene in the stable tie into Lauren Conway's disappearance?

Don't you mean her death?

Face it, Trent, you don't believe she's alive.

He told himself that he wasn't certain what had happened to her, but he knew in his soul that her parents wouldn't see her alive again. He had a gut feeling that Lauren was dead, as was Nona Vickers.

And now you have to worry about Jules.

"Damn it all to hell," he muttered, angry at the world. The last thing he needed was Jules damned Delaney messing up things. He didn't need to be worrying about her on top of everything else.

But, then, he would bet a year's salary she wouldn't be any happier to see him than he was to see her.

He couldn't imagine being near her again, didn't want to think about the last time they'd been together.

Hell, had it been five years?

He felt a moment's regret, then shoved it aside, irritated as hell that his years of not seeing Jules Delaney—no, make that Julia Farentino—were about to end.

* * *

As she turned up the fan on the defroster, Jules worked to find the narrow road beneath the mask of white that covered the earth. Talk about wishing the miles away.

She urged her car up the slippery hills, slowing as the road turned treacherously, her fingers gripping the steering wheel. As the car climbed, the thermometer for the outside temperature showed thirty degrees and the defroster struggled to keep the windows clear and the inside temperature comfortable.

Dusk hung heavy in the snowy landscape when the beams of her headlights splashed over a sign with BLUE ROCK ACADEMY in bold letters. An arrow indicated she should turn onto a private lane guarded by tall fencing that was partially masked by snowy stands of heavy-boughed fir, pine, and madrona trees.

"Here we go," she whispered, just as the phone jangled in the empty cup holder. Expecting to hear Rhonda Hammersley's voice again, she picked up without checking the number. "Hello?"

"Jules!" Shay's panic whispered over the faulty connection. "You have to get me out of here! This place is a frickin' horror movie!"

Jules felt immediate relief. "Shay!" Her sister was alive and well, not fighting for her life in a hospital. "Thank God you're okay!" Tears of relief burned behind her eyelids. "I was worried. I thought . . . I mean, Dr. Hammersley called. I know there's been an accident."

"Accident? Are you out of your mind? It wasn't an accident. No way!" Shay was talking fast, her voice anxious. "If she told you it was an accident, then she lied!"

"Lied about what? What are you talking—"

"Oh, I get it. They're whitewashing it for the families. Right. Claiming some sort of accident so that the parents don't go nuts. Crap! Edie probably believes it, too."

"Wait a minute. Slow down," Jules said, trying to concentrate on driving and the conversation. "What's going on?"

Shay's voice was small. "Oh, God, Jules, the cops have been here all day, and did you know it was my roommate? My roommate, Nona, was killed in the stable."

"Killed?" Jules nearly drove off the road. Her heart was pounding, a million questions screaming through her mind. "Wait a minute. No one said anything about anyone dying. And it was a boy. I thought he was going to pull through—"

"That's Nona's boyfriend. Drew. He's in the hospital, but Nona's dead! And, yeah, she was killed! Friggin' hanged! Either she killed herself or her boyfriend Drew did it, and he's in the hospital on life support or something, and it's . . . it's friggin' scary!" Shay was talking so rapidly that her voice had elevated an octave, her words tumbling out. "You have to get me out of here, Jules. This place . . . this place is worse than jail. I swear to God, everyone here is psycho!"

"Just calm down." Jules was frantic, Shay's anxiety infectious. But she had to take charge and somehow staunch Shaylee's runaway fears.

"I can't. People are dying!"

"Okay, okay, just listen," Jules said, slowing for another curve as the defroster fought the condensation on the windows. "Try to pull it together, okay?" She wasn't going to buy into Shaylee's paranoia, her melodrama.

"Didn't you hear me? Nona's dead!"

"Shhh." The connection was going bad again, and the snow that started as a white powder had turned into icy flakes. "Look, I'm working on getting you out. Trust me."

"Well work faster!"

"Slow down. Take a deep breath. I'm just glad you're okay," Jules said, hoping the connection hadn't been broken.

"I am definitely *not* okay!" Shay insisted. "Get me out.

Call Edie, tell her this is a big mistake. If she won't do any-thing, phone Dad. Tell Max I need the lawyer to make a deal—"

"It's probably too late for that," Jules said as her right tire hit a rock in the rutted road and the sedan bounced, jar-ring her already-pounding head. She gripped the wheel harder.

"Even when some whack job is killing kids?"

"I don't know, but we'll sort it out soon. Look, I'm al-most there."

"What?" Shay whispered. "Almost where?" After a pause, she said, "Here? As in . . ." The rest of what she said was garbled.

"I'm on my way to the school."

"You are? This school? But I don't . . ."

The connection was horrid. The snow came down in heavy, thick flakes, dancing in the beams of her headlights. She couldn't see the sky, could no longer make out the ridges high over this ever-narrowing canyon.

"Listen to me, Shay. Can you hear me?"

"What?" Shay snapped, the connection clear again. "What are you talking about?"

"I'm going to be at the school soon, so do not blow my cover, understand?"

"What the hell are you talking about? What cover?"

Her tires slid a bit, breaking through the new layer of snow, finding packed snow and ice below. She clutched the steering wheel with one hand and told herself, despite the tense conversation, to not overcorrect.

"Blue Rock hired me as a teacher. So I'll be at the school within the hour, I think, maybe less."

"What? Here?"

Nothing again, just fading, sputtering noise. "Damn it!"

She wanted to throw her cell phone out the window for all the good it was doing.

"You are joking, right? You did not take a job here! Come on, Jules, tell me this is your idea of a really, really bad joke."

"I'm not kidding."

The wireless connection was clear again, and Shaylee wasn't having any of Jules's scheme. "No! No way! Listen. You just need to get me out of here and fast! Detectives have been questioning me, because I was the last one to see Nona alive or something. . . . I don't know what that means. Am I a suspect?"

"Why would you be a suspect?"

"I don't know. Just because she was my roommate. I'm telling you things are fu-friggin' weird down here."

"So how did you get to a phone? I thought they were restricted." She fiddled with the heater and realized that she hadn't seen another vehicle on this road for miles. Just how isolated was this place?

"It's Nona's cell. I don't know how she got it, maybe from some black market thing that goes on here. It's not all that great . . . one of those prepaid things and . . . I swiped it last night."

"You did what?" Jules's mind was racing. Things were getting worse and worse by the second. The cell phone connection was disintegrating again as the canyon walls rose higher, the private road following the course of a frozen river far below.

"I saw her stash it in her jacket pocket. When she wasn't looking, I took it so I could call."

"Oh, God, Shay, you have to give it back. Give it to the police so they can check the records and find out who she talked to."

"I thought you didn't want me to blow your cover. Your

number will come up on the screen, you know, since I called you. And then where will you be? Not exactly up for Teacher of the Month."

"No reason to be sarcastic."

"I don't have time to worry about the damned phone," Shay reminded her. "Look, I gotta go!" Her voice was fading, the connection worsening. "I can't hear you anyway. The detectives are talking with some of the other teachers and kids, but they'll be back. You just have to get me outta here." Shay sounded beyond desperate, more than scared out of her mind.

Shay was freaked. Of course. Her roommate had been killed.

"Just hear me out. You know my ultimate goal is to get you out of there, but I need a little time, and you need to be a model student, got it?"

"Like I ever was."

"If I can find out what's happening, prove this school is negligent or criminal or whatever, you have a better shot of leaving there for good and not going to jail. So don't make any trouble while I figure out what's going on down here."

"Make trouble? I'm already in trouble. And now I'm locked up with a psycho killer on the loose."

"Shay, I'm doing everything I can. Just hold tight, okay?"

"Hold tight. My roommate is dead, and I'm supposed to hang out and wait for you to do something? Thanks but no thanks. I'll be waiting till I'm ninety."

"Right now, Shay, I don't think we have any choice. So, when you see me, be cool, okay? Pretend that we never met."

"Like that's going to help anything. Oh, crap! I think . . . someone's coming!"

The faulty connection was instantly severed.

With a groan of frustration, Jules dropped the phone into her purse, gripped the steering wheel, and pressed on into the blowing storm.

God only knew what she'd find when she finally made it to the academy.

CHAPTER 17

Jules was coming here? To Blue Rock? As a teacher? What good was that? Shaylee stashed Nona's phone in her book bag and sauntered into the rec area. The deputies had taken most of the students' statements, and kids were collecting in groups throughout the large hall. All were talking excitedly, all speculating on what had happened to Nona.

"I think she killed herself," Maeve Mancuso said smugly. With eyes as wide as pathetic dolls, Lucy and Nell listened intently, as if Maeve actually knew what had happened. The three girls stood in a circle away from the conversation pit, in a more private corner filled with overstuffed chairs and end tables with lamps. One wall was windows, the other lined with bookcases.

"And I think Drew tried to kill himself, too." Maeve stared off dreamily as she snapped the bracelet on her wrist. Always snapping at the band there, that one. What a freak. "It was a double suicide," Maeve went on. "Kind of like Romeo and Juliet."

"Really?" Nell was eating this up, like it was some great

romantic tragedy. She flipped her dark hair over her shoulder and leaned closer to Maeve. "That's just sooo—"

"Awful!" Shay cut in; she couldn't help it. These ninnies were getting it all wrong. "It's not romantic, or cool, or anything but sick!"

Maeve's little face crumpled, and she glared at Shay as if she were Satan incarnate. "Of course it's really, really, really sad about Nona. She was my friend. But I know for a fact that she and Drew were in love."

"You mean really, really, really in love?" Shay mocked. Maeve was acting like an idiot!

"Who knows how it went down?" Eric Rolfe, a major tool in Shay's estimation, sauntered over. Zach and Ethan were hanging with him. "Or who went down on whom?" he added with a nasty grin, thinking he was clever. "Could be that Nona fucked him, then tried to off him. Then, once she realized what she'd done, she took a flying leap." Eric crooked his neck at a weird angle and stuck out his tongue with an ugly expression as he held his fist over his head as if he were hanging from an imaginary rope.

"Gross!" Maeve recoiled, waving her hands spastically. "She's dead, Eric! God!"

"Show some respect," Nell agreed, repulsed.

Shay's anger simmered. Rolfe was such a dirtbag.

"Just trying to lighten things up." Eric let his "noose hand" drop as he made another goofy face. "Everyone's so emo and down about it. BFD. She was a psycho, anyway, a real nutcase, always sneaking out. And now everyone acts like it's the damned end of the world."

"Because a friend of ours died, dick-wad!" Lucy Yang stood and got into Eric's grill. "Get a life!"

"I bet that's what Nona's saying!" Eric laughed in a grating, high-pitched cackle, a wheezing laugh, so at odds with his football-player physique.

Lucy slugged him. Hard. In the belly.

"Ooof!" He doubled over, and she rounded as if she planned on bringing her knee up into his crotch. "You bitch!" One of his fists balled.

"He's not worth it." Shay took hold of Lucy's arm and kept her from taking a second strike.

Lucy rounded on Shay, her face a mask of disgust, her short black hair flying. "Did you hear what he said about Nona?"

"Shows how dumb he really is," Shay said, deliberately goading Eric. Instinctively, she rolled onto the balls of her feet just as she'd learned years before from Mr. Kim, her martial-arts instructor.

Eric growled, incensed. "You sick twat." His nostrils flared, his lips curling. "You're going to regret that."

"I doubt it." Shay kept him in her sights, measuring, calculating. Electricity crackled in the air as everyone turned to the center of the action. Kids cheered and jeered.

From the corner of her eye, Shay saw two people hurrying across the room. "Hey!" one of them, a woman, shouted, but Shay couldn't turn away from Eric; she couldn't break her concentration.

"Eric!" a male voice boomed.

As if on cue, Eric lunged, his right fist coiled, ready to lay Shay flat. At the last possible second, she sidestepped the attack, grabbing his arm and catching him in midair.

"Wha—?" He gaped as she flipped him onto his back in one quick motion.

Thud! The building shook as his back smacked into the hardwood floor.

The initial impact was followed by a smaller jolt as Eric's head smashed against the floor. He let out a yowl of sheer agony.

Maeve screamed.

"You twisted bastard!" Lucy cried as Eric tried to climb to his feet.

"Fight!" One of the boys, probably that pansy-ass Ollie Gage, yelled in excitement.

The circle of students widened as Eric staggered to his feet, crouching like a boxer, his fists clenched.

Shaylee remained alert, ready for him to come back at her. *Just try it, prick,* she thought.

"Stop!" Dean Hammersley yelled while that stupid Maeve screamed and screamed.

Eric's face turned nearly beet red. "Jesus Christ!" he hissed, springing to his feet with surprising agility. "You little bitch! You can't get away with this!" Again he ran at her, swinging wildly.

Shay feinted.

His fist glanced off her upper arm.

Pain shot through her.

He spun and pulled back, both fists curled, his bared teeth glistening. She noticed spittle had collected in the corners of his mouth. Bastard!

"I said stop this, now!"

The pounding of running footsteps almost caused Shay to take her eyes away from Rolfe. Almost.

"Did you hear me? Stop!" a woman yelled.

On the balls of her feet, circling, Shaylee focused on Eric. "Try it," she goaded, ready for another round. He kept his face toward her, his disgusting snarl in place, his eyes as dark and hard as onyx. Good. If he thought he could take her, he had another thing coming.

"I said, stop, this instant!" The woman again.

Suddenly Dr. Hammersley and Mr. Taggert cut between Shay and Eric, barricading them from hitting each other. Some of the other kids receded, only to linger a little farther away but close enough to watch the action.

"What do you think you're doing?" Dean Hammersley demanded in a harsh whisper, her gaze riveted on Shaylee. Her bird face was flushed, anger radiating from her slim body.

"Dealing with a loser." Shay wasn't backing down.

"Fighting isn't the answer, Shaylee, and you know it. Nor is name-calling."

Shaylee rolled her eyes at that.

"Hey!" Father Jake was running across the room, and Shay saw that his face, usually charming and friendly, had turned deathly serious. "What's happening here?" He glanced at Taggert and Hammersley. "Let them go." He turned his gaze to the group that had gathered. "Anyone want to explain?" he asked calmly.

"It wasn't Shaylee's fault!" Lucy Yang stepped forward from her group of friends, leaving Nell and Maeve to gape at her. In an act of honesty Shaylee couldn't believe, Lucy added, "Shaylee's right. Eric was being a real jerk about Nona. He wouldn't shut up about it, wouldn't quit making sick jokes, and I snapped. I slugged him in the gut."

Way to have my back, Lucy, Shay thought.

"Is that so?" Father Jake said, folding his arms over his chest, his gaze on Eric.

"See. It wasn't my fault," Eric said with a sneer as he swiped at his mouth with the back of his hand. "Yang started it."

Lucy sent him a withering glare, then turned to Hammersley. "Before he had a chance to hit me back, Shay stepped in and stood up for Nona."

"You were gonna coldcock me!" Eric accused, pointing at Lucy, his face twisted in hatred.

Father Jake held up a patient hand. "Slow down."

"You deserved it!" Lucy wasn't backing down an inch.

"We aren't here to judge." Wade's goateed jaw was rock solid as he glared at Eric Rolfe.

"That bitch slugged me!" Eric said, motioning toward Lucy.

"So she admitted," Wade agreed.

"I was just defending myself when she"—he hooked a thumb at Shaylee—"butted in and came at me!"

Hammersley studied Lucy Yang. "You put your hands on him first. Is that what you said?"

"That's right!" Still enraged and trying to hold on to some of his bravado, Eric sniffed and touched the corner of his mouth again. "Stupid, fuckin' cunt!"

"Hey!" Father Jake was having none of the swearing.

"That's it!" Wade grabbed the TA by one arm and escorted him out of the building.

Hammersley's eyes narrowed. "Anyone else witness what happened?"

Of course all the students turned away, afraid to be drawn into the fray. Shay didn't really blame them; it wasn't their fight.

"Lucy's right," Ethan finally said. "Eric was mocking the details of Nona's death. Lucy told him to knock it off, and when he didn't, it went down just as she said. She, uh, Shaylee"—he pointed at her—"was just helping Lucy out."

"Doesn't seem like she needed any help," Hammersley observed as an exit door opened and one of the deputies in full uniform, holster unbuckled, sidearm within his grasp, hurried inside the building.

"Is there a problem here?" he demanded.

"I think we're cool," Father Jake said, and then to Hammersley, "We can handle it."

Nodding, she said to the deputy, "Everything's under control. Right?" she asked Shay.

"Right," Shay said quickly, eager to be out of trouble, but that, of course, was impossible. She felt Father Jake's gaze following after her as she left the room, but she wasn't kidding herself that things were okay here.

She knew in her heart that she'd just made an enemy for life out of Eric Rolfe.

"I need a favor," Trent said, praying that his cell phone connection wouldn't fail as he drove on the winding road to the gatehouse.

"What's that?" Larry Sparks's voice was interspersed with static but was still audible. Sparks was an old friend and a detective for the Oregon State Police. When the OSP had needed assistance locating an escaped prisoner who'd crossed both the Oregon and Idaho state lines, ending up in Montana, Trent had helped track down the suspect and send him back in cuffs to Oregon. Sparks owed him at least one, maybe more.

"I'm down at Blue Rock Academy; there's been trouble," Trent explained, downshifting again for a sharp curve.

"I heard. Bad news. One dead, the other critical."

"That's right. I don't know what's going on, but I'm hoping you can help me out. Get official info for me if I need it, 'cause down here all I'm getting is double-talk. It would be legit. I'm going to try and get myself deputized by the local sheriff, a yahoo named O'Donnell. I'll give him your name as a reference."

"Got it," Sparks agreed, one step ahead of him. "Once you're officially on the force, we'll talk."

Where the hell was the damned school? It had been over thirty minutes since she'd turned off the main road, five since her connection to Shaylee had been severed.

Her muscles were beginning to ache, her eyes straining from following the narrow tunnel of her headlights in the snowy darkness.

All her worries converged on her as night closed in.

Jules passed another sign, and finally the open space of a lit parking lot loomed ahead. She steered the Volvo around a corner of the parking lot toward the guardhouse. She drove slowly, awed by the sight.

Security lights blazed, illuminating a massive stone wall and guardhouse built at the narrowest point of the gulch. There were two wide steel gates that swung open on either side of the gatehouse, the entrance to what appeared to be a fortress.

A few vehicles, covered with four inches of snow, were scattered near the edges of the parking area while a dirty news van with the logo and call sign for a television station from Medford was parked near the gate. Inside the idling van, visible through the windows, two people sipped from thermoses. The last vehicle parked near the guardhouse was a cruiser from the Rogue County Sheriff's Department.

Stomach in knots, Jules nosed her car into a spot in the area marked STAFF and told herself everything was going to be all right.

A door of the sheriff's vehicle opened. A deputy climbed out and headed her way.

Here we go, Jules thought, hoping she didn't have to stretch the truth with the police. She cut the engine and rolled down the window, the warmth of the interior immediately chilled.

The deputy was short and stocky, his thick jacket adding extra weight, a broad-brimmed hat covered in plastic protecting his head. His name tag identified him as Frank Meeker.

"I'm sorry, ma'am," he said through her open window. "The school is closed tonight."

"I understand." She flashed him her most sincere smile.

"I'm a member of the faculty." God, it was cold. The wind cut through her sweater, and she clenched her jaw to keep her teeth from chattering.

Meeker frowned. "Then you'll be on the list." It wasn't a question.

"I assume so, yes. Julia Farentino. I was hired only this week. Dean Hammersley called and said someone would meet me here."

"Did she mention the school is part of a crime scene?"

"She said there was an accident."

His eyebrows rose over the tops of his glasses as he leaned closer to the open window, his gaze sweeping the dark interior of her car. "I'd like to see your ID."

"Sure." She dug through her purse, found her wallet, and managed to wiggle her Oregon driver's license from behind its plastic window.

"Just a minute." Meeker turned back to his cruiser. Shivering, Jules grabbed her jacket from the passenger seat, slipped her arms through the sleeves, and hastily zipped it. Too late. Her insides felt like ice, and she turned her car on again, cranking up the heater as she found an old pair of knit gloves in her pockets and pulled them on just as she heard the rumbling sound of an engine in the distance. She looked toward the sound and spied headlights cutting through the darkness on the far side of the gate.

Her ride.

A Jeep appeared through the curtain of snow, slowing at the window of the gatehouse. Rolling down his window, the Jeep's driver slowed to talk to the officer in the gatehouse. A moment later, the gate swung open and the Jeep rolled through, headlights heading straight for her. The Jeep wheeled to a sliding stop next to her car, and the door popped open. Jules turned casually to look at the driver, and her heart sank. Something about his profile seemed familiar.

Jules's heart clutched as she squinted against the swirling snow.

She told herself she was imagining things. She had to be.

Cooper Trent was not crossing the parking lot!

Not in a million years.

Her tired, distraught mind was just playing tricks on her.

Nonetheless, her heart was trip-hammering, her pulse jumping, her nerves strung to the breaking point.

It was just her subconscious dragging him up again as it did in her nightmares, or her headache giving her eyestrain.

He was out of her life.

As in forever.

Right?

It couldn't be.

No way, no how.

But no amount of denial could erase the fact that Cooper Trent now stood outside her car, looking better than any man had a right to look and acting as if the past five years were just a heartbeat.

Gone were the dusty chaps, ratty old Stetson, and cocky cowboy grin. Instead he wore faded Levi's, a pair of worn boots, and a sheepskin jacket. Bareheaded, snow collecting in his hair, he stared downward.

Her foolish heart knocked.

"What the hell are you doing here?" she demanded through the open window.

He hesitated a second, glanced over his shoulder to make sure the deputy couldn't hear him, then met her gaze again. "You know, Jules," he drawled in a low voice she'd once found so sexy it had turned her inside out, "that's just what I was gonna ask you."

CHAPTER 18

Jules decided that the nightmare had just taken a turn for the worse. What were the odds? Out of the billions of people in the world, how did she end up face-to-face with the one man she'd never wanted to see again?

So God did have a sense of humor after all.

And a wicked one at that.

"You know why I'm here," Jules said. "Someone—probably Dean Hammersley—sent you to get me."

"That she did. And that's when she dropped the bomb that you were the new history teacher."

"Perfect," she said with sarcasm as bitter as the wind chasing down the mountainside.

"And the funny thing about that," Trent observed, "is, I've already got a job here."

"Yeah, real funny," she said. "You're not listed on the Web site."

"They're updating. I'm the newest person on staff. Well, I was until you showed up."

Great, just damned great! All her scheming and plotting and lying were for nothing. She'd been afraid that Shaylee might blow her cover or that Lynch's wife might figure out that she was related to Shaylee, but she hadn't thought—couldn't imagine—that Cooper Trent would be here. She rolled up the window, opened the door, and stepped onto the icy parking lot where the wind, like a frigid knife, cut through her jacket. "I didn't see that they were teaching bronc busting or bull riding down here, so what's your job?"

"I'm the phys ed teacher."

"Why?" she demanded, wondering why her pulse still pounded at the sight of him. "The rodeo circuit run out of bulls?"

"Change of profession."

"Oh, right. You traded in your spurs for Nikes. Don't think so."

Deputy Meeker glanced over at them. Frowning, he started heading across the lot again.

"Don't ruin this for me," she whispered. "I need this job."

"Deal. You do the same." He was waiting. When she didn't respond, he added, "Does Lynch know your sister is one of the students? I think there's some rule against family members—"

"Shh!" she warned, feeling heat in her cheeks. She had to stay cool, to calm down. She couldn't blow it with the deputy.

"Is there a problem, Officer?" Trent asked, and it was all Jules could do not to kick him in the shins. Instead, she pasted on a smile that she didn't feel.

"Just checkin'," the deputy said, and handed Jules back her ID. "Your license expired two days ago."

"Yeah, I know. I've been busy. I thought once I moved down here and took the job and had a permanent address I'd renew it." Oh, God, she hoped the deputy was buying her lie.

He studied her with eyes used to sorting fact from fiction, but finally he nodded. "All right, then. You take care of it. There's a DMV in Cave Junction. It's quite a bit closer than Medford." The deputy's cell rang, and he answered, turning his back to them.

"Thanks," she said, relieved.

"Great. So we're good to go?" Trent asked, but Meeker was deep in conversation.

"Sounds like a go to me," Jules said.

"Let's get your things out of your car and into the Jeep."

She popped the trunk and pulled out the smaller of two bags, her pillow, and a laptop computer case. He-Man could get the larger roller bag.

They loaded up the Jeep quickly and stopped at the gate, where Trent waved to the guard. All this was done in relative silence, questions pounding through her head.

Stupidly, her mind flashed to another time and place, when she was not quite twenty, still a virgin, and Erin's brother had introduced her to him. She'd expected he'd be brash, loud, and all macho; she'd discovered he was quiet, thoughtful, but with a sharp sense of humor that matched her own.

Now, five years of pent-up fury and bitter disappointment gnawed a hole in her gut. She'd thought she would never see him again, much less end up in a vehicle with him as he drove her to a school where, if Shay could be believed, a murder had recently been committed.

What kind of cruel twist of fate was at play here?

"Okay," she said, once they were completely alone on the precipitous road leading deeper in the mountains. "Why don't you tell me how you went from bull rider to teacher in one fell swoop?" She still couldn't believe it.

"Better yet, let's start with you," he countered. His cocky smile slid from his face, and his gloved fingers clenched the steering wheel. The temperature in the Jeep seemed to drop ten degrees. "Your sister's already here and up to her eyeballs in trouble," he admitted, his face grim. "Her roommate was murdered, or possibly killed herself—that hasn't been determined yet—and another boy is probably going to die from his injuries." He let his breath whistle through his teeth. "The sheriff's department is still trying to sort it all out, but whatever happened, it was brutal."

"Shaylee called. She warned me."

"Called? How? I thought—"

"Don't ask." She held up a hand. "But she's freaked."

"We all are."

"But you said that she was in trouble."

He nodded, glancing down at the gauges for a second. "Shaylee claims she knows nothing about what happened, but her baseball cap was found at the scene."

"Her cap?" Jules repeated, stunned. "Wait . . . let's just start from the beginning. Shaylee's a suspect?"

"Everyone is."

"Including you?"

He slid her a look. "Probably. But my college team baseball hat wasn't found at the scene."

"So Shaylee's number one on the list?"

"Don't know, but she's up there. The last person to see Nona Vickers alive, it seems."

"So what? Look, Shaylee couldn't kill anyone! And attack a second person? Get real! Besides, I think another student might be dead, too, the one who no one can find."

"Lauren Conway," he said. "I know."

"You know?"

"I don't know that she's dead, but she's certainly still missing." He downshifted as the Jeep slid around an icy corner. Jules grabbed the door handle to brace herself. "Let's start over. Why are you here?"

She wanted to lie. To tell him that it was all coincidence,

but he wouldn't buy it, and unless she somehow got him on her side, Cooper Trent could ruin everything. "How far is it until we get to the school?"

"Five, maybe six miles."

"Drive slowly," she said, "and you go first."

He slanted a hard look in her direction, then stared out the windshield. "I needed a job."

"Bull! You don't have the patience, temperament, or desire to teach kids badminton."

"Maybe I've changed."

She let out a disbelieving breath. "Sure." How much more complicated could this get? She twisted in the seat to stare at him harder. "Let's cut to the chase. Both of us, obviously, have ulterior motives for being at Blue Rock."

Beneath his beard shadow, his jaw tightened. "Okay I'll bite. What's yours?"

"I want to get Shaylee out of here."

"So yank her."

"Can't. Nor can Mom. Judge's order."

He swore under his breath, but she had a feeling she wasn't telling him anything he didn't already know. "Isn't her father rich? Can't he hire some hotshot attorney to spring her?"

"Max seems to think being at the academy will be good for her," Jules admitted, all the tension of the day seeping into her bones. "For once Edie agrees."

"But you don't."

"I've done some research. Things here aren't all they're cracked up to be, and all this pseudo-Christian rhetoric doesn't ring true. I've seen the mansion on Lake Washington. Someone's making big bucks off of messed-up kids. It all seems about as real as Disneyland."

"And then there's Lauren."

"You got it," she agreed. "The girl no one seems to want

to find." She thought of her phone conversations with Cheryl Conway. "Except for her mother."

He grimaced. "You've talked to Cheryl?"

"Yeah. Have you? Wait a second," she said, putting some of the ill-fitting pieces of the puzzle together. She'd read that he'd once worked for a sheriff's department in Montana. "Is that why you're here? You're trying to find her, right? Come on. Your turn, PE teacher. What brings you to the Blue Rock Academy locker room?"

"I can't really talk about it."

"Why not? I was straight with you; I expect the same." Really she didn't. Hadn't he proved what a jerk and liar he was once before? Why should she trust him now?

Because you don't have much of a choice. You're committed now, backed into a pretty tight corner. On top of all that, now Cooper Trent knows you're lying. You have to trust him, Jules. You'd better get him to keep your secret!

"Damn," she swore. If she'd thought things were bad before, she now knew how much worse they could get.

He stared straight ahead. "I'm being as straight with you as I can."

"Sure." She glanced out the window, wondering at the mountains she'd seen in the brochure, invisible tonight. Snow fell fast and hard, piling on the windshield before the wipers brushed it away.

"I can't tell you anything else," he said. "Really."

"Then maybe I can help you fill in the gaps. I read about you working for some sheriff's department in Montana." Her eyes narrowed as she remembered Cheryl Conway indicating that sometimes it wasn't enough to rely on the police to do their jobs; sometimes a person had "to do more." Meaning what? "So are you working undercover? Is that it?"

"As far as you're concerned, I'm a teacher here," he said slowly as he cranked on the steering wheel. The Jeep rounded a sharp corner, tires shimmying on ruts from the winter's storms. "And it would make what I'm trying to accomplish here so much easier if you'd refuse your position."

"What?"

"Tell Hammersley and Lynch you changed your mind. No one would blame you."

"I'm not backing down now!" she said.

"It's dangerous." A tic was working near his eye as he tried to hang on to the threads of his temper. She remembered that telltale sign from the past.

"So I should just abandon my sister?"

"You're not abandoning her."

"Damned straight. So don't waste your breath trying to talk me out of it!" She was seething now, her blood pressure climbing. "Until Shaylee is out of this place, I'm on staff!"

His lips drew into a blade-thin line. "You always were stubborn."

"So don't try to talk me out of it, okay? It won't work."

"I don't want you getting in my way."

"Fine!" she said, years of anger roiling deep inside. "Then you stay the hell out of mine!"

"Jules . . ."

Her heart cracked a little at the sound of his voice saying her name, but she wasn't going to let some long-forgotten, stupid, and oh-so-childish romantic fantasy deter her.

"I don't want you getting hurt."

"Didn't I just say I'd keep my distance?"

He winced a little at her harsh words, but she had to make him see she was serious and strong, not the weak, fragmented girl he'd known five years ago. "I'm not going to hurt you."

"You got that right, Cowboy," she vowed. No one had

ever had the ability to wound her like Cooper Trent. She'd make damned sure it didn't happen again.

"Look, I just don't want to worry about you."

"Easy solution: don't."

"Goddammit, Jules—"

"Julia. It's Julia. Get it straight! There just may be a test tomorrow." She arched an eyebrow, and as angry as he was, his lips twitched a bit.

"You're impossible," he said without a hint of admiration.

"One of my finer traits."

"What happened to kind, honest, loving?"

She flipped a hand dismissively. "Overrated. Let's not go there."

"Fair enough." Was there just a spark of humor in his eyes? She felt herself warming to him again and gave herself a swift, silent mental kick.

"So give me the rundown on the school. And don't sugarcoat anything."

"Yes, ma'am!" He barked out a laugh, and she didn't blame him. In all the time she'd known him, Cooper Trent was a straight shooter, telling it like it was and damn the consequences.

"Well, since I can't talk you out of resigning . . ."

"You can't. Forget it."

He frowned. Seemed to wrestle with a decision and finally appeared to accept the fact that, like it or not, he had to deal with her. "Well, to start off, you said something about there being a test about you? That's really not too far from the truth. If we've got anything, we've got rules, regulations, and tests at Blue Rock." He shook his head and swore again, but some of his ire had dissipated.

"Is that bad?"

"Probably not. These kids who come to the academy,

they do need structure. No doubt about it. They need to understand and accept authority. And most of all, they have to
be kept busy all the time."

"Idle hands are the devil's workshop?"

"At least," he admitted. "A lot of these kids are smart.
Most of 'em basically good, just out of control."

"And the rest?"

He thought. "I don't necessarily think it's the students,
but I get a hint at the school, a feeling, of something darker
going on, something . . ."

"Evil?"

He shook his head but said, "I don't know. What happened last night wasn't pretty." He glanced over at her. "I
found the kids. The boy in a crumpled heap, losing blood,
barely alive, and the girl . . ." Trent stared at the road where
the headlight's beams lit up the snow. "She was strung up
on the crossbeams of the stable, naked, bloody, and just
hanging in the cold."

Jules shivered inside. She'd known that Cooper Trent
was a realist, a man who knew that death was just a natural
part of life. Even so, he was bothered by what he'd seen last
night. Seriously bothered.

"There's talk of suicide, that she flipped out and rigged
this noose over the beam and threw herself from the
stacked bales or a ledge higher up, but I don't see it."

"You think she was murdered?"

"I'd bet my best horse on it." He nodded. "Since the
Prescott boy isn't talking, there are no witnesses, so we
can't be sure. Yet. But once the ME takes a look at the body,
does the autopsy, we'll know more." He slid her another
glance, and this one cut to her soul. "Just for the record?
My money's on murder."

CHAPTER 19

Maeve Mancuso reached under the wide bell sleeve of her black shirt and snapped the band against her skin, once, twice, three times. Over and over again until her flesh stung, until it felt real. Real pain. Real life.

Things were getting monstrously boring in the rec hall, waiting for the cop guys to do whatever they had to do out there. Nell yawned, suppressing a little peep.

They can't make us read all day, Maeve thought, though it had sort of been how the day had gone. Reading and waiting. Stuck in the rec room so long, some of the students had nodded off, and for once the teachers didn't seem to care. But Maeve didn't want to sleep, not with Ethan nearby. With her luck, she'd doze off and snore up a storm or drool on her books. She needed Ethan to see her in the best possible light if she was going to get him back. She snapped the bracelet again—a fat rubber band, really—and then let her fingertips smooth up toward her elbow, bumping along the ridges of scars that lined her arms. On bad days she used to pick and scratch, try to make them bleed, but not anymore. Ever since the day she'd kissed Ethan after he'd helped her cart her kayak to the water, that fall day when diamonds danced on the lake and the sun still had the power to warm through her clothes, she had vowed to stop cutting. A guy like Ethan didn't want a girl with bloody speed bumps covering her arms. She had promised herself never to cut again and actually started applying vitamin E to the scars, because her doctor said that would help them heal.

She dreamed of the day when she and Ethan would get out of here, when they would have the freedom to go to college together, maybe get their own place. Of course, she had to make him love her again, but it was going to happen. She was sure of it. Looking down at the stack of books in front of her, she picked up the fat Shakespeare volume she'd checked out of the library and opened it to *Romeo and Juliet.* Now, there was a love. Someday, Ethan would want her with the same passion and intensity. Someday, they'd be free of slutty girls like Shaylee Stillman. Girls who got off on stealing away other girls' boyfriends.

Now that the fight was over and the three kids had been marched off, Maeve had a better view of Ethan, who sat across the way writing something in a notebook. His head was tipped down, light glinting off his dark hair. He wore a plaid flannel shirt that showed off his shoulders and broad chest, and she thought of the way his arms had felt when they'd kissed, his biceps rounded and tight. He was a solid guy, strong and caring, and she could lose herself in those dark eyes.

And at that moment, as if he sensed her, Ethan looked up, his gaze searching the room, locking on her.

Oh, God.

She gave a halfhearted smile, wishing she were close

enough to tell him how sad she felt about Nona, wishing she were close enough to lean on his shoulder and rest in his arms, even if it were only for a brief hug.

He nodded at her, his expression an enigma. Was there love and support in those dark brown eyes, or was she imagining that because she wanted it so, so much?

She broke the connection, staring down at the Shakespeare compilation, which was open to the page with a soliloquy she'd memorized for Dean Hammersley's class. "But soft, what light through yonder window breaks?" Romeo said. "It is the east, and Juliet is the sun. Arise fair sun, and kill the envious moon. . . ." She curled her fingers around the edge of the book, letting the binding dig into her fingertips until it was painful.

Someday, Ethan would love her this way. She would be his sun, and he would kill off envious moons for her. Theirs would be a love like Nona's and Drew's—a love that would surpass death. Someday . . .

Jules was still trying to wrap her brain around the fact that she and Trent would be working together at the school. The snow was coming down hard now, tiny flakes coating the road, creating a curtain that the headlights had trouble permeating.

"Okay," she said, breaking a silence that had lasted for the last two miles. "Since we're in this thing together, how're we going to play it?"

"So the deal is this: You don't know me; this is the first time we've met." His eyebrows drew together in concentration. "So far, Shaylee hasn't put two and two together. She told me once that she thought she knew me, but that was a few days ago, and since then she's dropped it."

"I only hope she doesn't panic in all this and call Edie."

"Would she?"

"Normally no, but now, who knows?" Jules said, not elaborating. Shay was already on Trent's suspect list; Jules wasn't going to give him any more ammunition by admitting that her sister was using Nona Vickers's cell phone. God only knew what conclusions he'd draw from that.

"I really think you should resign your position," he said as he checked the rearview mirror.

"Resign? I haven't even started yet."

"Good. Then you're not involved."

"I want to be involved."

"It's dangerous."

"Really?" she mocked. "Thanks for the big tip!"

"I'm serious, Jules."

"So am I! And you'd better start calling me Julia or people will start to wonder."

"Oh, for the love of God." He found a wide spot in the road and pulled over, letting the Jeep idle near the trees. "Look, I don't have time for games, and I don't want to worry about you on top of everything else."

"So don't."

"Have you heard a word I've been saying?"

"Yeah, I get it. But I'm not leaving." The windows of the Jeep were fogging, the warm interior much too close. "Look, if I can find out and prove that Blue Rock isn't what it claims to be, that the administration is covering up what happened to Lauren, that some of its practices border on barbaric, then I have a shot of convincing a judge to move Shay."

"Where? To juvie? I've read her file. Shaylee's lucky to be at Blue Rock."

"You believe that?" she asked, noticing the wet strands

of his hair where the snow had melted. "I don't think any kid is 'lucky' to be here."

"Your sister isn't exactly lily white."

"Oh, please. Are any of the kids enrolled here completely innocent?" she demanded, angered by his attitude and the intimacy of this warm, tight Jeep.

"Of course not."

"So these students are no angels. But I know Shaylee's innocent; she told me about her cap. She told me she'll be cleared because the school has cameras everywhere, including the dorm rooms, which, I think is damned illegal."

Trent rubbed a hand around the back of his neck. "I'm not sure there are cameras. I sure as hell haven't seen any tapes."

"Would you?"

"Probably not. I'm not in what I think of as the inner circle."

"Which is?"

"Reverend Lynch and his cohorts, the school deans. They're all pretty tight—Hammersley, Williams, Burdette—and they're all women. The second tier is Flannagan, Taggert, and DeMarco, all men, by the way; they don't seem to be as tied in to the administration."

"Where do you fit in?"

"That's the trouble, I don't."

"I still can't see you teaching girls how to shoot hoops."

"It's a challenge," he admitted, "but, at the time, the PE job was the only one I was qualified for. I would have preferred working with the horses, but Bert Flannagan beat me to it. He's a piece of work; haven't figured him out yet. Retired military. DeMarco and Taggert seem to like him. I think they're attracted to Lynch's iron-fisted, by-the-rules policy."

"And the women?"

"Burdette and Williams are definitely drinking the reverend's Kool-Aid, but I can't get a bead on Rhonda Hammersley; she doesn't fawn all over Lynch like the others, but she seems earnest."

Jules was listening. "You're sure about the cameras? Shaylee seemed convinced that everything that happens at the school is filmed."

"Well, there are some security cameras, of course. They're mounted on the building entrances and on some of the paths, all pretty visible, but I think the cameras in the rooms might just be part of an urban legend."

"Really? A rumor started by someone who wants to keep the kids in line?"

"Or a student who gets off scaring others." He glanced into the rearview mirror and frowned. "Someone's coming."

"Who?"

"Don't know, but there have been cops going up and down this road all day." He didn't have to say that neither of them would want to explain why they hadn't driven directly back to the school. He shoved the Jeep into gear, the tires sliding a little as the tires spun over the crusted piles of ice and snow that had been pushed to the side of the road by a plow.

They hadn't driven a mile when the headlights that were bearing down on them closed in, casting the interior of the Jeep in a harsh, white glow. "More police?" Jules asked, glancing over her shoulder at the low beams of the vehicle behind.

Trent squinted at the mirror. "Can't tell, but probably. If they wanted to pass, they'd turn on their emergency lights."

"Is it much farther?"

"We're almost there."

Jules's stomach twisted. She'd passed the first unexpected hurdle with Trent, and they'd come to an uneasy truce. The past, a nasty demon, still haunted them, but at least for the moment it hid in the shadows.

Jules didn't kid herself. Issues still hung in the air between them. This man beside her had abandoned her at the most painful time in her life.

But you threw him away, remember? You told him you never wanted to see him again. He just respected your decision.

Her right hand curled into a fist, gloved fingers scraping her thigh. That was her problem—always expecting too much of those she loved. Hadn't she wanted her father to adore her, to remarry her mother and create a perfect little family, an idyllic existence? And what had happened there? Sheer disaster!

No, there were no happy endings. Parents did not remarry and suddenly parent their children. A man like Cooper Trent did not come charging back on his white horse, pledging his love, fighting for his woman against all odds.

No, Trent had simply followed her orders and left her.

For good.

Leaving her wounded, scarred from her father's murder, lost in misery and pain.

She'd been nineteen at the time; she should have known better. She glanced at Trent and felt a pang of regret. She had loved him. With the foolhardy, crazy, enthusiasm of a teenager, she had loved him. She had thought him capable of transforming her life, when he only had the power to walk out of it.

The story of her life.

She slid a glance his way and wondered if his own thoughts had tracked hers, if he, too, had replayed their disaster of a love affair and breakup. If so, he'd no doubt come to the same conclusion: They should never have gotten together in the first place and could never rekindle that short-lived flame again.

"Okay, brace yourself," he said as the Jeep crested a hill, and suddenly, through the falling snow, Jules caught a glimpse of lights glowing boldly in the white night. "It's showtime."

CHAPTER 20

If there was chaos inside the compound, it was well suppressed by a blanket of falling snow. The only real sign that things were amiss on this beautiful campus were police vehicles parked at odd angles in front of buildings with lights blazing.

"Where are all the students?" Jules asked as Trent parked the Jeep near a garage.

"The students were herded into the rec hall, at the heart of the campus. The sheriff's department is probably still interviewing people." He cut the engine, and they both watched as the vehicle that had been following them, a Range Rover, slid to a stop near a large cottage on the fringe of campus.

With a broad front porch, lights burning in the windows, and dormers peeking from a sharp-sloped, snow-covered roof, the house looked like something out of a Currier and Ives lithograph. A man stepped out of the driver's side, then hurried to the passenger door to help a bundled-up Cora Sue out of the vehicle.

"Let me guess, that's where the reverend lives," Jules said, eyeing the homey house.

Trent nodded. "When he's here."

"How often is that?"

"Most of the time. But wifey usually isn't."

"I bet. I saw her place on Lake Washington," Jules said, thinking of the massive estate with its separate wings, grand staircase, marble floors, and manicured grounds. The boathouse in Seattle was fancier than Lynch's home near Lake Superstition.

As more lights snapped on inside the house, a man came out of the house, and Jules recognized the pilot, Spurrier, half-jogging back to the Range Rover. He opened the rear door, and Jules half expected the black poodles to leap out and pee on the surrounding pines. Instead the pilot pulled two massive Louis Vuitton roller bags from inside the SUV. Without allowing either piece of luggage to touch the snowy ground, he carried them both inside.

"What do you think of Lynch?" she asked.

"Pompous and self-serving come to mind."

"Then we're on the same page."

"That," he said with a half-grin, "might be a first. Come on, let's not arouse any suspicion. There's enough of that to go around as it is."

He helped Jules haul her things into an office in the administration building, where a sheriff's deputy and Dean Hammersley searched through Jules's bags.

Rhonda Hammersley's strength was apparent as she hoisted a heavy bag to the table. Brown corduroy slacks and a hand-knit sweater did not soften her sinewy runner's frame. Her short, streaked hair was meticulous, every fingernail perfectly manicured, but there were smudges beneath her eyes, dark circles of worry that no amount of makeup could hide. She didn't even bother trying to smile as she apologized, "You understand we can't be too careful. Especially now."

Jules didn't buy it. She had the distinct feeling that

Rhonda Hammersley enjoyed going through other people's belongings. Maybe she just liked having that right, being superior in some small way.

Hammersley found Jules's cell phone and computer, and told her that they should be locked in Jules's private quarters at all times. Once both she and the deputy were satisfied, the dean directed Trent to show the newest member of Blue Rock Academy's staff to Stanton House and the studio apartment that would be Jules's home. Located on the uppermost floor, the unit was spacious yet rustic, with pine walls, warm sconces, and a bank of windows that overlooked the campus.

"Not bad, eh?" Trent said as he left her luggage near a small walk-in closet.

"All the comforts of home," she said, eyeing the kitchen area, which consisted of a microwave oven, a sink, a few cupboards, and a small refrigerator. "Except for my cat." She thought of Diablo, wondering how he was doing under the watchful eye of Mrs. Dixon. "Not that he would want a change of venue. Agnes Dixon, my neighbor who's watching him, will spoil him rotten. And he'll lap it up."

Standing near the door as if he wanted to make a hasty retreat, Trent checked his watch again and frowned. But before he could say anything, footsteps sounded on the stairs.

Trent glanced over at Jules, his gaze connecting with hers. "Nice meeting you, Ms. Farentino," he said, loud enough so that whoever was ascending the stairs would be sure to hear him.

"I go by Julia."

"Everyone here calls me Trent," he said as Rhonda Hammersley clipped through the open door, wearing a dark jacket with the school's logo emblazoned on it. "Dean," he said, tipping his head. Then he clambered noisily down the wooden stairs.

"Settled in?" Hammersley asked as Trent's footsteps faded.

"Just getting there." Now what did the dean want? "I have some unpacking in my future."

Hammersley folded her arms across her chest, defensive. "I have to apologize again," she said. Twice in half an hour; Jules guessed that might have been a record. "Things here, as you can see, aren't normal. Until the sheriff's department has concluded their investigation, I'm not at liberty to discuss the events of last night." She gave Jules the cleaned-up sound bite for the "tragic situation," even mentioning that one student, Nona Vickers, had died, but she didn't elaborate. Just that no one really knew what happened in the stable last night, and the school was doing everything possible to "get to the bottom" of the tragedy while ensuring the safety of all its students and staff. "Some of the students are really upset, as you can guess. We already had an altercation, one of the TAs and a new student," she admitted.

Jules's fears crystallized. Shay had to be the newest kid enrolled in the school.

"An altercation?"

"It's all sorted out now. No one was seriously hurt, thank goodness. One of the TAs got out of line, and the new girl, Shaylee Stillman, took care of it with some martial-arts moves."

"But no one was hurt," Jules repeated.

"Just Eric Rolfe's bruised male ego. Man, she did a number on that." Hammersley seemed amused. "Shaylee got hit, a deflecting blow, but Nurse Ayres said both of them will live. Another girl was involved. Two girls landing blows in one day. I've never seen that in my tenure here. The three students will have to be written up, of course, but we're giving them more latitude with all the anxiety over Nona's death."

Jules breathed a little easier. At least Shay wasn't hurt. Nor, it seemed, was she in serious trouble.

Hammersley went on to say, "Reverend Lynch has called for a vigil tonight, in the gazebo. He sent apologies; he usually greets new faculty personally, but under the circumstances . . ." She shrugged. "Anyway, the reverend would like you to stop by his cottage before dinner so that he can escort you to the dining hall. You'll have a few minutes to talk with students after dinner, before the prayer vigil." She pointed out the gazebo on a map that was framed and hung on the wall of the living area, then explained about meal procedures, common areas, and ground rules. "Tomorrow morning, Charla King will give you a complete tour of the school and curriculum guidelines, notes, and student rosters for your classes. You'll have the weekend to prepare a few lesson plans."

"I'm eager to get started," Jules said, steeling herself for the coming weeks. On Monday, she was expected to hit the ground running.

"So, what else? Oh, yes!" Hammersley walked to a chair where some items had been placed. "Here's the school-issued book bag, backpack, and jacket. It's a medium. If it doesn't fit, just talk to Charla King about getting a different size. It seems a little over the top, I know, all the mugs and toothpaste holders and flashlights with the school logo, but it's just one more way to solidify our sense of community here. We like to show school support as much as possible." The dean checked her watch and informed Jules that dinner would be served in the cafeteria in forty-five minutes, later than usual, due to the disruption, and that she shouldn't keep the reverend waiting.

Hammersley hurried away, the heels of her leather boots clicking on the hardwood as Jules closed the door behind her. *Disruption,* Jules thought. That was the academy's code word for the death of one student, the near-fatal injury of another? Disruption? Walking to the cathedral window, she stared out at the night. She was willing to bet that last night's events were more than a disruption to the victims' families.

Jules washed up, dabbed on another coat of lipstick, and touched up her mascara. Good enough. Throwing on her long coat, she gave herself a mental pep talk; then, after grabbing her Blue Rock monogrammed flashlight, she left her new suite and hurried down the stairs.

She nearly slipped on the icy walkway to the reverend's cottage, where smoke was curling from the chimney. From a distance, the cottage was quaint, but close up, the building showed its age. The gutters were stained black with mold, and as she climbed the porch steps, she noticed that one of the sidelights was cracked.

"I don't care, Tobias," Cora Sue said, her voice escaping through a window that wasn't quite latched. "It was humiliating. Not even first class. Me, the wife of a revered reverend and doctor. It just wasn't right."

Jules paused, her hand raised to knock on the door.

"They were the only seats available, and there aren't any first-class tickets into Medford. That's not how it works. The commercial planes are all small. I would have had Kirk fly you in the private plane, but it's not safe in this—"

"The private plane. The seaplane isn't exactly a Lear, now, is it? I don't know why you insisted I come down here; the weather's supposed to only get worse."

"Cora Sue, please . . ."

Jules hesitated, then eased away from the glass so that no one could see her from the inside, though anyone passing would see her lingering on the porch as she eavesdropped.

"Please what? Pretend that everything's fine?"

"I can't have this conversation now, not on top of everything else. The staff is nervous, and the students are a mess. We caught some students in a fistfight today."

"And you'll probably have more. You know it, Tobias! You're the one who accepts the students. It's your decision. Just like it is with all the staff members!"

Jules leaned over, as if retying her bootlaces, just in case anyone could see her.

"It's my Christian duty to help those who need it most. Try to understand."

"I'm trying, Tobias, but you just keep punishing me, don't you?"

"Never."

Punishing her? For what?

"I would never," he repeated.

"It's the look in your eyes. I see you try to disguise it, but I know you, Tobias Lynch, and I see how you watch me. Do you know what it feels like to be treated like a leashed pet, a tethered dog? You trust Esau and Jacob more than you do your own wife!"

"The dogs? Oh, Cora, I can't do this right now," he said, his voice stronger.

"You seem to gain some perverse pleasure in persecuting and torturing me," she said softly. "And you do it under the guise of executing God's will. That's sick, Tobias. And you, with your damned degree in psychology, should know it!"

"Cora, you misunderstand."

"Do I? Do I?" she demanded, her voice rising. Jules imagined the woman was blinking back tears of frustration. "I've tried, Tobias. Lord knows I've tried. Just remember that Jesus forgave those who sinned. You need to take a lesson!"

"Stop. We can't have this discussion. Not here. Not now!" His voice, too, was filled with fury. "The school is already reeling. I've got parents threatening to pull out their kids and reporters on me like vultures on a dying sheep. The weather service is saying we're in for a blizzard, which at least will keep visitors away for a while. On the other hand, our campus will be isolated by the storm. But any minute I'm expecting Julia Farentino, so please, let's attempt to look like we're getting along. You know, sometimes God gives us challenges that really try us."

"Every day," she agreed. "Every damned day."

Jules wanted to listen further, but a flurry of sound just a few feet down the lane caught her attention. Her heart nearly stopped as she thought she'd been found out. Stepping back from the door, she saw a flash of navy blue as two boys raced by, hurrying toward the chapel.

They didn't so much as glance in her direction as they passed.

Julia caught her breath, slowed her rapidly beating heart.

So much for her sleuthing skills.

As she stomped on the porch loudly and rapped on the door, she turned her head to see who was behind her. From the corner of her eye, she caught a dark figure darting into the shadows, disappearing under the low-hanging bough of a spruce tree. *What?!*

Her heartbeat went wild again.

Had someone been watching her as she eavesdropped?

A man?

Woman?

She thought of Shay's concerns that a killer was on the loose, of Trent's convictions that Nona had been murdered. Fear skittered down Jules's spine as she swept her gaze over thickets of fir, hemlock, and spruce that sheltered the cottage from the rest of the campus.

Did she hear footsteps?

The faint sound of snow crunching beneath boots?

Calm down, nothing is wrong. You're jumping at shadows. All because of Shay. Pull yourself to—

The door to the cottage swung open. "Ms. Farentino," Reverend Lynch said, his voice booming into the night. Cora Sue, on her invisible string, stood next to him.

"Call me Julia."

"Come in, come in," he said. "I apologize for how hectic things are down here . . . such a tragedy."

"I heard. Yes."

"You've met my wife, Cora Sue."

More than once, Jules thought, "Yes. In Seattle. Hello."

The other woman's eyes were cold, her mouth tight, the remnants of the argument with her husband still hanging in the air. "Welcome," the reverend's wife said without inflection as she stepped out of the doorway, allowing Jules to pass. "I'm sorry that you've come under such horrendous circumstances."

"Me too. I only hope I can help."

Cora Sue looked at her as if she was certifiable, but the reverend bought it. "That's the kind of can-do attitude that makes Blue Rock Academy the elite institution it is," Lynch said, and for the life of her, it seemed he really believed it.

Even with Lauren Conway missing, Nona Vickers dead, and Drew Prescott's life hanging by a thread.

CHAPTER 21

"So you didn't leave the filly out in the cold the other night." Trent pushed away from his desk and fixed Bernsen with a look that said the kid would not squirm out of this one.

"No." Zach Bernsen shook his head as if the idea was ridiculous. He stood in front of Trent's desk, his blond hair mussed, his jaw set in defiance.

"You were in charge."

"All of the horses were penned when I closed the stables. I counted twice. Rolfe was with me. He can vouch for me."

"I'll get to him." Eric Rolfe was currently cooling his jets on one of the plastic folding chairs outside Trent's office in the short hallway that branched to the gym and locker rooms. "But you're the senior TA."

"All the animals were accounted for." Zach wasn't about to budge.

"The horse got out somehow."

"That's just it—she got out on her own or someone let her out."

"Who?"

"How the hell should I know?" Bernsen's face, usually so calm, was flushed. "What is this, anyway? Doesn't the school have bigger problems? I mean, Nona Vickers is dead and Drew . . . Oh, hell, who knows?" His mouth clamped into a firm, angry line, and his cool blue eyes flashed with a silent rage.

"Okay, so you didn't do it. You won't say or don't know who did." Trent tented his fingers, considering the next move. Though he didn't admit it, he agreed with Bernsen. The filly was left out, but she survived. Nona Vickers had not. Could the two incidents be tied together? "Let's say I believe you. The filly was locked up before curfew. That means someone came by later and let her out, or else she got out when someone else came to the stable. I'm thinking that the hayloft has been used before Drew and Nona went up there. I can't believe that Drew Prescott had the time, energy, or foresight to pull it together by himself."

Was there a flicker in Zach's cool eyes?

"A couple of nights ago, I came up behind two people out after curfew, down by the garage. They took off before I could catch up with them. You know anything about that?"

"No!" Quick denial.

"Did you know that Drew Prescott and Nona Vickers were a couple?"

"Hell, no! Drew flirted with all the girls, wanted to get into their pants. He didn't care who. I don't think Nona was anything special to him."

"Real nice."

"Hey, you asked."

"Do you know anything more?"

Zach closed down. "I told the cops and I'll tell you—I don't know anything about what happened to those two. And that goes double for the freakin' horse! I do not know how Nova ended up locked outside."

Trent wasn't convinced. Zach was a player. "Okay, but if you change your mind and suddenly remember something, it would be wise to tell me about it, because Mr. Flannagan is pretty pissed about the whole thing, seeing as the stable is his responsibility. He's ready to rip you and Rolfe new ones with the business end of a pitchfork, so I'd think real hard about what you know and either tell me or the detectives."

Zach cocked his head, the tough facade cracking. "About . . . the horse, right?"

"About anything." Trent skewered the kid with a hard-ass glare. "You got something to tell me, Zach?"

The kid looked away, sucked in a breath, shook his head. "No. I don't know anything."

"Think about it, Zach. You've worked hard here. You wouldn't want to mess up."

"I haven't."

Trent didn't believe that for an instant. "You can leave now. Tell Rolfe he's up."

Zach couldn't get out of the room fast enough. A few seconds later, Eric Rolfe walked in, hands in his pockets, face set in a bring-it-on-punk expression. "What is this?" he demanded, standing in front of the desk, rolling on the balls of his feet, looking like he was itching for a fight. "It's time for dinner."

"Not yet. Sit." Trent had already pegged Eric as a hot-head. With little provocation, the guy would take a swing at him. And then there was the fight he'd already started with Shaylee Stillman. Yeah, a loose cannon.

"I don't get it," Rolfe demanded. "I already talked to Lynch and the cops. So now you've got more questions?"

"I just want to know why the filly was left out the other night."

"She wasn't, okay? Jesus, who cares?"

Trent leaned back in his chair, studying the tower of fury that was Eric Rolfe. "I care. I take it seriously when someone messes with animals. And the condition of the stables shows me that people are messing around. Someone's been using the hayloft as a bedroom. Last night probably wasn't the first time, and the way things go, I'm willing to bet that if one couple was using it, others knew about it, too. Kinda like a free, no-tell motel. One of them could have, by mistake, left the filly out because they were too interested in each other to realize they'd left the back door open and her stall was unlatched."

"I wouldn't know about that."

"No?" Trent leaned forward. "I thought that was part of your job description as a TA, that you help the teachers and the administration ride herd over the younger kids. I mean, you're an esteemed TA, first line in the campus security force."

Rolfe snorted. "You don't know Jack shi—"

"Don't I?"

Rolfe's eyes narrowed a fraction; his pupils focused hard on Trent. "You know, my old man's an attorney. Big firm in San Francisco. He wouldn't like you harassing me."

"Don't kid yourself, Rolfe. Your old man sent you here for a reason—because you had gotten yourself into a pile of trouble. What was it? B and E? Meth?"

"I don't do street drugs."

"That's right. Pills. Vicodin. Percocet. OxyContin. Doesn't matter what it was; you even stole from your grandmother to get 'em."

"I'm clean now."

"Clean but picking fights with new students. Slugging girls. Not smart, Rolfe. You're pushing it. Lynch might not have decided what your punishment should be, but I'll give him some advice. You should either be kicked out of the program or assigned to the stables to shovel manure for the next three months."

"I was just making fun. That girl went all psycho on me!" Rolfe declared.

"The way I heard it, you were being pretty obnoxious about Nona's death."

"Just tryin' to lighten things up."

"Sure." Trent eyed the kid. "The next time you want to mix it up, come up here. Don't embarrass yourself by picking on some girl half your size."

"She was the one who looked bad."

Trent snorted. "I'm just reminding you not to mess up. Don't mock the dead. Don't pick fights, and if you know something, spill it. Tell me, tell the cops, whoever. You've had a pretty clean slate until today. So chill."

Fury darkened Rolfe's eyes as he pressed his fists into the desk and leaned forward. "I don't know anything, Mr. Trent, so get off my case." He straightened, his balled fists at his side. "Can I go to dinner now?"

Trent waved him off. "Yeah. Go."

In seconds he was out of the office and down the hallway. A moment later, Trent heard the exterior doors bang shut behind Rolfe.

"Moody son of a bitch," Trent said, unsatisfied as he tapped his pencil on his desk. He'd decided to push the kids about the filly being left outside, hoping they'd scramble around and admit that other people knew about the makeshift bed in the hayloft. It was hidden well, behind stacks that would be pulled down, but eventually, within a week or two, it would have been discovered. So Trent wondered who knew about it and figured it could well be whoever left the filly outside.

But Bernsen and Rolfe hadn't cracked.

He put in a call to Sheriff O'Donnell, was patched to his

cell, and did something that was way out of his comfort zone: He kowtowed to the big man. "I know the department's strung thin," he said when O'Donnell asked gruffly what he wanted.

"So what?" The man's baritone voice was as big as he was.

"I worked in the Pinewood County Sheriff's Department in Montana; I know the ropes. You can check with Sheriff Dan Grayson or Detective Larry Sparks, Oregon State Police. I think, sir, with everything that's happening here, you might want to deputize me."

"What?"

"I'm already on staff. No one would know."

"Oh, I see, an undercover deputy. Hell, maybe I should just promote you to detective while I'm at it. Hell of an idea, Trent. You want a pension, too?"

"No pay."

"You're just an interested civilian trying to help his fellow man? Sure. And you'll probably try to sell me land in Florida, too. You can't be serious. I've got enough problems without some buff sporting a damned badge." He paused, then muttered, "Shit," under his breath.

"I'm just saying I could help." It was all Trent could do to hold on to his temper. Working for this prick wouldn't be a picnic, but he needed to get closer to the investigation, learn information only the cops would have. And, truth be told, he would be an asset to the overworked sheriff's department. "The weather service is predicting a blizzard. Up to three feet of snow. You think about it, Sheriff. Call Grayson."

O'Donnell snorted his disdain and advised, "Don't hold your breath, Trent. I got a job to do, and I'm going with my trained professionals. I can't afford to have another dead body on my hands. Now, if you'll excuse me, I've got to go make a show of reassuring the entire student body that they're safe here."

"And you believe that, Sheriff?" Trent asked.

A raspy breath, and O'Donnell muttered, "What do you think?" before ending the call.

CHAPTER 22

"Everyone." Reverend Lynch rose from his seat and spread his arms wide.

From her seat at the head table, Dr. Williams clicked her spoon against a glass to garner all the residents' attention.

A foot above the main floor and perpendicular to the other tables in the hall, the head table's placement reminded Jules of a medieval feast, where the lord and his privileged guests sat higher than his serfs and freemen—a not-so-subtle reminder of who was in charge.

Jules sat on one side of the reverend, wedged between him and Dean Williams. Cora Sue sat on the other side of her husband, her face pinched and stern, as if she were sitting next to the director of Blue Rock because of some detested duty. It wasn't hard for Jules to envision Reverend Lynch's huge poodles sitting in front of the table, proud as lions in the service of their master.

But the poodles weren't here.

And apparently, Reverend Lynch's wife wished she wasn't.

"I know this is a difficult time for all of us," Lynch said, standing tall in his black suit and white clerical collar. "What happened here is very disturbing. After tonight's meal, we'll have a vigil and prayer service in the gazebo, so bring your prayer books, candles, and bold spirits." He smiled beatifically, as if campaigning to be a twenty-first-century saint. "We will be strong and weather this recent tragedy together.

"And, please, know that we are taking every precaution for your safety. We have the deputies, detectives, and even Sheriff O'Donnell himself." He motioned to a big man standing near the door. At six five and possibly two hundred fifty pounds, the sheriff reminded Jules of a bull mastiff. Hat in his hands, he didn't crack a smile as his shaved head shone under the lights. "Sheriff O'Donnell has assured me that his deputies and detectives will serve and protect us."

The room remained silent, and Jules sensed that people on this campus weren't feeling so secure, despite the presence of law enforcement.

The corners of Lynch's mouth twisted upward, an odd, pious smile. "Now, I'd like all of our students to know that counselors are available to speak with you round the clock. If there's anything you'd like to discuss, please come directly to me or to Dr. Williams or Dr. Burdette. If you need to speak to family members, we'll arrange it. This is a loss we share together, but in our darkest moments, we must remember, my brothers and sisters, that we have God on our side."

Now the silence was broken by the sudden whimper of a girl off to Jules's left and the sound of sniffing as people tried to hold back tears.

"We have some new business that cannot wait." Lynch turned toward Jules, his small, dark eyes fixing on her. "Let me introduce the newest member of our staff, Ms. Farentino, who joins Blue Rock from Bateman High School in

Portland, where she recently taught a variety of subjects, including history, art, and sociology. Ms. Farentino will be teaching some of our social and environmental classes. I trust you will show her the spirit and sense of community that is so much a part of Blue Rock Academy. Ms. Farentino?" He held out his hand to her, cuing Jules.

She stood, lifting a hand. As she did, she spied Shaylee, sitting at a table with half a dozen kids, no doubt her pod. Shaylee sat apart from the others, a wide space between her and the next student, a black girl with cornrows. Nonverbal language that said Shay was not welcome. Shay's mouth drew into a deeper pout as she met her sister's gaze.

Jules's heart wrenched, but she couldn't acknowledge Shaylee. She stayed on her feet while Reverend Lynch invited all the students and staff to meet her, then asked everyone to stand for a prayer.

The meal was served family style and consisted of a hearty beef stew, crusty homemade bread, coleslaw, and apple pie. Jules was starving by the time she sat down, and every bite was delicious. Swabbing a last bite of bread with butter, Jules decided that any complaints Shay had made about Mrs. Pruitt's cooking were just as unfounded as her feelings of persecution. But, then, that was the glass-is-completely-empty Shay.

Reverend Lynch and Dr. Williams engaged her in conversation centering around the school. Cora Sue ate little and seemed pissed when the pie was passed. She shook her neatly coiffed head almost imperceptibly, as if the server, one of the students in Adele Burdette's pod, should know instinctively that there were far too many calories in a wedge of Dutch apple pie.

Flatware clicked, conversation was kept to a low, somber hum, and Jules felt the glances from the students. Curious. Wary. Anxious. They were sizing her up, wondering how much they could get away with if they ended up in her class.

Once the meal was finished, people cleared their plates and began moving toward the prayer vigil. Jules caught Shay's eye and knew she wanted to talk, but this was not the time. All eyes were on Ms. Farentino, the newcomer, who was supposed to be meeting staff and students right now. A few of the kids came up and introduced themselves, mumbling a quick greeting, and Jules nodded, smiled, and eased her way through the group.

Wade Taggert, one of the counselors who also taught psychology, was one of the first to extend a welcome. His handshake was firm, almost too hard. His thin goatee showed hints of gray that matched the glacial shade of his eyes. His gaze held no warmth as he said, "Glad you're on the team. We need you. I've been covering some of the history classes for a while, and it'll be good to settle back to a normal workload."

His words were kind enough, but his tone seemed hollow, soulless. There was something unfathomable about him.

Salvatore DeMarco was next in line, and he seemed a bit more sincere, with his dark good looks and quick, if slightly forced, smile. He was strong and fit and taught math, science, and survival skills. "You'll like it here," he predicted, his near-black eyes glittering.

As they introduced themselves, the other teachers insisted that Jules would fit right in.

Jules was pretty sure she wouldn't.

Reverend McAllister was quick to grab her hand, smile at her, and joke that she'd brought the bad weather. He had to be in his midthirties but looked younger, one of those faces that would always hold a hint of the boy he once was.

"This is a great place," he told her, "once you get to know us. I'm really sorry you came at such a bad time."

Bert Flannagan's handshake was a grip of steel, his expression intense. Jordan Ayres was friendly enough, a real take-charge woman who seemed to be sizing her up during their brief conversation. Jules then made small talk with Adele Burdette and Tyeesha Williams, both somber as they acknowledged the tragedy of losing a student to such violent means.

Jules was just about to extricate herself from the group as a whole when Cooper Trent approached her. "Hope you're settling in," he said as they were within earshot of the other instructors.

"Not quite, but I'm getting there."

"It takes a while, you know, as we're so isolated, but I think you'll find Blue Rock interesting."

"I'm sure I will," she said, meeting his gold-hued eyes and remembering how they darkened with the night, how his pupils would dilate when he stared at her.

She swallowed hard and folded her arms, afraid she might reach for his hand. Being close to him was not a good idea. She couldn't take these memories of how she'd once loved him. She had to suppress the quicksilver flashes of their passion that burst inside her whenever he was near.

"Let me know if you need anything," he said.

A little too late . . . no, make that a lot too late.

"Thanks," she said through lips that barely moved. Of all the men in the world who were qualified for the PE instructor job at Blue Rock, what twist of irony was it that brought Cooper Trent here? Talk about bad luck!

As if reading her mind, he stared at her a second too long, then turned away, leaving her to bob and weave her way past a few others on her way to the door.

Once outside, she took in a huge breath of air. Her

nerves were as tight as piano wire from the ordeal of keeping up her facade, and she'd just arrived! Maybe it would get easier as she went along. She'd never been a great liar, and now she had to stay on her toes, not let anything slip.

Lost in thought, she followed a dark path toward Stanton House and nearly jumped out of her skin when a box hedge shook, a dark figure rising behind the snow-covered green.

"What the hell!" Jules backed away, nearly falling into a mound of snow at the edge of the walkway. She caught her balance as she recognized her sister. "What're you doing?"

"We have to talk," Shay said in a stage whisper as she fell into step beside her. "Just keep walking and tell me how you think taking a job here is going to get me out." Her greenish-gray eyes flashed with anger beneath the brim of a watch cap with the Blue Rock insignia on it.

"I told you already."

"My roommate died last night." Shaylee's lower lip wobbled on a sob. "They're thinking that somebody here killed her!"

"I know that, Shay. I'm so sorry."

"So let's go."

"We can't just walk out of this place. Remember: A judge put you here."

"I know, but people are being killed!" Shay sniffed, starting to hyperventilate.

Jules put a steadying hand on her sister's back. "Hey, calm down. Just hang in there."

"I thought you were going to help."

"I am."

"Is anything wrong?" Trent's voice boomed from behind them, and Shay actually darted away from Jules as Trent approached.

"I'm handling it," Jules said. Dear God, she didn't want Shay to see her with Trent and somehow put two and two together. Shay might remember him. "Thanks, Mr. Trent."

"No problem. Shaylee's one of the students in my pod."

"Everything's cool," Shay said without an ounce of conviction.

"You're sure? I know this has been traumatic for you, what with Nona being your roommate and all."

"Hey, I don't need this. I've already had the interrogation from the cops and some 'counseling' from Dr. Williams, so don't go there with me, okay?" Her eyes narrowed as she stared at Jules and Trent standing so close together. "What is this, some kind of tag team?"

"Hey!" Trent said, but Shaylee was already jogging off toward the dorm.

Jules whirled on him. "What the hell do you think you're doing?" she demanded, her voice low, all her pent-up rage and frustration exploding. "Did you really think you could help? I was handling things!"

"Didn't look that way."

"She's my sister," Jules hissed.

"Not here she isn't," Trent fired back. "Remember that. If you insist on playing this charade, then do it right. You don't know me, and you damned well don't know her. She's in my unit, so it's only right that I would step in, Jules. Get it straight."

"Look, Shay's scared to death, and I don't blame her. You don't seem able to do much about that, do you? Wasn't the girl who died, Nona, one of the students in your pod or unit or group or whatever the hell you call it?"

He just stared at her.

"I thought so." So angry she was shaking, she stepped closer to him. "We can work on this together, or we can fight about it, but don't tell me how to deal with my sister. I've had a hell of a lot more practice at it than you have!"

She noticed a couple of students, prayer books and candles in hand, heading in their direction and decided to end the conversation.

"I'll see you at the vigil," she said, forcing a lightness in her voice.

Trent didn't answer as she turned away and headed to her quarters. Once at Stanton House, she clambered up the stairs and into her room, where she shut the door and leaned hard against it.

Oh, God, what a day!

Her head was throbbing.

What were the chances of having to deal with Cooper again. Holy crap, what a catastrophe.

She rubbed her eyes, thinking of her next move. No matter what tack she decided to take, she knew the wise choice would be to include Cooper Trent.

He used to be a cop.

He's smart.

God knows he's brave.

Work with him instead of against him.

"Yeah, right." She walked to the bathroom and splashed cold water on her face, then stared at her reflection as she patted her skin with a towel. Her eyes were still snapping fire, her hair dark and curling with melting snow.

Maybe Shay was right, she thought as she dropped her towel into the sink, then quickly finger-combed her hair and twisted it into a ponytail.

She snapped a rubber band into place. Maybe coming here, taking the job, was a mistake.

But it was too late to change that now. And she couldn't afford to be late for the vigil, unless she wanted to draw unwanted attention to herself. No, the more invisible she was, the more innocuous-seeming, the better.

She'd somehow gotten through the fifteen-minute meeting with the reverend and his wife, though Cora Sue had simmered throughout her husband's we're-all-just-one-big-happy-family conversation, which seemed ridiculous in light of what was going on.

And Lynch bugged her. Jules didn't consider herself particularly religious, but she had her own feelings about God and had met a few preachers that she really liked, whose faith was secure and solid, not overblown and dramatic. Those youth ministers had a sense of humor, an overflowing wealth of compassion and a deep-seated trust in God.

Those men and women saw people's foibles and, with care and love, laughter and hope, helped the misguided or forlorn. They prayed and gave sermons, joined baseball teams, and helped in hospitals. They were part of bazaars and golf tournaments and giving of themselves to their community and others worldwide. Within each and every one was a happiness in their faith and a sense of purpose to do God's will with an easy smile and a strong, helping hand.

Those men and women held deep convictions, and Jules respected them for it. If she were to guess, though she hadn't had much time with him yet, she thought the younger man, Reverend McAllister, was someone with whom the kids might relate, a minister whose relationship to them wasn't out of the Dark Ages.

Not so Tobias Lynch, at least from what she'd observed here to date. Granted, things were tough, and maybe her first impression was off or colored by Shaylee's jaded reactions to anything that happened at the school.

So far, it appeared that Reverend Lynch was always on-stage, performing an act. For all his big talk, there was no way he could connect with his students here. It was almost as if the man were from a bygone time and place.

And he was in charge. Unbelievable.

Returning to the living area, she bundled up against the cold and grabbed the prayer book and fake, battery-powered candle that had been left for her. "In for a penny, in for a pound."

She flew down the stairs and joined the throng heading along recently shoveled paths leading to the gazebo. Snow was still coming down like crazy, piling on rails and streetlamps, causing fir boughs to droop and giving the campus an otherworldly glow. All trails seemed to end in the mass of bobbing white pin dots, the lights of battery-powered candles held by students and faculty spilling out of the gazebo. Only a handful of faculty fit in the small structure, where Reverend Lynch stood atop a platform, his wife and Dr. Burdette flanking him. *Yin and Yang,* Jules thought. In her stocking cap, down jacket, thermal pants, and hiking boots, Burdette was the direct opposite of Lynch's wife in her designer ski outfit with fur trim.

Decidedly un-PC.

Not that Cora Sue would care how many ermine or snow leopards had to give their lives for the trim on her hood and high-heeled boots.

Jules had hoped that Trent would be nearby, but he stood on the fringe of the crowd, close to a path that led away from the central campus to the barns and outbuildings, a walkway she'd seen on the map in her room. He didn't catch her eye, and she chastised herself for feeling disappointed when she should be relieved.

Although she saw Shaylee in the large group, she did not meet her sister's eyes but let her gaze sweep over the sparkle of white lights and ruddy faces. Staff members were interspersed with the students, and she recognized them all, from Bert Flannagan to Father Jake.

"Thank you all for coming," Reverend Lynch said.

"This is a service for the passing of Nona Vickers's soul and a request to our Heavenly Father for Andrew Prescott's speedy recovery. . . ." He led off with a prayer, then a talk about tragedy and triumph. Another prayer and then, with one of the kids strumming her guitar, a final song. Voices, old and young, rose in a short rendition of "Amazing Grace," the thrumming melody rising to the snow clouds pressing low in the heavens.

If it was a show, it was a good one.

Even Jules was impressed, and she'd been privy to the harsh words between Lynch and his wife, words that seemed at odds with the image of the perfect, loving couple they attempted to project.

During the hymn, someone from the crowd ascended the steps of the gazebo and approached the reverend. Jules squinted against the mesmerizing dots of light to make out Sheriff O'Donnell. What was he telling Lynch?

When the hymn ended, the reverend lifted his arms to the crowd. "My brothers and sisters in Christ, I have some uplifting news from the hospital. Our good friend Andrew awakened after his surgery, and he was able to speak with his family and with the police."

A murmur passed through the crowd, a collective sigh amid the sniffing and teary eyes.

"That is good news, indeed," Lynch said, pinching his goatee. "However, from Andrew's statement, it is clear that both he and Nona Vickers were attacked by a third person."

The crowd grew silent as the realization set in: Then it was murder. For certain. No more doubts: Nona Vickers had been killed.

Taking in the young faces around her strained with fear, eyes dark sockets in the candlelight, Jules suspected that everyone else was drawing the same horrible conclusion.

"Which leads me to remind you all to take caution here

on campus," the reverend said slowly, sincerely. "Honor our curfew laws, and please, travel in groups after dark." His arms swept wide, embracing his flock. "Let us pray . . ."

As Jules bent her head, her gaze fell on Deputy Meeker, standing off at the edge of the crowd, his sidearm on his hip, below the waist of his jacket.

A silent reminder that a killer walked among them.

CHAPTER 23

Jules was exhausted, her head throbbing as she sorted through the events of the day. The long drive, the frantic calls from Shaylee, the stress over two students victimized on campus, one still fighting for his life, and now this—a killer in their midst.

She eyed her pain medication and took three rather than two, washing them down with water from the sink in her kitchenette. Peering in the cupboards, she found prepackaged coffee, tea bags, hot cocoa, and a small coffeemaker, similar to those in airport hotels. She heated water, planning to make some herb tea after her shower.

In the bathroom, she stripped out of her clothes and stood under the hot, steamy spray until some of the heaviness eased. She thought of Shay, hunkered over, following the path back to the dorm. For now, while she and Shay were trapped on this campus with the other students and faculty, Jules needed to protect her sister, first and foremost.

What had happened to her sister? The four-year-old who had come running to her as Jules's bus had stopped at the corner near their house, the eager grade-schooler who had at first idolized her older sister, then used her to help with homework. Shay had always been smart, and Jules had wondered if her little sis was sometimes manipulating her into helping with the homework, just to get out of it herself or to weasel more time with Jules. They'd been together through Edie's divorce from Max and her remarriage to Rip, seeing their mother's emotional ups and downs, feeling the burn of her anger or the warmth of her love. They'd stuck together. Even after Jules had moved away, going off to college, she'd tried to stay close to Shaylee, but somewhere along the way, her little sister had veered off the straight and narrow, worrying their mother and Jules as well.

So Jules was here.

And she would help Shaylee any way she could.

After she pulled on some pj's, she paused in front of the mirror and wondered what Trent had seen when he came face-to-face with her in the parking lot. God, she'd been driving for hours at that point, no makeup. She was still under twenty-five, just barely, but everything she'd gone through had aged her. What had her mother called her? An "old soul." Of course, that was ludicrous.

"You're still a baby," she told herself as she heard her cell phone ringing in the main room. Certain it was Shay again, she flew barefoot into the main room and scooped her cell from the dresser. "Hello!"

"Oh, thank God, I found you!" Edie said, her voice shaking. "Have you heard the awful news? Oh, God, it's so horrible! I think I've made a horrid mistake!"

"Mom, slow down." Jules had expected the call, though she could never be totally prepared to handle Edie. "Take a deep breath."

"I can't calm down! Your sister is at Blue Rock Academy, and there was a murder down there!" She was ranting, barely stopping to draw a breath. "Didn't you see it on the news?"

"Mom, I know," Jules said calmly. "I talked to Shaylee."

"Oh, my God, did she know the victims?"

"Yeah. I'm not sure about the boy, but the girl was her roommate."

There was a squeak on the other end of the phone.

"But Shay's all right for now. Shaken up, of course, and she wants to leave. But as I understand it, that's impossible not only because of the court order but also because right now there's an investigation by the local sheriff's department. They're interviewing all of the staff and students."

"Oh, my God! Oh, my God!" Edie was nearly hyperventilating. "I thought I was doing the right thing. I thought she needed the structure of that school. I thought . . . Oh, Lord, Jules, I know you tried to talk me out of this, but I believed Reverend Lynch and Analise and—"

"Mom, it's okay," Jules said, though she knew it wasn't. The only good news was that Edie possessed a scintilla of maternal love. "Shay is fine for now, but maybe you should lay the groundwork to get her out of the school."

"I can't do anything. It's a court order." She let out a long, trembling sigh, and Jules imagined her chewing on the end of a brightly tipped fingernail.

"Then talk to the judge. Get the attorney back."

"First I need to talk with Reverend Lynch. I tried earlier but couldn't get past his secretary."

Charla King. Jules had met her in passing.

"Keep trying, and even if you do get through, don't be talked out of it. Have your attorney file a motion or something."

Edie was calming down a bit. "And then what? Where will the judge send her? Juvenile detention? A psych ward?"

"Maybe she can attend some kind of day facility in a place where kids aren't getting killed," Jules said, trying to get the seriousness of the matter across. "Mom, you need to get Shaylee out of Blue Rock as soon as possible."

"You're right. I'll call Max," Edie decided.

"He hasn't exactly been the most dedicated father," Jules pointed out.

"Oh, I know, but he certainly has the money to . . . what?" Her voice softened and was suddenly muffled as she tried to disguise the fact that she was talking with someone else in the room—no doubt Grantie-Boy, the latest sycophant in her life. "Oh, sorry," Edie finally said, her attention returning to the phone conversation. "Did Shaylee leave a number where she could be reached?"

"No. You know the school doesn't allow calls normally." Jules walked to the tall windows overlooking the campus. Outside, the night was quiet, though she spied a deputy standing near the gazebo. "But she did say that Blue Rock had beefed up security and that there were officers from the sheriff's department at the school."

"Thank goodness! That makes me feel a little better. If she calls again, have her phone me, would you? And I'll keep trying to reach Reverend Lynch."

You and every other decent parent of the kids here, Jules thought, hanging up and letting out her breath. Dealing with Edie had never been easy, but it was worse in times of crises. It crossed her mind that Edie, if and when she ever got through to Tobias Lynch, might learn more than she bargained for. Especially if Lynch got on his soapbox and started telling her about how the school was coping, providing grief counseling and new security measures, how they'd even recently hired a new teacher in a never-ending quest for quality education, Ms. Julia Farentino . . .

For now, Jules would have to take that chance. Looking outside again, she saw a deputy in his car smoking a cigarette, the tip glowing red while the heavy snow continued to fall, as if to bury all the secrets of Blue Rock Academy.

Over the years, Shay had lost a lot of faith in her older sister. In many ways Jules was a screwup. She'd messed up her marriage and jobs, and Jules just never seemed able to get her act together. She was always nursing migraines and complaining of sleepless nights; she'd seemed weak to Shay, or at least a victim of her own neuroses, the kind of person who always shot herself in her own foot.

Incompetent.

Too nice. Too worried about what other people thought. Too much like their mother.

But, Shay had to hand it to her older sister. When push came to shove and Shay was in trouble, Jules came through. Who would have thought she'd have the nerve to lie and find a position at the school?

Certainly not Shay.

Not that Shay was convinced Jules could do anything while employed at Blue Rock. So she was here—to do what? Jules was planning to play some kind of detective to prove that the school was shady? First, Jules was not a crafty liar. And second, well, the school was already on shaky ground with some serious security problems right now. A girl had been killed. What more did Jules need to prove that Blue Rock wasn't a safe place?

On the other hand, Jules was fighting a losing battle. Reverend Lynch and his henchmen had too much at stake. He was on a power trip, there was big money to be made from the parents of rich juvie Ds, and Shay doubted he and the others would just admit anything even if Detective Jules found something fishy.

For now, Shay decided, as she opened the door to her new room, she'd play along. The room she'd shared with

Nona was now being treated as a crime scene, so she'd been moved, after everything she owned had been sifted over by the cops.

Great.

She fell onto one of the twin beds, thinking of all those kids crying at the prayer vigil. Some of them probably didn't even know Nona. Hypocrites. And she had been the girl's roommate, and did anybody cut her a break? Not a chance.

She sighed and found herself wishing for her laptop, a TV, or a real cell phone with apps instead of Nona's stupid bare-bones phone with limited minutes and no charger.

She was going out of her mind. And where was Dawg? Her boyfriend.

Forget him. Deep down you know that he was intrigued with you because of Max.

She hated to think that, but it was true. Once Dawg had realized she was Max Stillman's daughter, he'd become really interested. As if Max cared a bit about Shay.

Ridiculous!

Refusing to think of Dawg and all the trouble he'd caused her, she eyed the stack of books she was supposed to read for her classes.

Nuh-uh. She wasn't that desperate yet.

For a second, she thought about Father Jake and wondered what it would be like seriously talking to him. He seemed like a good enough guy, but, then, what did she know about him?

Nothing.

And besides, he couldn't help her with her problems. No one could.

Stretching on the bed, she heard voices, getting louder in the hallway.

Rap. Rap. Rap.

"Shaylee?" Knuckles banged on her door half a second before it swept open.

Shaylee shot up into a sitting position. "Hey!"

"Hi, Shaylee," Dr. Burdette said as she walked into the room without waiting for an invitation. She was carrying two big, overflowing plastic bags.

On her heels, obviously unhappy, was Crystal Ricci, the thin girl with the dragon tattoo on her neck. She was loaded down with a sleeping bag in her arms and still managed to wheel a roller bag behind her.

Burdette said, "I didn't want you to be alone, being as you're new and all, so Crystal is going to be your roommate for the next month or two. You girls know each other, right?"

"*Know* is subjective," Crystal said, scowling at Burdette.

"Semantics." Burdette waved off Crystal's back talk. "This is just a temporary arrangement."

"Great." In flannel pajamas, the sleeping bag trailing on the floor, Crystal looked as ticked off as anyone could get. "I thought I'd earned my privacy."

"And now you have a chance to help someone else to earn hers," Burdette said. "We have a serious problem here, Crystal, and we all have to pull together. Desperate times call for desperate measures. This is the academy's desperate time, and you having to accept a roommate again is your desperate measure."

"I don't need to be babysat," Shay said, cutting through Burdette's BS.

"That's not what this is about," Burdette insisted, dropping the plastic bags onto the bed.

"Sure it is." Crystal sent Shaylee a new look of respect. "Let's face it, no one trusts the new kid, especially when her roommate turns up dead."

Shay tried to stay cool, though every muscle in her body had gone tight. "You think I had something to do with Nona's death?"

"Did you?"

"Enough!" Burdette stepped in. "All things considered, you should both be happy to have a roommate. More security."

"Why do we need a bathroom buddy," Shay asked, "when there are cameras and spy equipment all over the friggin' school? In fact, you should know exactly who killed Nona. Isn't it all on tape? Hasn't the school turned the tapes over to the cops? That would make it pretty easy, wouldn't it? Check the tapes, see who attacked Nona and Drew in the stable."

"It's not that easy." Burdette's face was stone cold.

Shay shook her head. "This is basic stuff, Dr. Burdette. You can see it on any episode of *CSI* or *Law and Order* or *Forensic Files.*"

"Things are easy on television, all neatly tied up in forty-eight minutes." Burdette glanced up at the sprinkler head for a second, as if to make certain the camera was in place, then said, "Good night, ladies."

The door whispered shut behind her, and Shay was left staring at Crystal. "There are no cameras, are there?"

The girl with the dragon tattoo finally grinned. "So all the hype about you was right. You are smart, aren't you?"

"Is there a meeting tonight?" His right-hand man's voice crackled over a walkie-talkie.

Hidden in the shadows of the tree line, the Leader glanced around the campus. Dressed in black ski clothes that cut the windchill, he made note of the changes, security measures that had been enforced faster than he'd anticipated.

Despite the chaos around him, despite his need to be with his followers again, despite the roar of blood pulsing in his ears whenever he saw Shaylee Stillman, he decided a meeting of the disciples would only put those he cared for in danger. He would have to be strong. Patient. Clear-thinking.

"Not tonight." It was too dangerous. The sheriff's deputies were combing the campus on horseback, in four-wheel vehicles, even with cruisers and boats on the frigid lake. Armed with shotguns, rifles, scopes, pistols, night-vision equipment, and dogs, law enforcers were out in full force. That would die down, of course. The small, rural department didn't have the manpower to keep up the full-frontal attack for long.

"What about the inner circle?" asked his most trusted assistant, his voice so eager. So ready. So burning with fire for the cause . . .

Or was he? Perhaps this subordinate had his own ambitions. Perhaps he, the person he trusted most, was the reason things were spinning out of control.

"Soon. We just have to wait a few days. We can't arouse suspicion. I'll let you know when the time is right." He clicked off, the static receding, the wail of the wind filling his ears.

Fortunately, the weather was on his side, emergency personnel working around the clock. The sheriff's department would have to limit the number of personnel they sent to the campus when there were desperate calls for help elsewhere—downed wires, blown transformers, car accidents, people freezing in their homes, abandoned vehicles, and stranded travelers. Even the Oregon State Police had their hands full in the arctic blast that dropped temperatures far below freezing and dumped snow and ice all over the state.

Still, he had to be careful.

For now, he couldn't risk being followed or exposed.

The snow on the ground would make tracking much too easy, though the more powder that was predicted to fall in the next few days, the harder for the dogs, horses, and vehicles to get around. Even the frantic parents wouldn't be able to reach their darling delinquents.

He glanced to the sky, where opaque clouds blocked the stars. More snow was predicted, the pressure system bearing down in what newscasters were calling "the storm of the century."

That, he liked.

If things got worse and the concern about Nona Vickers's death died down, then he could get back to work. It depended upon Andrew Prescott, he supposed, whether he made it or not. He squinted into the night, not understanding how all of his plans, so well formulated, seemed to be unraveling.

Be patient. You can handle this.

The wind picked up again, whispering through the woods, slapping at his face, cooling his blood, forcing clarity to overcome passion. The flakes of snow had become tiny, icy pellets that indicated a blizzard on its way.

Good.

The more the campus was cut off from the rest of the world, the better.

Tonight, he would force himself to remain quiet. Tonight he would rein in his emotions. Soon there would be time for his ultimate goals.

He walked with purpose to his own quarters.

No one would think twice about him being out at this hour, as long as he was alone. Which was just the way he wanted it. Until he sorted things out.

Drip. Drip. Drip.

Jules made her way to the den, where the flickering gray light of a television drew her like a magnet, pulling her closer. She knew that something was wrong in the room. It felt empty and cold, as if the dark spirit of bad luck had passed through.

The French doors were open, a breeze playing with the

gauzy curtains. The red light for the VCR indicated the machine was playing, the clock stuck at two forty-seven.

Goose bumps pimpled her arms as she stared at the television screen, where muted images danced, a study of light and shadow.

And still the drip. Jules looked down at the knife in her hand. Beads of blood splashed onto her foot, pooled around her toes, trailed to the body of her father lying on the floor.

A scream ripped through the room, and she jerked up, saw Edie standing in the hallway, her face ashen.

"What have you done?" Edie cried.

Jules's eyes flew open.

For a second she didn't know where she was.

The school. That's right. Blue Rock Academy. She glanced at the clock and her heart stopped.

Two forty-seven.

"Oh, Lord," she whispered, trying to calm her racing heart. Rolling onto her side, she took in deep calming breaths as the dream receded into the dark corners of her mind. She was sweating, her muscles cramped, though the room was as cold as death.

She heard a squeak on the stairs outside her door, and for a second she thought that someone had been in the room. Someone stealthily rifling through her things, standing over her as she slept.

A shudder ripped through her body, and she pulled the covers to her chin, curling into a ball. She was imagining things. The vestiges of the dream were still scraping at her, teasing her.

Her robe sat in a mound at the foot of the bed, just where she'd flung it. She wrapped it around her body, walked to the window, and opened the blinds.

Sometime during the night, the snow had stopped. The deputy's cruiser was gone, tracks indicating that the car had driven away from the heart of the campus. There were mashed trails of snow on the paths to the various buildings, solitary tracks made while most of the residents were asleep.

Tracks to Stanton House.

That was nothing in and of itself. The deputies were still on duty, and Reverend Lynch had promised that the staff would be more vigilant.

Still, with the feeling that someone had been in her room, she couldn't help the shiver of fear that slid down her spine.

"Ninny," she told herself even as she walked to the door of her apartment. She checked the lock and the dead bolt for the tenth time that night. Locked tight.

But the dream . . .

She pulled the robe tight around her and huddled on the sofa. Had it been a warning? Or just a trick of the mind?

She wondered if she'd ever know.

CHAPTER 24

As the harsh winds of February swirled around him, the Leader crossed the campus and thought of the new teacher who had been hired at the academy.

Julia Farentino.

She was beautiful.

Hauntingly so.

With eyes the color of a stormy northern sea and a tongue that was as sharp as a razor; he'd heard it a time or two and had been intrigued. Tempted.

He'd noticed the way she walked, purposeful, her strides long, her ass . . . Oh, God, he'd seen it tighten beneath her jeans as she'd taken a step, and in his mind's eye, he envisioned her tight little cheeks, split perfectly, begging him to enter that warm, seductive valley.

Even now, in this frigid winter, his cock twitched as he thought of plunging into her sweet, slick warmth. Of reaching around her and feeling her breasts fill his hands, her nipples hard. Her neck would arch, a low moan of pleasure coming from her lips. He would pinch those nipples, make her gasp and buck and scream in pleasure and pain. And he would take her as she'd never been taken before, press his lips and teeth into the back of her neck, push harder and faster!

And then what?

When it's over and you're spent, after you've spilled yourself into her, what then? In the end, you know that she is little more than a whore, like Lauren and the others. A seductress sent here to test your faith.

Fists clenching, he tried to force the image of Julia's naked body, one he had not yet seen, out of his mind. But the demons inside him, the insatiable sexual appetite that consumed him, could not be quieted.

Julia Farentino was not the only one who filled his mind and caused the sheets on his bed to be sweat-soaked and wrinkled.

And what about the Stillman girl? Shaylee? His mind was ruthless with its cruel reminders of his weakness. Wasn't she the "one" you chose to join the others? Isn't her thick, dark hair a turn-on? Don't you see it splayed beneath you? And those eyes, greenish gray, don't you imagine them rounding in surprise, her pupils dilating as you hold her down and drive into her? Don't you imagine her tongue licking your body everywhere? Isn't she, too, seductively tempting?

He frowned slightly, the two women melding in his mind, becoming one, arms and legs surrounding him. He fantasized about having them both at the same time, almost heard their combined wails of pleasure and pain in the song of the icy wind.

Don't tread there.

Remember what they are, those two who look so much alike.

Distractions.

Tests of your will.

Nothing more.

Do not waver.

For they are dangerous, just as Lauren was.

He squeezed his eyes shut as he remembered her.

Lauren Conway.

A demon disguised as an angel.

God, he'd been a fool. A damned fool.

For a woman.

A classic mistake.

And stupid.

Hadn't he too, been played for a fool by another man's wife? And yet, he had let down his guard again.

Not that she had been any woman, Lauren Conway. Oh, no.

She'd been a beautiful girl just on the threshold of womanhood, or so he'd thought. But, of course, he'd been wrong. Her treachery had been so disguised in innocence he'd come to trust her.

Completely.

Madly.

Stupidly.

He'd allowed her into his inner circle.

For all the wrong reasons.

Mainly because of his ego.

And because he'd wanted to sleep with her.

He'd made that mistake and couldn't risk another, not with Shaylee Stillman or Julia Farentino or any other temptress who might cross his path. He closed his eyes, concentrated on the bitter winter night, and forced the heat in his blood to cool.

Pull yourself together.

You have work to do.

A sudden peace moved over him, and all the doubts were chased away as if they never existed.

Trent stood under the heavy spray of a shower so hot it damn near burned his skin. But the needles of hot water felt good, the steam in the room clearing his head after a sleep-less night spent spinning scenarios for what might have happened in the stables. Trying to think like the killer. Try-ing to focus on what happened to Drew and Nona without picturing Jules walking alone across this dangerous cam-pus.

Damned woman.

Seeing her again was a jolt back to another lifetime when he was still riding bulls, still thinking he could grab the world by the tail, still naive enough to believe in love.

"Get real," he told himself now, blinking the water from his eyes, feeling lather slide down his body. They'd had a shot; it hadn't worked out. End of story.

Except she's back and looking better than ever.

Her hair was shorter now, but still a deep, rich brown that waved as it brushed her shoulders. But it was her eyes that got to him. Surrounded by thick lashes, guarded by arched eyebrows, her eyes were between a steely gray and silver, depending on the light.

Did she look like her sister? Oh, yeah. But more refined, her lips a little fuller, her eyebrows more arched, her cheek-bones bolder than her younger sister's. Half sister, he re-minded himself.

But Jules . . . He lifted his face to the spray, trying to wash her from his mind.

Why now? Why did she have to appear now, when all hell was breaking loose? The last thing he needed was to worry about her or her damned sister!

As he reached for the faucet to turn off the water, he heard his cell phone ringing over the creak of old pipes.

Who would be calling him at six in the morning?

No one bearing good news, that much was certain.

He stripped a towel from the bar, then marched barefoot and dripping into the bedroom. "Trent," he said on the fourth ring, holding the cell between his ear and shoulder as he wrapped the towel around his waist.

"Sheriff O'Donnell. Hope I didn't wake you." O'Donnell's voice was rough from cigarettes or not enough sleep or, Trent figured, both.

"Been up a while."

"Figured as much. I took your advice and called Dan Grayson in Grizzly Falls."

Sheriff Dan Grayson.

"And I also put in a call to Larry Sparks, with the state police up in Portland," O'Donnell went on. "Grayson said you were a stand-up guy. Reliable. Sergeant Sparks confirmed it and told me he'd trust you to have his back."

"Good to know." Trent shoved his wet hair from his eyes and waited, knowing where this was going.

"According to Grayson, you're on the bull-headed side, but that's not a problem for me. Thing is, my deputies and me, we barely made it out of the mountains last night, what with the storm. And now that our investigation has turned to homicide, well, I'm going to need some inside help. So, if you're still willing, I'm deputizing you, here and now. Probably add a few others to the list out there, so I'll need your input on who at Blue Rock would be good, who you could trust."

That list was sure to be short.

"I won't kid ya," O'Donnell said, and paused for a second. Trent heard the click of a lighter and a deep intake of breath as the sheriff fired up a cigarette. "The storm has really stretched us thin. Deputies working around the clock. Had to pull a few of my guys away from the school to field other emergencies. Hell, I had to cover a few jobs myself."

Which explained the early hour.

"We just don't have the manpower to handle everything, even with help from the OSP, city police, and emergency crews. We could use a man like you."

"Count me in," Trent said, relieved to have access to some information, albeit limited, from the sheriff's office.

"I will, then."

"Just let me know what you want me to do, where I should start."

"Deputy Meeker will bring you up to speed. He's up there at Blue Rock now." O'Donnell took another drag. "Listen, Trent, don't go rogue on me, okay? This is still my county, and my ass is on the line. You're working for my guys, got that? The detectives are still in charge. Ned Jalinsky and Tori Baines. You report to them."

"Got it. But I take it they're not here now?"

"No, and they won't be up today. The roads were treacherous when we cut out last night. Good thing the crime scene crew handled everything yesterday, got what they needed." Trent remembered the techs who had taken pictures, dusted for fingerprints, collected trace evidence, searched for footprints, and scoured the stable and surrounding area while the interrogations had been going on.

O'Donnell was saying, "I understand no one can make it up to Blue Rock until the snow lets up. My detectives will get back up there just as soon as Mother Nature gives us a break. For now, you'll deal with Meeker. He's on campus, sort of trapped up there."

"Along with the rest of us."

"The storm will let up soon," the sheriff said, though they both knew the weather service predicted more snow.

"How's the Prescott kid doing?" Trent asked, dropping his towel and using it to wipe up the puddle that had formed around his feet.

"Still critical. The docs were real positive when he came to, had that burst of consciousness, talking with everyone, but it seems he's lapsed back into a coma again."

Trent hated to hear it. "Too bad."

"Yeah. The hospital is supposed to call the minute he

wakes up again, but he's still in the ICU. They're talking about brain and spine injury." After a brief pause, during which Trent hoped to God for a miracle, the sheriff wrapped things up. "I gotta roll. If you have any more questions, talk to Meeker, or call Baines or Jalinsky." O'Donnell hung up, giving Trent the green light to investigate what had happened in the stable.

About time. He kicked his towel into a corner and added the sheriff's number along with those for Jalinsky and Baines into his phone, then got dressed in heavy layers and headed to the stable. He had a couple of hours before he was expected in the gym for the group of kids who played pickup basketball or worked out on the equipment on the weekends, and he wanted to see the crime scene again.

Most of the stable had been off-limits while the sheriff's department worked the scene. Since the crime scene investigators and the detectives were finished, Trent ignored the yellow crime scene tape that was already broken and flapping in the breeze and let himself into the stable.

He found Flannagan leading Omen, a black gelding, through the back door and into his stall. Omen was pulling on his lead, prancing and tossing his head, his black coat gleaming under the lights. The other horses had already returned to their boxes.

Trent reached into a stall to pat Arizona's gray muzzle, and the gelding in the next stall snorted impatiently.

"Take it easy, Scout," he said, scratching the paint behind his ears. He turned to Flannagan. "Need help?"

Dressed in camouflage pants and a Blue Rock down jacket, Flannagan shook his head. "Nah. This is the last one. Besides, I got extra hands today, the three from yesterday's tussle. The new girl, Stillman, Lucy Yang, and Eric Rolfe. They've been assigned to muck out the stalls this weekend—that is, when they're not shoveling snow." His lips twisted in a smile that was more menacing than amused. "Guess that's the start of their punishment for their little spat yesterday."

"Start?"

"Hmm." He locked Omen in his stall, then unclipped the lead from the gelding's halter. "Usually the two involved would be left out in the wilderness for a day or two, separately, of course, just to give each of 'em time to think about what they've done, how they disrespected the school and all that." Slipping through the door to the stall, he walked to the area where the feed was kept. While the horses nickered and whinnied impatiently, Flannagan twisted off the top of a barrel of oats. "Because of the blizzard, Reverend Lynch is raining down a little mercy on the sinners' dark souls."

"So they're sinners?" Trent asked.

"Isn't everybody?" Flannagan snorted a laugh as he slipped through the gate. Trent's eyes were drawn to the man's hunting knife sheathed but at his side. An odd accessory for a man who worked with juvenile delinquents, but it was part of Flannagan's persona and was definitely a necessity working with farm animals.

As Flannagan climbed up the ladder to the loft, Trent stared down at the floor, at the spot where Andrew Prescott had lain, crumpled and unconscious. Although someone had washed the area, the old, porous floorboards had soaked up the blood so that the stain remained, a patch of rusty brown. Farther away was the smaller stain, the one that had looked like another patch of blood, one the detectives had photographed, discussed, and taken samples from to ensure that it was either Nona Vickers's or Drew Prescott's.

"Stand clear," Flannagan called as he dropped a couple of hay bales through the chute. Swinging down from the opening, he landed on the floor and deftly, one knee placed on the bale, used his knife to slice through the string holding the pressed hay together.

In his mind's eye, Trent envisioned Prescott on the floor and Flannagan standing over him, wielding that wicked hunting knife.

Except Andrew hadn't been stabbed.

"What?" Flannagan asked, grabbing a nearby pitchfork. "This bother you?" He pointed the tines at the bloodstain visible beneath the loose hay.

"Yeah, a little."

"I tried to wash it down, but the damn stain is stubborn. Blood is hard to remove, you know," Flannagan said, as if he'd had experience with trying to clean up like stains. He shook forkfuls of hay into the mangers, and the horses shuffled and snorted as they shoved their noses into the loose, dried grass.

"I guess it seems disrespectful to just pretend it isn't there." Trent measured rations of grain.

"Life goes on," Flannagan said, flashing his razor-sharp grin. "Don't get me wrong, I hope the boy survives. I hope Sheriff O'Donnell tracks down the killer and all. But I got stock to feed, barns to keep clean, kids to teach. I can't worry about a little spilled blood. Seen enough in my lifetime, let me tell you. Nothing we can do to change what happened; we can only hope to make sure it never happens again."

Finally, they agreed on something, Trent thought, as Flannagan returned the pitchfork to its hook on the wall, then walked out of the stable on his way to the barn.

Once the door shut behind Flannagan, Trent scowled at the faded bloodstain and climbed up the ladder to the hayloft. A familiar spidery feeling slipped up his back, an eerie sensation that had hit him in the gut the night Nona Vickers died. He stared up at the rafters, remembered her swinging, nude corpse. If only these walls could talk . . .

He climbed up to the spot where there had once been sleeping bags and a pile of clothes. The wall of bales had been dismantled, and there was a small stack of bales and loose hay in disarray from the investigation. It was cold up here, the small round window still open a few inches. He thought about closing it, then remembered the owl who nested in the rafters and left well enough alone.

Standing there, in the place where terror had reigned in the deep cold, he took out his cell and called the detectives he'd met yesterday. The line clicked through to Ned Jalinsky's voice mail, so he tried Tori Baines.

"This is Baines." Her voice was low and had a bite to it, as if she were too busy to talk.

"Cooper Trent, at Blue Rock. We met at the crime scene yesterday, and I spoke to O'Donnell this morning. He deputized me."

"Yeah, I heard." She didn't sound happy about it. "You've been a deputy for all of ten minutes, right? Not wasting any time, are you?"

"I want to get this guy before he gets someone else. Sheriff O'Donnell told me to refer questions to you. Is this a bad time?"

She sighed. "Fair enough. I guess this is as good a time as any, since I'm sitting at a roadblock. You wouldn't believe how many drivers think they've got the skill to beat snow and ice just because they have four-wheel drive."

"I believe it. I used to do police work." Trent looked up at the rafters and caught another memory flash of Nona swinging there. "I'm wondering if you've gotten any forensics back on Nona Vickers. Did they do an autopsy yet?"

"The coroner fit the autopsy in before end of day yesterday," she said. "I've got the report on my BlackBerry here, and no matter how it was staged, this was not a suicide."

"That would confirm what Drew Prescott said." Cell phone in one hand, Trent turned away from the loft and climbed back down to the stables.

"But you suspected as much, right? You pointed out the

signs of petechial hemorrhaging. Looks like the hanging was just for show. The victim died from asphyxiation."

"Someone strangled her," Trent said.

"Bruises on the neck consistent with fingertips," she said. "Also, a few broken ribs. You put it all together, and it looks like a strangling. Someone got on top of her and squeezed her neck until she died."

"Son of a bitch," Trent said, wanting a cigarette now more than ever. "Son of a goddamned bitch."

CHAPTER 25

Jules stood at her window drying her hair with a thick towel while she watched opaque clouds roll over the mountains. Though the night had been as quiet as death, this morning the storm was back with a vengeance. Those mountains would be impassable. For today, at least, they would be trapped here without the support from law enforcement.

Trapped with a killer on the loose.

The howl of the wind, as forbidding as Satan's laugh, shrieked through the canyon before licking the icy edges of Lake Superstition and roiling the center of the lake, which was too deep to freeze through. Steely clouds collided overhead, and snow fell in tiny, hard flakes of ice that clicked frantically as they hit the window.

After the nightmare, Jules had slept poorly, her mind filled with images of death. The dream with her father lying in a pool of blood had been followed by a nightmare in which the naked body of a young woman swung from a noose in a dark stable. Poor Nona.

As for her fears that someone had been in her room or

lingered in the hallway, she saw no evidence of anything out of place. Apparently her vivid, macabre imagination had been working overtime again. "Paranoid," she whispered under her breath as she walked into the bathroom. "That's what you are." She plugged in the dryer and finished with her hair, then added lipstick to her pale face. She made herself a cup of orange pekoe and dialed Mrs. Dixon, an early riser who answered on the first ring, saying, "You'll never get him back."

"What?"

"I saw it was you on the caller ID, and I'm just warning you, I'm in love with this cat. You'll have to pry him out of my arms!"

"You've had him what, two days? Let's see how much you love him in a week or so, after he's brought you headless mice as trophies, then clawed your drapes and hissed at any friends you have over."

"Sweet little Diablo?" the older woman said with a laugh.

"He has that name for a reason, you know. He earned it."

Mrs. Dixon chuckled, and they chatted for a few minutes while Jules sipped her tea and Agnes Dixon regaled her with cute stories of the cat. When she hung up, Jules felt a little more grounded. The hot tea had warmed her from the inside out, and any concerns she had about her pet had been quieted by her neighbor in Seattle. Diablo, that little traitor, appeared to be doing just fine without her.

After she bundled up against the cold, she set out to explore the campus on her own, trusting that she was safe navigating on her own in the light of day. She tried to memorize the location of buildings and the way paths connected them. A walking trail that cut through the campus led past the barns and into the wooded slopes in one direction and followed the shoreline of the lake in the other. This, she decided, would become her jogging path when the weather broke. If she was here that long.

Right now it was impossible to run due to the icy conditions, but she figured she could work out in the gym, where, according to all the literature she'd read, there was plenty of exercise equipment.

Even if it meant dealing with Cooper Trent.

She had to start thinking of him as an ally rather than an adversary. The heartbreak between them was long over; they both had to deal with the here and now.

No more tripping down memory lane to that summer when she'd first met him. He'd smelled of dust, tobacco, and horses, a three-days growth of beard had shaded his strong jaw, and an irreverent smile that touched his eyes had slowly crept across the lower half of his face. She'd been caught up in the mystique and pure, sexy maleness of him.

"Fool," she said under her breath, but even so, her stupid heart was racing at the memory.

Forgetting about their time together was easier said than done, Jules decided, and found out she was right a few hours later.

She caught her first glimpse of Trent that day at breakfast when he took a seat at the table with his pod. A glum Shaylee sat next to him, picking at her muffin. Each time Jules glanced Trent's way, she saw him dealing with his students. She never caught him looking in her direction, which was just as well. Still, that didn't improve the taste of her oatmeal, fruit, and coffee.

On the other hand, Shaylee nearly stared a hole right through Jules, which wasn't smart. Jules tried and failed to ignore the plea in her sister's eyes. It wasn't that Jules didn't want to talk to her sister; she simply couldn't risk it. Not with the faculty and student population of Blue Rock Academy looking on.

Before the meal, Reverend Lynch had given his prerequisite prayer about trusting God for their safety. "Psalms twenty-seven five tells us, 'For in the day of trouble he will keep me safe in his dwelling, he will hide me in the shelter of his tabernacle and set me high upon a rock.'"

High upon a rock? Jules mulled that one over, wondering if he'd chosen the Bible quote because the academy was called Blue Rock.

The meal itself was strained, with students and staff still reeling from the attacks on campus, still worried that the killer had not been found.

As students began clearing their plates, Lynch went to the podium again and moved on to housekeeping, breaking down chores by pod. Then, to Jules's surprise, he called up Shaylee, Lucy Yang, and Eric Rolfe. He asked them to hold hands and "break through the wall of misunderstanding" that had put them at odds.

Jules tried to ignore the snickers that punctuated the room as Lynch placed a hand on each of their heads and led a prayer asking the Lord's forgiveness for their sins. At the last "Amen," he insisted everyone in the dining hall link hands and say a kind word to each of the people they were touching.

Just the kind of thing Jules abhorred.

"I'm glad you're a part of the staff," Rhonda Hammersley said to her. "We need a few more women."

Jules, forcing the lie over her lips, responded in kind, that she was happy to be at Blue Rock.

On her other side, Wade Taggert, with his ever-worried expression, told her she was a welcome addition to the school and that he was looking forward to working with her. The whole scene seemed surreal, even scripted. Hoping she sounded a hell of a lot more sincere that she felt, Jules repeated what she'd said to Hammersley. As soon as Taggert dropped her hand, he rubbed nervously at his goatee.

She couldn't hear what Shaylee, Lucy, and Eric said to each other, but the set of Shay's jaw didn't bode well in the forgiveness department, but Jules couldn't worry about it. Not now.

Even though it was technically the weekend, Jules was busy. First up, she had to complete employment forms for her personnel file. As soon as breakfast ended, Jules headed over to the office in the admin building and located Charla King, Lynch's secretary, who looked a little like a former beauty queen—very faded and slightly unhappy. With manicured fingernails, Charla pointed out where Jules was to sign on insurance, retirement, and tax forms. The process was tedious, but Jules scanned the documents as she signed them.

"Almost done," Charla promised, as if reading Jules's mind. She slid the final form across her desk. "This is about privacy for the school. It ensures that you won't disclose anything about Blue Rock Academy during your tenure or after you leave us. As you know, we value the privacy of our staff and students."

Jules's toes wiggled in her boots as she looked down at the form. This one would be a problem, but what the hell?

Charla smiled as Jules read the short document quickly, then scribbled her name in the appropriate box.

"Perfect." Charla scooped up all the pages, tapped them on the top of her desk to straighten them, then carefully placed them in a file and locked the slim folder inside one of a bank of file cabinets.

"Okay, then." Charla dropped the key in her purse, then reached for her wool coat and scarf. "Let me take you on a quick introductory tour, though the campus is going to be quiet today. All this snow, and our students will be kept inside for the most part. Everyone's still worried about what happened to those two kids."

Somehow, Charla's tone minimized the severity of the situation. Jules shrugged her coat on, grabbed her hat, and followed the woman out into the cold wind.

Animated, the tip of her nose and cheeks turning red, Charla pointed out buildings, paths, and shortcuts, most of which Jules had seen on the map in her room.

"Reverend Lynch runs a tight ship and helps hundreds of troubled kids every year," Charla said, her breath fogging in the air, as if powered by her faith in the man who was, in her mind, the backbone of Blue Rock Academy.

Jules followed her on the shoveled path, which was quickly being covered by new snow. With more force than had been predicted, the arctic storm was ripping down from Canada, tearing through British Columbia, Washington, Oregon, and even parts of Northern California. News reports indicated that parts of I-5, the lifeline of the western states, were closed. Jules was glad to have made it here yesterday before the blizzard set in.

Jules stared at the edges of the frozen Lake Superstition, where the seaplane was tethered in ice. In this weather, there really was no way in or out of here.

Charla followed her gaze. "I've never seen that much ice on Lake Superstition, though we get our fair share of snow. This area of the Siskiyou Mountains is always inundated."

"You don't mind the isolation?" Jules asked, feeling the spit of tiny crystals of ice against her face.

"I can honestly say it's cozy in the winter. Blue Rock Academy might be geographically challenged, but we're prepared for anything. We could probably even survive a nuclear attack."

Prepared for anything except missing students and mur-

der, Jules wanted to say. The woman seemed ridiculously smug about Blue Rock's resilience.

"I even think at one point there was a fallout shelter on campus, though I've never seen it." Charla laughed and explained that the campus was self-contained, with stores of food, two generators, extensive tanks of propane, and gasoline. There was a radio/communications station as well as a clinic. Though there was no doctor on staff, Jordan Ayres was soon to become a nurse practitioner, and Kirk Spurrier, the pilot, had once been an EMT.

Glasses fogging, Charla seemed to think that the school's medical bases were covered. Jules didn't agree, but she held her tongue, nodding in all the appropriate conversation lapses while holding the hood of her ski jacket tight at her chin. Even in her boots, with her warm socks, her toes were starting to feel numb.

As they made a circuit of the campus, Jules asked, "How long have you been here?"

"Eighteen years in April," the woman said proudly. "I was the first person Reverend Lynch brought on board. I helped him organize and hire the teaching staff. Back then, when the school was new, there were only a few of us."

"And before that?"

"Oh, the property was in disrepair." She waved a gloved hand toward the buildings. "Horribly so. It had been donated to a church in the late forties to be used for family retreats and counseling, but the facilities were neglected and run-down. I think the reverend's father came here as a child, then later brought Reverend Lynch here when he was a boy. Hunting and fishing, that sort of thing. Years later, when Reverend Lynch came up with the idea of the academy, he thought this would be the perfect spot. Isolated and idyllic, close to God. He found some investors and worked hard to fulfill the dream. Now the academy is a standard for learning institutions throughout the country, probably the world," she said proudly.

"And Mrs. Lynch, she's a part of this?" Jules asked, thinking of the angry conversation she'd overheard between the reverend and his wife.

"Oh, of course." Charla's face lost a little of its animation, but her smile returned, as if on cue. "Mrs. Lynch's father, Radnor Stanton, was a major investor in Blue Rock Academy. He was a philanthropist. An entrepreneur. Made his fortune in shipping, I think." She waved a gloved hand, as if Stanton's occupation was of no consequence.

But it explained the mansion in Seattle. "I take it he's passed on?"

"Ten years ago and it's too bad," she said. "He was a good man. Far-sighted, like the reverend."

"And maybe Reverend McAllister?" Jules prompted.

Charla sighed. "He's . . . different. The board of directors wanted to have someone more youthful on the staff, I guess, and he was available, but he believes the students should, you know"—she made air quotes—"do their own thing. Have their own personal relationship with God. He seems to disdain order and doctrine." She slid Jules a look. "As I said, different."

"I know what you mean. Nontraditional."

"That's one way of looking at it."

"But the two ministers, they work well together?"

"Reverend Lynch says 'there are many paths to God.'"

"And Mrs. Lynch agrees?"

"Cora Sue? Who knows?" Charla said hotly.

"And their marriage? How is it? What with him being here most of the time and she in Seattle."

"It makes it easier for her," Charla said with a trace of bitterness.

"And him. Without the wife around, well, he can . . . do whatever he wants."

Charla turned horrified eyes on Jules. "Are you suggesting that Tobias would cheat on Cora Sue?" Her back was really up. "*He* would never do anything of the kind. *He* is not an adulterer."

"And Cora Sue?"

Charla stopped dead in her tracks. "This is none of your business or mine," she said. "Reverend Lynch is a good man! Kind, just, and extremely forgiving . . ." There was a hint that she wanted to say more but thought better of it.

Jules pushed, "Even when his wife . . . ?"

"Cora Sue isn't as . . . dedicated as the reverend is." Charla glanced sharply at Jules. Disapproval was evident in her eyes. She knew the marriage was strained and that the problem was with the reverend's wife. She kept walking, her cheeks red with the cold.

Jules kept up and decided to test the woman even further. "I could see from my first interview that Doctor Lynch is a doctor as well as a preacher, right?"

Charla beamed again. "Double Ph.D. Psychology and religious studies. Extremely well educated—one of the most honored theologians on the West Coast. Absolutely dedicated to the students."

Jules guessed the besotted secretary was stretching things a bit but said, "I knew he was a true man of God. That's one of the reasons I took the job. Like Reverend Lynch, I'm committed to helping young people." At least that much was true, and Charla seemed to believe her. "But there are some gaps in the curriculum I received from my predecessor, Ms. Howell."

Charla visibly stiffened. "She's been gone for a while. Dean Hammersley and Mr. Taggert filled in for her until you were hired. If there are gaps, you should speak with them."

"I just thought that since you seem to be the coordinator

of the entire school, you might have some idea where I'd find Ms. Howell's class notes and detailed lesson plans."

"I don't know," she said, but there was a little gleam in her eye, as if she were dying to pass on a tidbit of Blue Rock gossip. "I'm sure everything the school has is in the file you were given."

"I got the book and the syllabus, but I thought you might give me some insight into the woman. She worked with the kids I'll be teaching. She must have known them well."

Charla sighed. "I really shouldn't talk about her."

So much for subtlety or beating around the bush. "Because of the lawsuit?"

"That was dropped," she snapped fiercely, then caught herself. "Just recently . . . It's no secret, I guess. Maris was caught with one of the students, Ethan Slade. Understandably, his parents were upset."

"But he's still here," Jules pointed out.

"Oh, yes. And he became a TA and is going to college through the school, all gratis—part of the deal his parents worked out. Maris was let go, but even the DA backed off. Charges dropped." Obviously Charla didn't approve. As if realizing she'd said more than she should, she picked up the pace. "This is our gymnasium." She motioned grandly to the huge building with its soaring, curved roof. "Every student is required to take physical education courses along with survival training. You've met the instructor, Mr. Trent. He's relatively new to his position but works with each of the kids, and the curriculum isn't limited to indoor sports. Mr. Trent spends a lot of his time outdoors. Everything from soccer to archery, to horseback riding, yoga, and windsurfing.

"Reverend Lynch, he's quite an athlete himself, a boxer, and he believes in physical fitness, that the body and mind are God's gifts. Each student is taught to take care of both."

Back to the good reverend. Boy, Charla had it bad.

They passed several groups of students who were helping clear walkways, and Charla waved to a big man wearing an insulated hunter's cap with earflaps. "Hi, Joe!" At six-foot-four or five, he was built like a lineman for a professional football team. "Joe Ingersoll, our maintenance supervisor."

Appearing perturbed, he nodded but never stopped instructing three of the teachers' aides whom Jules didn't know by name yet.

Charla held a gloved hand up to her mouth. "We were talking about Ethan Slade. He's the one next to Joe." She pointed to an earnest boy, the one supposedly caught up in a scandal with Maris Howell. Jules made a note to talk to him. "The kids with him are TAs as well," she added, "Roberto Ortega and Kaci Donahue."

"You know all the students by name?" Jules asked.

"Of course." Charla's breath was a puff of white. "Some of the TAs take instruction from Joe before leading teams to work on the grounds or in the buildings."

"And the TAs also help with security, right?" Jules asked.

"Yes, under supervision, of course."

"Whose supervision?"

"We hire people, like the guard at the gate, but ultimately, if you have a problem, you need to talk with Bert Flannagan or Kirk Spurrier. Flannagan was solely in charge until one of the students went missing," she said nervously. "Since then, he and Spurrier have been a team."

"You're talking about Lauren Conway," Jules said, seeing a way to switch to the topic. "I read that she disappeared without a trace."

Charla stiffened. "There's all sorts of speculation, I know. But, if you ask me, she ran away, plain and simple. The press, they wanted to make it look like something horrid had happened to her, and I can't say that it didn't, but she was a manipulator, that one. Came down here, begging to be part of the TA program to help her pay for school." She shook her head. "I had her pegged from the start, you know. Knew she was up to no good."

"You think she had another reason for being here."

"I can't prove it, of course. But there was just something not right about the entire situation." Then, as if realizing she'd again said too much, Charla made a sweeping gesture toward the administration building and effectively changed the topic. "Here we are, back where we started. If you want coffee, tea, or cocoa, it's available all day at the cafeteria.

"And it goes without saying that if you have any questions, I'm usually available." She added, "The reverend wanted me to remind you that you have a meeting with him tonight. Seven o'clock in his study at the chapel."

"Wouldn't miss it for the world," Jules said, trying to keep the bite out of her words.

As Charla hurried up the snowy steps of the admin building, Jules wondered about the secretary and her relationship with her boss. Charla obviously had no love for Cora Sue Stanton Lynch, and Jules thought there might be a grain of envy. Because of Cora Sue's wealth? Or the fact that she was married to the Reverend Tobias Lynch?

It was hard for Jules, head bent against the wind, to think of the preacher in sexual terms, but then, what did she know? She'd been involved with Cooper Trent when he was a low-down rodeo rider, and truth to tell, she still found him attractive.

"Idiot," she muttered under her breath as she stomped snow from her boots on the porch of Stanton House. Glancing behind her to make sure no one was watching or following, she proceeded inside, wondering what Trent would be doing today.

Stop that. It's over.

Whatever fascination you had with him should have died years ago.

But there it was.

Like a damned toothache, one you hoped would go away if you ignored it, though it just got worse.

CHAPTER 26

There had to be some kind of law against this kind of inhumane treatment, Shay thought. Didn't shoveling horse manure fall under the category of cruel and unusual punishment? There had to be some child labor laws against this kind of abuse on the books!

Standing in the gray mare's stall, Shay rammed her shovel under the steaming manure and dirty straw and scooped the dung into a half-full cart. Though it was freezing, she was beginning to sweat, probably because she was seething inside. Shoveling horse dung with Lucy and Eric was the worst!

She had hoped Jules had a plan to get her out of here. But it seemed pretty lame. What was it again? Join the staff and poke around and tell Shay to "be patient."

She pushed her shovel again and heard it scrape against concrete. A good sign. At least this box was almost done.

But the stable was huge. There had to be thirty boxes, all of them needing to be cleaned while the horses milled around the indoor arena.

It would take forever to get it clean and spread new

straw. Meanwhile, the horses would just keep fouling the place up.

Even though she was wearing thick leather gloves, she still felt the sting of blisters forming. But she didn't dare stop or complain. Not with Flannagan popping in and out and Eric and Lucy ready to rat her out if she didn't keep working. Her shoulders and back ached. Even her arms were protesting, though she kept herself in great shape. Worse yet, she stood ankle-deep in horse manure.

Could the juvenile detention center be worse than this? Shay doubted it. She flung another shovelful into the cart positioned in the aisle behind all the stalls and thought about sending a stray pile of dung straight at Eric's face. But she didn't. He was working twice as fast as she was, which only made less work for her.

"This is so unfair!" Lucy hissed from the stall of Roscoe, a dun gelding. She slid a dark look in Eric's direction.

"I know," Shay agreed.

"Oh, shut up, you wusses!" Eric straightened, sweat running down his face. He was about finished cleaning out Scout's stall. "It could be worse."

"No way!" Lucy said, always quick with a challenge. "How?"

Rolfe smirked, wiping his forehead with his sleeve. "Try it in summer, when it's over a hundred degrees. It smells a thousand times worse, and there are flies everywhere, not just buzzing but stinging. Sometimes the shit has worms in it. Or grubs."

"Are you trying to gross me out?" Lucy asked.

Eric snorted. "Just work and stop complaining."

Creaking on freezing casters, the sliding door to the pasture opened, and Flannagan strode inside. "Is there a problem here?" Snow covered the shoulders of his jacket and the brim of his hat. "I hope not, because if you think I don't have better things to do than babysit your sorry backsides, then you've all got another thing coming."

"I'm fine," Eric said, and picked up the handles of the cart to wheel it outside. "It's just the girlies. They don't know how to handle hard work." He pushed the cart down the aisle and out the open door.

"He is such a pain." Lucy sighed as the men left the building. "It's the TAs. They all get big heads." Lucy sent a withering look at the door. "Think they deserve to be treated differently. Like they've earned it or something." Her nose wrinkled. "It's weird, you know. Like they're part of a secret club or something."

"It's no secret," Shay said.

"I'm not talking about *just* being a TA. I think it's something different. Something . . . I don't know, more intense. Maybe it's not all of them." Lucy frowned, her pencil-thin eyebrows drawing together. "Lauren Conway, the girl who disappeared before Thanksgiving? She said there was something going on, like a cult or something, and she should have known because she was one of them."

"A cult of TAs?" Shay almost laughed.

"Hey, I'm serious. I think that's why she disappeared," she said, leaning on the handle of her shovel. "I think she knew too much."

"So now they're a *deadly* cult?"

Lucy mopped the sweat off her brow with the back of her hand. "I know it sounds crazy, but maybe it's not so far off base. I mean, what do you really think happened to Nona and Drew?"

"I don't know, but I don't think a lunatic group of TAs attacked them. I mean, come on, Drew Prescott *is* one of them! Don't tell me you think they all ganged up on him because he's, like, a rogue TA or something? And the same with Lauren Conway. She didn't fit in, so they what, killed her and got rid of her body somehow?" Shay rolled her eyes. "You know, Lucy, this is right up there with Maeve's great Shakespearean tragedy."

"I know it sounds out there, but I'm tellin' ya. There is something going on here."

Wind whistled around the building, and overhead the timbers creaked. Lucy glanced up, and Shay knew what she was thinking, that this was where Nona and Drew were attacked. Where Nona had lost her life.

"That's how they do it, you know," Lucy said. "This"—she motioned to the half-cleaned stalls and their shovels—"this isn't the real punishment. It's the psychological stuff. Lynch's specialty."

"What do you mean?"

Lucy looked around to make sure no one overheard. "We could have been assigned to the kennels, or the barns, or the pigpens. Right? Wouldn't that have been worse, the pigs? But, no, we're here in the stable"—she looked up toward the loft—"right where Nona was killed."

"So?" Shay said.

"Think about Reverend Lynch's last name. Lynch. As in noose. As in hanging." Lucy actually shuddered. "You think that's a coincidence?"

Before Shay could respond, the lights flickered ominously.

"Oh, for the love of God," Lucy whispered, and the sound of angry voices swept into the stable.

"And I expect you to maintain focus," Flannagan was saying, obviously irritated. "We didn't handpick you so you could go punching girls, *Mister* Rolfe. Don't screw up again."

Lucy met Shay's eyes and lifted a shoulder, as if to say, *Didn't I tell you?*

"Oh, so now what? Flannagan's involved, too?" Shay laughed. "I hate to tell you this, Yang, but Flannagan's a little old to be a TA. And so is Lynch."

With a grim slash of a frown, Lucy moved on to another stall. Shay bent into her task as Eric, his face red from the cold and a dressing-down, wheeled the cart down the aisle.

He stepped into Omen's stall. "I hate that old man," he said under his breath as he scooped up another shovelful of straw and manure. "I wish the son of a bitch were dead."

Jules stomped the snow from her boots before pushing open the door to the empty chapel. She had left the dining hall with the dinner meal in full swing, wanting to be on time for her appointment with Dr. Lynch, though the thought of crossing the campus alone after dark had given her some pause.

Once inside, she pressed into the shadows of the nave. The tile floor reflected the glow of battery-powered candles placed strategically to light the way up the center aisle to the altar. Behind her, recessed lights illuminated the massive cross built into the window.

Her footsteps hushed by the red floor runner, Jules made her way to a side door and down a short hallway to Reverend Lynch's private office. She knocked, listened. When no one answered, she tried the door.

Of course it was locked.

It seemed she was alone in the building.

A shiver ran down her spine at the thought. What would prohibit him, the killer, from walking into a building like this and striking again?

Keep moving, she told herself. *Moving and exploring.*

She made her way to the main staircase and descended.

Downstairs was a warren of a basement where, she knew, some of the theology, psychology, and religion classes were taught. She snapped on lights as she looked into the rooms with their egress windows, whiteboards, overhead projectors, and flickering fluorescent fixtures.

Nothing sinister or suspicious.

At the end of the hall was a set of restrooms and a locked door marked CUSTODIAN, which she assumed was a janitor's closet or furnace room. She felt a jab of disappointment that she'd discovered nothing spectacular or out of the ordinary, but then, if Blue Rock had dark secrets, they would be well buried.

Discovering a secondary, narrow staircase, she climbed and bypassed the first floor, heading to a choir loft situated high above the nave. This elevated position offered an eagle's-eye view of the rows of pews below and, through the soaring windows divided by a massive crucifix, a wide panorama of the campus. As she turned around, noticing windows on all four sides of the loft, she realized every portion of the campus could be observed. Lake Superstition and the women's dorm were visible, as were the cluster of main buildings, the gazebo, and the cafeteria, even the road leading to the stable and garages. Nearly three hundred sixty degrees. This place was like some kind of sacred watchtower.

"Breathtaking, isn't it?" a deep male voice whispered from the shadows.

Jules gasped. Her heart clutched. She nearly tripped as she spun around.

Tobias Lynch stood at the edge of the loft, leaning against a bookcase.

She pressed a hand to her chest, as if that would still her pounding heart. Had he been here all along? Standing alone in the dark? Watching over his beloved campus from the shadows?

"You should see it in the moonlight," he said as he crossed the loft noiselessly. Suddenly he stood so close to her that she felt the warmth of his body. She had to fight her instinct to cringe away.

This was creepy. Jules wanted to step away, put some distance between them, but she held her ground.

"The view is spectacular under a full moon," he went on. "The lake and grounds cast in silver. Such a glorious example of God's work."

"It is beautiful," she admitted, trying to keep her voice even, despite her racing pulse. What was he doing here in the dark? "I went to your office and you weren't there. I hadn't been up here, so . . ."

"You checked things out." Was there a trace of judgment in his tone? "I understand, and I didn't mean to startle you. We've all been under an undue amount of stress."

In shadow, his face seemed darker, the hollows of his eyes and lines of his face more defined, almost sinister.

"I've had a lot on my mind as well." He touched her shoulder, and his fingers lingered a millisecond too long. "Such tragedy and loss. A waste. Even though I know we have to take solace in the fact that Nona is with God now, it's difficult to let go of her, bright star that she was." He checked his watch, the illuminated dial glowing blue. "I see that I've kept you waiting. My apologies." He motioned toward the main, open staircase that wound downward behind the altar.

She hurried down to the main level, his even footsteps behind her. He unlocked his office, chatting about the reasons why he kept this second office here in the chapel. All the while, she wondered if he'd been in the loft alone or if he'd followed her. Had her exploration been caught on a security camera and he'd been warned that she was poking around the building, or was it all just coincidence? Not that it really mattered, at least not this time.

"Come in, come in," Lynch said, holding the door open for her and reaching inside the doorway to hit a switch. A desk lamp suddenly cast golden light into the small room with its floor-to-ceiling bookcases, a small brick fireplace, wide desk, and credenza. Upon the desk were several files, one open enough that she caught a glimpse of a picture of Cooper Trent, another labeled FARENTINO, JULIA.

Her heart jolted.

Why was Lynch looking into Trent's file? And hers? Had he noticed that her maiden name was Delaney, which was the same last name of Shay's mother? No, no . . . Delaney was a common name, and she doubted that the parent application would have asked for maiden names. Maybe he'd connected her to her cousin Analise . . .

So many worries. Jules knew that, with a little digging, he could find the truth, and her lie that she wasn't related to anyone connected to Blue Rock would be exposed.

It's nothing. Just a coincidence. He has no idea you're involved.

He waved her into a rocker tucked into a corner, then quickly slipped both files into a cabinet behind his desk. Before he settled into his leather chair, he lit the fire, turning on a gas jet that ignited the kindling and logs stacked in the grate. "There we go." Once the fire was crackling to his satisfaction, he turned off the gas and slid into his chair. "Sorry . . . organization is one of my strong points, but it's been difficult keeping up with the recent turn of events here."

He did seem a little flustered. Off.

"I wanted to talk to you alone, to personally welcome you to the staff, to assure you that we're all a team and you can feel free to ask me any questions."

"So you said," she reminded him.

"I know. Last evening at my home." *Meaning: with my wife around.* "But I wanted to share something personal with you."

Warning bells went off in Jules's head. He leaned back in his chair and stroked his soul patch with a finger. A sensual, thoughtful gesture.

She forced herself to remain seated.

In brief, he shared his testimony, explaining how once he'd been on "the wrong path," when his negligent actions had put him and two others in the hospital. He'd been unconscious when his Lord and savior had come to him, told him that this time he'd spare Tobias and his friends, but from that point forward, he was to spread the word of God.

And he had listened to the Lord, he told her soberly. His friends survived, though one had been confined to a wheelchair, and Tobias Lynch had turned his life around, accepting God into his life and dedicating himself to doing his will. It was his hope that this school, Blue Rock Academy, would survive him as an institution dedicated to helping troubled youth reclaim their lives.

"The purpose of this school—the academy's mission—is a wonderful thing," Jules said with forced conviction, and a part of her wanted to believe him. He seemed sincere. Even troubled. She looked down at her lap, thinking, *The mission is good; the way you carry it out is what's questionable.*

"But? Do I detect a note of reticence?" He had a knack for reading between the lines. "You've been asking questions about Maris Howell."

So Charla had already gotten to him. Word traveled fast.

"I'm taking over her classes. It's natural to want more information."

"Julia," he said softly, his voice like an arctic chill against her skin. "It's more than that, isn't it?"

She felt like a trapped butterfly, alive and being pinned to a Peg-Board for observation. "Yes . . . ," she said slowly, thinking fast. "I wanted a better sense of what went on, who was affected. I want to be sensitive to the students' needs. I couldn't walk blindly into a situation where students had been hurt in some way."

He was watching her carefully, his hands tented under his chin. "That's rather insightful, but next time, come to

me. Talk to me in person. We don't want to stir up ill feelings on campus, do we?"

She nodded and he rose, signifying the meeting was
over. "I hope you share our dedication and vision," he said.

"I'm all about helping kids," she said, which was the
truth.

"Good, good. That's what I want to hear." Rounding the
desk, he clasped her hand in both of his. "I'm just sorry
that you had to come amid this trying time. But we will get
through it with God's help." He gave her hands a squeeze.
"Welcome, Julia Farentino." His smile was wide, almost
knowing.

Warnings sizzled through her brain, hairs lifting on the
back of her arms. She forced a smile and somehow kept up
the lie. "I can't wait to get to work," she said as he finally
released her hand. "Say hello to your wife."

"My wife," he said under his breath, as if Cora Sue were
the furthest thing from his mind. "I will, yes."

Jules thanked him for the opportunity to work with
these students and slipped on her coat, all the while wondering what it was about him that set her nerves on edge.

As Jules left the building, she thought of the files she'd
seen him slip into his credenza. Were they duplicates of the
files Charla King kept in the admin building, or something
more? It would be a waste of time to maintain duplicates.
No, she suspected that Tobias Lynch kept his own files on
every staff member, unofficial files that ignored the ethics
of most human resources departments.

Out in the gathering snow, she kept her eyes on the path
and moved quickly from one pool of lamplight to the next.
She knew Lynch was watching her from the window; she
had seen his silhouette.

A man of God?

Of true faith?

Jules wondered.

CHAPTER 27

Warming the back of his legs on the fire, Trent sipped coffee reheated from yesterday's pot and turned Nona's murder over in his mind. He'd tried and failed to connect Nona's homicide to Lauren Conway's disappearance, but somehow, he was certain, the two mysteries were linked.

He'd spent hours going over everything he'd learned about the events leading up to Nona's fateful trip to the stable. He figured she'd worn Shaylee's cap, probably just as she had on the night he'd discovered the filly caught outside. The way he saw it, the yearling had slipped out when Nona and Andrew had sneaked into the stables for a quick hookup. Then, later, Trent had stumbled upon them as they were leaving.

At the moment, he was going with the theory that Shaylee Stillman's hat had been part of Nona's disguise. He figured Nona had "borrowed" the cap, just in case any cameras had been rolling or in case anyone in authority caught a glimpse of her. In bulky sweatshirts, school-issued jackets, and jeans, the only identifying piece of clothing would have been the hat.

Too bad it had been left in the hayloft, and Shaylee Stillman had to take the heat.

Draining the cup, Trent thought about the two kids and the conversation he'd overheard that night. He remembered the girl being in a near panic and the boy trying to calm her down, promising to keep her safe. If it had been Drew and Nona, then he'd let her down. Big-time.

What was it she'd said?

This is getting out of hand. . . . I mean . . . when I agreed to this, to be a part of it, I thought it would be fun, a thrill, and I believed in him.

The more he considered it, the more he was certain the voice had belonged to Nona.

I believed in him.

Who? Who did she believe in?

A man. Trent didn't think she was talking about God or Christ in the same sentence as "fun" and "a thrill." He considered Reverend Lynch, but again, it didn't fit. He couldn't see anyone thinking the somber, self-important, God-fearing Lynch was fun. Or thrilling.

Puzzled, he poured himself the last of the coffee, heated it in his microwave, and, as the cup warmed, tossed the old grounds out.

Right now, Trent was going with the theory that there was a third person in the loft, one who, for whatever reason, killed Nona after getting his jollies watching the kids make love. Then somehow, he'd strung Nona up in some kind of statement.

To make it appear a suicide?

Or for theatrical effect?

It would have been so much easier just to leave her strangled body in the hay, instead of rigging a noose, looping it over the rafters, and hoisting her body up.

Unless that was what got him off.

Some kind of sick torture.

But only the girl. Drew had been hit over the head and tossed through the ladder's hole.

The microwave dinged, and he picked up the cup gingerly. Staring out the window to the storm, still raging, still dumping more snow, he thought of the information he'd gotten from the sheriff's department and sipped the bitter blend.

Detective Baines had informed him that Nona didn't have defensive wounds, though the coroner had found skin cells under her nails. They were waiting to see if the cells matched Andrew Prescott's DNA—a possibility, since the two were naked and entangled. But that analysis would take some time. There was still trace evidence being studied, fingerprints to be matched, but nothing firm yet.

And meanwhile, this whole community was trapped here, trapped and scared.

He took a final swallow from his cup, then tossed the remainder down the sink. Now that he was a damned deputy, he'd better get to work and find out what really happened in the hayloft.

For once, Jules awoke from a dreamless sleep. Thankfully she'd been exhausted enough to keep the nightmares at bay, and her headache had receded, no longer pounding.

"Clean living," she whispered to herself before taking a quick, hot shower, then changing into thermal underwear, jeans, a sweater, and a thick, insulated parka.

She was reaching for the handle of her door when she caught sight of a small piece of white paper near the threshold, a page that hadn't been there earlier.

She picked up the single sheet and turned it over.

HELP ME!

The frantic message was scrawled at an angle in black ink.

She nearly dropped the page.

"What the devil?" Was this some kind of a joke? A prank the kids pulled on the new teacher? Or something else? Hadn't she felt as if someone had been in her room the other night? Possibly standing over her and watching her as she slept.

Her skin crawled as she threw open the door and stepped into the outer hallway.

Empty.

The two other doors on the floor shut tight. Who had left the desperate plea?

Shay.

Of course.

But it wasn't her sister's style to be so coy.

Tucking the bit of notebook paper into her pocket, she hurried down the flight of stairs, looking for anyone who might have slipped the page under the door. *So you got a note, so what?* She tried to make light of the situation, but because of the murder, she couldn't.

She climbed down the stairs and came across no one.

At this hour, Stanton House was quiet.

She checked the main level, where a few couches, tables, and lamps created a seating area, but again, she was alone, the only sounds in the house the soft purr of a hidden furnace forcing warm air through the building and the quiet tick of an old clock mounted on the wall.

For now, there was no telling who had left the note or whether it was a serious plea or some kind of prank.

Get over yourself!

Yanking on her gloves, Jules made her way outside, where the night wind howled as it battered the campus, dumping snow, churning the dark waters of Lake Superstition.

Pulling the hood of her jacket tight against her face, she muttered, "Just another day in paradise," and trudged through a new layer of snow to the stable. The pathway was covered with six inches of the white stuff, and the drive, where some of the school's vehicles were parked, hadn't yet been plowed.

So much for the Arcadian, sun-dappled shoreline and serene Alpine vista that she'd seen on the Web site. Even the winter photographs had been of kids sledding or snowshoeing in a wintry but sunny forest. There had been shots of the interior of the rec center, the panes of glass frosted, students gathered around a cozy fire burning in the grate. Another photograph had showed a twenty-foot Christmas tree glowing with hundreds of tiny lights as students in stocking caps gathered, hymnals in hand.

Like angels . . . Oh, sure.

Jules shivered.

There were no warm and fuzzy photo ops today, not with the windchill factor driving the temperature into the teens and the pall of a student's gruesome death hanging over the school.

Wind whistled around the door as she stepped into the stable. The interior was warm with incandescent lighting and the smells of horses and fresh straw, a haven from the outside world.

Curious, the horses peered over the gates to their stalls. With dark, liquid eyes, flickering ears, and snorts of disapproval, the animals appraised her. She walked along the aisle, petting muzzles, feeling hot breath on her hands, a little wary just in case some of the animals weren't as friendly as they seemed.

Then she saw it. The rust-colored stain on the floor below the ladder to the hayloft. Someone had tried to clean it up, but the stain seemed indelible. Covered by stray wisps of hay, the evidence of Andrew Prescott's fall caused her to stop dead in her tracks.

There must have been so much blood. . . .

She stepped backward, shivering.

Scraaape.

What was that?

The sound of leather against wood.

She wasn't alone!

Heart hammering, she backed up, ramming into a post just as scuffed cowboy boots and long, jean-clad legs appeared on the ladder. "Someone here?" Trent called, just as he hopped to the floor, his boots avoiding the stain. He saw Jules and one side of his mouth lifted. "Lookin' for me?" he asked, a bit of humor glinting in his brown eyes. He was still unshaven, his mouth a razor-thin line, his deep-set eyes cutting right to her soul.

"Definitely not looking for you to scare the hell out of me," she said, hand over her heart.

"But you *were* looking for me." A smile tugged at the edges of his mouth, and the corners of the stable seemed to grow closer. Tighter. The atmosphere suddenly thick.

"You tell me."

"Nah." He shook his head. "What's the fun in that?"

She grinned, not able to believe him. "Wait a second, Cowboy. Are you flirting with me?" she asked, secretly pleased, even though the entire situation was surreal, considering the circumstances.

"Flirting? I don't think so." But the glint in his eyes told her differently. Her heart raced a little faster as she remembered exactly how it felt to kiss him, how his tongue touched the roof of her mouth and caused a tingle deep inside. How the crush of his lips brought heat to the back of her neck. How he'd made her go weak, her knees giving way of their own accord.

As if reading her thoughts, he said, "So what is it you want, Jules?"

"I hate to burst the bubble that's your incredible ego, but I really didn't think I'd find you here."

One doubting eyebrow cocked.

As if she were challenging him. The way it had often raised just before he pulled her into his arms and kissed her hard, to prove the point that she wanted him.

She had to fight the urge to back up a step.

A paint with a white face and blue eyes pushed his head over the top of the box and snorted, sniffing. Jules moved toward the stall to stroke the gelding. "You think I have a treat," she said to the horse to break the tension, "but I don't."

"Scout's always looking for something," he said.

"Typical male."

"Yeah, well, don't tell him, but he's been gelded."

"Oops." She glanced at the horse. "Sorry, boy." She felt Trent's eyes on her, studying her. "You know, I really didn't think I'd run into anyone in here."

"So, what, you just came to the crime scene to look it over?"

"I guess." She scratched Scout beneath his black forelock. It was hard to explain. She didn't want to think she was the victim of morbid curiosity, but there was a part of her that wanted to know what had happened, to see for herself and connect with the victims. "I thought maybe if I saw where it happened, I'd have some idea of why and how it connects, if it connects to Lauren Conway's disappearance. Don't tell me the same thought didn't cross your mind."

"Okay, I won't."

"I came to Blue Rock to see what was going on and to get Shay out of here if I found out that the academy wasn't the answer it was supposed to be." She shook her head and bit her lip, thinking. "But even before I got here, things turned upside down, a girl killed. It just doesn't make any sense."

"Nothing does," he admitted.

"Well, then, let's add another cryptic note to the mix."

Jules retrieved the note from her pocket and handed it to him. "I found this under my door this morning."

Trent read the simple message and frowned. "From Shay?"

"I don't know. But I don't think so."

"Mind if I keep it?"

"Sure, but why?"

"I'm a deputy now," he said, then told her about O'Donnell's call.

"So it's official." It seemed to underline the feeling of safety she had near Trent, physical safety, even if her emotions scattered wildly when he was close by. "Does Lynch know?"

"We haven't talked about it, but I'm sure O'Donnell has."

"Tell me about our fearless leader," she suggested.

"Lynch? All I know is that he's been here from the get-go and has a vision of this school being an example for others; he sees Blue Rock as his mission."

"What about his wife?"

"Cora Sue?" He shook his head. "Piece of work, that one. I'm not sure she shares her husband's vision. Avoids this place like the plague."

"She's here now."

"Well, Cora Sue comes when she's called." He leaned over the rail of one of the stalls and patted the head of a dark horse with a burst of jagged white on its forehead. "She makes it very clear that she'd rather be anywhere else, but she comes and he shows her off, they're together, but if you read her body language, she's just doing her duty."

"Why is that?"

"I don't pretend to understand marriages, but if I had to guess, I'd say they stay together because of the money, or their vows."

"They don't love each other?"

"Who knows?" he said as the dark horse turned away from him.

"You think he cheated on her?"

"Possibly, or maybe the other way around," he thought aloud. "But don't ask me; I'm not exactly batting a thousand when it comes to relationships, but he's definitely got some kind of influence on her. As I said, when he calls, she comes running."

"Like a dog to her master," she said, remembering the conversation she'd heard while eavesdropping on the reverend's porch.

"Who knows what goes on in people's relationships," he said, his gaze touching hers.

For a second, she remembered how much she'd loved him. *Thought you loved him. Remember? It didn't work out.*

The conversation was taking a dangerous path, so she said, "I take it, this"—she motioned to the stained floor beneath the opening to the hayloft—"is where Drew Prescott was found? I heard he suffered from a head wound." Her stomach curdled as she imagined the boy lying on the dusty floor.

"That's right."

She leaned down, studying the discoloration, though what she thought she'd find, she didn't know. She wasn't an investigator and knew nothing about blood spatter or body position or anything that dealt with murder.

About an arm's length from the large blotch was another stain about the size of her spread hand. "What's this?"

"Blood. Smeared," he admitted. "The crime scene investigators took samples and pictures."

"That stain happened the night of the murder?" He was nodding as she rocked back on her heels and stared at the small stain. "Odd."

"Any theories?"

She shook her head and looked up at him. "Sorry. Fresh

out." But it was strange. Had the blood come from Andrew? Nona? Or someone else? She glanced up, through the opening to the darkened hayloft. Dear God, what had happened up there?

Trent said, "You can go up if you want."

"I'm not sure I want to," she admitted, but was already walking to the ladder, avoiding stepping on the bloodstain and trying like crazy to ignore the trepidation chilling her soul.

Gripping the steel rungs, knowing she was following the same path that Nona had taken only nights before, she ascended into the loft. From below, Trent snapped on the lights, bare bulbs mounted high overhead. They added an unworldly glow to the old crossbeams and soaring, drafty ceiling rising high over the loft, where hundreds, maybe thousands, of bales had been stacked.

Jules heard Trent climbing to the loft as she walked along a wide path between fat, cubed bales, some of which were strewn haphazardly, others split open, spilling dry stalks, obviously torn apart during the investigation.

Near the far wall, Jules paused and looked up at the single window, high overhead, snow lining the glass. It was cracked a bit, and evidence of an owl drizzled down the plank walls.

In her mind's eye, Jules saw the nude body of a girl hanging from one of the crossbeams. Swinging slowly. Skin a gray-white, eyes fixed.

Jules shook her head to shake off the image. God, she didn't need more death in her psyche. But the girl's ghost had touched her now and would probably haunt her forever.

"What the hell happened here?" she whispered, suddenly cold to the bone.

Trent was beside her, shaking his head, raking stiff fingers through his hair. He stared up at the rafters, as if he, too, could see her. "Two kids meet in the stables." He nodded toward the corner of the loft. "They had sort of a love nest built out of bales over there. Apparently it was set up in advance, though for how long I don't know. Flannagan doesn't take any shit from these kids."

"Rumor has it they were found naked," she said, and he nodded. "So they were attacked while they were having sex . . . or possibly afterward?"

"Yeah. Prescott gave a statement to the detectives. He claims he and Nona were going at it, about finished, he on top, when the world exploded. He can't even remember any pain, just that one minute he was having sex, the next he found himself waking up in a hospital."

Jules thought aloud, "So someone came in, hit him, kicked him through the hole in the floor, and then hung her? Really?" That didn't sound right.

"No weapon was found. The cut on the back of Andrew's head was deep, probably from a sharp rock, but the police haven't found it yet. Until the storm breaks, they might never." He glanced down at her. "For all anyone knows, it could be at the bottom of the lake or buried under two feet of snow." He squinted upward to the wooden ceiling. "As for Nona, she was probably already dead when the killer strung her up." He glanced down at Jules, his eyes dark in the watery light, his jaw set. "The details are ugly."

"I can deal with ugly." Painful memories flashed through her mind: her parents' vile fights, nights spent huddled in her bed, wishing it would just stop, and then, ultimately, discovering her father's body in a pool of blood. Yes, she had endured the ugly, worked beyond it, or at least tried. "What I can't take is being blindsided."

He hesitated, as if unsure how much he should divulge.

"I'm a big girl," she reminded him.

"This I know," he said, nodding. "I suppose if you're going to stay here, you should be armed with the truth." He told her about the severity of the attack, about how the coroner found that Nona's hyoid bone was crushed, her larynx damaged, her vagina showing signs of rough sex. Hers had been a violent, painful death, and from the bruises on her neck, it was obvious that she'd been face-to-face with the person who had taken her life, had watched and struggled as he'd cut off her air, then, using a winch usually used in stacking the bales and a rope Flannagan had for the horses, he'd strung Nona's nude corpse high above.

"What kind of sick mind would do that?" she asked, almost wishing she didn't know the truth.

"Someone extremely disturbed." Trent let his boot scrape at a wad of hay, and they both watched as golden strands of straw tumbled through the opening and fluttered down to the floor far below. "Someone here at the school."

"So does the sheriff's department think this is an isolated case?" she asked. "That Nona and maybe Drew were targets, that there's a motive for the killings?"

"That's the million-dollar question, isn't it?" Trent said. "I guess time will tell."

CHAPTER 28

Sundays, Shay had heard, were usually quiet on the campus, but today was different than most. Half the students were whining about being scared, and the administrators were freaking out and keeping everyone pent up in annoying group activities.

Reverend Lynch's sermon had been less than inspired, but Father Jake managed to make the service a little more interesting and lively, and the kids responded to him. Shay had witnessed it herself and so had Lynch; he'd pretended not to notice that the younger preacher had everyone listening, but Shay had seen the reverend's jaw tighten.

It probably had made things worse that his Barbie Doll of a wife had sat on the edge of her seat when Father Jake stood at the altar.

All in all, the church service had been a lot more interesting than Shay had expected.

Now, in the dining hall, along with everyone else, Shay was picking at her lunch, which consisted of chili, corn bread, coleslaw, and, afterward, ice-cream sundaes. "Sundaes for Sundays," Lynch had proclaimed, and some of the kids thought that was clever.

Jules was seated on the far side, three tables away from Shay. Since Jules was no longer the guest of honor, she'd lost her spot at the head table. Also, Jules didn't have a pod to oversee, so she could choose her spot. She'd taken a chair with some of the staff. Brawny Nurse Ayres sat to her left. On the other side was Spurrier, the friggin' Red Baron, who was elbow-to-elbow with Flannagan, the creepy horse guy who was the essence of military macho. Shaylee had put up with enough of that jerk yesterday.

The math teacher Mr. DeMarco was a little more interesting. He had some of the same qualities she fell for with Dawg, a dangerous edge. She frowned at the thought of Dawg. He was the first of her boyfriends who had really gotten to her, but she'd been cautious. Wouldn't Edie be shocked to learn that Shay hadn't slept with him, hadn't taken that step.

Shay hadn't heard a word from him since she'd landed here, and though she told herself that was all part of the process, that he wasn't allowed to call her from jail, she'd still been hurt.

What do you expect? That he would be different from every other man in your life?

"Yeah," she whispered, dipping her straw in and out of her iced tea. Raw blisters lined her palms from hours spent shoveling manure and snow. Glancing up from her hands, she caught a glimpse of DeMarco's smile, that sexy, faintly dangerous quality. She lifted the straw to her lips, sucked out a bit of tea, and chewed the end. Not that she would ever go for a math teacher like DeMarco. How stupid would that be? And how against the rules. If she was caught with him, maybe she'd be expelled.

Was it worth it?

Would juvie or another school be any better?

As Jules pushed her chair back, Shay let her gaze drift to the other woman at Jules's table, that bossy secretary who couldn't keep her eyes off Reverend Lynch. At least in the time when she wasn't shooting daggers with her eyes at Lynch's fussy little wife.

The good news? Shay knew her way around Ms. Charla King's domain, including access to computers and files and records of the school. It was amazing what could be bought in the Blue Rock black market.

She saw Jules reach the hallway.

The second her sister rounded the corner, Shay dropped her straw into her glass, then knocked over the remains of her chili into her lap. She let out a little screech as she turned to Cooper Trent, who sat at the head of the table. "Sorry." Man, she hoped he bought her act of being a klutz. Quickly dabbing at her lap with a paper napkin, she pushed her chair back and hurried off to the ladies' room. The fake accident might be overkill, since no one really cared if a person used the facilities, but the mess on her clothes would gain her time in the bathroom, time she could use to talk to Jules.

Besides, even though she didn't think there were cameras in the private dorm rooms, she wasn't certain about common areas. Surely they had some security cameras on campus. Maybe mics, too. For all she knew, there could be microphones in the bathrooms.

The short hallway was empty as she slipped into the restroom. Still rubbing her shirt, she turned on the tap, soaked a paper towel, and scrubbed at the stains. A toilet flushed. Within seconds, the door to a stall opened and Jules stepped into the washroom.

Their gazes met in the mirror.

Jules started to say something, thought better of it, and taking a cue from Shaylee, turned on the tap.

"I saw you come in here," Shaylee said in a low voice, her lips barely moving as she worked on her shirt. "Have you talked to Edie again?"

"No."

"Damn it, Jules." Shaylee kept rubbing the stain with the towel, which was starting to shred.

"Take it easy." Thankfully Jules was playing along, pumping the soap, eyeing her reflection, smiling appropriately at Shaylee but keeping her voice nearly inaudible. "No one is getting in or out right now. Some parents want their kids home right away, but it's out of the question. I heard that the road is impassable. I was one of the last people in. And with this storm, the seaplane and helicopter are grounded."

Shaylee's heart sank. She didn't know how much longer she could stay here without losing her mind. "There has to be a way."

Jules was shaking the water from her hands, though the tap was still running. "I'm working on it."

"Well, work faster!" Shay urged as she tossed the disintegrating towel into the trash and noisily yanked out another from the dispenser. "I got to talk to Edie, you know." From Jules's deer-in-the-headlights expression, she obviously hadn't heard. "Yeah, the administration let us each call one of our parents and tell them that we're 'fine.'" She made air quotes with her fingers while hanging on to the wadded-up towel. "Well, I'm not 'fine,' and I told Edie as much. But Reverend Lynch must have gotten to her, smooth-talked her into believing the school is safe. All that crap about extra security guards and police so nothing else can go wrong." She skewered her sister with a can-you-believe-this-crap? stare. "He also told her that I had 'anger issues' and that I got into a fight."

"You did."

"It wasn't my fault! God, Jules, friggin' Eric Rolfe started it. And now I'm stuck shoveling horse crap and snow for the weekend, probably longer."

"So learn a lesson. Stay out of trouble."

"Oh, sure. Should I just sit back like a wuss and let him diss Nona? Maybe you'd let him trounce on you, but that's not me."

"Shaylee, listen to me. I'm doing all this for you, so you might think twice about picking a fight with me."

"Or what?" She glowered at Jules. "You'll never stand up to Lynch. You're too much of a wimp."

Jules turned to face her, and her eyes blazed. She was stung at the insult. Good. Shay needed her sister on board.

"Just be smart, Shay. Prove that your IQ is as high as Mom thinks. And don't leave me any more notes. You'll get caught; we both will."

"What're you talking about?"

"The message under the door this morning."

"Are you crazy?" Shay demanded. "What message?"

"Someone—I thought it might be you—left me a note, that's all," Jules said in a pissy tone.

"Who?"

"Would I ask you if I knew?"

Shay bit her lower lip, not liking this at all. "What did it say?"

"'Help me.'"

"That's it?"

"Yes."

"It wasn't me, okay?" Shay had to find a way to get through to her sister, to get her off the lame note. "I don't know who left it, and I don't care." She tried another tack. "So, you're just letting me be stuck here, in this school of the damned; is that what you're saying?"

"'School of the damned'? Like the title for a really bad horror flick? Come on, Shay! Stop with the drama and get your act together. Quit getting into trouble, or you'll never get out of here."

"Are you kidding me? You think they'll release me because of good behavior?" The thought made Shay's stomach sour, and the indigestible chili burned through her. Jules was drinking the Kool-Aid. Time to let it rip. "I heard some of the kids talking. They think the TAs are part of some secret cult or something."

"A cult . . . really? Who said so?"

No way was Shay going to give up Lucy, not even to her sister. "It doesn't matter. The point is, this place isn't safe for anyone. You have to do something, Jules. For God's sake, call Edie again and—"

The door swung open and laughter bubbled in. Missy Albright and Kaci Donahue entered, talking loudly. The TAs sent a cursory glance at the sinks but didn't really seem to pay attention to anyone but themselves. Kaci hurried into one stall while Missy stood at the mirror and fiddled with her hair. She plumped the pale strands with expert fingers and twisted her head this way and that for a better look at herself. What a head case! As if anyone here cared how she looked.

Nonetheless, Shay couldn't take a chance that Missy thought she and Jules knew each other. After all, Lucy Yang seemed to think these TAs were in some secret, ominous cult. Probably sealed in blood.

Shay swore under her breath at the thought of the stain. Giving up, she wadded the paper towel, tossed it into the trash, then stormed out, unafraid to share her pissed-off mood with the world. She didn't look over her shoulder but figured Jules could deal with the two stupid TAs.

Maybe.

So far, Jules was proving to be a big disappointment.

CHAPTER 29

Bam!

A rubber ball smacked into the back of the last remaining student on the green team, a short, smooth-faced boy, quick on his feet but not quite fast enough. Before he could step out of the way, two more balls hit him in the midsection. The kid made a fist, hit an imaginary target, and tried not to swear as his teammates, lined against the wall and already out, groaned in unison.

On the other side of the court, their opponents, wearing yellow mesh pinnies, whooped, hollered, and gave each other high fives. Several of the guys raised their hands, jabbing a single finger in the air. Their team was "number one."

From the Olympics to a mini dodge ball tournament at Blue Rock Academy, the thrill of victory and the agony of defeat never changed, Trent thought as he blew the whistle. At least the tourney had provided a distraction from the pall that had settled over the school. "Okay, yellow team wins this round!"

More shouting and jumping from the students in the yellow vests.

The green team fell morosely quiet, as if the tourney really mattered. Two kids grabbed stray balls and started shooting hoops.

"Hey! Balls in." Trent blew his whistle and caught everyone's attention again. "That's it! We'll call it a day. So tomorrow is the dodge ball finals, and Wednesday we start martial arts." Neither of the two sports were Trent's favorites. He preferred canoeing and rafting and horseback riding, even snowshoeing, over indoor activities. But because of the blizzard and security concerns, they were stuck inside.

He heard a few boys on the yellow team taunting the losing team. "Enough! Now listen up. Pick up the balls and hit the showers!" A few of the younger kids on the green team tossed the balls into the cart, which they rolled into a closet while others took off at the speed of light to avoid any extra work. Finally, the kids who'd helped him ran off the court to catch up with their classmates.

As he locked the closet and was about to snap off the lights to the gym, Trent noticed Reverend Lynch standing in the doorway near the front entrance. He'd probably been watching all along. That's the way it was with the school's director, always observing or dropping into class unannounced. Usually he reminded Trent of Ichabod Crane from *The Legend of Sleepy Hollow,* but today, bundled in a ski jacket and insulated pants, he seemed less gangly as he strode across the gym.

"Mr. Trent." Lynch smiled, though there was little humor in the lines of his face. He crossed the glossy gym floor in his boots, tracking water and snow. *Clueless.* "Do you have a minute?"

"Sure," Trent said, though he felt a tightening in the back of his neck. This was the first time since he'd been hired that Lynch had searched him out. In the past, he'd been summoned to the reverend's private office, usually with a group of teachers. "Careful with the shoes."

"What?" Lynch looked down and sighed, finally noticing the wet tracks. "Oh. Sorry."

"What can I do for you?" Trent walked with Lynch into the wide hallway that was the main entrance to the building.

"I was told by Sheriff O'Donnell that you've been deputized."

Trent gave a quick nod. "That's right."

"And you worked as a deputy for a sheriff's department in Montana. That's in your file."

"Pinewood County."

"Good. Well, then, it only makes sense. I think Blaine O'Donnell might want a few more deputies, and if he asks, I'm going to suggest Bert Flannagan and Kirk Spurrier. They're already in charge of security."

"No women?" Trent grabbed a folded towel from the cart near the shower room.

"Oh." Lynch's mouth twitched. "You're right. Guess I'm old school, and I suppose that could be construed as sexist these days. Which, by the way, I am not. If push comes to shove, I think Dr. Burdette would make an excellent deputy."

Trent wasn't sure he agreed, but he kept his opinion to himself.

Lynch frowned and waited as Trent shook the folds from the towel. "So as things develop, I want you to not only report to the sheriff, but to me as well."

"You?"

"You are employed by the school," Lynch reminded him with the supercilious smile that bugged the hell out of Trent.

"I am, and I take my teaching job seriously," Trent said, thinking of the information he'd already obtained in conversation with detectives. Certain details were not to be spread around campus; it would compromise the investigation. "But the teaching gig is different from police work."

"Of course. But I'm counting on you to keep me informed."

Trent wasn't one to sell out, even if he was on a payroll. "Tell ya what. If I find out anything that you, as the director of the school, should know, I'll fill you in. But I can't compromise the case."

"Oh. Well, of course, I wouldn't want you to do that," Lynch said as a gust of wind rattled the double doors at the end of the hall.

Trent didn't buy the minister's pout—all that wounded integrity.

"I just need to be informed for the safety of the students," Lynch explained.

Trent held the reverend's gaze, knowing full well there was more to it. "I'm sure the sheriff will keep you updated," Trent said, wrapping the towel over one hand.

Lynch's beatific countenance shifted just slightly, and for a millisecond, Trent caught a glimpse of the calculating man behind the clerical collar. "We'll be talking," Lynch said. And with a few long strides, the reverend pushed open the heavy glass doors and disappeared into the night.

Trent took the towel and mopped up the gym floor, all the while considering the reverend's request. There was something off about the guy. Not that he wasn't pious enough; he didn't seem a fake that way. It was just that Reverend Tobias Lynch seemed to enjoy the role of benevolent dictator a little too much. Nicholas II had Russia. Lynch had Blue Rock Academy.

Shaylee was right.
Edie wouldn't budge.

"Blue Rock may be one of the best things that's ever happened to Shay," Edie said over a poor connection.

Jules leaned a hip against the desk of room 212 in the education hall and switched her cell phone to the other ear. She could hardly get a word in edgewise as Edie sang the praises of Blue Rock.

Reverend Lynch had assured Edie that Shaylee was doing "better than expected." She was fitting in and had made lots of new friends, despite her altercation with one of the students. Though it was a tragedy that Shaylee's roommate had died, Shaylee was "handling the extraordinary emotional challenge with spirit and bravery." Edie had loved that.

Jules stared out at the snowscape as Edie droned on. Located on the second floor of the education building, her classroom afforded a view befitting a ski resort. This side of the building, housing the language and social studies departments, looked over the water. On the other side of the staircase, the math and science departments faced the rolling campus and the mountains. For a moment, she felt a twinge of guilt, pretending that she was off in another state just to keep her mother calm.

And Edie was definitely in her happy place today. After hearing so many negatives about her second-born, the fact that the head of a school was actually praising Shaylee had gone far to make Edie feel that her daughter was right where she should be. No matter that Shaylee, forever overly dramatic, was pleading with her to be set free; Edie felt good about her decision to leave her daughter under the watchful, caring eyes of Blue Rock Academy's administration.

"So for now, Shaylee stays right where she is," Edie insisted. "Even Max agrees. The roads are impassable anyway. When the weather warms up, we'll reassess. If Shay still wants out and my attorney can meet with the judge, then so be it. But for now, Shaylee will just have to buck up."

"But she's so unhappy," Jules said.

"Shaylee is always unhappy, and I've been through this a million times. In fact, I just told her all this," Edie insisted, then turned the conversation to Jules. "So, where, exactly, are you again?"

"Not far from San Francisco," Jules lied smoothly, glancing out the window at the ice-glazed edges of Lake Superstition.

"Still looking for a job?"

"As it turns out, there are possibilities at several districts, at least for next year, so I'll be here a while."

"What about your cat?"

"No worries. My neighbor is taking care of Diablo and picking up my mail, so everything's fine."

"Good. Look, I've got to run. We'll talk soon."

"Okay, Mom. Take care." Jules clicked her phone closed and locked it, a precaution she'd practiced since arriving at Blue Rock. Stashing her phone in her purse, she found her lesson plan and prepared for her last class of the day, the group of students from Cooper Trent's pod, which included Shay. The subject was U.S. history, and according to the syllabus, the class should have been studying the years surrounding the Great Depression and comparing that era to the recent economic downturn.

The kids began to file into the room, some laughing and talking, others more reserved.

Shay, of course, brought up the rear, but at least she wasn't alone. Lucy Yang, the girl with whom she'd spent the weekend shoveling snow and manure, walked into the classroom and took a seat next to her.

Progress? Had the girls bonded through the incident?

Jules hoped so.

She introduced herself for the fourth time that day, then broke the ice by saying, "I know this is a hard time for everyone. I didn't know Nona, but I understand she was from your pod, so this must be particularly difficult for each of you. So, let's kick back a little. We'll catch up later in the week, but why don't you tell me what you've been studying and bring me up to speed. As I understand it from Dean Hammersley's notes and Ms. Howell's syllabus, you're working your way through the early nineteen hundreds."

No one seemed interested.

She didn't blame them.

They were under so much stress right now, and eighty years ago was ancient history to them. "Hey, I need your help." A few heads lifted, a couple sets of eyes sparked. Jules managed a smile and saw that she'd caught some of her students' attention. "I'm the newbie here, right? So, come on, help me out. We're talking about the Great Depression, and as ancient as I might seem to you, I didn't live through it, either."

A few kids snickered. Good. A start.

She thought she'd see how this played out. Find out who the leaders were, who engaged, who didn't. In her experience, the discussion would start slowly, with only one or two students offering anything up. Midway through the period, a few more kids would warm up to the discussion. Usually by the end of class time, most of the students would be engaged.

And so it was with the kids in Shaylee's pod. When she asked if anyone could compare what was going on in the economy now to the years of the Great Depression, a few kids actually spoke up.

Lucy Yang, Keesha Bell, Nell Cousineau, and Ollie Gage were the most talkative, Ollie admitting that his father had lost his job in the dot-com crash, and Keesha worried that her parents might have to turn their condo back to the bank. Shay kept her eyes on her desk, and Jules had to ask Chaz Johnson to remove his hood and stay awake. Although Maeve Mancuso kept her eyes down as she fidgeted at something under her sleeve, when called upon, she was able to answer a question. JoAnne Harris, aka Banjo, shared her sense of guilt. Though her family was doing well, she felt bad that her grandfather was scooping up foreclosed homes, kicking homeowners out, then renting the houses, sometimes to the same people, actually making money off of someone else's misfortune.

"That's really messed up," Ollie said. "But it's not on you. You know what I mean? Not your fault, Banjo."

Eventually Crystal Ricci raised her hand. "So what's really the difference between a depression," she asked, looking more bored than engaged, "and a recession?"

"Good question," Jules said. "Why don't you tell me?"

Surprisingly, the kids suggested a wide range of answers, some of which led to more questions. Finally, with only ten minutes until the end of class, even Shay and Chaz gave up their ticked-off expressions and seemed somewhat interested.

Jules found herself loosening up a bit. If it hadn't been for the violence that had been perpetrated on this campus, she might have even enjoyed herself. Yes, she would have had to deal with her conflicted feelings for Cooper Trent. Yes, she would be barraged by Shaylee to get her out of the school. And, yes, there were still unanswered questions about Blue Rock Academy and its practices. All those things were true, but she had always loved teaching and could see that many of the "problem" or "troubled" kids here were bright and insightful.

"It looks like we're about out of time, so read chapter seventeen tonight. We'll discuss it tomorrow, and we'll get started on outlining essays. You can focus on any era you've studied so far this term, so pick a time period and a social topic by Friday."

"It would be a lot easier if we had e-mail," Lucy complained.

"That it would. But we don't, so you'll have to do it the old-fashioned way."

Crystal and Ollie groaned theatrically as everyone began to file out of the room. Keesha grabbed her books and hooked up with BD, who was waiting for her by the door. Once the kids had filed out, Missy Albright stepped into the classroom.

Shay, the last student in class to leave, cast a guarded look over her shoulder. Her eyes met Jules's in silent warning: *Be careful!*

Missy didn't seem to notice as she set her purse on a side counter near Jules's book bag. "Reverend Lynch assigned me to be your assistant," she said in her tiny, falsetto voice that didn't quite fit her body.

"Really?" This was a surprise. "He didn't mention it to me."

"He will. He just told me to come and talk to you, so here I am." She gave an exaggerated shrug, the kind cute girls do when they are trying to appear even cuter and sweeter and more innocent. "Anything you want me to do—I mean, for tomorrow?"

"Tomorrow. Huh. To tell you the truth, I haven't thought that far ahead," Jules admitted, a little irritated that Lynch hadn't clued her in first before assigning the girl as her personal aide. "I've seen what the previous teacher planned, but it's a little dry. Lecture. Discussion. Questions. Test." She glanced at Missy. "Pretty boring."

"It's history," Missy said, as if that explained everything.

"I know and I'm just learning the ropes around here, not quite sure how I want to do things, but I'd like to make the class a little more interesting."

"Good luck."

Jules was already thinking aloud as she straightened the room, repositioning the desks into a semicircle that faced her desk. "Right now, this class is studying the nineteen thirties and the Great Depression. I think that's a great opportunity to tie into what's going on in the country today. I'd also like to make it real by studying day-to-day struggles. Real life in the thirties."

"I thought you didn't want it to be boring."

Jules grinned a bit. "Okay, so give me a break. What if we came up with some kind of guessing game about life back then. Questions like, How much money did the average person make in a month? What did a loaf of bread cost? What movies were popular?"

"Did they have movies back then?" Missy asked, leaning against the counter as she watched Jules.

"Yeah, Missy, even in the dark ages of the twentieth century there were movies," Jules mocked. "You've even seen some, I'll bet."

Missy was shaking her head, her blond hair almost white under the fluorescent light.

"How about classics like *Gone with the Wind* or *The Wizard of Oz,* or Disney's *Snow White and the Seven Dwarfs?*" The head shaking stopped. "And then there were movie icons like the Marx Brothers and Shirley Temple. We can talk about books that were written around that time. Off the top of my head, I think of the Dr. Seuss books, Agatha Christie mysteries, and classics like *The Grapes of Wrath.*"

Missy was unimpressed. "The kids probably won't care."

"Come on, they all read Dr. Seuss as kids, and they know who Agatha Christie is. And don't tell me they never watched a Disney movie growing up." Jules felt her blood pumping. "I bet they even played Monopoly or watched the Yankees, which were both big in the thirties. Yes, there was the Dust Bowl and hobos riding the rails and extreme poverty, but there was also Albert Einstein and Joe DiMaggio and Lou Gehrig and Duke Ellington and Bette Davis. Twinkies and Spam—the food, not bad e-mail."

"I know," Missy said, rolling her eyes at Jules's enthusiasm.

Jules was really getting into it and remembered for the first time in a long while why she took up teaching and how much she loved history. She was all wound up, excited as she walked by the desk in which Maeve had been sitting and saw the letters *ES* written in pencil on the top. Ethan Slade's initials.

Jules knew she'd have to reprimand the girl for defacing school property, but for now, she took a tissue from her pocket and wiped away the scribbled initials. As she did, she was aware of Missy watching her every move.

Was she a teacher's aide or a spy? Who knew? Either way, Jules was going to put Missy to work.

"Let's set up some kind of guessing game and see what the kids know about sports, fashion, inventions of that era."

"If you say so."

"I do." Jules stuffed the tissue into her pocket and rubbed at the trace of writing with her finger. "And I think we can present the positive side. We should show that even during times as bleak as the Great Depression, some people achieved great things." She pointed at her new helper. "I assume you can access the Internet?"

"Sure." Missy lifted a shoulder. "I'm a TA. We can get on anytime we need it."

"Really?"

"Yeah. At the computer lab." She wrinkled her nose. "I wish we could have our own laptops or cell phones, but you know they're taboo."

"Even for the TAs?"

"Yeah." She sighed. "It's all a major control issue."

Jules gambled and pushed her a bit. "I would have thought that there would be a way to get online other than the lab."

"How?" Missy asked innocently enough, but her easy smile faded a bit, as if she were sizing Jules up.

"Oh, come on. It wasn't that long ago that I was your age. I'm sure there are plenty of opportunities for kids to smuggle in USB modems, devices that tap into cell towers, or even phones." When Missy didn't reply, Jules added, "There has to be a black market for that kind of thing."

"I don't know about that," Missy said tentatively, but the glint in her eye suggested she was lying.

"Well, maybe I'm wrong." Jules didn't believe Missy, but she decided not to press the issue. Not right now. "Since you can get access to the Internet through the lab, that's good enough. For tomorrow, come up with twenty-five items or events that are attributed to the thirties, then add in some other decades, anything from the forties to the nineties, to make it fun. Come up with about fifty or sixty in total. Then print them out and bring the list to me. Do we have an overhead projector? One of those electronic ones, or if not, an older one? Oh, and can you print on clear plastic?"

"I guess . . ." Missy didn't seem sure.

"Good. If you can, do it and see that I get a projector or whatever it is you use now. Tomorrow, we'll play a guessing game. The winner gets . . . oh, I don't know. Maybe a can of Spam or a package of Twinkies or a comic book."

"But you can't offer anything like that as a prize." Missy looked at her as if she'd gone nuts.

"Why not?" Jules asked.

"Well, I don't think Dr. Hammersley will go for it, do you? And no way would Reverend Lynch allow us to have Twinkies here. Uh-uh."

Jules wasn't going to be derailed. "I'll deal with Dr. Hammersley and the director. You just make the list."

"O-kay." Missy's tone indicated that she thought Jules had a screw or two loose and was on the fast track to getting herself fired.

Which was kind of funny, as Jules was certain she'd be fired for other, far darker reasons. "I'm telling you, this assignment is going to be fun. Talk to me before class tomorrow."

Missy nodded as Jules returned to her desk. From the corner of her eye, she watched the blond fiddle with her oversized bag, zip it shut, then hurry through the open door to the hallway, where the sounds of shuffling feet and young voices were beginning to fade.

Missy seemed to be following instructions, Jules thought, snagging a pen from her drawer and making some quick notes to herself.

So why didn't Jules trust her new assistant?

Because of Shay.

What was it her sister had said? That the TAs were part of some kind of cult?

How ludicrous was that?

Who was to say that Shaylee, with her rock-solid bad attitude, was the goddess of knowledge of all things at Blue Rock Academy? First off, Shay hadn't lived on campus long enough to learn the school's inner workings. The rumor was just some teenaged gossip, campus mythology.

Jules tapped a pencil against her planner, wondering if Trent knew anything about the alleged cult.

He just might.

She glanced out the window to the coming night.

Maybe it was time for a teachers' conference.

CHAPTER 30

The invisible cloud of cigarette smoke hit Trent before he saw Meeker walk into the gym. From his perch atop a ladder where he was reattaching a basketball net, Trent knew the officer was on a mission.

Frank Meeker looked like hell. His uniform was wrinkled, the bags beneath his eyes heavy, his jawline in serious need of a razor. He'd camped out at the school for three days, taking a small room on the main floor of Stanton House, which he'd used as his office and bunk. Trent figured that Meeker was making good use of the time, considering he was trapped at the school until the plows could get through.

They were alone in the cavernous gym, but the sound of weights clicking regularly indicated someone was pumping iron in the room up a half flight of stairs.

"Got a minute?" Meeker asked grimly.

"Yeah. Just a sec." He finished hooking up the net, climbed down, and snapped the ladder shut, then locked it in one of the equipment closets. "We can talk in here." He motioned toward his office.

Meeker nodded, and Trent knew it was bad news. He

could see it in Meeker's body language. Trent closed the
door behind Meeker, then waved him into a side chair.
"What's up?"

"The Prescott boy didn't make it."

"Hell." Trent's stomach turned to stone. All along he'd
expected Drew, a young, strapping boy, to pull through.

"Just took the call. The sheriff wanted me to tell you.
He's phoning Lynch now." He sighed heavily and licked his
cracked lips. "And he was doing so well after surgery.
Woke up, talked to people. Remembered everything that
went down in the barn. Then he goes back to sleep and it's
over." He snapped his fingers. "Just like that. Shit." He
rubbed his jaw with a fleshy hand and looked at the floor. "I
got a kid about that age. Goes to the community college.
Plays football. If anything like this happened to him . . ."
His voice trailed off, and the only sound was the regular
click of weights being lifted and dropped in the next room.

"It's hard. I didn't know Drew well, but it never seems
right when a kid dies." Trent went quiet, recalling the sight
of the young man, crumpled on the floor of the horse barn.
And Nona, dead as she dangled from a rope in the loft.
"Hard to take."

Meeker looked up quickly, meeting Trent's gaze. He
swore and rubbed his knuckles. "Poor damned son of a bitch."
He placed his hands on his knees and stood. "Baines got it all
on tape, and the kid seemed fine. And suddenly, couple of days
later, his heart just stops beating." He squared his hat on his
head. "Couldn't be revived. Flatlined."

The weights had stopped clanking, and now Trent's office was as silent as a tomb. "Makes you want to nail the
son of a bitch who would take down two kids," Trent said
grimly, a dark fury sweeping through him. He met
Meeker's tired eyes. "No way can we let that bastard get
away with it."

"You're right about that." Meeker rubbed a hand around

his unshaven jaw. "Looks like we've got our work cut out for us," Meeker said as the lights flickered eerily. "Let's catch that son of a bitch."

Still working at her desk, Jules reconsidered her sister's wild accusations.

Shay wasn't exactly the barometer for reality.

How had her father summed up Shay when he and Edie had remarried? If Jules thought hard enough, she could almost hear Rip Delaney's deep baritone voice as he'd told Edie, "You know, hon, if there was an emotional tidal pool anywhere in a three-state radius, Shaylee would find the deep end, jump in feetfirst, then call for help."

Edie hadn't been amused.

Rip Delaney's attitude about his stepdaughter had been a sticking point in an already unhappy union.

So, Jules advised herself, *don't take everything Shay says at face value.* Unfortunately, Jules hadn't been here long enough to evaluate any of the teachers' assistants' motives or actions. Nor had she gained their trust to the point that they would confide in her.

She was the outsider. As was Shay, who hadn't been here much longer than Jules.

For now, Jules decided, she'd follow that particular point of law that considered all suspects innocent until proven guilty. Even the malevolent TAs. Good God, Shay could be such a drama queen.

The apple doesn't fall very far from the tree, she thought, and made a mental note to give Edie another call. Even if the teachers' aides were innocent, there was still something very wrong here. One student dead, another missing, and a third—who happened to be a TA—seriously injured, all within five months.

Nona Vickers had been a student for almost a year, and

Lauren Conway had been on campus only a few months. She wasn't sure of Andrew's tenure, though he would have been at Blue Rock for a while before being promoted to the level of graduate student and TA. There was also Ethan Slade, the boy who had been supposedly sexually molested by Maris Howell. Ethan was still on campus, his parents settling, his education here at Blue Rock Academy oddly ensured.

She clicked her pen nervously. Her attempts at getting information from other staff and students had been unsuccessful. It took a while for people to warm up here, staff and students alike.

So what did that leave?

The student and faculty files.

Glancing out the window, she saw the corner of the admin building where all the records were kept. Not all, she reminded herself, and replaced her pen in the drawer. Some of the records were kept in Reverend Lynch's office, the one in the chapel.

Could she do it?

Break into the file drawers or the computers, then, if she were caught, drum up some excuse?

The bottom line was she had to.

Before someone else was hurt.

She just had to come up with a plan.

Her mind still half on her mission, she spent another half hour trying to focus on the next day's lesson plans.

Finally, she gave it up for the night. She could do more prep after dinner. Once she was settled into her pajamas at home, she might even come up with a way to get a peek at the student and faculty files. She gathered up her notes, books, and a couple of computer disks, then shoved them into her Blue Rock Academy book bag and zipped it closed.

Hitching the strap of her bag over her shoulder, Jules

made her way to the door of this fishbowl of a classroom. Darkness had already settled over the mountains, snow still falling hard. As she snapped off the lights, she wondered when the storm would break, when this school wouldn't be so isolated. As it was now, not only the police and supplies weren't able to get through the passes, but also families of the students, rescue workers, and the police were blockaded by the blizzard. It was as if the fates were conspiring against them, the whistling wind nearly laughing as everyone at Blue Rock dug in.

Don't be ridiculous, she silently chastised herself, but couldn't stop a little drizzle of dread from dripping down her spine.

She closed the door behind her.

Drained of students, the hallway was eerily quiet. Jules's boots rang on the tile floors, echoing in her ears. *Just stay calm,* she told herself as she hurried down the empty staircase, intent on heading back to her room for a little time alone. Although the crimes against Nona and Drew were vile, Jules had no reason to think someone would attack her or any other teacher on this campus.

Despite her case of nerves, Jules thought about the evening ahead. She intended to call Analise again since Eli had been a TA. What was it he'd said to Jules the last time they'd spoken?

Analise was afraid you might go poking around.

Why?

Jules had considered her cousin's concerns weird at the time. She'd thought Eli and Analise were worried about themselves and how they'd left the school, but maybe that hadn't been it. Maybe they'd been afraid of what Jules might find. . . .

She turned the corner and nearly ran over Maeve.

In tears, her shoulders braced against the wall, Maeve slowly slid to the floor, where she dissolved into horrid, heart-wrenching sobs, the books she'd been carrying falling onto her lap.

Jules was at the girl's side in an instant. "What's wrong?" Jules bent down on a knee to touch Maeve on her shoulder. "Maeve?"

Startled, as if she'd been in her own private world, Maeve looked up sharply and pulled back. "Nothing." A bald-faced lie. She blinked back a fresh onslaught of tears and hiccupped, her eyes filled with despair as they met Jules's.

"Oh, honey, you can talk to me."

Maeve was sniffing and hiccuping, blinking like crazy. "I . . . said . . . I'm okay." She scooted away, her right hand under her left sleeve and fidgeting—a motion Jules had noticed during class. "I'll be all right. Really. Just leave me alone."

Click, click, click!

"I don't think so," Jules said softly as she realized that Maeve was repeatedly snapping a rubber band against her wrist. Her face was flushed beet red, and tears drizzled from her eyes, tracking down her cheeks.

"Maeve . . . you know you shouldn't be moving around campus alone, but . . ." Jules respected the girl's space, but she wanted to help. "I'm here to help, okay? Is there anything I can do?"

"No!" Maeve was emphatic. She sniffed and scrambled onto her feet, losing hold of her bag.

The contents of her open purse tumbled out, scattering across the floor. She lunged for her purse and the books on her lap, and fell onto the floor, sliding on the shiny tiles. "Oh, crap!" Quickly she began retrieving items, a pink eye-glass case, a package of tissues, her wallet, keys, a plastic tampon case.

"Oh, God," she whispered, mortified as she scooped a pack of breath mints and a pink knit cap into the purse.

More tears. Black streaks of mascara. A quivering lower lip.

Jules couldn't let this go on. "I'll walk you where you need to go." She tried to help, scraping up a couple of pens and a piece of paper that read *OMEN*. She handed them to Maeve, but the girl was suddenly furious. "Maybe you should talk to your counselor or Dean Burdette."

"Just leave me alone! I'm fine! It's not so weird to be upset, is it, not with everything that's happening here." Grabbing her wallet and eyeglass case, she sniffed loudly again, then shoved the items into her bag. She wiped the tears from her cheeks, then retrieved her notebook—the cover completely covered by ink doodles of faces, stars, hearts, and swirls of Ethan Slade's initials—which had landed near a watercooler.

Maeve tucked the notebook under her arm, then swept the pens and note from Jules's outstretched palm. "I don't want your help. I don't need your help." But there was something in her eyes, a glimmer of self-doubt, a deep-seated sadness.

"I'm serious. I think you should talk to Dr. Williams," Jules suggested, knowing that Maeve, like everyone else here, was caught in an emotional tidal wave, but she wondered if there was another reason other than her grief for her classmate that caused her complete emotional melt-down. "You know, Maeve, we're all here to help."

"You think anyone can help me?" she mocked, her face distorted by her ruined makeup. "Are you out of your mind? There's nothing a counselor or you or anyone else can do, okay? So just leave me the hell—" She started, then caught herself, blinking and swallowing back her anger. "Please," Maeve pleaded, holding out one hand, fingers splayed in Jules's direction. "Just go away."

"Hey! You okay?" another voice chimed in, and Jules

looked over her shoulder to see Roberto Ortega hurrying down the stairs from the second floor.

"I'm fine!" Maeve sniffed loudly and shook her head.

"You sure?" Roberto's face was pinched with concern.

"Didn't I just say so?" Quickly she stuffed the rest of her belongings into her purse, snatched up the remaining scattered books, and bolted outside into the storm. Cold air swept into the education hall, the slap of winter catching Jules off guard as she watched Maeve through the closing glass door. Hair streaming behind her, her gait encumbered by her bags, she ran through the falling snow. Clumsily reaching into her bag, she forced her pink knit cap over her head.

"Girls!" Roberto snorted, shaking his head as the door clicked shut. Then, as if realizing Jules had heard him, he flashed a self-deprecating smile as he checked his watch, frowned, then headed for the far end of the building. "Sorry."

"It's okay," she said, but Roberto, who had picked up his pace, was already past the doors to the science labs and pushing open the exit located closest to the dorms.

Bang! The latches of the far door clicked into place, and once again Jules felt as if she were alone in the tall glass building.

Zipping her coat, she walked outside. From a distance, through a shifting curtain of snow, she watched Maeve catch up to someone standing under the overhang of the breezeway. A boy? Or a man? She couldn't see his face, catching a glimpse of only jeans and the back of one of the blue jackets issued by the academy.

It was already dark outside, though not yet five in the evening, the dead of winter draping the mountains with early nightfall.

Maeve's companion wrapped a comforting arm over her

shoulders, then shepherded her toward the path leading past the chapel.

For a second, Jules thought he might be Ethan Slade, the boy she assumed Maeve was crying over.

Or was it someone else who was comforting her?

For half a heartbeat, she thought Maeve's companion might be Father Jake, but he seemed much too familiar to be the youth minister.

They disappeared into the night, and Jules was left wondering about Maeve Mancuso.

Truth to tell, Jules didn't know why the girl had been reduced to tears. Her emotional state might have had nothing to do with unrequited love. Perhaps, as she'd claimed, grief over Nona was setting in. In any case, teenaged girls were known to have extreme highs and lows, elated one minute, depressed the next.

Still, Jules was bothered, though she didn't know how to help Maeve.

She remembered the glimpse of Maeve's note and thought of the one that had been left for her. Both on lined paper, but in different hands.

HELP ME, the first had pleaded. *OMEN* was the warning in Maeve's possession. Had the girl written it, or had she received it?

Jules would probably never know, but those three simple words, written on two scraps of paper, bothered her, and all of Shay's fears, real or imagined, slid through her brain.

Get over it. So you saw some notes. So Shay thinks there's some deep, dark conspiracy on campus. Big deal.

As the wind shrieked over the lake, Jules walked toward Stanton House. With each step, she told herself she was letting her imagination run away with her, that Shay was wrong, but as she walked by the chapel, a shudder ripped through her soul.

CHAPTER 31

"**D**amn!" Jules couldn't find her cell phone. Her gloved fingers scrabbled through her purse but came up empty as she turned on the snowy path leading to Stanton House.

She'd planned on phoning Adele Burdette, the headmistress for the girls. According to all the Blue Rock Academy literature she'd skimmed, as a member of the staff, she was supposed to help with emotional or physical trauma as well as report all "incidents" with students, including physical altercations or verbal confrontations or emotional problems.

Maeve Mancuso's meltdown in the hallway probably qualified, but Jules didn't want to create a tempest in a teapot. She figured she'd let Dean Burdette know what happened, but downplay it. So, after she got hold of Burdette, Jules planned on calling Analise and her husband. She needed to find out more about the TAs, and she decided a good source of information would be her cousin. Eli had been a TA; he hadn't revealed much before, but if she confronted him now, she felt sure he would give her more information if there was some kind of secretive cult.

Or laugh in your face.

Since her phone wasn't in her purse, she checked her book bag. Nothing. Her pockets, too, were empty. "Can't be," she said to herself, remembering that she'd had it just before class when she'd talked to Edie.

The phone was definitely missing.

Had she left it in the classroom? She knew she had it there; she'd been talking to Edie.

Oh, great. A killer on campus, and now she didn't even have a cell phone to call for help. Some example she was setting for these kids.

As Jules turned on her heel and headed back to the education hall, she thought of the information on that phone. The calls that had come in from Shaylee on Nona's prepaid cell, the menu of numbers that included Shaylee's old cell phone and Edie's home and cell. Analise and Eli's number would show on the recent calls. Though she remembered locking the phone, any techie type would make fast work of unlocking the phone and retrieving all of the data stored inside.

"Damn."

Her heart began to race, and she had to fight a looming sense of panic. "Don't go into orbit yet," she cautioned herself, her breath fogging with the cold. The phone wasn't really lost or stolen, just misplaced. However, the knot twisting painfully in her stomach reminded her of how much she had at stake.

She flew into the building and ran up the stairs. Her boots rang in the hollow hallway, melting snow dripping onto the tiles. On the second floor, she nearly skidded around a corner, then stopped short when she spied Missy Albright just closing the door to room 212 behind her. Loitering in the empty hallway, as if he was standing guard while waiting for Missy, was Zach Bernsen.

What?

For a split second, they both appeared startled; then matching grins quickly slid into place. Just like clockwork. "Hi!" Missy said brightly. She held up her calculator as Jules approached. "I'm sorry, but I lost my stupid calculator. It must've fallen out of my purse when I was in your class."

"Is that right?" Jules couldn't keep the disbelief from her voice. "You know, I didn't see it when I was straightening up the room." *And now I'm missing my phone.*

"I know, I know." Missy rolled her eyes in a silly-me-I'm such-a-goose expression. "When I started looking around the classroom, Zach came up here and found me. I'd left it in the science lab when he and I were doing calculations for a chemistry experiment." She stretched her mouth and lifted her shoulders in an exaggerated shrug while starting to walk toward the elevators with Zach. "I'm really sorry."

"Wait a sec. While you were in there," Jules said, motioning toward the door to her classroom and not letting the girl escape so easily, "did you happen to see my cell phone?"

Missy's face collapsed into an expression of confusion. "Nuh-uh," she said, shaking her head and keeping her gaze locked with Jules's. "But I wasn't looking for it."

"I just thought you might have come across it while searching."

"Sorry." Again she lifted her shoulders as if that said it all. Other than calling the girl an out-and-out liar or stripping Missy of her bag and searching it, Jules was out of options. As for Zach, he seemed almost bored with the exchange.

"Then it must still be in the classroom," Jules said as the two students retreated for the bank of elevators.

She opened the door to her room, and it appeared just as she'd left it, the desks rearranged into a semicircle, all the surfaces clean.

Jules searched for ten minutes, opening drawers, looking in the closet, eyeing the floor, but she came up empty-handed. Her cell phone wasn't anywhere to be found. Had Missy taken it? Someone else in the classroom? Or had Jules lost it during the time she'd spent dealing with Maeve?

She realized that a cell phone was like gold to these kids; most of them would jump on the chance to swipe it, either for personal use or for trade. The reasons didn't necessarily have to be nefarious.

And yet . . .

Once again she turned off the lights, but this time, before she actually stepped into the hallway, she detoured to the window and looked across the campus, where snow glittering under the security lamps offered a peaceful vista.

Warm lamplight glowing from the chapel added to the appearance of serenity. *All an illusion,* she told herself.

If she didn't believe it, all she had to do was ask Nona Vickers's father.

She spied Missy and Zach as they walked rapidly from the education building toward the chapel. Zach's arm was slung over Missy's shoulders, as if he were shepherding the tall girl.

Just as they reached the arched doors, Missy dared to look over her shoulder. Her face turned upward, her gaze centered on the very spot where Jules stood in the darkness.

She froze, wondering if the girl could see her.

Don't make more of it than it is, the voice of reason nagged at her, but she felt a whisper of fear just the same.

With a word from Zach, Missy slipped through the door of the chapel, and Jules was left with the disturbing notion that despite all the accolades about Blue Rock Academy, Shaylee might be right. It could very well be the school of the damned.

If so, Jules was going to find out.

Tonight.

* * *

Trent caught Jules as she was leaving the education hall. Head bent against the wind, apparently lost in thought, she was walking quickly in the direction of Stanton House. "Hey, Ms. Farentino," he called, just in case anyone saw him flagging her down. "Wait up!"

"What?" She looked up quickly, startled as she slowed in the light of a tall lamppost. Snow swirled around her, catching on the wisps of hair that had come free of the hood of her long coat.

It could have been a trick of light, but for a fraction of a heartbeat, the corners of her mouth lifted a bit, as if the sight of him was a welcome distraction. "I want to talk to you about one of our students," he said, and resisted grabbing the crook of her elbow.

"Which one?" she asked as he reached her.

"Andrew Prescott," he said, his voice lowered as they walked along the path. "I just got the word a couple of hours ago—he didn't make it. Lynch will be making an announcement a little later."

Jules paled under the lamplight, her gray eyes darkening with sadness. "Another one," she whispered. "Dear God, I was hoping he'd recover."

"We all were."

She let out a long breath as he brought her up to date on what Meeker had told him about the deaths. She listened, shivering slightly, worry straining her features. He added, "In some ways, I don't know how these kids are bearing up under the strain. A killer on the loose, and we're all pent up here in the storm. Unless the son of a bitch got out that first night, after he attacked Nona and Drew and before the blizzard hit, he's trapped here."

"With us. I know."

He witnessed her shudder and wanted like hell to wrap a comforting arm around her, to hold her close, to press his lips into her frozen hair and whisper that everything would be all right. But he didn't. First, he couldn't give anyone else a glimpse that he knew her more than as a new colleague. Secondly, he'd sworn long ago that he wouldn't try to keep close contact with any woman who'd made it clear she wasn't interested.

Jules qualified. Big-time.

Right after Rip Delaney's murder, Jules had been adamant that she didn't want anything to do with him.

Thirdly, he now knew that despite all of his rules and vows to himself, he couldn't trust himself near Jules, because, like it or not, he'd never gotten over her. Being near her, staring into her concerned eyes, watching the thoughtful pout of her lips, he realized with heart-jolting clarity that he still wanted her.

What the hell was wrong with him?

For a heartbeat, he considered throwing caution to the wind and leaned closer to her.

"Mr. Trent!" a young voice called, shattering the moment. He looked over his shoulder and spied Banjo Harris running toward them.

Oh, hell!

He'd forgotten that he'd promised to meet with her to resolve some questions about her schedule.

"I have to go," he said.

"Wait! I need to talk to you!" Jules was insistent, grabbing his arm.

He couldn't risk lingering any longer. Too many people were watching. He stepped away, breaking contact. "Then come by my place tonight, say ten, ten-thirty," he whispered, anxious not to be overheard. "You know which one it is?" She nodded. "The porch light will be off." God, what was he thinking? Inviting her to his cottage? Inviting disaster.

"I'll be there," she said softly just as Banjo bounded up

to them, her guitar case banging against her back with each stride.

"Thanks," he said to Jules, then turned on his heel.

Being any closer to her was dangerous.

Dangerous in a million ways.

"You're wrong!" Maeve insisted. Her insides were shredding as she walked toward the cafeteria with Nell, Lucy, and that awful new girl, Shaylee. Just because Shaylee was in their pod didn't mean that they had to hang out with her.

Not that it mattered now.

The rumor was that Andrew Prescott had died. He'd really died. And although Maeve had given up the romantic notion of a suicide pact between Drew and Nona, once she'd learned that there'd been an attack, she had desperately wanted Andrew to live. As if his survival was a valiant act, a way to defy the killer who'd taken his beloved's life.

Drew's death, on top of Maeve's own problems, made life here at Blue Rock unbearable. For the past couple of days, her friends had been trying to convince her to give up on Ethan, to deny that which was the most important, the most vital part of her.

She knew in her heart that Ethan was her true soul mate, the only man she would ever love.

God, she was so miserable, and she couldn't keep from crying. Her tears froze on her face, tiny diamonds in her eyelashes, and the night wind blew so hard it made her lungs feel frozen. Maeve didn't know how she'd get through dinner. Of course, she felt a little zing of anticipation because Ethan would be there, but she feared that he wouldn't spare her a look. He wouldn't wink, wouldn't give her any indication that she was special to him, even though he'd said it dozens of times before.

Hadn't she been there for him during all those awful,

ridiculous accusations about him and Ms. Howell? Hadn't she stood by him? Given him an alibi if he needed it? Didn't he know that she'd do anything for him? *Any*thing?

Their boots crunched in the snow that was crusting over. She'd never been so cold in her life. But this, the chill of winter, was nothing like the ice that threatened her heart when she thought of losing Ethan.

Ethan loved her, he did. He'd told her so. Every time they'd gone to the hayloft where . . . Oh, God, she couldn't think of Nona, how she'd died dangling from the end of a rope.

The lump in her throat was so large she could barely breathe, and the thought that Ethan could be with anyone else was like a thousand daggers in her heart.

"I'm just saying that I saw him with Kaci Donahue," Lucy said. "It's not that big of a deal."

But it is! It's my life! He's everything to me! She blinked hard, pretending the snow on her eyelashes was bothering her, when, in truth, she was fighting a losing battle with tears. She loved him. She'd proven it. Letting him touch her and kiss her and make love to her. She would have risked everything for him.

"No guy is worth this," Shay said, as if she had some experience with this kind of pain. Yeah, well, who needed her opinion anyway?

"Ethan is," she whispered fervently as they reached the cafeteria and pushed open the doors. The bright lights blinded her, and the smell of Mrs. Pruitt's shepherd's pie made her gag. Bile rose up her throat, and it was all she could do to swallow it back. She couldn't let any of the staff know how she felt. She cleared her throat and whispered, "I don't want to talk about it. Not now."

"Uh-oh." Nell's gaze swept across the wood-paneled interior to a far table, where Ethan was seated alone with

Kaci. "I can't believe he has the balls to show up here with her."

"They're both TAs," Lucy pointed out.

Maeve wanted to disappear through the floor. She grabbed the band on her wrist and snapped it hard, harder. She needed to feel a pain to drown out the bleeding in her heart.

"Bastard!" Nell hissed.

Shay said, "She doesn't want to talk about it, okay?"

"Well it's right in her face!"

For his part, Ethan glanced at Maeve, gave her a quiet, innocuous smile, then turned back to Kaci. Just like that. As if she were just another student he barely recognized, a nobody in Mr. DeMarco's calculus class. Someone he had to help understand logarithms.

Nothing more.

Zach and Missy joined the other couple, and Maeve thought she might be sick. The two couples looked like they were on some kind of double date.

Maeve took her seat at Mr. Trent's table. Wedged between BD on one side and Nell on the other, Maeve tried not to focus on Ethan, but it was damned hard. Why didn't he understand that their love was something so special, something priceless? Under the table, she snapped at her wristband, letting the sting keep her in the moment.

The rest of the students took their places, and Reverend Lynch confirmed that Andrew Prescott had died. Somberly, he led them in a prayer while a glum silence fell over the stunned students.

Everyone had known that Drew might die, but it was still weird. Surreal. For a while, out of respect, or just because it was expected, everyone was quiet, the shepherd's pie and salad passed around the tables with very little conversation.

That changed midway through the meal as people began to talk in hushed tones, then with more animation over the clatter of flatware and clink of plastic glasses. Maeve had taken a serving of the pie and a slice of bread, but when it came to actually eating, she couldn't manage a bite. And the buzz of conversation faded into white noise, punctuated by Kaci Donahue's trilling laughter.

Tears welled in Maeve's eyes, and she had to fight to keep them from streaming down her cheeks, so she squished her bread into small dough balls and thought of ways to make Ethan love her again.

What would it take for him to realize that she, not bony Kaci, a girl who was a female version of a daddy longlegs spider, was the woman he was meant to be with?

"You need to be chillin', Maeve." BD grinned, his dark eyes dancing as he stared at her torn and flattened dinner roll. "You've already killed it!"

On the other side of him, Keesha laughed.

That did it! Maeve's stomach lurched and she didn't care about the rule that everyone was supposed to wait until after another prayer before leaving the dining hall. No one understood her. No one! Not even Nell.

And not even Ethan, she thought miserably.

She scooted back her chair and took off, wending her way through the tables toward the hallway and restroom. She felt the prying heat of curious eyes upon her and hoped beyond hope that Ethan saw her pain and would come looking for her.

He didn't, of course.

To her absolute mortification, the next person who pushed open the door to the restroom was Kaci Donahue. Maeve wished she'd hidden in one of the stalls.

"Hi," Kaci said lightly, as if there was nothing wrong. She leaned close to the mirror and studied her reflection, dabbing at the corner of her lips as if to wipe away an errant bit of lip gloss.

But Maeve detected satisfaction in Kaci's gaze and knew the older girl had just come into the bathroom to rub it in.

How mortifying.

Without making a sound, Maeve left the restroom and walked into the hallway, where Mr. Trent stood leaning against the far wall, waiting for her.

Great!

Arms crossed over his chest, he caught her eye, then fell into step beside her. "You okay?" he asked.

She wanted to dissolve into a thousand pieces. "Yeah," she lied. *Don't make me talk, please, please, please. I can't talk about it!*

"Sure?"

"Mmm." She nodded her head frantically, anxious to get rid of him. The last thing she needed was her semihot pod leader watching as she imploded, self-destructing. Her throat was still thick, but she forced out the words, "I, uh, think I'm coming down with a cold or something," she said, the lie tripping off her tongue.

"Okay."

He was buying it? Really?

"I know all this is difficult."

What? He knows? Was she that transparent?

Then she got it. He was talking about Andrew and Nona being killed.

"We've got grief counseling set up. Private and group. And you know that if you want to talk, I'm here. . . ."

"I know," she said, forcing brightness into her tone that she didn't feel. Mr. Trent didn't understand it, of course, but she was way beyond being saved by talking.

Talk was useless. She needed action.

CHAPTER 32

In a throwback to his youth, Father Jake made the sign of the cross over his chest as he stared at the altar in the chapel.

He hadn't been a Catholic in a long, long while, but old habits died hard, especially when confronted with great tragedy, hard times.

He'd seen more than his share of heartache, fear, and humiliation in his thirty-six years, and throughout it all, his faith had been unshaken. He knew the emotional pain of losing a wife, of watching her slowly die and realizing that her death was the result of his own actions.

He'd felt despair as great as any and guilt that had been unbearable. He'd made mistakes during his lifetime, had been a liar, a cheat, and he had done things for which he'd had no pride.

Throughout it all, however, he'd held on to his faith. Sometimes it had been hard, nearly impossible, but he'd always felt the spirit of the Lord with him.

But that was changing, he realized. Ever since he'd come to Blue Rock Academy, his faith had been tested.

Now he wasn't sure it would survive.

He fell to his knees and prayed for guidance, for divine intervention. All the while, he felt the cold metal of the Glock tucked into the waistband of his pants, pressed hard against his back.

Jules stood at the window of her darkened room and hoped no one could see her looking over the campus. Pulling her hands into the warmth of her sweater sleeves, she kept her eyes on Reverend Lynch, a dark slash of a figure. Bent against the wind, he walked on the path from the chapel, veering off from the main walkway, as if he was headed toward the house he shared with Cora Sue. She couldn't see the house through the curtain of snow, but she was convinced he was going home for the night.

She could only hope he stayed there.

Keyed up, she threw on her jacket, scarf, and boots and grabbed a flashlight and keys, both of which she figured could qualify as weapons. There was no way she could stay in this room and do nothing, just sitting behind a locked door and praying that she was safe. Not with a killer on the campus. Not with her sister at risk.

Locking the door behind her, she told herself to calm down and get a grip, but she knew full well that nothing short of the killer being brought to justice would ease her mind or anyone else's. Everyone at the school was jumpy.

She hurried down the stairs to the cozy nook that served as the common area for Stanton House. Clusters of tables and chairs were situated around warm, earth-toned rugs that had been tossed over the hardwood floor. Reading lamps and half a dozen battery-powered candles added to the ambience.

However, no one relaxed on the soft leather cushions or curled up in the corner of the couch angled near the win-

dows. The place was empty and quiet except for muted
notes of some Spanish ballad drifting from an upper floor.

Jules adjusted her scarf.

The door closet under the stairs opened.

She nearly jumped out of her skin as Keesha Bell, a disgusted look on her face, a dust rag dangling from the back
pocket of her jeans, pushed a vacuum cleaner into the
room. An empty bucket was swinging from the fingers of
her free hand.

"You scared me!" Jules admitted, then laughed.

"Sorry." Keesha didn't even pause or crack a bit of a
smile. "Sometimes I scare myself. 'Specially in the morning." She stopped to straighten a stack of magazines resting
on a glass coffee table before she plugged the cord of the
vacuum into an outlet.

"You must have late duty tonight."

The furrows in Keesha's forehead deepened. "Yeah," she
said with a roll of her expressive eyes. "Lucky me."

"Every night, right?"

The girl nodded as she unlooped the vac's cord. "That's
the way Dr. Lynch wants it."

Jules thought about the note that had been slipped under
her door the other night. She didn't know if it was a prank
or a sincere plea for help, but she intended to find out.
"Have you been doing this all week?" Jules asked, walking
into the living area.

"No, thank you, God. We rotate," Keesha said, snapping
the rag from her pocket to swipe at a cobweb hanging from
the shade of a floor lamp.

"Were you working here last Friday?"

"Nuh-uh." Keesha shook her head, cornrows rubbing the
back of her neck.

"Do you know who was?"

"Uh . . . Nell. Maybe." Puzzled, she walked to the janitorial closet again and opened the door to expose a duty list posted on the back panels. "Let's see." Squinting, Keesha ran a long finger down the list. "Yeah. I thought so. Nell was scheduled over the weekend. What happened? She miss your room?"

"No, no, nothing like that," Jules said, glad for a name. If Nell hadn't slid the note under her door, she might have seen someone else loitering on the floor. She tucked the ends of her scarf into the lapel of her coat. "I was just wondering how the rotation went."

Keesha closed the closet door and walked back to the vacuum cleaner again just as the song from above changed tempo. "Well, things have changed a little this past week. Used to be one person was in charge of cleaning each of the buildings, but with what's happened around here . . . you know, Nona and Drew being killed and all . . ." She rubbed her arms as if suddenly chilled. "Now we work in teams of two."

Jules surveyed the first floor. "You've got a partner?"

"If ya can call it that. Banjo's up on the third floor." Keesha jabbed a finger toward the ceiling. "Listen. Can't you hear her?"

"Yeah, I do."

"You think she's gettin' much cleaning done?" Keesha asked, then snorted her own reply. "No way. I bet I have to go up there and scrub the damned toilets myself." She let out another disgusted huff of air. "Don't know why I was teamed up with her. I asked if BD and I could work together, but oh, no, Mr. Trent wasn't about to have that. No, sir! No 'coupling up' I think he said." Obviously agitated, she smacked the rag over the back of the sofa, as if snuffing out insects. "But we're only here for a couple of nights, then, oh, joy, our entire pod gets cafeteria duty."

"I take it you're not big on working in the kitchen."

"You got that right." Keesha nodded emphatically. "It *really* sucks. Makes cleaning this place look like the damned garden of Eden." She winced as she heard herself. "Sorry about that. It's just that thinking about the cafeteria . . . yeck! All that gross food and dirty plates and spilled stuff on the floors? Dishes and trays piled to the ceiling? Who needs it?" As if suddenly realizing she was ranting to a staff member, she shut up, tossing her dusty rag into the empty pail. "Well, as my grandma always says, 'there just ain't no rest for the wicked.'" Keesha forced a smile, caught somewhere between amusement and deceit. "I say a big amen to that." She reached for the handle of the vacuum. "I still think it would have been safer for me to be hangin' out with BD, you know, rather than with Senorita Jewel up there." She swept her gaze toward the stairs, where the plaintive notes echoed in the stairwell.

"Just be careful."

"Oh, I will!"

"Good." Jules pushed open the doors against a blast of icy, arctic air. In fierce gusts, the wind screamed through the night, rushing through the campus and rattling the chains on the flagpole.

Jules's already ragged nerves tightened. Mentally she chastised herself for being an idiot. She'd be fired if she was found trying to break into Lynch's office, but the thought of the files locked away in his credenza bothered her. Why a second set of information? Why not on the computer?

Face it, Jules, the reason you're worried is that you saw your name and Trent's picture. You're thinking Lynch is putting two and two together.

No matter what, she was not about to second-guess herself now. She made a beeline toward the chapel, only pausing to double-check Lynch's cabin with its windows glowing bright. "Stay there," she muttered as the wind stole the breath from her lips and icy flakes of snow melted against her face.

Gaze skating over the frozen landscape, ears straining to hear even the slightest sound of a footstep behind her, she hurried to the main doors and reached for the handle.

"Ms. Farentino?" a male voice asked, and she literally jumped, spinning to face two large men, both dressed in ski jackets, hats, and masks. She clutched her chest, her heart exploding in fear.

"Julia?" One of the men peeled back his ski mask— Wade Taggert, one of the psychology instructors.

Damn!

Her gloved fingers tightened over her flashlight.

"Where's your partner?" he asked as the second man, too, lifted his mask, and she recognized Tim Takasumi, a TA who, she'd learned, was studying computer engineering.

"Oh, Lord! You scared me!" she said, still nervous. "And, yes, I know I'm supposed to buddy up when I'm out, but I just thought I'd spend some time alone in the chapel."

Taggert's eyebrows drew together. "The rule is that no one crosses the campus after dark unaccompanied. It's for your own good."

"I know. I'll just be a few minutes. It's been a hard first week, and I needed some time alone. I thought I'd light a candle or two." She offered a wavering smile but didn't give up her death grip on the flashlight.

Who knew who you could trust?

Taggert, blinking against the storm, seemed to accept her explanation. "You want us to stay with you?" he yelled over the shriek of the wind.

"No, thanks. You have rounds." She had to raise her voice to be heard, too. "I'll be fine in here. I'll just be a few minutes."

She was afraid Taggert would say they would be willing to wait for her, but his eyes caught a movement by the gazebo. Jules saw it, too. Someone seated within the lattice-work decorated with hundreds of tiny lights. "What the—?" He glanced at Jules again. "You're sure you'll be okay?"

"Yes."

Wade hit Takasumi on the arm. "Let's go."

They pulled their masks down and took off, half-jogging against the brutal, gusting wind.

Now that they knew she was here, she didn't have much time. Quickly, heart hammering in her ears, she moved through the nave and to the hallway leading to Reverend Lynch's office.

She tried the door.

Locked.

Of course.

Damn!

She wasn't a thief, didn't know how to pick a lock to save her soul. She could try the outside window, she supposed, but she would run the risk of the security teams seeing her.

Her only hope was the bathroom, one that was accessible from the hallway and from the reverend's office. She'd caught a glimpse of it earlier and silently prayed that it was open, the connecting door unlocked.

Noiselessly, she slid into the restroom and locked the door behind her; then she tried the connecting door, which opened, of course. The lock was on the inside.

But that was only half the battle. Now there was the file cabinet to break into. She drew the shades down and turned off her flashlight, afraid the vigilant eyes of the new legion of security guards might see the moving illumination and come into the chapel to investigate. After a minute, her eyes grew accustomed to the fading red glow from a dying fire.

She rounded the desk and tried the top drawer.

It was locked tight.

Great. Now what? Snow was melting from her shoes,

leaving puddles on the carpet, puddles she hoped would dry before Lynch returned in the morning. Dressed as she was, the chill of the night had worn off, the heat in the office chasing away the cold.

She yanked at her scarf, allowing a little breathing room around her neck, but she didn't remove her gloves. Stealthily, her heart pounding a nervous tattoo, she opened the desk drawers one by one, searching for small keys that would fit the cabinet. Nothing. It was possible, she supposed, that he kept the key with him at all times, but most people kept a spare in the office.

Somewhere.

Yeah, like in Charla King's possession.

No, that didn't make sense. Jules doubted Lynch would trust anyone, even King, with the key to his private files.

Bam!

The fire popped suddenly, sounding for all the world like the sharp report of a gun.

Jules bit back a scream, her knees nearly giving out, her pulse skyrocketing. She was just no good at this cloak-and-dagger stuff, no good at all. She wasn't cut out for this.

Every muscle tense, she did a quick search, touching the underside of drawers, looking under plants, even flipping up the corners of the carpet. Again, she came up dry.

Frustration ground through her.

Where, where, where would he hide them?

Maybe they weren't in the office. But, then, where?

She'd never been a quitter and hadn't come this far to give up, but she was running out of ideas. And time was against her. Soon, she knew, Taggert and Takasumi would check the chapel. Would they think she'd just left and returned to her suite, or would they search for her? She couldn't be sure.

Sweat dampening her palms, she found a letter opener in the top drawer of the desk, but it was too large to slip into the lock. Ditto, the nail file. All of her own keys were too large.

"Damn, damn, damn," she whispered.

Maybe there was nothing in the files. Maybe her pathetic attempts at sleuthing weren't worth the time. And yet . . . she reached around the back of the file cabinet, running her fingers down the flat back and came up with nothing. Short of prying the damned drawer open with a hammer and breaking the lock, she thought there was no way to open the damned cabinet.

Creeeak.

A footstep sounded in the hallway.

Jules's heart leapt to her throat.

She froze, praying she'd imagined the sound.

Then the quiet, steady thud of footsteps, getting louder, coming closer.

Oh, God!

Keys jangled in the hallway on the other side of Lynch's office door.

Oh, no!

She eased even closer to the bathroom as the reverend's muffled voice penetrated the door. "Well, I hope to high heaven that the FBI does show up," he said as Jules slid from behind his desk toward the bathroom door. "Someone has to do something!"

Who was he talking to? Hopefully someone who would keep him distracted long enough for her to escape.

"Absolutely!"

The door was shouldered open just as Jules slipped into the restroom, the door whispering shut behind her.

"Yes, yes, I know. Trust me, I'm aware that we've got a serious problem," Lynch was saying.

The lock clicked softly under her fingertips. Her heart raced madly as she listened to Lynch's footsteps thumping through his office. Should she stay? Or should she try to leave now, out the door to the hallway and, if he found her, use the same excuse she had given Wade and Takasumi?

Lynch was still talking, his voice rising to be heard, but no one responded, and she guessed he was on his phone. "I know that! Just get someone up here . . . What? Sheriff? You're cutting out! Can you hear me?" A pause. "Sheriff O'Donnell? Can you hear me?" Another long pause and Jules hardly dared breathe. "Sheriff? Oh, heavens. Blaine? If you can hear me, I can't hear you. I'm hanging up now. Call me back!"

Then only silence.

Jules didn't dare move as sweat dripped down her back. She stood, ear to the door, listening hard, every instinct in her body insisting she run.

Be patient.

Just wait.

Maybe you'll learn something.

She closed her eyes.

Concentrated.

Through the door she heard a click—a lock—then the rumble of a large drawer being opened. She bit her lip, tried to slow her breathing.

Slap! Papers being tossed onto his desk?

Slap! Again.

"That should do it," he said, his voice lower as his footsteps crossed the room again, coming closer. Jules hardly dared breathe. She took a step back only to hear a creaking, metallic noise, the sweep of metal against metal. "Here we go."

Whoosh!

Air? What was that?

Closing her eyes, she pressed her ear to the space where the bathroom door fit against the jamb. She willed her loud heartbeat to slow and heard a soft hiss and crackle . . . the fire. He was messing with the fire.

In her mind's eye, she saw flames. Where only minutes before there had been merely glowing coals.

So why would he stoke the . . . Oh, God. With a sinking feeling, she understood—he was burning something, not for heat and not because he was housecleaning in the middle of the night, but to destroy whatever it was. No doubt the sheriff's call had propelled him back to the office to get rid of . . .

The damned files!

Heartsick, she understood: There was something damaging in the files, so Lynch had decided to get rid of them before the sheriff's department or some other law enforcement agency returned to the school. Once the storm abated, Blue Rock Academy would be inundated with parents, police, and the press.

There would be no quick double-talk or platitudes. The school would be put under a microscope. Two students had been brutally murdered, the killing ground a macabre scene that would have investigators and reporters crawling all over the campus.

And Lynch was taking pains to get rid of some of his private papers in the middle of the night. Evidence of something was being destroyed. If she'd only come back here earlier . . .

Faintly, she heard music. Strains of the "Hallelujah Chorus."

"Hello? . . . What?"

His cell phone. Of course.

"I'm sorry, Cora Sue. I can't hear you. I'm in the office. It's the connection . . . What? . . . Are you there?" A long pause as the smell of smoke slipped under the door. "I don't know what you expect me to do! Just turn the water off under the sink . . . Oh, for the love of Mike. Fine, fine! I'm on my way. I don't know! A mop? Towels? Hold on. I'll be home in two minutes!"

A few seconds later, she heard him stride out of the room, slamming the door to the office so hard the building shuddered.

Now was her chance!

She started counting to ten to make sure he wasn't returning but stopped at five and unlocked the bathroom door.

The room was awash in shifting golden light. Deep in the fireplace, flames consumed the sheaves of paper tucked into manila files. Black smoke rolled up the chimney as the pages curled and burned.

Jules threw open the screen of the fireplace and grabbed a poker from the hearth. Leaning close to the fire, feeling its heat, she used the tool to push the pages apart, separating the stack of files, easing each manila folder away from the center of the blaze, trying to save as many of the documents as she could.

"You bastard, what were you up to?" she said under her breath, and wondered what information the files had contained. A clue to the killer's identity?

Unlikely.

But surely proof of the school's complicity in something that wouldn't bear scrutiny in the light of day.

She managed to drag the papers onto the stonework, then used the small shovel to stamp out the flames curling over the corner.

"Come on, come on," she urged, leaning over the smoldering, smoking papers. Some of the pages were untouched, others completely consumed.

All were files on the staff and students at the academy; there were no accounting ledgers, no proof of a second set of books.

So what did it all mean? she wondered, soot on her gloves and jacket. Somehow she had to find out, and the only way was to haul these files, half burned as they were, out of here.

A brass wood carrier sat empty on the hearth. It might just do the trick. Using the thick leather gloves left near the utensils on the hearth, Jules carefully pulled out the papers she could salvage from the firebox. The edges of the pages were blackened, some still glowing red, but she kept at it, blackening the fingers of the gloves, carefully laying the pages and files, some still with clasps, into the carrier.

She had started adjusting the screen when she heard a noise in the hallway.

She froze. Oh, God, no. Not when she was so close. Sure enough, voices carried through the door.

"She could still be in here?"

Wade Taggert!

Damn!

She straightened, left the gloves on the hearth, and slid silently toward the bathroom.

The doorknob rattled.

Her heart nearly stopped.

Lynch hadn't locked the door when he'd flown out in a rage.

Not the dead bolt, but the lock in the knob might always be turned to the locked position.

The door didn't open immediately, but she didn't dare draw a breath. What if they had a key? How would she explain herself? The carrier of burned pages?

Heart in her throat, she backed up, caught the corner of Lynch's desk with her thigh, and bit her tongue to keep from crying out.

"You smell smoke?" Takasumi asked.

"Always. Lynch burns a fire every day, rain or shine. Kinda like Nixon." Taggert laughed. "I heard he built a fire and ran the AC."

"Did you believe the girl's story? That she'd gone to the gazebo for meditation?" Takasumi asked.

"Don't know. She's disturbed."

"Weird if you ask me, but then aren't they all? Talk about a fantasy world. I mean, out in the gazebo in the middle of a damned blizzard, clicking that rubber band at her wrist. It just doesn't make a whole lotta sense."

"Maeve has issues; let's just leave it at that."

Oh, yeah, ever the good therapist. What was Wade thinking, discussing a student, his client, with Takasumi?

Jules eased into the bathroom just as the door to it clicked loudly.

"This one locked, too? It's not supposed to be, right?" Takasumi asked.

Jules's knees went weak. How could she explain herself being in the office, carrying a load of half-burnt papers? How many laws was she breaking?

"It's the only way his office is secure, really, so Lynch locks it. Come on. She probably got done with her prayers and went back home."

The "she," no doubt, meant Jules.

Dear Lord, she hoped they didn't check at Stanton House.

Tense, ears straining, Jules waited. Footsteps retreated. Finally, far off, a door closed. She didn't know which direction they'd gone, out the front or the back of the chapel, so she waited longer, giving them a head start, the seconds slowly stretching to minutes.

When she could stand it no longer, she opened the door. The hallway was empty, nearly dark, the only illumination coming from night-lights in the chapel. Fearing she'd be accosted at any instant, Jules quickly hauled the carrier with its stack of smoldering papers down the short corridor.

At the back door, she sent up a quick prayer.

Then she let herself out and stepped into the night.

CHAPTER 33

"I told you she was trouble," his right-hand man said as he flipped a cell phone through the air, the slim instrument glistening under the lamplight as it arced in the snowfall.

The Leader caught the phone on the fly and jammed it into the pocket of his ski jacket. "I unlocked the security code. Piece of cake."

Cocky son of a bitch. "I'll check it out."

"Just give me the word," his minion insisted, teeth flashing. "I'm ready. We're ready. Whatever you want."

That was better. "Soon." They had a plan, but it might have to change if Julia Farentino became a serious problem. And his right-hand man was correct—things were spinning out of control. "You're not going rogue on me?"

"Never," the kid said, but there was an undertone to his words, and if one of those he trusted ever struck out on his own, started taking matters into his own hands . . .

"Trust me." Another flash of white and the kid took off, disappearing into the thick veil of snow. Was he lying? A master at deception? If not he, then who? *Some*one was definitely playing by his own rules.

The Leader just had to find out who was deceiving him.

There was restlessness in the night, the precursor to what was to come, what he would decide. He felt a thrill at the prospect, a sizzle in his bloodstream, but there were worries as well.

Like the snow spinning fast and wild as it fell, the winds of change were swirling, winds that he needed to control. Was his right-hand man correct? Did the problems begin and end with Julia Farentino, or did they run deeper?

Darker?

Was she more dangerous than he imagined? All of his fantasies about her and the Stillman girl, the two women who resembled each other, would have to be tamped down until he was certain about her.

Clutching the phone, welcoming the sharp slap of the wind on his face, he made his way across the snow-covered lawns, the blizzard nearly a whiteout, the lights on campus barely discernible until you were nearly upon them, but he had no trouble navigating, not here, not in the one place on earth he thought of as home.

At the breezeway, he stomped snow from his boots, though the concrete was already covered with snow and ice, carried by the raging wind. Even the long roof shuddered under the weight of the heavy accumulation.

Inside the admin building, he walked quickly down the hall, then slipped into his private office, a place where he wouldn't be disturbed, a spot he rarely used, as he had a much more private one.

Tonight, he was certain, he wouldn't be disturbed. Nonetheless, he locked the door behind him. He unzipped his jacket and pulled off his gloves, the interior feeling warm, though his thermostats were set in the low sixties for the night hours. He drew the shades quickly and hung his jacket on a coatrack, then got down to business at his desk.

He turned on Julia Farentino's phone. As the kid who'd

stolen the phone had said, the cell was already unlocked. He had free access to menus of text messages, lists of contacts and calls that had been received, sent, or missed. Then there was the contact list, which proved without a doubt that Julia Farentino was at the very least a fraud, at the worst an undercover cop, though he doubted that. He saw her as a lot of things, but a detective?

Unlikely.

He gleaned what he could from the slim device and stared at the glowing menu of names and numbers, making note of each. His teeth gnashed in frustration. How he would love to squeeze the life out of the damned cell! Or, better yet, her long, sensual neck. In his mind's eye, he envisioned confronting her. Or better yet, gaining her trust. Finding a way to isolate her from the rest, get her alone, flirt with her a bit. Toy with her emotions.

That part of seduction was easy.

He imagined pricking that part of her that found danger attractive and tapping in. Touching her cheek, catching her gaze, offering her the smallest of smiles as his eyes held hers. She'd get the message.

They would be somewhere secure, a place where she would feel safe letting down her guard.

Flipping the phone in his hands, he imagined the look of excitement in her gray eyes, the tease of her naughty smile as she realized he was dangerous, but, she would tell herself, only slightly.

That bit of false knowledge would be her undoing.

But he had no time for fantasies, not tonight. He studied the information on the phone.

Several names on the contact list caught his attention: Shay, for example. Not a common name but the same as the newest student, the one who resembled Julia. And then there was Analise. Again, not common, though neither were rare. Yet he wondered . . . Unfortunately, Julia hadn't added pictures of those she called into the phone's memory; her screen saver was of a gray cat, sitting on his haunches, batting at some unseen item with one paw.

He dialed each number. The first—for "Shay" with an area code he recognized as that of Seattle, where Shaylee Stillman lived—hadn't gone through. The storm again. He tried again, and this time, the call went to voice mail, with no instructions, just the flat voice of a prerecorded message from the cell phone company instructing him to leave his name and number.

He clicked off. Drummed his fingers on the desk. This wasn't good, not good at all.

He dialed the number for Analise. Again, no last name. But this time the call was picked up on the third ring.

"Hey, Jules," a woman greeted, obviously reading the caller ID. "Oh, good, I want . . . talk to . . . can't . . . hear . . . Jules? Oh, rats! Try . . . call again."

With dead certainty, he recognized the voice. So Julia "Jules" Farentino possibly knew both Shaylee Stillman and Analise Delaney. A contradiction. A niggle of fear slid through him. Heretofore, he had been certain there was no indication that she'd known anyone who'd ever attended Blue Rock Academy.

An outright lie?

Or an omission?

Lie? Omission? What did it matter?

No, not Analise Delaney. He corrected himself as he remembered that the pretty girl had married Eli Blackwood. Another mistake. He'd trusted Eli, though he had not entrusted him with too many secrets. Good thing, as the boy had failed him.

How did she know Analise and Eli Blackwood?

Scowling, he dialed the number marked as "home," with its Seattle area code, and heard her voice, though the connection was fading. "Hi! You . . . reached . . . Jules . . .

out right now . . . know . . . drill . . . leave . . . -sage and I'll call you back as . . ." The call was disconnected, but there was no mistake. He recognized her voice. Julia Farentino, who had sworn she lived in Portland, Oregon. Why would she have a Seattle exchange? Had she moved? Kept her service in Seattle, Washington, because it was easier? Friends and family knew the number?

There were lots of possibilities.

But it was just too much of a coincidence to think she'd been hired soon after Shaylee Stillman had become a student. . . .

And they resembled each other.

He took another chance and dialed the number marked "Mom."

The phone rang several times before it was answered by voice mail. "You've reached Edie. Sorry to have missed your call. Please leave . . ." And blah, blah, blah.

He didn't have Shaylee Stillman's file in front of him, but he remembered that her mother was Edith Stillman, the same woman whom Julia had tagged as "Mom."

So they were sisters?

He stared at the certificates on the walls of his study, an impressive and vast array of documents proclaiming him "excellent" or "exceptional," degrees that proved his natural intellect and ability to work hard against the disadvantages of his early years. And yet, sometimes he erred. His sharp, clinical mind could be clouded by lust, by envy, by greed, sins of the soul that he'd tried so hard to tamp down.

He leaned back in his chair so far that it squeaked in protest.

Why would she lie?

To get the job?

To be near her sister. No wonder he'd blended the two women in his mind, fantasized about both.

Or was she here for a darker purpose?

It didn't matter. The bottom line was that he couldn't take a chance with her. And her death was the only sensible answer. Confronting her, exposing her as a liar, might ensure that she was thrown out of the school. But intuition burned deep in his gut, telling him that there was more to her deception.

And he couldn't take any chances.

The phone jangled in his hand. Analise's number showed on the screen. He clicked on. Didn't say a word.

"Jules?" Analise's voice was clear this time, but he didn't respond. "Can you hear me? Oh, God, I hope so. Jules? *Jules!* Listen, Eli would probably kill me if he knew I told you this, but there is something going on at Blue Rock—can you hear me? Oh, God. I didn't want to tell you, didn't think you'd be in trouble or danger or, oh, God. Neither Eli nor I are sure of what it is, but there's some kind of secret club there. I know it sounds weird, but I feel they could be . . . I don't know, *dangerous* sounds so over the top, but that's what I feel . . . Jules? Are you there? I thought the place would be good for Shay, but I don't know. I love the school, believe it really helped me, but . . . you're right. Oh, darn, I should have warned you. Look, I'll try to call back. I hope you're doing okay, that you've got power. We're out here . . . Jules? Damn it all anyway!" She clicked off, and the Leader stared at the phone. All of his plans, all of his dreams, all of his ideals flashed like lightning through his mind.

So why was Jules here?

To spy? To get her sister, under court order, out of here? To expose him?

The Leader's heart went cold as stone. Lauren Conway's face shot through his mind, and he touched his pocket, reassuring himself that the small flash drive with its incriminating pictures and information was still safely tucked away. She, too, had thought she would expose him, and she'd found out the hard way that it was impossible to thwart God's will.

It had been the last time his followers had met him at the old church, a forgotten building going to ruin. Adjacent to a cemetery, tucked into the forest near the Blue Rock caves, the nearly dilapidated church had provided much-needed secrecy and had been a perfect, secure place to hold his meetings, to praise God, to gather and mold the minds of those most ready to serve the Lord, or so he'd thought.

But as he'd orated, he'd caught a glimpse of her face in the watery panes of a narrow window and had realized then that she'd been spying on him.

A traitor.

Just like the first woman he'd ever truly loved. That first one, she would soon see her mistake, would soon know as he rose in power what a fool she'd been, but Lauren had been another matter.

That night, he'd pretended that he hadn't caught a glimpse of her, that he hadn't known of her lies, but she'd found out. Before any real damage had been done.

Again, he touched the small lump in his pocket, reassured himself that the information was secure and reminded himself that he could trust no one. The flash drive was a silent, constant reminder.

He had to be vigilant. He bit on the corner of his lip. As the Lord's soldier, he needed to take care of any threat to his mission, to make this school the best in the country. He saw himself being elevated, lauded for his good deeds. Blue Rock would be the first of many like academies whose purpose was to aid the disenchanted youth, to turn them to Christ, to mold them into soldiers, an army for God. He thought of his mission much like the kings and emperors of Europe who had organized the Crusades to the Holy Lands, considered himself a warrior like King Richard I of England, the Lionheart.

Yes, blood had been spilled.

But it was necessary in the fight for God's word to be spread.

In his mind's eye, he saw himself in the house on the shores of Lake Washington, so much like a castle. Perfect. But he was getting ahead of himself. There was much to do here first, and his soldier was right—the storm provided perfect cover to get rid of the traitors who had infiltrated the academy.

For the time being, here in southern Oregon, travel was still impossible. Planes were grounded, trucks, cars, and buses stranded on the interstate, the local roads impassable. Drifting snow had closed the main gate to the school, and supplies were limited to what was held in the larders.

So far, the electricity was still operational. If and when a transformer blew or a utility pole snapped, there were generators in place, though power would be limited.

So he had to work fast.

Deal with traitors.

Julia Farentino was the first on his list.

Why was it that the women he always found the most fascinating turned out to be the most deadly?

The cell phone jangled in his hand, and he smiled as he clicked it on and lifted it to his ear. A frantic voice on the other end of the line hissed, "Jesus, Jules, what're you doing here? Doesn't it totally freak you out that students are dying here? I mean dying! As in dead! I . . . I thought you came down here to get me out of here—well, do it already. You have to! Whatever it takes, do it ASAP! Call Edie! Call Dad! Call the damned president! Just get me out! Oh, damn, I think someone's coming. . . ."

The line went dead.

He swore under his breath.

Things were worse than he'd thought. Belatedly, he realized that his right-hand man was right. He had to act swiftly. Vengefully.

There was no time for a meeting in the small church; it was too far away, would take away precious time from their purpose. But there was another place within the campus.

It was more dangerous to meet there, but he had no choice.

A gust of wind slammed against the building, shaking the timbers, rattling the windows.

The Leader took it as a sign from God.

Omen.

The note had said *Omen.*

And it had been.

Maeve knew what she had to do, where she had to go.

But she was afraid.

She snapped the band on her wrist, the sting calming the frantic part of her mind so that she could think straight. Had Ethan sent her the note? The romantic part of her had hoped so, had prayed that he still loved her. Desperation tore at her heart. She so wanted to believe that he, her soul mate, had realized that they were meant to be together.

Her dreams had shattered, though, after spotting him with Kaci. Flirting with her. Rubbing it in Maeve's face.

Maybe it was a test.

To see just how deep her love was, her adoration.

Didn't he know that she would do anything for him, even if it meant sacrificing herself?

Wasn't that the way love worked?

Maeve was no longer sure. She had gone to her group counseling session with Dean Williams and tried to participate, but the discussion about the strength of a woman in a relationship had cut too close to the bone tonight.

And even though she was supposed to go with her part-

ner back to the dorm, she'd ducked out. Her "security partner" hadn't cared. That's the way it was with Crystal; she
didn't really give a damn about anyone but herself.

Which worked out just fine, because Maeve didn't need
any prying eyes or questions.

She felt the knife tucked deep in her boot and smiled to
herself. If things didn't work out, there was always the
comfort of the sharp little blade, a special glinting solace in
seeing her own blood ooze in a perfect line against her skin.

Her hand was cold, getting numb, because she had to
push up her sleeve to snap the rubber band at her wrist. But
she could wait. She let the sleeve fall down now, knowing
there would be satisfaction.

Either Ethan.

Or the blade.

She only hoped that he would prove himself tonight, that
he would truly be Romeo to her Juliet. She remembered a
quote, dark, jeweled words that touched her as she walked
through the snow and thought of Ethan . . . perfect, handsome Ethan.

"These violent delights have violent ends. . . ."

CHAPTER 34

Run! Run! Run!
Jules ran through the thick drifts of snow.

She felt as if she was being chased, run to the ground, that someone *knew*.

"That's crazy," she whispered to herself, but couldn't help thinking Taggert or Takasumi or even Lynch might be on her trail.

Did she hear footsteps behind her?

Oh, God, please no!

She propelled herself even faster, her boots slipping, the handle of the carrier cutting through her gloves.

Skirting the pools of light cast by the security lamps, Jules, breathless, hauled the damned firewood carrier down the path as she raced toward Trent's cabin. Briefly, scared out of her mind, she considered ditching the carrier, but the pages were still too hot to tuck under her jacket and might fly away in the gusting, screaming wind.

So she took a chance, one hand curled in a death grip over the handle, the other stabilizing the top file so that she lost none of the precious, probably damning, pages.

What would they reveal?

What secrets did they hold that the director of the school had tried to destroy them?

Keep moving! Don't think about it.

At every corner, she tensed, certain someone would leap out from behind a snow-covered hedge or up from beneath a bench where a deranged killer lay in wait. Or she would be accosted by one of the teams of security guards roving the grounds.

Gun-shy after being confronted with Takasumi and Taggert, she was doubly careful as she threaded her way through the trees.

Even so, she still felt as if someone was watching her, following her. Biting her lip, not giving in to the fear, she kept running and prayed that the harsh curtain of snow falling steadily from the heavens would conceal her.

Crunch!

Oh, God, she was certain she heard footsteps.

She ran faster, plowing through the snow.

If she could just get to Trent.

She would be safe.

Right?

Crunch. Crunch.

Oh, dear God . . .

She flew by a thicket of pine trees and her heart raced ever faster as she thought about the murders. Why would anyone kill Nona and Drew?

Because of what they knew.

And maybe what you're carrying in these files might shed some light on the killer's motive. Keep running! For God's sake, keep running!

Her lungs burned, arctic cold searing her airways. What if the files told her nothing? What if Nona and Drew had been killed for revenge? It was possible. Drew could have thrown someone over to be with Nona. The jilted girlfriend, a troubled teen who had a history of violence, could have snapped. Or had Nona Vickers really pissed someone off? Had they both been targets, or had one gotten in the way of the other, been in the wrong place at the wrong time?

Nona's body had been obviously staged to gain attention. Drew's had been almost tossed aside. Except for that small, smeared bloodstain away from the pool from his head wound. Something about that tiny puddle, smeared as it was, bothered her.

Don't go there! Don't even think about it. Just run as you've never run before. Maybe the files will have the answer.

"Hey!" a deep male voice yelled.

Oh, no! She kept running.

"Jules! Slow down!"

She whirled, ready to swing the carrier at her attacker's face, only to spy Trent, hands buried deep in the pockets of his sheepskin jacket, collar turned up to the wind as he jogged through the blizzard to catch up to her.

"You scared the liver out of me!" she cried, relieved nonetheless to see his sharp features. "For the love of God, what were you thinking? I nearly clocked you with this!" She held up the wood carrier with its fragile contents. "You bastard, you've been following me!" She was instantly hot.

"Just keep walking. And don't yell, okay?"

"But I was scared to death."

"Good, you should be." He grabbed her by the arm and propelled her forward. His breath fogged in the night, and snow had collected on the shoulders of his jacket. The strands of hair that had escaped from beneath his hat were frozen, icy and white. "What the hell have you got?"

"Lynch's files. He was starting to burn them."

"What?" He glanced at her as if she'd gone mad. "So you, what, stole them?"

"Yep."

"Son of a bitch."

"I said he was burning them," she said as they trod through the heavy snow. "I figured I just saved him the trouble of disposing of them."

"He won't like it."

"Definitely not. I thought we were meeting at your place."

"We were," he agreed, his free hand digging in his pocket as he retrieved a small key chain. "But I didn't think it was smart to let you walk in the dark all by yourself, so I waited outside Stanton House, then saw you cut into the chapel after being accosted by Tweedledee and Tweedledum."

She smiled, thinking of Takasumi and Taggert.

"So I had to wait outside, damned near freezing to death, until I saw you sneak out the back. Here, let me take that." He grabbed the carrier with his free hand. His jaw was set stubbornly, his muscles tense as he surveyed the ice-crusted shrubbery flanking the buildings as if he expected the killer to leap out from the shadows at any second.

"What has the sheriff's department found out?"

"Nothing new."

"Damn." They rushed past the stables, and she thought of the murder scene, the hayloft and floor of the stable where Drew Prescott had lost his life and so much blood. Again, she flashed on the secondary stain, the smaller indication of blood. It bothered her, pulled at her conscience, and she felt there was something to it that she should understand, but the thought drifted away again. "What about the bloodstains?"

"Still working on them."

They were jogging together, slogging through the snow, bending their bodies against a wind so harsh it froze her skin. She glanced up, noting the tense lines of Trent's face, the unforgiving line of his jaw, and a long-forgotten memory flashed, a ridiculous recollection of warmth and love in this frigid February night.

Like tonight, they had been running through the woods, but it was summer and warm, sun dappling the dried grass under their feet, a startled rabbit leaping into the scrub oaks and pine. Trent had grabbed her hand then, strong fingers twining with hers as he'd pulled her toward a hidden spot near a river, where the water eddied into a clear pool and the branches of a willow formed a canopy over the banks. Dragonflies had snapped over the surface of the water while trout had flashed silver in the depths. An osprey had circled high overhead in a sky as blue as all of June.

They'd skinny-dipped in the water, splashing and laughing. Afterward, they made love on the banks while the sun baked the dry earth and cast shimmering sparkles over the water.

For a few precious months, she'd felt alive and in love and assured that the future was golden.

And then Rip Delaney's life had been cut short and everything had changed.

And now she was running for her life through a frigid winter, Trent's gloved hand urging her along a darkened path that had once been shoveled but now was thick with new snow. Her ears were frozen, her nose running as the blizzard just kept whistling through the mountains.

And, on top of everything else, a murderer was in their midst. A killer holed up here, beyond the reach of any arm of the law.

A far cry from that long-ago idyllic summer.

Trent hurried her along the edge of a building that held equipment, to the row of old, ramshackle cottages that were home to some of the teachers at the school.

Wade Taggert resided in one. Kirk Spurrier, when he was on campus, lived in another, and Salvatore DeMarco in a third. Bert Flannagan had his own quarters in a loft of the tack room near the stable. Charla King, too, had her own place while most of the other members of the staff lived in suites at Stanton House.

As snowflakes stung her face, she thought of those who had elected to become a part of Blue Rock Academy. Teachers, counselors, and administrators who had supposedly been recruited by Reverend Lynch for their leadership and scholarly capabilities.

Or for other unknown reasons?

Then there was the group of teachers' assistants, kids who had elected to stay on and be a part of the Blue Rock Academy college program, smart students who Shaylee was certain were part of some kind of dark, secret cult. Their faces flashed before her eyes. Missy Albright, Zach Bernsen, and Kaci Donahue, members of a deadly secret society? What about Eric Rolfe? Ethan Slade? Half a dozen others? Who among them possessed the qualities of a cold-blooded killer?

What about the students who were trapped here? Could one of them be the murderer, a sociopath? Every one of the students at the academy had psychological problems, some worse than others, some with streaks of violence.

Maybe the answer lay in the files she'd rescued from being incinerated. Maybe not.

Who?

Why?

She shuddered as Trent guided her along the back side of the houses, along what could loosely have been called an alley. Lights glowed in the windows of several homes. Others, unoccupied and in various states of disrepair, were dark, windows boarded over, snow and ice accumulating over rusted spouts and porches.

Trent's cottage was the last in the row, a single-level

bungalow that looked as if it had been constructed in the thirties or forties and was in serious need of renovation. The back steps were atilt, and the roof sagged in spots.

"Welcome to the Ritz," he muttered under his breath as he unlocked the door. Once they were inside, he threw the bolt behind them and snapped on a few lights. Even though the temperature inside the cabin couldn't have been much more than sixty-five degrees, the air felt warm, a distinct difference from the frigid outdoors.

"You okay?" he asked, and set the carrier on the short bench in the enclosed porch.

"Just great," she said sarcastically. "Couldn't be better. Cut off from the world in the worst snowstorm of the decade, maybe the century, and trapped with a homicidal maniac on the loose. Seriously, could things get any worse?"

"I'm here," he reminded her.

"My point exactly," she shot back, then caught his slow-spreading smile. "This has to be as bad as it gets."

"Is that right?"

"Absolutely!" She tossed him a don't-mess-with-me look. "So don't you dare think of yourself as some kind of Western-type hero, okay? You can peddle, but I'm definitely not buying."

He grinned, a devilish twinkle in his eye. "Aw, shucks, ma'am, and here I was givin' it my best damned shot."

"Not good enough, Cowboy." But she couldn't help smiling, some of the tension broken. He was right, she thought as they both kicked off their boots, leaving them under the bench on the porch; she felt safer with him, somehow sensing she could trust him—despite the fact that she'd sworn years ago to never see him again.

Fool. You knew better. Even when you married Sebastian. Inwardly cringing, she watched as Trent hung his hat on a peg, then peeled off his coat.

A pistol was tucked into the waistband of his jeans.

"Wait a second," she said. "You're carrying a gun?"

He hooked his jacket over a free peg. "I figured it might be a good idea."

"I guess, considering."

"Yeah. It's legal. Meeker and O'Donnell know. They're okay with it."

"And Lynch?"

He snorted. "Trust me, Jules, there are enough weapons locked in gun closets around this campus to arm a small country."

"Really?" she said. "So much for peace, love, dove."

"Not the motto of Blue Rock," he said. "Flannagan's team alone could take a stand at the Alamo."

"His 'team'?"

"Almost like special-ops, only no one ever says anything like that, of course. However, Flannagan's team could be construed as an elite force; you'll remember they were the first that Lynch asked to help tighten up security around here."

"I guess I didn't catch that," she said. "So they work as internal vigilantes?"

"Sometimes." He eyed her jacket. "You keeping that on?"

"For now, yeah." Though the temperature was warmer in the cottage, Jules was still cold to the bone, her toes tingling as they warmed deep in her socks.

"Let's see what I can do about that." He retrieved the carrier from the mudroom, and she followed him into the attached kitchen, little more than a nook with a sink, a tiny refrigerator, a two-burner stove, and a few cupboards that had seen better days. The floor was cracked linoleum and stopped at the edge of an archway that opened to the dining room and living area to be replaced by scuffed hardwood. He paused for a second at the thermostat and cranked it up.

"So who gets to play with guns?" she asked as he set down the carrier on the counter. She reached into the charred remnants of the files, the first of which had lost its tab. She flipped open the seared manila folder and saw the first document with the name *Slade, Ethan* visible in bold type.

"All the usual suspects are legal, have permits. You know, Eric Rolfe and Missy Albright, Ethan Slade, Zach Bernsen."

He drew the shades throughout the house, then went through the motions of making coffee, tossing old grounds into a trash can under the sink, then filling the pot with water.

"All TAs?"

"Nah. Mostly, though, I suppose." He paused as he measured coffee into a new filter. "I think Drew Prescott was being considered."

"Really?"

"Only Flannagan knows for sure."

She leaned against the short bank of cabinets. Ideas were gelling in her mind as she thought of everything she'd learned recently. "You know, Shay told me she thought that there was a secret cult among the TAs. That's what I wanted to talk to you about."

"Really? A secret cult that does what?"

"I don't know, but Shay thinks they might be tied to the murders of Nona and Drew."

His eyebrows knitted as he hit the ON switch, and the Mr. Coffee machine gurgled to life. "She's sure?"

"Sure enough to mention it to me."

"Far-fetched." He shook his head, but she could almost see the wheels turning in his mind, considering Shay's theory. He lifted the wood carrier and its charred contents, carrying it into the nearby dining area. "So let's see what you risked your life to retrieve. You know, Lynch is gonna be pissed as hell when he walks into his office tomorrow and sees that the ash has been disturbed. He's gonna know by the color, content, and amount of debris in the fireplace that something's up."

"And the carrier's gone. I'll worry about that later."

"Takasumi and Taggert saw you. There's gonna be hell to pay."

"I said later."

For once he didn't argue and led her through an archway that branched in two directions, one to bedrooms and a bath, the other to the living area where a square oak table surrounded by mismatched chairs occupied a space near the windows. Nearer to the front door, a faded love seat and beat-up leather recliner were grouped around a blue rock fireplace flanked with bookcases. Within the grate, a fire was banked, red embers visible through a thick layer of ash.

Trent kicked out a chair and placed the carrier on it, allowing Jules to sort through the charred remnants of Lynch's private documents.

"Cozy," she remarked as he double-checked that all the shades were drawn.

"That's one word to describe it." He almost smiled, relaxing a bit as he fiddled with the thermostat again while Jules willed the warmer air to heat the chill in the marrow of her bones. Slowly she started to thaw.

As Trent worked on the fire, Jules tackled the files. Her jacket was bulky, so she stripped it off and tossed it over the back of one of the dining chairs. Warm air was humming through the air vents, chasing away the cold.

She began working by separating out the pages that weren't totally destroyed, placing them in some kind of order. The files that were intact were easy. Other loose pages were singed and blackened, some falling to pieces when she touched them. That part of the job was tedious, those fragile pages taking much longer to sort.

"Find anything?" he asked, looking over his shoulder as he knelt at the fireplace.

"Don't know yet."

He tossed thick lengths of oak from a stack that filled a metal carrier, which was identical to the one she'd stolen from Lynch's office—apparently standard issue here at Blue Rock. The wood caught quickly, the fire beginning to pop and crackle against the mossy oak. Soon the smell of wood smoke mingled with the tantalizing aroma of hot coffee.

Trent brought her a steaming mug as she sorted the pages, but she was suddenly not interested in the coffee, not when she was starting to see a pattern emerge.

At first she wasn't certain.

Surely not . . .

But as she worked, she became more and more certain she was right, and if she was, then evil truly reigned at Blue Rock Academy.

All of the Leader's worst fears were confirmed.

He stood in the shadows outside Cooper Trent's cabin and knew that he and Julia Farentino were inside. He'd caught them together, Trent chasing her down, Julia running as she carried what looked like a heavy basket. Only metal. It had glinted a bit, catching in the light of a lamp-post she'd tried to avoid. But he'd seen it, that little metallic flash.

What was it?

And why was she carrying it to Trent's bungalow?

Whatever was going on, it wasn't good. Wasn't planned.

Worry tangled his insides.

The Leader had observed the way Trent had taken the crook of her elbow in a proprietorial fashion, shepherding her toward his cottage. He'd noticed how they huddled close, as if they'd known each other a long time, even though she'd been at the academy only a few days.

But Trent had called her cell phone, had her private number.

The Leader had listened to his message.

It had been curt and professional, just a quick, "This is Cooper Trent, Ms. Farentino. Would you please call me as soon as possible?" Trent had left his number, as if Julia didn't already have it in her memory, and certainly it wasn't an entry on the contact list of her cell.

The message had bothered the Leader, like an itch under his skin that he couldn't quite scratch. He'd told himself not to think too much about it. He had bigger things to worry about.

Now, of course, he'd changed his mind.

From his hiding spot in a copse of redwood and madrone, he observed the snug little cottage. There hadn't been much to witness, just Trent squinting into the darkness as he'd drawn the shades and the smell of wood smoke from a fire. Lights glowed from within. Shadows played upon the shades, fuzzy silhouettes that moved but offered him little in the way of knowing what was going on within the walls of the cabin.

Whatever it was, he had to stop it.

Tonight.

CHAPTER 35

Jules couldn't believe her eyes.

Was it possible?

Was Reverend Lynch—a man of God who always portrayed himself to be the benevolent guardian of troubled youth, a paragon of faith—a fraud? Worse than that, could he really be a twisted, cruel madman, a duplicitous pious Dr. Jekyll and Mr. Hyde?

What was it his wife had said the night that Jules had listened at the preacher's door?

You seem to gain some perverse pleasure in persecuting and torturing me.

Now Jules understood.

Insides quivering, she scanned the burned pages quickly, gently swiping away ash, reading what she could, stacking the information in piles. Despite the papers singed in the fire, there were enough legible documents to paint a sick, almost diabolical picture of Blue Rock Academy.

"This is a little scary," she whispered to Trent, who was tossing another log onto the fire as she looked at a file that proved even more disturbing. "I think I'm beginning to understand what's going on around here."

He stood and dusted his hands, the fire burning even brighter. "So show me what you've got, Nancy Drew."

"Very funny."

"I know, but humor me." He stood behind her, reading over her shoulder.

She reached for her coffee, and cradling the mug in her fingers, she said, "You're not going to like it."

"I figured that much."

She took a sip, turning her attention to the information in front of her, and summed up what she'd found. "From what I can decipher, Lynch kept a file for each student and teacher, separate from the administrative files Charla King locks away in a file cabinet in her office at the admin building." She motioned to the blackened documents in front of her. "These files, or dossiers or whatever you want to call them, are separate and hold very different information such as personal material, arrest records, and psychological data that's been collected on the kids. These"—she tapped a finger on a blackened page with the name *Bernsen, Zachary* typed across the top—"are not your standard personnel files. That's why they were locked away."

He was listening, his brow furrowed as he scanned the documents. "There's no crime in keeping a second set of more detailed files."

She nodded, ignoring a gust of wind that rattled the windows and caused the fire to dance. "No crime in that, right, but here's the kicker: These files contain information deliberately excluded from Charla King's computerized files. For example, if you look here"—she indicated a few pages that, aside from singed corners, were intact—"we have a psychological profile for Eric Rolfe. Right?"

"Yeah?"

"Here are his test scores and grades, all neatly computerized and printed out. There's even some sketchy information about his family and a quick assessment of his social problems."

Trent nodded, eyes dark, as he studied the printout.

Jules said, "I'll bet this is what shows up in Charla King's files, what the parents or prospective colleges or doctors or lawyers see."

He took a sip of coffee. "So?"

"It doesn't even scratch the surface." She felt that buzz of adrenaline zinging through her veins, nervous energy that came with discovery. "Look here." She flipped open another page, written in Lynch's handwriting. "This is a different report. Not even typed, and it goes into much more detail. Rolfe's psyche is dissected and studied."

He shrugged. "Again, not illegal. Looks normal to me."

"Except that it was kept from the main files. What if . . . what if Lynch was taking those kids with the raw proclivity for violence, you know, picking them and culling them out, for something other than to help them."

"What?" He eyed her as if she were sprouting a third eye. "Why?"

"Because no one else will take them," she said. "Because this would keep them out of institutions or psych wards in hospitals and because their parents will pay him well to take them off their hands."

"I don't follow."

"Okay, let's start with Eric," she said, pushing Rolfe's file to one side of the table. "He's a good one to think about, because he's so antisocial, his feelings right out in the open."

"For which he's being counseled," Trent argued, but scooted out a chair and straddled it as he gently lifted the pages and read the notes, Lynch's personal profile on Rolfe, showing how Lynch regarded the boy as a sociopath. Even as a child, Eric Rolfe's pattern of behavior was noticed. He'd wet the bed until junior high, his older brother noted for making fun of him publicly. At a very young age, he'd been caught harming small animals for the pure enjoyment of it, and when in school he'd bullied and fought with younger, weaker kids as a thrill and had been kicked out of half a dozen schools. Eventually he'd beaten up a classmate so severely the boy had to be hospitalized.

There was even a charge of rape in Rolfe's file, though that case had been dismissed. Somehow, though, Lynch had gotten his hands on a picture of the victim, a girl of thirteen who had changed her mind about who had attacked her on that dark playground. DNA evidence had somehow been compromised. The case never got before a judge.

"A real charmer," Trent said, his coffee long forgotten, his eyes dark with a quiet rage.

"And supposedly, from his test scores, brilliant."

"Who cares? He could be as smart as Einstein, but he's still a sociopath."

"Right." Jules, too, was stone-cold sober. "You see this red tape on the inside of the file?" Carefully, so as not to have the charred pages crumble, she spread open the information on Missy Albright and Roberto Ortega. "These have the same strip of tape and similar observations. There might be other files as well, but these are the only ones whose covers weren't burned, the information the most complete."

As Trent compared the files, the corners of his mouth twisting downward, Jules added, "These two, Missy and Roberto, are like Eric and some of the others. They, too, have a long history of violence, and because of it, I think, they got special attention from the reverend, lots of notes in Lynch's handwriting. He was fascinated by them." She pushed some of the pages toward Trent, then indicated the detailed, handwritten notes in each of the files. "The common theme is that these kids are smart, but very, very disturbed. At a deep, core level. They've got uncontrollable rage, just beneath the surface. They're cruel without any morsel of empathy."

Jules met Trent's dark gaze. "They're sociopaths, a danger to society. To themselves." She lifted her fingers one by one as she listed several symptoms of a sociopath. "They're charming, even glib; they show no remorse; they think the world revolves around them; they lack empathy; they live on the edge; and they don't give a damn about others." Letting out a deep breath, she added, "They can't be redeemed, but that's not what Lynch is about. I'm just not sure if he's brought them here for the money, or if there's some other motive. Maybe he thinks he can harness their evil somehow? I don't know."

"Jesus," Trent whispered. "Most of them are as smart as whips, off the charts. That's how they ended up here in the first place."

"But they're not all cruel. That's why the weaker ones become victims." She felt sick inside, horrified at her discovery, but she was certain she was right.

"Nona Vickers and Drew Prescott? What about them?" he asked, absently scratching at his jaw. "You think there's a group of kids that Lynch culled out because they're sociopaths, and somehow Drew and Nona got caught in the cross fire? Or became targets?"

"I don't know," she admitted, her darkest fears congealing. "But I think that it's worse than that. I think that this group of sociopaths, put together, with so many of them having such a broad history of violence, they could very well be identified as homicidal."

"You think they would kill willingly?"

"Some of them even eagerly." She had to get up, walk from one end of the room to the other to release some of the tension deep inside.

"Lynch knowingly brought a group of them together. Psychopaths."

Just the sound of the word, spoken aloud, seemed to echo through the room. Suddenly cold again, she walked to the fire and warmed the back of her legs, all the while trying to make sense of what she'd discovered. "What if no one else had identified them? What if Lynch was the only one who had?"

"So why bring them all together?" he asked.

"Worse yet, why arm them? You said some of those kids had access to weapons, permits to carry guns."

His face drained of all color. "An army?"

"I don't know. But you mentioned Flannagan had an 'elite' fighting force almost like special-ops. These are the kids who are guarding us—you know, the group that leads other students. How nuts is that?" She was really thinking hard. It was too bizarre, too far beyond the bounds of reason to think that Lynch would seek out rich psychopaths, give them weapons—all for what? Then again, who knew if he was sane.

"What about Lauren Conway?" he asked as the lights flickered, throwing the room into darkness for a second, the fire their only source of light.

"God, I hope we don't lose power," she said.

"We'd better be prepared." He had already scooted his chair back and was rummaging in a sideboard drawer for a lighter. "How do you think Lauren fits into all of this?"

"I don't know, but it can't be good; otherwise, she would have surfaced and called her folks, or someone she knew, at the very least a girlfriend."

"No one's seen or heard from her since she went missing." He lit the kerosene lanterns.

"I know." Sighing, Jules glanced over the files spread upon the table, none of which were identified by Lauren's name. Had there ever been a file? Or had it been destroyed in the fire, or earlier when she disappeared? "I hate to say it, but I think Lauren's probably already dead. Either she got caught up in something she couldn't have gotten out of, or she died while trying to make her escape, or something. I think if there had been an accident, say, she was lost in the woods or hurt on campus somewhere, her body would have been found."

"I think so, too," he admitted as the lights winked again. He placed one of the lanterns on the table and sat in his chair again. "But, from my understanding, she wasn't weak, wouldn't have been an easy victim. She was tough, smart, athletic." His eyes narrowed as if he were exploring the possibilities. "Do you think that she knew too much? Maybe she stumbled on what was happening here?" He picked up Missy Albright's file. "Missy was one of the TAs who was supposed to take Lauren under her wing, show her the ropes. If you're right about all this—"

"I am." Jules felt it. She finally got what was happening here at Blue Rock as the lantern glowed brightly.

"Then she probably is dead." His scowl was deep, the lines in his face deep furrows as he studied the charred notes strewn upon the table.

She said, "Some of these files are not tagged with red tape. For example, two kids from your pod, Chaz and Maeve, their folders aren't marked that way."

"Great. So we've got two normal but 'disturbed' kids, is that what you're saying?"

"There are probably more. A lot more. But either Lynch didn't bother creating files on them, or they burned. I didn't find a file for Shay or Ollie Gage or Crystal Ricci, to name just a few." For that much she was relieved.

"Okay, I'll play along with this. I've got nothing better. But unless he's planning a military coup—of what, Medford? Oregon?—why would Lynch want all these kids here? To observe them? To try and mold them? What?" he asked, picking up file after file. "And why promote them to teachers' aides?" He turned to Roberto Ortega's file. "It just doesn't make any sense."

"Sure it does," she said, the implications of what she was thinking causing her stomach to sour. "When you cross-reference the psychological information with these," she said, handing him several singed pages.

"What're those?"

"Financial forms."

He'd chosen Eric Rolfe's parents' financial report and studied the asset statement. He let out a long, low whistle, which was magnified by the moan of the wind.

"I know. I was surprised, too. Eric's father is a multimillionaire, a German industrialist. And he's not alone. Take a look." She handed him Missy Albright's family's financial records. "Missy just happens to be the firstborn daughter of a socialite shipping heiress and her third husband. Sick as it sounds," she said, pointing out the obvious, "it seems that most of the TAs have parents with a lot of money."

"And social connections," he thought aloud, eyeing Roberto Ortega's file. The Ortega name was synonymous with a chain of fast-food restaurants stretching from El Paso, Texas, to Seattle, Washington.

"Lynch would never want anyone to make these connections, at least not easily. I'm sure the authorities would be able to put it all together, just like Lynch did, but it would be a helluva lot more difficult with these files destroyed."

"And he wouldn't want his private notes about the students' mental conditions made public."

Jules rubbed the back of her neck, trying to work out the knots of tension that had developed as she'd pored over files that had survived the fire. "It makes sense for the parents in a perverse way. Enrolling the problem kids here at Blue Rock into the college programs would be a way to keep them out of trouble and jail."

"And their names out of the papers. Less media attention, less scandal," he said.

"It's a win-win situation. The parents believe their twisted little darlings are safe and"—she made air quotes with her fingers—"'getting help.' Their kids can graduate from college and appear 'normal.'"

"Sick, that's what it is."

Jules agreed. But there was still a lot to learn. All of the puzzle pieces weren't dropping neatly into place; there were lots of holes she couldn't quite fill. "I'm just wondering if these 'red-taped' kids are placed in that elite force you told me about, the one run by Bert Flannagan."

He considered. "It's possible, I suppose. Hell, after what you've shown me, anything is."

She was already thinking hard. "It only gets worse, I think."

"How could it possibly get any worse?"

"I already told you that Shay suspects there's a secret cult on campus. What if it's not just TAs? What if members of the staff are involved? Probably Lynch. Maybe others."

"Wait a second." He tossed her a look that accused her of finally going around the bend.

"Just hear me out. I know it sounds really out there, kinda insane, but think about it. The cult would need a leader."

"Come on, Jules. These are qualified educators with degrees and awards and years of experience. Just because you might not like any of them doesn't mean they're criminals."

She felt as if the weight of the world had settled on her shoulders, but she was certain she was on the right track. "Hey. I'm not making this up. Look for yourself." She scooted another slim stack of blackened pages his way and pointed to the top file, where the name *Flannagan, Bert* was visible. Near his name was a piece of singed red tape. "Some of the faculty files are marked, too."

"You're right. It's worse." He shoved his chair back and stood. "Lynch sure knows how to pick 'em."

"That he does." She reached over the table for a stack of files, suddenly conscious of her arm brushing his, the rising heat in the room, the clean smell coming off his skin, a mixture of soap and sweat. "I'd be willing to bet my cat's nine lives that they were recruited for just that purpose."

"Then he's as sick as the rest of 'em."

"Sicker," she said, "if that's possible."

"A mighty fortress is our God, a bulwark never failing . . ."

Maeve's voice was the barest of whispers as she sang a song from her youth group and trod steadily through the snow. It seemed as if she'd been walking for hours, but the truth of the matter was she'd chosen to plod along at a slow pace. She had to be wary. Already she'd dealt with Mr. Taggert, convincing him and Tim Takasumi that she was returning to her room, when, really, once they were out of sight, she'd left the dorm again.

Did they really think they could stop her? No one could stop love.

She knew that Ethan would have trouble getting away. He was on security detail, so she'd had to kill time, walking in the snow, thinking about what she'd say to him, how she'd confront him, how she'd make him love her again.

He does, he does, he does love you. You just have to show him, prove it.

Now she was at the stable, and she let herself into the building that smelled of horses and hay. This hadn't been her choice. Why would she want to meet where Nona and Drew had been killed? Or maybe it was fate to be here, where they had made love for the last time.

There was something romantic about that, right?

It wasn't creepy or weird.

Dimmed security lights gave off an eerie blue glow, illuminating the aisle between the stalls like runway lights. It was warmer inside, but darker without the snow's white reflection. Rakes, harnesses, brushes, brooms, buckets, and feed bags became dark figures, fuzzy in the umbra of the unlit corners. She saw embodiments of evil in the shadows. The bit of a bridle reflecting the blue light, the tines of a pitchfork glinting evilly as Lucifer's weapon.

For a second, she thought she heard the mocking refrain of "A Mighty Fortress" in the creak of the floorboards overhead, from a chorus of lost souls who had died before her.

"The Prince of Darkness grim, we tremble not for him. His rage we can endure, for lo, his doom is sure. . . ."

She ran the words in her head, driving the evil out, pushing the bad things from her mind. She'd always liked that line about the Prince of Darkness, imagining herself plunging a sword into a black-caped demon. Yeah, that would be tight.

Then the rafters creaked overhead, and her resolve faded. The music in her head died, and she felt her skin crawl. Maybe this was a bad idea, coming to the place where two people had died.

She snapped the band on her wrist and moved forward, slowly, half-expecting the snarling ghosts of Nona and Drew to leap out at her. Nona, without clothes, her head perched at an impossible angle upon her long neck, and Drew, naked and wide-eyed, blood dripping from his head wound, could appear at any instant.

Maeve's heart grew still.

Stop freaking yourself out! You're here to meet Ethan, your Romeo! There are no ghosts. No ghouls. No one here to do you harm. Only Ethan if you're lucky.

She kept tugging and releasing the rubber band at her wrist as she forced herself to get a grip, to pull herself together.

The horses were as restless and edgy as she was, as if they, too, sensed a lurking presence of evil. They shuffled nervously in their stalls, snorting and pawing. Tails switching, hooves clomping, they neighed and refused to quiet.

Maeve swallowed back her fear and found comfort in the knife hidden within her boot, its razor-sharp blade touching her ankle, teasing the skin beneath her sock. She felt a bit better knowing she could retrieve it in a second.

Knives.

Scissors.

Razors.

Hated, beloved friends.

It's all right. It's all right. Just be patient. Ethan will come. He has to.

And yet, the moan of the wind brought goose bumps to the back of her neck, a crinkle to her scalp.

From the corner of her eye, she caught a glimpse of movement over by Scout's box.

She froze.

Ethan?

Was he playing games with her?

Again, a shadow darted near the feed bins.

Was it Ethan, come to meet her? Or someone else, someone who had stalked her, Nona's murderer come back to haunt the scene of the crime?

Dear God.

Her heart beat as wildly as the wings of a thousand frightened bats.

Her throat closed, and she slowly bent down, intent on retrieving the hunting knife.

But now there was no movement at the feed bins. No homicidal maniac.

And really, maybe one of the freakin' horses moved.

Oh, get over it. There's nothing evil here! No Satan with his pitchfork. No ghosts of schoolmates past.

Arizona, the gray mare, snorted as Maeve passed. She nickered softly, obviously wanting attention, but Maeve didn't have time. Now that she was here, she was on a mission, had to keep moving. She ignored Plato, the dun gelding who observed her suspiciously from the back of his stall, and Scout, the paint with the white face and eerie pale eyes. A gust of wind pounded the building, rattling the panes in the windows and howling eerily from the hayloft high above.

The spot where Nona's nude body had hung, twisting in the winter wind.

Again, Maeve swallowed back her fear. She was here to see Ethan. Meet him. Vow her love.

Finally, she reached Omen's stall. The big black horse was inside, standing toward the back, the muscles of his sleek coat seeming to quiver.

"It's okay, boy," she said, but was unable to convince herself as the hymn replayed in her mind. *The body they may kill, God's love abideth still . . .*

This was the place Ethan meant; she was sure of it.

The note she'd received, tucked in her math book during the class where Ethan was a TA, had been only one word: *OMEN.*

She turned to Omen, who snorted suspiciously. "He'll be here," she whispered to the pitch-black gelding. "I know it."

In the past, they'd met here when Ethan got off duty, around eleven. This had to be right.

She reached for the latch of the stall and opened the gate.

She'd hide inside with the big black horse standing guard.

Ethan would find her.

He would.

CHAPTER 36

A cult?

Jules was trying to sell him on some secret society led by one of the teachers or even Reverend Lynch himself, but Trent was still a little skeptical. Her reasoning was sound, to a point. Why, he wondered, would Lynch need a cult when he already ruled this tiny little enclave?

Trent thought of the grisly scene he'd witnessed in the stable. Could it be part of some kind of initiation? A macabre sacrificial rite?

If so, the sheriff's department would be stunned. They were working on the premise of a lone killer, someone psychotic enough within the school to pull off the double homicide, someone with a history of violence. Detectives Baines and Jalinsky were doing background checks on the students and faculty; however, considering the type of student Blue Rock attracted, the investigations had hit on dozens of juvenile arrest records. The suspect list in the sheriff's investigation was not narrowing yet.

And he knew that Jules wouldn't want to hear who was at the top of that list.

Guilt gnawed at him as he watched her go through the

motions of trying to prove her theory—and Shaylee Stillman's—that the murders of Drew Prescott and Nona Vickers were part of some elaborate plot devised by a fanatical cult. That the murders and the cult were somehow linked to Lauren Conway's disappearance.

But Trent listened to Jules's theory. To her credit, she was putting together a pretty good case as they sat at the old oak table in his quarters. As much as he had doubted her, Trent saw where Jules was going with her theory of what was happening at the academy.

He'd pushed his chair next to hers to read over her shoulder, glad for an excuse to be close. As the fire burned in the grate, they went over the information together.

Jules had sorted the faculty records into stacks on the table. Most of the information was standard: résumés and references, awards and degrees. But the handwritten notes in the red-taped files, they were disturbing. As with the student files, it was the personal notes in files marked with red tape that gnawed at him, pricking that instinct that something wasn't right.

From a partly singed paper, he learned that Salvatore DeMarco, while an accomplished math teacher, was also an ex-Marine who had been thrown out of the corps for fights that sent him to the brig and his combatants to the hospital with knife wounds. After the Marines, he'd served six months in jail for beating a woman who'd cut him off in traffic.

"Lynch notes that DeMarco has anger-management issues," he said. "That's putting it lightly."

"Scary stuff, huh?" Jules said, biting her lower lip in that manner he found so distracting. It made him think of nuzzling her lips with his teeth. . . .

He placed a hand at the back of her neck and felt her tense until he rubbed the exposed skin gently. "Yeah, it's real scary." He turned back to the files, trying to understand where all of this was going. Why would Lynch hire anyone he considered remotely unstable or volatile to deal with at-risk kids? What was his purpose?

Kirk Spurrier's folder had been destroyed, except for the bottom notes on a couple of pages. Trent was able to make out part of his résumé, where he'd listed that he'd been a pilot in the Air Force and was adept with weaponry. On the other partially legible page, Lynch had noted that Spurrier was sometimes passive-aggressive.

"Passive-aggressive. Isn't that what we do to keep from lashing out at people the way DeMarco does?" he said as Jules pushed her chair back and walked to the kitchen.

"Sometimes," she agreed. "But there are extremes."

Jordan Ayres's file was intact, and the only comment by Lynch was that he considered her extremely capable but felt she was someone who had authority issues. Trent read "bossy" between the lines.

Jules returned with what was left of the coffee. She re-filled each of their cups from the glass pot, then carried it back to the kitchen.

As she did, the lights blinked again. Hell. The last thing they needed was to lose power. He watched the incandes-cent bulb in the fixture over the table begin to glow again.

"Looks like we're on borrowed time with the electric-ity."

"There are backup generators, aren't there?" she asked, the empty pot still in her hand as she stood at the archway to the kitchen.

"Yeah, but they won't help here. The generators have enough juice to power up the dorms, education hall, chapel, rec hall, and some of the outbuildings like the stable, but that's it. Stanton House will have power; I won't. None of these cabins will. So we'd better get ready." He pushed back his chair and set to work stacking wood near the fire-place, enough for the night. He also lit three candles in glass jars to give light where kerosene lanterns might fail. Inside the small closet off the hall, he found a couple of flashlights and flipped them on to make sure the batteries were strong. Both lights fired up with steady beams. "We might freeze," he said, "but we sure as hell will be able to see."

"How comforting." Jules stretched, placing her hands over her head and arching her back as she moved her head from side to side.

Her breasts were thrust forward, the hollow of her throat revealed, and he had to drag his eyes away, force his concentration to the remnants of the documents on the table. Did she have any idea how sexy she appeared, her dark hair cascading down her back, her eyes closed as her lean runner's body stretched?

The woman had to realize what she was doing.

With an effort, he tore his eyes from her, turning back to what was left of Rhonda Hammersley's file. No red tape here. This woman seemed on the level—solid, conscientious, religious. Lynch's only note was that she internalized too many problems and was an overachiever, which Trent found odd. Wasn't that what Lynch wanted? Wasn't it what he preached to the kids?

So why the notes about the violent tendencies of the other staff members? Why hire these ticking time bombs? True, Lynch needed strong, tough teachers. Leaders, not psychos.

Bert Flannagan's dossier noted that he'd been dismissed from several colleges and had an attraction for weaponry. After his stint in the U.S. Army, he'd been denied two jobs in law enforcement. The word *mercenary* was written with a question mark beside it.

Wade Taggert's file was almost completely burned; just one note suggesting he had delusions of grandeur could be deciphered when Trent held a magnifying glass and flashlight close to the browned page.

"Here's a really scary one," Jules said, pushing some nearly illegible pages toward him. Trent read his own file and saw that Lynch had noted that Trent had once been employed by the Pinewood County Sheriff's Department, was an ace marksman, and was licensed to carry a gun. All true.

"Funny woman."

"Just trying to keep things light."

"It's nice to know that you're not only an idiot for sneaking around Lynch's office all by yourself, but also a comedienne."

"We got the information, didn't we?"

"You should have told me. I would have come with you."

"You would have tried to talk me out of it," she said, her eyebrows rising, daring him to argue.

"Probably."

"So don't go calling me an idiot."

"How about bullheaded?"

"Maybe."

He leveled his gaze at her as she held her coffee cup in two hands and placed her lips over the rim. "From now on, you don't go anywhere without me."

"Don't go all macho on me, Trent."

"I'm serious."

"I know, but think about it. Don't you have security duty? I do. With Hammersley and DeMarco."

"I don't trust him. DeMarco."

She let out a nervous laugh and shook her head. "Me neither, Cowboy. But for the record," she said, pointing to the burned pages, "I don't trust anyone."

"Except for me."

"You?" she said in mock horror, glints of light in her

gray eyes. "No way. The not-trusting thing, it goes double for you!"

Maeve was tired of waiting.

She was freezing in the stall, and Omen, the big black gelding, wasn't happy that she was there. He'd even pissed near her, the smell so acrid and disgusting she was about to retch.

She tried to hang on to her sense of hope. Ethan would be here any minute, as soon as he was off patrol. Then the wait would be worth it.

But right now, hugging the manger in a huge animal's smelly stall, freezing her butt off, didn't seem like such a great idea.

She checked her watch, the illuminated dial showing that she'd been waiting only twenty minutes.

Give him time. He'll be here!

Still she was jumpy, her nerves on edge and that stupid hymn running in circles through her mind. She tried thinking of something newer, a song by Fergie coming to mind, but always, no matter what, the refrain of "A Mighty Fortress" came back to haunt her.

She wiggled her toes in her boots, hoping to get the blood flowing, as her toes were beginning to turn to ice. Maybe she should get up and walk around. She'd been afraid to move, because she'd thought she'd seen the bogeyman in the shadows, Nona and Drew's killer hiding between the bags of oats and bales of hay.

Which was ridiculous.

No bloodthirsty maniac had jumped out at her.

She wasn't in a *Scream* movie, for God's sake.

She slid up along the wall to a standing position and plucked the straw from her jacket, hoping none of it had been fouled by the horse. Wouldn't that be great? When Ethan finally got here, she'd smell like horse pee.

Giving the big black animal a wide berth, she eased her way to the gate. Over the sound of the rustling straw, she heard something else. Footsteps? Or one of the horses shuffling in his stall?

Don't freak yourself out! Come on, Maeve, you've been down this road before. You're alone.

Still . . . Didn't she feel a hidden set of eyes watching her, squinting at her through the gloom of the stall?

Cut it out! No! There's no one. Got it?

But she stopped. Squinted into the darkness, held her breath and listened. Hard.

Did she hear footsteps near the door? She swung her head in that direction. The hairs on the back of her neck stood straight on end.

"Ethan?" she whispered nervously.

Click!

A flame shot up in front of her eyes.

Gold, with a blue base, the flame from a barbecue lighter nearly singed her nose.

Maeve screamed, jumping back.

The horse snorted nervously. Hot breath streamed down her back.

"Ethan, this isn't fun—"

But the cruel, gleeful eyes behind the flame didn't belong to Ethan Slade.

Maeve whispered, "Oh, God. What the hell are you doing here?" Her heart beating like a drum, panic shot through her.

"Guess." A hiss.

Oh, Jesus. Fear curdled Maeve's insides. She scrambled for the latch to the stall, fingers scraping the smooth wood, but the gate was jammed tight.

At that second, the lighter swept in a shimmering arc to the floor.

Whoosh!

Straw, strewn across the box stall and into the aisle, ignited. Crackling, bursting into a string of growing flames, the dry grass was quick tinder.

"What the hell are you doing?" Maeve squealed. She was stomping on the crawling, horrid flames like crazy, pulling wildly at the gate, trying to get out. "Are you freakin' crazy? This place will go up in a flash!" She wrestled with the latch, but the gate was held tight by strong, determined fingers. "Stop this! Let me out!"

Flames sizzled.

The horse behind her went berserk. Screaming shrilly, Omen reared up, his front legs slicing the air, his eyes white, rimmed with fear.

Maeve slammed her body against the wall of the box. Scout, the paint, was going nuts on the other side of the stall. *Bam!* He kicked the stall and whinnied.

"Are you a lunatic?!" she cried, cowering away from the horse, then flinging herself to the rails and trying to climb over. Smoke was growing thick in the air. She would leap on her attacker if she had to.

Surely someone would come! Someone had to hear all this commotion!

But the whistle of the wind outside drowned the frantic noises from within.

"Get back!" Maeve tried to climb out.

Her attacker swung the lighter.

Flames brushed over her face, a whisper of heat searing her scalp. She shrieked. Wavering flames took hold in the bits of yarn of her stocking cap, racing through her hair.

"What are you doing?" Maeve screeched, pain searing her scalp as she dug at the cap, ripping it from her head and screaming. She fell back into the stall, landing hard, flames burning in front of her face, the big horse kicking and rearing in terror.

Why was this happening?

Why, why, oh, God, why?

She forced herself to her feet, choking, the damned horse shrieking.

"Are you crazy?" she yelled, climbing the rails again. "Let me the fuck out of here, you freak!" Fear pounded through her skull.

"Don't ever call me a freak!" Maeve's tormentor's face twisted cruelly.

Omen reared again, his nostrils wide, his black coat a sheen of nervous sweat.

Maeve cowered.

Steel-shod hooves slashed through the air. Close. So damned close! Smoke swirled and rose. Deadly flames crackled like Satan's laugh.

Freaked and desperate, Maeve tried vainly to escape. She pushed and pounded on the gate, shoving into it, but the latch wouldn't budge an inch. She climbed but was pushed back into the maniac horse's box. "Oof!" She landed hard and scrambled away from the horse and the flames.

Crying from the smoke, choking, heat tingled up her legs as the hem of her pants caught fire.

"No! No! Let me out! Help! HEEELLLP! Oh, God, please, don't do this!" Maeve begged on her hands and knees. She pulled herself up again.

Behind her, Omen shrieked wildly. Kicking. Trapped.

"Oh, God . . . Oh, God!"

Omen reared again.

From the corner of her eye, Maeve caught a glimpse of a horseshoe reflecting the fire's shimmering light. "No!"

She lunged to one side.

Too late.

Bam!

A steel-shod hoof crashed into her back.

Crrraaack!

Bone splintered. Beneath her jacket, skin ripped away from flesh.

Pain, hot as fire, tore down her spine.

Maeve howled and tried again to thrust herself over the gate. She surged forward, but her legs gave way, crumpling beneath her. Her arms clung to the gate as flames crawled over her, engulfed her. "Help me," she begged, her throat raw, tears streaming down her face. "Please, please . . . Oh, God!"

But her tormentor only smiled.

The panicked horse ran in circles, trying to escape. He lunged forward, another hoof grazing her shoulder.

The pain . . . It was all too much. Her world started to go black.

Maeve slid down the gate, her weight dragging her into the flames. Sheer terror streaked through her. "You've got to help me, please!" But her voice was just a dry whisper.

"Why not?"

What? Her attacker had experienced a change of heart?

The latch clicked and the gate opened.

Maeve dropped like a stone to the floor. Maybe now, oh, God, please, she was going to be helped.

Omen shrieked again.

He bolted for the open gate.

She braced herself.

Omen soared, trying to leap over Maeve. His body scraped one side of the stall.

Bam! A heavy, deadly hoof caught her head.

Maeve hit the floor. Pain exploded behind her eyes. For a second, everything went black, only to come back in clear, sharp focus.

Instinctively, she tried to get up.

Nothing happened.

Her legs wouldn't move, not an inch.

Paralyzed? She was paralyzed?

No, oh . . . no . . .

She tried to turn to see her tormentor, but couldn't; the smoke was too thick. She felt herself being lifted by her shoulders. A moan tore from her throat. It felt as if she were being ripped in two.

"Call someone," she said, her mind fuzzy. Was her attacker really trying to save her? "An ambulance . . ."

"Shut up!" The voice was guttural, feral, as she was dragged past the stalls of frightened, terrorized horses.

Through pain-glazed eyes, Maeve looked down the aisle. She was being dragged away from the fiery stall, and through the smoke, at the far end of the stable, the black horse was pacing, quivering, pawing at the big door to the rear.

I'm sorry, she thought, knowing she was responsible for his impending death . . . and her own.

Where the hell were the sprinklers? Why wasn't water raining down on the stalls? And the smoke detectors, why weren't they shrieking more loudly than the terrified horses?

Not working.

Her assailant had seen to that.

Maeve thought of Ethan as she was dropped unceremoniously into a heap. Maybe he would come and save her. She tried to whisper his name, but her voice failed her.

In a surreal moment, she watched from the floor as her tormentor calmly located a fire extinguisher, pulled it from its hook, and with expert precision sprayed the flames with a foaming retardant.

Then, just when Maeve thought she might be saved, her attacker threw down the canister, returned, bent over Maeve's broken body, and reached into her boot to extract the hunting knife.

The knife . . . Oh, God. No.

"You're left-handed, right?"

The rubber band at her wrist was snapped, then sliced cleanly. Coughing, smoke still heavy in the air, Maeve watched in mesmerized fascination as the blade was drawn across each of her wrists several times. Her heart raced, the pain throbbing through her body fading as blood began to flow, slowly seeping out of the neat lines.

The knife was shoved into her left hand, her fingers curled over its hilt.

"You know, Maeve, Ethan isn't worth it." The voice was casual now.

Warm blood oozed, dripping to the floor.

Maeve mewled, helpless, and she could do nothing but watch her brutal killer take her wrist and hold it aloft, moving it ever so slowly as drops of blood fell to the floor in what appeared to be a precise pattern. Then her arm was dropped, the blood smeared with the toe of a boot, and her killer walked calmly out the door.

Maeve tried to push herself to her feet, but her body wouldn't work, her legs leaden, as if her spine had been severed. It was over. She swallowed a small sob, knowing she was going to die.

Words from the last hymn she'd ever sung slid through her mind. *Let gods and kindred go, this mortal life also; the body they may kill . . .*

Light-headed, she felt herself crashing, the bluish lights wavering in front of her eyes. "Ethan," she whispered as darkness overcame her, "Oh, love . . ."

CHAPTER 37

Jules couldn't look at the damning evidence another second. She scooted her chair back and walked into the living room. Something was in the air tonight.

She shivered inside, feeling as if a ghost had just passed through her soul. "I should really check on Shay," she said, frustrated that her cell phone was missing.

"Shay is safe. She's in the dorm, with her roommate and security guards."

"As if that's any consolation. The security around here is about as solid as a sieve. Kids come and go at will. Escape artists and sociopaths—no wonder there's a killer on the loose."

There was an underlying sense of panic among the students. Dormitories had been fitted with new locks, and staff members were taking turns sleeping in extra rooms in each of the buildings housing students. Security teams had been formed under the guidance of Deputy Meeker, who had deputized Bert Flannagan, Wade Taggert, and Rhonda Hammersley, but now that she'd read Lynch's files, Jules worried that one of those faculty security groups could be harboring the killer.

"Do you want me to call over to the dorm?" Trent offered. "Ask someone to check on Shay?"

"Yes . . . no. That would draw attention to her, and she's already under suspicion, with her hat being found at the crime scene." She twisted her hair into a knot at the base of her skull and held it there for a second. "What set the killer off? Why now?"

"I don't know."

"We need to talk to Meeker or the sheriff. Or maybe we should confront Lynch ourselves."

"We're not confronting anyone, but I can track Meeker down," Trent decided. "The problem is, once I tell him you broke into Lynch's office and took the files, we're opening a new can of worms."

"Technically I didn't break in," she argued, frustrated and edgy. "But I'm not sure I'm ready to have my cover blown. Once it gets out that I'm Shay's sister . . ." She walked to the window but didn't dare peek outside, so she ended up pacing back toward the fire. "Oh, God, they might know who I am already. Someone stole my cell today. If they get into my directory, it won't take long for them to start piecing relationships together."

"Someone stole it?" Trent was bending low, working on the fire again.

Letting her hair fall to her shoulders, she watched as Trent poked at the hissing logs, somehow soothed by it. "I think maybe it was Missy Albright or Roberto Ortega. They both had access." She explained what had happened earlier in the day. How she'd found Missy in her classroom, how she'd run into Roberto while trying to help Maeve. "If someone looks through the phone, they could put two and two together and realize that I know Shay. Her name would come up on my contact list."

"That's a lot of assuming, but it gets worse," he admitted as the fire began to sizzle and pop again. "I left you a message earlier, before I knew you'd be sleuthing around Lynch's office. In my message I said I'd be waiting outside Stanton House."

"No one picked up?"

"No. But it doesn't mean they didn't see that you had a missed call from me. Or they might have accessed your voice mail."

"I've got a security code—"

"That probably wouldn't be too hard to break. These kids are smart, and some of them have been working with cell phones and iPods and computers from the time they could walk and talk."

"Damn." But it was true. The teachers, too. Hadn't she, herself, been at a computer keyboard from the time she could sit in her father's lap and pretend to type?

He leaned a shoulder against the mantel. "Why do I feel things are gonna get a whole lot worse before they get better?"

"Because you're psychic?" she teased, though she didn't know why she was making light of the tense situation.

"If only."

Outside, the wind continued to batter the house while inside the fire crackled and the electricity winked. They talked about the message she'd received and the one she'd seen in Maeve's possession. "I want to talk to Nell Cousineau. She was on duty at Stanton House the night someone left me the note. If she left the note, I'm wondering how she wanted me to help her."

Trent nodded. "Right. The note was vague." He rubbed the back of his neck. "It's frustrating when an investigation hits a wall like this. The snow hasn't helped."

"But the sheriff's department collected all that forensic evidence before the snowstorm. Haven't they heard anything?"

"Nothing new, at least not that I know of. There's a lot of

pressure on the state crime lab to produce. We're hoping to glean something from the analysis that will lead to the killer. But it takes weeks for DNA evidence to be deciphered, despite what they show on television. No murder weapon was found, but the ME says the wound on Drew's head was consistent with some kind of hatchet or ax, none of which has been located."

"Maybe the killer still has it," she said, her stomach twisting a bit. "Maybe he plans to use it again."

"So why not on Nona? Why go to all the trouble of trussing her up? Hanging her body?"

"Final revenge of a sort? To debase her? Part of the cult's sick rituals?"

"If there is a cult," he reminded her.

"God, Trent, I wish you would stop saying that. Can you honestly look at those files and tell me there isn't something sick and dysfunctional going on here?"

"You're definitely on to something, Jules, but I'm not buying into a conspiracy theory that came from one of those dysfunctional students. I know Shay is your sister, but she's no angel." One thick eyebrow lifted, questioning her. "In the end, if Shay's notion is a big lie, I just don't want you to be disappointed."

"I think I can handle it," she said, remembering another place and time, where once they had been a strong, vibrant couple, believing in the strength of their love. They had ended up fractured, apart, not trusting each other. They both knew all about disappointment.

She caught his gaze, wondered if his thoughts were traveling that old path that went to nowhere.

Long-buried feelings resurfaced, and she imagined for just a second what it would feel like to kiss him again. To touch him. To feel the strength of his corded muscles beneath her fingertips.

God, she was a fool. One minute furious with him, the next minute fantasizing about him.

Get a grip, Jules.

Being close to him was just plain nerve-racking. Old memories had taunted her. Often, tonight, while working with him, for just a heartbeat, she had lost sight of the reason she was with him, why she was here.

And it was happening again.

Suddenly warm, she pushed up the sleeves of her sweater and cleared her throat. "Okay, let's regroup here," she said, feeling time racing by, worried sick that the killer would strike again. "We're still not sure how the kids' murders are linked to Lauren's disappearance."

"Or if they are."

"What about the business between Ethan Slade and his teacher, Maris Howell, the one I'm replacing?"

"If you believe him, nothing happened. The situation was misinterpreted and overblown. By his parents and the school. Maris was run out of town on a rail."

"But not prosecuted?"

"Right." He returned to the table, resting a hip against one scarred corner. "Maybe all the events aren't tied together."

"Smoke screens?" she asked, looking up at him, his eyes dark.

"Or coincidence."

"What? No? If so, Blue Rock Academy has the worst luck of any school in the nation."

He laughed then. "Well, that's not melodramatic," he said sarcastically. Firelight played upon his features, casting his cheekbones and deep-set eyes in shadowy gold. His jaw was still as strong as it ever had been, his blade-thin lips as sexy as she remembered. He was worried. And sexy as all get-out.

"Here's the upside." Trent looped his thumbs into the pockets of his jeans. "The news is that the storm should break tomorrow."

"Really?"

"Meeker talked to the sheriff and told me before I came looking for you. If that's true, a helicopter might be able to fly in."

She listened to the howl of the wind. "A pretty big if. I wouldn't count on it." But in her heart, she felt a ray of hope. If they could connect to the outside world, get the kids to safety, have the resources of law enforcement, there was a chance they would catch this maniac.

She stretched again, lifting her hands high over her head and twisting her neck to release some of the tension.

Trent said, "When the detectives get here, I think they'll want to talk to Shaylee again."

"Along with everyone else."

Trent nodded slowly, but she read his hesitation and caught on.

"Wait a minute," she said, instantly hot. "Don't tell me you really think my sister is guilty?"

"She hasn't been ruled out yet."

"Oh, for the love of God. Then what about Lauren Conway? Is Shaylee a suspect in her disappearance, too, even though it happened months before Shay came here?"

"You're assuming the events are related, remember?"

"Aren't they?" she tossed back, desperate to make him see that Shay was innocent. "Other than a scandal concerning a teacher and a student, this school hasn't lost any of their students. Ever. Until November. Then, four months later, two other kids are killed!"

"I'm just saying that Shaylee is going to be looked at. Hard."

"Because of her damned hat. That's ridiculous! Nona

had worn it before. As for the cell phone, big deal. She took Nona's phone. When she was alive! Her biggest crime is petty theft!"

"Nona's body was dragged. The abrasions on her back and rump are consistent with being dragged across the hay bales to the spot where she was hoisted over the beams."

"She and Drew were making love."

"On a sleeping bag, not straw," he said quietly, "and Shay was the last person to see Nona alive."

"Wrong!" Jules was incensed now. "Drew was the last person, and we don't know that Nona didn't come into contact with someone between leaving her dorm room and meeting Drew!" Breathing fire, she shoved back her chair, the legs scraping noisily against the hardwood. "I can't believe you're buying into this . . . this easy and ridiculous answer. Especially after what I showed you here," she said, jabbing a finger at the seared records. "For crying out loud, she's only seventeen, barely a hundred and twenty pounds."

"So you're saying she would have trouble hauling Nona's body?"

"No! She knows the fireman carry. Good Lord, she's taken all kinds of martial arts and strength-training and . . ." She let her voice fade away, knowing she was only digging a deeper hole for her sister. "Listen to what you're saying," she hissed as he rose to face her. "You're accusing her of murder. Double homicide at the very least."

"No one's accusing anyone of anything." He came to her, closing the space between them. "I just think you should be aware of what's happening."

"Forewarned is forearmed?" she said, incensed.

"Just that you need to be prepared."

She nearly slapped him then. Her hand jerked backward, recoiling as if to strike.

He stared down at her. "I wouldn't."

"Wouldn't what?" she taunted, blood pumping through her. God, he was close. Too close. She thought of stepping backward but was already as close to the fire as she dared.

He glanced down at her hand, still poised as if to strike. "Hit me." His breath was warm against her face. "I might hit back." His eyes were dark as night. "Or worse."

"Worse?"

His gaze dropped to her lips. "Uh-huh."

Her pulse was pounding, her gaze focused on his, every sense aware of the tiniest shifting in the atmosphere. "I think you're bluffing," she said.

One side of his mouth twisted upward in that crooked, self-deprecating smile that had always scraped her soul. "I think you are."

She had trouble taking a breath; it was impossible to process anything beyond the warmth coming off his skin or the smell of coffee and a hint of aftershave reaching her nostrils. His sheer presence caused turmoil deep inside her. The back of her legs were warm with heat from the fire, and she felt a flush crawl up her spine.

"Seems as if we're at an impasse," he said.

"Aren't we always?"

"We should be talking about the case."

"That's right. We should," she said, but right now, all thoughts of their discussion were scattered. She found herself wanting and, for just a tiny bit of time, needing to forget the nightmare that had become their lives, needing to escape to somewhere safe and warm.

Which was ludicrous.

"I just think you should consider other suspects," she forced out.

"I am."

"And the police?"

"They'll pursue every suspect, every possibility." His

gaze slid over her face; she felt its warmth. Oh, Lord, she couldn't go there . . . wouldn't!

"Then give Shaylee a damned break," she said, her voice lower than she'd intended, the heat between them nearly palpable. "Trust me on this one, Trent. I know I'm right." Resolve coursed through her; she couldn't let her sister be railroaded for murders she didn't commit.

"For once, Jules, let's turn this around," he said, and placed his hands against the mantel on either side of her head, trapping her there. "You trust me."

For a heart-stopping moment, she thought he might kiss her. Instead he pinned her with his eyes.

"I don't know if I can," she admitted, her heart pounding wildly.

"That's a problem."

"Only one?" she asked, the night seeming to thrum around them. Dear God, she'd missed him.

"You're right. We've got a bigger one."

"Which is?"

"This, damn it." As quick as a lightning strike, his arms wrapped around her and his lips found hers. He kissed her hard, holding her close, nearly crushing her body to his.

She didn't resist. Instead, she slid her arms around his neck, her fingers catching in his hair. Her mouth opened to him, and as the kiss deepened, the years that they'd been apart disintegrated into thin air. Her skin heated, her blood ran wild, and deep inside, in the very center of her, she began to feel a want that had been dormant for five years.

Sadly, no man had ever touched her the way Cooper Trent had; she'd never let any other man close enough to reach her or to wound her.

She didn't protest when he lifted her from her feet and carried her along the short hallway and into his bedroom. He fell with her on the mattress, which squeaked beneath them.

"This is a big mistake," he whispered, still holding her close.

"You're right."

"Oh, hell." His mouth found hers again, and there was no stopping. His hands slid beneath her sweater, pulling it over her head, while hers worked at the fly of his jeans. He buried his face in the cleft of her breasts, his breath warm, his lips eager as he nibbled at the edge of her bra, then slid the strap from her shoulder. One breast spilled from its cup, and he kissed her nipple, causing the ache deep inside to grow. She moaned, arching to him as he teased and nipped, circling the areola with his tongue, causing her nipple to harden.

With a moan, she cradled his head to hers as he suckled, and she arched her neck and back.

"I forgot how beautiful you were," he said against her skin, the warm air from his mouth ruffling across her flesh.

"And I forgot how adept you were at bull," she replied, giggling a little.

He kissed her belly then, his nose pressing deep into her skin. "You are trouble, Jules."

"As are you." She forced his jeans over his hips, scraping the hard muscles of his butt and thighs, reminding her that he'd once ridden rodeo, that his body was honed by years of hard work. There were scars along his back, old injuries that her fingers skated over after he flung his shirt onto the floor.

He made short work of her ski pants and snapped her panties off in one deft stroke.

"You sure about this?" he asked once they were naked and he was levered above her, balanced on one bent arm while his free hand stroked her, fingers exploring her ribs and waist, lingering at her hips.

"I'm not sure about anything," she admitted.

His smile was a slash of white. "Me neither." He kissed

her again and rolled atop her, his weight welcome, his skin warm against hers. She told herself a thousand times that this was a mistake, that she would regret making love to him, but the scent of him was too powerful an aphrodisiac, the feel of his body welcome relief.

She closed her eyes and gave in to the moment, feeling his hands twine in her hair as he pressed a wet trail of kisses from her nape, across her neck, to the circle of bones at her throat.

Her body responded, and she kissed him in kind, feeling the stubble of his beard against her lips, tracing her fingers along his spine, cupping his muscular buttocks.

She moaned as he slid his knees between hers and arched upward when he caressed her with his mouth and tongue, sliding downward, exploring and breathing hot air against flesh already on fire.

He parted her gently, then touched her in the most intimate of places, creating a swirling pool of need deep within until she cried out. He kissed. He touched. He licked. And she wanted more.

"Trent," she whispered, her voice cracking as he slid upward, coming to her, his hardness rubbing gently against her belly. He kissed her and tried to slide between her legs, but she moved lower, intent on pleasuring him as he had her. The bedsheets crumpled beneath her back as she positioned herself, kissing him, feeling his back muscles tense as she offered featherlight touches that made him groan and gasp above her.

The smell of sex was heavy in the air, beads of perspiration rising on her skin.

"Jules . . . Jules . . . ," he rasped.

"Mmmm."

"I don't think I can . . . hold back."

"Don't," she whispered, but pushed herself upward to find his mouth with hers.

"Jesus, God, woman!" He pushed himself inside her, and she wrapped her legs around him as he thrust. Once, twice, three times. Faster and faster. Jules clung to him, arching up, her mind spinning crazily.

She was here.

With Trent.

In his bed.

She felt the first wave wash over her. Hot. Violent. A spasm that caught her in its heated grip.

He cried out.

The second wave was stronger still. She bucked upward, holding fast to this man she'd once loved, once trusted. Tears burned at the back of her eyes, but she refused to give in and crumple to fear and doubt. Let the winds howl and whistle, the frozen sting of snow battering the ramshackle cottage, the breath of evil whispering over the school grounds. For this moment, she was riding the storm with Trent, proud and strong, loving and loved. With Trent.

CHAPTER 38

God was testing him.

That was it.

Finally the Leader understood that God was throwing down his immaculate gauntlet and observing, watching to see if the leader he'd chosen would take up the battle. And he would. Oh, yes, he would.

"I will not fail you," he whispered as he moved across the campus through the blizzard, a storm that God had provided, the perfect cover. The Leader realized that now; God was testing him, yes, but aiding him in his ultimate purpose. Everything was becoming clear.

As always, God's wisdom was complete.

Avoiding the pathetic security patrols, he smiled to himself as he hurried behind the rec hall. Weren't his own people on each and every team appointed to oversee the safety of the academy?

It was a joke really.

He was in control.

God was on his side. The rest of the world would see. *She* would see, the woman who had so callously cast him aside.

Surely God would reward him and those who had helped him along the path of his holy mission; those who had misused the word of God, twisting it for their own purposes, would be exposed. Punished. Ultimately face their master for their sins.

Yes, there were a few bumps in his plan, but they could be smoothed easily, the Leader thought as he slipped into the chapel, the smell of smoke lingering in the air. He hurried to the staircase and flew down the steps, moving without a sound, his heart beating fast, adrenaline fueling his blood.

Not bothering to switch on a light, he strode quickly along the familiar hallway to the janitorial closet that was rarely used, the equipment within gathering dust.

Once the door was closed behind him, he flipped on the light, a dim bulb overhead; then, nearly kneeling, he reached behind a long-forgotten bucket and brush on a low shelf. Behind the bucket was a hidden keypad. He quickly pressed in the code, and the shelves popped open, swinging noiselessly toward him on a hinge to reveal stone steps leading downward.

Single bulbs offered pale light as he descended into what had once been a cave. Sometime after World War II, in the early fifties, the space had been fitted as a fallout shelter, complete with reinforced walls and ceiling, an underground generator, an air-filtration system, and a vented stove. A natural spring provided water. Fortunately, Radnor Stanton, Cora Sue's dear, deceased father, had been a man with vision, he thought with more than a trace of bitterness. When Stanton, a Cold War survivor, helped with the construction of Blue Rock Academy, he made sure to preserve this perfect sanctuary.

But Radnor Stanton was long dead, his idiosyncratic underground shelter forgotten over the years. Gone were the ancient canned foods, transistor radio, metal cots, and huge flashlights that had been part of the essentials over half a century earlier. Now the space was filled with an altar, pews, and lanterns, but it was vented as it had been, allowing in fresh air, filtered by the original components.

There was a locked cabinet as well, an arsenal where rifles, handguns, and walkie-talkies were stored. Cell phones were helpful, but not completely reliable here in the mountains. He did a mental inventory of the ammunition, night-vision goggles, and knives, along with ski masks, armored vests, and extra academy jackets.

He was ready.

For Armageddon.

His followers, carefully selected, were eager and fervent, anxious to put the plan into motion. Already, some had carried out his orders; others were on their way to get their instructions.

A tingle of anticipation swept through him as he realized that all of his plans, all of his dreams, were about to be realized. There would be ramifications, he was certain, but in the end, he would prevail.

He had to.

He had God on his side.

To calm himself, to show God his humility and reverent dedication, he knelt at the altar and prayed. He asked for guidance, knowing that God would provide him the true path, that he wouldn't be lured away from his mission.

He thought of Lauren Conway, a beautiful, seductive Jezebel. How she'd outwitted and outrun him to the banks of the river. Everything he'd worked for had nearly been destroyed.

There was a reason her body had never been found, would never be. As he stood, he touched his pocket again, reassuring himself that the tiny flash drive he'd taken from her backpack, wrapped in several ziplock bags, was now with him and always would be. He hadn't destroyed the tiny flash drive with its pictures and data about him, about his mission neatly documented, instead keeping it with him. Always. A reminder of how insidious lust could be.

Her face came to him. He remembered chasing her down, desperately running after her in the night, determined to stop her. But she'd been more clever than he'd anticipated, and only after an hour of dashing through the moon-washed landscape had he tracked her to the edge of the river. There her footprints in the snow had vanished, and he'd had to assume that she'd been swept away in the frigid, whirling current of the icy river.

No one could have survived.

He'd cursed her for eluding him and sent a prayer up for her damaged, traitorous soul.

At dawn, before a true search had been organized, on one of the rare occasions when he'd been a passenger in the seaplane, he'd stared out the window and caught a bit of the dark blue of her backpack. A small swatch of color on the snowy shores of the river. He'd said nothing, but later had ridden by horseback to the remote canyon and found her body caught in a snag of logs and brush at the river's edge. Ashen gray and bloated, she lay on the side of the river, washed upon the shore. He'd wanted to spit on her dead body but instead had kissed her blue, blue lips for the last time. It had been a struggle, but he'd loaded her corpse onto Omen's back and returned to the little, forgotten church where he'd caught her looking through the frosted panes, spying on him.

Though the earth had been frozen and hard, he'd dug a quick, shallow grave with a pickax. He had dropped her body into it and buried her, replacing the sticks and twigs over the frozen chips of earth, thanking God for the snowfall that would hide the burial plot in a cemetery that no one visited.

The headstone read:

LILY CARVER, IN LOVING MEMORY.

How fitting. A perfect grave. Above the rotted casket and ancient bones of Lily Carver, he'd buried Lauren Conway, her initials the same so that he could always remember where he'd laid her to rest, visit her if he wanted.

She was a traitor, remember that. Her soul will burn in hell.

As much as he now hated her, he would never forget the trill of her laughter, the glint of merriment in her eyes, the graceful way she walked away from him, casually looking over her shoulder and winking at their great secret. He'd remember always the sensual lift of those provocative lips; the memory of that smile still caused a reaction in him.

Julia Farentino could do the same.

Imagine how the feel of her supple mouth upon your skin would twist you inside out. You could have her—she's given herself to Cooper Trent after only a few days; you could take his place, strip away her clothes, make her kneel in front of you. You have the power.

His blood raced. He licked his lips and reminded himself that lust was a sin, that the hardness swelling between his legs was a distraction. Though he would like nothing more than to screw the living hell out of her, he would wait.

For now.

He couldn't risk another mistake.

And she, like Lauren, would surely only betray him.

Footsteps alerted him that they were coming. His disciples. Tonight this underground shelter was more war room than church. He waited, not saying a word as they entered in twos and threes, following the orders of the academy to always travel with a partner.

They didn't speak but took their places, eager and avid, the fervor of youth in their eyes. They were rabid, this cadre of bright, talented soldiers. Dedicated to God's cause, ready to cross any line.

Crusaders.

A few followers cast glances at the open cabinet door, eager to get their hands on weapons, keyed up and ready to do his bidding. He wondered if one of them could be a rogue, more interested in his or her own agenda than the greater good.

He dismissed the idea quickly as they stared up at him, if not in adoration, then at the very least awe.

The Leader gave a nod, and the sergeant at arms swung the door shut. Once he'd returned to his seat on the pew, the Leader said, "You've been patient long enough. Some of you already know this, but tonight we strike. The plan we've discussed for so long has already been set into motion.

"A few of you have already begun your tasks, as have I, but now all of us need to unite and go with purpose. You know what your assignments are." He moved his gaze over each of the faces staring up at him, caught a few of them nodding, anxious, ready. "We may suffer casualties, but not if we are precise.

"As you leave here, take the equipment you've been allotted and go forth with fervor and faith." A few feet scuffled on the hard rock floor as they prepared to stand. "First," he cautioned, "let us pray."

In her dream, Jules walked through the den, past the flickering screen of the television to her father's body. Rip lay in a pool of blood, the knife deep in his body.

"Dad . . . Dad!" She bent over and pulled out the knife, and Rip's eyes opened wide, staring at her.

Somewhere nearby a woman screamed.

She turned, saw her mother in the archway, Edie's face twisted in horror. "You killed him!" she accused, and ran into the room to drop onto the floor.

"No, I didn't. Mom . . ."

Edie, kneeling in her husband's blood, turned to look over her shoulder and stare at her firstborn. "Why?" she demanded. "Why would you kill your father?"

"I didn't . . . Mom, you gotta believe me."

"You're to blame." Rip's voice thundered, though his mouth didn't move, and somehow Jules knew he was talking about Edie. "You let her do this."

"I didn't!" Jules insisted, the drops of blood dripping onto the floor.

Jules sat bolt upright in the darkness, the strange room closing in on her. Where the hell was she?

"Hey. You okay?" Trent was beside her in the bed. His strong arms surrounded her, dragging her close. She blinked hard, remembering where she was and how she'd gotten here, fool that she was.

"No." She was shaking her head; she was definitely not okay on so many levels. Good Lord, she was an idiot, and the memory of the nightmare still caused goose bumps to rise on her skin. "It's . . . it's everything. I get this recurring nightmare about Dad's murder. It just keeps coming back, and it changes just a little each time. I always hear a disturbing dripping sound. And I check around and know it's coming from the den."

She let out a breath, shivering a little, though Trent's arms surrounded her.

"And that's where it changes. I walk into the den, and the TV's always on and Dad's always on the floor, blood pooling around him, but sometimes he's still alive and he talks to me. Sometimes my mother is nearby; other times Shaylee is cowering and . . . and it all gets so blurry. All the people I cared about at that time in my life are nearby, but it's as if they're acting, playing different roles." She shook her head in the darkness. "Oh, I don't know what it means, *if* it means anything." She let out a soft breath, ruffling the hairs on his chest. "To tell you the truth, it scares me to death."

"Shhh." He kissed her hair. "Let it go."

"Believe me, I've tried, but . . ." She sighed, wishing that horrid night would stop haunting her. *It won't; not until the memory is clear.* Her recollections of the night of her father's death had changed with time, aged a bit, in shattered little pieces that she'd formed into a smooth montage. She was living at home, the marriage between Rip and Edie disintegrating by the day. They were continually sniping at each other, the arguments escalating. She and Shaylee had taken refuge upstairs, listening to music with the volume turned up to mute the painful words her parents thrust at each other.

Seeing them destroying each other took its toll on Jules and her half sister. And the aftermath of Rip's death had been worse. Jules had scrapped her plans of moving away to college and had forced Trent from her life. Shay had started getting into trouble at school, and Edie . . . Edie had nearly lost it, falling into a horrible depression that had only lifted with the advent of Grant Sykes into her life. She'd felt a failure with two divorces, widowhood, and the loss of any considerations of wealth. Max Stillman was determined that she never get one more dime of his money to the point that he'd nearly turned his back completely on his own daughter, doting instead on Max Junior. So they'd both lost their fathers that night. Though Shay's relationship had always been tenuous with Max, Rip had doted on Jules. Once Rip was killed, the murderer, a robber who had taken his wallet and fled in smooth-soled, size 12 shoes, according to partial impressions in the mud, their lives had changed forever. Had it been random? A business partner who had been taken? The husband of one of Rip's girlfriends finally taking revenge?

No one knew.

All in all, it had been a disaster, the night of Rip Delaney's death changing the course of Jules's life and haunting her dreams.

"I think," she said, blinking in the darkness, "the nightmare is never going to go away. It'll always be with me."

"Hey." Trent's voice was low. Steady. "I'm here."

She snorted a laugh, finding a hint of macabre humor in his single statement. "And?"

"And this time I'm not going away."

A lump formed in her throat, and she let his strong arms comfort her. "Even if I push?" she asked.

"Especially then."

"Need I remind you that 'here' is in the middle of a madhouse of a boarding school where people are being killed?"

"It won't always be this way." God, he said it with such conviction.

Jules wanted to take comfort in his strong belief, she supposed, but it was difficult. As she roused and the nightmare skittered away to hide in the murky corners of her mind, she was faced with what she and Trent had discovered in Lynch's partially burnt files. Also, now there was the heart-jarring realization that she'd made love to Cooper Trent again.

As quick as lightning, she'd slid willingly between the sheets of the ex–bull rider's bed, and they had become lovers again in a heartbeat.

She hadn't even put up a fight, and then had fallen asleep in his arms.

Stupid, stupid, stupid!

What was wrong with her?

Had she just taken solace and comfort for a few hours? Needed a reaffirmation of life and love in the middle of this chaos?

What an inane rationale.

Sleeping with him would help nothing. Tears stung the back of her eyes, but she fought them back. "You're a fool, Cooper Trent."

"At the very least."

"I'm serious."

"So am I." He kissed her then, his lips claiming hers, and she felt as if she'd finally come home. She felt the heat of his body, the pounding of his heart, the sheer strength of him.

"I'm sorry," she finally whispered. "I blamed you for something that didn't have anything to do with you."

"Water under the bridge."

"No, it's not. I think what scared me the most back then was how much I depended on you, how much I loved you."

"Tell ya what," he suggested, and she almost felt him smile in the darkness. "Let's give it another go."

She cleared her throat. "I don't know how that will work."

"As my father used to say, we'll make it work. He was a firm believer in positive thinking. So am I." He squeezed her and kissed her forehead again, and for a second in the darkness, she trusted that things would be all right, that they actually had a chance to overcome this nightmare they were living in.

"Listen."

She did, and over the pounding of her heart, she heard nothing. Not even the rumble of a furnace.

"The power's out," he said, and she was finally awake enough to realize how dark the room was. There was no glowing digital readout on a clock, just total, pitch blackness, and the room was getting colder by the minute. "And the wind's died down." Trent reached over to the nightstand, and a moment later she saw the flash of his cell phone as he tried to make a call. "Out of luck."

Jules huddled back under the quilt, shivering.

"Hey. Come on." Trent was already swinging out of bed. "You'll freeze in here. Wrap up," he instructed, coiling a quilt around her as she tried to wake up, to think clearly.

She couldn't stay here all night. Not with everything that was happening. Still half-asleep, she let him guide her out to the living room, close to the fire.

Naked, he poked and prodded the fire, his muscular silhouette in stark relief against the bloodred coals. He added several chunks of oak and fir, and as the mossy wood caught fire, he returned to the bedroom, then dragged his mattress and a pair of jeans to the living room. He dropped the mattress onto the floor and stepped into his jeans. "I have to go and check on the animals, make certain there's heat in the stable, but stay here. I'll bring the pillows out and you can sleep by the fire."

"What? No!" She didn't want to be left alone. Not tonight. *Why? Come on, Jules, don't be one of those men-dependent women you hate.*

"Seriously. You'll be safe here." But there was a hint of trepidation in his voice. "Look, I'll be gone less than twenty minutes, and I'll leave the pistol with you."

"You think the killer is after me?" she asked, and felt another sliver of fear.

"I don't know who he's after, or even if he's still hunting, but I want to know that you're safe."

"Well, hey, me, too. I think that's a great idea, but what about Shay?"

"She's in the dorm with a buddy; she'll be fine," he reminded.

"We don't know that. We don't know if anyone here is 'fine.' It would be comforting to think that the murderer is finished with his work, that Nona and Drew were his only targets, that the murders were personal. But then there's Lauren Conway."

"Okay, point taken."

"And you were going to leave me with the gun. For safety. Because in your heart of hearts, you have a feeling this killer isn't done. And we could be targets, right?"

"Right."

"I just need to know that Shay's safe. That's the reason I'm down here, you know. To take her home." She was already unwrapping the quilt. "But there have been a few obstacles in my way," she said, tossing the quilt aside. She snagged a flashlight from a side table, flicked it on, and started toward the bedroom. What had she been thinking? With everything else going on, she had no business sleeping with Trent. No business at all.

And all his words about sticking around, about trying again, these were empty phrases until they were out of the trap that was Blue Rock.

Crossing the bedroom, she tripped on her boots and stubbed her toe. Swearing under her breath, she located her damned panties and bra where they'd been flung into a corner. Her jeans and sweater were on the other side of the room, testament to how fast and anxiously they'd been stripped from her body.

Refusing to consider how foolish she'd been, she got dressed as quickly as possible.

"For the record," Trent said, "I think this is a bad idea."

She looked up and found Trent in the doorway, adjusting the waistband of his jeans.

"Well, lately I haven't had a lot of great ones," she muttered, wondering why he'd returned to the bedroom. "What're you doing?"

"What does it look like?" Buttoning his jeans in the thin, watery light from the flashlight, he grinned. She tried not to notice how low his faded Levi's hung on his hips. "I've decided we should stick together. We'll check on the animals, make sure they've got heat, then head to the dorms."

She hated the rush of relief that swept over her. "Sounds like a plan."

"A bad one," he said, "but all we've got."

In the living room, by the glowing embers of the fire, they slipped into their snow gear and boots. Trent was still shrugging on his sheepskin coat as he locked the door behind them.

The snowscape was eerie and still. After days of the wind screeching through the hills, the night was deathly quiet, a half-moon glowing bright and casting everything in a silvery glow.

"That's odd," Trent said, eyeing the campus. "The generators should be on, but there are no lights."

He was right: no security lighting in the buildings, no twinkling Christmas lights in the gazebo, no lampposts illuminating the paths.

Their flashlights were the only swaths of illumination visible in the night.

It was too quiet. Too still.

Fear prickled the back of Jules's neck.

"Cut off the flashlight," he whispered abruptly, clicking his off. As if he felt the great unlikely quietness, too. "We don't want to be sitting ducks."

"Where are the security patrols?" she asked.

"Good question."

Her heart turned to ice. "I don't like this."

He pulled the pistol from the holster inside his jacket. "Neither do I." He took her hand in his free one, gloved fingers linking with hers, his sidearm pointed ahead.

Wary, Jules kept her eyes on the shadows, the drifting piles of snow, the darkened corners as they trudged past several dark outbuildings, their roofs laden with snow, their windows like a myriad of ghostly reflective eyes.

Jules clung to Trent's hand as they turned onto the path leading to the stable. Though there was no wind, the temperature was below freezing, the air frigid as she dragged it into her lungs. The frozen air had a burnt odor, as if someone has just doused a campfire.

"Do you smell that?" she said. "Is it just wood smoke?"

"Maybe." His voice was hard.

The stable was as dark as the other buildings, but the main door was open slightly, hanging ajar. "Hell," Trent whispered, and waved her to stand behind him as he walked inside, flicking the light switch.

Click.

No flash of lights followed.

"Something was burning in here," he said under his breath.

The hairs on the back of her arms raised as Trent stepped inside, sweeping the arc of his flashlight over the stalls where horses were stomping nervously and the heavy smell of smoke lingered.

What had gone on in here?

A horse neighed loudly.

"What the hell?" Trent turned the flashlight to the far wall, where a huge black horse was pacing, his coat lathered, his eyes wild.

Trent lowered the light. "Hey, boy, it's all right. Shhh." He kept the flashlight directed toward the floor, and Jules followed, the scent of smoke and something else, something metallic . . .

"Trent—" she whispered.

"Holy shit!" The beam of his flashlight swept over the body of Maeve Mancuso. He was on his knees in an instant, Jules one step behind. "What the hell?" He handed Jules his gun. "Just in case," he said. "Keep an eye out." He propped his flashlight on the floor, training its beam on the poor girl.

Maeve was propped up against a post, blood pooled

around her on the dusty cement floor. He touched her neck and shook his head. "Hell." Still, he listened for the sound of the faintest breath whispering through her lungs, but shook his head. "She's gone," he said, almost inaudibly, and Jules felt something break deep inside her as she stared at the girl's pale, lifeless face.

CHAPTER 39

"It's been staged to look like she committed suicide," Jules said, not fooled for an instant despite the long, thin slash marks visible inside Maeve's wrists. The bloody knife lay on the floor beneath the fingertips of her left hand, her dark hair singed. "But there was a fire in here . . . doused. God, what happened?"

"That son of a bitch got her. That's what happened." Trent was still beside the girl, shining the beam of his flashlight over the surrounding area.

Angry, he rocked back on his heels. "Look at this." He shined his flashlight over the death scene to a small puddle of blood not far from the wide dark pools coagulating beneath Maeve's open palms. The puddle had been scuffed and smeared, just like the one Jules had seen close to the spot where Drew Prescott had been left for dead. Not twenty feet from this very spot. Without thinking, she glanced to the area under the ladder to the hayloft.

Two smeared stains . . . apart from the bodies. So much alike. Snake-like, but blurred. A chill slid down her spine. "Was anything like this found near Nona? Up in the loft?" she asked.

He shook his head, then stopped. "I don't know. If it was, I suppose, it could have been on the sleeping bag, but I never saw it as it was taken to the lab. But it sure wasn't anywhere else in the hayloft; I looked over the place myself."

"Why?"

"I'm not sure." Jules stared at the spot near Maeve and felt as if it should mean something, an idea forming that couldn't quite gel. What was it?

From the far end of the aisle, the big horse snorted and pawed the ground, instinctively staying away from the scent of death. Jules didn't blame him. She, too, wanted to step away from reality, away from the killing, away from this horrible school with all its dark secrets.

She coughed. The smell of smoke hung heavy in the air and horses in surrounding stalls shuffled and whinnied. Jules shined the beam of her flashlight over the floor of the stable where the cement was marred by blackened straw and bloodstains. The big black horse that had gotten loose was still trembling at the far end of the aisle. What in God's name had happened here? What kind of evil?

Trent slowly guided his flashlight's beam down Maeve's body, pausing on her torso and legs. "Jesus. Even with her snow gear on you can tell she was worked over. She's got other wounds." He glanced up at Jules and when they connected, she felt sure they had the same soul-numbing thought.

The killer could still be here.

Inside.

Waiting.

Jules's insides quivered. Dear God, even now, the beast who had attacked Maeve could be watching their every move. Silently Trent touched Jules's shoulder gently, and she, understanding, released the gun to him, an "ace" marksman according to Reverend Lynch's records.

Jules's heart was knocking so wildly it echoed in her brain, pounded against her skull. Who had done this to Maeve? And why? Oh, God, why? Swallowing back her fear, she stared deep into the darkest corners of the stable. Anyone could be hiding in the weird, unearthly shapes of the equipment and tools tucked against the walls and hanging from the rafters. The killer could be crouched low. Waiting. Observing. He could be in one of the stalls, or in the shadowy feed bins or above, in the hayloft . . .

She glanced upward, imagining the crime scene, seeing, in her mind's eye, the very space where Nona Vickers had been so viciously and cruelly hung from the rafters, her naked body displayed almost as if the killer were mocking them. She shuddered, spying Trent who was already on the ladder, pistol in his hand.

Jules cringed as he climbed to the next rung. If the murderer had a gun, they were easy targets with their bobbing flashlights. She took a step toward him, but he shook his head, silently urging her to stay put.

She froze as he reached the top and disappeared into the darkness, leaving Jules, nerves stretched to the breaking point, to listen to his footsteps moving across the old floorboards above her head.

She started to follow.

The black horse snorted loudly and she froze. She saw his muscles quiver and instantly turned, searching for a sign of anyone else in the stable. The other animals, too, were anxious, pawing and whinnying, nervous in their stalls.

She took a step toward the ladder again.

"No one up here," Trent said, then dropped to the floor, landing on the spot where Drew Prescott had been left for dead.

Jules let out the breath she'd been holding and rubbed her shoulders.

The big horse began to pace, steely hooves scraping the concrete of the stable floor near the far wall.

"He's not happy," Jules said, forcing a joke that fell flat.

"None of us are. Stay here." Trent started for the horse. An easy target. Jules's stomach was in knots. At any second she expected a shot to ring out and Trent to fall to the floor. "I'll take care of him," he said without raising his voice. To the gelding, he added, "Take it easy, big guy. It's okay. Sure it is."

Like hell, Jules thought but held her tongue as Trent reached the frightened animal and ran experienced hands over the black horse's quivering hide.

"It's all right," Trent said in a low tone to the horse, lying through his teeth again. It wasn't all right; nothing was. Nothing would ever be.

"That's it . . . everything's okay, Omen."

Omen? Hearing the gelding's name triggered the memory of the note she'd seen in Maeve's purse earlier in the day when the girl had been so distraught over Ethan Slade. Could the note have been about the horse? She glanced at the girl's dead body again and felt cold as death.

"There ya go . . . see? It's not so bad," Trent said as he reached the horse, grabbed Omen's halter, and clucked softly. "Come on, now." To Jules, he said, "He's got a shallow cut, bleeding on his right shoulder, probably where he scraped the edges of the stall gate." To the horse, he added, "You'll live." *Unlike Maeve. Or Drew. Or Nona. Or, probably, Lauren.* Still standing so near the dead girl, Jules couldn't help but wonder who would be next. Whom would the killer target? Like pictures in a kaleidoscope, the students' faces slid behind her eyes, morphing into each other: little Ollie Gage, brooding Crystal Ricci, Keesha Bell with her neat cornrows and quick smile, or Shay, her misunderstood sister. Jules swallowed hard, her fear mounting, dread racing through her bloodstream.

"We have to stop him," she whispered and even as she said it, she wondered who the killer was, her brain racing to connect the dots of a puzzle that wasn't yet making any sense: Who? Why? To what damned end?

The questions blazing through her mind, she watched Trent latch the big gelding into a stall.

Once Omen was secure in his box, Trent paused to sweep his light over the next stall, the one from which, presumably, the terrorized gelding had broken free.

Who would do this?

Take the time to stage the scene? Blood on the floor, burned straw, twin trails of heel marks visible, evidence that Maeve had been dragged from the door of the open stall to the spot where she died.

None of it made any sense. If the killer wanted Maeve dead, why not just kill her and be done with it. Instead, the whole murder seemed drawn out and orchestrated.

"The fire was in here," Trent told her, his flashlight's beam still crawling along one stall. "In Omen's box." He was staring at the floor, his frown barely visible in the dark. "But it looks like it was contained to this area, not allowed to burn any further. The killer took the time to set it and then douse it with the fire extinguisher."

"Unless Maeve lit the fire."

"Or someone else? A third party? Shit, who knows? But there's blood in here."

"From the horse?"

"Nah. It's too much; his scrape wasn't that deep." Trent slid the beam of his flashlight over the opening to the stall. "Horsehair here, caught on the side rails. And . . . oh, what's this?" he asked, then said, "Looks like a knit cap, half burned."

"Pink?" Jules asked, knowing the answer. "Maeve was wearing one earlier."

"Bingo."

Jules shuddered. A graphic, painful image of Maeve's hat, perched upon her head, being set afire to singe her scalp and burn her hair came to mind. Dear God, what cruelty. What kind of deranged monster would do such a thing? The cold of the night, the evil that lurked in this building, seeped deep into her soul. "So the blood in the stall is Maeve's?" she asked, hazarding a glance at Maeve's dead body. Poor, poor thing.

"Or her killer's."

As he walked down the aisle Trent swept the beam of his flashlight into each of the stalls. Absently, he touched the noses of the nervous horses who plunged their heads over the top rails as he passed. Their large eyes were nervous, white rimmed, their nostrils flared at the lingering scent of smoke and metallic odor of the spilled blood.

"It's gonna be fine," he said to Scout, whose pale blue eyes looked eerie in the darkness. He tossed his white head and snorted as if calling Trent the liar he was. "Hey . . . Shhh." He scratched the pinto's forehead until the horse calmed a bit.

Satisfied that the animals were safe, Trent found his cell phone, and said to Jules, "I've got to call Meeker." He punched in the number, waited, then swore under his breath. "Oh, hell. Still can't get through. Guess we can't count on the cavalry."

Jules's heart sank. Was the killer finished? Or, she wondered in horror, were there more bodies?

The door to the stables flew open. A rush of frigid air swept inside, tossing bits of hay into the air and cutting through Jules's jacket.

She jumped and bit back a scream.

"Get down!" Trent yelled at her. Crouching swiftly, he leveled his gun at the doorway.

A dark figure carrying a large battery powered light in front of him. "Hey!"

"Stop!" Trent warned, his gun and flashlight trained on Bert Flannagan's shocked face.

"What the hell?" Flannagan stopped dead in his tracks, a large survival lantern in one hand, his rifle strapped across his back. "What's going on in here? A fire?" The lantern's harsh glow washed over the burned straw on the floor to stop at Maeve's ashen-faced corpse and the blood puddled around her. "Holy Christ!" His Adam's apple worked, then he swung his dark gaze at Trent. "What the fuck happened here?"

"You don't know?"

"Hell, no!" His lips tightened, and he appeared agitated, even desperate. "Why don't you fill me in?"

"We just found her," Jules said, wary.

"You have any idea why there was a fire in Omen's stall?" Trent cut in.

"Fire?" Flannagan repeated, as if just noticing the singed straw and the strong odor of smoke that wafted through the stalls. "What the hell?" Flannagan's features pulled tight, his mouth twisting down at the corners as he shot a look at the box where the big horse was usually housed. "Omen wasn't hurt?"

"Just a scratch. Cut himself escaping. We found him outside the gate." Eyeing Flannagan cautiously, Trent motioned to the opening of Omen's stall with the beam of his flashlight. "It was hanging wide open."

Jules remembered Lynch's notes in Flannagan's file. *Affinity for weaponry. Military background. Not hired by several law enforcement agencies.* Flannagan, with his military buzz cut and honed wrestler's physique, worked with the animals every day. Here. The stable was his milieu. All three kids who had died, had been attacked in his domain. He could have murdered Maeve earlier and returned in an attempt to throw suspicion away from him.

Jules's skin crawled. She didn't trust this man, plain and simple. Was he a cold-blooded killer?

Flannagan glanced again at the dead girl and a muscle worked in his jaw. "I suppose we'd better get hold of Lynch."

"Get him," Trent suggested, "and while you're at it, round up Deputy Meeker, send him out here. We'll need to cordon off the stable until the detectives and crime investigators get here."

"So we're just going to leave her?" Flannagan was incredulous as he lifted his lantern higher, spreading more light over the area, illuminating Maeve's gray corpse. Ghostly shapes disappeared, transforming into feedbags and dangling bridles; lumpy, distorted images became saddles stretched across sawhorses.

"For now we leave her as we found her. Until the crime investigators have a look. We'll have to keep everyone out of the stable to preserve the integrity of the scene."

Flannagan frowned down at the body and sighed through his nose. "You don't think she just slit her wrists?"

"After setting a fire in Omen's stall and setting him free, then dousing the place with retardant?" Trent asked. "No, I don't think so."

Flannagan looked over at Jules. Silvery eyebrows formed one suspicious line. "So what were the two of you doin' in here?"

"Checking on the stock after the power went out," Trent replied without missing a beat.

"Yeah?" Flannagan wasn't buying it.

Trent didn't seem to notice. "I'll find the battery-powered heater and set it up, keep the place from freezing. But the temperature's already dropping in here. Let's get winter blankets on these horses." While Flannagan was still eyeing Jules, Trent opened a cupboard and began hauling out blankets. Jules was right beside him. Flannagan, too, went to work, snapping blankets on each of the animals in their stalls.

"Let me get this straight. You two were together when the fire broke out, is that what went down?" Flannagan asked as he stepped out of Scout's stall, his harsh gaze riveted to Jules, as if he wanted her to feel that she might be wearing some kind of scarlet letter.

"That's right," she said.

"In the middle of the frickin' night?"

"Yes." She wasn't backing down an inch. Let Flannagan think what he damned well wanted.

Trent nodded as he latched the gate to Arizona's box, then scratched the mare's nose as she shoved it over the top rail. "We were working on a project for my pod when the power went out."

"Were ya, now?" Flannagan's smile was a humorless white slash in the semidarkness, his sneer audible as he repeated, "A project?"

"That's what I said."

"After lights-out?" Flannagan said. "I'll remember that one."

"Do. In the meantime, just find Lynch and Meeker. You got walkie-talkies, Flannagan?" Trent double-checked the latch on Nova's stall.

Flannagan nodded. "Back at my place."

"Bring them," Trent instructed. "We need to be in contact. I've got a set that I'll pick up later."

Flannagan pointed out, "The security patrols are already using them." He glanced around the stable. "What the hell happened to the backup generator?"

"Don't know. Bring that up with Lynch as well. And leave the lantern. You can have this." Trent tossed Flannagan his flashlight, and the rumored ex-mercenary snagged it easily out of the air. "Let's move."

"You got it." Flannagan left the lantern with its harsh light washing the area in white light on the floor near one of the stalls.

Jules watched him leave, his rifle still slung over his back, as quickly as he'd strode in. She didn't trust him one little bit. After all, he was rumored to be a mercenary, a soldier who sold his loyalty to the highest bidder. Could he have done the same here? Was it possible that he was one of Lynch's henchmen, hired to fulfill the reverend's fanatical need to kill?

But why would Lynch want to kill off another student? That didn't make any sense!

Didn't Lynch have the ultimate say as to who was enrolled? If he made a mistake, taking in the wrong kid, why not just expel the student on a trumped-up charge? Why sink to murder?

For the thrill?

To make a point?

To make certain the victim never talked?

Quivering inside, Jules looked at the dead girl again. Propped up against the wall, her wrists slit, her hair burned, scrapes on her body, Maeve, like the horses, had been terrorized. Threatened. Burned. Someone was sick enough to have gotten off on her fear.

"What happened to you?" Jules whispered, then, hearing Trent's boots, snapped out of her reverie and helped him drag two huge battery-powered heaters from storage. They placed the heat sources about twenty feet apart in the aisle, then switched them on to bathe the center aisle of the stable in a weird, unworldly glow.

"That should do it for now," Trent said, looking around one last time.

Jules couldn't take her eyes off the dead girl. "You know, I think Maeve was here to meet Ethan Slade," she confided, then explained about the note she'd witnessed spilling from Maeve's bag and how distraught the girl had been earlier: ". . . she was really upset, nearly incoherent and crying her eyes out." Guilt tore through Jules at the memory. "I should have insisted she see a counselor. If I had, she might be alive now."

"Don't beat yourself up about it; this isn't your fault."

"But I should have stepped in," Jules said. "I had a feeling that something was wrong."

"We all knew she had a thing for Slade, that she was obsessed. She'd been counseled by Dr. Williams and Lynch, too, I think." He touched Jules on the shoulder gently, his gaze holding hers. "We don't have time for this—no blame game, okay?"

"But—"

"I know what you're going to say, but we have to work past it. For Maeve. To find out what happened to her. So, now, tell me, do you think Ethan's a suspect?"

"I think everyone is," she said, trying to push aside the guilt that clung to her. She remembered the comments in Lynch's files, all scribbled in his strong hand. "And that includes Dr. Tobias Lynch himself. No, check that. I think he's at the top of the list. After all he's the one who made all the notes, seemed to realize that some of the people he was hiring had their own sets of mental or emotional problems." She glanced toward the doorway where Flannagan had disappeared. "Take our buddy Bert Flannagan, for example. Turned down by a couple of police departments, but fine with Lynch. Good enough for Blue Rock. Flannagan had been in the military, was good around weapons, flew planes, saw combat, even maybe was a mercenary, all according to Lynch's notes. Doesn't sound like the best influence around troubled kids, now, does it? Only if the institution is really into discipline and warfare and the like.

"So why would the reverend, the director of the school, hire people he knew weren't completely sound, huh?" She asked. "Why not hire those applicants who are one hundred percent above board, those without even a hint of a problem? Lynch needed teachers and counselors, a whole staff of educators to deal with seriously troubled kids. And Lynch knew how deep these kids' issues are. So it really doesn't make sense, right? If you ask me, it's a lot like bringing together high octane gasoline and a lit match."

Trent scowled as his eyes glanced around the interior of the stable one last time. "I read Lynch a little differently," Trent said. "I think he's a man of conviction. Believes he's doing the right thing, following God's course. I don't think it's an act."

"Maybe not. But there are graveyards filled with dead soldiers, all who died in the name of religion. Leaders from the dawn of time have twisted their faith into their own personal vendettas." She eyed Maeve's corpse again and shuddered. This was no place for a discussion on theology or religion. "Look, I have to get out of here," she said. "I need to talk to Nell Cousineau, for one. I'm almost certain she sent me that note asking for help. She knows something. And then there's Ethan Slade. I'd like to hear what the hell he knows!" Her mind was spinning ahead. "Also, I need to talk to my cousin Analise and her husband, Eli. He was a TA here. He might have heard something when he was enrolled at Blue Rock and—"

"Jules!" Trent cut her off, then softened his voice and hugged her. "Slow down, would you? This is police business. It's dangerous!"

"That's not exactly a news flash!"

"Yeah, but, listen," he said, "I don't want you hurt. I'll take you back to Stanton House. You go back to your suite and lock the doors. I'll—"

"What? Are you crazy? After finding Maeve?" she asked incredulously. What was he thinking? "No way can I just sit still and wait around."

"There's not much else you can do." He was emphatic. "The phones aren't working, so you won't be able to get through and you won't accomplish anything running around the campus in the middle of the night with a god-damned killer hiding nearby!"

"But I have to do something! I—we—can't just sit around and wait. The last time he killed two people! How do we know that there isn't another dead kid somewhere?" she said, her panic rising again.

Trent shook his head. "We don't. But if someone's dead, we can't do anything about it now. It'll be daylight in a few hours."

"I don't think we should wait," she said, thinking of Shay. Was her sister safe? God, what if the killer were, at this moment, extracting his own special vengeance on her? Jules's stomach turned sour and the night seemed so, so long. "What time is it?"

"Don't know. Probably close to four."

"Still two, maybe three hours before dawn," she thought aloud. "The last time he hunted, he killed two people. Before that, if he did kill Lauren, only one, but maybe he's escalating, one, two, and tonight maybe three? What if poor Maeve is just the first of many?" She looked down at the dead girl once more, and her stomach threatened to heave.

Trent took hold of her arm. "You're jumping to conclusions," he warned. "Don't go off the deep end on me. Okay? I need you to think straight. Got that? You have to be clear."

She was nodding but trying to step toward the door, to get out, away from the gloom and death that lingered here.

"Just wait," Trent said, fingers tight over her arm. "Hold the lantern up. High. Like this." He wrapped her fingers over the handle of the lantern he'd suspended over Maeve's body. "There. Hold still." Retrieving his cell phone from his pocket again, he flipped it open, hit a button, and began taking pictures of the dead girl.

Each time the camera in his phone flashed, illuminating Maeve's fixed gaze and gray face, Jules cringed.

Click. Another image of death.

"I might not be able to call on it yet, but this damned phone can still serve a function." He took two more shots as a nervous horse whinnied. "Just in case we have to leave, I want a record of how things looked when we got here."

Click. Click. Click. Three new, ghastly images.

Trent continued. "I would hate to leave and come back to find the girl moved or missing or I don't know what." Walking away from the body, telling Jules where to redirect the lantern's beam, he took some photos of Omen's damaged stall, then returned with a measuring tape, which he pulled out to the length of one foot. He lay the tape by Maeve's hand, near the knife. "Just for some idea of perspective," he said before snapping several more images.

Footsteps sounded outside.

Jules's heart leapt to her throat.

Trent grabbed his pistol and trained it on the door just as it opened. Frank Meeker, weapon drawn, eased inside. "Police!" he said, as Trent lowered his pistol.

"Glad you're here," Trent said as Meeker's gaze slid around the stable to land on Maeve's body.

"Another one?" he asked as Jules, eyes turned from the death scene, nodded. "Son of a bitch." Meeker shook his head sadly and holstered his sidearm. "Son of a goddamned bitch."

CHAPTER 40

Cooper Trent!
Shay, lying on her twin bed in the dorm, remembered why he seemed so familiar.

Jules had dated him. It had been during that weird time when the whole family was off-kilter. Max had just remarried and had a new baby, pushing Shay even further away from him. Edie had snagged all that she could of Max's money, then retreated, going back to Rip Delaney, a son of a bitch if there ever had been one. It had been obvious to everyone, except love-besotted Edie, that Rip Delaney had only started seeing her and married her again for a shot at her part of the Stillman fortune, the pittance she'd received from divorce number two.

Greed, greed, greed. It had always come down to money with Edie. Same with Rip.

Then there was Max Stillman, dear old Dad. No, make that Max Senior as now there was a Junior for him to dote on. At six, Max, the younger, Shay's half brother, was rumored to be hell on wheels. Good. Served her father right. It had always bothered Shay that Edie had been pregnant when she'd married Max and it had crossed Shay's willing mind that Edie had trapped Max with her pregnancy with Shay and that was the reason he'd never been close to his only daughter.

"Who cares?" she muttered now, but felt heat at the back of her eyelids. The truth of the matter was that Maxwell Octavius Stillman was just another self-indulgent creep who had cast Shaylee aside like last night's leftovers once he became a father to stupid little Maxwell Junior.

Even before "Maxie" was born, Shay's dad had never really had much to do with her, and she couldn't even say it was to get back at Edie. Nuh-uh. Max just didn't give a damn.

Not like Rip Delaney had with his kid. Yeah, he'd been a loser with a capital L, always screwing around and getting into debt because he gambled, but at least he'd loved Jules. Sickeningly so.

Disturbed, Shay brought her thoughts back to the present; reined in those old emotions that were too painful to think about. Especially when Shay fantasized that her father had never met Hester, wife number 2, had never conceived her half brother . . .

Quit thinking about it! So your old man's a prick, so what? Just focus on the here and now.

Shay was keyed up tonight, unable to sleep. Unlike Crystal. Shay's roommate was currently dead to the world, her head buried under her pillow, her neck exposed, the odd-looking dragon tattoo barely visible in the half-light as she softly snored.

Earlier, Shay had heard the power go off, the rumble of the furnace fading into stillness. She'd clicked on her flashlight, just so the darkness wouldn't close in on her. So she wouldn't feel so alone.

When the backup electricity had powered on half an hour later, she'd gone to the window and spied two people walking swiftly along one of the campus paths, Jules and

Cooper Trent, Shay's pod leader, huddled together. Trent had touched the crook of Jules's arm as they slogged through the drifts in the predawn hours, when no one except the security patrols was supposed to be out.

So what did it all mean?

Nothing good, that was for sure.

And why hadn't Jules confided to her about Trent, that he was the same bull rider she'd once thought she'd marry? Sure, Jules had never admitted that she'd planned to wed the cowboy, but Shay had known, had sensed the change in her. Shay understood her older sister so much better than Jules understood her.

Now, though, why was Jules keeping secrets?

As a sense of foreboding slid through her, Shay had watched through the window as near the chapel Trent leaned over and brushed a kiss across her sister's cheek.

Like he cared for her.

A stone forming in the pit of her stomach, Shay wondered if Jules had known that Trent was part of the staff when she'd taken the job. Maybe Jules had come to Blue Rock not to help Shaylee but because she wanted her old boyfriend back. Maybe Shay was just an excuse.

That was crazy, wasn't it?

Jules, though no genius, had loved her, had always protected her younger sister.

Until now.

Shay had been about to turn away from the window when she'd spied another figure against the snowy landscape. Tall. Alone.

What in the world, Shay had wondered. Had the loner been following Jules? No, that didn't make any sense. He had paused, as if contemplating his next move, then turned, and in a split second, his face had been illuminated by the moon's frail light.

Father Jake?

Shay's heart had nearly dropped.

Why in the world had he been out in the middle of the night?

Probably not writing next week's sermon.

Shay had stepped away from the window and spied her backpack in the corner of the room. She hadn't called Jules, as the damned cell phone she'd taken off Nona had nearly run out of battery, and Shay didn't have the charger.

So, she'd stretched out on the bed, contemplating her next move, thinking about how she could get out of this damned prison.

Finally, she'd decided, she would have to confront her sister the old-fashioned way: face-to-face.

As for a killer on the loose?

She wasn't worried.

She could handle herself.

Now, smiling to herself, she dressed in the dark, adding another thermal layer beneath her jacket. Ski pants slid over her jeans, and she stepped into boots. Gloves in her pocket, she was ready.

Quietly, she eased out of the room and down the hallway. So what if she set off any alarms? She was no longer worried about the stupid security devices; so far, they hadn't caught her coming or going at will. She knew that the cameras in the rooms didn't exist. As for the hallways, she'd take her chances.

Down the stairs and into the basement.

Though, supposedly, each building had been double-checked and made more secure, it was a joke. Just like everything else around here.

Quickly, she made her way to the window and unlatched it with the screwdriver she'd hidden in an old dilapidated bookcase. Pushing the glass open was easy; hoisting herself upward and through, her escape was a piece of cake. Once outside, she felt alive again. The night air was crisp and bracing, the snow a thick white blanket, the moon a bright orb in a black sky speckled with stars.

While the twinkling lights in the gazebo shined no longer, a few security lamps offered some illumination, enough so that she could navigate easily.

She stayed on the shoveled, trampled paths, hoping to keep her tracks hidden now that no new snow would cover them. The brittle air burned in her lungs, bringing with it a faint scent of smoke.

With a sense of urgency pushing her, Shay hurried forward, across the lawn, under an awning and around the corner of the admin building. She eyed Stanton House and the area around the gym and cafeteria, scoping out the area, hoping to dodge the idiot nerd patrols. She just didn't want to have to explain herself to Missy Albright or that freak show of a teacher, Flannagan.

Nothing.

She was alone.

She let out a breath and took two steps forward.

Crunch!

Hell! She froze. Was that a footstep? Where?

Her heart trip-hammered.

She inched her way to the side of a building and tried to calm down near a snow-draped rhododendron. Slowly, noiselessly, she turned, her eyes sweeping the serene white landscape. Everything was so still, eerily peaceful, the wind that had screamed through the canyons silenced, the icy pellets of snow that had stung her cheeks for days no longer.

The campus was empty.

Not one person around.

Not even a security patrol making rounds.

Nonetheless, her nerves tightened, the muscles in the back of her neck stiffening. She *felt* someone observing her; unseen eyes watching her every move.

Stop it! Don't fall for any of the paranoia going around! Just get to Jules. Find out what the hell she's got planned, how she intends to get you out of this freakoid school!

She started forward.

Crunch!

That was definitely a footstep.

Damn!

Instinctively, she whirled, snow kicking up behind her as she fell into a crouch, her muscles tense and ready, all her martial arts training clicking in. If she had to, she would attack.

She caught a glimpse of someone by the dorm.

The hairs on the back of her neck raised.

This was it!

The person looked her way.

Nell Cousineau?

The ninny was standing alone, shivering by the side of the dorm.

Seriously?

"Shaylee?" Nell said, spying her, relief evident in her small face. The girl's teeth were chattering loudly, her breath a cloud.

What a moron! Nell wasn't even wearing a ski coat, just some kind of flimsy flannel jacket.

"Shhh!" Shay hissed.

"Can you help me?" Nell said, moving closer.

"What?" This was the *last* thing Shay needed.

"I'm locked out," Nell said, her big eyes pleading.

Great! "What the hell are you doing out here?" Shaylee was pissed as she stood up and took a step toward the idiot of a girl. "Don't you know it's dangerous to be outside? That's why they've got the beefed up patrols."

"I know, I know," Nell said, rubbing her arms and looking scared as a trapped rabbit. "It all freaks me out so bad. I—I can't stand it here anymore. I've tried to get people to help me. Counselors and teachers and my mom . . ." Her voice faded for a second and Shay thought the goose might break down into a puddle of tears. Instead she sniffed loudly. "I—I just want to get away from here and go home."

"Yeah, well, I get that." Boy did she ever, but she didn't have time for Nell's ridiculous antics. "Look, what were you thinking? What did you think you could do? Walk through the blizzard?"

"It's not snowing now," Nell said, hugging herself, and blinking like crazy. "I thought maybe I could steal one of the snowmobiles and drive it out of here. I know where the keys are."

Snowmobiles? "You do?" Shay was suddenly intrigued. This was the first she'd heard of snowmobiles, but it made sense. Of course Blue Rock Academy would have them. And they would be the answer to her prayers, a way to navigate through the snow-crusted hills and escape. For the first time in days, hope swelled inside her. "Where are the keys?"

"Here." Nell actually held up her gloved hand and opened her palm to show off a tiny ring with two keys dangling from it. "I ripped off a set."

"Really?" For an instant, Shay's esteem for Nell shot to the heavens. How great was this? But Nell? Really? Wimpy Nell jacking anything, much less something as cool as a set of keys, was definitely a surprise. A good one.

Shaylee could use Nell's idea to her own advantage, if that was what it took. She stepped around the corner of the building again, past the rhododendron with its snowy leaves. "Let me see." She was still trying to wrap her mind around what Nell's real agenda was. "So you were going out riding in subzero temperatures without a jacket?"

Wait a minute!

That didn't make any sense!

Oh, crap! Could Nell be part of some kind of a—?

She felt hot breath on the back of her neck. *Oh, God! NO!* Fear spurted through her bloodstream. Instinctively, she started to run. Rough, strong arms clamped around her from behind, nearly knocking her down.

Oh, Jesus, please no!

He smelled like sweat. A pig.

Panic shot through her brain.

She twisted, started to scream, tried to round on this huge, burly maniac holding her. Too late! One steely arm forced her upper body and shoulders against him, a gloved hand over her mouth.

Shay bit. Tasted leather!

She felt the cold muzzle of a gun pressed hard against her temple. Instantly, she stopped moving.

"One move, one little sound," he snarled against her ear, his breath foul and warm. "I swear, bitch, I'll blow your fuckin' brains out."

CHAPTER 41

Her captor yanked Shay's arms back, angrily forcing her hands behind her.

Click! A pair of handcuffs were locked over her wrists. Cold, hard steel bit into her wrists.

"How does it feel, bitch?" he growled against her ear again, and then, just because he could, he twisted the handcuffs a bit. She nearly fell to her knees. Pain burned up Shay's arms, screamed through her shoulders, ground into her spine. She gasped, the agony excruciating, then wrenched herself away, desperate for a look at his face.

Moonlight washed against his handsome, cruel features.

Eric Rolfe!

Satan incarnate.

His eyes glittered with a deep-seated, evil glee that twisted his lips into a cruel grin. "Gotcha."

Screaming wouldn't work. He'd kill her before anyone noticed and then claim he'd thought she was the killer.

Hell!

If only she could get out of these restraints! All she needed was a little room to spin, gain some momentum, and she'd kick that sick smile off the bastard's face. He'd go down cold. She could take care of him, she could. She only needed a few feet of space.

But the monster knew what she planned and held her fast.

"I'm sorry," Nell whispered, tears running down her face as she shivered with the cold.

What a wimp!

"They said . . ." Her teeth were chattering crazily, not so much from the cold but from the fear that was eating her up inside. ". . . They said that if I did this, I would be safe." She was sobbing now as Missy Albright, part of the security patrol with Eric, showed up and snatched the keys from Nell's shaking fingers.

Missy pocketed the keys.

Nell mewled forlornly.

"Shhh!" Shay couldn't believe what a weakling Nell was. But she also couldn't believe that she herself had been stupid enough to be caught off guard, to be lured into this ridiculous trap. And the fact that Eric Rolfe had caught her only made it worse.

"Let's go," Missy said, nodding to Eric. "Before anyone else shows up." She glanced up at Stanton House, where a few lights were burning as Eric pushed Shay forward and Nell, sobbing, was herded by Missy.

Shay was nudged along, the barrel of Eric's gun now placed firmly against her spine, reminding her that he'd gladly shoot through her spinal cord and leave her dead or paralyzed. "Don't trip," he whispered softly, "or make any sudden moves, or I promise you, you'll never get off another round kick or any of that tae kwon do shit again."

The backup power had returned, but Jules wasn't about to sleep.

Not after Maeve's murder.

She'd allowed Trent to walk her, first to the chapel, where he'd kissed her gently enough to break her stupid heart, then here, to Stanton House, to what? Wait for the damned dawn? Well, that wasn't going to happen.

She paced from one side of her suite of rooms to the other and all the while, the image of Maeve, lying in a puddle of her own dark blood, burned through her mind. It was the same kind of mental picture of her father that she'd carried with her since the night he died.

What was it her shrink had said? That she had the unique ability to block out impressions she didn't want to face, but also to dwell on those that were the most repulsive. He'd been fascinated by her case and had told her that she'd locked Trent away from her life because she was afraid that if she trusted him too much, he'd leave. Just as her father had left her the first time Rip and Edie had divorced. Just as her stepfather, Max Stillman, had after his short marriage to her mother. Then her father, after remarrying Edie, dying as he had . . . Rip's death had been the ultimate abandonment.

He hadn't wanted to leave, though, had he, Jules?

He left because someone took his life.

You pushed Trent away because you were afraid of loving him too much, of being hurt, of him leaving you . . . You were a coward.

"Stop!" she ordered, her voice ringing louder than she'd expected. Too bad. She wouldn't listen to the arguments that raged in her mind, the stressful battles that always brought with them pounding, merciless headaches. Just like the one that was forming behind her eyes right now.

Think, Jules, think. Figure this out, damn it!

Before something happens to Shay!

She walked into the bathroom, found her bottle of Excedrin and tossed back four pills before dipping her head under the faucet for a swallow of water. Standing, wiping her mouth with the back of her hand, she caught her reflection in the mirror, witnessed her own fear, her own frustration in her own eyes.

Who was behind these murders, the brutal killings, all with separate MOs? She and Shaylee had spent night after night watching *CSI* and *Law and Order* and anything forensic on what was then Court TV. She knew how things worked, and it seemed odd, out of character, for the murderer to kill Drew with an ax or hatchet, to strangle Nona and dangle her from the rafters, and then to slit Maeve's wrists, after burning her hair. Nona and Drew had been naked, Maeve fully clothed, but then Nona and Drew had taken their own clothes off presumably while having sex.

The killer hadn't undressed them.

There had to be a connection between the killings, one she was missing. One that was deeper than the fact that the killings had been committed in the stable.

Or was that just a line from TV? She stared at her reflection in the mirror over the sink. Who was killing off students? And why those particular students? Were the killings random, the victims' deaths a matter of opportunity, or had the murders been meticulously planned, the victims chosen and stalked? That seemed more likely, considering the methods of death.

Or was that, too, something she'd learned from watching too much television crime?

She threw cold water on her face, willing the headache to subside, then yanked the hand towel from her face and patted her skin dry.

How had the killer known Maeve would be in the stable?

Because he'd lured her there with his note. Remember? The piece of paper with OMEN scrawled upon it?

She glanced at her reflection one more time, and confirmation parked in her mirrored gaze.

There was only one reason Maeve would go out in the

middle of the night: to meet Ethan Slade. Hadn't she said as much to Trent earlier?

Snapping off the bathroom light on the fly, Jules walked into the living area and stopped at her desk. She rifled through a few papers stacked haphazardly in the corner near her computer and found the schedule for the security patrols. Her eyes skimmed down the list of assignments, stopping when she came to the guards listed for the time span when she assumed Maeve had been killed.

"You guys are toast," she said aloud, reading that Ethan Slade and Roberto Ortega, under the guidance of Salvatore DeMarco, had been on security duty early in the night.

Jules didn't doubt for a second that Ethan made plans to meet up with Maeve after his shift ended.

She checked further, running her finger down the security detail. After Ethan and Roberto, Missy Albright and Eric Rolfe were up. Bert Flannagan was supposed to have been their supervisor. Except Flannagan was alone when he'd appeared at the stables. He'd gotten caught up in dealing with the aftermath of the fire and Maeve's murder.

Which conveniently left Missy and Eric to their own devices . . .

Was it possible? Had he been covering for them? Or had they given him the slip earlier to do their horrific deed? Or, more likely, had he been the killer and had only returned to the scene of the crime to make it appear that he knew nothing about it? Could he be that good of an actor? His reaction to Maeve's body had seemed legit.

Jules's skin crinkled at the thought of that particular security team, the mercenary guiding smart but secretive Missy and hothead Eric. Hadn't Flannagan appeared in the stables carrying a rifle? For protection on the security detail or to lead a group of TAs on a murderous rampage? Ice collected in her soul.

Nothing was making sense, all the pieces of this horrific

jigsaw puzzle not quite fitting, the edges and corners close together but refusing to snap together. What was she missing?

Think, think, think! You're running out of time. Again, she swept her gaze over the security roster. After Missy and Eric, Zach Bernsen and Kaci Donahue were on patrol with Kirk Spurrier as their guide. What had Lynch mentioned about Spurrier in his files? That he'd been in the Air Force and was passive-aggressive? Again, a man who was in his element around weaponry. Just the kind of guy you wanted teaching the kids a few theology classes. Bernsen, Donahue, and Spurrier. Another suspect group, if there ever was one. Zach Bernsen was a know-it-all to the nth degree and Kaci seemed to be a follower, with little mind of her own. Then there was Spurrier, a handsome, athletic man who didn't say much, who held his cards close to his vest.

And he wasn't the only one who was suspected.

Everyone in the damned school seemed to possess a serious psychological dysfunction. As if Lynch had chosen them for their flaws, rather than their attributes.

And it's worse than just a case of dysfunction; at least one of them is homicidal.

Too bad there hadn't been a file on Lynch himself, she thought. No doubt he was the headmaster of death and destruction in what so many people believed was an idyllic institution of rehabilitation, education, and hope.

"Such BS." Jules muttered, frustrated. "A total load of bull."

Feeling as if sand was slipping far too quickly through the hourglass, she walked to the window and peered outside to the calm night. In the center of Lake Superstition, the waters were dark as obsidian. Closer to the shoreline, the edges of the lake were glazed with ice and snow. The seaplane was still moored, cast in ice. She remembered spying Spurrier on the dock earlier in the day. God, it seemed a lifetime ago when she'd last cast a glance in his direction and watched as he, along with help from some of the students, had brushed and shoveled snow from the wings, fuselage, and floats. Several of the TAs had been called into duty: Tim Takasumi, Ethan Slade, and Zach Bernsen had been the last crew she'd witnessed working on the plane. Now it sat unmoving, shackled in the ice.

She looked to the center of the lake again and wondered if the weapon that had killed Drew Prescott was lying deep in its dark waters.

Worse yet, was it possible Lauren Conway's body was hidden deep in those still, dark waters? Reduced to bones, weighed down by anchors or cement blocks or any damned thing, was her corpse lying upon the lake's bottom?

God only knew.

Jules rubbed at her temples, forcing the headache back as she squinted into the night. With the main source of power out, the campus was darker than usual, but the snow, cast silver by moon glow, helped illuminate the grounds.

Where was Trent?

Her heart twisted at the thought he might be in danger, outside alone, looking for a killer. "Be safe," she whispered and tried to convince herself he would be careful, that he had police training, that he would be all right. And then there was Shay. At least Shaylee was secure in her dorm room.

Right?

Something felt wrong about that.

If only Jules could get in touch with her, confirm that she was okay. The damned cells were out, but there had to be a way to find out that Shay was safe.

Of course the sane thing to do was to wait it out, until dawn when the sun chased away the shadows and the doors on the campus were unlocked.

The less sane thing to do was to chance it; go outside,

cross the expansive, snow-covered lawn that separated the buildings and pound on the door of Shay's dorm until someone let her inside. Or, Jules supposed, she could chase down Adele Burdette, headmistress for the girls. Surely Burdette would allow Jules to see Shay, but if so, she'd have to tip her hand, admit that they were sisters.

For God's sake, who cares? People are dying! Being murdered! You have to do something. Anything.

Jules couldn't just sit here, safe and sound, while those she loved—Trent and Shay—could possibly be in danger.

Without a second thought, she found her snow gear and didn't consider how easily she'd put Trent into the category of loved ones as she stepped into insulated pants and zipped her jacket.

It wasn't really a surprise.

Hadn't her ex-husband, Sebastian, accused her of that fact over and over, for the short period of her marriage? Hadn't his perception of her "never getting over that damned bull rider" given Sebastian an excuse for his affair with Peri? Hadn't her best friend thrown that very fact in her face when Jules had found them in her marriage bed?

"Oh, hell," she said. This was no time to dwell on ancient history. Pocketing Trent's pistol, she left her room and hurried down the stairs. She was out the front door, flashlight in her hand, when she stopped to catch her breath.

First things first; she'd connect with Trent, no matter how pissed he was that she hadn't sat still. Lord, he should have known her better than that! If she and her sister had anything in common, it was that they never sat idly by.

She started for his cabin, took two steps, then stopped as if yanked by invisible reins.

From the corner of her eye, she saw movement. In that split second, she realized she wasn't alone in the darkness. She slid backward, into the shadows, her gaze fastened on the knot of people heading in the opposite direction. Huddled against the cold, their faces in shadow, their breaths mingling in the arctic air, they trudged through the snow to the chapel.

Not a word was spoken.

The silence was like an unheard knell of death.

Her fingers tightened over the pistol. Was this a security patrol?

She didn't think so.

There were too many of them. Five? No, four! All walking as rapidly as they could, as if they were bound by a single purpose. Which was what? Murder?

Her heart stone cold, she inched forward. For a second, she thought she recognized Shay in the group. One of the members was the right size, and moved in the same manner Shay did . . . but that was impossible. Right? Two of the others were taller, dressed in thick, dark clothes, pressed shoulder to shoulder, the smaller ones in front. The fourth member of the group was different, though. She was walking in front of the larger ones and appeared to be a girl, her long hair visible, her figure slim, not bulked up by thick clothing. Bareheaded and vulnerable, she stumbled forward, her shoulders shaking. From the cold? Or was she sobbing?

She, and the person who resembled Shaylee, were being prodded forward, urged onward. The bareheaded girl tripped.

Jules stepped forward, opening her mouth to yell out, when one of the taller ones yanked the girl to her feet as they passed under one of the few lights that glowed in the darkness. A glint of silver flashed in the bigger person's hand, the man behind the girl who looked like Shay.

Jules's heart nearly stopped as she recognized a pistol.

Of course, for the security detail. But . . .

The bareheaded girl, stumbling but on her feet again, her arm now held firmly by the tall, thin member, turned and looked over her shoulder. Her face was pale, her eyes round with panic.

Oh, God, it was Nell Cousineau!

The girl who had left Jules the note.

The student who had pleaded for her help.

In that moment, Jules realized that the two larger people were not members of the security patrol, but killers. She didn't doubt for a second that the larger, stronger people were marching these girls to their ultimate doom.

In the bluish light, she caught a glimpse of the girl with the gun pressed against her back.

Jules felt sick inside as she recognized her sister.

Her worst nightmare had come true: The killers had Shay!

Crackkkkk!

Somewhere glass shattered.

Trent froze in his tracks. He turned, straining to listen, trying to figure out from which direction the sound of cracking glass had come.

He'd been running back to the stable to meet with Lynch and Meeker when he'd heard the distinctive sound of glass breaking, the sound echoing through the stillness.

"What the devil?" he whispered under his breath.

Of course, it was quiet again. Deathly quiet. Not a noise to break the silence.

Even with Maeve's murder, there was a deceptive serenity and calm over the white-blanketed buildings of Blue Rock Academy.

That was changing, of course. Though Lynch had decided to withhold information from the students until the morning, hoping to contact Maeve's family first, the word was getting out.

Some of it came from the staff, most of whom Lynch and

Flannagan had contacted while Meeker guarded Maeve's grisly death scene. Then there were the patrols of students who also knew what was going on. Trent had noticed lights in dorm rooms flickering to life. Yeah, the word was getting around that the killer had struck again.

And so why the sound of shattering glass?

Thud!

He spun, turning quickly toward the direction of the sound. And his house. Running now, he was certain that the noise emanated from the direction of the row of cottages.

Who would be breaking windows in the middle of the damned night? In a second, he flashed on the table in his house and Lynch's private files, spread out and open.

If someone stole them . . .

"Hell!"

Speeding through the thick snow, he cut across the back of the admin building and along a thicket of pines to the alley behind the row of cabins where darkness prevailed, still no backup power reaching this string of old cottages.

All the houses were dark, no signs of life visible.

All except his.

Through the drawn shades of his cabin he saw firelight shifting, brightness illuminating the interior.

His insides clenched. The fire he'd left smoldering in the grate should have died by now, and all the lanterns had been turned down. His house, too, should appear nearly dark but now offered up an eerie orange glow behind the shades.

Silently, he reached for his pistol before remembering he'd given his weapon to Jules.

He rounded to the back of the house without making a sound. Sure enough, the window in the back door was broken, jagged shards of glass visible in its frame, the door itself hanging ajar, the smell of burning oil escaping with a thick cloud of smoke.

Damn it!

Through the broken glass, he spied a wall of flames. Hot and wild, crackling hungrily, they ran through his home. "Son of a bitch," he muttered, flicking on his walkie-talkie as he climbed the short flight of stairs to the back porch.

"Yeah?" Bert Flannagan said.

"It's Trent." He kept his voice low but firm. "I need backup. ASAP. I've got a fire in my cabin. You hear me, ASAP!" Trent clicked off, wondering if he'd just alerted the enemy. Not really giving a damn, he picked up a piece of oak from the back porch, the only weapon at hand.

It didn't take a brain surgeon to figure out why his cabin had been broken into: Someone was dead set on destroying Lynch's damning files.

Who?

Had Tobias Lynch figured out the files hadn't been burned the first time?

So much for being the man of God and faith.

He burst through the door to the kitchen.

A wave of heat assaulted him. Black smoke stung his nostrils as he crossed the kitchen floor.

Bang!

Through the archway to the living room, he witnessed a shower of flame exploding as another window shattered. Sparks rained. Heat billowed.

No damned way would he let this happen!

Through the kitchen he propelled himself, expecting someone to leap out at him and knock him flat. His gloved fingers dug into the chunk of oak, his makeshift weapon.

No assailant sprang from the shadows.

No dark figure pointed a gun at him.

Without thinking twice, he yanked the fire extinguisher from the wall in the hallway.

Still no assailant.

Maybe he'd gotten lucky.

Trent dropped the chunk of wood to free his right hand.

Deftly, he engaged the extinguisher, setting off a fume of CO_2 throughout the hallway and living area.

As black smoke billowed and coiled around him, dancing crazily and searing his lungs, he headed farther into the shambles that had been his house. Fire was crawling along the living room floor, catching in the upholstery. Eagerly, the flames ate through a blanket that had been spread from the fireplace to the mattress he'd left in the middle of the floor. Clearly someone had worked to make it look as if the fire were a careless accident.

Heat swelled and shimmered as he sprayed the fire.

Another window popped, glass spraying.

The dining room table was a pyre. Already blackened pages were turned to ash, once legible files burning wildly. A broken kerosene lantern, the source of the blaze, lay in the middle, shards of glass glinting bloodred.

It was all destroyed. All of Lynch's damning notes. All the proof Jules had risked her life procuring. All up in smoke!

"Goddamned son of a bitch!" Trent muttered as he kept extinguishing the flames, fighting the ever-encroaching fire. He trained the nozzle on the table, a hissing spray of CO_2 clouding the air.

He coughed and tasted smoke. His eyes watered. Still he sprayed, forcing the flames down, killing the fire, trying to salvage something, anything from Lynch's damning notes.

Something moved in his burning, peripheral vision.

He blinked, disbelieving, but there it was again, just out of focus, caught by the corner of his eye. Spinning, he pointed the nozzle warily. What had he seen? Was someone inside? Had Flannagan arrived?

"Hey!" he called out.

Crunch. Glass splintered as if someone had stepped on it.

Oh, crap!

Bam!

Pain exploded in the back of his skull.

His knees buckled.

Trent fell to the floor, his head slamming against the floorboards. The fire extinguisher clanged as it banged against the floor beside him and rolled away. Flames and smoke rose before his eyes and a deep, searing blackness threatened to pull him under.

Stay awake! Don't pass out! For God's sake, Trent, hang the hell on!

His eyes swam. He blinked as the fire swept closer, shimmering, slithering waves of flame.

He tried to get up, to roll over and get his knees beneath him, to gut it out and stand, but his body wouldn't move an inch.

Still fire crept closer. Teasing. Toying. While he lay motionless.

Get up! Get up! For the love of God . . . Move!

But he couldn't. His brain couldn't connect with his muscles and in a last instant of clarity, Cooper Trent knew he was a dead man.

CHAPTER 42

Jules, hiding in the shadows of the frigid night, watching Nell and Shaylee being marched into the chapel, took off after them. Too many kids had died already, been murdered, and now her sister was being marched to her death, a gun pressed to Shay's back. No way could she let this happen.

Fingers clenched over the pistol Trent had given her, Jules kept the small group in sight following at a distance. Shay was walking strangely, her hands behind her back, the person with the pistol shoving her, steering her.

Maybe she should shoot into the air to alert someone—anyone!—but she couldn't. Shaylee's captor could lose control, fire and kill her sister in an instant. The same horrible ending would happen if she tried to bluff her way and aim her pistol at the man pushing Shaylee forward. The way Jules saw it, she had no choice but to follow them into the chapel.

God help me. Oh, please, and be with her.

Prodding Shaylee, the biggest of them, a tall man or boy, herded the group inside. He was confident, knew his way around, didn't bother with any lights.

Jules was only a few steps behind. She moved swiftly

and silently, managing to catch the door before it slammed shut. Quickly, she slid into the shadowed warmth of the interior, the door clicking, uninterrupted behind her. She caught her breath as she got her bearings, then softly she crept through the nave. She heard footsteps ahead of her, the sound of feet shuffling along the hallway, then onto the staircase, muted by the carpet. She reached the landing, and thought the footsteps were heading down to the basement rather than up to the loft.

What was down there?

A dead end. Be careful.

Pistol clenched in her fingers, Jules started down the stairs, keeping a short distance between the group of four and herself. At the bottom of the stairs, someone clicked on a flashlight and she stopped midway down, barely daring to breathe. If the light were shined upward, she would be caught in its thin, hard beam.

"Let's go! Move it!" a gruff voice ordered and the flashlight's beam turned away from the stairs, bobbing along the hallway as the group navigated through the dark, tangled corridors.

Heart in her throat, Jules inched along the hallway behind them. What were they planning to do to Shay? Flashes of Maeve's dead body cut through her brain, and she vowed nothing so vile would happen to her sister, the girl she'd loved and protected, despite all of Shay's flaws. Jules wouldn't allow a fate as brutal and macabre as Nona's or Maeve's to happen to her sister. Or anyone else. She had to stop the obscene killing spree and stop it now.

Nervous sweat collected on her spine as she inched forward, pressed against the wall, trailing behind as they proceeded through the warren of offices and halls.

Farther and farther into the darkness.

Her gaze fixed on that bobbing, weaving light ahead.

She swallowed back her fear and cast aside worries that

she would stumble or in some way alert the attackers that she was on their heels.

Keep your cool, just be steady, she told herself, but was reminded of her nightmare, of walking through a darkened house, slowly following the sound of dripping water until, at last, she came across her father's dead body.

In the dream she held a knife.

Tonight she had a pistol, and damn it all to hell, she'd use it if it meant saving Shaylee.

Just as she would have used the knife to save her father.

No way was she going to replay the same scene with its new cast of characters. Jules wasn't about to come across her sister's dead body. Not tonight.

She noticed the light disappear, as if it had turned a corner, outlining the wall in a faint, eerie glow. It's now or never! Heart racing, dread propelling her, her gloved fingers trailing against the wall until she touched nothing, she followed.

At the corner she turned.

Took one step.

A bright, glaring light flashed in front of her eyes.

She gasped. Lashing out with the gun, she struck the flashlight down.

"Bitch!" a deep voice snarled. *Eric Rolfe.*

Blinded, she tried to back away. Someone jumped her from behind. Her attacker's weight pushed her face down on to the thin carpet. She tasted dust and fibers, but fought. Twisting. Flailing. Hitting with the damned gun. Her attacker was breathing heavily, but wouldn't give an inch. Jules's eyes were still struggling to focus, the flashlight trained on her.

A girl screamed, the horrid sound echoing down the corridors.

Jules struggled.

She connected once with the butt of the gun.

Her attacker let out a wounded, frustrated howl, then easily pried the pistol from her fingers.

Oh, God, no . . .

In the stark beam of the flashlight, Jules found herself staring down the barrel of the very gun Trent had given her. Breathing hard, blood drizzling from the corner of her mouth, Missy Albright gloated.

"No," Jules said, not really believing that the girl who had been assigned to her class was capable of murder.

Smiling with smug hatred, her platinum hair shimmering white, Missy seemed to read her mind. Swiping at the blood, she taunted, "So, Ms. Farentino, why don't you name some of the things from the 1930s that are the same as today?"

"What?" Jules said, her head thundering. God, what kind of sickness was this?

"Hey, I know," Missy said, grinning more widely, blood showing between her teeth. Her little-girl voice irritating. "How about starting with Bonnie and Clyde in the thirties, and today? Uh, how about Missy and Eric?"

"Oh, shut up!" Eric ordered, but he did laugh, that nasty humorless chuckle.

Nell Cousineau trembled like a leaf, looking ready to throw up, and Shay, hands behind her back, glowered with pure hatred as she stared at Rolfe.

"Ms. Farentino," he mocked, taking the gun from Missy. "I figured you would join us. You know," he said, wagging the pistol in front of her nose, "you're just so damned predictable."

She met his stare without flinching.

"I'm thinking," he continued.

"That would be a first," Shay said and was rewarded with Missy jabbing an elbow into her side. "Bitch!" she muttered, doubling over in pain and Jules couldn't help her.

"Shh," she warned, hoping Shaylee would take heed.

"As I was saying," Eric said, a little more agitated. "I think maybe we can have some kind of family counseling tonight. You know, a little sisterly one-on-one? You've both got dad issues, right?"

So they knew that she and Shaylee were related. Jules should have guessed.

"You're a dick, you know that, don't you?" Shaylee said. "A real piece of work."

"That may be, bitch, but guess who has the gun?" Eric was really rubbing it in now. "So if I were you, I'd shut the fuck up and start pleading for your pathetic life." He glanced at Missy and his sadistic grin widened. "Not that it will help. You're as good as dead already."

The fire was spreading, Trent was vaguely aware of the shimmering wall of heat, the acrid smoke and the crackling sound of voracious flames.

He blinked, trying to keep from blacking out, and saw the toes of heavy boots in front of his face. Glancing up, feeling blood ooze from the back of his head, his eyes focused on not one, but two dark figures looming above him, surrounded by creeping, shifting fire.

The room spun. He thought he was seeing double, but, no, they were different, not twins, not some melded dizzying image. Dressed in black, the men stood together, glaring down at him. Through the smoke, he recognized Kirk Spurrier, the pilot, his dark silhouette outlined by flames, as he said, "This is what you get when you go nosing around where you're not wanted." Spurrier grinned with a sense of satisfaction, the smile of a demon.

Spurrier was behind the murders? Not Lynch? Something was wrong here. Pain pounded in Trent's head as he clung desperately to the conscious world.

The pilot's accomplice was no big surprise, a kid Trent knew well. Tall, athletic Zach Bernsen was shoulder to shoulder with the older man. The piece of oak Trent had dropped now swung from one of Bernsen's big hands. As Trent struggled, Bernsen raised the bloody stick as if all too ready to bash Trent's head in once again.

"You bastard," Trent spat at the pilot as blackness pulled at the corners of his vision.

"Make that 'you superior bastard,' seeing as you're on the floor." Spurrier's smile twisted evilly and he snorted an amused laugh. "Welcome to your own personal hell, Trent. It's better than you deserve. I know who you are, that you were hired by Lauren Conway's parents to find out what happened to her. And I know about Julia Farentino as well." As if noticing Trent tense, he added, "That's right, I saw you together tonight, and it didn't take a genius to realize that the two of you are involved. Then there's that little fact everyone kept forgetting to cough up, that Julia Farentino is related to Shaylee Stillman." Before Trent could respond, Spurrier said, "No worries, though, that's a bit of information that's going to die here, tonight, with you and Lynch's files." He started to laugh, but coughed instead, the smoke getting to him.

"We have to get out of here," Bernsen said nervously, covering his face with the crook of his elbow. Zach wasn't quite as brave as he wanted to appear.

Another window shattered, hot glass splintering and spraying, but Spurrier barely noticed, not when he had someone to brag to. Eyes glowing like the true zealot he was, Spurrier wasn't finished gloating.

"They'll think it was an accident, you know," he said as if he'd planned everything, including the damned storm.

Trent's head cleared a bit.

Spurrier motioned to the burning living area. "The

spilled lantern fuel, the burnt mattress. You and your lover caught in an inferno. Unable to escape. That's how it will look."

"That . . . that's nuts." Trent said. "No one will believe anything of the sort." But inside he was panicking. Where was Jules? Already in this megalomaniac's clutches? Terror ripped through him. God, please, let her have stayed locked in her room at Stanton House. He raised his head, ignoring the pain and skewered Spurrier in his gaze. "You're a damned psychotic."

"Most men with vision are misunderstood." Spurrier found a lantern that hadn't yet cracked, and he smashed it onto the floor, next to Trent. Kerosene ran crazily over the hardwood toward the flames already burning bright.

"Misunderstood?" As battered as he was, Trent pushed up to his elbows. He couldn't believe the man's ego. "Give me a break."

"Really, we gotta go!" Bernsen was starting to feel real terror. "This place is going up fast."

Spurrier didn't seem concerned. "Lynch is going to be blamed for everything that happens here, all the deaths," he told Trent in a calm voice. "It's only fair. They weren't my fault, you know."

"Sure." Trent spit out the word.

"Blue Rock will need a new director, someone with vision, someone who understands God's will."

"You?" This guy was certifiable!

"That's right. And everyone will see. Everyone including her."

"Her?" Oh, God, Jules," Trent realized. The sick bastard had plans for her.

"She married the wrong man," Spurrier said, his mask of calm slipping a bit.

Was he talking about Sebastian Farentino? That didn't make sense.

"Trust me," Spurrier added, "She's going to know the mistake she made. That's what the bitch will get for listening to her father."

What the hell was he talking about? Not Jules, thank God. "Oh, don't tell me. Some woman got smart and dumped you?" Trent mocked. "Now, there's a surprise. What do you bet, she didn't see Blue Rock as a stepping stone for taking over the world."

Anger flared bright in Spurrier's eyes.

Who did this guy think he was?

"Cora Sue will finally understand," he said.

"Cora Sue? As in Lynch's wife?" Trent coughed, the smoke burning into his lungs. "You and her? Was that before or after she married the reverend?" One corner of Trent's mouth lifted, he couldn't help it and pushed hard. "You're sick, Spurrier. Twisted. You know that, don't you? Lynch was right. He called it. I saw it in his notes."

"Lynch is a fraud!" Spurrier snarled.

"But not a killer, right? You're the one. And you started with Lauren Conway."

Spurrier's eyes narrowed, his lips twisted downward. "Lauren was a traitor. She wasn't who she claimed to be. You didn't know that, did you? She wasn't here for an education, to learn about God, to follow! She had her own plans. Cameras. Flash drives. Stealing information. She came here to expose the school and Lynch for what he was."

"I would think that would have fit right into your plan," Trent taunted.

"We gotta get out, man," Zach cut in, nervous and trying to back out the front door where flames were chewing through the casing.

But Spurrier couldn't let it lie. "She should have stayed with her original purpose. If she'd stayed on course—"

"For the love of God, just tell him you fucked her and

let's get out of here!" Zach was frantic now, his face twisted in fear. "Before someone sees the damned fire. Before we're trapped!"

"It was more than that," Spurrier said, ignoring the flames, a fanatic defending himself.

So he'd been played for a fool, falling for a woman who had used him. "What happened, Spurrier? She throw you over for someone more her age?"

Spurrier's lips pulled into a snarl. "She thought she would expose me. *Me!*" He hooked a thumb at his chest in rage while flames started crawling around the arch to the hallway, framing his head. "She became confused and . . ."

"You killed her." Damn, but Trent hadn't even had Spurrier on his radar until tonight, until he'd read Lynch's files.

"I killed no one, you Cretin!"

"'Course not," Trent said, coughing. "You're a coward! You sent one of your crazy followers to take care of it for you."

"You don't know anything!" Spurrier raged.

"So where's her body, huh?"

The heat was intense, flames soaring, smoke roiling upward. Trent could barely breathe.

"Her death was an accident."

"Come on, man! This is insane!" Zach was heading for the kitchen and the back door as the front entrance was now engulfed, the heat sweltering.

"A convenient accident. Right," Trent mocked, goading the egomaniacal bastard. "She tossed you over and you killed her. You're no great leader, Spurrier, just another idiot whose woman dumped him. Maybe she didn't want to be with a hypocritical killer. Probably found a better lover."

"You idiot. You've got it all wrong!" Spurrier swung his foot back and kicked, hard. The toe of his boot was aimed straight for Trent's face.

Trent rolled.

Heavy leather bashed into his shoulder. "Ooof!"

He wrapped his hands and arms around Spurrier's pant leg and threw his weight the opposite direction.

The pilot hopped once, then fell, landing hard on his back.

Thud!

The house rocked.

Flames shimmied.

Spurrier sent up a howl of pain.

Trent flung himself upward and rolled atop the pilot. Balling a fist, he let fly, smashing Spurrier's jaw, jarring his own hand, the two of them wrestling over broken glass and flames.

"Oh, shit! Oh, shit, oh, shit!" Bernsen edged through the archway and leveled his rifle at the two of them. "Stop it! Let him go! Holy goddamned shit!"

Trent ignored the TA and his damned weapon. Furious, his fists punching wildly, he straddled Spurrier as he would have a fifteen-hundred-pound Brahman bull.

"Get him off me!" Spurrier ordered, eyes rolling toward his minion.

Trent slammed his fist into Spurrier's nose.

Crack!

Bones splintered. Cartilage became mush.

Blood sprayed from Spurrier's nostrils.

The pilot writhed and screamed.

Trent hit him again, his fist aching.

"Enough!" Bernsen, eyes round with terror, pointed a rifle straight at Trent's head. "Get off him! Now!"

In that moment's hesitation, Spurrier rolled to one side, bucked up, and landed a fist against Trent's jaw, knocking him back. Trent swung again.

Bam! The rifle's barrel cracked into the back of his head. He collapsed.

Spurrier disentangled himself, climbing on wobbly legs. "Good job," he said. "I was afraid you would shoot him."

"You said to make it look like an accident. Let's get the fuck out of here!"

"Yeah!" Spurrier scowled down at Trent. "Don't you know you can't thwart God's will?" He was sniffing, trying to staunch the blood gushing from his nose.

On the floor, Trent moved slowly, his hands surrounding a piece of glass from the lantern. It was a struggle to sit up, and the hot glass cut his hand, but it was his only chance, his only weapon, a lousy piece of glass in this hellish inferno.

His fingers tightened over curved glass probably from the bell of the lantern. Miraculously, it still held enough oil to leak through Trent's fingers. He held on tight, trying to keep the precious liquid from drizzling out.

The air was thick with smoke, flames rising higher. Bernsen was frantic. "Come on, man, let's just break the fucker's legs and get the hell out of here!"

"We can't be blamed for this! It has to look like an accident," Spurrier insisted, coughing, his fury radiating in waves as Trent watched from the floor.

"It will," Bernsen insisted. His eyes moved restlessly, anxiously watching the ever-growing fire. He grabbed the wooden club again. "I'll crack his knees. He won't be able to move. Then everything will burn here. No evidence. An accident. Like you said. It'll look like he tripped and fell, hit his head on the table, and, trying to get out, broke his damned legs. Then we get the fuck outta here before anyone comes." Hyped up on adrenaline and fear, Bernsen was practically bouncing on the balls of his feet.

"I'll do it," Spurrier insisted, regaining some of his power over the kid as the fire crept closer, across the floor. Enraged, he spat a broken tooth toward a window, then wrested the club from Bernsen's hand.

To Trent, he said, "Here's an example of God's will you'll appreciate."

"God's will? Oh, yeah, right. One more murder on your hands. Lauren, Drew, Nona, and Maeve aren't enough. God would be so proud."

"I already told you that wasn't me. Why would I bother with Prescott and Vickers and, what, now Mancuso? I had nothing to do with them." His eyes burned bright with a rabid fervor. "They weren't part of the mission."

"We *have* to go!" Bernsen was frantic.

The flames were closer, circling. Burning crazily.

With the rifle still trained on his heart, Trent watched as Spurrier squatted, the chunk of bloody oak in one hand, flames gathering around him. "One at a time, Trent," he promised, loving the power he was wielding. "You're gonna hear each of them shatter. The pain will be excruciating." He grinned with the satisfaction of the truly self-deluded.

"Again, God's will," Trent taunted, fingers clutching the glass so hard he felt his own blood flowing.

Spurrier's temper flared. "You'll be thankful to die, rather than suffer."

"Will I?" It was Trent's turn to grin. "Don't bet on it!" Striking as quick as a rattler, Trent flung the piece of glass and its oily contents into Spurrier's face.

"What the fuck!" Bernsen cried.

Spurrier recoiled, dropping the chunk of oak, his hands going to his eyes. Blinded, he backed up toward the fully engulfed mattress. "Kill him!"

Bernsen hesitated. "What?"

"Kill him now!" Spurrier ordered.

"Gladly!"

Trent slid to one side.

Bernsen fired.

Blam! The report rocked the building.

Hot pain sizzled through Trent's shoulder.

Before the kid could get off another shot, Trent rolled across the floor.

Spurrier howled in pain as flames crawled up his pants. "Help! Oh, for the love of God, help me!"

The kid turned toward his leader.

Pain rattling through his body, Trent rolled toward the kid and swept Bernsen's feet out from under him.

Crack!

The rifle fired again as the kid went down with a heavy thud. "You bastard!"

The bullet went wild, ricocheting through the room.

Bernsen scrambled to his feet.

Spurrier was yelling in pain, the flames climbing up his body. Howling, digging at his eyes, he fell to his knees, a burning pyre.

"Oh, God!" Horrified, a true coward, Zach crawled frantically toward the kitchen. Abandoning his leader, leaving the damned rifle on the floor, he ran.

Trent lunged at the fleeing kid.

Zach dodged quickly. Terrified, the TA took off through the back door.

And straight into the muzzle of Frank Meeker's gun.

"Stop. Police!" the deputy ordered, Bert Flannagan at his side. Trent, trying to climb to his feet, witnessed it from the hell of the living room.

Zach was pinned against the porch wall. "Oh, fuck!"

"You okay?" Flannagan asked Trent, sliding by Meeker, unintimidated by the wall of flame in the living room.

Trent turned to Spurrier. "I'll live," he said, forcing himself to his feet.

"Help!" Spurrier, blinded, screamed. Fire climbed up his clothes and caught in his hair. Anguished howls erupted from his throat.

Trent spied the fire extinguisher under a flaming chair and dived for it.

"Don't!" Flannagan warned. "It'll blow!"

"We can't let him die!" Trent grabbed the cannister, the hot metal burning his hands. Spurrier was trapped behind an ever-climbing wall of flame, his body afire, his face a blackened, horrified mask, his shrieks of pain echoing over the roar of the flames.

"Oh, hell, let me." Flannagan ripped it out of Trent's hands and turned the hose on Spurrier and the surrounding flames. CO_2 filled the air.

Spurrier fell to the floor where he screamed and writhed. "Take me, Father," he cried desperately as the smell of burning flesh rose to the heavens. "My God, my God, why have you forsaken me?"

As if he truly thought he were Jesus Christ.

CHAPTER 43

"So now we wait," Eric Rolfe said smugly. "The others should be joining us, once they've finished their missions." He glanced over at Missy, and she nodded, her blond hair pale in the fallout shelter, her expression one of supreme satisfaction. She'd cleaned her teeth of blood and now seemed confident that whatever horrid plan they'd all hatched together was working.

"What missions?" Jules asked from a hard folding chair, the one she'd been forced to take.

Whimpering Nell sat to one side of her, and Shay, belligerent, her eyes hot with fury, was seated on the other. They were trapped in a small subterranean room that, Jules guessed, was the fallout shelter from the fifties, the one Charla King had mentioned. It apparently had been recently fitted with a state-of-the-art security system and backup power and had been converted into some kind of weird underground chapel that housed not only an altar but also a floor-to-ceiling cabinet that held guns, rounds of ammunition, night goggles, and God only knew what else. It was certainly enough firepower to arm a secret militia. The place gave her a serious case of the creeps; the kids holding guns on them scared her to death.

"You don't need to know anything else," Missy said in her grating voice. Nonchalantly studying the nails on one hand while pinning the three captives down with a handgun with the other, she seemed at home in her position as prison guard. "The Leader has it all planned out. Perfectly."

"Your leader is a murderer," Jules said.

"Hey, don't!" Nell shook her head, afraid to make any waves. Eyes round with terror, she said, "I'm sure . . . I'm sure he's a great guy."

Shay let out a huff of disbelief, and Jules couldn't take the naive, desperate girl's rationale. "A great guy? Get real. Three people are dead. Probably a fourth if you count Lauren. The one thing he isn't is 'a great guy.'"

"There are always sacrifices," Missy said blithely as if the people who had died were meaningless.

"Four people dead?" Nell repeated, swallowing hard, her voice a frantic squeak. "But I thought just Drew and Nona . . ."

"And Maeve," Jules said, "We found her mutilated body in the stable tonight."

"Maeve, too?" Nell cried, horrified, shaking, a fresh spate of tears running down her cheeks. "Oh, no, no, no."

"Who cares who's dead?" Missy really wasn't interested. "We just do what he tells us to."

"No questions asked? Even murder?" Jules tried to get through to these kids. "Taking innocent lives?"

"God's will," Missy insisted. "And I don't know about any murders."

"There's gonna be more," Eric predicted. His smile was wide, an evil grin meant to remind them that they were in his control. He could do anything he damned well pleased with them, and there would be no consequences.

Nell whimpered.

Eric loved intimidating the poor girl. "If you ask me," he said slyly, "we're already a few shy."

Missy shot him a look, warning him to be quiet.

Eric, however, was on a roll. "But I think we'll make up for it tonight."

"Shut up," Missy advised.

Eric scoffed at her. "They want to know, so let's tell them." To Jules, he said, "I told him he should have taken out Howell, too, but he went soft on her."

Maris Howell, the teacher Jules replaced?

"She was nosing around, like Lauren, and he let her go. Stupid." Eric's nostrils flared and his fingers tightened over his handgun. "I would have taken her out. Got rid of the problem once and for all."

"Maris Howell?" Jules said. "Because of her affair with Ethan Slade?"

Again Missy and Eric exchanged glances, their smiles telling all. "What affair?" Eric finally said, and laughed brutally, the horrid sound intensified by the small, confined space. Missy, too, giggled in her tiny voice as they shared a private little joke.

"She was caught with Ethan Slade," Jules pressed, trying to understand.

"A setup." Rolfe was enjoying himself now, thinking he was smarter than everyone. "Because she was spying, the Leader came up with a story to get her out of the school. Ethan really played it up, crying on her shoulder, convincing her that he needed special attention." Eric pulled a tragic face, rubbing at an imaginary tear in his eye. "Boo-hoo. She bought it. Comforted him. Embraced him." Rolfe was nodding, enjoying bragging about how smart they all were. "We took pictures and Ethan worked it so that when she showed up to talk to him, he was half naked. With a little cutting, pasting, and editing, it looked like she was seducing him—at least to Ethan's parents."

"Poor darling," Missy added.

"*Sick* darling," Shay corrected.

Nell whispered, "Don't! Shay, for the love of God!"

"That's why we're here," Eric said. "For the love of God."

"I don't think so," Jules said, sickened at the depths of their depravity, of how easily they twisted other people's lives, of how ruthlessly they killed. All in the name of God.

Eric shrugged, and Jules doubted that he cared one iota about God or Christianity or even the Leader. Eric Rolfe was all about Eric Rolfe. "So, we all backed Ethan, she got the boot, Slade is now in a college program. A win-win."

"Except for Maris Howell," Jules pointed out, wondering at the depths of this group's penchant for evil. "Her reputation was ruined. But this 'great' leader. Who is he?"

"Hey." Eric leaned closer. "Howell got off lucky." His eyes glittered like hard stones. "I would have killed her."

"But, then, you're a prick," Shay said.

Without thinking, Eric swung a meaty fist. His knuckles bashed into Shay's jaw. Her head snapped back. Blood slid from the corner of her mouth.

"Stop it!" Jules cried, jumping up from her chair, only to be pressed back by the barrel of Missy's gun.

"You're one sick bastard!" Shay spat, and Nell began to cry again, sobbing loudly, wailing in terror.

"I'm gonna love seeing you die," Eric snarled at Shay as hurried footsteps sounded on the other side of the door. "You, Nell, shut up!"

The scared girl bit her trembling lower lip and blinked, but her tears still rained down her cheeks.

A sharp rap on the wall separating the fallout shelter-cum-place of worship resounded.

"Showtime," Eric said eagerly as he opened the door.

Jules felt all hope die as she watched the enfolding scene.

Tim Takasumi, Kaci Donahue, Roberto Ortega, and Ethan Slade appeared in the doorway. They were all nervous and twitchy, high on adrenaline or God knew what else, all suited in black, all carrying weapons.

"They've got him," Kaci cried, her face a mask of concern. "They've got the Leader!" She was freaked, gesturing wildly with her gun.

What? Jules wondered; maybe there was still a chance . . . She exchanged glances with Shay.

"Who?" Eric demanded. "Who's got him?"

"That fuckin' Trent, that's who!" Ortega said, his eyes dark with fury. "The Leader, he's fucked up, too. Burned to hell." He, too, was freaked. Squirrely. "There's more. They've got Zach, too."

"No!" Missy cried, her smug face dropping into horror. "No way."

"It's true!" Takasumi said, nodding his head violently.

They were all charged up, feeding on each other's anxiety.

Ortega glanced at the hostages, then back to Rolfe. "I'm tellin' ya, man, he's locked up. In the clinic. Guarded by that pig Meeker."

Good, Jules thought, a crack in their defenses, but she wondered how it happened that the Leader was captured. Whoever he was, he wouldn't have gone down without a fight, and that might mean Trent was hurt. Although Ortega said Trent got the better of their precious freak.

"What do we do now?" Slade demanded, nervous and edgy. "We can't just sit here."

Rolfe's hateful gaze scraped the room to land on his hostages. His eyes narrowed and his lips flattened in renewed determination. "We get him back, that's what we do." He hooked a thumb at the hostages. "We've got bargaining chips. Either they release him, or we start shooting our little bitches here. And we'll start with this one," he said coldly, a spark in his eyes as he leveled his pistol at Shay.

"No!" Jules cried.

With a wicked grin, he pulled the trigger.

Jules screamed.

But he caught the hammer before it hit. "Pop," he whispered to Shay in dark delight. "You're dead."

The clinic became their fortress.

With Zach Bernsen locked in one of the detox rooms and Spurrier on an IV that knocked him out in the infirmary, Trent sat on a gurney in the hallway. Nurse Ayres, lips compressed, glasses perched on the end of her nose, deep circles under her eyes, worked steadily to dislodge the bullet in Trent's shoulder using only local anesthesia and sterile tweezers.

It hurt like hell.

"You're lucky," she said. "Just missed the brachial artery."

"Lucky," Trent repeated, not exactly feeling as if the Fates were shining on him. "What about Spurrier?"

She shook her head. "Doubt if he'll make it." Grumpy and efficient as ever, she frowned under the bright fluorescent lights as she worked, swathing his upper arm and shoulder in bandages.

"Keep him alive," Trent told her. "Whatever you do, don't let him die."

"I'll mention it to God," she said with a wry twist of her lips. "Next time He asks."

Trent could barely manage a smile. His body ached; he was bruised and battered, but he could deal with the physical pain; none of it much worse than what he'd suffered during his days in the rodeo. What troubled him was far deeper, a dark pain deep in his soul: Jules was missing. He'd heard the news from Deputy Meeker who had checked.

Her missing wasn't good.

Not with the maniacs who followed Spurrier on the loose. If only she'd stayed put . . . no, strike that, if only he'd stayed with her, protected her. Guilt, so often his companion, had found him again.

But he wouldn't lie idle. Somehow, by God, he was going to find her. Save her. He wasn't going to lose her again. Nuh-uh. No way in friggin' hell!

They'd learned from a near-dead, pain-wracked Spurrier that he had thought he would take over the school, that Tobias Lynch was a fraud, misinterpreting God's will. Though Lynch liked a challenge and willingly took the most mentally troubled students to Blue Rock, encouraging and rewarding them, he was failing. Spurrier had known about Lynch's private records, had read them himself when Tobias was in Seattle with the wife that Spurrier had once coveted. Cora Sue and he had been lovers, even after Lynch's marriage to her. She, Trent gleaned, had always regretted marrying Lynch, but she'd followed her father's suggestion, fearing that Radnor Stanton would cut her out of his will should she disobey and hook up with the more radical, younger man.

In the ensuing years, Kirk Spurrier had vowed to show Stanton and Cora Sue that she'd made a mistake of monstrous proportions. Lynch had even hired him, trusting that forgiveness, not bitterness, was the right path.

His error.

Trent, testing his shoulder, couldn't believe that one man could be so delusional. But Spurrier was. Worse yet, he'd convinced a small army of brilliant, if sick, young people to follow him. While Lynch had wanted to help those who were the most ill, Spurrier had used them to his advantage.

Now, Meeker, with help from Bert Flannagan and Wade Taggert, supposedly had the campus on lockdown. The students were locked in their dorms, staff members guarding the lobbies. The fire at Trent's house still smoldered and the cabin next door, DeMarco's, singed. DeMarco, it seemed, could sleep through Armageddon and had been found in his house, head under the covers, totally unaware of the chaos ensuing around him.

Some of the TAs were missing—the usual suspects, it seemed, all of whom had already been named by Bernsen who was giving up information grudgingly, trying like hell to work a deal to save his own pathetic hide.

Frantic, knowing he was going down in flames, Bernsen swore he had nothing to do with the deaths on campus. Then again, he was a lying son of a bitch.

Meeker was with him now, reading him his rights, explaining how this was Zachary Bernsen's last chance to do the right thing and possibly work some kind of a deal with the DA, though Meeker was making no promises.

Worried sick, Trent couldn't stand being cooped up. He'd agreed to have his shoulder worked on, but he was anxious about those who were still missing, eager to find them and flush out the other members of Spurrier's grossly delusional band. Not only was there no trace of Jules, but Nell Cousineau and Shaylee Stillman hadn't been found.

For a second Trent closed his eyes, fear consuming him. To be this close, to make love to Jules for hours . . . only to have her stripped away. His fist clenched. He wouldn't let this happen; not while there was a breath of life in his body.

If those bastards killed Jules, then they would pay. Each and every one of those twisted sickos. Trent had no sympathy. "Troubled teens" were one thing, psychopaths another.

The door to the detox room holding Bernsen opened. Meeker stepped into the hallway, then locked the door behind him.

"Where are they?" Trent demanded.

Meeker, looking tired as hell, shook his head. "Don't know. Yet." Meeker's tired gaze met Trent's. "Bernsen won't budge. He'll only talk, he says, if he gets to walk away scot free. No prison time."

"Then he needs to be convinced."

"Won't be."

Trent felt his lips twist. "Let me talk to him." Then to Ayres he said, "We're done here, right?"

"I've given it my best shot," she said, smoothing tape over his bandage.

"Good." He climbed off the table and walked across the polished tile floor to the locked detox center.

Meeker apparently read the set of Trent's jaw, the narrowing of his eyes. "You think this is a good idea?"

"You got a better one?" They both knew they were on their own; communication with the outside world still only a wish and a prayer.

"No."

"Then stay out," he warned, ignoring the pain in his shoulder. "And lock the door."

Shay wanted to scream, but she held her tongue. She couldn't let that jerk-wad Rolfe see how he'd humiliated her. How had she been so foolish as to fall into his trap? She was smarter than this! Damn it all to hell! Not taking her eyes off the creep, she struggled in her handcuffs, trying to wiggle her fingers free, determined, once she'd slipped out of the manacles, to not only lift the snowmobile's keys from Missy but to personally deal with Eric Rolfe.

He had no idea who he'd crossed, but he was about to find out. She watched him carefully. Felt the sting on her cheek, where he'd punched her, tasted her own blood. Saw the fear in Nell's eyes.

Shay met Jules's gaze. Silently communicated. Neither one of them would go down without one helluva fight.

Bernsen eyed him warily as Trent walked into the detox room, the door clicking loudly behind him.

Puffing up, trying like crazy to look as if he were still in command, Zach stood in a corner, his hands cuffed behind his back, his jaw thrust forward, his lips compressed. Challenge sparked in his eyes.

Trent wasn't buying the bravado. Not for a second. The kid was scared; putting up a fake front. With his back pressed to the door, Trent waited for a few minutes, not breaking the silence, Bernsen caught in his uncompromising glare.

Finally he pushed off from the door and didn't wince, though his shoulder ached as the anesthesia was beginning to wear thin. "Look, Zach," he said evenly. "I'm not messin' around, you got it? Either you tell me where the rest of your group is, or I'm going to handle you the way I did your goddamned leader."

"You wouldn't dare."

"Like hell. Try me." Trent stared the kid down with dead calm. "You remember what that leader of yours looks like, right? His face is damn near melted off, his lips peeled back, his eyes slits and he's still on fire, you know. Wishing that God he keeps talking about will take his wretched, ugly soul."

"So what?" Bernsen snarled, holding onto his pride, not flinching a bit. Just like some of those fake bad ass cowpokes he'd dealt with during his days riding bulls.

"I'll tell you what." Trent didn't raise his voice. "You see, Frank Meeker, he's a family man, a paid deputy, sworn to uphold the law and play by the rules."

Zach paled a little; saw where this was going.

"But I'm not," Trent said. "I can do anything I want to you."

For a second, the boy's eyes flickered with fear.

"And it's worse than that." Still standing near the door, a good twelve feet of space between him and the kid, Trent felt a tic in his jaw, knew the kid saw how hard it was for him to hold on to his patience. "Meeker, out there"—Trent cocked his thumb toward the thick panels of the door—"he's takin' a break, so I'm in charge. So, that means, we're going to do things my way."

Bernsen swallowed hard. He was getting the message.

"So here's how it's going to go down. You're going to tell me what I want to know and if you put up a fight"—Trent shrugged, as if he didn't care how the kid reacted—"well so be it." He managed a thin, humorless smile. "If you cry foul and put me up on assault charges, you know, that would be just fine with me. I don't really give a rat's ass."

Bernsen spat on the polished tile. "Big deal!"

That was it. Trent snapped. His cool fled. He sprang, lunging forward, pushing the big kid up against the wall, ignoring the sound of ripping tendons in his shoulder, the anesthetic saving him from serious pain. "It *is* a big deal. A real big deal." He breathed hard in the boy's face, his words spitting through tight lips, his arm over Bernsen's throat. "I've dealt with Brahman bulls and rodeo broncs and cowboys who thought they were tough as old leather. I've been in more emergency rooms than you have fingers. So, you don't scare me a bit, you pansy-assed rich kid." His nostrils were flared, every muscle tight, ready for a fight. "Go ahead, show me your store-bought martial arts, and I'll show you how to fight with your fists and fight dirty." He gave the kid a shake, rattling his teeth.

Bernsen tensed.

Good.

Bring it on, Trent thought, bring it the hell on!

"No one here's gonna help you, Zach. Your leader, he's done for. I got you on a charge of attempted murder, so unless you want to play Russian roulette and lose, you're gonna tell me where your friends are holed up."

"Nice try," Bernsen snarled, spitting in Trent's face. "I think I'll take my chances."

"It's your funeral, kid." He grabbed the boy's left arm and twisted both cuffed arms upward, behind his back, inching them toward the ceiling, stretching ligaments, waiting to hear them pop and break free.

Bernsen squealed in agony, then fell to his knees.

Trent backed off, breathing hard. "Think about it," he warned, shaking inside.

"Hey!" Meeker poked his head in, his expression dark. "We got company," he said, ignoring Bernsen as the kid climbed to his knees, "And it's not good."

Bernsen spit on the floor, blood and spittle splashed against the tiles.

Trent backed out of the room, then locked the door behind him.

"Who?"

"The followers," Meeker said in frustration, his balding pate glinting under the fluorescent lights. "And they brought hostages."

CHAPTER 44

Jules shivered in the night as she was marched across the silent campus, the muzzle end of a gun shoved tight against her spine, her captors urging her, Nell, and Shaylee onward. Jules couldn't let whatever this bunch of deranged, fanatical maniacs had planned happen. She'd heard them talking and knew they'd hoped for some kind of exchange, their lives for the damned Leader's, whoever the hell he was.

As she trudged through the snow, her hands cuffed behind her back, her boots making fresh tracks, she tried to think of some means of escape. She, Shay, and Nell were walking abreast just far enough apart as to not touch each other, the leader's rabid followers armed and urging them forward in the moon-washed night, one step behind.

All those tales that Shay had told her, of rogue teachers' assistants, the worries Shay had voiced and Jules had scoffed at were true. These kids were beyond troubled; they were a tiny army of trained, fearless fanatics, ready to give their lives for their leader and his "cause," whatever the hell that was.

Think, Jules, think. Don't give up! There has to be a way to escape; you have to make it happen.

Shivering, her soul numb, they plowed forward in the predawn hours, crossing the white landscape that surrounded the school's clinic. The moon was still visible, a pale orb, while to the east, the first gray streaks of dawn were beginning to lighten the sky.

A tiny ray of hope, she thought fleetingly.

But deep in her heart she knew, this gray light of morning might be the last sunrise she would ever witness.

Trent's guts turned to water. In his mind's eye, he saw a vision of Jules on his bed the night before. "What do you mean, hostages?" he asked Meeker.

The deputy walked him to the darkened front of the clinic. "Take a look."

Trent peered through the blinds.

His heart became stone.

Sure enough, standing knee-deep in the snow, Eric Rolfe was pointing a rifle right into the middle of Jules's spine. She stood straight, looking at the door of the clinic. If she was afraid, she didn't show it, her beautiful face was without emotion.

No! he thought, fear curdling through him, *No, no, no!*

Shay, her hands behind her back, stood to one side of Jules, Nell Cousineau on the other. Missy Albright was prodding Shay, whose lips were tight, her expression dark and rebellious. Nell was shaking uncontrollably as if she might pass out while Roberto Ortega goaded her with the nose of his weapon.

"Damn," Trent whispered, his worst nightmare unfolding. Grabbing the pistol Meeker had given him, he didn't think too hard about what he was going to do; just went into survival mode. Jamming the Glock into the back of his jeans, he started for the door.

Frank Meeker stepped in front of him. "Wait, Trent," he ordered, his ruddy face dark and worried as he saw what Trent had in mind. "Hold up. You just can't walk out there."

"Like hell."

"I mean it; those kids are more than insurgents, they're rabid fanatics. For all we know they could be on a suicide mission. They'll shoot you without thinking twice."

"We'll see."

"I'm serious, Trent."

"So am I. Call Flannagan on the walkie-talkie. Get him and Wade and whoever else out here. Then cover me!" Trent didn't bother with a coat, just pulled out the tail of his flannel shirt, then, one hand in the air, the other at an angle because of the bandages, he walked outside into the bitter light of coming dawn.

He saw Jules gasp, her calm destroyed in an instant as she saw him. For a second she looked as if she might collapse. *Don't,* he said silently. *Hang tough.* His gaze found Rolfe. "What the hell is going on here?"

"We want Spurrier." Rolfe was all bluster and pride, menace radiating off of him as he stood behind Jules. A tough man with a gun pressed hard against a woman's back. The new leader, now that Spurrier was out of commission.

All three of the hostages' heads snapped at the mention of the pilot's name. As if they hadn't known.

"And Bernsen," Rolfe added, his voice booming across the icy, too-quiet landscape. "In exchange, you get her"—he pushed Jules so hard she stumbled a bit before catching herself—"and the two others." He nodded at Shay and Nell, including them in the deal.

Missy Albright gave Shay a shove with her rifle. Jules's sister didn't so much as flinch.

Roberto Ortega had Nell Cousineau in his crosshairs

and Nell looked like she expected to die at any second. When he nudged her, she mewled plaintively.

Trent didn't flinch, though he was dying inside. Instead, he stared straight at Rolfe, the bully. "You're making a big mistake, Eric."

"Oh, right."

"I mean it."

"Oh, yeah! And blah, blah, blah." Rolfe wasn't buying it and Trent wondered how he, alone, with a single pistol tucked in his jeans, would be able to take out three of the psychos and somehow save all of the hostages. Even with Meeker behind him, no way would this turn into anything but a bloodbath. There could be no good ending and Eric, the brute, smiling despite his cold, murderous eyes, knew it. "Look, man, you're outnumbered and outgunned," Rolfe said, getting antsy. "And we're freezin' our asses off out here, so let's cut to the chase. I already said we want an exchange. But since you're fuckin' around, I think I'm changing the terms."

"How?" Trent asked, seeing the situation deteriorating. Still, he had to keep the guy talking, buy more time.

"You give us Bernsen and Spurrier, and you can have this one." Again he prodded Jules with his gun. "And Cousineau. She's about to pee all over herself anyway. She's yours. But we keep Stillman until we're safe, then we'll let her go."

"No!" Jules cried.

"Shut up, bitch," he growled.

It was all Trent could do not to grab his weapon and take aim at the bastard's head as he walked toward the group. "I can't promise that."

Rolfe wasn't listening. He was already thinking ahead, past his negotiated exchange of prisoners. "We'll need the helicopter and the seaplane. That's part of the deal."

"And go where? Roseburg? Or Medford? Come on,

man, Spurrier's in no condition to leave, much less fly," Trent said, trying to reason with a maniac. "Give it up, Eric. It's over. Spurrier needs medical attention ASAP or he won't make it, and Zach's singing like a bird, naming names, giving all of you up."

Missy shook her head. "No way," she said. "He . . . he wouldn't." But there was a seed of doubt in her high-pitched voice.

"Way." Trent was still walking forward, ignoring the slight shake of Jules's head, the fear in her eyes.

"You know that he'll do anything to save his own skin. He's got a father or an uncle or someone in the family who's a lawyer or a judge. Anyway, he's already demanding to speak to the DA. Wanting immunity so that you can all rot in prison for the rest of your lives."

"Trent's lying!" Missy cried, desperately disbelieving.

"I know." Eric wasn't bullied.

"How do you know?" Ortega demanded, sending a worried glance to Rolfe. So Ortega was the crack in the armor. Good. The anxious boy licked his chapped lips and his nerves were evident in his drawn face. "Zach could turn."

"He wouldn't!" Missy was insistent as a bit of wind kicked up, ruffling her hair.

"Don't let this loser rattle you," Eric advised.

Trent's eyes found Jules's, and he saw the terror within, knew she'd read his mind that he was going to take Rolfe out. *No*, she mouthed.

Rolfe grinned. "I guess we're at an impasse, aren't we?" He shifted the barrel of his gun away from Jules and aimed directly at Trent's head. "Too bad. I kinda liked you, Trent."

Trent reached for his gun.

Craaaak!

A rifle shot echoed through the canyon.

Jules screamed.

Rolfe's head spun. Blood sprayed, red spatter on the snow-white ground. Twirling, dropping his weapon, Rolfe fell into the snow, blood and gray matter darkening the pristine ground.

"What? No!" Missy shrieked, her eyes rounding. "Eric! No! Jesus Christ, what have you done?"

Trent jerked his pistol from the back of his pants.

Behind him Deputy Meeker, standing near a skeletal oak, turned the muzzle of his deadly weapon from Eric's dead body to aim at Roberto Ortega.

Nell screeched in pure terror. Stumbling, she ran through the snow heading toward the clinic, her hands bound behind her, her hair streaming in the clear night.

With no hostage in front of him, Ortega was an easy target.

"No, oh, God, no!" Missy was out of her mind with panic.

Jules dived into the snow, falling on Eric's rifle, picking it up behind her, trying with frozen, awkward fingers, to aim the gun at Missy.

Roberto Ortega saw her and lifting his rifle to his shoulder, pointed its deadly barrel directly at Jules.

"Watch out!" Trent yelled, running forward, pistol in hand. Aiming at Ortega, he sailed through the air, landing on Jules and covering her body with his own.

Ortega squeezed the trigger.

Trent fired.

Blam!!!

A shot whizzed past Trent's head, missing him by a hair's breadth.

Squealing in pain, Ortega went down.

Out of the corner of his eye, Trent spied Shay, spinning, leg in the air, catching Missy's chin and sending the blond girl's weapon twirling, end over end, into the air.

Only wounded, Ortega lifted his head, and with his elbows buried in the snow, aimed his weapon at Trent. "Die, bastard!" he snarled, squeezing the trigger.

Trent rolled, pulling Jules with him into the drifts.

The bullet went sizzling through the snow, missing them by inches. In a second, still covering Jules's body with his own, Trent lifted his good arm and took aim with his pistol.

Roberto, struggling to stand, pulled the trigger again.

Blam!

Ortega went down in a heap, his shot going wild, his blood oozing dark against the snow.

Meeker was running forward, the sight of his weapon now trained on Missy Albright as she struggled to climb to her feet in the slick snow. Shay, breathing fire, dancing on her toes, hands still uselessly cuffed behind her back, was ready to kick the living hell out of her.

"Don't even think about it, bitch!" Shay snarled, her eyes bright with hatred.

"No . . ." Missy started to argue but took one look around, to Roberto gasping for breath and Eric obviously dead. "Oh, God," she whispered, defeated. Tears slid down her face as she crumpled, disheartened, to the snow. Curling into a fetal position, snow clumping in her hair, she whispered, "This is all wrong. It's not the way it was supposed to be."

"Too friggin' bad," Shaylee said.

The other soldiers in Spurrier's sick little army, Takasumi, Slade, and Donahue, stared at the muzzle of Meeker's gun and the bodies littering the snow. One by one, they dropped their weapons and raised their hands. Takasumi was stoic, Slade defiant, and Kaci Donahue shaking, her teeth chattering so loudly they rattled. "Don't shoot!" she yelled. "Please, please! Don't shoot!"

None of these three, the second tier of soldiers, it appeared, had gotten off a shot, nor been part of the action.

Thank God. If they'd started shooting, the outcome of this battle might have turned out far, far worse.

As far as Trent was concerned, they all deserved to face a judge and long prison terms.

Thank God, Jules and Shaylee were safe. Finally. He rolled to one side, looking down on Jules, her dark hair fanned in the snow, her face pale in the moonlight. "Are you okay?"

"Depends on what you mean by 'okay.'" She managed a bit of a smile, then looked toward her sister. Tears filled her eyes as she saw that Shay was alive and unhurt. "Have I ever been okay?"

"Never."

"Didn't think so." She pushed herself to a sitting position where she could see the damage. "Such a horrid waste," she said as if to herself, then to Trent, "I could've taken care of myself, you know. You didn't have to tackle me and pin me to the ground."

"Maybe I wanted to. Couldn't control myself."

"Give me a break."

"I think I just did!" He winked at her as sunlight began to stream over the mountains, the long-awaited dawn chasing away the night.

"Okay, okay, so you saved my life," she mocked, somehow pulling herself together. "I suppose now I'm on the hook of owing you for the rest of my life."

"You got that right." Trent gave her a squeeze with his good arm, helping her to her feet. He spied Meeker, still training his gun on the group of TAs who had survived. "We okay?"

"Yeah. These are good kids," he mocked. "They do what they're told and right now, they're cuffing each other. Just like I ordered." Sure enough, he was standing close enough to the group so that they wouldn't run and make a break for it, while watching them place handcuffs over their peers. He'd already collected their weapons and stood over the rifles and handguns.

Trent asked, "So why didn't you stay put, safe at Stanton House, huh? What the hell were you thinking?"

"That maybe I could help. If you haven't noticed I'm not all that great about just sitting around when there's trouble." She shook some of the snow from her hair. "Your turn. What the hell were you thinking, taking off and trying to take down Spurrier?" she said.

"Actually he was taking me down, I just got lucky. But what I was thinking was just one thing. That if we ever lived through this nightmare, I was going to make damned sure that I never lost you again."

"Oh, yeah, right."

"Seriously," he said, sunlight catching in his eyes.

"Funny, I was thinking just the opposite," she teased. "I told myself that if I had any brains at all and if I got through this and saw you again, I should run the other way as fast as my feet would carry me."

He arched a skeptical brow. "I'd catch you, you know."

"Oh, I know." She buzzed his grizzled cheek with a quick kiss. "In fact, Cowboy, I was counting on it!"

"Save me," Shay groaned as she approached, nearly stumbling over Eric Rolfe's dead body. She glanced down at him and her expression turned dark. "Serves you right, bastard," she said just as Flannagan, astride Omen, burst across the lawn.

The black horse plowed through the snow, sending up a spray of powder. Behind him, the entire herd ran wildly through the grounds, kicking up more snow, dark legs flashing, eyes bright.

"What the hell?" Trent said, but got it. In desperation, Bert Flannagan had come up with the harebrained idea that a stampede would stop the ensuing attack. Eyes bright, Flannagan held a gun in each hand and the reins in his teeth, like some damned Hollywood version of an anti-hero riding to save the day.

Like an avenger from hell, he headed straight for the weak group of TAs who were surveying the bloody scene, then climbed off his horse and scooped up all their weapons.

"Hey!" Meeker said. "Leave everything. We got it."

Flannagan did as he was told and eyed the small cluster of remaining TAs. "Guess I missed the action," he said.

Trent said, "A day late and a dollar short."

"Always these days, it seems," Flannagan said, stuffing his pistols into holsters and eyeing the carnage as if he were sorry not to have been a part of it.

Meeker looked at the vigilante. "You're in time for clean up."

"My luck," Flannagan said unhappily.

"Who would have thought?" Jules whispered as she eyed the bloodied snow. Ortega, still alive, was whimpering.

"I've got him," Flannagan said, no doubt a trained medic, though Jordan Ayres, the nurse, dressed in a snow-suit, had left her post in the clinic and, with a bag in hand, was hurrying toward the injured students.

Trent inspected the body of Eric Rolfe. The kid was dead, staring sightlessly upward, his face still showing signs of the hatred that had burned deep in his guts. Trent wondered what had happened to the boy to make him such easy fodder for a homicidal fanatic like Spurrier. Had Rolfe been hard-wired wrong from birth? He reached into the stiff, frozen pockets of Rolfe's jacket and discovered a set of keys to the handcuffs.

"Here we go." Trent planted a kiss on Jules's forehead as she rubbed her wrists and took the key to Shaylee, who, now that she had no one to kick to hell and back, was breathing hard, staring at her sister in disbelief.

"You and the cowboy? Really?"

"Looks like." Jules hazarded a glance at Trent. No man on earth had the right to appear so damned sexy, especially after the hellish night they'd just endured. Quickly Jules unlocked Shay's wrists. "How about that?"

"Yeah," Shay said rubbing her wrists and managing a fake, unhappy grin, "How about that?"

Jules hugged her fiercely. The sky was lightening rapidly now, the sun chasing away the stars and reflecting on the churned snow. "God, I'm glad you're okay."

"Me too."

"I was afraid . . . really scared that they had . . ." She swallowed hard, the words hard to say. "I mean I thought they might have killed you, too. When I saw Maeve I was sure there were others and you . . ." Jules blinked hard, tears burning her eyes.

"Hey. I'm okay." Shay said. "But I told you this place was sick and twisted. You get it now, right? So why don't we get the hell out of here? Take me home."

"As soon as I can," she promised, swallowing the lump in her throat. "As soon as I can."

Shay was nodding to herself, the aftereffects of being held at gunpoint, in fear for her life, taking hold. "Good. That's good. I have to get out of here. Hey, why don't you give me those," she said, indicating the small key that unlocked the cuffs. "I'll spring Nell."

"Sure." Jules handed her the keys.

"First things first, though." Shay marched up to a whimpering Missy Albright, pulled a pair of handcuffs from Tim Takasumi's hands and clipped the cuffs on the taller girl herself. "Serves you right, you bitch!" Shay said, giving Missy a push, then catching her by the pockets.

"That's enough!" Meeker ordered and Shay, fists clenched, grudgingly backed away.

"I hope you get what you deserve," she said to Missy, then took off after Nell as Trent draped an arm over Jules's shoulder and hugged her close. "Once a rebel," he said, watching Shay, "always a rebel."

"Are you talking about Shay?" Jules asked. "Or yourself?"

He smiled. "Both." Then he kissed her forehead.

CHAPTER 45

Hours later, Jules relaxed a little. She and Trent had ended up in the school's cafeteria where they were drinking coffee while still trying to figure out some of the loose ends that hadn't yet made sense.

At least her sister was safe.

Shay, along with Nell Cousineau, had been taken to the clinic to be checked for injuries by Nurse Ayres. Afterward they were to meet with their counselors to help them sort through their war-torn emotions and the trauma of being held hostage, their lives continuously threatened.

As far as Jules knew, Shay seemed to be handling the situation, at least outwardly, for the moment. Nell, however, was an emotional wreck, might be scarred forever, and was under the watchful eye of Rhonda Hammersley until her parents could arrive.

Meeker, with the help of Flannagan, Taggert, and Burdette, had locked the offenders in the clinic, the new makeshift jail. Ayres helped with the wounds. Eric Rolfe was dead, Roberto Ortega clinging tenaciously to life, Spurrier fast slipping away, the leader no more.

Earlier, from her suite at Stanton House, Jules had

watched as a sheriff's helicopter was able to land long before the roads were cleared. Detectives Baines and Jalinsky had already taken both Trent's and her statements and were in the process of interrogating Spurrier's followers. The sheriff and a few deputies, who had arrived via helicopter, were talking to the students, taking statements one by one in a long, grinding process.

Through it all, while the detectives were going over the crime scenes of the stable, clinic, campus lawn, and retrofitted fallout shelter, Jules and Trent had pieced together what had happened.

It was unthinkable, really, Jules thought now as she took a swallow of tepid coffee. She'd been blown away to learn that Kirk Spurrier, the pilot and sometimes teacher, had put into action a plan to take over the school. In his deluded vision of the world, he'd seen his control of Blue Rock Academy as the ultimate revenge against Reverend Tobias Lynch and his mouse of a wife, Cora Sue. Spurrier's plans had been more far-reaching, though, according to some of the TAs who were talking. The academy was just a stepping stone for a far bigger area of influence that included other schools where he would gather his flock of fanatics. He'd seen himself as a true crusader, one who would eventually lead a huge congregation as a televangelist with political influence.

Jules reached for the pot of coffee on the table and refilled her cup. Trent was looking through the windows, his good arm draped over her shoulder. He, too, seemed lost in thought, his coffee forgotten.

Jules lifted the pot and he nodded, so she topped off his cup and thought of the TAs who had become Spurrier's followers. The police were still sifting through all the members of the program, talking to Lynch and those they knew about, trying to determine how deep was Spurrier's influence.

His inner circle of Rolfe, Bernsen, Albright, and Ortega had been told most of his plans. Bernsen and Albright, the remaining inner-circle members who were still conscious, had reluctantly told of Spurrier's mission, though they'd vehemently denied any part of the killings of Drew Prescott, Nona Vickers, and Maeve Mancuso.

They wouldn't budge on that issue—their beloved leader was not a killer! However, they did claim that Spurrier had worried that there was a "rogue" in their midst. Missy was convinced that Eric Rolfe was the killer as he was always pulling at the bit, anxious for bloodshed, pushing Spurrier to become more violent.

Who knew?

Spurrier was nearly dead, Rolfe already gone to meet his maker.

Meanwhile, a couple of the investigators were going over the stable, hoping to find some bit of forensic evidence to connect Rolfe with the killings. Fortunately, cell phone service, though spotty, had been restored.

"I don't know about you, but I'm about ready to leave this place," Trent finally said. He twisted his neck, stretching tight muscles.

"The sooner the better. I just want to wait so that I can take Shay with me."

"That might be a while." Trent's gaze skated over the group of students at tables near the far wall. They were all quiet, their faces pale. The survivors. Jules wondered how much each of them had known, how many had suspected the evil that had been a part of Blue Rock.

An outside door opened and Father Jake found his way into the cafeteria. Spying Jules and Trent, he wended his way through some empty tables. "Long night," he said, and kicked back a chair. "Mind if I join you?"

"Not at all," Jules said.

The preacher was somber as he upended one of the unused cups on the table and poured himself a thin stream of coffee. "Since you two were so involved in this mess, I thought I should explain myself, why I'm really here."

Trent snorted. "Even you have a secret agenda?"

"Don't we all?" The preacher managed a half smile and leaned back in his chair.

All true. Jules had lied to help spring Shaylee from the academy and Trent was really undercover trying to determine what had happened to Lauren Conway. They both had fessed up and now, it seemed, it was Father Jake's turn.

"So, here's the deal," he said and launched into his story. He explained that he'd been hired by Blue Rock Academy's board of directors to double-check on Lynch. After Lauren Conway's disappearance, the members of the board, unsatisfied with the reverend's explanations, had wanted another viewpoint on the school."

"Yours," Trent guessed. "So what did you conclude?" Trent asked.

"Obviously, I think that Lynch should step down." Jake McAllister smiled. "And don't look at me. I know my limits as a clergyman, and I don't belong here. But Lynch has been convinced that he should resign. It should happen this afternoon. I told the board that I'll stay on until they find a more suitable replacement."

Jules was having trouble taking it all in. "Do you think Blue Rock will shut down?" she asked, her coffee forgotten.

McAllister lifted a shoulder. "Who knows? Maybe. But, under the right direction, I think it could work. I hope it can." He offered up a thin smile. "There's always a need for troubled kids."

Jules knew it. Shay was a perfect example. God only knew if, after this terrifying experience, she would ever return to that happy little girl she remembered.

The doors opened again and a few more students, after

being interviewed, were filing into the cafeteria where Martha Pruitt had put together a long buffet of sandwiches and cold drinks. They were sober and pale, not the excited, eager group she'd first met . . . Dear Lord, had it only been a few days earlier?

Several of her students caught her eye and she held up her hand, waving to them as they found trays and silverware. Ollie Gage looked at her with owlish eyes, and Keesha Bell offered up her free hand, the other linked tightly with her boyfriend's. Even Crystal Ricci gave her a nod. As in any tragedy, people were drawing together. With minimal conversation, they filed through the line and congregated at the tables at the far side of the room. A few counselors were interspersed with them, but today, for once, there were no assigned tables; no strict rules and most of the students seemed content to hang together in a large group.

A few seconds later the door flew open and Shay walked in. She took a quick look around the cafeteria, spied Jules and made a beeline to the table.

"I thought you were being counseled," Jules said as her sister approached.

"I was. But I'm okay." Shay was nodding, agreeing with herself. "I think we can leave now."

"Just like that?" Jules asked, dubious. "You're 'okay' and the school is releasing you? Now?"

"They think I've been through enough." Shay was actually smiling for the first time in a long, long while. It wasn't the infectious, eager grin from her youth, but it was a smile just the same.

"Wow. I'm surprised, but I guess that it's all good," Jules said, though Shay's release, considering everything that had happened in the last forty-eight hours, seemed a little premature.

As if reading her thoughts, Shay added, "Dr. Hammersley wants me to see someone, a counselor up in Seattle, maybe do some outpatient stuff and, of course, I'll have to deal with the judge." She was talking fast now. Excited. Ready to finally get out of the school she considered a prison. "I figure Edie will straighten all that out, you know, because of everything I've gone through. Being a hostage, seeing people killed." She shuddered and Jules noted both Trent and Father Jake were watching her sister, as if trying to understand Shay. Which, of course, was impossible.

"I'm sure Edie will try. I've talked to her, explained that I was coming to get you, but I haven't admitted to working here yet. I thought that would best be said face to face."

"Yeah, I guess." Shay wasn't really listening, too keyed up. "If Edie has to, she can talk to Max. There has to be a way to convince the judge to let me go home."

"You'll need a counselor's recommendation, I would think, and a letter from someone here at the school as well as a good attorney," Father Jake said.

Shay shrugged. "Then it should be no problem."

"We'll work on it." Jules said, still not wholly convinced. That was the problem with Shay; she thought if she believed something strongly enough, she could make it happen by the sheer force of her will. "Why don't you get something to eat until all the paperwork's ready?" When she saw Shay about to argue, Jules said, "You know the drill. *Every*thing takes time."

"Fine." Shay rolled her eyes. "But I'm not hungry. I'll just get something to drink and take it back to the dorm. I really want to pack and get out of here."

"Wait a sec. Are there any special forms that need to be signed, so that you can leave with me? Since I'm not your mother."

"Hammersley said you have to go prove who you are. That you're my sister, or something like that. She said that the secretary, Ms. King, has all the release forms." She turned her eyes on Father Jake. "And then someone in authority has to sign them."

"We'll see," Father Jake said.

"Without a judge's release, or your parents' say so?" Jules asked. "The school will let you out of here?" Boy, Shay was pushing it!

"Of course not, but we'll get that, right? Since the phones are working, we can call Edie and Max and the attorney can find the judge and convince him. Right? I asked Detective Baines during my interview."

Jules glanced at Father Jake.

He nodded, though he didn't crack a smile. "That's basically how it works and everything's amped up because families are clamoring to get their kids out of Blue Rock."

Jules wasn't convinced. "I don't know, Shay, you've been through a lot and—"

"And I'm fine!" Shay rolled her eyes as if Jules were thick-headed and couldn't see the obvious. "Really. Everything's okay!"

Jules still had trouble with the concept that everything could easily be forgotten and swept under the rug, but maybe this was Shay's way of dealing with trauma. She was also dead tired and didn't want to argue. "All right. But whatever Dr. Hammersley advises and whatever the judge orders, you'll do, right? Promise."

"Scout's honor!" Shay said, "Yeah, okay, 'I promise.'"

"I'll hold you to it." Jules wasn't going to be buffaloed.

Shay was smiling. "I know, I know. Okay?"

Jules gave in. "Then I'll meet you in your room in a little bit and we'll wade through the paperwork together," she said.

"Just hurry. I am soooo outta here," Shay said, then was off to snag a can of Coke from the cooler before heading outside.

As if nothing had happened.

Weird.

But that was Shay. Unpredictable.

Jules turned to Father Jake. "Does this really sound legit to you? It seems all too easy somehow." She glanced at Trent whose gaze was fastened to Shaylee as the doors shut behind her.

Father Jake said, "It's a little fast but we're not exactly on real time, not after everything that's happened. Everyone on staff knows that a lot of kids will be leaving as soon as the Sheriff's Department gives its okay. There'll be a mass exodus, I assume, because of the murders." His eyes clouded a bit. "Parents and judges alike won't make the kids stay here. It's too traumatic, would do more harm than good. Lawyers are probably already making noise to get the students released to other, safer institutions and I can't say as I blame them." He looked at the group of students gathered at tables, some somber, a few others talking and joking loudly, as if nothing had happened.

They, like Shay, seemed to have developed a thick shell, a guard against letting any of the horror of the last few days touch them.

Trent asked, "What's the update on Spurrier?"

"In a coma." Father Jake rolled his lips in on themselves. "Life flight's on its way, but no one thinks he'll pull through."

"Hell is too good for him," Trent said.

"Agreed." Father Jake nodded.

"What about Roberto Ortega?" Trent was still looking at the door, then turned his attention to the preacher.

"He has a chance, but it's slim. A pity about the kids." Father Jake looked at his watch, sighed, then rapped on the table with his knuckles. "Thanks for everything. Without the two of you, I'm not sure Spurrier would have been flushed out. Duty calls. I'd better attend to it." He stood abruptly, kicking his chair back, then moving swiftly through the surrounding tables, his footsteps taking him out the very door through which Shay had exited only minutes before.

A few kids watched him leave.

The rest didn't appear to notice.

But Trent had. His eyebrows slammed together thoughtfully, he stared at the preacher. "What do you think of Father Jake?"

Jules glanced over her shoulder. "That he's too good looking to be a minister."

"Be serious."

"I am." She reached across the table and took his hand. "But maybe not quite as handsome as a certain bull rider I know."

"Has-been bull rider. Remember?"

"That's what I meant." She grinned and he squeezed her hand, but his eyes remained on the door as it slammed behind the preacher.

Things were changing, and fast, Jules thought. Her unexpected relationship with Trent was one thing; a positive force, and now her mission, to rescue her sister, to spirit Shaylee away from whatever dark presence was lurking here, was about to be fulfilled.

As for the school, now that Spurrier and his twisted followers had been ferreted out, Blue Rock Academy would likely fail. Another example of the unexpected outcome of the best laid plans gone so far awry.

"Okay, I guess I'd better pack my things, too, and resign," she said, pulling her fingers from his as she scooted back her chair. "You know, this might be the shortest tenure of a teacher at the school."

Trent laughed. "I'll be right on your heels. I'm resigning as soon as I get through to Lauren Conway's parents. You heard that Meeker found a flash drive in Spurrier's pocket, right?"

"I didn't know what it meant."

"We're not sure yet, but we think the drive might hold information Lauren gathered—Rhonda Hammersley put it into one of the computers in the clinic—and though it was partially burned, some of the info seemed intact; the Sheriff's Department will get their lab to try and retrieve it."

"In lieu of Lynch's files."

"In addition to whatever wasn't destroyed in the fire. Deputies are already searching through the rubble of my house."

"What about Lauren's body?"

"Bernsen thinks he knows, but he's holding out. Wants immunity."

"Great. Just what we need, Zach Bernsen, a free man." She rotated her half-drunk cup on the table, then realized she was fiddling and let it be. "So what about you, Cowboy?" she asked. "Once you're out of here, what then?" she asked.

"You have to ask?"

She arched a brow. "With you? I think so."

"I thought I explained all this right after we were nearly killed in the snow. Remember? If not, I'll fill you in: What I intend to do as soon as I get out of here is chase you down. So don't think you'll be getting away."

She winked. "Catch me if you can."

"I can," he said confidently. "And trust me, I will."

So her life was going to make a major left turn, she thought, imagining a future with Cooper Trent. Who would have thought?

Buoyed that at least this nightmare was about to be behind her, Jules left the cafeteria and walked across the campus for one of the last times. Now, the campus seemed serene, even peaceful. The sun was shining brightly, rays glinting off the ice collecting around the edges of Lake Superstition. The campus once again had that idyllic appearance captured in so many of the photographs on the Web site, an Eden-like setting filled with promise for teens with problems.

The mountains spired into the blue, blue sky and she heard the *whomp, whomp, whomp* of the medivac helicopter before she saw it slowly descending onto the snowy campus.

The seaplane bearing the academy's logo was still locked in ice and was a sober reminder of Spurrier and all of his diabolical plans. How could one man affect so many? Shuddering, she headed toward Stanton House.

Life here at Blue Rock Academy would never be the same.

Would Spurrier survive?

Ever admit to the murders?

She doubted it. Even Zach and Missy were screaming that their leader had no intention of killing anyone. But then they were blind and trusting, almost as if Spurrier were part of their family, like children who refuse to see the evil side of their parents.

Family loyalty was usually deep; sometimes to the point of the ridiculous. Just look how much she, herself, had gone through, the lies and deception, all for her sister.

She glanced at the area in front of the clinic, the trampled snow, the blood that still remained. The horses had been rounded up and were back in their stalls, once again safe under Bert Flannagan's care. But the students involved in the attack would never forget, be changed forever.

As would she.

And Shay.

She changed her mind about returning to her suite and decided to check on her sister instead. There was something false about Shay's reactions to the ordeal, and Jules wanted to be certain her sister was okay, that she would be able to put all this horror to rest and live a normal life.

Well, as normal a life as Shay could sustain.

Truth to tell, Jules was bothered by something else. Shay's being able to leave today, within the hour, just didn't ring true, despite Father Jake's rationale.

Shaylee was known to lie, to bend the truth to her own way of thinking, to work Jules into doing what she wanted and damn the consequences. Her track record spoke for itself.

Shay might believe she was miraculously "cured" of the horror of being confined and kept hostage by Eric Rolfe, but Jules knew it would take years of therapy, if that, before her sister stopped playing the people around her, pretending that she was "just fine." Deep in her heart, Jules wondered if Shay ever would be normal, whatever that was. Ever since Edie had remarried Rip Delaney, Jules's father, Shay had been acting out, adolescence stealing the sweet child within. As Father Jake had said, "A pity."

Jules hurried up the stairs of the empty dorm. It was still, other-worldly quiet with most of the students either being questioned in the admin building, or gathering in the cafeteria. Jules knocked on Shay's door. "Hey, are you about ready?" Unlatched, the door opened of its own accord, swinging into the hallway.

Shay, alone, a cell phone jammed against her ear, jumped. Startled, she turned around to face the open door. "What the hell?" she demanded, angry, one hand knocking over her half-drunk can of soda. "Shit, Jules, you scared me!"

"Sorry," Jules said, realizing her sister wasn't as calm as she'd pretended. Jules pulled the door shut behind her as the Coke continued to gurgle from the can. "I thought—"

"I'll call ya back, Dawg," Shay said into Nona's cell phone, the one she'd never returned, as she clicked off and turned to face Jules. "He's out, you know. On bail," she said with a grin.

"Maybe you should avoid him." Jules walked to the desk, searching for something to clean up the mess.

"Right." Without thinking, Shaylee grabbed a towel from her desk, dropped it over the spreading stain of dark soda, then placed her foot atop the towel and smoothed it over the floor.

Nudging the towel with her toe.

Sopping up the liquid. Slowly.

In an *S* formation.

As natural as if she did it all the time.

Jules, standing near the window, stared at Shay's foot. The circular motion. Familiar. Dark.

Her heart nearly stopped beating.

In a flickering memory, one that she'd repressed for years, she saw her sister's small boot-clad foot on another towel, dropped onto the floor near Rip Delaney's body, covering a small stain of blood. Not blood that Jules had spilled from pulling the knife from her father's body, but from the wound already there.

"Oh, God," she whispered. In her mind's eye, in jagged pieces she caught a glimpse of her father, lying dead, the knife in his leg, bleeding out from his femoral artery. She was already too late as she'd walked into the room with the flickering television screen and found Shay mopping up the blood with her foot. Jules had screamed and yanked out the butcher knife, but it had been too late.

What had been Shay's excuse? She was trying to help?

The memory, so long a blur, was clear as glass.

Jules's insides turned to ice.

It couldn't be!

And yet the motion that Shay did so naturally was identical to the one in her mind's eye.

No way! She had to be imagining things! Her head began to pound painfully as she remembered the bloodstain near Andrew Prescott's body in the stable. Swiped over, as if someone had spilled his blood and tried to wipe it away in a smooth, swirling motion, the darker "S" shape visible.

Another flash of memory: the small smeared pool by Maeve Mancuso's corpse. Again, smooth, sure strokes. A snake-like shape darker in the wiped stain.

And, no doubt, on the sleeping bag where Nona Vickers had lost her life there was the same bloody signature: Shay's signature. The snakey, blurred *S*.

Jules swallowed hard, her head screaming denials.

She focused again, back in the moment, her gaze fixed on Shay's foot. *God help us.* Glancing up, Jules saw her sister staring at her, a knowing smile playing upon Shay's full lips. "For the love of God, Shay," Jules whispered, her voice trembling. "What did you do?"

This couldn't be happening! Couldn't! Shay wasn't a killer! There had to be something else, someone else . . . But the light in her sister's gaze in that moment burned bright with triumph and something else, something far more sinister and evil-bred.

In that instant of recognition, Jules knew. But she had to hear it from her sister's lips. "You killed them?"

No, not Shay. NOT SHAY!

"Nona? Drew? Maeve? You murdered them?" she asked again, hoping beyond hope that she was wrong. *Please deny it. Please. I'll believe you!*

"How else was I going to get you to believe me?" Shay asked innocently, an undercurrent of satisfaction in her voice, not a trace of denial. "How else would you have gotten me out of here?"

"No, you couldn't have," Jules whispered, shaking her head, refusing to think her sister was a monster, horrified to believe Shay capable of cold-blooded, premeditated murder.

"Are you too stupid to see that you would never have gotten me out of here unless you thought there was danger to me and my life?" Shay asked, anger sparking. "You thought I should be locked up; you just came down here to make yourself feel better about it."

"I don't . . . no . . ." But that much was true. They both knew it.

"Right, and it wasn't bad enough! That was the problem. So someone had to die. I figured it should be someone who thought they were smarter than I was, someone who got off on being mean to me. Nona and Maeve, they were a good start. Andrew; he just got in the way. You know, that same old problem: Wrong place, fucking the wrong girl."

"What! Wait a minute. Don't lie, Shay," Jules said, clinging desperately to the belief that Shay's talk was just bravado; that she'd snapped when Eric Rolfe and Missy Albright had trained rifles at her back. "You didn't kill them! You couldn't!" Jules argued, trying to get through to her. "Lauren Conway disappeared a long time before you even got here." That was it; proof that her sister was confused.

But Shay didn't bat an eye and Jules's blood was pulsing through her body with the knowledge that there was an explanation. "You really are naive, aren't you? God, Jules, I would hate to be you. Of course I didn't kill Lauren! I think Spurrier or his band did. Maybe it was even an accident, but I knew it could work to my advantage and it did, didn't it?"

Jules saw the hatred in her sister's expression. "And Dad?"

"Rip? That perv? Are you kidding? Of course I killed him, because you couldn't! You were so blind when it came to him! Do you know how he looked at me? At you?" she demanded, her lips curling in disgust. "I did us both a favor!"

"What? No—"

"So he didn't touch me, big deal! It was only a matter of time. And he was half in love with you."

"What?" Jules couldn't believe her ears.

"Always hugging you, hanging on your every word, acting like you were so damned special."

"He was my father."

"Well, he wanted something more." Shay's face contorted in disdain, her psychosis visible in her features.

"You're nuts," Jules whispered. This was unbelievable! Yes, Shay and Rip hadn't gotten along, yes, Shay had never understood a father's devotion, but this sick delirium was so far gone . . . "So you killed him?" Jules whispered, horrified to the marrow of her bones. She couldn't believe what was happening here.

"Oh, what did you think? That somebody broke in and stabbed him in the leg for what? His Visa card?" She rolled her eyes.

"But why?"

"I told you, he freaked me out!"

What kind of monster was she?

"He was so shocked . . . and I guess I was, too. But I watched him bleed out and I felt this . . . this rush of power. It was funny really—" Shay said, her voice trailing off, as if she were lost in the memory.

"Funny? My father's murder was 'funny'?" Jules couldn't believe she'd been duped for so many years, that the chameleon who was her sister had fooled her so completely.

"You know what I mean, I was kinda transfixed," Shay said, "just watching the blood flow out of his body. There was so damned much of it. Everywhere . . . and I had to keep away from it, of course, so I did. I even pretended to dial nine-one-one as he lay there, trying to reach for the phone."

"But there was an intruder . . ."

"Sure there was!" Shay was nearly laughing, enjoying the look of horror on Jules's features. "He'd left his wallet on the table, so that part was easy. I just hid it from Edie and ditched it with a homeless guy on the street on my way to school the next day."

"But there were footprints," Jules argued, realizing the depths of her sister's depravity, that she was enjoying the fact that she'd gotten one over on Jules, on Edie, on Rip, on the police.

"The same size as his own. Did the police even notice? Odd thing about that. Remember the good shoes that Edie had tucked away into some sacks for Goodwill?" She lifted her shoulders as if to say, "Easy."

Jules felt sick inside, starting to believe the mind-numbing truth.

"And then you came in and I had to wipe up . . . with the towel, to make it look like I'd just found him, too. I had to start crying and screaming, but you didn't even notice. One glance at him and you really freaked out, lost your damned mind." Shay grinned. She was almost giddy! "Man, did I luck out!"

"But you were so young . . . oh, God, why did you do it?" Jules asked, trying like crazy to wrap her mind around the depths of her sister's depravity.

"Duh! Can't you figure anything out. I already told you I was saving us and I knew if he was gone, if Edie and I were left alone, you wouldn't leave." She was studying Jules carefully now, her bravado melting into suspicion. "You were going to. I knew it and you were the only one who really cared about me. At least that's what I thought. But I was wrong. It all changed. You had plans to go away for college and you were hooked up with some boyfriend that I'd never met, the same son of a bitch who became my pod leader down here . . . how's that for bad luck?"

Trent. "I can't believe this."

"Of course you can't, Miss Goody Two-shoes." Shay snorted a laugh. "You never believe anything bad about anyone. I was afraid I wouldn't be able to convince you the school was rotten, but I got lucky with Spurrier and his band of lunatics." She was pleased with herself. Gloating again, though still wary. "You know, I wondered if you'd ever put two-and-two together. Those bloodstains near Andrew's and Maeve's bodies were a pretty big clue. I was just testing you and you failed, Jules. Really failed. I mean, how dense are you?"

So it was true. Jules had to accept the truth.

Shay was a cold-blooded killer. And standing between her and the door. This girl who had once adored her, now a woman who, in so many ways, resembled Jules, was planted firmly in the middle of the room as if she intended to block her sister's escape. Had planned it. Dear God, what had happened to Shay? Where was that sweet little girl she'd once loved? How had she become this monster?

Shay's lips twisted as if she were reading Jules's mind. Her eyes glimmered with a hideous light. "You still don't 'get' me, do you, Jules?"

"No." It was the truth. Maybe she never had.

"And you never will." In a heartbeat, Shay's eyes went blank, no emotion visible. Whatever connection they'd once had had been severed years ago and now, for the first time, Jules felt a tremor of fear.

"It's time to go," Jules said firmly, one eye on the door.

"Go where? Do you think I believe you're interested in helping me? No way."

"Shay, there's a chance with the right attorney—"

"Fuck the right attorney!" Every muscle in Shay's compact body tensed. In a second she transformed into a heartless murderer. Her gaze narrowed on Jules as she crouched, a position Jules recognized, one that indicated Shay was about to strike.

At that moment Jules knew the truth: Shay would kill her. And she wouldn't think twice about it.

Eyes focused, Shay rounded.

Damn! Automatically, Jules feinted toward one of the twin beds.

Her sister adjusted. Aimed a kick square at Jules's face. "Shay, don't!!"

Too late! Teeth bared, Shay spun rapidly, her booted heel slicing through the air near Jules's head.

Jules ducked.

Bam! Shay's heel hit her shoulder. Pain sizzled up her spine.

"For the love of God, Shay, stop!"

"No way." She was already setting up again.

Jules yelled. Sprang for the door!

Shay, eyes dark with a bitter hatred, refocused.

Jules had to get away!

Again, she leapt, her hands scrabbling for the door handle.

Shay anticipated her move.

She adjusted. "I've been waiting for this for a long time," she said with evil satisfaction. She set up as Jules yanked on the door handle.

Shay spun again, her toe sliding on the towel still lying on the floor. "Shit!" she yelled, her balance off. Still, she managed to kick out.

Jules dropped. Hit the floor.

Shay's leg swooshed over her head and Jules grabbed Shay's calf.

With a squeal, Shay hit the floor. Her head thudded against the floor.

Footsteps pounded down the hall.

"In here!" Jules screamed.

Shay struggled. She was strong, fighting and kicking, determined to kill her sister. They rolled across the floor. Jules's back hit the leg of one of the twin beds and she cried out, screaming in pain.

Hadn't she heard someone in the hallway?

"Help!" she yelled desperately. Pinned against the bed's leg, Jules held fast to her sister's deadly leg. Wouldn't let go. Just like she had never let go of her stupid vision of her sister, held fast to the notion that Shay, troubled, could be redeemed. But the monster wrestling with her, swearing, spitting, clawing and raging, was too far gone, had crossed the frail line between rational thought and insanity.

Shay's free leg clamped down hard on Jules's waist, pinning her against the bed leg. Strong fingers twisted in Jules's hair, yanked hard, drawing her head back. Breathing rapidly, panting like an animal, Shay kicked and twisted, trying desperately to dislodge Jules's grip, while doing damage with her own.

No way would Jules release her. Shay had won too many competitions, had bragged to Jules in the past about how easy it was to take down an opponent.

Shay arched her back. Fingers clawed Jules's scalp, twisting her hair, and pulling up, stretching Jules's neck. Shay's free hand became a weapon. Fingers glued tightly together and stiff, as if she intended to give Jules a karate chop to her exposed throat!

"God, I hate you!" Shay said, raising her hand, taking aim.

Jules couldn't move.

She watched in horror as Shay swung down.

Instantly, she let go of Shay's leg and threw up a hand to deflect the blow.

Too late!

Shay's hand sliced against her throat.

Jules went limp. Coughed. Blinked as the world spun. Couldn't breathe, couldn't speak. Blackness closed in around her as Shay stripped her fingers from Jules's hair and, breathing hard, rolled away. "Die, you miserable bitch," she said as Jules dragged in a breath with difficulty, one hand at her throat, the other on the floor where the towel still stretched across the floor. "I talked to Dawg. *He's* going to help me. All I have to do is jack one of the snowmobiles that Nell told me about and I'm home free." She reached into her pocket and showed off the keys, letting them dangle from her fingers as Jules tried desperately to drag in a breath. Shay's eyes glowed triumphantly. "I took these from that bitch Missy when I cuffed her. Things are gonna be different now. You'll see!"

She straightened, satisfied that her job was done, then, as Jules watched helplessly, snagged her backpack from the corner of the desk and started for the door.

Jules's fingers tightened on the towel as she gasped for breath.

Shay didn't notice. She had to step over Jules before she got there, and she couldn't resist. Standing with one foot on the damned towel, she aimed the toe of her other boot so that it would smash into Jules's face.

"If you can find your voice, say 'hello' to Rip for me," Shay taunted with a nasty laugh and swung her leg backward.

Closing her eyes, Jules yanked hard on the towel.

With all her strength, throwing her weight backward, she pulled, dragging the soggy terry cloth toward her.

Shay teetered. Her mask of hatred gave way to surprise. "Shit!" Flailing, arms finding nothing to grab onto, Shay lost her balance and fell, hitting the floor hard, her backpack flying.

More footsteps on the other side of the door!

Shay landed. Hard!

"Help!" Jules tried to cry, but had no voice.

The door banged open.

"Hold it right there!" a male voice commanded.

From the floor, Shay, looking over Jules's shoulder,

scrambled to her feet, not ready to give up. Her teeth were bared, her lips pulled back into an awful grimace.

Trent threw himself into the room. He tackled Shay. She went down again! Jules scooted away, trembling, the demons of the past becoming the present, morphing into one body, that of her little sister.

"Let go of me!" Shay was kicking wildly, trying to roll away as Trent pinned her down.

"Not on your life." His body was stretched over hers, his hands trying to grab her wrists. But she was quick and determined, fists flying, booted feet striking out!

"Bastard!" she cried.

He caught one wrist and she bucked up, trying to kick him.

"Get off of me or I'll scream rape!"

He grabbed her second wrist. She spat upward, spittle hitting him between the eyes.

He growled, "You'll have to do better than that."

"Cocksucker! No good fucking cowboy!" she raged and Jules curdled inside. This shrieking, struggling psycho was her sister?

"You okay?" Trent asked, looking over his shoulder as Shay fought and snarled beneath him.

Jules could only nod. Of course she wasn't okay. She never would be. Spying her sister like this was killing her.

"Stop! Now!" Father Jake, weapon drawn, strode into the room. "Let her go!" he ordered, pistol trained on Shaylee.

Trent, looking as if he were making the worst mistake of his life, breathed hard and rolled away from Jules's sister. "Careful," he warned the preacher as he swiped a sleeve over his face.

"I will be." Father Jake's eyes were steady, his face set as he hauled Shaylee to her feet, then forced one of her wrists backward so that she squealed in pain and fell to her knees. Once she was on the floor, subdued, he clipped a pair of handcuffs on her. "It's over."

"It will never be over!" Shay said defiantly, spittle running from the corner of her mouth, her hair a mess, her eyes crazed. She looked from Trent to Father Jake before her gaze landed on her sister. "As long as I'm alive, Jules, it will never be over!" she raged.

"Then take it up with God," Father Jake advised, before marching her from the room.

Jules watched her sister disappear through the door.

Trent knelt beside her and she was shaking, tears running down her face. She collapsed into his arms. "Shay's right," she whispered, grateful for Trent's strength, but knowing the chilling truth deep in her heart. "It'll never be over. Never."

EPILOGUE

Seattle, Washington
May

Sweating in the spring sunshine, her legs aching from her workout, Jules unlocked the door of her condo. She walked inside and found Diablo curled on the sofa, only deigning to lift his gray head to greet her.

"Lazybones," she accused, rubbing him beneath his chin as she caught her breath. Her voice was still a little bit raspy, her larynx having been damaged in her struggle with Shay months earlier. But she was healing. Both inside and out.

"So what do you think about a move, eh?" she asked as she eyed the mess that was her home. Every room was littered with boxes, some packed, some empty.

Despite her mother's trepidations, Jules knew moving in with Trent was the right thing to do. The only thing. Even if it was a major life change.

He'd bought a ranch outside of Spokane and was settling in. Jules would join him and they'd start their new life together. Trent was in the process of buying rodeo stock, horses and cattle that he would breed on nearly a hundred acres of rolling farmland. Jules had already started sending out applications and hoped to land a teaching position.

"Just not one that deals with troubled teens," she told Diablo.

Grabbing a hand towel, she dabbed at her face. Her friends Erin and Gerri applauded her move away from the city and her only regret was that she'd lost her sister. Not, she reminded herself, that they had ever been close. It had all been a mirage, nothing more.

"Guess you won't be a 'city cat' anymore," she said to Diablo, walking to the kitchen and flipping on the radio. "And it might get tough. I'll expect you to keep the rat and mice population down in the barns. Got it?"

Diablo, uninterested, stretched and yawned, showing off his pink tongue and white teeth as pop music from the eighties filled the rooms. The first few notes of a familiar song filled the kitchen and Jules smiled as Rick Springfield began singing passionately about "Jessie's Girl."

Jules turned on the tap and filled a glass. She gulped down the chilled water and felt better. Her nightmares had receded, and she no longer needed handfuls of Excedrin. She'd spent the last three months, her throat healing as she'd visited a counselor, retrieving all her repressed memories and her conflicting feelings about her sister.

Rip Delaney's murder case was reopened, and Shaylee was the prime suspect. Jules still didn't remember the night with crystal clarity, but the images were becoming sharper. Scarier. How had she blocked out Shaylee's guilt?

As for the horror at Blue Rock Academy, Shaylee was the only suspect in the murders of Nona Vickers, Drew Prescott, and Maeve Mancuso. The prosecution was still putting its case together and Max Stillman had ponied up for the best lawyers money could buy to defend his only daughter.

Both Kirk Spurrier and Roberto Ortega had died from their wounds, but with Zach Bernsen's help, along with cadaver dogs and the spring thaw, the sheriff's department had located Lauren Conway's bones, buried in a shallow grave in the deep woods of the campus, in, of all things, a long-forgotten cemetery.

For the moment Shaylee was ensconced in a mental hospital in Oregon, awaiting trial, though whether she was competent to stand trial was still unclear, psychiatrists and psychologists on both sides of the courtroom trying to prove or disprove her sanity.

Max Stillman's money was being spent on her treatment as well as her defense, more, Jules assumed, to save his name and reputation than his daughter's freedom.

Not that he should.

Shay was guilty.

Jules knew it in her heart.

Was her sister psychotic? Absolutely. But calculatingly so. Shay had left her cap at Nona's murder scene intentionally—to throw off the police by intentionally incriminating herself. No one knew why she'd staged the murders as she had. All part of her game, Jules supposed.

"Yep," she said, glancing at the cat again, "We all need a new start." Through the open window, she heard the familiar rumble of Trent's truck and she couldn't help her stupid heart from kicking into a faster beat.

Knocking once, he let himself in. From the kitchen, Jules spied Diablo scurrying to hide under the couch, but he didn't seem to notice.

"How're we doing?" he asked, as he found her by the sink. From behind, he wrapped his arms around her waist.

"*We're* not doing anything. *I'm* doing fine, except that I'm sweaty and gross."

"Just the way I love you." To prove his point, he nibbled her neck.

She wrinkled her nose. "Ew."

"A dirty, sweaty woman is the best."

"Spoken like a true cowboy," she teased, but leaned against him.

"Mmm. Just wait until after you move in and I come into the house after dealing with the livestock."

"Let's not even go there," she warned, but chuckled despite herself.

The song ended and an announcer's sober voice filled the room. "Is your teen troubled? Acting out? Has he been arrested? Is she disruptive to your family?"

Jules froze.

A worried woman's voice said, "My daughter was having trouble in school and running with the wrong crowd. She was failing all her classes and sneaking out at night. I was at my wit's end, and then I heard about Blue Rock Academy, and it changed my life, *our* lives, forever. . . ."

Shay sat in a corner. Rocking. Pretending that she didn't see anything going on here at Halo Valley Security Hospital. Acting like she was just as out of it as most of the other deranged patients trapped inside these walls. She was on Side B, where all the real loonies, the scary ones, were housed, but she knew how to deal with them.

They thought she fit right in with Alice May, the mumbler who had wielded a machete against her husband, and Sergio who never said a word, but had been found naked, covered in blood, in a forest near Tillamook. The blood hadn't been his, but that of an unidentified female who'd never been found. Orville, probably fifty, sat in the corner, sucked his thumb, and watched everyone with a weird look on his face. Someone said he'd burned down his own house, with his family inside. Shay didn't know if any of it were true or not and she really didn't care.

Oh, sure, she belonged here. Not! God, the authorities

were ridiculous. She was way too smart to be confined in the asylum. Didn't they know she was a genius? She looked at the psychos in this ward. Homicidal maniacs.

But she wasn't scared.

She could handle herself.

The truth was that nothing scared her.

Nothing ever had.

She stared out the window, watched a rainstorm coming in from the coast, the trees with their new leaves bending in the wind, the sky a dismal iron gray.

Another prison; no better than Blue Rock Academy.

Rock, rock, rock.

She pretended to swing.

Keep up the movement; let them think you're lost in your own little world. Don't let them guess for a minute you have any idea what's really happening.

"Time for your pills," an apple-cheeked nurse said. Jesus, she was a pain. Her name tag read: Amy Dryer, L.P.N., and she was an idiot who droned on and on about her fiancé. If Shay heard Merlin's name one more time, she thought she might get sick.

Dressed in purple today, pants and matching V-neck top that didn't disguise how soft her hips were, the nurse offered Shay her sickeningly plastic smile along with the cup of pills, all pre-measured, all precisely counted out.

Shay didn't look away from the window, only saw Nurse Amy's pale reflection in the glass as she noted the first splatters of rain drizzling down the panes.

"Shaylee?" the nurse said, her voice upping an octave as she was starting to get really agitated.

Perfect!

Swallowing a smile, Shay kept rocking while one of the aides adjusted the music that played from hidden speakers. Today: country. Taylor Swift. Again.

"Please, honey," Nurse Amy said, "it's time."

Shay didn't respond.

"Shay!" Her name was spat now, Apple-Cheeks was really pissed off. Shay slowly turned her head and looked into the consternation on Nurse Amy's face. She kept her own eyes blank, didn't let the fire of hatred burning deep in her soul shine through, even managed a bit of drool to show on the side of her mouth.

"Didn't you hear me, honey?"

Oh, I heard you, you cretin, I just didn't want to answer.

"It's time for your meds."

Trying to appear dull, Shay accepted the cup of pills and slowly pretended to take them as Apple-Cheeks, frowning now, moved off to the next imbecile of a patient.

Idiot!

Shay always pretended to take the pills, faking swallowing, then stuffing them into her shoes when no one was looking. She hid the pills, of course, couldn't run around and mash them, but they were safely tucked away. Who knew when she might need them? The pills, a knife from the cafeteria, a small pair of scissors from craft time and the tiny screwdriver she'd lifted off the maintenance man's tool belt he'd laid on the floor when he'd tried to fix the cable TV. All her precious items secreted away in a makeup bag, which was taped to the bottom of a rolling cart holding Connie's belongings.

If the contraband was ever discovered, it would look like Connie, a forty-something real whack who had kleptomaniac tendencies, had stolen it. That's right, folks, blame it on Connie the Klepto.

All in good time, Shay thought, forcing herself to be calm. She hated being locked up, but it wouldn't be forever, and she knew exactly what she would do once she escaped.

She had some scores to settle: Edie was on the list, along with Cooper Trent, that rodeo-riding son of a bitch. But the one she really wanted to deal with was her sister: Jules.

Shaylee's blood boiled at the thought of her sister. She'd counted on her and Jules, true to form, had let her down, mortified her, caused her to end up here in a hospital with maniacs and morons. Jules was the reason she was here. Make no mistake.

Yes, Shaylee thought, Jules would have to pay and pay with her life.

The Taylor Swift song ended with a familiar guitar chord, then faded into an advertisement for Blue Rock Academy. Her insides went stone cold as Shay listened hard to the ridiculous mother spouting her worries about her daughter, and finally, the daughter, in a younger, cheery voice saying something inane about the school turning her life around.

"Save me," Shay muttered, one fist clenching.

"And now, I have my daughter back," the mother assured the listeners in a bright, confident voice.

Shay remembered the campus, the mountains, the icy waters of Lake Superstition, and all of the people who had sworn to help her. They'd all only made things worse.

Even Jules.

Especially Jules.

Idly, Shay wondered who was running the academy now.

Not that it mattered.

She was never going back.

Never!

Not even when she escaped, she thought, smiling inside, her watery reflection leering back at her in the glass, because she knew that her escape would happen very, very soon . . .

Dear Reader,

I can't tell you how much fun I had writing WITHOUT MERCY with its whole set of new characters and the setting of Blue Rock Academy deep in the mountains of Southern Oregon. Such a beautiful place, even if the academy is all in my imagination. I originally wrote the book as a stand-alone novel with no plans for a sequel, but, after reading so many letters, e-mails, and Facebook postings from readers, I'm wondering if, perhaps, there is another book to be written about Blue Rock and some of the characters you met in the story. What do you say?

For now, though, I've got another couple of books coming out. The first is DEVIOUS, my next Montoya/Bentz novel set in New Orleans! It's a hardcover that will be out in April 2011. This time there's a killer who's targeting young, novice nuns at St. Marguerite's Cathedral. The first victim, Sister Camille, is the sister of Valerie Renard Houston, an ex-cop who's going through a messy divorce from her husband, Slade Houston. Slade is a sexy rancher who just doesn't seem to get it that Valerie wants out. He, who has a history with Camille, shows up on Val's doorstep the very night Camille is killed. Coincidence? Valerie doesn't think so. Nor can she stand to sit around and let Detectives Rick Bentz and Reuben Montoya try and hunt down her sister's killer. Despite everyone's warnings and her mixed emotions for Slade, Valerie gets involved, more deeply than she should and before she knows it, she becomes the next target of a twisted psychopath.

It was great returning to New Orleans and catching up with Rick Bentz and Reuben Montoya—there's even a new character, Cruz, who is Montoya's younger and oh, so sexy, motorcycle-riding brother. I think you'll like him.

Hot on the heels of DEVIOUS is my next book written with my sister, Nancy Bush. WICKED LIES is the sequel to WICKED GAME and yes, you'll visit the creepy "cult" known as The Colony again, where everyone has a secret worth dying for. You'll also catch up with the killer from WICKED GAME whose mission of destruction is stronger than ever. WICKED LIES will be available in June 2011, so look for it!

Then, finally in August of 2011, it will be time to check in on Detectives Pescoli and Alvarez in BORN TO DIE, the next book in the Montana series. If you read LEFT TO DIE and CHOSEN TO DIE, or even if you haven't, you'll want to return to Grizzly Falls where the colorful locals are as plentiful as blueberries in the pies served up at Shorty's Diner! There's a whole new mystery unfolding in the Bitter-root Mountains, and bodies are piling up around Dr. Acacia "Kacey" St. Lucien. From L.A. to Grizzly Falls, the killer spares no one in his path. Once again Pescoli and Alvarez have their hands full with a killer darker and more evil than anyone could ever imagine. Again, I'm sure you'll love this one.

So you see, I've been busy doing what I love. You can find out more about all these books (and more!) on my website www.lisajackson.com and I've got some fun interactive things happening there as well as on Facebook where I've got a fan page up and running. For now, for a sneak peek of DEVIOUS, just turn the page. . . .

Lisa Jackson

Please turn the page for an exciting sneak peek of Lisa Jackson's newest Rick Bentz/Reuben Montoya thriller, DEVIOUS!

"**I**t's time." The voice was clear.

Smiling to herself, Camille felt a sublime relief as she finished pushing the last small button through its loop. She stared at herself in the tiny mirror and adjusted her veil.

"You're a vision in white," her father said . . . but he wasn't here, was he? He wasn't walking her down the aisle. No, no, of course not. He'd died, years before. At least that was what she thought. But then her father wasn't her father . . . only by law. Right? She blinked hard. Woozy, she tried to clear her brain, wash away the feeling of disembodiment that assailed her.

It's because it's your wedding day; your nerves are playing tricks on your brain.

"Your groom awaits." Again, the voice propelled her, and she wondered if someone was actually speaking to her or if she was imagining it.

Silly, of course it's real!

She left the small room where she'd dressed and walked unsteadily along the shadowed corridor, lit by only a few wavering sconces. Dark, yet the hallway seemed to glisten.

Down a wide staircase with steps polished from thousands of feet scurrying up and down, she headed toward the smaller chapel where she knew he was waiting.

Her heart pounded with excitement.

Her blood sang through her veins.

What a glorious, glorious night!

One hand trailed down the long smooth banister, fingertips gliding along the polished rail.

"Hurry," a harsh voice ordered against her ear, and she nearly stumbled over the dress's hem. "You must not keep him waiting!"

"I won't," she promised, her voice reverberating from a distance, as if echoing through a tunnel. Or only in her own head.

She picked up her skirt to move more quickly, her feet skimming along the floor. She felt light, as if floating, anticipation urging her forward.

Moonlight washed through the tall tracery windows, spilling shadowed, colored patterns on the floor, and as she reached the chapel, her legs wobbled, as if she were wearing heels.

But her feet were bare, the cold stone floor penetrating through her soles.

Poverty, chastity, obedience.

The words swirled through her brain as the door to the chapel was opened and she stepped inside. She heard music in her head, the voices of angels rising upward through the spires of St. Marguerite's Cathedral on this, her wedding day.

Night . . . it's night.

Candles flickered at the altar and overhead a massive crucifix soared, reminding her of Christ's suffering. She made the sign of the cross as she genuflected, then slowly moved forward.

Poverty. Chastity. Obedience.

Her fingers wound around the smooth beads of her rosary as the music in her head swelled.

As she reached the altar, the church bell began to toll and she knelt before the presence of God. She was ready to take her vows, to give her life to the one she loved.

"Good . . . good . . . perfect."

Camille bowed her head in prayer, then, on her knees, looked up at the crucifix, saw the wounds on Christ's emaciated body, witnessed his sacrifice for her own worldly sins.

Oh, yes, she had sinned.

Over and over.

Now, she would be absolved.

Loved.

Forever.

Closing her eyes, she bent her head with difficulty . . . it seemed suddenly heavy, her hands clumsy. The chapel shifted and darkened, and the statuary, the Madonna and angels near the baptismal basin, suddenly stared at her with accusing eyes.

She heard the scrape of a shoe on the stone floor and her lightheartedness and joy gave way to anxiety.

Don't give in. Not tonight . . .

But even her wedding dress no longer seemed silky and light; the fabric was suddenly scratchy and rough, a musty smell wafting from it.

The skin on the back of her neck, beneath the cloying veil, crinkled with anxiety.

No, no, no . . . this is wrong.

"So now you know," the voice so near her ear reprimanded, and she shrank away from the hiss. "For the wages of sin are . . ."

"Death," she whispered.

Sheer terror curdled her blood. Oh, God! Scared out of her mind, Camille tried to scramble to her feet.

In that instant Fate struck.

The rosary was stripped from her hands, beads ripping over her fingers and flesh, only to scatter and bounce on the floor.

Camille tried to force her feet beneath her, but her knees were weak, her legs suddenly like rubber. She tried to stand, pushing herself upright, but it was too late.

A thick cord circled her throat and was pulled tight.

NO! What was this?

Needle-sharp shards cut deep into her flesh.

Panic surged through her.

No, no, no! This was all wrong.

Help me!

White hot pain screamed through her body. She jerked forward, trying to throw off her attacker as her airway was cut off. She tried to gasp, but couldn't draw a breath. Her lungs, dear Jesus, her lungs strained with the pressure.

Oh, God, what was happening?

Why?

The nave seemed to spin, high-domed ceiling reeling, the monster behind her back drawing the deadly cord tighter.

Terror clawed through her brain. Desperately, Camille tried to free herself, to kick and twist again, but her body wouldn't respond as it should have. The weight against her back was crushing, the cord at her throat slitting deep.

Blood pounded behind her eyes, echoed through her ears.

Her fingers scrabbled at the cord around her neck, a fingernail ripping.

Her back bowed as she strained.

She fought wildly, but it was useless.

Please, please, please! Dear Father, spare me! I have sinned, but please . . .

Her feet slipped from beneath her.

Weakly she flailed, her strength failing her.

No, Camille. Fight! Don't give up! Do not! Someone will save you.

Her eyes focused on the crucifix again, her vision of Christ's haggard face blurring. *I'm sorry . . .*

She was suddenly so weak, her attempts frail and futile.

Her strong body grew limp.

"Please," she tried to beg but the sound was only garbled and soft, unrecognizable.

The demon who dared set foot in this chapel, the monster who had defiled this holy ground, held her fast. Pulling on the cord. Unrelenting. Strong with dark and deadly purpose.

Camille's lungs were on fire, her heart pounding so loudly she was sure it would burst. Through eyes round with fear, she saw only a wash of red.

Oh, Dear Father, the pain!

Again, she tried to suck in one bit of air, but failed.

Her lungs shrieked.

Brutal strength, infused by a cold dark wrath, cinched the garrotte still tighter.

Agony ripped through her.

"Whore," the voice accused. "Daughter of Satan."

No!

Eyes open, again she saw the image of Christ on the cross, a film of scarlet distorting his perfect face, tears like blood running from his eyes.

I love you.

The deluge of sins that was her life washed over her—quicksilver images of those she had wronged. Her mother and father, her sister, her best friend . . . So many people, some who had loved her . . . the innocents.

This was her punishment, she realized, her hands falling from her neck to scrape down her abdomen and linger for a second over her womb.

In the name of the Father, and the Son, and the Holy Spirit, wash my soul clean. . . . Forgive me, for I have sinned . . .

them know I saw PLYR 1 stab Lisa. But what if they had a way of tracing the phone and PLYR found out and went after me?

Who saw me and gave them my face for that picture?

No, I'll just keep my mouth shut. If I dream about Mom again, I'll try to figure out what it is I want to convince her of.

CHAPTER 64

■

LAND OF THE FREE, HOME OF THE STUPID.

In the cramped storage room behind the souvenir shack, Vladimir Zhukanov finished the vodka and wondered if he'd been an asshole to leave Russia.

At least there he had a uniform, a purpose. There was always someone who needed controlling. Even more now, since capitalism was sinking its claws in. The gangs were taking over, and half the gangsters were ex-police. He could've found something.

In America, he had no respect, only stupid dolls. Stupid nigger cop ignoring him, then taking his information to the TV, the black bastard.

Anonymous tip. Meaning they didn't want to pay him.

One thing: It proved he'd been right about the kid. Like there'd been any doubt—that dimple in the chin, just like the drawing. Scratches on his face, what you'd expect in someone hiding in a forest. Zhukanov's father had told him stories about forests, the war. Militiamen chasing Yids through clumps of wintering birch. Bare trees, iron sky, the marriage of bayonet and flesh, crimson stains on snow.

Anonymous tip. The TV news meant competition for the twenty-five thousand. Only one competitor so far, but he was trouble enough. Fat guy in filthy leather, walking up and down the walkway with the kid's picture.

From his station behind the counter, Zhukanov watched

the big pig. Up and back, up and back, walking laboriously, breathing hard in the heat. Growing visibly pissed off as the day wore on and he got nothing but head shakes and blank stares.

The first time the guy waddled toward the souvenir shack, Zhukanov made sure to be in the back room, examining the day's receipts, trying to figure out how much he could skim and get away with. The second time, though, he was up front, counting trolls, making sure no one had ripped *him* off.

The big pig said, "Hey, man," and shoved the picture in Zhukanov's face. Zhukanov shook his head dismissively—it wasn't even worth talking about—but the guy just stood there.

"You didn't even look at it, man." Breath like a toilet. Zhukanov refused to dignify the question, picked up a Malibu troll. "Want to buy something?" His tone making it clear that the guy couldn't afford a lousy toy.

The fat guy tried to give him the evil eye. Zhukanov almost laughed out loud. Big but flabby. Back in Moscow, he'd trampled runny-shit like this half-drunk.

Finally the guy jiggled off. What an imbecile.

Still, it was competition. He'd have to be sharper than ever.

Now it was dark and all the retail shops were closed; the only things open were the cafés on the north end of Ocean Front. And the Yid church a few stores south. Bunch of old Yids in there wailing, plotting, whatever the hell they did when they got together.

He had skim money in his pocket, the vodka had awakened his senses, and he was hungry and horny and getting angrier by the minute at the nigger cop and everyone else who was conspiring to deprive him of what was rightfully his.

Tomorrow, he'd call the newspapers and tell them the truth about the anonymous tip, how stupid cops didn't respect dutiful citizens.

No, no, not yet—that would focus more attention on the walkway, bring in more problems. He'd give the nigger one more chance. What was his name, he had the card, somewhere . . . not in his pockets. Maybe he'd left it in the back room.

Slipping behind the curtain, he searched among the clutter but didn't find it. No matter, he'd ask around, a bald nigger detective, someone would know him. Then a man-to-man talk.

Maybe offer him a piece of the twenty-five. If that was the only way.

If the nigger *still* didn't cooperate, he'd go to the papers— no, the TV stations. Get in touch with one of those blondies who read the news, tell her the truth. Maybe some big-shot movie producer would be watching and say, "Hey, this is a good idea for a movie." Arnold Schwarzenegger, a Russian cop, comes to America to show the stupid Americans how to— Did they do that one already? It sounded familiar. No matter. With movies, you had something good, you did it again.

Publicity. That was what he needed.

On top of the money, he'd be the hero, trying to find the kid, solve a crime, but no one listened and—

"Hey, man," said a voice from up front.

Fatso.

How had he gotten in? Then Zhukanov realized he'd forgotten to pull down the shutters and lock up. He took another swallow of vodka.

"*Hey!* You back there, man?"

Stupid asshole. Get rid of him and find some place to eat and drink. Zhukanov put on his Planet Hollywood jacket and tapped his front pockets. Cash in the right front pocket, knife in the left. Cheap Taiwan blade—he carried it with him for the walk from the shack to his car, sometimes with an unlicensed 9mm. Part of the back-room arsenal: nunchucks, a sawed-off baseball bat, age-blackened brass knuckles he'd inherited from his father. So far, the only thing he'd had to use was the bat, as a warning to kids with itchy fingers, but you never knew. The gun was back home. Cheap junk. It had jammed, and he had it on the kitchen table, trying to figure out what was wrong with it.

"Hey!"

Zhukanov bolted the rear door before parting the curtains. The fat bastard had his elbows on the counter, scratching a blubbery chin, sweating, eyes raw-looking and swollen. Hulking silhouette against the black beach sky, maybe tough-looking to some tourist, but all Zhukanov saw was a vat of grease.

"Hey, bro, din' you hear me?"

Zhukanov said nothing.

"Listen, man—"

"Can't help you."

"How can you say that, man, you don't know what I'm asking."

Zhukanov started to slide down the front shutter. The fat man reached up and stopped it.

Zhukanov pulled. The fat man resisted. Flabby, but his weight gave him strength.

Zhukanov said, "Move, fatso."

"Fuck you, shithead!"

That brought the blood to Zhukanov's face. He could feel it, hot as winter soup. His neck veins throbbed. His hands ached from gripping the shutter.

"Go away," he said.

"Fuck *you*, man. I got a question, you could at least try a fucking answer."

Zhukanov went silent again.

"No big deal, bro," said the fat man. "Maybe you've seen this kid since I was here. You say no, fine. So why you giving me shit?"

The shutter wouldn't budge. The fat guy's resistance enraged Zhukanov. "Go away," he said very softly.

The fat guy pushed at the shutter and it shot up. Daring Zhukanov to try closing it. A bully, used to having his way.

Zhukanov remained in place, smelling him. The stench wasn't just his breath, it was all of him. A walking garbage heap.

"Seen him?"

"Go away, asshole."

Now it was the fat man's turn to go red. Pig eyes bulged; spittle bubbled at the sides of his mouth. That soothed Zhukanov's anger, turning it warm and smooth. This was starting to get funny. He laughed, said, "Stupid fat-ass piece of shit."

The fat guy made a deep, fartlike, rumbling sound, and Zhukanov waited for the next insult, ready to throw something back, laugh in the bastard's face again.

But the fat guy didn't say a word, just went for him, faster than he thought possible, one huge hand shooting out and snagging him by the throat, pulling him up so hard against the counter he thought his ribs had broken. The pain nearly blinded him and he thrashed helplessly.

The fat guy's other hand was fisted, zooming at him for a face-pulverizing punch.

Zhukanov managed to jerk his face away from the blow, but the hand around his neck kept squeezing and he could feel all the breath go out of him, hear the fat guy snarling and cursing. Ocean Front was dark, abandoned, just the waves, no one around to watch this monster strangle him to death— no one but the Yids, yards away, doing their Christ-killing chants; they wouldn't help him anyway.

He tried to tear at the strangling hand, but his hands were sweat-slick, so weak, and the fat man's arm was moist too, and he couldn't get a purchase. Slipping and flailing as his field of vision funneled to a pinpoint of light, he saw the fat man's enraged face, another fist coming at him.

A spasm of panic saved his face but brought the blow along the side of his head, hard enough to rattle his brain pan. His arms continued to wave around uselessly. He didn't remember the knife until he'd nearly lost consciousness.

Then he remembered: pocket, front pocket, left side for the quick draw, just like they'd taught him in hand-to-hand. The fat man began shaking him harder, feeding off the pain and terror on Zhukanov's face, not noticing as Zhukanov reached down.

Zhukanov floundered, found it, grabbed too low. Cold metal, a sting, grope-grope, finally he touched the warmth of wood.

He yanked upward. Pushed the blade. No strength, not even a thrust, just a weak, womanish poke and—

Must have missed, because the fat man was still choking him, cursing . . . gargling. And now the shaking had stopped.

Now the bastard wasn't making any sounds.

A look of surprise on his face. The blubbery lips formed into a tiny O.

Like saying, "Oh!"

Where was the knife?

Suddenly, the hand around Zhukanov's throat opened and air rushed into his windpipe and he retched and choked; finally realized he could breathe, but his throat felt as if someone had used it for a lye funnel.

The fat man was no longer facing him; he was flopped down on the counter, arms hanging over.

Where was the knife?

Nowhere in sight. Losing everything. Must be the vodka.

Then he saw the slow red leak from under the fat man's shoulder. No gush, no big arterial spurt, just seepage. Like one of those summer tides when the waves got gentle.

He took hold of the fat man's hair and lifted the massive head.

The knife was still embedded in the guy's neck, just off-center from the Adam's apple, tilting downward. Diagonal slice through jugular, trachea, esophagus, but gravity was pulling the blood back down into the body cavity.

Zhukanov panicked. What if someone *had* seen?

Like the kid in Griffith Park, watching, thinking he was protected by darkness.

But there was no one. Just this fat, dead piece of shit and Zhukanov holding his head up.

A hunter with a trophy. For the first time in a long time, Zhukanov felt strong, territorial, a Siberian wolf.

The only bad thing was the size of the bastard, and now he had to be moved.

Letting the head flop down again, he turned off the lights in the shack, checked the cut on his hand—just a nick—vaulted over the counter, and scanned the walkway in all directions just to make sure.

The stained-glass window in the Yid place was a multi-colored patch in the darkness, but no old Yids out in front. Yet.

Removing the knife, he wiped it with his handkerchief, then eased the corpse down to the ground. Wiping blood off the counter, he stuffed the kerchief into the neck wound. Having to roll it up into a tight ball, because the slash was only a couple of inches wide.

Small cut but effective. Small blade—it was the angle that had done it, the fat guy leaning forward to strangle him, Zhukanov giving that little girly poke upward and then suddenly the guy's weight had reversed the trajectory, forcing the knife down into his throat, severing everything along the way.

Making sure the handkerchief plug was secure, he inhaled deeply and prepared himself for the tough part. Mother of Christ, his neck hurt. He could feel it starting to swell around the neckline of his T-shirt, and he yanked down, ripping some elastic. Looser, but he still felt like the fat guy was choking him.

Another look around. Dark, quiet, all he needed was old Yids flooding out.

Okay, here goes.

Taking hold of the fat guy's feet, he started to pull the corpse.

The damn thing only budged an inch, and Zhukanov felt horrid pain in his lower back.

Like dragging an elephant. Bending his knees, he tried again. Another vertebral warning, but he kept going—what was the choice?

It took forever to get the bastard out of view, and by then Zhukanov was sweating, out of breath, every muscle in his body aflame.

And now he could hear voices. The Yids coming out.

He yanked, dragged, breathed, yanked, dragged, breathed, frantic to get the corpse well back from the walkway. Had he gotten all the blood off the counter?

He rushed back, found a few stains, used his shirt, turned off the lights, and slammed down the shutter.

Now he could hear them louder, old voices jabbering.

He got the corpse halfway to the back of the shack. Stopped when his chest clogged up. Bent his knees again, resumed.

Yank, drag, breathe.

By the time he reached the alley, all he could hear was the ocean, no voices; all the Yids gone home.

He dragged the corpse next to the shack's garbage bins. Not a commercial Dumpster, because the boss was too cheap. Two wooden shipping crates that some Mexican illegals emptied every week for ten bucks.

Okay . . . now what?

Leave him there, concealed by darkness, fetch the car, load the bastard in it, and take him somewhere to dump—where did the West Hollywood guys go for that?—Angeles Crest Forest. Zhukanov had a vague notion where that was; he'd find it.

Another forest. If the old man could see him now.

David had finished off Goliath, and soon Goliath would be rotting in some gulley.

No, wait, before that he had to triple-check for bloodstains— inside the shack and out, along the side of the shack, where the pig had been dragged.

He'd get the car, load the guy, keep him there while he gave the shack a thorough going over. Ditch the knife, the clothes he was wearing. The nunchucks and the baseball bat, too? No. No reason to panic. Why would anyone connect him to the fat bastard, even if they found the corpse?

Just the blood, the knife, his clothes.

Get it done before sunrise.

The guy would leak all over his trunk, but he'd clean it. Running it through again, he decided it was a good plan.

He stretched, fingered the tender, hot flesh of his neck. Slow down, slow everything down, it's over—why had the bastard invited trouble like that?

Zhukanov thanked him for starting up. He hadn't felt this good since leaving Moscow.

Okay, time to get the car. He'd taken three steps when light caught his eye.

The back door of the synagogue opening—someone still there!

He pressed himself against one of the wooden bins, tripping over the corpse's legs, nearly falling on his ass.

Forcing himself not to curse aloud, he breathed through his nose and watched as an old Yid came out of the synagogue. Zhukanov could see him clearly, illuminated by the light inside. Short, thickset, one of those beanies on his head.

The Yid reached in and the blessing of darkness returned. But just for one second, because now the guy was opening a car door.

Not the driver's door, the left rear door. Someone in back of the car sat up. Got out. Stretched. Just like Zhukanov had just done. The Yid talked to him.

Shorter than the Yid—a kid.

Hiding in back—had to be *the* kid. Why else would he be hiding?

The right size, and he'd been lying low—who else could it be?

The kid got back in the rear seat, lay down, disappeared.

So he'd been here all along. Hidden by the Yids—made sense; twenty-five grand would make them come in their pants.

We'll see about that.

The Yid's car started up and the headlights went on. Staying in the shadows, Zhukanov ran toward it. The Yid started backing out just as Zhukanov got close enough to read the license plate.

Bunch of letters and numbers. Zhukanov mouthed the magic formula soundlessly. At first his brain refused to cooperate.

But the old Yid helped him, taking a long time to back the car out and straighten up, and by the time he finished, Zhukanov had it all memorized.

No time to get his old car to follow. He'd write the number down, call the Department of Motor Vehicles. Giving out addresses was illegal, but he knew a clerk at the Hollywood branch, wiseass louse from Odessa who'd do it for fifty bucks.

Given the payoff, an excellent investment.

CHAPTER 65

BY 10 P.M. THE SEARCH OF THE MONTECITO house had turned up nothing.

"The place is just about empty," Sepulveda told Petra. "A little furniture in the living room and one bedroom; the rest of the rooms have nothing."

"Check for secret passages?" she said, only half in jest.

Sepulveda stared at her. "I'll let you know if the Phantom of the Opera shows up."

She and Ron headed back to L.A. She'd been running up his cell-phone bill, talking to airline supervisors, some of them impressed by her title, others skeptical. So far no, no flights under Balch's name had turned up, and a 9:50 call from Wil let her know he was meeting with the same results. Thoroughness would demand paperwork, the proper forms. Tomorrow. She was exhausted, angry at Schoelkopf for keeping the news about Balch under wraps.

The kid he publicizes, but this scares him.

She and Ron talked about it till they got to Oxnard. Bosses

were always easy targets. When they reached Camarillo, the car turned silent and she saw he had his eyes closed.

He awoke when she stopped the car in front of his house.

"Rise and shine," she said.

He smiled groggily, apologized, then leaned over to kiss her. She shifted her hips in the seat and met him halfway. One of his hands passed behind her head, pressing gently. The other found its way to her breast. He was smoother when fatigued.

He squeezed her softly then began to remove his hand. She held it in place. The next kiss lasted a long time. He was the first to pull away, and now he looked wide awake.

She said, "Some first date."

"Second. The first was the deli."

"True." She realized she'd thought of that as getting acquainted.

He said, "Well, you've got plenty to do. I won't keep you."

She initiated a third kiss. He didn't try to feel her; kept both hands above the neck. Then he cupped her chin. With Nick she hadn't liked that—too confining. He did it differently. She traveled his mouth with her tongue, and he made a small, baritone noise of contentment.

"Oh, man," he said. "I really want to see you again—I know it's not a good time to be thinking about going out."

"Call," she said. "If I say I'm too busy, it'll be the truth."

He kissed the tip of her chin. "You are *so* pretty. The first time I saw you, I—" Shaking his head, he got out, groped in his pocket for his keys, and waved.

"Wait," she called out as he turned and started toward his front door.

He stopped.

"Your phone."

He laughed, returned to the driver's side, took it.

"Make sure you send me the bill," she said. "It's going to be huge."

"Sure," he said. Then he kissed her again.

※

Back on the 101, she could barely keep her eyes open. Exhaustion even in the face of all that adrenaline meant she was severely sleep-deprived. She'd go home, take some caffeine, squeeze in another hour or so of phone work, then enough.

By the time she reached her apartment, it was 11:23. One message on her machine. She let it sit there, changed into a flannel nightie, and got extra-strong coffee going. Realized she still hadn't called Stu. Too late now. She felt lousy. One day this case would be over, but Kathy's experience would last forever. Would Stu remember her as being neglectful during his crisis?

The message turned out to be him, phoning at 11:09, and asking her to call back up to midnight. The St. Joe's operator was reluctant to put her through this late, but finally she heard Stu say, "Petra?"

"So sorry for not calling sooner. How's Kathy?"

"Fine," he said. "Resting." Someone who didn't know him would have thought he sounded okay.

"Everything went smoothly?"

"Very smoothly—they did a mastectomy. One breast. The surgeon says she'll have total recovery."

"That's great."

"I got through four years of *TV Guide*—"

"Don't worry about that, Stu. How can I help?"

"Thanks, but we're okay," he said.

"You're sure? Do the kids need anything?"

"Just their mom," he said, and his voice changed. "They'll get through it, Petra. We'll all get through it."

"I know you will." One breast . . .

"Anyway," said Stu, "how was *your* day?"

Apart from that, Mrs. Lincoln, how was the play? Keeping her at arm's length. He'd cried once in her arms, probably vowed never to lose it again.

"Actually, a huge amount of stuff hit the fan, Stu." She told him about Estrella Flores, the bloodstained Lexus, Balch's attempt to rabbit by charter. Then William Bradley Straight, ID'd but still unaccounted for, left without a mother.

"Poor kid," he said. "I leave you alone for one day, and look at all the trouble you get yourself into."

Everything coming together, and he had nothing to do with it. She wanted to tell him it was okay, but it wasn't.

"Balch," he said. "He fits that well?"

"As well as Ramsey does."

Stu didn't pick up on that. He was the veteran. Maybe she should focus.

"So we track Balch," she said.

"Any idea where he is?"

"My bet is some other state or out of the country, but S. says we can't publicize it, yet. Near arrest of an innocent man, and all that scared the hell out of him. But it's nuts, right? With the Straight kid we go media-wild, but on Balch we're gagged, giving him a head start. Oh yeah, something else: Karlheinz Lauch died a year ago, but the similarities between Lisa and Ilse Eggermann got me thinking. Eggermann was picked up in Redondo and dumped in the Marina. Balch lives in Rolling Hills Estates, right down the coast."

"A serial?"

"Wouldn't it be weird if he was some big-time creep and this is just the tip of the iceberg?"

Silence. "The number-two man strikes out to achieve dominance . . . another inadequate psychopath."

"Exactly."

"Hold on," he said, and Petra heard him talking to someone. "That was the night nurse. Okay, what can I do to help?"

"Right now? Just stay with Kath—"

"She's sleeping," he said sharply. "I want to work tonight, Petra. What airlines have you checked?"

"Wil and I split them up. We haven't gotten through to some of them. They want paper. I figured—"

"What about international carriers?" he said. "Does Balch have a passport?"

"Don't know—"

"I've already made contact with the passport office on Eggermann. I'll do international—and the domestic carriers you haven't reached. You sound bushed, get some sleep. I'll talk to you in the A.M."

CHAPTER 66

LET THEM THINK HE'D RABBITED TO VEGAS.

Let them think they were dealing with someone stupid.

It would help him tie everything up. He liked being neat.

Not as bad as Lisa. She was compulsive, wanting everything just so. Irregularities set her off. That vicious mouth . . .

She hated surprises. So he gave her one.

The German girl too. Little stupid Sally.

One more surprise left, and the stupid cops were making it a little easier, leaking "anonymous tips." Venice Beach. Ocean Front Walk. Could the kid still be there? Maybe. Sometimes those runaways bunked down.

How far could a street kid go? If he'd tunneled deep, could he be found?

Should he forget about the kid? Was he overreacting? Obsessing? Sometimes he did that, like the way he'd worry a hidden pimple till it got infected and festered and he'd have to lance it himself, coat it with Neosporin, live with the pain. No one knew that about him.

Maybe the kid hadn't even been in the park. If he'd seen something, wouldn't he have turned himself in, tried to collect the reward?

But that assumed he read the papers, watched TV, knew what was going on in the world. Some of those kids were so stoned-out or brain-damaged, they didn't have a clue.

Not much of a witness. Should he just let it ride? Live with the uncertainty?

He considered it for a long time. The idea bothered him. *Big* loose end.

He could at least check it out. He thought a long time about how to do it without putting himself in danger, finally came up with the plan.

Perfect. And ironic. The hardest thing to pull off, irony, according to the bullshit-artist acting coaches.

What's my motivation?

Self-preservation.

CHAPTER 67

▧

SAM'S HOUSE HAS A LIVING ROOM, A KITCHEN, two bedrooms with a bathroom in between. I got a real bed. The sheets felt new. Sam slept in the other room, and I could hear him snoring through the wall.

It's only a few blocks from the shul, on what Sam calls a walk street. Instead of a road to drive through, there's a sidewalk, maybe twice as wide as a regular one.

"I should walk," said Sam, driving there. "But at night there are too many nuts out." He parks in an alley around the back.

He's got an alarm with panels on the front door and the door to the kitchen. I looked the other way while he punched the code, so he wouldn't think I was up to something. He said, "I'm ready to hit the hay," and showed me my room. On the bed were a new toothbrush and toothpaste and a glass.

"No pajamas, Bill. Didn't know your size." He looked embarrassed, standing in the doorway, not coming in.

I said, "Thanks. This is great. I mean it."

He clicked his teeth together, like his false teeth didn't fit. "Listen, I want you to know I don't usually have guests—never did before."

I didn't know what to say.

"What I'm getting at, Bill, is you don't have to worry about something funny going on. I like women. Stick around long enough and you'll see that."

"I believe you," I said.

"Okay . . . better get some sleep."

The bedroom is painted light green and has old, dark furniture, a gray carpet, and two pictures on the wall hanging crooked. One's a black-and-white photograph of a woman with her hair tied up and a guy with a long black beard. The other one's a painting of some trees that looks like it was cut out of a magazine. The room has that old-guy smell and it's a little hot.

I brush my teeth and look in the mirror. The scratches on my face aren't too bad, but my chest hurts, my eyes are pink, and my hair looks nasty.

I strip down to my underpants, get under the covers, and close my eyes. At first it's quiet, then I hear music from Sam's room. Like a guitar, but higher. A mandolin. A bluegrass band at the Sunnyside had one of those.

He plays the same song over and over; it sounds sad and old.

Then he stops and the snoring begins. I think of Mom. That's all I remember till morning.

Now it's Saturday, and I wake up before he does and go into the living room. The curtains are closed and the house is dark. I pull a living room curtain aside and see a couple of metal chairs on Sam's front porch, then a low wall, houses across the walk street. The sky is getting blue and some gulls are flying. It's weird, but I swear I can smell the salt through the windows.

The living room has more books than any place I've seen except a library. Three walls are covered with bookshelves, and you can barely walk 'cause of all the magazines on the floor. In one corner's a couch with a knitted blanket thrown over it, a TV, and a music stand holding a song by some guy named Smetana.

I sit down on the couch and dust shoots up. No morning stomachache. It's the best sleep I've had in my life, and I decide to say thank you by making breakfast.

In a box on the kitchen counter I find whole wheat bread and I toast four slices. There's a coffee machine, but I don't know how to use it, so I just pour milk and orange juice into glasses and set them out on the table, along with paper napkins, forks, spoons, knives. In the refrigerator are fruits and vegetables, butter, some sour cream, eggs, and a big jar of something silvery-looking, like out of a science lab. Pickled herring. I take out the eggs, hoping Sam likes them scrambled.

They're frying up when I hear him coughing. He comes in, wearing this light blue bathrobe, rubs his eyes, and pushes at his teeth. "Thought I heard something—what, you're a gourmet?"

"Is scrambled okay?"

He turns his back on me, puts his hand to his mouth, and coughs some more. "Excuse me. Yeah, scrambled is great. Usually I don't cook Saturday—it's my Sabbath. I'm not that religious, but I usually don't cook. Maybe 'cause my mother never did."

"Sorry—"

"No, no, this is good, why should it apply to you?" He comes closer, looks into the pan. "Smells good. I could use something hot—you know how to make coffee?"

"No."

He explains how to use the machine and leaves. When he comes back, the coffee's poured and he's dressed in a tan suit and a white shirt with the collar open; his hair's brushed and he's shaved. By now, the eggs are pretty cold.

"Okay, let's chow down," he says, unfolding his napkin and putting it on his lap. "Bon appétit—that means 'eat up' in French." He tastes the eggs. "Very good. Very gentlemanly of you to do this, Bill. Maybe there's hope for the younger generation."

He finishes everything on his plate, has two cups of coffee, and lets out a big sigh. "Okay, here's my schedule: I go to the shul for Saturday services, should be back around eleven, eleven-thirty, noon at the latest. You want to leave the house, I'll keep the alarm off."

"No, I'll stay here."

"You're sure?"

"Yes." Suddenly my voice is tight. "I'll read."

"Read what?"

"You've got a lot of books."

He looks over at the living room. "You like to read, huh?"

"Very much."

"You work and you read . . . I'm a reader, too, Bill. Once upon a time I wanted to be a lawyer. Back in Europe. No one in my family was a professional. We were farmers, miners, laborers. My father knew the Bible by heart, but they wouldn't let us get an education. I was determined to get one, but the war interrupted—enjoy the books. There's nothing in there a guy your age shouldn't see."

He wipes his hands, carries his plate to the sink, and checks himself in a little mirror over the faucet. "Sure you want me to leave the alarm on?"

"Yes."

"I just didn't want you to feel like you were in prison." He touches his shirt collar, smooths it out, pats his hair. "Here I go, ready for God. Hope He's ready for me. If you get hungry, eat. I'll bring something back, too. See you eleven, eleven-thirty."

※

He's back at 11:27, pulling the Lincoln behind the house and getting out in a hurry, carrying something wrapped in aluminum foil. He opens the passenger door and a skinny old woman with red hair gets out. The two of them talk for a while and then they disappear.

He comes through the front door fifteen minutes later. "Escorted a friend home." He puts the foil thing on the table and unwraps it. Cookies with colored sprinkles on them. "Here you go."

I nibble one. "Thanks."

"You're welcome—listen, I appreciate manners, but you don't have to thank me for every little thing. Otherwise we'll be standing around here like Alphonse and Gaston—two very polite French guys." He puts one hand behind his back, the other over his stomach, and bows. "*You* first—no, *you* first. It's an old joke—they're so polite, they stand there all day, never cross the street."

I smile.

He says, "So what'd you end up reading?"

"Magazines."

Most of his books turned out to be fiction; the real stuff I found was mostly catalogs of sinks and toilets. The magazines were interesting, though—really old, from the fifties and sixties. *Life, Look, Saturday Evening Post, Time, Popular Mechanics.* Presidents back to Eisenhower, stories about the Korean War, movie stars, animals in the zoo, families looking happy, weird ads.

"You hungry?"

"No thanks."

"What'd you eat?"

"The cookie."

"Don't be a wise guy."

"I had some milk."

"That's it?" He goes to the refrigerator and takes out the jar of herring. Pieces of fish are swimming around in this cloudy-looking juice. "This is protein, Bill."

I shake my head.

"It's fish. Don't like fish?"

"Not very much."

He opens the jar, takes out a piece, eats it, opens the refrigerator again, and looks inside. "How about some salad?"

"I'm fine, Mr. Ganzer. Really."

He puts the herring back and takes off his jacket. "I'll go out later, get us a couple of steaks—you're not one of those vegetarians, are you?"

"Meat's fine."

"What an agreeable fellow—you play chess?"

"No."

"So learn."

❖

It's basically war, and I like it. After six games I beat him, and he says, "Very good," but I'm not sure he's happy.

"Another one, Mr. Ganzer?"

"No, I'm gonna take a nap." He reaches out to touch my head but stops himself. "You've got a good brain, Bill."

I read while he sleeps, getting comfortable on the dusty couch with the knitted blanket over my legs. A few times I get up, look outside, see a beautiful sky. But I don't mind being inside.

He wakes up at 6:15 P.M., takes a shower. When he comes out of his bedroom, he's wearing another suit, brown, a blue shirt, tan shoes.

"I'll go get the steaks," he says. "No, wait a second—" Opening the freezer compartment above the fridge, he pulls out a package of chicken. "This okay?"

"It's fine, Mr. Ganzer, but I'm not really hungry."

"How could you not be hungry?"

"I'm just not."

"You don't usually eat much, do you?"

"I do fine."

"How long you been on your own?"

"A while."

"Okay, okay, I won't pry—I'll defrost it and broil it, it's healthy that way."

By 7:20 the chicken's done, and I'm eating more than I thought I would. Then I notice Sam has barely touched the drumstick he put on his plate.

"You need protein, Mr. Ganzer."

"Very funny," he says. But he smiles. "I'm taken care of in the cuisine department. Got an appointment tonight for dinner—you going to be okay alone here?"

"Sure. I'm used to it."

He frowns, puts the drumstick on my plate, gets up. "I don't know when I'll be back. Probably ten, ten-thirty. Normally, I might entertain here, but I didn't figure you'd want to meet anyone. Right?"

"It's your house. I could stay in the bedroom."

"What? Hide like some . . . no, I'll go over there. If you need me, it's six houses down, the white house with the blue trim. The party's name is Kleinman. Mrs. Kleinman."

"Have a nice time," I say.

He turns pink. "Yeah . . . listen, Bill, I been thinking. That twenty-five thousand. If it's rightfully yours, you should claim it. That's a lot of money for anyone. I could make sure no one swindles it from under you—there's a fellow across the street, used to be a lawyer. A Communist, but smart, knows the angles. He wouldn't take a penny from you, could make sure you're protected—"

"No one can protect me."

"Why do you say that?"

"Because no one ever did."

"But, look—"

"No," I say. "There's no way they'd let a kid keep all that money. And I can't help them anyway, I didn't see the guy's face, all I saw is a license plate—"

"A license plate? Bill, that could be very helpful. They've got ways of tracing license plates—"

"No!" I shout. "No one ever did anything for me, and I don't care about any of it—and if you think that makes me a bad citizen and you don't want me around, fine, I'll leave!"

I get up and run for the door. He grabs my arm. "Okay, okay, calm down, take it easy—"

"Let me go!"

He does. I reach the door, see the alarm's red eye, stop. Here comes a stomachache.

"Please, Bill, relax."

"I am relaxed." But it's a lie. I'm breathing fast and my chest is really, really tight.

"Look, I'm sorry," he says. "Forget it, I just thought . . . you're obviously a good guy, and sometimes when good guys don't do the right thing, they feel— Ah! Who the hell am *I* to tell *you*? You know what to do."

"I don't know anything," I mutter.

"What's that?"

"Every time I try to learn, something gets in the way—like with you and the war."

"But, look, you're making it. Like I made it."

I want to cry again, but no way—no damn way! Words start pouring out of me: "I don't know what I'm doing, Mr. Ganzer. Maybe I *should* call the police—maybe I'll do it from a pay phone, tell them the license plate and then hang up."

"If you do it that way, how do you collect the money?"

"Forget the money, they'll never give me the money. Even if they do, my mom will find out, and then Moron—he's the guy she lives with. He's the reason I left. He'll end up with it, believe me, there's no way I'm going to get a penny and I'll be right where I started from."

"Moron, huh? A dim bulb?" He taps his head.

I laugh. "Yeah."

He laughs. I laugh harder. I'm not really happy, but it's a way to get out the feelings.

"A smart guy like you and a dim bulb," he says. "I can see why there'd be problems— Okay, I'm gonna give you the alarm code. Just in case you want a breath of fresh air. One one twenty-five. Think of January first, 1925. My birthday—I'm a New Year's baby."

"I'm not going out."

"Just in case." He punches the numbers, the light goes green, and he opens the door. "Relax, take it easy—try the herring."

"Not a chance," I say, and he leaves smiling.

The chessboard is still out on the kitchen counter. I think I'll experiment with different moves. See things from both sides.

CHAPTER 68

![decorative square]

SATURDAY MORNING AT 6:46, THE PHONE WOKE Petra. Schoelkopf's voice played havoc with her brain waves.

"Got comprehensive warrants on Balch's office and home. You and Fournier go over both with a fine-tooth before we put a bulletin out on him. I've messengered the paper and keys to you, should be there any minute. Get it all done today so we can cast the net on the bastard."

"Why do we have to wait to cast?"

"Because that's the way upstairs *wants* it, Barbie. The fact that we came so close to tunnel-visioning on Ramsey scares them shitless. No more questions. Get moving."

"Does Fournier know about the assignment?"

"You tell him."

The doorbell rang just as she was stepping out of the shower. Drying off frantically, she wrapped herself in a bath sheet, ran to the door, saw a patrolman through the peephole, and stuck her hand out through a crack in the door for the manila envelope containing the warrants and the keys. The uniform, a tall guy, grinned, checked her out, and said she'd have to sign a form.

"Slide it under the door." After I slam it in your face.

She roused Wil at 7:15. He sounded half dead, and she thought she heard a woman in the background.

"All right," he said. "Where first?"

"Up to you."

"Balch's office is closer. How about . . . nine? Make that nine-thirty."

"Want me to pick you up?"

He didn't answer immediately. There was definitely a woman there, talking low and rhythmically, almost singing. "No," he said. "I'll meet you."

※

With no traffic, the drive to Studio City was fifteen minutes of morning breeze, and she had time to stop at DuPars near Laurel for takeout coffee and an apple cruller. In the lot fronting the brown building was a gray Acura but no signs of the driver. The license plate said SHERRI. She pulled up next to it and was eating in the car when Wil arrived in his civvy wheels—black Toyota Supra. He wore an off-white linen suit, black polo shirt, perforated black shoes, looked ready for a Palm Springs weekend; she'd put on the usual pantsuit.

He looked at the building. "What a dump."

"Ramsey lives like a king but treated him like a serf. Maybe the guy finally exploded."

"Didn't know you were a shrink," he said. "Actually, that makes sense."

"Want more? This occurred to me last night: the way Lisa's body was left out in the open, no attempt at all to conceal. Same with Ilse Eggermann. It's as if he's boasting—look what I can get away with. All his life, Balch is subservient to Ramsey, eating dirt, taking verbal abuse. What better way to undo that psychologically than by taking Ramsey's woman, then discarding her and announcing it to the world?"

"Taking her," said Wil. "You think Balch and Lisa were making it?"

"I think Balch wanted to. He's no Adonis, but she dated him once, and we know she likes older men. Whether or not she agreed to start up again, only Balch knows. Unless we find something in there."

They had their guns in their hands as they approached the door. Basic procedure: Detectives did little shooting, but a good deal of it took place while serving warrants.

Petra unlocked the door and went in first. Someone was sitting at the desk in the front room and she brandished her 9mm.

A young woman in a budget power suit working the morning crossword. The sight of the gun painted her face with terror. Pretty brunette, very short hair, dark eyes, maybe Hispanic.

"Who are you?" said Petra. Wil was behind her. She could hear him breathing.

The woman's voice dribbled out, nearly inaudible. "Sherri Amerian—I'm an attorney."

The Acura in the lot.

"Mr. Balch's attorney?"

"No," said Amerian. "I work for Lawrence Schick." Stronger voice now, a little brassy with resentment, and the eyes had turned chilly. "Am I allowed to show you my ID? It's in the purse over there. I mean, I don't want to get shot in the process."

"Go ahead," said Petra.

Amerian produced a driver's license and her business card from Schick and Associates. The license made her twenty-seven years old. Fresh out of law school. Doing Schick's scut work on a Saturday.

"Okay?" she said imperiously. Junior associate, but to look at her body language, she was arguing before the Supreme Court. Didn't take long to get that lawyer 'tude going. "Will you please put those *guns* away?"

Not waiting for a reply, she came around from behind the desk. Great figure.

Wil holstered his piece. "What are you doing here?"

"Representing Mr. H. Cart Ramsey's interests, Officer . . ."

"Detective Fournier. This is Detective Connor."

Amerian's shrug said their names didn't matter. "Our firm was informed that you intended to conduct a search of these premises related to possible evidence pertaining to Mr. Gregory Balch. May I see the warrant?"

"Why?" said Wil.

"Because the premises are owned by Mr. Ramsey, and we represent his—"

"Here." Petra slipped her gun back into her purse and gave her the Studio City paper.

The young lawyer studied it. "Exactly right: material pertaining to Mr. Balch. Not Mr. Ramsey. This office contains numerous documents of a confidential nature pertaining to Mr. Ramsey's finances, and we insist that they not be tampered with. As such, I'll be remaining here while you conduct your search. In order to accomplish that, our suggestion is that we set up a procedure in which you indicate a given drawer and/or shelf and I review the contents beforehand—"

"If I have to blow my nose," said Wil, "are you going to review the tissue?"

Amerian frowned. "I really don't see the point of—"

"Fine," said Wil. "Cut to the chase. The top drawer of this desk first. And no chitchat or coffee breaks. Fold your puzzle and put it away."

❋

They took three hours to search every inch of the suite. After the first hour, Amerian got bored with her role as gatekeeper and started to say, "Sure, sure," whenever Wil or Petra pointed out a book on a shelf or a box on the floor. Short attention span, the *Sesame Street* generation.

The only remnants of Balch's presence were fast-food cartons, take-out menus from local restaurants, and a top drawer full of office-supply flotsam. No family photos—Petra supposed that made sense: Balch was a two-time marital loser.

Man with no attachments? Something about him that got in the way of relationships? So what? The same could be said for millions of people who didn't kill.

She kept going. All the papers were Ramsey's. Now Amerian was paying attention again. Rent books, tax returns, folders listing deductions, business contracts. Documents Petra would have loved to see a few days ago. Balch had worked here for years but left nothing of himself behind.

Did that say something about the way he viewed his job?

She removed a California Tax Code from the shelf, flipped pages, turned it upside down. Nothing. Same for the next ten books. The place was even messier than when she'd interviewed Balch. For a guy with such a disorganized mind, he'd proved a canny killer—so many steps, carefully laid out.

Then why had he been sloppy enough to call Westward Charter and alert them to the rabbit?

The usual psychopath's self-destructive behavior?

Or a ruse . . . where *was* he?

❋

They left at 1 P.M., stopped for lunch at a seafood place on Ventura. Not much conversation. Wil had started off grumpy, and four hours of futility hadn't improved his disposition. He ate his sand dabs slowly, drank a lot of iced tea, looked out the window. Petra's crab cakes went down like deep-fried hockey pucks, and by 3 P.M. they were in separate cars on the 101 headed for the 405 interchange and the one-hour ride to Rolling Hills Estates and Balch's home on Saddlewax Road.

He got ahead of her at Imperial Highway, and she'd lost sight of him when she thought of something. Speeding up, she managed to spot the Supra just past Hermosa Beach and waved him off at the Redondo Beach exit. They both pulled onto the shoulder. Petra jogged to his car.

"Humor me," she said, "but I want to take a look at the place on the pier where Ilse Eggermann was last seen, then go to Balch's."

"Fine," he said. "Good idea. I'll stick with you."

A fifteen-minute westerly cruise down Redondo Beach Boulevard took them to the former site of Antoine's, now a Dudley Jones Steak House franchise with a harbor view. Deepred room full of weekend brunchers and noise, blond surfer/waiters sailing past with platters of rare flesh and melon-size baked potatoes.

Petra allowed herself a second to visualize Ilse Eggermann feuding with Lauch. Leaving the restaurant, descending wooden steps off the pier—just as she and Wil were doing now. Continuing down to the parking lot. Late at night, deserted, the place would be spooky.

The drive to Rolling Hills Estates chilled her.

Six-mile straightaway on Hawthorne Boulevard, it began as a swath through the usual mash of car dealers, malls, and office-supply barns, then narrowed just before Palos Verdes Drive, where a median strip appeared, planted with eucalyptus and pine and black-trunked shaggy trees that resembled willows. A white wooden sign welcomed her to Rolling Hills Estates, and low white corral fencing appeared along both sides of the road.

Ten minutes from Redondo, driving leisurely. This was Balch's turf.

She pictured him coming home from a long day as Ramsey's slave, stopping off for a drink, noticing Ilse and Lauch fighting. He follows them out, sees Lauch drive off, picks up Ilse, promising to drive her to her hotel near the Marina, but they never get there.

Open dump in a parking lot.

Look what I can get away with!

Then back home. So simple.

A day at the beach.

CHAPTER 69

BEAUTIFUL OCEAN, BUT TOO MANY PEOPLE.

He wore a top-quality, real-hair false beard, similar to the one he'd used for the German girl, a wide-brimmed straw hat, a long brown ratty raincoat over a frayed white shirt, and cheap gray cotton pants. Running shoes, relatively new, but dirtied-up to stay in character.

The gait he adopted was a clumsy, stiff-legged shuffle. When he walked, he pretended to stare at the ground but was able to sight upward without being obvious, because the hat did a good job of concealing his eyes. If someone made eye contact, he could half lower the lids and focus on nothing.

Mr. Mentally Disordered Homeless. Ocean Front Walk was full of them, sitting on benches, lurching along with the crowd, staring at the sand or the palm trees or the ocean, as if something important were happening out there. What? Imaginary whales? Mermaids with big tits flapping around on the beach?

His mother had gone crazy when he was fourteen. He'd never wondered what she thought about. Just stayed away, as if she were contagious.

He walked up and down Ocean Front very slowly. Every so often he'd sit, make like he was dozing off, while examining passersby.

No one paid attention to him. The bicycle cops were on the

lookout for violence, so if you kept to yourself, they were happy to ignore you. Same with the tourists—anything to avoid being panhandled.

The problem was the quantity of people. Nice, warm Saturday, everyone flocking to the beach, the slow-cruising walkathon along Ocean Front so dense you could barely make out individuals.

Plenty of kids, but not *the* kid. After an hour, he was able to classify them into two groups: the well-scrubbed spawn of the tourists and clots of dark-skinned, big-mouthed local brats weaving in and out of the pedestrian stream, probably looking for pockets to pick.

Why would *the* kid be out in broad daylight?

Why would he be here, period, after the "anonymous tip"?

Waste of time, but considering all he'd accomplished, he didn't feel that bad.

Beautiful day; go with it. Long time since he'd been here, and the walkway had gotten more commercial, lined with shops, snack stands, restaurants, even a synagogue—that was odd. Some of the buildings ran through to the alley and, beyond it, the Speedway. Others occupied the ground floors of multistory prewar apartment buildings. The boy could be in one of those buildings, and how could you find him?

The boy could be anywhere.

He'd give it a few more hours. The beard and hat and coat were heating him up. A cold drink would be nice, and he had ten bucks in his pocket—more back in the car, parked six blocks away. But a crazy bum fishing out money might attract attention, so he decided to settle for water from a fountain.

There was one down at the other end, near the synagogue. He'd shuffle clear to the northernmost end of Ocean Front, turn around, come back, drink, repeat it a few times, take a pseudo-nap on a bench, call it a day.

Forget about the kid. He told himself it was okay, but it stuck in his throat. Big, hot pimple full of pus, just itching to be squeezed.

He preferred to give in to his compulsions. Avoiding them built up tension.

His mother had been unbelievably compulsive before going completely bonkers. Smoking five packs a day, picking at her face, rocking when she sewed, going on food binges, then starving herself for days. When they put her in the hospital, she began to bang her head against the wall, like one of those autistic kids, and they forced her to wear a football helmet. Flowered dress and a helmet—what position do you play, Ma? She looked ridiculous, and he did everything he could to avoid visiting her.

She'd died ten years ago, and he was sole surviving kin. Through a local attorney, he'd instructed the hospital to cremate her, bury her on the grounds.

Thinking about her evoked no emotion. He was hot, discouraged, not happy about abandoning the loose end. Mostly the heat right now. That was the biggest part of what he felt.

He took an hour to cover the walkway two more times, getting more and more uptight about not succeeding.

No kid who looked anything like the picture. He reached the water fountain, filled his belly with water, wiped the beard. A tourist about to drink changed his mind. Talk about a convincing performance.

The nearest bench was occupied by a young couple in spandex. He stumbled over, muttering, perched his butt on a corner, and the couple got up and left.

This was good!

The synagogue must have just let out, because he saw old people milling around outside the front door, then dispersing. He had nothing against any group, even Jews, just wished those who couldn't take care of themselves would die and make room for everyone else.

Someone else didn't like the Jews, though.

Guy working the souvenir stand a couple of stores down. Look at how he stared at them—real hostility.

Ugly guy, mid-forties, long greasy-looking blond hair, probably tinted. Bad skin, skinny arms sticking out of the sleeves of a really hideous purple CALIFORNIA HERE I COME T-shirt.

The stand stocked similar shirts, hats, sunglasses, toys and banners and postcards, a tiny little place crammed with junk. No one was buying, probably because the proprietor was about as welcoming as a piranha.

Hostile *and* jumpy. Looking up and down Ocean Front, too. Interesting.

A pair of cops walked their bicycles past the stand, and the

ugly guy's eyes widened and his body shot forward; he almost
threw himself over the counter.

Wanting to tell them something?

But he stopped himself, picked up some kind of doll, pretended to be checking the price.

Strange . . .

The cops must have thought so too, because they stopped
and talked to the ugly guy. He produced a sick-looking smile
and shook his head. The cops didn't leave right away. Something about the guy was making them wonder. The guy kept
smiling, fingering the doll, and finally they did leave.

The guy stood there for a long time watching them before
returning to his old routine: looking north, then south, north,
then south. Not a glance at the beach.

Looking for something in particular. Some*one*?

Anonymous tip. Could it be? Was God that good?

He studied the souvenir vendor for another twenty minutes,
and the pattern never altered: pace, check out the walkway, take
a doll down, squeeze it, put it back, pace . . . Suddenly, the
guy altered his routine, going behind the cheap chintz curtains
that backed the souvenir stand. Probably a rear stockroom;
maybe a bathroom break.

For five minutes, the stand was left unattended and some
local kids cruised by and pulled postcards from the rack. When
the long-haired guy came out, he was wiping his lips.

A drink break. Here he goes again: up and down, up and
down. Definitely on the prowl.

Could it really be? Maybe he was waiting for a dope deal.

Then again, the tip had come from somewhere.

To a loser like this, selling crap no one bought, twenty-five
thou would be a helluva lot of Saturdays. Good reason to be
jumpy.

He observed the guy some more. Same routine; one more
booze break. The guy was robotic, on autopilot, just like the
nuts he used to see when he visited his mother.

Definitely worth looking into—what did he have to lose?

He got up, walked a hundred yards south, reversed direction, and shifted closer to the storefronts, passing close to the
stand and looking for posted hours. There it was:

SUMMER HOURS: 11 TO 5 M–F, WEEKENDS, 11 TO 8.

He'd leave, come back close to 8; hopefully the crowds

would be gone. Hopefully the guy wouldn't close up early or go off shift; if he did, there was always another day.

Given no other leads, it was all he had and he decided to be hopeful.

Optimism, that was the key. Long as you didn't lose the irony.

CHAPTER 70

SADDLEWAX ROAD WAS A QUARTER MILE IN from the Palos Verdes turnoff. Along the way, Petra saw two little girls in full equestrian dress riding gorgeous brown horses. A woman on a black steed trailed them, scrutinizing their posture or the horses', or both.

Balch's house was three-quarters up the shady street, a one-story apricot stucco ranch atop a high bed of devil ivy. That same white corral fencing cordoned the property and all its neighbors. Boys shot baskets; a man in a bright green polo shirt hosed down a vintage Corvette. The neighborhood had that aura of families with bright futures.

Strange place for a man living alone. Maybe the remnant of one of the marriages.

There was a basketball hoop atop Balch's garage, too. No cars parked outside. The few roses planted next to the house were leggy and browning, and the roof shakes were warped. Bound stacks of mail—four days' worth—sat in front of the screen door. A very small notice stapled to the screen said the local sheriffs had assumed jurisdiction over the property; no one was to trespass. The locals hadn't taken in the mail.

Wil phoned them, and they said it was okay to enter; if he and Petra removed anything, make a list and send a copy. He got evidence bags and recording forms from the trunk of his car, Petra picked up the mail, and they went in.

The living room was dark, rancid, littered with unfolded newspapers, dirty clothes, empty cans of beer and Pepsi, bottles of orange juice and vodka. A screwdriver man.

A sty, just like the office. Unlike the Lexus. As Petra read the mail, Wil got to work on the sofas, removing cushions, unzipping them, yanking out the foam.

Four days of post yielded utility bills, junk ads, coupons. Three days ago, he'd been spotted at Montecito switching cars, after burying Estrella Flores. Where had he cut the maid's throat? Probably somewhere in the hills above Ranch-Haven. Petra's best guess was he'd overpowered Flores in the house, driven her out through the fire road, found some nice quiet kill spot. Then, wrapping the body in plastic, stashing her in the trunk, he made the forty-five-minute drive to Montecito, entombed the body, left the Lexus behind—because he thought it was clean, and why would the cops check out Ramsey's weekend house?

Picking up the Jeep because that had been Lisa's murder vehicle and he wanted to make sure *it* was clean?

She recalled his demeanor during the interview. A little downbeat, self-effacing. No edginess, but if he was that psychopathic, why would there be?

Slipping in Lisa's bad temper, how she took it out on Cart. Brand-new running shoes. A clever bastard, Mr. Gregory Balch. So why had he stayed a lackey all his life?

Embezzling cash from the boss, waiting for the right moment to bolt? Original plans to do it with Lisa, but something had gone wrong . . . was Balch somewhere in Brazil with suitcases of cash, the satisfaction of having destroyed Ramsey's life in more ways than one?

She went into the kitchen. The food in the fridge was sad bachelor fare: beer, wine, more orange juice and Smirnoff, more take-out cartons. Beef lo mein and ribs from a Chinese place on Hawthorne Boulevard; KFC crispy chicken bucket— no address, but she'd seen an outlet along the way, on Hawthorne. Half a gigantic pizza from a place called DeMona's in Studio City. Ventura Boulevard, just a few blocks from the office. All the food was long past edibility. The pizza looked petrified.

In the living room, Wil worked grimly and silently, upending couches, slitting burlap bottoms, pulling a clock off the wall and shaking it hard enough to do serious damage, peering up the fireplace.

She decided to get an overview of the house, found three bedrooms, two bone-empty, one a disgusting mess, a pair of bathrooms, a dining area off the kitchen, and, next to the living room, a paneled den that looked out to the backyard, nothing in it but a brown leather recliner and a sixty-inch TV. An illegal black box sat atop the television. Petra switched on the set and was assaulted by five feet of penis entering vagina, a lazy synthesizer score, moans and grunts.

"Oh, those men," said Wil, laughing.

She turned off the TV, opened the curtains. The yard was nice-sized, with several mature trees and an oval swimming pool, but the grass was ten inches of hay; the pool, a sump of algae-streaked soup. High block walls and shrubbery blocked the neighbors' views. Lucky for the neighbors.

Light-years from Ramsey's princely lifestyle. All those years of being nothing like Ramsey.

She decided to tackle the disgusting bedroom first. It smelled like the bottom of a laundry basket. King-size bed, cheap headboard, black sheets and pillowcases flecked with oily gray stains. Gloving up, she bagged the linens. The mattress was a mildewed ruin. Even protected by surgical rubber, she found handling Balch's linens repulsive.

Facing the bed was another TV, same size, and a second black box. Same porn station. Wadded tissues and stroke books in a nightstand added to the picture of Balch's solitary sexual life. She flipped through the magazines, hoping for some really nasty S&M to build up the bad-guy psyche, but most of it was straight hetero male fantasy; the worst, some lightweight bondage.

The porn went into a bag, duly noted.

Piles of dirty underwear and socks created a lumpy rug between the wall and the left side of the bed. Balch probably slept on the right side, tossed his junk across. The closet was crammed with sweat suits in varying colors, drawstring lounging pants, jeans, shirts, all with Macy's labels. A plastic bag with a ticket from a dry cleaner—on Hawthorne Boulevard—contained two pairs of pants and three shirts, including the bright blue silk he'd been wearing the day of the notification call.

She removed the plastic-wrapped garments. He leaves dirty laundry on the floor for days but chooses to clean these.

Probably the stuff he'd worn while murdering Lisa. Two pants, three shirts.

If they were bloodstained, why hadn't the cleaner noticed? She tagged and bagged, moved on to the shelf above the closet. Thirteen file boxes up there. Balch's tax records. She took her time with them.

His salary from Ramsey was his sole income. Ramsey'd started him off twenty-five years ago at $25,000. Regular raises had brought him to $160,000. Nice, but nothing compared to the boss's millions.

The forms listed little by way of investment. He'd deducted depreciation on the Saddlewax house, which had been purchased fourteen years ago, and his car leases—Buicks, then Caddies, now the Lexus—but no other real estate. For thirteen years, alimony had been paid monthly to Helen Balch, of Duluth, Minnesota. For the last nine, he'd also divvied up to Amber Leigh Balch.

Helen's name conjured up a middle-aged woman, the dutiful first wife. The house bought fourteen years ago—right after the marriage? If so, dissolution had taken place one year later.

Amber Leigh sounded like an industry pseudonym. Petra saw a homewrecker with big hair, long legs—probably blond, because Lisa and Ilse said he liked blondes. Big-chested bimbo, a face not quite pretty enough. That hadn't lasted long, either.

Two thousand a month to Helen; fifteen hundred to Amber.

His take-home was a little over eight thou a month. Lease payments on the Lexus were six hundred. Take away that and spousal support, and he cleared thirty-nine hundred a month. For the last few years, he'd received tax refunds of twenty grand or so. Not poverty, but chicken feed by industry standards. By Ramsey standards.

No obvious signs of big-ticket hobbies or conspicuous expenditures. Did he play the track? Sniff coke? Had he accumulated a money stash? Augmented it with skim?

She searched every corner of the room, found no bankbooks or investment material. Unlike Lisa, no plans. Had *she* been his launderer?

Then she'd demanded more. Or tried to blackmail Balch. Money and passion; had to be.

A door slammed. She looked out the window and saw Wil heading for the garage. He pushed a remote and the door slid open. No car that she could see. She returned to the tax files, labeling each carton. Onward.

The first of the empty bedrooms was just that. In the second, though, she found more booty on the closet shelf: three shoe boxes of loose photos. First came thirty-year-old professional shots of football teams, high school and college, the faces too small to make out, then home-camera jobs showing Ramsey and Balch in full athletic gear, giant padded shoulders, tight waists.

Tall, Dark, and Handsome and his flaxen-haired buddy, both grinning, cocky, ready to take on the world.

After that came wedding snaps, Balch still lean and tan, wearing a powder-blue tux, a ruffled shirt, and an unsure expression. Helen turned out to be slender, attractive, with short dark hair and a prim mouth. Later photos showed her aging well, staying slim, sometimes wearing glasses. Holding a baby.

Wrapped in pink. A daughter. Balch had never mentioned a child during the interview, but why would he, they'd been focusing on other people's lives. Petra remembered how he punted away personal questions. At the time, it had seemed aw-shucks. Now she understood.

Twenty or so pictures of the child, no name on the back of any of the pictures. A pretty dark-haired girl who favored her mother. Snapshots up till age eight or so, then nothing.

The divorce, or had it been worse—a death? Yet another loss in Balch's miserable life?

Box number two contained smaller versions of the celeb shots Petra had seen on Balch's office wall. Mostly Ramsey, a few of Balch. Various photographers, Hollywood and the Valley.

The last box was nearly empty. Just a wedding portrait, photographer's stamp from Las Vegas—a Vegas connection. Balch in a dark suit and white banded-collar shirt, pink-faced, puffy, slightly off-kilter, towering over Amber Leigh, who was tiny and Asian, with incredible cheekbones and breasts that screamed augmentation. Not what Petra had pictured, but definitely bimboistic.

He married dark-haired women but killed blondes.

Beneath the photo was an envelope dated three years ago.

Loopy childish handwriting addressed to Mr. G. Balch at the Saddlewax address. On the return side, Caitlin Balch, no address; Duluth, Minnesota, postmark.

The same handwriting on a single sheet of lined notepaper.

Dear Dad,

Well, Im graduating from Junior High and I won an award for band, but I don't think you care about that. You never call or come here anymore and you never send the alemoney on time and with Mom being sick that makes it really hard for us. Im only writing this because Mom said I should, you should know when your daughter graduates.

    You don't care. Right?

Your daughter (I guess)
Caitlin Lauren Balch

Pathetic. Had he ever answered? No further correspondence said probably not.

No shots of Lisa. Or Ilse Eggermann. That would have been too much to hope for.

If he'd been obsessed with either of the dead women, he'd probably destroyed the evidence. Or taken it with him to play with.

Petra bound all the shoe boxes with rubber bands and was carrying them out when she heard Wil shout.

※

He'd laid it all out on the floor of the garage.

Six handguns—two revolvers and four automatics—three rifles, two shotguns, one an expensive Mossler. Boxes of ammo for everything. The garage smelled of gun oil.

Tool rack on a wall above an empty workbench, two large toolboxes full of assorted gizmos, a pair of fishing-tackle boxes, six fishing rods, seven reels.

"Deep-sea and lake," said Wil, appreciatively. "Good lures, too. Hand-tied. And look at this."

Knives. Petra counted thirty-two.

Bucks, fighting daggers, long-bladed boning knives Wil said he'd taken from the tackle boxes.

"The man likes to shoot and cut, Petra. There's blood on the boning blade. Might be trout; then again, maybe not."

"Fishing and hunting," said Petra. "Maybe he's got himself a little cabin up in the woods."

"That's all we need, one of those nature boy–survivalist deals. Better take our time with all this. I'm gonna put on fresh gloves, get my video cam."

※

It was 8:14 when they finished. The house had grown almost unbearably hot, and Petra's nose had gotten accustomed to the smell.

Wil said, "We earned our keep," and clicked the TV on, again, switching channels from an oral-sex pretzel to local news. "Just in case something broke. It seems to be the way we find out anything."

The news was all crime—a nine-year-old girl abducted in Willow Glen, a drive-by in Florence, and another db out in Angeles Crest, but nothing on Lisa or William Bradley Straight.

"Work, work, work," said Wil, yawning and pulling down his sleeves. He'd folded his linen jacket and placed it on the mantel, over a protective layer of LAPD plastic. He looked as tired as Petra felt.

He yawned again, and she said, "I know we're supposed to start casting the net on Balch, but I for one need some food—"

He held up a silencing finger. Something on the TV had turned him wide-awake.

". . . white male," the reporter was saying. "No name has been released yet, but sheriff's deputies have described the victim as unusually large, over six feet and three hundred pounds or more. The body parts were separated, but hadn't yet been scattered in this remote area of the forest. The Boy Scouts who may have disturbed the killer report seeing a car drive off quickly, with its lights off. That's it for now, Chuck. We'll keep you posted."

Fournier gunned the remote, speeding through channels. Three other news shows, but either the dismemberment had already been covered or only one station had the story so far.

"What?" said Petra.

"Six feet, three hundred pounds," he said. "Maybe it's a coincidence, but that's real damn close to the size of Buell Moran, the fool who was looking for the Straight kid. The one who probably killed the kid's mother. I mean, I know this country's got an obesity problem, but . . . We were figuring he'd heard about the beach tip and headed west. If he did, maybe he met someone he thought could help him but didn't. I'm not saying it *is* him—lots of bikers get dumped in Angeles Crest, plenty of them are big—but it's too cute to ignore."

"Much too cute," said Petra. "Enter it in a baby contest."

"And here's another thing, Petra. Dismemberment and Angeles Crest reminds me of something I dealt with years ago, working on those Russian cases. Russians loved to cut up the bodies. We walked in on one of them doing it. They concentrate on the head and the fingertips, think it screws up IDs. And they were using Angeles Crest, had just discovered it. The guy who gave me the tip on the kid is Russian. First time I met him, I had a feeling about him. Con eyes."

"Why would he kill Moran?"

"How about competition for the twenty-five? Let's say both of them got a serious case of the greeds, both are lowlifes, no impulse control. The Russian—Zhukanov's his name—sees Moran showing the kid's picture around, gets worried. Or maybe Moran approaches him, tells Zhukanov he's the kid's father, has some rights here. Zhukanov says, Enough of this noise. Those Russians are mean, Petra. The guy we caught playing human jigsaw had been paid two hundred bucks. Imagine what twenty-five thou would motivate."

"If Zhukanov was threatened enough to kill Moran," said Petra, "it might mean he learned something new about the Straight boy's whereabouts, more than he told you. Let me phone in to see if any new messages came in on that."

The clerk said, "You've got messages, but it's crazy; can't go up to check." No one answered in the squad room. She hung up, and Wil took his jacket off the mantel. His forehead was as dark and slick as licorice and he wiped it and dialed the phone. A number she recognized: Downtown Sheriff's. Ron's HQ.

"Good old tans again," he said. "Their solve rate's about

twice ours, but they don't have to deal with the gangbanger-no-witness bullshi— Hello, this is Detective Fournier, Holly-wood LAPD. Could you please—"

Petra took the shoe boxes out to her car. In the dark, Balch's street was silent and peaceful, happy families cozy in front of the big screen. If they only knew. She filled her nose with warm, piney air. What was the weather like in Duluth, Min-nesota? What would Helen Balch think when the ex's face was all over the tube?

When she got back, Wil was smiling.

"No ID on the body, but they've got the head—thank you, Boy Scouts—and the description fits Moran to a T. I know we've been cranking up the overtime, and I was looking for-ward to some shut-eye, Petra, but I think we need at least to check this Russian out. Maybe we can't solve Lisa right away, but wouldn't it be nice to solve something?"

"It would be loverly," said Petra. "Do you mind if we stop on the way for some grub? There's a Chinese place on Haw-thorne that Mr. Balch patronized. I doubt he's got good taste, but who knows?"

CHAPTER 71

KATHY BISHOP AWOKE AT NINE, SWEATING, chilled, in terrible pain. Stu punched the call button and held her hand. She looked at him, but from her face he couldn't tell what she saw. Where the hell were the nurses—he wanted to run over to the station but didn't want to leave Kathy.

Finally they came, and he had to control himself from screaming at them.

Now Kathy was sedated, back asleep, and he realized it hadn't taken that long after all.

Get a grip.

The room felt like a cell; he'd left only for an hour, when Mother had vanned all the kids over at five-thirty and they'd gone for burgers and fries at a local McDonald's. All six were quieter than usual, even the baby. He assured them they could see Mommy soon, played around, told jokes, thought they were buying the Daddy-as-usual bit but wasn't sure. He felt out of it, some imposter inhabiting Daddy's body.

The kids started acting up, and Mother said, "Let's go, troops."

On the way out, Stu noticed other diners staring and he filled with anger.

What's wrong, turkeys, never seen a big family before?

He stayed hot all the way to St. Joe's. Weird; he'd never had a short fuse before.

Meanwhile, Petra and Wil were chasing what looked to be a multiple killer and he was calling airlines, catching guff and bureaucratese, turning up empty, no record of Balch booking any flights, but with all the turndowns he'd received, who knew?

He used to be able to worm stuff out of bureaucrats. Mormon charm, Kathy called it, kissing his forehead and favoring him with her come-hither wink. He loved that wink.

Not an ounce of charm in him tonight. He held Kathy's hand. Limp, lifeless. But for the warmth of her skin, he might have panicked.

Breathing evenly. The machines said she was fine.

No more airlines to call, not a damn thing to do but wait.

For what? More pain?

Too wound-up to sleep, he got up and paced the room. He needed to sleep, needed to be together for Kathy . . . the stack of *TV Guides* sat on an end table. Maybe stupid, derivative Dack Price plotlines would get him drowsy.

He was into the second volume when he felt his posture slacken and his eyelids droop. The third made the room grow dim.

Then something filtered through the fatigue.

Words, sentences—something a little different.

Now he was sitting up. Wide-awake.

Rereading . . . wondering . . . should he call Petra?

Strange—maybe nothing. But . . .

He didn't even know where Petra was. So out of touch. Could his judgment be trusted?

He'd try to find her. Worse came to worst, he'd have wasted some time.

Wasting time was his new hobby anyway.

CHAPTER 72

THE WHITE COP WAS TAKING HIM SERIOUSLY.

Finally. Which is what Zhukanov told him when the guy appeared at the counter, just before closing time, showing his badge and the picture of the kid.

"Finally."

"Pardon, sir?"

"I talk to one of you, but he don't call back. A black guy."

The white cop stared. "Yes, sir, I know."

"What do you want?" demanded Zhukanov.

"Double-checking on the identification, sir." The cop leaned his elbows on the counter and put the newspaper clipping down. Big guy, blond, ruddy, dark suit, dark tie. He reminded Zhukanov of a colonel he'd worked with on crowd control back home, a real sadist, loved to twist limbs, knew how to do maximal damage with just a flick of a wrist . . . Borokovsky. This guy looked a lot like Borokovsky. Was he of Russian descent? His card said Detective D. A. Price, but everyone changed their names.

"Double-checking? I already tell you he been here, no one calls me, it's on the TV."

"It's a homicide investigation, sir, we have to be careful," said the blond cop, looking over Zhukanov's shoulder at the shelves of toys.

Calling me sir but probably thinking I'm some kind of joke, a clown. The fat guy thought so too, and look where he was.

Having had several hours to think about it, Zhukanov felt good about killing the fat guy—great, even; the Siberian wolf dispatches its prey, paints its muzzle with blood, howls at the moon. While cutting the guy up, Zhukanov had *felt* like howling.

Moving him into the car, then dragging him out had been torture; Zhukanov's back and shoulders and arms still throbbed. Getting the bastard into pieces turned out to be not so easy, either. He should've sharpened the kitchen knives better; that cleaver should've gone right through the joints, not stuck like that.

The head, though, had been less of a problem than he expected. Rolling away like a soccer ball, eyes open. That was funny. He felt like kicking it, but you had to get rid of the head and the fingers, let the cops have the rest of the carcass. His plan had been to take the head somewhere it would never be found, but the Boy Scouts had ruined it, hiking through the forest, yelling like drunks. So now the cops had the head; maybe they'd learn who the fat guy was. Big deal. No connection to him; he'd cleaned all the blood. And here was a cop leaning over the very same counter, no clue.

Zhukanov fought not to smile. He'd tossed the knives into five separate storm drains from Valencia to Van Nuys. The fat man's clothing and billfold ended up in Dumpsters near Fairfax and Melrose—let the Yids get blamed.

No bills in the billfold, just a driver's license and a nice picture of a naked girl with her legs spread that Zhukanov pocketed. The license he slipped down another drain. The fat man's name was Moran. So what.

When he got home he washed his bloody clothes, took a shower, had something to eat, worked with the broken gun for a while, still couldn't figure out what was wrong with it. Then a few glasses of vodka and he was out like a light by three. Five hours later, he was back at the shack waiting for the Yids to return with the kid. If they didn't, he'd go over to the motor vehicle department on Monday.

But the car showed up, all right, pulling behind the Yid church at nine. Prayer time for the Yids, Zhukanov knew, usually till eleven or so. He kept going back to the alley every fifteen minutes; finally spotted the old guy who'd hidden the kid coming out with an old woman. They drove off, and he followed them in his car. They never noticed—too busy yapping.

And now he had an address without paying for it. Twenty-three Sunrise Court.

He didn't write it down, the way he had with the license number, because now he was smart; no one would get it unless they paid for it.

And now look how calm he was, facing the white cop. Though if the guy had just showed the badge, no picture of the kid, he might've figured it had something to do with Moran—what the hell would he have done then?

"I tell the black guy," he said. "He never call me back."

"I'm sorry, sir. We've been quite busy—"

"You busy looking for the kid," said Zhukanov, "but I see him."

"You saw him several days ago, sir."

"Maybe," said Zhukanov, smiling.

"Maybe?"

"Maybe I see him again."

The blond cop pulled out a little notepad. "When, sir?"

"I tell your black buddy the first time; he never call me back."

The blond cop frowned, leaned a little closer. "Sir, if you have information—"

"I don't know," said Zhukanov, shrugging. "Maybe I forget. The way the black guy forget to call me."

The pad shut. The cop was annoyed, but he smiled. "Sir, I understand your frustration. Sometimes things get busy and we don't dot every *i*. If that happened to you, I'm—"

"Dot every *i* is important," said Zhukanov, not sure what that meant. "But also money."

"Money?" said the cop.

"Twenty-five thousand."

"That," said the cop. "Sure. If we find the boy and he helps us, it's yours. At least that's what I was told."

"No one tell *me*."

"I've seen the forms, sir. My captain signed them. If you'd like to call him—"

"No, no," said Zhukanov. "I just wanna get it square, you know? Maybe I know something more than I told the black guy, but what if kid runs, you don't find him? What happens?"

"If your information's solid, you'll get partial payment," said the cop. "Part of the twenty-five thousand. That's the way we always do it. I'm not saying you could get all of it, but—"

"How much part of it?"

"I don't know, sir, but generally in these situations it's around a third to a half—I'd guess ten, twelve thousand. And if the boy is there, you'd get all twenty-five—why don't you speak to my captain—"

"No, no," said Zhukanov, thinking, If the old Yid did take the kid home with him, the kid could still run; better not dawdle anymore. "I want you should write it down."

"Write what?"

"What you say. Twelve, fifteen to Zhukanov just for telling, all twenty-five if kid show up."

"Sir," said the blond cop, sighing, "I'm not in a position— oh, all right, here you go."

Ripping a sheet out of his pad, he said, "How do you spell your name?"

Zhukanov told him.

The blond cop printed neatly:

This stipulates that to the best of my knowledge, Mr. V. Zhukanov is due $12,000.00 because of information he has offered about a missing boy, unknown identity, related to L. Ramsey, PC 187. Should Mr. V. Zhukanov's information lead directly to this boy and this boy's information lead to apprehension of a suspect, he would be due $25,000.00.
                              Det. D. A. Price, Badge # 19823

"Here," said the cop, "but to be honest, I can't promise you this means much—"

Zhukanov snatched the paper, read it, and stuffed it down his pants pocket. Now he had a contract. If the bastards gave him trouble, he'd hire Johnnie Cochran, sue the hell out of them.

"I know where he is," he said. "Enough for the twenty-five."

The blond cop waited, pen poised.

"The Yids—the Jews from over there got him." Zhukanov pointed south. "They got a church. The old Jew hid him in there, took him home."

"You saw this?" said the cop. He straightened and his shoulders widened.

"You bet. I looked for the car, followed it to the old guy's house this morning."

"Good detective work, Mr. Zhukanov."

"In Russia, I was policeman."

"Really. Well, it paid off, sir. Thank you. And believe me, I'll do everything I can to make sure you get every penny of that twenty-five thousand."

"You bet," said Zhukanov. The wolf triumphs!

The blond cop said, "What's the address?"

"Twenty-three Sunrise Court." Twenty-five-thousand-dollar address.

"That's here in Venice?"

"Yeah, yeah, right here." Idiot, didn't know his own city. Zhukanov hooked a thumb. "From alley, you go to Speedway, then to Pacific, then five blocks over."

"Great," said the cop, closing the pad. "You've been a tremendous help, sir—when you say the alley, you mean the one back there?"

"Yeah, yeah—I show you."

Vaulting over the counter—adrenaline-charged, despite his aching limbs, Zhukanov led the blond cop around the side of the shack, past the shipping-carton trash boxes. If the guy only knew what had been in there yesterday.

"Over there," he pointed, "is Jew church where I see car. Okay?"

"What kind of car, sir?"

"Lincoln. White, brown roof."

"Year?"

"Don't matter, I got something better for you." Grinning, Zhukanov recited the license number. The cop scrawled in the darkness. "Other way is where he went."

"North," said the cop.

"Yeah, yeah, right up to Speedway and then Pacific, five blocks."

The cop repeated the instructions, a real dummy.

"That's it," said Zhukanov. Go find him, you stupid bastard. I'm giving him to you on a platter!

The cop put his pad away and shot out a hand. "Thank you, sir."

They shook. Firm, manly shake. If the cop only knew the hand he was grasping had been bloody up to the elbow a few hours ago. Zhukanov tried to break the clasp, get the guy moving, but he couldn't pull away—the cop was holding on to him, yanking him close—what the hell was this? The cop was grinning, like he was going to kiss him, this wasn't right, this was wrong.

Zhukanov struggled, struck out.

A hand grabbed his wrist, twisted it, something broke, and pain devoured him from fingertip to the bottom of his ear. One quick move, just like Colonel Borokovsky. He cried out involuntarily, and something big and meaty exploded in the middle of his face and he went down.

Then more pain, even worse, burning, searing, like a fire igniting his bowels.

Starting right under his navel, then spreading upward, like a burning rope. Then he felt cold, a strange cold—cold air blowing . . . inside him, *deep* inside, and knew he'd been split open, filleted—the way he'd split the fat bastard and now it had happened to him and he couldn't do a damn thing, just lie there and take it.

The last thing he felt was a hand going through his pocket.

Fishing out the contract. Liar! Cheater! The money was hi—

CHAPTER 73

BEING ALONE HERE IS DIFFERENT FROM THE park. Different from Watson.

I've got all these rooms, these books, someone who trusts me. Once in a while I hear footsteps out on the sidewalk or someone talking or laughing, a car driving by. But they don't bother me; I'm here, locked in. I can sleep without waking up to see what's around. I can read without a flashlight.

I've thought about it a lot, and Sam's right. Tomorrow I'll find a phone and call the police, tell them about PLYR 1. Maybe I can call Mom, too. Tell her I'm okay, not to worry, I'm doing just fine, one day I'll come back, be able to support her.

What would she do? Cry? Get mad? Beg me to come back? Or worse: *not* beg me? She must miss me a little.

I stop thinking about it, stretch my feet out on the couch, pull the knit blanket up over my knees, start in on the next *Life* magazine. The main article's all about John Kennedy and his family, happy and handsome on the beach.

California beach, same sand that's just a little way up. I could walk over, look at it, pretend to be John Kennedy, come back. But I told Sam I'd stay here, and he gave me the alarm code.

1-1-2-5. I get up and try it. Green light.

Red light, green light, red light.

Green light. I open the door, smell the salt, that beach smell. No one's out; most of the houses are dark.

I go out to the porch. Feel cold, scared.

Back in the house. Why does just going outside scare me?

I'll try again later. Back to the Kennedys.

CHAPTER 74

THE OWNER OF THE CHINESE RESTAURANT HAD no memory of Balch. Petra and Wil ordered some spring rolls to go, ate them in her car, agreed to drive separately to Venice, meet on Pacific and Rose, walk to Zhukanov's stand together.

She called the desk at Hollywood station.

"Detective Bishop for you half an hour ago," said the clerk. Had Stu gotten hold of flight information on Balch?

This operator refused to put Petra through. "No calls to surgical patients past nine, ma'am."

"I'm a police detective returning another detective's call. Stuart Bishop."

"Is Mr. Bishop the patient?"

"No, his wife is."

"Then I'm sorry, ma'am, I can't put you through."

"Let me speak to your supervisor, please."

"I am the supervisor. The rules are for our patients' welfare and comfort. If you'd like, I can have a message slip sent up to the room telling him you called."

"Fine, I'll wait."

"Can't do that, ma'am. It'll take time. We're understaffed, and I need to keep all the lines open. If it's important, I'm sure he'll call back."

"Sure," said Petra. "Have a nice night."

She got back in the car, drove on, hoping it wasn't that important. Even if they found a flight reservation, she had doubts Balch had actually shown up. The call to Westward Charter had to be a fake-out. Balch had been too careful about everything else to slip up like that.

Meaning what?

He was anywhere *but* Las Vegas. Site of his second wedding. Tomorrow, she'd try to get hold of Amber Leigh. And Helen. Find out why they'd divorced the guy. His kinks, bad habits, what might lead him to murder blondes.

Anywhere but . . . the cabin in the woods? Homicidal Thoreau? If no leads showed up soon, Schoelkopf would probably go straight to *America's Most Wanted*. Maybe that was the best way to handle it. Take the heat off her and Wil. Off William Bradley Straight, now motherless, poor, poor kid.

And now the guy who'd probably turned him into an orphan had been butchered like the squalid ton of pork he was.

One less felon heard from. Petra felt grim satisfaction about that.

Not that it would stop her from going after the butcher.

CHAPTER 75

DINKY LITTLE HOUSE. LIGHT ON IN THE FRONT room, but dim. The Lincoln parked in back.

So the old man was home with the kid. Was he married? Zhukanov hadn't mentioned anything about seeing a wife, but that didn't mean anything; the old guy could've gone to temple, left her behind. Maybe she was sick, an invalid.

Easy.

On balance, the walk street was probably an advantage. No cars to hide behind, but no drivers interrupting. No pedestrians either during the half hour he'd watched the house from three different spots.

He tried the back alley again, rubber soles swallowing his footsteps. The newish running shoes; he'd walked around in them, made sure there was no squeak.

Out of the cheap-suit cop getup and into black sweats and a black windbreaker with pockets. The van, rented from a fly-by-night place down near the airport, a perfect dressing room. He'd paid cash, used no ID, leaving the guy who ran the rental lot five hundred in cash as collateral. Five hundred he'd never see again. Worth it. The van was parked four blocks away, east of Main, on a residential street.

Pleasant stroll to Sunrise Court; the beach air was tangy, invigorating. He'd never lived on the beach. Maybe one day . . .

From the back he could see that the kitchen light was still on. Ten thirty-eight. Someone up, or just a security measure? Probably the latter; he'd seen no trace of any movement.

Why had the old guy taken the kid in? A relative? The drawing didn't show a Jewish-looking kid, but you could never tell. No, if it was a family thing, wouldn't they be pushing the kid to collect the money?

A good samaritan? Religious convictions? Giving the kid sanctuary in the temple? Did Jews believe in that? He had no idea. Returning to the front, he hid behind a clump of shrubbery, continued to watch the house.

How to do it?

The only way was a blitz. Home invasion. Gangbangers were getting into that, especially the Asians. A small place like this, how many rooms could there be?

A knife would be best because of the sound factor, but running from room to room stabbing was risky; even with weak prey, there was the risk of escape.

The alternative was the Glock, but that meant noise. Venice was high-crime, he'd heard about gangs on Ocean Front, had seen gang types during today's surveillance. So the neighbors were probably used to hearing gunshots at night. But a street like this, the houses close together, bursting in, doing it, ditching the gun, taking the escape route he'd plotted back to the van.

Risky.

But fun—admit it. The risk was *part* of the fun. That and simply being able to do it.

A zapperoo commando blitz then—one hand on the knife, the other on the gun. If it was just the kid and the old man and they were close together, the knife would probably work. So he'd start with the knife, have the gun ready for complications.

One thing he'd decided for sure: Rear entry was best. Ha ha.

Another advantage of the walk street: Everyone parked in back, so walking through the alley wouldn't be viewed as deviant. If he was spotted, he'd affect a relaxed stroll, pretend to belong, jangle his keys, and head for one of the cars. The way he looked—white male, sweats—wouldn't be threatening, he hoped.

His knees hurt. Too much squatting. The Percs were no longer doing the trick. Lisa had claimed coke was a good anesthetic; dentists used to smear it on gums. Always wanting him to try it. Screw that. He bought it for her, *spooned* it up her cute little nose, tried to get some satisfaction from her body while she was high, but no way would he do it—Percs were as far as he went.

Maintain the upper edge.

He waited. Nothing. Okay, back again, ready to blitz.

He was just about to leave when the front door opened and someone came out.

On the patio, looking around.

The kid!

Perfect! He'd sprint across the sidewalk, grab him, cut his throat, be off—God *was* good!

But just as he got ready to spring, the kid ran back inside.

Scared?

You've got good reason, sonny.

CHAPTER 76

"THAT'S THE PLACE," SAID WIL, WAITING, THE phone to his ear.

Ocean Front Walk was dark and deserted, and Petra could barely make out the souvenir stand. As they got closer, she saw it was a tiny, ramshackle thing, roll-down shutter over the front.

"Okay," Wil said to the phone. To Petra: "Got a home address for him. West Hollywood. Of course."

They were twenty feet away from the shack. No one on the walkway for at least a hundred yards. They'd passed one homeless guy at the corner of Paloma and Speedway, and Petra saw another sitting on a bench to the north, but he got up and shuffled away. The tide whispered secrets and the beach looked like ice.

They were about to turn around when she noticed something. Two inches of space beneath the shutter. Closed but not locked?

Gun out, she hurried over, Wil following. Loops for a lock were welded to the lower-right-hand corner of the steel roll and a ring was bolted to the counter. But no lock in sight. She peered through the two inches. Dark, but she could make out

stuff wrapped in plastic hanging from racks . . . Postcards.
Hats. Just like the kind William Straight wore.

She backed clear across Ocean Front, watched the stand
while talking to Wil in a low voice: "Clear sign of illegal entry,
our duty to investigate."

"Absolutely," he said. "But what if the guy's some nut and
he's lurking inside there—let's check the back first."

Whipping out penlights, they snaked along the north side of
the stand. Too damn dark, too damn quiet. Petra liked using her
brains, psyching out bad guys. She could do without this TV
cop stuff.

Behind the building were two huge wooden packing crates,
slats over plank sides. Her penlight said they came from the
docks at Long Beach.

The stand's back door was bolted, a nice big padlock
in place. Off, definitely off. Unless it hadn't been a thought-
out burglary, just something impulsive . . . the packing crates
stank of garbage. The neighboring buildings all utilized
commercial Dumpsters. City regulations—the Russian saving money?

One good thing about the crates, though—the slats offered
an easy foothold. She got a toe in, hoisted herself up the first
one, looked inside. Nothing.

She found Zhukanov in the second crate, lying on his back
atop a heap of trash, mouth open in the dead man's stupid gape,
one arm spread, the other pinioned under his head at an angle
that would have been excruciatingly painful had he been alive.

Bisected, disemboweled. The penlight turned his intestines
into overfed eels.

Same killing wound as Lisa.

Balch had never left town at all; the charter call, a fake-out
just as she'd suspected—so what had *Stu* phoned about?

No time to think about that. She ran the light over the trash,
saw the blood now, a huge crimson oblong, spattered on paper
refuse.

Wil had found blood, too. Specks and drips on the front of
the crate, another large stain on the ground. She'd been standing right in it, damnit! How could she have missed it?

They phoned it in to Pacific Division, were told to safe-
guard the scene—it might be a while before anyone showed

up, because a shooting had just gone down in Oakwood and some of those victims were still breathing.

Inside the stand, they found no evidence of break-in, just crappy toys, a rear stockroom with a chair and a card table full of receipts and sales slips, no apparent system. A Planet Hollywood jacket hung from a nail in the wall. On adjoining nails were nunchucks, half a baseball bat with a leather thong, tarnished brass knuckles.

The Russian, equipped for battle. Someone had taken him by surprise.

Several bottles in the corner might explain it. Cheap-looking Russian labels, cloudy vodka. One of the bottles was nearly empty. Zhukanov drunk, his defenses down? Bolstered by booze when he killed Moran?

If he *had* killed Moran. Maybe he'd been Moran's crime buddy, a drug connection, whatever, and the two had colluded to collect the twenty-five thousand.

Somehow, Balch had figured it out and finished them both off.

But then why bother taking Moran to Angeles Crest while leaving Zhukanov right here where he was sure to be found?

Look what I can do!

Zhukanov's gut wound matched Lisa's and Ilse's. But Moran didn't fit. So the Russian probably *had* dispatched Moran. And Balch had finished off Zhukanov.

There could only be one reason: The Russian knew something vital about William Bradley Straight.

All Zhukanov had told Wil was that the boy had bought a hat from him.

Not enough to kill for.

Had the Russian held back? Did he know more?

She shot her theories at Wil, who was up in front, examining the inside wall beneath the counter, looking for more bloodstains.

She was talking at manic speed, couldn't believe the edge in her voice. Wil listened, said, "You think Zhukanov saw the boy again? Got a fix on his location? But how would Balch find out?"

"I don't know—but if it was him, he took Zhukanov by surprise. Maybe force. Or Zhukanov was plastered. Or he pulled some kind of scam on Zhukanov. The guy was crazy for the reward. It could have clouded his judgment."

"A scam," said Wil. "Someone who'd be legit asking about the boy?"

"Yes," said Petra. "A social worker—a cop. Maybe Balch impersonated a cop."

Wil thought about that. "A suit and a fake badge is all it'd take. Yeah, Zhukanov's greed would do the rest. But for Balch to risk killing him now, when he knows we're going to be looking for him?"

"We haven't caught him. He may not even know we're on to him," said Petra. "And if it leads to the boy, it could seem worth it. That tells me Zhukanov may very well have learned something more about the boy."

She returned to the stockroom, searching nervously, frantically. Toys, stupid toys—imagine a hairbasket like Zhukanov peddling playthings to little kids . . . nothing in the pocket of the Planet Hollywood jacket . . . the card table, the receipts— she grabbed them all up, started scanning.

Ten slips in, she found an invoice form, no sale marked, no date. Just a single line of shaky printing.

2RTRM34

License number? Had the Russian seen William Straight in a car and copied down the plate? Everyone knew you could bribe info out of DMV. The papers had covered a big bribery scandal a few months ago. A guy like Zhukanov would know his way around that sort of thing. Pay up, get the address.

She looked for a phone in the shack. None in either room. What a hovel. Fournier was still looking for blood. She borrowed his phone—what was the night number for DMV traces . . . yeah, yeah, she remembered it. When the clerk came on, she had to fight from barking orders at the woman. This one was a stickler for regulations.

Lord save me from rule books.

But a little assertiveness finally made her cooperate, and a few computer clicks later Petra had it: Samuel Morris Ganzer, 23 Sunrise Court, Venice.

Birthdate in 1925.
An old man.
Had William found himself a protector?

CHAPTER 77

THE LINCOLN WAS PARKED INCHES FROM THE
back of the house, and its front bumper gave him a great boost
to the window.

Drapes on this one too, but not drawn tightly; he had a perfect view of the kitchen, helped along by a small light over the
stove. The living room, too, separated only by a waist-high
counter. A floor lamp there cast charcoal shadows on gray
carpet. Enough light to see the front door. Red glow off to the
right side. Alarm. Too bad. But better to know up front.

Three doors to the left, probably bedrooms and bathroom. Not much space between them. Small rooms, better
for stabbing.

And that was the entire layout. Excellent . . .

No sign of the boy since he'd first ventured out onto the
porch. The old guy, either. Both bedroom doors closed. The
boy and the old man—with or without wife—fast asleep?
Or maybe the old guy was a queer and the boy was sleeping
with him.

That would sure explain taking him home.

Sleep made it a helluva lot easier: Burst in, throw the bedroom doors open, boom boom boom, gone even before the
time delay kicked in on the alarm.

Knock stuff over on the way out, maybe steal something, to
make it look like a gang thing.

He got down from the car, checked the alley for intruders,
examined the house's rear door. Two dead bolts. Bad. But
putting a little weight on the wood, he felt some give. One or

two good shoves would take it off the hinges. Probably ruin his shoulder, but he was used to pushing his way through obstacles. The door was nothing compared to a defensive line.

Okay, then. Here come da blitz. The knife if it worked, the gun ready for backup. Either way, he could do it in seconds, run out the back, fade into the night.

One last look through the kitchen window.

He was scared, had to admit it. This was different, not like Lisa, the German girl, Sally, the stupid Russian. All those times, he'd set up the scenes.

But there were times you had to improvise.

He climbed up on the Lincoln's bumper again. Nothing different, but still he hesitated. Up again, down again. Compulsive. When his anxiety rose, he handled it with repetition. Like his mother's head banging. The stupid bitch. She deserved to die in that stupid helmet.

Okay, one last look—this time, he saw the boy—see, it pays to be thorough!

Coming out of the middle door to the left. A bathroom, just as he'd guessed.

Skinny little thing, light enough to drop-kick. He watched him emerge, go into the kitchen, open the refrigerator, take something out—a carrot.

Would he wash it? The sink was right below the window. *Duck.*

Crouched next to the outer wall, he heard plumbing kick in. Hygienic little sucker.

The water stopped. He waited, finally raised his head, peeked in, again. The kid was standing in the living room, back to the kitchen window, eating the carrot. Finishing half of it, he walked to the front door, punched the alarm panel—damn, too far to make out the code.

Opening the door, the kid stepped out again. But only for a few seconds, and here he was again, back inside, closing the door, turning, about to face the window.

Could he see anything out here in the darkness? Probably not, unless it was right up against the glass, but be extra careful, duck again.

Another thirty seconds passed before he dared another look. The kid was still standing in the living room, munching on the carrot, visible in profile.

Just another face.

The kid finished the carrot, bent, and picked something up. A magazine. He eats healthy, washes, reads. Such a good little citizen.

But not careful. Because the light on the front alarm panel was green.

He'd forgotten to trigger the goddamn alarm!

God was *wonderful*!

The blitz was on!

CHAPTER 78

"SUNRISE COURT," SAID PETRA, THUMBING through her *Thomas Guide*.

Wil took his penlight out of his mouth. "I know it, one of the walk streets." He was outside the stand, recording the details of the Zhukanov crime scene.

"Which direction?" she said.

"North, five, six blocks."

The license number and Samuel Ganzer's name hadn't impressed him. "Could be Zhukanov's boss, a customer. Zhukanov could've recorded the license for a check authorization."

"Could be," said Petra, having only instinct to back her up. She closed the map book. "So you'll stay here, keep Zhukanov company?"

"Sure. Maybe he'll teach me Russian."

CHAPTER 79

It's almost eleven. Sam should be back soon. I thought I'd stay up till he got here, but now I'm tired; guess I'll go to sleep.

He's probably having a good time with Mrs. Kleinman. I could eat another carrot, but I'm not really hungry . . . maybe I'll take another shower. No, I already had one, don't want to use up too much of Sam's water.

I go to turn off the living room lamp—maybe I'll take some magazines to bed—uh-oh, I forgot to switch the alarm back on.

I head for the panel, reach out for the buttons, and from behind me comes an explosion, then a crash—from the back of the house. *Oh no, did I leave the stove on or something?*

But I don't smell gas or anything burning, and when I turn, I see a big black space where the kitchen door was and the door's down on the floor and a guy's coming through the space, he's in the house, now, seeing me, throwing open the door to Sam's room, looking in, coming out—

Coming at me.

Dressed all in black.

Weird orange-pink skin and yellow hair.

Big.

He looks right at me. I don't know him, but he knows me! PLYR 1!

How?

Oh God, no oh no—he's coming right at me and he's got a knife—a big pink man with a knife. I want to scream, but my mouth is frozen. I reach for the doorknob, touch only air, and he's coming faster, closer, such a big knife—I run to the left, but that just puts me in a corner, nowhere to go, bookshelves behind me. I have to do something—*throw* something, that worked before—books.

I start pulling them off the shelves and heaving them at him as hard as I can. A few hit him, but he keeps coming, walking slower, smiling, taking his time, holding the knife out in front of him, waving it back and forth.

I keep pulling out books and throwing them, they hit him in the face, the chest, the stomach, he laughs, pushes them away, keeps coming, the room's dark, but he can see me, he keeps coming straight at me.

I try to shove the dusty couch at him, but it's too heavy.

He laughs.

I pick up the music stand and throw *it*.

That surprises him. He loses his balance, and I run around him into the kitchen, toward the back door.

Suddenly I'm down on the floor.

Something around my leg.

He's pulling me by the ankle, I see his knees bend, see the bottom of his chin, his arm, the knife's coming down—

I twist around like a snake, just keep moving, moving, maybe if I move he'll miss and I can get out through the back door. He's squeezing my ankle, hurting it, I punch at him, keep twisting, get close enough to the arm that's holding my ankle and bite it, bite it hard, Billy Snake Billy Viper.

He shouts and lets go and I want to run out the back, but he's blocking the way—where where where—the only choice is fake him out, move to the left then the right, into the bathroom, next best thing get in there, lock myself in.

I jump up, run faster than I've ever run before across the kitchen he's running too breathing hard I make it into the bathroom slam the door lock it squeeze in between the toilet and the bathtub cold floor breathing fast my chest hurts so bad—

No sound.

Then he laughs again. I hear footsteps. Slow footsteps; he's relaxed. I'm trying to breathe slower, but every breath makes a squeaky sound.

Through the door I hear: "Stupid little shit. You cornered yourself."

He's right.

The bathroom has no window.

Now he's kicking the door it shakes the wood swells like a balloon that cracks right in the middle I jump up open the medicine cabinet feel in the darkness for something sharp a razor blade scissors anything no razor blade no scissors here's something pointy a nail file I think it's not sharp but I grab it he kicks part of his leg comes through black sweats black tennis shoes I stab down at the pants the nail file hits bone but it slides off doesn't go in he yells calls me a little bastard—

Another explosion much louder.

Something comes through the door flying by me the mirror on the medicine cabinet door shatters I feel pain in the back of my head put my hand there warm and sticky needles glass needles.

A gun—he's got a gun, too.

I throw myself into the tub he shoots again now the door is full of holes splintering and now I can see part of him on the other side his legs and shoes and his pants he's still shooting I'm lying facedown in the tub as low as I can go but a bullet hits the tub and the porcelain shatters and part of the wall falls off this is it I'm trapped finished I did my best it wasn't good enough I hate you everyone—another explosion the bullet goes into something above my head stuff falls down on me dust tiles I'm getting buried.

Now there's no door just him big huge the knife in one hand the gun in another.

He turns on the light.

I've still got the nail file. He sees it and laughs.

Puts the gun in his pocket.

Oh no the knife.

I curl up don't want to see it just don't let me feel it.

He takes hold of my hair pulls me up so I'm on my knees pulls my head back.

I piss my pants and shit slides out of me running down my leg thank you God for nothing you don't exist you liar—

Another explosion.

More and moreandmoreandmore I can't stand the noise I don't get it what's he doing—

He drops me and I fall into the tub hard.

A woman's voice says, "My God!"

Then: "It's okay, honey."

A hand touches the back of my neck.

I scream.

CHAPTER 80

RED PUFFS SPARKED FROM BALCH'S BACK, NECK, posterior skull. Later, Petra learned she'd shot him nine times within a two-foot diameter, each bullet lethal, a tight little circle of death.

He fell on his face next to the bathtub, stayed there, the gun at his side. She kicked the weapon across the floor. Kicked him to make sure he was dead, though maybe that wasn't the only reason. The knife had fallen to one side. Big ugly commando thing with a black hard-rubber handle. She kicked it away, too, stepped over the black-sweat-suited corpse. Bits of blood-pinkened bone gritted the tile floor. The bathroom door was a splinter of frame barely hanging from one hinge.

The boy was huddled fetally in the tub.

What was left of the tub. Ragged chunks of porcelain had been torn loose; glass shards and dust and broken tiles were everywhere. Blood had flowed over Balch's back and wormed onto the floor. The place looked as if it had been through a war—how could the idiot think he'd get away with this?

He'd come close.

She'd had trouble finding a space within eyeshot of the house, and even though she saw no sign of intrusion, something pinged in her gut and she double-parked around the corner.

She got out of the car, smelling sea air, expecting another dead end.

Then gunshots raped the silence and she pulled out her gun and ran around to the back, found the door kicked in, a dimly lit kitchen beyond the threshold, off to the left another ravaged door, black-sweat-suited bulk nearly filling the opening—an upraised knife, a child's limp legs.

"Stop!" she screamed, but it was no warning; she was already shooting.

When she got to the boy, he refused to uncurl, whimpered when she talked to him, screamed when she touched him. Such a skinny little thing! His long hair was bloodstained, porcupined with glass fragments. Twelve, but the size of a ten-year-old. A yellow pool had spread underneath him. She smelled feces, saw the stain covering the seat of his jeans.

The urge to pick him up, hold him, rock him in her arms was so strong it made her palate ache. She got down on the floor, talked to him, finally managed to stroke his hair without repulsing him.

He stopped shaking, went rigid, then limp. She cradled his head, and now he let her. She knew how to comfort. At that moment she thought, crazily, of Nick. You were wrong, you prick.

When the boy was breathing regularly, she lay him down gently in the tub and called for an ambulance and uniformed backup, Code 3. Returning, she stayed with him, picking glass out of his scalp, getting splinters in her finger—it didn't matter; it felt okay. Calling him William, using a soothing tone, not really knowing what she was saying, wanting to calm him down, but how could you comfort a kid who'd been through this?

She heard sirens. Pacific Division cops burst in; then came the paramedics. Only when the boy was up on a stretcher did she allow herself to leave him. Fetal again, so small under the shock blanket. An old man rushed in, looking stunned. The paramedics seemed pained as they carried the boy out.

She watched them carry him away, ignored the old man's questions. The uniforms' too. Walking straight to Balch's body, she turned it over.

Not Balch. A stranger.

The shock punched her in the heart, and she broke out into a sweat.

A second jolt hit her, even stronger. Recognition.

Ramsey.

His mustache was gone and his skin was different—some kind of salmon-pink theatrical makeup was smeared all over his face and down his neck, flaking around his nostrils. Dark shadows around his eyes—gray makeup. The bushy blond wig had been jarred loose, revealing a crescent of black curls. Blond tint in the eyebrows—he'd even done the eyebrows.

Blue eyes, dull as sewer water.

Mouth open, the same old death gape. She looked down his mouth, saw the tongue curled back, blood collecting at the bottom of his throat.

Thinking about what he'd put the boy through, Lisa, Ilse, the Flores woman, she would have welcomed the chance to kill him again.

CHAPTER 81

THEY FOUND GREGORY BALCH'S BODY THE NEXT day, buried under dirt, hay, and horse manure in the barn behind the Calabasas house, his throat cut, just like Estrella Flores's.

Entombed in dung. You didn't need to be a shrink to interpret.

After tearing the pink palace apart, the closest they got to a motive was a single piece of notepaper in Ramsey's bedroom rolltop. One of those FROM THE DESK OF things. In the center, he'd written:

L and G?

Lisa and Greg. A sweat stain beneath the inscription indicated stress, according to a department shrink. Very profound. The psychologist was light on facts, heavy on pomposity, suggested he be the one to see Billy Straight for "debriefing."

Petra had other ideas, and she stood her ground.

Stu's find added another layer: ten-year-old *Adjustor* plot out of *TV Guide*.

A football player attempts to frame his best friend for murder, and Dack Price investigates.

Maybe eventually it would help Stu feel he'd played a part. Right now he had Kathy's recuperation to deal with; she'd finally gotten realistic, agreed to his thirty-day compassionate leave.

L and G? Had Lisa and Balch tumbled? Or was it all in Ramsey's paranoid mind? Or maybe it was money, Lisa and Balch conspiring to skim. No way to know till all the financial records were pried loose from Larry Schick. Maybe never. Petra really didn't care.

Same for the specifics of Lisa's murder—just paperwork now. Her best guess was the original scenario: Ramsey had doped up Balch on Sunday night, snuck out, followed Lisa, abducted her. Using the Mercedes, not the Jeep. Because Billy had seen the plates. PLYR 1.

Turned out that's *all* he'd seen. Not enough to point a finger at anyone—the boy had been turned into quarry for nothing.

Or maybe Ramsey had switched plates, used the Jeep after all. Or some other set of wheels. He had so many; let the techs logic it out.

Killing Estrella Flores up in the hills because she'd seen him sneak out. Or might have. Borrowing Balch's Lexus for the Flores kill. Or maybe Balch had been in on it, after all, friend to the end. Whatever. Ramsey'd used him, tossed him away.

A football player attempts to frame an old friend . . . pilfering from a script that hadn't been very good in the first place. No imagination. The industry.

Industry big shots called themselves players.

Ramsey styling himself a player, knowing he really wasn't one. Because his ratings were low, his acting was a joke, and his penis wouldn't harden.

To hell with him. Billy was her concern.

The boy was beginning his sixth day at Western Pediatric Hospital, where he'd proved a difficult patient at first. Petra neglected her paperwork, ignored Schoelkopf's calls, spent most of her time bedside. When she left, a hospital play therapist filled in. At first, Billy ignored both of them. By the third day, he was accepting the books and magazines Petra brought him.

On the fourth day, Ron came and took her to dinner at the Biltmore, downtown.

Nice dinner—great dinner. She found her hand seeking his. The way he listened to her turned her on. Till then she'd wondered if what had happened between them was due to the tension of the case.

To her great pleasure, now that things were calming down, she wanted to be with him more. Maybe soon she'd get to meet his girls.

Sweet fantasies ... she harbored no illusions of healing the boy's emotional wounds, had phoned Alex Delaware, a psychologist she'd worked with and trusted, friend of Milo Sturgis's, a man who'd been willing to go undercover for something he believed in. But he was out of town with his girlfriend, would be returning today.

Meanwhile, Billy stayed in the hospital for antibiotic treatment and nutrition, a police guard sitting ten feet down the hall. No reason Petra could see for that, but Schoelkopf had ordered it. Maybe he was feeling guilty, so why not?

The uniform at the door to Billy's room had been called into action only once, dealing with Sam Ganzer, who insisted on visiting. Feisty old guy, standing on his tiptoes, facing up to the uniform, fingers pointing, things getting loud until Petra interceded, said Ganzer could see Billy, took him for coffee in the family lounge first, to calm him down.

He wanted to know what would happen after Billy left the hospital. Telling Petra she was brave, a "real hero," but no way would he allow her or anyone else to send the boy to some "stupid juvenile hall, I can tell you about institutions—hell, I'll adopt him myself before I let you get away with that."

Petra promised she'd take care of Billy. Adoption fantasies had filled her head, too.

Billy needed to be hospitalized for at least three weeks. He'd emerged from the nightmare encounter with only superficial scratches, but medical tests revealed a low-grade bacterial infection in his lungs, foot fungus, slightly elevated blood pressure, and a pre-ulcerous stomach. The doctors pronounced the last two symptoms as probable stress reactions. No kidding. The infection was their main concern, and they had him on IV antibiotics. No one had told him about his mother yet.

Delaware said he'd handle it, and Petra was grateful it wouldn't be her.

Ilse Eggermann would never be solved officially, but Petra was sure Ramsey had done her, too. How close she'd come to being fooled—okay, humility was good for the soul. Good for the career, too. In the future she'd be careful about assuming anything.

She thought about how Ramsey and Ilse could have gone down: Ramsey visiting Balch in Rolling Hills Estates, couple of beers between friends, then on the way home, nice, easy drive up Hawthorne, he decides on a stopover at the pier. Had he used a disguise that night, too? Had he been planning something all along? Or had Ilse's foreigner status protected him from recognition? *The Adjustor* had never made it over to Europe.

That kind of M.O. indicated he might've killed other women. She'd beg off that part of it—let the feds have their fun, anyone else who wanted the glory. Schoelkopf was already holding press conferences, talking about *his* investigation.

No news on the reward yet. Dr. and Mrs. Boehlinger had returned to Ohio to finalize Lisa's funeral arrangements, and they hadn't returned Petra's calls. Whether or not Billy deserved the reward legally, he certainly deserved it morally. Boehlinger would probably try to avoid paying. After what he'd put Billy through, Petra wanted to lean on him, but what could she do? Maybe an anonymous leak to the papers. Or perhaps Mrs. B. would come through.

All secondary. For now, Billy slept, helped along by a big dinner and sedation.

Angel face, white and smooth, so peaceful.

She bent down, kissed his forehead, left the room, went to get the play therapist.

On her way out of the hospital, one of the administrators, a middle-aged suit named Bancroft, snagged her.

"How's our little hero, Detective Connor?"

"Fine."

Bancroft caught her arm, let go quickly when she stared at his hand. "If you have a moment, Detective, I have someone who'd like to speak with you."

"Who?"

"In my office, please."

❖

His office was big, done up in blue tweed and fake Colonial. Two women in their sixties sat in overstuffed chairs. One was chunky, broad-shouldered, with wiry gray hair uncoiling under a small charcoal pillbox hat, an ancient, no-nonsense tweed suit, a melt-the-glacier stare. The other was very thin, with coiffed hair the color of brandy, tasteful jewelry, light makeup. Navy suit that looked like Chanel, matching shoes. Her face was longish, painfully angular. She'd probably been beautiful once. She looked frightened. Petra was baffled.

"Detective," said Bancroft, "this is Mrs. Adamson. She and the late Mr. Adamson were among our most generous benefactors."

Slight inflection on the past tense. Bancroft winced. The thin woman smiled. Her hands were white, blue-veined, slightly liver-spotted. Petra noticed one index finger making tiny circles atop her purse. Gorgeous shoes, gorgeous suit, but, like the stocky woman's getup, the outfit looked old, gave off a clear sense of history.

No introduction of the other woman. She was examining Petra like a fishwife rating mullet.

"Well, I'll leave you to talk," said Bancroft. He left.

The chunky woman got up too, looking none too happy.

"Thank you, Mildred," Mrs. Adamson told her. Mildred nodded grimly before closing the door.

Mrs. Adamson turned to Petra. Her mouth worked. Finally, she said, "Please call me Cora. I'm so sorry to take your time, but . . ." Instead of continuing, she removed something from her purse and held it out.

Color snapshot of Billy. A little younger—maybe eleven. He stood on a boat dock, waving.

"How did you get this, ma'am?"

"It's mine. I snapped the picture."

"You know Billy Straight?"

The bottom half of the woman's mouth trembled, and her eyes pooled with tears. "This isn't Billy Straight, Detective Connor. It's Billy Adamson. William Bradley Adamson, Jr. My son. My late son."

Petra examined the back of the photo. A handwritten inscription said: *Billy, Arrowhead, 1971.* The colors were a little faded; she should have noticed. Some detective.

The boy was smiling, but something was off—the smile required effort.

A handkerchief had flown to Cora Adamson's face. She said, "Perhaps there are things I could've done differently, but I wasn't— How could I know for sure?"

"Know what, Mrs. Adamson?"

"Forgive me, I'm not making sense, let me organize my thoughts . . . Billy—*my* Billy—was an only child. Brilliant, he taught himself to read at four. He graduated from Cal law school thirteen years ago, immediately began doing legal work for the Farm Workers Union. My late husband was convinced it was a stage, rebellion, getting back at the corporate world. But I knew better: Billy had always been caring, kind. Even as a small boy, he refused to hurt anything—he wouldn't fish. Bill senior loved to fish, but Billy refused. The day I shot that picture, he and Bill had had a tiff about that. Bill insisted he was going to show Billy how to fish once and for all. Billy cried and insisted he wouldn't get in the boat, refused to kill anything. Finally, Bill told him if he couldn't be a man, just to stay behind with his mother. Which he did. But he was upset—he loved his father. I took the picture to cheer him up."

Petra stared at the photo. Same eyes, same hair. Same cleft chin. Jesus, even the expression was a clone.

"At twelve he became a vegetarian," said Cora Adamson. "Again, Bill thought it was a phase, but Billy never touched meat or fish again—I'm wandering, forgive me—where was I—the farm workers. Billy could have gotten a job with any firm in the country, but he chose to travel around the state with the farm workers, looking for violations, living the way they lived. He seemed happy, then suddenly he showed up at home and announced he'd quit, gotten a job with the public defender's office. But he wasn't happy there either, and left soon after.

"After that, he started to drift, driving around the state in an old car, growing his hair long, a long beard, doing legal work for various free clinics, never settling down. I knew something was bothering him, but he wouldn't tell me what it was. He wasn't around long enough to tell me. His father was so angry at him . . . he just kept wandering, leaving me no phone number, no address—I knew he was lost, but he refused to be found."

Sitting up straighter, she twisted the handkerchief. "Then one weekend he showed up at our place in Arrowhead. We had guests—business associates of his father—and Bill was embarrassed about the way Billy looked. Billy didn't care—it was me he wanted to talk to. He came to my room late at night, brought a candle and lit it. He said it was confession time. Then he told me he'd had an affair with a girl in Delano, one of the migrant girls, a young girl, underage. And she became pregnant. Or claimed to. Billy never saw a child, because he panicked when she told him, being a lawyer. Her age—statutory rape. He was also worried some grower would find out and use it against the union. Instead of shouldering his responsibility, he gave the girl every dollar he had with him and left town. That's when he joined the public defender's office. But it never stopped bothering him, and he began driving around California trying to find her—he said her name was Sharla and that she wasn't sophisticated but she had a good heart. He never found her.

" 'But let's face it, Mom,' he told me. 'If I'd wanted to badly enough, I would've, right? I'm not sure I want to know—Father's right, I am a coward, spineless, no use to anyone.' I told him the fact that he was telling me now showed he was extremely courageous—he still had a chance to buck up. I promised to do everything I could to help him find the girl, make financial arrangements for the child. If there *was* one—because I was skeptical, thought the girl was out for money. That infuriated him. He began pounding the bed, shouting that I was just like all the others, everything was money, money, money. Then he blew out the candle and stomped out. I'd never seen him like that and it shocked me. I thought I would let him cool down. The next morning, he was found floating in Lake Arrowhead. They said it was an accident. I never looked for the girl. I was never sure it was true. I did wonder from time to time . . . and then I saw the picture in the paper. And I knew. And now you've found him, Detective Connor."

Petra took another look at the photo and handed it back. Too close to be anything but righteous, and the time line was right. William Bradley Adamson. William Bradley Straight.

"What is it you want me to do for you, Mrs. Adamson?"

"Detective, I know I have no right to—maybe legal rights, but morally . . . but this child. He must be my grandson. There's no other rational explanation. I'm sure we can prove it with genetic tests. But not now, not with all he's been through—I want to . . . help him."

Suddenly, she looked down at her lap.

"I don't have the resources I used to have. My husband ran into some . . . misfortune before he passed away."

Petra found herself giving a sympathetic nod.

"The truth is," said Cora Adamson, still averting her eyes, "I've been living off savings for several years, but I know how to budget and I'm by no means penniless. Learning about Billy—this Billy—has crystallized my plans. I live in a grotesquely oversized house that I've been thinking of selling for some time. Until now, I lacked the incentive—and the will—to make the change. Now, it's clear. There's no mortgage on the house. Once I sell it, even after taxes, I should have enough to support myself and my grandson in a reasonable manner."

A pleading note had entered the woman's voice. Here she was, Chanel suit and all, applying for parental rights. What do you say to that?

Cora Adamson's head rose. "Perhaps it's all for the best. Too much privilege can create its own difficulties."

Petra wanted to say, I wouldn't know. Instead, she nodded.

"I love children, Detective Connor. Before I was married, I taught school. I always wanted *lots* of children, but Billy's birth was difficult and the doctors forbade it. Other than the loss of Billy and Bill and my parents, learning I couldn't have more children was the saddest moment of my life."

A thin white hand clutched her sleeve. "What I'm saying is I sincerely believe I have something to offer. I make no excuses for the lack of— Detective Connor, can you see it within yourself to help me?"

The woman's eyes locked onto Petra. Hungry, desperate.

Delaware was flying into town tonight. Why couldn't he be here *now*?

"Please," said Cora Adamson.

Petra said, "Let's talk about it."

CHAPTER 82

YESTERDAY, DR. DELAWARE TOLD ME ABOUT Mom. My stomach caught fire and I wanted to rip the IV line out and punch him in the face.

He sat there looking sad. What right did *he* have to be sad?

I rolled over and ignored him. No way would I let him see me cry, but the minute he left, I started crying and I went on crying all day and all night. Except when someone came into the room, and then I pretended to sleep.

Sometimes when they thought I was sleeping, they'd discuss me—nurses, interns.

Poor kid.

He's been through so much.

Tough little bugger.

I am *not* tough. I'm here because what's my choice?

Thinking about Mom made me want to be dead, too, but then I thought, What good would that do? There probably is no God, so I wouldn't get to see her anyway.

That first night I dug my nails into my hands, made them bleed. A little extra pain felt right.

It's the next day and I still can't believe it, I keep thinking she's going to walk through the door. I'll say I'm sorry for running away, she'll apologize, too, we'll hug—then it hits me. She's gone. That's it. Never again. *Never! This hurts so much!*

I cry a lot, fall asleep, wake up, cry some more.

Haven't cried for an hour. Maybe I'm all dried up, no more tears.

Hey, Doc, put some tears in the IV.

I spit on the floor. If I could empty my mind the way the orderlies empty my trash can. Out with all the garbage.

When I'm alone I think of her. Even though it hurts. I *want* to hurt.

Being alone is what I'm used to; I don't get enough of it. With all the doctors and interns and the nurses, sometimes I can't stand all the noise and the sympathy; want to punch all of them.

Not Sam. He comes every morning, brings me candy and magazines, pats my hand and talks about how we're two peas in a pod, tough, survivors. How he won't let anyone "mess" with me—don't worry, he's got connections. He repeats things, and sometimes his voice puts me to sleep. I fight to stay awake, don't want to make him feel bad. He was my friend when no one else was. One time he came with Mrs. Kleinman, but she annoyed me, touching my cheek, bringing food I didn't want to eat, trying to feed it to me. I was polite to her, but maybe Sam could tell, because he never brought her again.

Petra brings me books. She's very pretty, not married, not a mom, and I think maybe she likes me because it gives her mom practice. Or it's a vacation from being a detective.

She killed him. She's a serious person, doesn't tell jokes, doesn't try to cheer me up when I don't want it. Even when she smiles, she's serious.

Even if I'm totally exhausted, I can't be anything but nice to her.

She's about Mom's age—why'd Mom have to take that idiot Moron in, let him run her life, let him put a split in our family?

Why couldn't Mom learn to be *alone*?

Dr. Delaware said it was probably an accident, he pushed her and she fell, but that doesn't make her any more alive.

I keep thinking: If I'd been there, I could've saved her.

Dr. Delaware talked to me about guilt, how it was normal but it would pass. How it was the parents' job to take care of children, not the other way around. He said Mom did love me, she meant well, but she'd hit some bad luck. He also said that what happened to her was terrible—no way would he try to tell me everything was okay, because it wasn't.

He was certain, though, that Mom would be proud of how well I'd done on my own.

Maybe.

He considers me very "impressive."

At first I thought he was full of it, the way he'd just sit, not saying much. At first I thought he didn't care. Now I think he probably does. He shows up every day at 6:00 P.M., stays with me for two hours, sometimes more, doesn't mind if we don't do anything.

Before he left, he noticed the chessboard that Sam left and asked if I wanted to play. He's about as good as Sam, and I beat him two out of three. He said, "Okay, next time," and I said, "Prepare to lose." He laughed and I asked him who's paying him to play games and he said the police, don't worry, he'd collect, he always does.

Sometimes he tells jokes. Some of them are funny. The nurses seem to like him. I heard one nurse ask another if he was married and the other one said she wasn't sure, she didn't think so.

He and Petra would make a good couple.

I can imagine the two of them in a nice house, a good car, some kids, a dog. Or even one kid, so he could get all their attention.

Nice happy family, taking trips, going to restaurants.

Maybe it happens. I don't know. I'll never stop thinking about Mom—the door's opening and for a moment I think it's her.

It's Petra and she's wearing a red suit.

That's different, she always wears black. She's carrying a bag, and she gives it to me.

Inside is a book.

The presidents book. Not the one from the library. A brand-new one—clean cover, crisp white pages. It has that new-book smell. The colors in the illustrations are very bright. This is very cool.

"Thanks," I say. "Thanks a lot."

She shrugs. "Enjoy. Who knows, Billy, someday you might be in there."

"Yeah, right." It's a crazy idea. But an interesting one.

Alex Delaware is back! Coming in hardcover from Random House in December 1999, a riveting and devilishly ingenious story about an asylum inmate who seems able to predict grisly slayings in the outside world.

MONSTER

To read the first chapter, please turn the page...

THE GIANT KNEW Richard Nixon.

Towering, yellow-haired, grizzled, a listing mountain in khaki twill, he limped closer, and Milo tightened up. I looked to Frank Dollard for a cue. Dollard appeared untroubled, meaty arms at his sides, mouth serene under the tobaccoed gray mustache. His eyes were slits, but they'd been that way at the main gate.

The giant belched out a bass laugh and brushed greasy hair away from his eyes. His beard was a corn-colored ruin. I could smell him now, vinegarish, hormonally charged. He had to be six eight, three hundred. The shadow he threw on the dirt was ash-colored, amoebic, broad enough to shade us.

He took another lurching step, and this time Frank Dollard's right arm shot out.

The huge man didn't seem to notice, just stood there with Dollard's limb flung across his waist. Maybe a dozen other men in khaki were out on the yard, most of them standing still, a few others pacing, rocking, faces pressed against the chain link. No groups that I could see; everyone to himself. Above them, the sky was an untrammeled blue, clouds broiled away by a vengeful sun. I was cooking in my suit.

The giant's face was dry. He sighed, dropped his

shoulders, and Dollard lowered his arm. The giant made a finger gun, pointed it at us, and laughed. His eyes were dark brown, pinched at the corners, the whites too sallow for health.

"Secret service." He thumped his chest. "Victoria's Secret service in the closet underwear undercover always lookin' out for the guy good old Nixon RMN Rimmin, always rimmin wanting to be rimmed he liked to talk the walk cuttin outta the White House night house doing the party thing all hours with Kurt Vonnegut J. D. Salinger the Glass family anyone who didn't mind the politics heat of the kitchen I wrote *Cat's Cradle* sold it to Vonnegut for ten bucks *Billy Bathgate* typed the manuscript one time he walked out the front door got all the way to Las Vegas big hassle with the Hell's Angels over some dollar slots Vonnegut wanting to change the national debt Rimmin agreed the Angels got pissed we had to pull him out of it me and Kurt Vonnegut Salinger wasn't there Doctorow was sewing the Cat's Cradle they were bad cats, woulda assassinated him any day of the week leeway the oswald harvey."

He bent and lifted his left trouser leg. Below the knee was bone sheathed with glossy white scar tissue, most of the calf meat ripped away. An organic peg leg.

"Got shot protecting old Rimmin," he said, letting go of the fabric. "He died anyway poor Richard no almanac know what happened rimmed too hard I couldn't stop it."

"Chet," said Dollard, stretching to pat the giant's shoulder.

The giant shuddered. Little cherries of muscle rolled along Milo's jawline. His hand was where his gun would have been if he hadn't checked it at the gate.

Dollard said, "Gonna make it to the TV room today, Chet?"

The giant swayed a bit. "Ahh . . ."

"I think you should make it to the TV room, Chet. There's gonna be a movie on democracy. We're gonna sing 'The Star-Spangled Banner,' could use someone with a good voice."

"Yeah, Pavarotti," said the giant, suddenly cheerful. "He and Domingo were at Caesars Palace they didn't like the way it worked out Rimmin not doing his voice exercises lee lee lee lo lo lo no egg yolk to smooth the trachea it pissed Pavarotti off he didn't want to run for public office."

"Yeah, sure," said Dollard. He winked at Milo and me.

The giant had turned his back on all three of us and was staring down on the bare tan table of the yard. A short, thick, dark-haired man had pulled down his pants and was urinating in the dirt, setting off a tiny dust storm. None of the other men in khaki seemed to notice. The giant's face had gone stony.

"Wet," he said.

"Don't worry about it, Chet," Dollard said softly. "You know Sharbno and his bladder."

The giant didn't answer, but Dollard must have transmitted a message, because two other psych techs came jogging over from a far corner. One black, one white, just as muscular as Dollard but a lot younger, wearing the same uniform of short-sleeved sport shirt, jeans, and sneakers. Photo badges clipped to the collar. The heat and the run had turned the techs' faces wet.

Milo's sport coat had soaked through at the armpits, but the giant hadn't let loose a drop of sweat.

His face tightened some more as he watched the urinating man shake himself off, then duck-walk across the yard, pants still puddled around his ankles.

"Wet."

"We'll handle it, Chet," soothed Dollard.

The black tech said, "I'll go get those trousers up."

He sauntered toward Sharbno. The white tech stayed with Chet. Dollard gave Chet another pat and we moved on.

Ten yards later, I looked back. Both techs were flanking Chet. The giant's posture had changed—shoulders higher, head craning as he continued to stare at the space vacated by Sharbno.

Milo said, "Guy that size, how can you control him?"

"We don't control him," said Dollard. "Clozapine does. Last month his dosage got upped after he beat the crap out of another patient. Broke about a dozen bones."

"Maybe he needs even more," said Milo.

"Why?"

"He doesn't exactly sound coherent."

Dollard chuckled. "Coherent." He glanced at me. "Know what his daily dosage is, Doctor? Fourteen hundred milligrams. Even with his body weight, that's pretty thorough, wouldn't you say?"

"Maximum's usually around nine hundred," I told Milo. "Lots of people do well on a third of that."

Dollard said, "He was on eleven migs when he broke the other inmate's face." Dollard's chest puffed a bit. "We exceed maximum recommendations all the time; the psychiatrists tell us it's no problem." He shrugged. "Maybe Chet'll get even more. If he does something else bad."

We covered more ground, passing more inmates. Untrimmed hair, slack mouths, empty eyes, stained uniforms. None of the iron-pumper bulk you see in prisons. These torsos were soft, warped, deflated. I felt eyes on the back of my head, glanced to the side, and saw a man with haunted-prophet eyes and a chestful of black beard staring at me. Above the facial pelt, his cheeks were sunken and sooty. Our eyes engaged. He came toward me, arms rigid, neck bobbing. He opened his mouth. No teeth.

He didn't know me but his eyes were rich with hatred.

My hands fisted. I walked faster. Dollard noticed and cocked his head. The bearded man stopped abruptly, stood there in the full sun, planted like a shrub. The red exit sign on the far gate was five hundred feet away. Dollard's key ring jangled. No other techs in sight. We kept walking. Beautiful sky, but no birds. A machine began grinding something.

I said, "Chet's ramblings. There seems to be some intelligence there."

"What, 'cause he talks about books?" said Dollard. "I think before he went nuts he was in college somewhere. I think his family was educated."

"What got him in here?" said Milo, glancing back.

"Same as all of them." Dollard scratched his mustache and kept his pace steady. The yard was vast. We were halfway across now, passing more dead eyes, frozen faces, wild looks that set up the small hairs on the back of my neck.

"Don't wear khaki or brown," Milo had said. "The inmates wear that, we don't want you stuck in there—though that would be interesting, wouldn't it? Shrink trying to convince them he's not crazy?"

"Same as all of them?" I said.

"Incompetent to stand trial," said Dollard. "Your basic 1026."

"How many do you have here?" said Milo.

"Twelve hundred or so. Old Chet's case is kinda sad. He was living on top of a mountain down near the Mexican border—some kind of hermit deal, sleeping in caves, eating weeds, all that good stuff. Couple of hikers just happened to be unlucky enough to find the wrong cave, wrong time, woke him up. He tore 'em up—really went at 'em with his bare hands. He actually managed to rip both the girl's arms off and was working on one of her legs when they found him. Some park ranger or sheriff shotgunned Chet's leg charging in, that's why it looks like that. He wasn't resisting arrest, just sitting there next to the body pieces, looking scared someone was gonna hit him. No big challenge getting a 1026 on something like that. He's been here three years. First six months he did nothing but stay curled up, crying, sucking his thumb. We had to IV-feed him."

"Now he beats people up," said Milo. "Progress."

Dollard flexed his fingers. He was in his late fifties, husky and sunburnt, no visible body fat. The lips beneath the mustache were thin, parched, amused. "What do you want we should do, haul him out and shoot him?"

Milo grunted.

Dollard said, "Yeah, I know what you're thinking:

good riddance to bad rubbish, you'd be happy to be on the firing squad." He chuckled. "Cop thinking. I worked patrol in Hemet for ten years, woulda said the exact same thing before I came here. Couple of years on the wards and now I know reality: some of them really *are* sick." He touched his mustache. "Old Chet's no Ted Bundy. He couldn't help himself any more than a baby crapping its diaper. Same with old Sharbno back there, pissing in the dirt." He tapped his temple. "The wiring's screwy, some people just turn to garbage. And this place is the Dumpster."

"Exactly why we're here," said Milo.

Dollard raised an eyebrow. "*That* I don't know about. Our garbage doesn't get taken out. I can't see how we're gonna be able to help you on Dr. Argent."

He flexed his fingers again. His nails were yellow horn. "I liked Dr. Argent. Real nice lady. But she met her end out there." He pointed randomly. "Out in the *civilized* world."

"Did you work with her?"

"Not steadily. We talked about cases from time to time, she'd tell me if a patient needed something. But you can tell about people. Nice lady. A little naive, but she was new."

"Naive in what way?"

"She started this group. Skills for Daily Living. Weekly discussions, supposedly helping some guys cope with the world. As if any of 'em are ever getting out."

"She ran it by herself."

"Her and a tech."

"Who's the tech?"

"Girl named Heidi Ott."

"Two women handling a group of killers?"

Dollard smiled. "The state says it's safe."

"You think different?"

"I'm not paid to think."

We neared the chain-link wall. Milo said, "Any idea why someone in the civilized world would kill Dr. Argent? Speaking as an ex-cop."

Dollard said, "From what you told me—the way you found her in that car trunk, all cleaned up—I'd say some sociopath, right? Someone who knew damn well what he was doing, and enjoyed it. More of a 1368 than a 1026—your basic lowlife criminal trying to fake being crazy 'cause they're under the mistaken impression it'll be easier here than in jail. We've got two, three hundred of *those* on the fifth floor, maybe a few more, 'cause of Three Strikes. They come here ranting and drooling, smearing shit on the walls, learn quickly they can't B.S. the docs here. Less than one percent succeed. The official eval period's ninety days, but plenty of them ask to leave sooner."

"Did Dr. Argent work on the fifth floor?"

"Nope. Hers were all 1026's."

"Besides total crazies and ninety-day losers, who else do you have here?" said Milo.

"We've got a few mentally disordered sex offenders left," said Dollard. "Pedophiles, that kind of trash. Maybe thirty of 'em. We used to have more but they keep changing the law—stick 'em here, nope, the prison system, oops, back here, unh-uh, prison. Dr. Argent didn't hang with them, either, least that I noticed."

"So the way you see it, what happened to her couldn't relate to her work here."

"You got it. Even if one of her guys got out—and they didn't—none of them could've killed her and stashed her in the trunk. None of them could plan that well."

We were at the gate. Tan men standing still, like oversized chess pieces. The faraway machine continued to grind.

Dollard flicked a hand back at the yard. "I'm not saying these guys are harmless, even with all the dope we pump into them. Get these poor bastards delusional enough, they could do anything. But they don't kill for fun—from what I've seen, they don't take much pleasure from life, period. If you can even call what they're doing living."

He cleared his throat, swallowed the phlegm. "Makes you wonder why God would take the trouble to create such a mess."

JONATHAN KELLERMAN

SAVAGE SPAWN

Reflections on Violent Children

What makes children kill?

In such places as Jonesboro, Arkansas; Springfield, Oregon; and Littleton, Colorado, kids are killing kids. In this powerful, disturbing book, bestselling author and noted child psychologist Jonathan Kellerman examines the socio-pathology of today's youth, attempting to make sense of the bloody rampages that have taken over today's headlines. In such chapters as "Dissecting Evil," "The Scapegoat We Love to Hate," and "The Biology of Being Bad," Kellerman discusses the history of childhood violence, takes a hard look at antisocial children, and, most important, offers warning signs and solutions to stop the spread of these devastating tragedies that we all think can—pray will—never happen in our town.

LIBRARY OF
CONTEMPORARY THOUGHT
Published by Ballantine Books.
Available in bookstores everywhere.